PRAISE FOR THE DUNE CHRONICLES

DUNE

"An astonishing science fiction phenomenon." —*The Washington Post*

"Powerful, convincing, and most ingenious." —Robert A. Heinlein

"Herbert's creation of this universe, with its intricate development and analysis of ecology, religion, politics, and philosophy, remains one of the supreme and seminal achievements in science fiction."
—*The Louisville Times*

"One of the landmarks of modern science fiction . . . an amazing feat of creation."
—P. Schuyler Miller

DUNE MESSIAH

"Brilliant. . . . It is all that *Dune* was, and maybe a little more."
—*Galaxy Magazine*

"The perfect companion piece to *Dune* . . . fascinating."
—*Challenging Destiny*

CHILDREN OF DUNE

"A major event."
—*Los Angeles Times*

"Ranging from palace intrigue and desert chases to religious speculation and confrontations with the supreme intelligence of the universe, there is something here for all science fiction fans."
—*Publishers Weekly*

"Herbert adds enough new twists and turns to the ongoing saga that familiarity with the recurring elements brings pleasure."
—*Challenging Destiny*

GOD EMPEROR OF DUNE

"Rich fare . . . heady stuff." —*Los Angeles Times*

"A fourth visit to distant Arrakis that is every bit as fascinating as the other three—every bit as timely." —*Time*

"Book four of the Dune series has many of the same strengths as the previous three, and I was indeed kept up late at night."
—*Challenging Destiny*

HERETICS OF DUNE

"A monumental piece of imaginative architecture . . . indisputably magical." —*Los Angeles Herald Examiner*

"Appealing and gripping . . . fascinating detail, yet cloaked in mystery and mysticism." —*The Milwaukee Journal*

"Herbert works wonders with some new speculation and an entirely new batch of characters. He weaves together several fascinating story lines with almost the same mastery as informed *Dune*, and keeps the reader intent on the next revelation or twist." —*Challenging Destiny*

CHAPTERHOUSE: DUNE

"Compelling . . . a worthy addition to this durable and deservedly popular series." —*The New York Times*

"The vast and fascinating Dune saga sweeps on—as exciting and gripping as ever." —*Kirkus Reviews*

THE DUNE CHRONICLES BY FRANK HERBERT

DUNE

DUNE MESSIAH

CHILDREN OF DUNE

GOD EMPEROR OF DUNE

HERETICS OF DUNE

CHAPTERHOUSE: DUNE

OTHER BOOKS BY FRANK HERBERT

THE DRAGON IN THE SEA

DESTINATION: VOID
(revised edition)

DIRECT DESCENT

THE DOSADI EXPERIMENT

EYE

THE EYES OF HEISENBERG

THE GODMAKERS

THE HEAVEN MAKERS

THE GREEN BRAIN

THE SANTAROGA BARRIER

SOUL CATCHER

WHIPPING STAR

THE WHITE PLAGUE

MAN OF TWO WORLDS
(with Brian Herbert)

ANGELS' FALL

A THORN IN THE BUSH

HIGH-OPP

A GAME OF AUTHORS

UNPUBLISHED STORIES

THE BOOK OF FRANK HERBERT

THE WORLDS OF FRANK HERBERT

HELLSTROM'S HIVE

THRESHOLD: THE BLUE ANGELS EXPERIENCE

THE OFFICIAL DUNE COLORING BOOK

BOOKS BY FRANK HERBERT AND BILL RANSOM

THE JESUS INCIDENT

THE LAZARUS EFFECT

THE ASCENSION FACTOR

DUNE

FRANK HERBERT

ACE
NEW YORK

ACE
Published by Berkley
An imprint of Penguin Random House LLC
penguinrandomhouse.com

ISBN: 9780593640333

The Library of Congress has cataloged the G. P. Putnam's Sons
hardcover edition as follows:

Herbert, Frank
Dune.
1. Title
PS3558.E63D8 1984 813.54   83-16030
ISBN 0-399-12896-4

G. P. Putnam's Sons hardcover edition / 1984
Ace hardcover edition / October 1999
Ace trade paperback edition / August 2005
Ace premium edition / December 2010
First Ace movie tie-in trade paperback edition / September 2021
Second Ace movie tie-in trade paperback edition / September 2023

Printed in the United States of America
1st Printing

Motion Picture Artwork © 2023 Legendary and Warner Bros.
Entertainment Inc. All Rights Reserved.
Interior art: Desert Cave © masher / Shutterstock Images
Book design by Kristin del Rosario

To the people whose labors go beyond ideas
into the realm of "real materials"—
to the dry-land ecologists, wherever they may be,
in whatever time they work,
this effort at prediction is dedicated
in humility and admiration.

CONTENTS

BOOK ONE

DUNE

A beginning is the time for taking the most delicate care that the balances are correct. This every sister of the Bene Gesserit knows. To begin your study of the life of Muad'Dib, then, take care that you first place him in his time: born in the 57th year of the Padishah Emperor, Shaddam IV. And take the most special care that you locate Muad'Dib in his place: the planet Arrakis. Do not be deceived by the fact that he was born on Caladan and lived his first fifteen years there. Arrakis, the planet known as Dune, is forever his place.

—FROM "MANUAL OF MUAD'DIB"
BY THE PRINCESS IRULAN

In the week before their departure to Arrakis, when all the final scurrying about had reached a nearly unbearable frenzy, an old crone came to visit the mother of the boy, Paul.

It was a warm night at Castle Caladan, and the ancient pile of stone that had served the Atreides family as home for twenty-six generations bore that cooled-sweat feeling it acquired before a change in the weather.

The old woman was let in by the side door down the vaulted passage by Paul's room and she was allowed a moment to peer in at him where he lay in his bed.

By the half-light of a suspensor lamp, dimmed and hanging near the floor, the awakened boy could see a bulky female shape at his door, standing one step ahead of his mother. The old woman was a witch shadow—hair like matted spiderwebs, hooded 'round darkness of features, eyes like glittering jewels.

"Is he not small for his age, Jessica?" the old woman asked. Her voice wheezed and twanged like an untuned baliset.

Paul's mother answered in her soft contralto: "The Atreides are known to start late getting their growth, Your Reverence."

"So I've heard, so I've heard," wheezed the old woman. "Yet he's already fifteen."

"Yes, Your Reverence."

"He's awake and listening to us," said the old woman. "Sly little rascal." She chuckled. "But royalty has need of slyness. And if he's really the Kwisatz Haderach . . . well. . . ."

Within the shadows of his bed, Paul held his eyes open to mere slits. Two bird-bright ovals—the eyes of the old woman—seemed to expand and glow as they stared into his.

"Sleep well, you sly little rascal," said the old woman. "Tomorrow you'll need all your faculties to meet my gom jabbar."

And she was gone, pushing his mother out, closing the door with a solid thump.

Paul lay awake wondering: *What's a gom jabbar?*

In all the upset during this time of change, the old woman was the strangest thing he had seen.

Your Reverence.

And the way she called his mother Jessica like a common serving wench instead of what she was—a Bene Gesserit Lady, a duke's concubine and mother of the ducal heir.

Is a gom jabbar something of Arrakis I must know before we go there? he wondered.

He mouthed her strange words: *Gom jabbar . . . Kwisatz Haderach.*

There had been so many things to learn. Arrakis would be a place so different from Caladan that Paul's mind whirled with the new knowledge. *Arrakis—Dune—Desert Planet.*

Thufir Hawat, his father's Master of Assassins, had explained it: their mortal enemies, the Harkonnens, had been on Arrakis eighty years, holding the planet in quasi-fief under a CHOAM Company contract to mine the geriatric spice, melange. Now the Harkonnens were leaving to be replaced by the House of Atreides in fief-complete—an apparent victory for the Duke Leto. Yet, Hawat had said, this appearance contained the deadliest peril, for the Duke Leto was popular among the Great Houses of the Landsraad.

"A popular man arouses the jealousy of the powerful," Hawat had said.

Arrakis—Dune—Desert Planet.

Paul fell asleep to dream of an Arrakeen cavern, silent people all around him moving in the dim light of glowglobes. It was solemn there and like a cathedral as he listened to a faint sound—the drip-drip-drip of water. Even while he remained in the dream, Paul knew he would remember it upon awakening. He always remembered the dreams that were predictions.

The dream faded.

Paul awoke to feel himself in the warmth of his bed—thinking . . . thinking. This world of Castle Caladan, without play or companions his own age, perhaps did not deserve sadness in farewell. Dr. Yueh, his teacher, had hinted that the faufreluches class system was not rigidly guarded on Arrakis. The planet sheltered people who lived at the desert edge without caid or bashar to command them: will-o'-the-sand people called Fremen, marked down on no census of the Imperial Regate.

Arrakis—Dune—Desert Planet.

Paul sensed his own tensions, decided to practice one of the mind-body lessons his mother had taught him. Three quick breaths triggered the responses: he fell into the floating awareness . . . focusing the consciousness . . . aortal dilation . . . avoiding the unfocused mechanism of consciousness . . . to be conscious by choice . . . blood enriched and swift-flooding the overload regions . . . *one does not obtain food-safety-freedom by instinct alone* . . . animal consciousness does not extend beyond the given moment nor into the idea that its victims may become extinct . . . the animal destroys and does not produce . . . animal pleasures remain close to sensation levels and avoid the perceptual . . . the human requires a background grid through which to see his universe . . . focused consciousness by choice, this forms your grid . . . bodily integrity follows nerve-blood flow according to the deepest awareness of cell needs . . . all things/cells/beings are impermanent . . . strive for flow-permanence within. . . .

Over and over and over within Paul's floating awareness the lesson rolled.

When dawn touched Paul's window sill with yellow light, he sensed it through closed eyelids, opened them, hearing then the renewed bustle and hurry in the castle, seeing the familiar patterned beams of his bedroom ceiling.

The hall door opened and his mother peered in, hair like shaded bronze held with black ribbon at the crown, her oval face emotionless and green eyes staring solemnly.

"You're awake," she said. "Did you sleep well?"

"Yes."

He studied the tallness of her, saw the hint of tension in her shoulders as she chose clothing for him from the closet racks. Another might have missed the tension, but she had trained him in the Bene Gesserit Way—in the minutiae of observation. She turned, holding a semiformal jacket for him. It carried the red Atreides hawk crest above the breast pocket.

"Hurry and dress," she said. "Reverend Mother is waiting."

"I dreamed of her once," Paul said. "Who is she?"

"She was my teacher at the Bene Gesserit school. Now, she's the Emperor's Truthsayer. And Paul. . . ." She hesitated. "You must tell her about your dreams."

"I will. Is she the reason we got Arrakis?"

"We did not *get* Arrakis." Jessica flicked dust from a pair of trousers, hung them with the jacket on the dressing stand beside his bed. "Don't keep Reverend Mother waiting."

Paul sat up, hugged his knees. "What's a gom jabbar?"

Again, the training she had given him exposed her almost invisible hesitation, a nervous betrayal he felt as fear.

Jessica crossed to the window, flung wide the draperies, stared across the river orchards toward Mount Syubi. "You'll learn about . . . the gom jabbar soon enough," she said.

He heard the fear in her voice and wondered at it.

Jessica spoke without turning. "Reverend Mother is waiting in my morning room. Please hurry."

THE REVEREND MOTHER GAIUS HELEN MOHIAM SAT IN A TAPESTRIED chair watching mother and son approach. Windows on each side of her overlooked the curving southern bend of the river and the green farmlands of the Atreides family holding, but the Reverend Mother ignored the view. She was feeling her age this morning, more than a little petulant. She blamed it on space travel and association with that abominable Spacing Guild and its secretive ways. But here was a mission that required personal attention from a Bene Gesserit-with-the-Sight. Even the Padishah Emperor's Truthsayer couldn't evade that responsibility when the duty call came.

Damn that Jessica! the Reverend Mother thought. *If only she'd borne us a girl as she was ordered to do!*

Jessica stopped three paces from the chair, dropped a small curtsy, a gentle flick of left hand along the line of her skirt. Paul gave the short bow his dancing master had taught—the one used "when in doubt of another's station."

The nuances of Paul's greeting were not lost on the Reverend Mother. She said: "He's a cautious one, Jessica."

Jessica's hand went to Paul's shoulder, tightened there. For a heartbeat, fear pulsed through her palm. Then she had herself under control. "Thus he has been taught, Your Reverence."

What does she fear? Paul wondered.

The old woman studied Paul in one gestalten flicker: face oval like Jessica's, but strong bones . . . hair: the Duke's black-black but with browline of the maternal grandfather who cannot be named, and that thin, disdainful nose; shape of directly staring green eyes: like the old Duke, the paternal grandfather who is dead.

Now, there was a man who appreciated the power of bravura—even in death, the Reverend Mother thought.

"Teaching is one thing," she said, "the basic ingredient is another. We shall see." The old eyes darted a hard glance at Jessica. "Leave us. I enjoin you to practice the meditation of peace."

Jessica took her hand from Paul's shoulder. "Your Reverence, I—"

"Jessica, you know it must be done."

Paul looked up at his mother, puzzled.

Jessica straightened. "Yes . . . of course."

Paul looked back at the Reverend Mother. Politeness and his mother's obvious awe of this old woman argued caution. Yet he felt an angry apprehension at the fear he sensed radiating from his mother.

"Paul. . . ." Jessica took a deep breath. ". . . this test you're about to receive . . . it's important to me."

"Test?" He looked up at her.

"Remember that you're a duke's son," Jessica said. She whirled and strode from the room in a dry swishing of skirt. The door closed solidly behind her.

Paul faced the old woman, holding anger in check. "Does one dismiss the Lady Jessica as though she were a serving wench?"

A smile flicked the corners of the wrinkled old mouth. "The Lady Jessica *was* my serving wench, lad, for fourteen years at school." She nodded. "And a good one, too. Now, *you* come here!"

The command whipped out at him. Paul found himself obeying before he could think about it. *Using the Voice on me*, he thought. He stopped at her gesture, standing beside her knees.

"See this?" she asked. From the folds of her gown, she lifted a green metal cube about fifteen centimeters on a side. She turned it and Paul saw that one side was open—black and oddly frightening. No light penetrated that open blackness.

"Put your right hand in the box," she said.

Fear shot through Paul. He started to back away, but the old woman said: "Is this how you obey your mother?"

He looked up into bird-bright eyes.

Slowly, feeling the compulsions and unable to inhibit them, Paul put his hand into the box. He felt first a sense of cold as the blackness closed around his hand, then slick metal against his fingers and a prickling as though his hand were asleep.

A predatory look filled the old woman's features. She lifted her right hand away from the box and poised the hand close to the side of Paul's neck. He saw a glint of metal there and started to turn toward it.

"Stop!" she snapped.

Using the Voice again! He swung his attention back to her face.

"I hold at your neck the gom jabbar," she said. "The gom jabbar, the high-handed enemy. It's a needle with a drop of poison on its tip. Ah-ah! Don't pull away or you'll feel that poison."

Paul tried to swallow in a dry throat. He could not take his attention from the seamed old face, the glistening eyes, the pale gums around silvery metal teeth that flashed as she spoke.

"A duke's son *must* know about poisons," she said. "It's the way of our times, eh? Musky, to be poisoned in your drink. Aumas, to be poisoned in your food. The quick ones and the slow ones and the ones in between. Here's a new one for you: the gom jabbar. It kills only animals."

Pride overcame Paul's fear. "You dare suggest a duke's son is an animal?" he demanded.

"Let us say I suggest you may be human," she said. "Steady! I warn you not to try jerking away. I am old, but my hand can drive this needle into your neck before you escape me."

"Who are you?" he whispered. "How did you trick my mother into leaving me alone with you? Are you from the Harkonnens?"

"The Harkonnens? Bless us, no! Now, be silent." A dry finger touched his neck and he stilled the involuntary urge to leap away.

"Good," she said. "You pass the first test. Now, here's the way of the rest of it: If you withdraw your hand from the box you die. This is the only rule. Keep your hand in the box and live. Withdraw it and die."

Paul took a deep breath to still his trembling. "If I call out there'll be servants on you in seconds and *you'll* die."

"Servants will not pass your mother who stands guard outside that door. Depend on it. Your mother survived this test. Now it's your turn. Be honored. We seldom administer this to men-children."

Curiosity reduced Paul's fear to a manageable level. He heard truth in the old woman's voice, no denying it. If his mother stood guard out there . . . if this were truly a test. . . . And whatever it was, he knew himself caught in it, trapped by that hand at his neck: the gom jabbar. He recalled the response from the Litany Against Fear as his mother had taught him out of the Bene Gesserit rite.

"I must not fear. Fear is the mind-killer. Fear is the little-death that brings total obliteration. I will face my fear. I will permit it to pass over me and through me. And when it has gone past I will turn the inner eye to see its path. Where the fear has gone there will be nothing. Only I will remain."

He felt calmness return, said: "Get on with it, old woman."

"Old woman!" she snapped. "You've courage, and that can't be denied. Well, we shall see, sirra." She bent close, lowered her voice almost to a whisper. "You will feel pain in this hand within the box. Pain. But! Withdraw the hand and I'll touch your neck with my gom jabbar—the death so swift it's like the fall of the headsman's axe. Withdraw your hand and the gom jabbar takes you. Understand?"

"What's in the box?"

"Pain."

He felt increased tingling in his hand, pressed his lips tightly together. *How could this be a test?* he wondered. The tingling became an itch.

The old woman said: "You've heard of animals chewing off a leg to escape a trap? There's an animal kind of trick. A human would remain in the trap, endure the pain, feigning death that he might kill the trapper and remove a threat to his kind."

The itch became the faintest burning. "Why are you doing this?" he demanded.

"To determine if you're human. Be silent."

Paul clenched his left hand into a fist as the burning sensation increased in the other hand. It mounted slowly: heat upon heat upon heat . . . upon heat. He felt the fingernails of his free hand biting the palm. He tried to flex the fingers of the burning hand, but couldn't move them.

"It burns," he whispered.

"Silence!"

Pain throbbed up his arm. Sweat stood out on his forehead. Every fiber cried out to withdraw the hand from that burning pit . . . but . . . the gom jabbar. Without turning his head, he tried to move his eyes to see that terrible needle poised beside his neck. He sensed that he was breathing in gasps, tried to slow his breaths and couldn't.

Pain!

His world emptied of everything except that hand immersed in agony, the ancient face inches away staring at him.

His lips were so dry he had difficulty separating them.

The burning! The burning!

He thought he could feel skin curling black on that agonized hand, the flesh crisping and dropping away until only charred bones remained.

It stopped!

As though a switch had been turned off, the pain stopped.

Paul felt his right arm trembling, felt sweat bathing his body.

"Enough," the old woman muttered. "Kull wahad! No woman-child ever withstood that much. I must've wanted you to fail." She leaned back, withdrawing the gom jabbar from the side of his neck. "Take your hand from the box, young human, and look at it."

He fought down an aching shiver, stared at the lightless void where his hand seemed to remain of its own volition. Memory of pain inhibited every movement. Reason told him he would withdraw a blackened stump from that box.

"Do it!" she snapped.

He jerked his hand from the box, stared at it astonished. Not a mark. No sign of agony on the flesh. He held up the hand, turned it, flexed the fingers.

"Pain by nerve induction," she said. "Can't go around maiming potential humans. There're those who'd give a pretty for the secret of this box, though." She slipped it into the folds of her gown.

"But the pain—" he said.

"Pain," she sniffed. "A human can override any nerve in the body."

Paul felt his left hand aching, uncurled the clenched fingers, looked at four bloody marks where fingernails had bitten his palm. He dropped the hand to his side, looked at the old woman. "You did that to my mother once?"

"Ever sift sand through a screen?" she asked.

The tangential slash of her question shocked his mind into a higher awareness: *Sand through a screen.* He nodded.

"We Bene Gesserit sift people to find the humans."

He lifted his right hand, willing the memory of the pain. "And that's all there is to it—pain?"

"I observed you in pain, lad. Pain's merely the axis of the test. Your mother's told you about our ways of observing. I see the signs of her teaching in you. Our test is crisis and observation."

He heard the confirmation in her voice, said: "It's truth!"

She stared at him. *He senses truth! Could he be the one? Could he truly be the one?* She extinguished the excitement, reminding herself: *"Hope clouds observation."*

"You know when people believe what they say," she said.

"I know it."

The harmonics of ability confirmed by repeated test were in his voice. She heard them, said: "Perhaps you are the Kwisatz Haderach. Sit down, little brother, here at my feet."

"I prefer to stand."

"Your mother sat at my feet once."

"I'm not my mother."

"You hate us a little, eh?" She looked toward the door, called out: "Jessica!"

The door flew open and Jessica stood there staring hard-eyed into the room. Hardness melted from her as she saw Paul. She managed a faint smile.

"Jessica, have you ever stopped hating me?" the old woman asked.

"I both love and hate you," Jessica said. "The hate—that's from pains I must never forget. The love—that's. . . ."

"Just the basic fact," the old woman said, but her voice was gentle. "You may come in now, but remain silent. Close that door and mind it that no one interrupts us."

Jessica stepped into the room, closed the door and stood with her back to it. *My son lives*, she thought. *My son lives and is . . . human. I knew he was . . . but . . . he lives. Now, I can go on living.* The door felt hard and real against her back. Everything in the room was immediate and pressing against her senses.

My son lives.

Paul looked at his mother. *She told the truth.* He wanted to get away alone and think this experience through, but knew he could not leave until he was dismissed. The old woman had gained a power over him. *They spoke truth.* His mother had undergone this test. There must be terrible purpose in it . . . the pain and fear had been terrible. He understood terrible purposes. They drove against all odds. They were their own necessity. Paul felt that he had been infected with terrible purpose. He did not know yet what the terrible purpose was.

"Someday, lad," the old woman said, "you, too, may have to stand outside a door like that. It takes a measure of doing."

Paul looked down at the hand that had known pain, then up to the Reverend Mother. The sound of her voice had contained a difference then from any other voice in his experience. The words were outlined in brilliance. There was an edge to them. He felt that any question he might ask her would bring an answer that could lift him out of his flesh-world into something greater.

"Why do you test for humans?" he asked.

"To set you free."

"Free?"

"Once, men turned their thinking over to machines in the hope that this would set them free. But that only permitted other men with machines to enslave them."

"'Thou shalt not make a machine in the likeness of a man's mind,'" Paul quoted.

"Right out of the Butlerian Jihad and the Orange Catholic Bible," she said. "But what the O.C. Bible should've said is: 'Thou shalt not make a machine to counterfeit a *human* mind.' Have you studied the Mentat in your service?"

"I've studied *with* Thufir Hawat."

"The Great Revolt took away a crutch," she said. "It forced *human* minds to develop. Schools were started to train *human* talents."

"Bene Gesserit schools?"

She nodded. "We have two chief survivors of those ancient schools: the Bene Gesserit and the Spacing Guild. The Guild, so we think, emphasizes almost pure mathematics. Bene Gesserit performs another function."

"Politics," he said.

"Kull wahad!" the old woman said. She sent a hard glance at Jessica.

"I've not told him, Your Reverence," Jessica said.

The Reverend Mother returned her attention to Paul. "You did that on remarkably few clues," she said. "Politics indeed. The original Bene Gesserit school was directed by those who saw the need of a thread of continuity in human affairs. They saw there could be no such continuity without separating human stock from animal stock—for breeding purposes."

The old woman's words abruptly lost their special sharpness for Paul. He felt an offense against what his mother called his *instinct for rightness*. It wasn't that Reverend Mother lied to him. She obviously believed what she said. It was something deeper, something tied to his terrible purpose.

He said: "But my mother tells me many Bene Gesserit of the schools don't know their ancestry."

"The genetic lines are always in our records," she said. "Your mother knows that either she's of Bene Gesserit descent or her stock was acceptable in itself."

"Then why couldn't she know who her parents are?"

"Some do. . . . Many don't. We might, for example, have wanted to breed her to a close relative to set up a dominant in some genetic trait. We have many reasons."

Again, Paul felt the offense against rightness. He said: "You take a lot on yourselves."

The Reverend Mother stared at him, wondering: *Did I hear criticism in his voice?* "We carry a heavy burden," she said.

Paul felt himself coming more and more out of the shock of the test. He leveled a measuring stare at her, said: "You say maybe I'm the . . . Kwisatz Haderach. What's that, a human gom jabbar?"

"Paul," Jessica said. "You mustn't take that tone with—"

"I'll handle this, Jessica," the old woman said. "Now, lad, do you know about the Truthsayer drug?"

"You take it to improve your ability to detect falsehood," he said. "My mother's told me."

"Have you ever seen truthtrance?"

He shook his head. "No."

"The drug's dangerous," she said, "but it gives insight. When a Truthsayer's gifted by the drug, she can look many places in her memory—in her body's memory. We look down so many avenues of the past . . . but only feminine avenues." Her voice took on a note of sadness. "Yet, there's a place where no Truthsayer can see. We are repelled by it, terrorized. It is said a man will come one day and find in the gift of the drug his inward eye. He will look where we cannot—into both feminine and masculine pasts."

"Your Kwisatz Haderach?"

"Yes, the one who can be many places at once: the Kwisatz Haderach. Many men have tried the drug . . . so many, but none has succeeded."

"They tried and failed, all of them?"

"Oh, no." She shook her head. "They tried and died."

To attempt an understanding of Muad'Dib without understanding his mortal enemies, the Harkonnens, is to attempt seeing Truth without knowing Falsehood. It is the attempt to see the Light without knowing Darkness. It cannot be.

—FROM "MANUAL OF MUAD'DIB"
BY THE PRINCESS IRULAN

It was a relief globe of a world, partly in shadows, spinning under the impetus of a fat hand that glittered with rings. The globe sat on a free-form stand at one wall of a windowless room whose other walls presented a patchwork of multicolored scrolls, filmbooks, tapes and reels. Light glowed in the room from golden balls hanging in mobile suspensor fields.

An ellipsoid desk with a top of jade-pink petrified elacca wood stood at the center of the room. Veriform suspensor chairs ringed it, two of them occupied. In one sat a dark-haired youth of about sixteen years, round of face and with sullen eyes. The other held a slender, short man with an effeminate face.

Both youth and man stared at the globe and the man half-hidden in shadows spinning it.

A chuckle sounded beside the globe. A basso voice rumbled out of the chuckle: "There it is, Piter—the biggest mantrap in all history. And the Duke's headed into its jaws. Is it not a magnificent thing that I, the Baron Vladimir Harkonnen, do?"

"Assuredly, Baron," said the man. His voice came out tenor with a sweet, musical quality.

The fat hand descended onto the globe, stopped the spinning. Now, all eyes in the room could focus on the motionless surface and see that it was the kind of globe made for wealthy collectors or planetary governors of the Empire. It had the stamp of Imperial handicraft about it. Latitude and longitude lines were laid in with hair-fine platinum wire. The polar caps were insets of finest cloudmilk diamonds.

The fat hand moved, tracing details on the surface. "I invite you to observe," the basso voice rumbled. "Observe closely, Piter, and you, too, Feyd-Rautha, my darling: from sixty degrees north to seventy degrees south—these exquisite ripples. Their coloring: does it not remind you of sweet caramels? And nowhere do you see blue of lakes or rivers or seas. And these lovely polar caps—so small. Could anyone mistake this place? Arrakis! Truly unique. A superb setting for a unique victory."

A smile touched Piter's lips. "And to think, Baron: the Padishah Emperor believes he's given the Duke your spice planet. How poignant."

"That's a nonsensical statement," the Baron rumbled. "You say this to confuse young Feyd-Rautha, but it is not necessary to confuse my nephew."

The sullen-faced youth stirred in his chair, smoothed a wrinkle in the black leotards he wore. He sat upright as a discreet tapping sounded at the door in the wall behind him.

Piter unfolded from his chair, crossed to the door, cracked it wide enough to accept a message cylinder. He closed the door, unrolled the cylinder and scanned it. A chuckle sounded from him. Another.

"Well?" the Baron demanded.

"The fool answered us, Baron!"

"Whenever did an Atreides refuse the opportunity for a gesture?" the Baron asked. "Well, what does he say?"

"He's most uncouth, Baron. Addresses you as 'Harkonnen'—no 'Sire et Cher Cousin,' no title, nothing."

"It's a good name," the Baron growled, and his voice betrayed his impatience. "What does dear Leto say?"

"He says: 'Your offer of a meeting is refused. I have ofttimes met your treachery and this all men know.'"

"And?" the Baron asked.

"He says: 'The art of kanly still has admirers in the Empire.' He signs it: 'Duke Leto of Arrakis.'" Piter began to laugh. "Of Arrakis! Oh, my! This is almost too rich!"

"Be silent, Piter," the Baron said, and the laughter stopped as though shut off with a switch. "Kanly, is it?" the Baron asked. "Vendetta, heh? And he uses the nice old word so rich in tradition to be sure I know he means it."

"You made the peace gesture," Piter said. "The forms have been obeyed."

"For a Mentat, you talk too much, Piter," the Baron said. And he thought: *I must do away with that one soon. He has almost outlived his usefulness.* The Baron stared across the room at his Mentat assassin, seeing the feature about him that most people noticed first: the eyes, the shaded slits of blue within blue, the eyes without any white in them at all.

A grin flashed across Piter's face. It was like a mask grimace beneath those eyes likes holes. "But, Baron! Never has revenge been more beautiful. It is to see a plan of the most exquisite treachery: to *make* Leto exchange Caladan for Dune—and without alternative because the Emperor orders it. How waggish of you!"

In a cold voice, the Baron said: "You have a flux of the mouth, Piter."

"But I am happy, my Baron. Whereas you . . . you are touched by jealousy."

"Piter!"

"Ah-ah, Baron! Is it not regrettable you were unable to devise this delicious scheme by yourself?"

"Someday I will have you strangled, Piter."

"Of a certainty, Baron. Enfin! But a kind act is never lost, eh?"

"Have you been chewing verite or semuta, Piter?"

"Truth without fear surprises the Baron," Piter said. His face drew down into a caricature of a frowning mask. "Ah, hah! But you see, Baron, I know as a Mentat when you will send the executioner. You will hold back just so long as I am useful. To move sooner would be wasteful and I'm yet of much use. I know what it is you learned from that lovely Dune planet—waste not. True, Baron?"

The Baron continued to stare at Piter.

Feyd-Rautha squirmed in his chair. *These wrangling fools!* he thought. *My uncle cannot talk to his Mentat without arguing. Do they think I've nothing to do except listen to their arguments?*

"Feyd," the Baron said. "I told you to listen and learn when I invited you in here. Are you learning?"

"Yes, Uncle." The voice was carefully subservient.

"Sometimes I wonder about Piter," the Baron said. "I cause pain out of necessity, but he . . . I swear he takes a positive delight in it. For myself, I can feel pity toward the poor Duke Leto. Dr. Yueh will move against him soon, and that'll be the end of all the Atreides. But surely Leto will know whose hand directed the pliant doctor . . . and knowing that will be a terrible thing."

"Then why haven't you directed the doctor to slip a kindjal between his ribs quietly and efficiently?" Piter asked. "You talk of pity, but—"

"The Duke *must* know when I encompass his doom," the Baron said. "And the other Great Houses must learn of it. The knowledge will give them pause. I'll gain a bit more room to maneuver. The necessity is obvious, but I don't have to like it."

"Room to maneuver," Piter sneered. "Already you have the Emperor's eyes on you, Baron. You move too boldly. One day the Emperor will send a legion or two of his Sardaukar down here onto Giedi Prime and that'll be an end to the Baron Vladimir Harkonnen."

"You'd like to see that, wouldn't you, Piter?" the Baron asked. "You'd enjoy seeing the Corps of Sardaukar pillage through my cities and sack this castle. You'd truly enjoy that."

"Does the Baron need to ask?" Piter whispered.

"You should've been a Bashar of the Corps," the Baron said. "You're too interested in blood and pain. Perhaps I was too quick with my promise of the spoils of Arrakis."

Piter took five curiously mincing steps into the room, stopped directly behind Feyd-Rautha. There was a tight air of tension in the room, and the youth looked up at Piter with a worried frown.

"Do not toy with Piter, Baron," Piter said. "You promised me the Lady Jessica. You promised her to me."

"For what, Piter?" the Baron asked. "For pain?"

Piter stared at him, dragging out the silence.

Feyd-Rautha moved his suspensor chair to one side, said: "Uncle, do I have to stay? You said you'd—"

"My darling Feyd-Rautha grows impatient," the Baron said. He moved within the shadows beside the globe. "Patience, Feyd." And he turned his attention back to the Mentat. "What of the Dukeling, the child Paul, my dear Piter?"

"The trap will bring him to you, Baron," Piter muttered.

"That's not my question," the Baron said. "You'll recall that you predicted the Bene Gesserit witch would bear a daughter to the Duke. You were wrong, eh, Mentat?"

"I'm not often wrong, Baron," Piter said, and for the first time there was fear in his voice. "Give me that: I'm not often wrong. And you know yourself these Bene Gesserit bear mostly daughters. Even the Emperor's consort had produced only females."

"Uncle," said Feyd-Rautha, "you said there'd be something important here for me to—"

"Listen to my nephew," the Baron said. "He aspires to rule my Barony, yet he cannot rule himself." The Baron stirred beside the globe, a shadow among shadows. "Well then, Feyd-Rautha Harkonnen, I summoned you here hoping to teach you a bit of wisdom. Have you observed our good Mentat? You should've learned something from this exchange."

"But, Uncle—"

"A most efficient Mentat, Piter, wouldn't you say, Feyd?"

"Yes, but—"

"Ah! Indeed but! But he consumes too much spice, eats it like candy.

Look at his eyes! He might've come directly from the Arrakeen labor pool. Efficient, Piter, *but* he's still emotional and prone to passionate outbursts. Efficient, Piter, *but* he still can err."

Piter spoke in a low, sullen tone: "Did you call me in here to impair my efficiency with criticism, Baron?"

"Impair your efficiency? You know me better, Piter. I wish only for my nephew to understand the limitations of a Mentat."

"Are you already training my replacement?" Piter demanded.

"Replace *you*? Why, Piter, where could I find another Mentat with your cunning and venom?"

"The same place you found me, Baron."

"Perhaps I should at that," the Baron mused. "You do seem a bit unstable lately. And the spice you eat!"

"Are my pleasures too expensive, Baron? Do you object to them?"

"My dear Piter, your pleasures are what tie you to me. How could I object to that? I merely wish my nephew to observe this about you."

"Then I'm on display," Piter said. "Shall I dance? Shall I perform my various functions for the eminent Feyd-Rau—"

"Precisely," the Baron said. "You are on display. Now, be silent." He glanced at Feyd-Rautha, noting his nephew's lips, the full and pouting look of them, the Harkonnen genetic marker, now twisted slightly in amusement. "This is a Mentat, Feyd. It has been trained and conditioned to perform certain duties. The fact that it's encased in a human body, however, must not be overlooked. A serious drawback, that. I sometimes think the ancients with their thinking machines had the right idea."

"They were toys compared to me," Piter snarled. "You yourself, Baron, could outperform those *machines*."

"Perhaps," the Baron said. "Ah, well. . . ." He took a deep breath, belched. "Now, Piter, outline for my nephew the salient features of our campaign against the House of Atreides. Function as a Mentat for us, if you please."

"Baron, I've warned you not to trust one so young with this information. My observations of—"

"I'll be the judge of this," the Baron said. "I give you an order, Mentat. Perform one of your various functions."

"So be it," Piter said. He straightened, assuming an odd attitude of dignity—as though it were another mask, but this time clothing his entire body. "In a few days Standard, the entire household of the Duke Leto will embark on a Spacing Guild liner for Arrakis. The Guild will deposit them at the city of Arrakeen rather than at our city of Carthag. The Duke's Mentat, Thufir Hawat, will have concluded rightly that Arrakeen is easier to defend."

"Listen carefully, Feyd," the Baron said. "Observe the plans within plans within plans."

Feyd-Rautha nodded, thinking: *This is more like it. The old monster is letting me in on secret things at last. He must really mean for me to be his heir.*

"There are several tangential possibilities," Piter said. "I indicate that House Atreides will go to Arrakis. We must not, however, ignore the possibility the Duke has contracted with the Guild to remove him to a place of safety outside the System. Others in like circumstances have become renegade Houses, taking family atomics and shields and fleeing beyond the Imperium."

"The Duke's too proud a man for that," the Baron said.

"It is a possibility," Piter said. "The ultimate effect for us would be the same, however."

"No, it would not!" the Baron growled. "I must have him dead and his line ended."

"That's the high probability," Piter said. "There are certain preparations that indicate when a House is going renegade. The Duke appears to be doing none of these things."

"So," the Baron sighed. "Get on with it, Piter."

"At Arrakeen," Piter said, "the Duke and his family will occupy the Residency, lately the home of Count and Lady Fenring."

"The Ambassador to the Smugglers," the Baron chuckled.

"Ambassador to what?" Feyd-Rautha asked.

"Your uncle makes a joke," Piter said. "He calls Count Fenring Ambassador to the Smugglers, indicating the Emperor's interest in smuggling operations on Arrakis."

Feyd-Rautha turned a puzzled stare on his uncle. "Why?"

"Don't be dense, Feyd," the Baron snapped. "As long as the Guild remains effectively outside Imperial control, how could it be otherwise? How else could spies and assassins move about?"

Feyd-Rautha's mouth made a soundless "Oh-h-h-h."

"We've arranged diversions at the Residency," Piter said. "There'll be an attempt on the life of the Atreides heir—an attempt which could succeed."

"Piter," the Baron rumbled, "you indicated—"

"I indicated accidents can happen," Piter said. "And the attempt must appear valid."

"Ah, but the lad has such a sweet young body," the Baron said. "Of course, he's potentially more dangerous than the father . . . with that witch mother training him. Accursed woman! Ah, well, please continue, Piter."

"Hawat will have divined that we have an agent planted on him," Piter said. "The obvious suspect is Dr. Yueh, who is indeed our agent. But Hawat has investigated and found that our doctor is a Suk School graduate with Imperial Conditioning—supposedly safe enough to minister even to the Emperor. Great store is set on Imperial Conditioning. It's assumed that ultimate conditioning cannot be removed without killing the subject. However, as someone once observed, given the right lever you can move a planet. We found the lever that moved the doctor."

"How?" Feyd-Rautha asked. He found this a fascinating subject. *Everyone* knew you couldn't subvert Imperial Conditioning!

"Another time," the Baron said. "Continue, Piter."

"In place of Yueh," Piter said, "we'll drag a most interesting suspect across Hawat's path. The very audacity of this suspect will recommend her to Hawat's attention."

"Her?" Feyd-Rautha asked.

"The Lady Jessica herself," the Baron said.

"Is it not sublime?" Piter asked. "Hawat's mind will be so filled with this prospect it'll impair his function as a Mentat. He may even try to kill her." Piter frowned, then: "But I don't think he'll be able to carry it off."

"You don't want him to, eh?" the Baron asked.

"Don't distract me," Piter said. "While Hawat's occupied with the Lady Jessica, we'll divert him further with uprisings in a few garrison towns and the like. These will be put down. The Duke must believe he's gaining a measure of security. Then, when the moment is ripe, we'll signal Yueh and move in with our major force . . . ah. . . ."

"Go ahead, tell him all of it," the Baron said.

"We'll move in strengthened by two legions of Sardaukar disguised in Harkonnen livery."

"Sardaukar!" Feyd-Rautha breathed. His mind focused on the dread Imperial troops, the killers without mercy, the soldier-fanatics of the Padishah Emperor.

"You see how I trust you, Feyd," the Baron said. "No hint of this must ever reach another Great House, else the Landsraad might unite against the Imperial House and there'd be chaos."

"The main point," Piter said, "is this: since House Harkonnen is being used to do the Imperial dirty work, we've gained a true advantage. It's a dangerous advantage, to be sure, but if used cautiously, will bring House Harkonnen greater wealth than that of any other House in the Imperium."

"You have no idea how much wealth is involved, Feyd," the Baron said. "Not in your wildest imaginings. To begin, we'll have an irrevocable directorship in the CHOAM Company."

Feyd-Rautha nodded. Wealth was the thing. CHOAM was the key to wealth, each noble House dipping from the company's coffers whatever it could under the power of the directorships. Those CHOAM directorships—they were the real evidence of political power in the Imperium, passing with the shifts of voting strength within the Landsraad as it balanced itself against the Emperor and *his* supporters.

"The Duke Leto," Piter said, "may attempt to flee to the new Fremen scum along the desert's edge. Or he may try to send his family into that imagined security. But that path is blocked by one of His Majesty's agents—the planetary ecologist. You may remember him—Kynes."

"Feyd remembers him," the Baron said. "Get on with it."

"You do not drool very prettily, Baron," Piter said.

"Get on with it, I command you!" the Baron roared.

Piter shrugged. "If matters go as planned," he said, "House Harkonnen will have a subfief on Arrakis within a Standard year. Your uncle will have dispensation of that fief. His own *personal* agent will rule on Arrakis."

"More profits," Feyd-Rautha said.

"Indeed," the Baron said. And he thought: *It's only just. We're the ones who tamed Arrakis . . . except for the few mongrel Fremen hiding in the skirts of the desert . . . and some tame smugglers bound to the planet almost as tightly as the native labor pool.*

"And the Great Houses will know that the Baron has destroyed the Atreides," Piter said. "They will know."

"They will know," the Baron breathed.

"Loveliest of all," Piter said, "is that the Duke will know, too. He knows now. He can already feel the trap."

"It's true the Duke knows," the Baron said, and his voice held a note of sadness. "He could not help but know . . . more's the pity."

The Baron moved out and away from the globe of Arrakis. As he emerged from the shadows, his figure took on dimension—grossly and immensely fat. And with subtle bulges beneath folds of his dark robes to reveal that all this fat was sustained partly by portable suspensors harnessed to his flesh. He might weigh two hundred Standard kilos in actuality, but his feet would carry no more than fifty of them.

"I am hungry," the Baron rumbled, and he rubbed his protruding lips with a beringed hand, stared down at Feyd-Rautha through fat-enfolded eyes. "Send for food, my darling. We will eat before we retire."

Thus spoke St. Alia-of-the-Knife: "The Reverend Mother must combine the seductive wiles of a courtesan with the untouchable majesty of a virgin goddess, holding these attributes in tension so long as the powers of her youth endure. For when youth and beauty have gone, she will find that the *place-between*, once occupied by tension, has become a wellspring of cunning and resourcefulness."

—FROM "MUAD'DIB, FAMILY COMMENTARIES"
BY THE PRINCESS IRULAN

"Well, Jessica, what have you to say for yourself?" asked the Reverend Mother.

It was near sunset at Castle Caladan on the day of Paul's ordeal. The two women were alone in Jessica's morning room while Paul waited in the adjoining soundproofed Meditation Chamber.

Jessica stood facing the south windows. She saw and yet did not see the evening's banked colors across meadow and river. She heard and yet did not hear the Reverend Mother's question.

There had been another ordeal once—so many years ago. A skinny girl with hair the color of bronze, her body tortured by the winds of puberty, had entered the study of the Reverend Mother Gaius Helen Mohiam, Proctor Superior of the Bene Gesserit school on Wallach IX. Jessica looked down at her right hand, flexed the fingers, remembering the pain, the terror, the anger.

"Poor Paul," she whispered.

"I asked you a question, Jessica!" The old woman's voice was snappish, demanding.

"What? Oh. . . ." Jessica tore her attention away from the past, faced the Reverend Mother, who sat with back to the stone wall between the two west windows. "What do you want me to say?"

"What do I want you to say? What do I want you to say?" The old voice carried a tone of cruel mimicry.

"So I had a son!" Jessica flared. And she knew she was being goaded into this anger deliberately.

"You were told to bear only daughters to the Atreides."

"It meant so much to him," Jessica pleaded.

"And you in your pride thought you could produce the Kwisatz Haderach!"

Jessica lifted her chin. "I sensed the possibility."

"You thought only of your Duke's desire for a son," the old woman snapped. "And his desires don't figure in this. An Atreides daughter could've been wed to a Harkonnen heir and sealed the breach. You've hopelessly complicated matters. We may lose both bloodlines now."

"You're not infallible," Jessica said. She braved the steady stare from the old eyes.

Presently, the old woman muttered: "What's done is done."

"I vowed never to regret my decision," Jessica said.

"How noble," the Reverend Mother sneered. "No regrets. We shall see when you're a fugitive with a price on your head and every man's hand turned against you to seek your life and the life of your son."

Jessica paled. "Is there no alternative?"

"Alternative? A Bene Gesserit should ask that?"

"I ask only what you see in the future with your superior abilities."

"I see in the future what I've seen in the past. You well know the pattern of our affairs, Jessica. The race knows its own mortality and fears stagnation of its heredity. It's in the bloodstream—the urge to mingle genetic strains without plan. The Imperium, the CHOAM Company, all the Great Houses, they are but bits of flotsam in the path of the flood."

"CHOAM," Jessica muttered. "I suppose it's already decided how they'll redivide the spoils of Arrakis."

"What is CHOAM but the weather vane of our times," the old woman said. "The Emperor and his friends now command fifty-nine point six-five per cent of the CHOAM directorship's votes. Certainly they smell profits, and likely as others smell those same profits his voting strength will increase. This is the pattern of history, girl."

"That's certainly what I need right now," Jessica said. "A review of history."

"Don't be facetious, girl! You know as well as I do what forces surround us. We've a three-point civilization: the Imperial Household balanced against the Federated Great Houses of the Landsraad, and between them, the Guild with its damnable monopoly on interstellar transport. In politics, the tripod is the most unstable of all structures. It'd be bad enough without the complication of a feudal trade culture which turns its back on most science."

Jessica spoke bitterly: "Chips in the path of the flood—and this chip here, this is the Duke Leto, and this one's his son, and this one's—"

"Oh, shut up, girl. You entered this with full knowledge of the delicate edge you walked."

"'I am Bene Gesserit: I exist only to serve,'" Jessica quoted.

"Truth," the old woman said. "And all we can hope for now is to prevent this from erupting into general conflagration, to salvage what we can of the key bloodlines."

Jessica closed her eyes, feeling tears press out beneath the lids. She fought down the inner trembling, the outer trembling, the uneven breathing, the ragged pulse, the sweating of the palms. Presently, she said, "I'll pay for my own mistake."

"And your son will pay with you."

"I'll shield him as well as I'm able."

"Shield!" the old woman snapped. "You well know the weakness there! Shield your son too much, Jessica, and he'll not grow strong enough to fulfill *any* destiny."

Jessica turned away, looked out the window at the gathering darkness. "Is it really that terrible, this planet of Arrakis?"

"Bad enough, but not all bad. The Missionaria Protectiva has been in there and softened it up somewhat." The Reverend Mother heaved herself to her feet, straightened a fold in her gown. "Call the boy in here. I must be leaving soon."

"Must you?"

The old woman's voice softened. "Jessica, girl, I wish I could stand in your place and take your sufferings. But each of us must make her own path."

"I know."

"You're as dear to me as any of my own daughters, but I cannot let that interfere with duty."

"I understand . . . the necessity."

"What you did, Jessica, and why you did it—we both know. But kindness forces me to tell you there's little chance your lad will be the Bene Gesserit Totality. You mustn't let yourself hope too much."

Jessica shook tears from the corners of her eyes. It was an angry gesture. "You make me feel like a little girl again—reciting my first lesson." She forced the words out: "'Humans must never submit to animals.'" A dry sob shook her. In a low voice, she said: "I've been so lonely."

"It should be one of the tests," the old woman said. "Humans are almost always lonely. Now summon the boy. He's had a long, frightening day. But he's had time to think and remember, and I must ask the other questions about these dreams of his."

Jessica nodded, went to the door of the Meditation Chamber, opened it. "Paul, come in now, please."

Paul emerged with a stubborn slowness. He stared at his mother as though she were a stranger. Wariness veiled his eyes when he glanced at the Reverend Mother, but this time he nodded to her, the nod one gives an equal. He heard his mother close the door behind him.

"Young man," the old woman said, "let's return to this dream business."

"What do you want?"

"Do you dream every night?"

"Not dreams worth remembering. I can remember every dream, but some are worth remembering and some aren't."

"How do you know the difference?"

"I just know it."

The old woman glanced at Jessica, back to Paul. "What did you dream last night? Was it worth remembering?"

"Yes." Paul closed his eyes. "I dreamed a cavern . . . and water . . . and a girl there—very skinny with big eyes. Her eyes are all blue, no whites in them. I talk to her and tell her about you, about seeing the Reverend Mother on Caladan." Paul opened his eyes.

"And the thing you tell this strange girl about seeing me, did it happen today?"

Paul thought about this, then: "Yes. I tell the girl you came and put a stamp of strangeness on me."

"Stamp of strangeness," the old woman breathed, and again she shot a glance at Jessica, returned her attention to Paul. "Tell me truly now, Paul, do you often have dreams of things that happen afterward exactly as you dreamed them?"

"Yes. And I've dreamed about that girl before."

"Oh? You know her?"

"I will know her."

"Tell me about her."

Again, Paul closed his eyes. "We're in a little place in some rocks where it's sheltered. It's almost night, but it's hot and I can see patches of sand out of an opening in the rocks. We're . . . waiting for something . . . for me to go meet some people. And she's frightened but trying to hide it from me, and I'm excited. And she says: 'Tell me about the waters of your homeworld, Usul.'" Paul opened his eyes. "Isn't that strange? My homeworld's Caladan. I've never even heard of a planet called Usul."

"Is there more to this dream?" Jessica prompted.

"Yes. But maybe she was calling *me* Usul," Paul said. "I just thought of that." Again, he closed his eyes. "She asks me to tell her about the waters. And I take her hand. And I say I'll tell her a poem. And I tell her the poem, but I have to explain some of the words—like beach and surf and seaweed and seagulls."

"What poem?" the Reverend Mother asked.

Paul opened his eyes. "It's just one of Gurney Halleck's tone poems for sad times."

Behind Paul, Jessica began to recite:

> *"I remember salt smoke from a beach fire*
> *And shadows under the pines—*
> *Solid, clean . . . fixed—*
> *Seagulls perched at the tip of land,*
> *White upon green . . .*
> *And a wind comes through the pines*
> *To sway the shadows;*
> *The seagulls spread their wings,*
> *Lift*
> *And fill the sky with screeches.*
> *And I hear the wind*
> *Blowing across our beach,*
> *And the surf,*
> *And I see that our fire*
> *Has scorched the seaweed."*

"That's the one," Paul said.

The old woman stared at Paul, then: "Young man, as a Proctor of the Bene Gesserit, I seek the Kwisatz Haderach, the male who truly can become one of us. Your mother sees this possibility in you, but she sees with the eyes of a mother. Possibility I see, too, but no more."

She fell silent and Paul saw that she wanted him to speak. He waited her out.

Presently, she said: "As you will, then. You've depths in you; that I'll grant."

"May I go now?" he asked.

"Don't you want to hear what the Reverend Mother can tell you about the Kwisatz Haderach?" Jessica asked.

"She said those who tried for it died."

"But I can help you with a few hints at why they failed," the Reverend Mother said.

She talks of hints, Paul thought. *She doesn't really know anything.* And he said: "Hint then."

"And be damned to me?" She smiled wryly, a crisscross of wrinkles in the old face. "Very well: 'That which submits rules.'"

He felt astonishment: she was talking about such elementary things as tension within meaning. Did she think his mother had taught him nothing at all?

"That's a hint?" he asked.

"We're not here to bandy words or quibble over their meaning," the old woman said. "The willow submits to the wind and prospers until one day it is many willows—a wall against the wind. This is the willow's purpose."

Paul stared at her. She said *purpose* and he felt the word buffet him, reinfecting him with terrible purpose. He experienced a sudden anger at her: fatuous old witch with her mouth full of platitudes.

"You think I could be this Kwisatz Haderach," he said. "You talk about me, but you haven't said one thing about what we can do to help my father. I've heard you talking to my mother. You talk as though my father were dead. Well, he isn't!"

"If there were a thing to be done for him, we'd have done it," the old woman growled. "We may be able to salvage you. Doubtful, but possible. But for your father, nothing. When you've learned to accept that as a fact, you've learned a *real* Bene Gesserit lesson."

Paul saw how the words shook his mother. He glared at the old woman. How could she say such a thing about his father? What made her so sure? His mind seethed with resentment.

The Reverend Mother looked at Jessica. "You've been training him in the Way—I've seen the signs of it. I'd have done the same in your shoes and devil take the Rules."

Jessica nodded.

"Now, I caution you," said the old woman, "to ignore the regular order of training. His own safety requires the Voice. He already has a good start in it, but we both know how much more he needs . . . and that desperately." She stepped close to Paul, stared down at him. "Goodbye, young human. I hope you make it. But if you don't—well, we shall yet succeed."

Once more she looked at Jessica. A flicker sign of understanding passed between them. Then the old woman swept from the room, her robes hissing, with not another backward glance. The room and its occupants already were shut from her thoughts.

But Jessica had caught one glimpse of the Reverend Mother's face as she turned away. There had been tears on the seamed cheeks. The tears were more unnerving than any other word or sign that had passed between them this day.

You have read that Muad'Dib had no playmates his own age on Caladan. The dangers were too great. But Muad'Dib did have wonderful companion-teachers. There was Gurney Halleck, the troubadour-warrior. You will sing some of Gurney's songs as you read along in this book. There was Thufir Hawat, the old Mentat Master of Assassins, who struck fear even into the heart of the Padishah Emperor. There were Duncan Idaho, the Swordmaster of the Ginaz; Dr. Wellington Yueh, a name black in treachery but bright in knowledge; the Lady Jessica, who guided her son in the Bene Gesserit Way, and—of course—the Duke Leto, whose qualities as a father have long been overlooked.

—FROM "A CHILD'S HISTORY OF MUAD'DIB"
BY THE PRINCESS IRULAN

Thufir Hawat slipped into the training room of Castle Caladan, closed the door softly. He stood there a moment, feeling old and tired and storm-leathered. His left leg ached where it had been slashed once in the service of the Old Duke.

Three generations of them now, he thought.

He stared across the big room bright with the light of noon pouring through the skylights, saw the boy seated with back to the door, intent on papers and charts spread across an ell table.

How many times must I tell that lad never to settle himself with his back to a door? Hawat cleared his throat.

Paul remained bent over his studies.

A cloud shadow passed over the skylights. Again, Hawat cleared his throat.

Paul straightened, spoke without turning: "I know. I'm sitting with my back to a door."

Hawat suppressed a smile, strode across the room.

Paul looked up at the grizzled old man who stopped at a corner of the table. Hawat's eyes were two pools of alertness in a dark and deeply seamed face.

"I heard you coming down the hall," Paul said. "And I heard you open the door."

"The sounds I make could be imitated."

"I'd know the difference."

He might at that, Hawat thought. *That witch mother of his is giving him the deep training, certainly. I wonder what her precious school thinks of that? Maybe that's why they sent the old Proctor here—to whip our dear Lady Jessica into line.*

Hawat pulled up a chair across from Paul, sat down facing the door. He did it pointedly, leaned back and studied the room. It struck him as an odd place suddenly, a stranger-place with most of its hardware already gone off to Arrakis. A training table remained, and a fencing mirror with its crystal prisms quiescent, the target dummy beside it patched and padded, looking like an ancient foot soldier maimed and battered in the wars.

There stand I, Hawat thought.

"Thufir, what're you thinking?" Paul asked.

Hawat looked at the boy. "I was thinking we'll all be out of here soon and likely never see the place again."

"Does that make you sad?"

"Sad? Nonsense! Parting with friends is a sadness. A place is only a place." He glanced at the charts on the table. "And Arrakis is just another place."

"Did my father send you up to test me?"

Hawat scowled—the boy had such observing ways about him. He nodded. "You're thinking it'd have been nicer if he'd come up himself, but you must know how busy he is. He'll be along later."

"I've been studying about the storms on Arrakis."

"The storms. I see."

"They sound pretty bad."

"That's too cautious a word: *bad*. Those storms build up across six or seven thousand kilometers of flatlands, feed on anything that can give them a push—coriolis force, other storms, anything that has an ounce of energy in it. They can blow up to seven hundred kilometers an hour, loaded with everything loose that's in their way—sand, dust, everything. They can eat flesh off bones and etch the bones to slivers."

"Why don't they have weather control?"

"Arrakis has special problems, costs are higher, and there'd be maintenance and the like. The Guild wants a dreadful high price for satellite control and your father's House isn't one of the big rich ones, lad. You know that."

"Have you ever seen the Fremen?"

The lad's mind is darting all over today, Hawat thought.

"Like as not I have seen them," he said. "There's little to tell them from the folk of the graben and sink. They all wear those great flowing robes. And they stink to heaven in any closed space. It's from those suits they wear—call them 'stillsuits'—that reclaim the body's own water."

Paul swallowed, suddenly aware of the moisture in his mouth, remembering a dream of thirst. That people could want so for water they had to recycle their body moisture struck him with a feeling of desolation. "Water's precious there," he said.

Hawat nodded, thinking: *Perhaps I'm doing it, getting across to him the importance of this planet as an enemy. It's madness to go in there without that caution in our minds.*

Paul looked up at the skylight, aware that it had begun to rain. He saw the spreading wetness on the gray meta-glass. "Water," he said.

"You'll learn a great concern for water," Hawat said. "As the Duke's son you'll never want for it, but you'll see the pressures of thirst all around you."

Paul wet his lips with his tongue, thinking back to the day a week ago and the ordeal with the Reverend Mother. She, too, had said something about water starvation.

"You'll learn about the Funeral Plains," she'd said, "about the wilderness that is empty, the wasteland where nothing lives except the spice and the sandworms. You'll stain your eyepits to reduce the sun glare. Shelter will mean a hollow out of the wind and hidden from view. You'll ride upon your own two feet without 'thopter or ground car or mount."

And Paul had been caught more by her tone—singsong and wavering—than by her words.

"When you live upon Arrakis," she had said, "khala, the land is empty. The moons will be your friends, the sun your enemy."

Paul had sensed his mother come up beside him away from her post guarding the door. She had looked at the Reverend Mother and asked: "Do you see no hope, Your Reverence?"

"Not for the father." And the old woman had waved Jessica to silence, looked down at Paul. "Grave this on your memory, lad: A world is supported by four things. . . ." She held up four big-knuckled fingers. ". . . the learning of the wise, the justice of the great, the prayers of the righteous and the valor of the brave. But all of these are as nothing. . . ." She closed her fingers into a fist. ". . . without a ruler who knows the art of ruling. Make *that* the science of your tradition!"

A week had passed since that day with the Reverend Mother. Her words were only now beginning to come into full register. Now, sitting in the training room with Thufir Hawat, Paul felt a sharp pang of fear. He looked across at the Mentat's puzzled frown.

"Where were you woolgathering that time?" Hawat asked.

"Did you meet the Reverend Mother?"

"That Truthsayer witch from the Imperium?" Hawat's eyes quickened with interest. "I met her."

"She. . . ." Paul hesitated, found that he couldn't tell Hawat about the ordeal. The inhibitions went deep.

"Yes? What did she?"

Paul took two deep breaths. "She said a thing." He closed his eyes, calling up the words, and when he spoke his voice unconsciously took on some of the old woman's tone: "'You, Paul Atreides, descendant of kings, son of a Duke, you must learn to rule. It's something none of your ancestors learned.'" Paul opened his eyes, said: "That made me angry and I said my father rules an entire planet. And she said, 'He's losing it.' And I said my father was getting a richer planet. And she said, 'He'll lose that one, too.' And I wanted to run and warn my father, but she said he'd already been warned—by you, by Mother, by many people."

"True enough," Hawat muttered.

"Then why're we going?" Paul demanded.

"Because the Emperor ordered it. And because there's hope in spite of what that witch-spy said. What else spouted from this ancient fountain of wisdom?"

Paul looked down at his right hand clenched into a fist beneath the table. Slowly, he willed the muscles to relax. *She put some kind of hold on me*, he thought. *How?*

"She asked me to tell her what it is to rule," Paul said. "And I said that one commands. And she said I had some unlearning to do."

She hit a mark there right enough, Hawat thought. He nodded for Paul to continue.

"She said a ruler must learn to persuade and not to compel. She said he must lay the best coffee hearth to attract the finest men."

"How'd she figure your father attracted men like Duncan and Gurney?" Hawat asked.

Paul shrugged. "Then she said a good ruler has to learn his world's language, that it's different for every world. And I thought she meant they didn't speak Galach on Arrakis, but she said that wasn't it at all. She said she meant the language of the rocks and growing things, the language you don't hear just with your ears. And I said that's what Dr. Yueh calls the Mystery of Life."

Hawat chuckled. "How'd that sit with her?"

"I think she got mad. She said the mystery of life isn't a problem to solve, but a reality to experience. So I quoted the First Law of Mentat at her: 'A process cannot be understood by stopping it. Understanding must move with the flow of the process, must join it and flow with it.' That seemed to satisfy her."

He seems to be getting over it, Hawat thought, *but that old witch frightened him. Why did she do it?*

"Thufir," Paul said, "will Arrakis be as bad as she said?"

"Nothing could be that bad," Hawat said and forced a smile. "Take those Fremen, for example, the renegade people of the desert. By first-approximation analysis, I can tell you there're many, many more of them than the Imperium suspects. People live there, lad: a great many people, and. . . ." Hawat put a sinewy finger beside his eye. ". . . they hate Harkonnens with a bloody passion. You must not breathe a word of this, lad. I tell you only as your father's helper."

"My father has told me of Salusa Secundus," Paul said. "Do you know, Thufir, it sounds much like Arrakis . . . perhaps not quite as bad, but much like it."

"We do not really know of Salusa Secundus today," Hawat said. "Only what it was like long ago . . . mostly. But what is known—you're right on that score."

"Will the Fremen help us?"

"It's a possibility." Hawat stood up. "I leave today for Arrakis. Meanwhile, you take care of yourself for an old man who's fond of you, heh? Come around here like the good lad and sit facing the door. It's not that I think there's any danger in the castle; it's just a habit I want you to form."

Paul got to his feet, moved around the table. "You're going today?"

"Today it is, and you'll be following tomorrow. Next time we meet it'll be on the soil of your new world." He gripped Paul's right arm at the bicep. "Keep your knife arm free, heh? And your shield at full charge." He released the arm, patted Paul's shoulder, whirled and strode quickly to the door.

"Thufir!" Paul called.

Hawat turned, standing in the open doorway.

"Don't sit with your back to any doors," Paul said.

A grin spread across the seamed old face. "That I won't, lad. Depend on it." And he was gone, shutting the door softly behind.

Paul sat down where Hawat had been, straightened the papers. *One more day here*, he thought. He looked around the room. *We're leaving.* The idea of departure was suddenly more real to him than it had ever been before. He recalled another thing the old woman had said about a world being the sum of many things—the people, the dirt, the growing things, the moons, the tides, the suns—the unknown sum called *nature*, a vague summation without any sense of the *now*. And he wondered: *What is the now?*

The door across from Paul banged open and an ugly lump of a man lurched through it preceded by a handful of weapons.

"Well, Gurney Halleck," Paul called, "are you the new weapons master?"

Halleck kicked the door shut with one heel. "You'd rather I came to play games, I know," he said. He glanced around the room, noting that Hawat's men already had been over it, checking, making it safe for a duke's heir. The subtle code signs were all around.

Paul watched the rolling, ugly man set himself back in motion, veer toward the training table with the load of weapons, saw the nine-string baliset slung over Gurney's shoulder with the multipick woven through the strings near the head of the fingerboard.

Halleck dropped the weapons on the exercise table, lined them up—the rapiers, the bodkins, the kindjals, the slow-pellet stunners, the shield belts. The inkvine scar along his jawline writhed as he turned, casting a smile across the room.

"So you don't even have a good morning for me, you young imp," Halleck said. "And what barb did you sink in old Hawat? He passed me in the hall like a man running to his enemy's funeral."

Paul grinned. Of all his father's men, he liked Gurney Halleck best, knew the man's moods and deviltry, his *humors*, and thought of him more as a friend than as a hired sword.

Halleck swung the baliset off his shoulder, began tuning it. "If y' won't talk, y' won't," he said.

Paul stood, advanced across the room, calling out: "Well, Gurney, do we come prepared for music when it's fighting time?"

"So it's sass for our elders today," Halleck said. He tried a chord on the instrument, nodded.

"Where's Duncan Idaho?" Paul asked. "Isn't he supposed to be teaching me weaponry?"

"Duncan's gone to lead the second wave onto Arrakis," Halleck said. "All you have left is poor Gurney who's fresh out of fight and spoiling for music." He struck another chord, listened to it, smiled. "And it was decided in council that you being such a poor fighter we'd best teach you the music trade so's you won't waste your life entire."

"Maybe you'd better sing me a lay then," Paul said. "I want to be sure how *not* to do it."

"Ah-h-h, hah!" Gurney laughed, and he swung into "Galacian Girls," his multipick a blur over the strings as he sang:

> *"Oh-h-h, the Galacian girls*
> *Will do it for pearls,*
> *And the Arrakeen for water!*
> *But if you desire dames*
> *Like consuming flames,*
> *Try a Caladanin daughter!"*

"Not bad for such a poor hand with the pick," Paul said, "but if my mother heard you singing a bawdy like that in the castle, she'd have your ears on the outer wall for decoration."

Gurney pulled at his left ear. "Poor decoration, too, they having been bruised so much listening at keyholes while a young lad I know practiced some strange ditties on his baliset."

"So you've forgotten what it's like to find sand in your bed," Paul said. He pulled a shield belt from the table, buckled it fast around his waist. "Then, let's fight!"

Halleck's eyes went wide in mock surprise. "So! It was your wicked hand did that deed! Guard yourself today, young Master—guard yourself." He grabbed up a rapier, laced the air with it. "I'm a hellfiend out for revenge!"

Paul lifted the companion rapier, bent it in his hands, stood in the *aguile*, one foot forward. He let his manner go solemn in a comic imitation of Dr. Yueh.

"What a dolt my father sends me for weaponry," Paul intoned. "This doltish Gurney Halleck has forgotten the first lesson for a fighting man armed and shielded." Paul snapped the force button at his waist, felt the crinkled-skin tingling of the defensive field at his forehead and down his back, heard external sounds take on characteristic shield-filtered flatness. "In shield fighting, one moves fast on defense, slow on attack," Paul said. "Attack has the sole purpose of tricking the opponent into a misstep, setting him up for the attack sinister. The shield turns the fast blow, admits the slow kindjal!" Paul snapped up the rapier, feinted fast and whipped it back for a slow thrust timed to enter a shield's mindless defenses.

Halleck watched the action, turned at the last minute to let the blunted blade pass his chest. "Speed, excellent," he said. "But you were wide open for an underhanded counter with a slip-tip."

Paul stepped back, chagrined.

"I should whap your backside for such carelessness," Halleck said. He lifted a naked kindjal from the table and held it up. "This in the hand of an enemy can let out your life's blood! You're an apt pupil, none better, but I've warned you that not even in play do you let a man inside your guard with death in his hand."

"I guess I'm not in the mood for it today," Paul said.

"Mood?" Halleck's voice betrayed his outrage even through the shield's filtering. "What has *mood* to do with it? You fight when the necessity arises—no matter the mood! Mood's a thing for cattle or making love or playing the baliset. It's not for fighting."

"I'm sorry, Gurney."

"You're not sorry enough!"

Halleck activated his own shield, crouched with kindjal outthrust in left hand, the rapier poised high in his right. "Now I say guard yourself for true!" He leaped high to one side, then forward, pressing a furious attack.

Paul fell back, parrying. He felt the field crackling as shield edges touched and repelled each other, sensed the electric tingling of the contact along his skin. *What's gotten into Gurney?* he asked himself. *He's not faking this!* Paul moved his left hand, dropped his bodkin into his palm from its wrist sheath.

"You see a need for an extra blade, eh?" Halleck grunted.

Is this betrayal? Paul wondered. *Surely not Gurney!*

Around the room they fought—thrust and parry, feint and counterfeint. The air within their shield bubbles grew stale from the demands on it that the slow interchange along barrier edges could not replenish. With each new shield contact, the smell of ozone grew stronger.

Paul continued to back, but now he directed his retreat toward the exercise table. *If I can turn him beside the table, I'll show him a trick,* Paul thought. *One more step, Gurney.*

Halleck took the step.

Paul directed a parry downward, turned, saw Halleck's rapier catch against the table's edge. Paul flung himself aside, thrust high with rapier and came in across Halleck's neckline with the bodkin. He stopped the blade an inch from the jugular.

"Is this what you seek?" Paul whispered.

"Look down, lad," Gurney panted.

Paul obeyed, saw Halleck's kindjal thrust under the table's edge, the tip almost touching Paul's groin.

"We'd have joined each other in death," Halleck said. "But I'll admit you fought some better when pressed to it. You seemed to get the *mood*." And he grinned wolfishly, the inkvine scar rippling along his jaw.

"The way you came at me," Paul said. "Would you really have drawn my blood?"

Halleck withdrew the kindjal, straightened. "If you'd fought one whit beneath your abilities, I'd have scratched you a good one, a scar you'd remember. I'll not have my favorite pupil fall to the first Harkonnen tramp who happens along."

Paul deactivated his shield, leaned on the table to catch his breath. "I deserved that, Gurney. But it would've angered my father if you'd hurt me. I'll not have you punished for my failing."

"As to that," Halleck said, "it was my failing, too. And you needn't worry about a training scar or two. You're lucky you have so few. As to your father—the Duke'd punish me only if I failed to make a first-class fighting man out of you. And I'd have been failing there if I hadn't explained the fallacy in this *mood* thing you've suddenly developed."

Paul straightened, slipped his bodkin back into its wrist sheath.

"It's not exactly play we do here," Halleck said.

Paul nodded. He felt a sense of wonder at the uncharacteristic seriousness in Halleck's manner, the sobering intensity. He looked at the beet-colored inkvine scar on the man's jaw, remembering the story of how it had been put there by Beast Rabban in a Harkonnen slave pit on Giedi Prime. And Paul felt a sudden shame that he had doubted Halleck even for an instant. It occurred to Paul, then, that the making of Halleck's scar had been accompanied by pain—a pain as intense, perhaps, as that inflicted by a Reverend Mother. He thrust this thought aside; it chilled their world.

"I guess I did hope for some play today," Paul said. "Things are so serious around here lately."

Halleck turned away to hide his emotions. Something burned in his eyes. There was pain in him—like a blister, all that was left of some lost yesterday that Time had pruned off him.

How soon this child must assume his manhood, Halleck thought. *How soon he must read that form within his mind, that contract of brutal caution, to enter the necessary fact on the necessary line: "Please list your next of kin."*

Halleck spoke without turning: "I sensed the play in you, lad, and I'd like nothing better than to join in it. But this no longer can be play. Tomorrow we go to Arrakis. Arrakis is real. The Harkonnens are real."

Paul touched his forehead with his rapier blade held vertical.

Halleck turned, saw the salute and acknowledged it with a nod. He gestured to the practice dummy. "Now, we'll work on your timing. Let me see you catch that thing sinister. I'll control it from over here where I can have a full view of the action. And I warn you I'll be trying new counters today. There's a warning you'd not get from a real enemy."

Paul stretched up on his toes to relieve his muscles. He felt solemn with the sudden realization that his life had become filled with swift changes. He crossed to the dummy, slapped the switch on its chest with his rapier tip and felt the defensive field forcing his blade away.

"En garde!" Halleck called, and the dummy pressed the attack.

Paul activated his shield, parried and countered.

Halleck watched as he manipulated the controls. His mind seemed to be in two parts: one alert to the needs of the training fight, and the other wandering in fly-buzz.

I'm the well-trained fruit tree, he thought. *Full of well-trained feelings and abilities and all of them grafted onto me—all bearing for someone else to pick.*

For some reason, he recalled his younger sister, her elfin face so clear in his mind. But she was dead now—in a pleasure house for Harkonnen troops. She had loved pansies . . . or was it daisies? He couldn't remember. It bothered him that he couldn't remember.

Paul countered a slow swing of the dummy, brought up his left hand *entretisser*.

The clever little devil! Halleck thought, intent now on Paul's interweaving hand motions. *He's been practicing and studying on his own. That's not Duncan style, and it's certainly nothing I've taught him.*

This thought only added to Halleck's sadness. *I'm infected by mood*, he thought. And he began to wonder about Paul, if the boy ever listened fearfully to his pillow throbbing in the night.

"If wishes were fishes we'd all cast nets," he murmured.

It was his mother's expression and he always used it when he felt the blackness of tomorrow on him. Then he thought what an odd expression that was to be taking to a planet that had never known seas or fishes.

YUEH (yü´ē), Wellington (weling-tun), Stdrd 10,082–10,191; medical doctor of the Suk School (grd Stdrd 10,112); md: Wanna Marcus, B.G. (Stdrd 10,092–10,186?); chiefly noted as betrayer of Duke Leto Atreides. (Cf: Bibliography, Appendix VII Imperial Conditioning and Betrayal, The.)

—FROM "DICTIONARY OF MUAD'DIB"
BY THE PRINCESS IRULAN

Although he heard Dr. Yueh enter the training room, noting the stiff deliberation of the man's pace, Paul remained stretched out face down on the exercise table where the masseuse had left him. He felt deliciously relaxed after the workout with Gurney Halleck.

"You do look comfortable," said Yueh in his calm, high-pitched voice.

Paul raised his head, saw the man's stick figure standing several paces away, took in at a glance the wrinkled black clothing, the square block of a head with purple lips and drooping mustache, the diamond tattoo of Imperial Conditioning on his forehead, the long black hair caught in the Suk School's silver ring at the left shoulder.

"You'll be happy to hear we haven't time for regular lessons today," Yueh said. "Your father will be along presently."

Paul sat up.

"However, I've arranged for you to have a filmbook viewer and several lessons during the crossing to Arrakis."

"Oh."

Paul began pulling on his clothes. He felt excitement that his father would be coming. They had spent so little time together since the Emperor's command to take over the fief of Arrakis.

Yueh crossed to the ell table, thinking: *How the boy has filled out these past few months. Such a waste! Oh, such a sad waste.* And he reminded himself: *I must not falter. What I do is done to be certain my Wanna no longer can be hurt by the Harkonnen beasts.*

Paul joined him at the table, buttoning his jacket. "What'll I be studying on the way across?"

"Ah-h-h, the terranic life forms of Arrakis. The planet seems to have opened its arms to certain terranic life forms. It's not clear how. I must seek out the planetary ecologist when we arrive—a Dr. Kynes—and offer my help in the investigation."

And Yueh thought: *What am I saying? I play the hypocrite even with myself.*

"Will there be something on the Fremen?" Paul asked.

"The Fremen?" Yueh drummed his fingers on the table, caught Paul staring at the nervous motion, withdrew his hand.

"Maybe you have something on the whole Arrakeen population," Paul said.

"Yes, to be sure," Yueh said. "There are two general separations of the people—Fremen, they are one group, and the others are the people of the graben, the sink, and the pan. There's some intermarriage, I'm told. The women of pan and sink villages prefer Fremen husbands; their men prefer Fremen wives. They have a saying: 'Polish comes from the cities; wisdom from the desert.'"

"Do you have pictures of them?"

"I'll see what I can get you. The most interesting feature, of course, is their eyes—totally blue, no whites in them."

"Mutation?"

"No; it's linked to saturation of the blood with melange."

"The Fremen must be brave to live at the edge of that desert."

"By all accounts," Yueh said. "They compose poems to their knives. Their women are as fierce as the men. Even Fremen children are violent and dangerous. You'll not be permitted to mingle with them, I daresay."

Paul stared at Yueh, finding in these few glimpses of the Fremen a power of words that caught his entire attention. *What a people to win as allies!*

"And the worms?" Paul asked.

"What?"

"I'd like to study more about the sandworms."

"Ah-h-h, to be sure. I've a filmbook on a small specimen, only one hundred and ten meters long and twenty-two meters in diameter. It was taken in the northern latitudes. Worms of more than four hundred meters in length have been recorded by reliable witnesses, and there's reason to believe even larger ones exist."

Paul glanced down at a conical projection chart of the northern Arrakeen latitudes spread on the table. "The desert belt and south polar regions are marked uninhabitable. Is it the worms?"

"And the storms."

"But any place can be made habitable."

"If it's economically feasible," Yueh said. "Arrakis has many costly perils." He smoothed his drooping mustache. "Your father will be here soon. Before I go, I've a gift for you, something I came across in packing." He put an object on the table between them—black, oblong, no larger than the end of Paul's thumb.

Paul looked at it. Yueh noted how the boy did not reach for it, and thought: *How cautious he is.*

"It's a very old Orange Catholic Bible made for space travelers. Not a filmbook, but actually printed on filament paper. It has its own magnifier and electrostatic charge system." He picked it up, demonstrated. "The book is held closed by the charge, which forces against spring-locked covers. You press the edge—thus, and the pages you've selected repel each other and the book opens."

"It's so small."

"But it has eighteen hundred pages. You press the edge—thus, and so . . . and the charge moves ahead one page at a time as you read. Never touch the actual pages with your fingers. The filament tissue is too delicate." He closed the book, handed it to Paul. "Try it."

Yueh watched Paul work the page adjustment, thought: *I salve my own conscience. I give him the surcease of religion before betraying him. Thus may I say to myself that he has gone where I cannot go.*

"This must've been made before filmbooks," Paul said.

"It's quite old. Let it be our secret, eh? Your parents might think it too valuable for one so young."

And Yueh thought: *His mother would surely wonder at my motives.*

"Well. . . ." Paul closed the book, held it in his hand. "If it's so valuable. . . ."

"Indulge an old man's whim," Yueh said. "It was given to me when I was very young." And he thought: *I must catch his mind as well as his cupidity.* "Open it to four-sixty-seven Kalima—where it says: 'From water does all life begin.' There's a slight notch on the edge of the cover to mark the place."

Paul felt the cover, detected two notches, one shallower than the other. He pressed the shallower one and the book spread open on his palm, its magnifier sliding into place.

"Read it aloud," Yueh said.

Paul wet his lips with his tongue, read: "'Think you of the fact that a deaf person cannot hear. Then, what deafness may we not all possess? What senses do we lack that we cannot see and cannot hear another world all around us? What is there around us that we cannot—'"

"Stop it!" Yueh barked.

Paul broke off, stared at him.

Yueh closed his eyes, fought to regain composure. *What perversity caused the book to open at my Wanna's favorite passage?* He opened his eyes, saw Paul staring at him.

"Is something wrong?" Paul asked.

"I'm sorry," Yueh said. "That was . . . my . . . dead wife's favorite passage. It's not the one I intended you to read. It brings up memories that are . . . painful."

"There are two notches," Paul said.

Of course, Yueh thought. *Wanna marked her passage. His fingers are more sensitive than mine and found her mark. It was an accident, no more.*

"You may find the book interesting," Yueh said. "It has much historical truth in it as well as good ethical philosophy."

Paul looked down at the tiny book in his palm—such a small thing. Yet, it contained a mystery . . . something had happened while he read from it. He had felt something stir his terrible purpose.

"Your father will be here any minute," Yueh said. "Put the book away and read it at your leisure."

Paul touched the edge of it as Yueh had shown him. The book sealed itself. He slipped it into his tunic. For a moment there when Yueh had barked at him, Paul had feared the man would demand the book's return.

"I thank you for the gift, Dr. Yueh," Paul said, speaking formally. "It will be our secret. If there is a gift of favor you wish from me, please do not hesitate to ask."

"I . . . need for nothing," Yueh said.

And he thought: *Why do I stand here torturing myself? And torturing this poor lad . . . though he does not know it. Oeyh! Damn those Harkonnen beasts! Why did they choose me for their abomination?*

How do we approach the study of Muad'Dib's father? A man of surpassing warmth and surprising coldness was the Duke Leto Atreides. Yet, many facts open the way to this Duke: his abiding love for his Bene Gesserit lady; the dreams he held for his son; the devotion with which men served him. You see him there—a man snared by Destiny, a lonely figure with his light dimmed behind the glory of his son. Still, one must ask: What is the son but an extension of the father?

—FROM "MUAD'DIB, FAMILY COMMENTARIES"
BY THE PRINCESS IRULAN

Paul watched his father enter the training room, saw the guards take up stations outside. One of them closed the door. As always, Paul experienced a sense of *presence* in his father, someone totally *here*.

The Duke was tall, olive-skinned. His thin face held harsh angles warmed only by deep gray eyes. He wore a black working uniform with red armorial hawk crest at the breast. A silvered shield belt with the patina of much use girded his narrow waist.

The Duke said: "Hard at work, Son?"

He crossed to the ell table, glanced at the papers on it, swept his gaze around the room and back to Paul. He felt tired, filled with the ache of not showing his fatigue. *I must use every opportunity to rest during the crossing to Arrakis*, he thought. *There'll be no rest on Arrakis.*

"Not very hard," Paul said. "Everything's so. . . ." He shrugged.

"Yes. Well, tomorrow we leave. It'll be good to get settled in our new home, put all this upset behind."

Paul nodded, suddenly overcome by memory of the Reverend Mother's words: "*. . . for the father, nothing.*"

"Father," Paul said, "will Arrakis be as dangerous as everyone says?"

The Duke forced himself to the casual gesture, sat down on a corner of the table, smiled. A whole pattern of conversation welled up in his mind—the kind of thing he might use to dispel the vapors in his men before a battle. The pattern froze before it could be vocalized, confronted by the single thought:

This is my son.

"It'll be dangerous," he admitted.

"Hawat tells me we have a plan for the Fremen," Paul said. And he wondered: *Why don't I tell him what that old woman said? How did she seal my tongue?*

The Duke noted his son's distress, said: "As always, Hawat sees the main chance. But there's much more. I see also the Combine Honnete Ober Advancer Mercantiles—the CHOAM Company. By giving me Arrakis, His Majesty is forced to give us a CHOAM directorship . . . a subtle gain."

"CHOAM controls the spice," Paul said.

"And Arrakis with its spice is our avenue into CHOAM," the Duke said. "There's more to CHOAM than melange."

"Did the Reverend Mother warn you?" Paul blurted. He clenched his fists, feeling his palms slippery with perspiration. The *effort* it had taken to ask that question.

"Hawat tells me she frightened you with warnings about Arrakis," the Duke said. "Don't let a woman's fears cloud your mind. No woman wants her loved ones endangered. The hand behind those warnings was your mother's. Take this as a sign of her love for us."

"Does she know about the Fremen?"

"Yes, and about much more."

"What?"

And the Duke thought: *The truth could be worse than he imagines, but even dangerous facts are valuable if you've been trained to deal with them. And there's one place where nothing has been spared for my son—dealing with dangerous facts. This must be leavened, though; he is young.*

"Few products escape the CHOAM touch," the Duke said. "Logs, donkeys, horses, cows, lumber, dung, sharks, whale fur—the most prosaic and the most exotic . . . even our poor pundi rice from Caladan. Anything the Guild will transport, the art forms of Ecaz, the machines of Richesse and Ix. But all fades before melange. A handful of spice will buy a home on Tupile. It cannot be manufactured, it must be mined on Arrakis. It is unique and it has true geriatric properties."

"And now we control it?"

"To a certain degree. But the important thing is to consider all the Houses that depend on CHOAM profits. And think of the enormous proportion of those profits dependent upon a single product—the spice. Imagine what would happen if something should reduce spice production."

"Whoever had stockpiled melange could make a killing," Paul said. "Others would be out in the cold."

The Duke permitted himself a moment of grim satisfaction, looking at his son and thinking how penetrating, how truly *educated* that observation had been. He nodded. "The Harkonnens have been stockpiling for more than twenty years."

"They mean spice production to fail and you to be blamed."

"They wish the Atreides name to become unpopular," the Duke said. "Think of the Landsraad Houses that look to me for a certain amount of leadership—their unofficial spokesman. Think how they'd react if I were responsible for a serious reduction in their income. After all, one's own profits come first. The Great Convention be damned! You can't let someone pauperize you!" A harsh smile twisted the Duke's mouth. "They'd look the other way no matter *what* was done to me."

"Even if we were attacked with atomics?"

"Nothing that flagrant. No *open* defiance of the Convention. But almost anything else short of that . . . perhaps even dusting and a bit of soil poisoning."

"Then why are we walking into this?"

"Paul!" The Duke frowned at his son. "Knowing where the trap is— that's the first step in evading it. This is like single combat, Son, only on a larger scale—a feint within a feint within a feint . . . seemingly without end. The task is to unravel it. Knowing that the Harkonnens stockpile melange, we ask another question: Who else is stockpiling? That's the list of our enemies."

"Who?"

"Certain Houses we knew were unfriendly and some we'd thought friendly. We need not consider them for the moment because there is one other much more important: our beloved Padishah Emperor."

Paul tried to swallow in a throat suddenly dry. "Couldn't you convene the Landsraad, expose—"

"Make our enemy aware we know which hand holds the knife? Ah, now, Paul—we *see* the knife, now. Who knows where it might be shifted next? If we put this before the Landsraad it'd only create a great cloud of confusion. The Emperor would deny it. Who could gainsay him? All we'd gain is a little time while risking chaos. And where would the next attack come from?"

"All the Houses might start stockpiling spice."

"Our enemies have a head start—too much of a lead to overcome."

"The Emperor," Paul said. "That means the Sardaukar."

"Disguised in Harkonnen livery, no doubt," the Duke said. "But the soldier fanatics nonetheless."

"How can Fremen help us against Sardaukar?"

"Did Hawat talk to you about Salusa Secundus?"

"The Emperor's prison planet? No."

"What if it were more than a prison planet, Paul? There's a question you never hear asked about the Imperial Corps of Sardaukar: Where do they come from?"

"From the prison planet?"

"They come from somewhere."

"But the supporting levies the Emperor demands from—"

"That's what we're led to believe: they're just the Emperor's levies trained young and superbly. You hear an occasional muttering about the Emperor's training cadres, but the balance of our civilization remains the same: the military forces of the Landsraad Great Houses on one side, the Sardaukar and their supporting levies on the other. *And* their supporting levies, Paul. The Sardaukar remain the Sardaukar."

"But every report on Salusa Secundus says S.S. is a hell world!"

"Undoubtedly. But if you were going to raise tough, strong, ferocious men, what environmental conditions would you impose on them?"

"How could you win the loyalty of such men?"

"There are proven ways: play on the certain knowledge of their superiority, the mystique of secret covenant, the esprit of shared suffering. It can be done. It has been done on many worlds in many times."

Paul nodded, holding his attention on his father's face. He felt some revelation impending.

"Consider Arrakis," the Duke said. "When you get outside the towns and garrison villages, it's every bit as terrible a place as Salusa Secundus."

Paul's eyes went wide. "The Fremen!"

"We have there the potential of a corps as strong and deadly as the Sardaukar. It'll require patience to exploit them secretly and wealth to equip them properly. But the Fremen are there . . . and the spice wealth is there. You see now why we walk into Arrakis, knowing the trap is there."

"Don't the Harkonnens know about the Fremen?"

"The Harkonnens sneered at the Fremen, hunted them for sport, never even bothered trying to count them. We know the Harkonnen policy with planetary populations—spend as little as possible to maintain them."

The metallic threads in the hawk symbol above his father's breast glistened as the Duke shifted his position. "You see?"

"We're negotiating with the Fremen right now," Paul said.

"I sent a mission headed by Duncan Idaho," the Duke said. "A proud and ruthless man, Duncan, but fond of the truth. I think the Fremen will admire him. If we're lucky, they may judge us by him: Duncan, the moral."

"Duncan, the moral," Paul said, "and Gurney the valorous."

"You name them well," the Duke said.

And Paul thought: *Gurney's one of those the Reverend Mother meant, a supporter of worlds—". . . the valor of the brave."*

"Gurney tells me you did well in weapons today," the Duke said.

"That isn't what he told me."

The Duke laughed aloud. "I figured Gurney to be sparse with his praise. He says you have a nicety of awareness—in his own words—of the difference between a blade's edge and its tip."

"Gurney says there's no artistry in killing with the tip, that it should be done with the edge."

"Gurney's a romantic," the Duke growled. This talk of killing suddenly disturbed him, coming from his son. "I'd sooner you never had to kill . . . but if the need arises, you do it however you can—tip or edge." He looked up at the skylight, on which the rain was drumming.

Seeing the direction of his father's stare, Paul thought of the wet skies out there—a thing never to be seen on Arrakis from all accounts—and this thought of skies put him in mind of the space beyond. "Are the Guild ships really big?" he asked.

The Duke looked at him. "This *will* be your first time off planet," he said. "Yes, they're big. We'll be riding a Heighliner because it's a long trip. A Heighliner is truly big. Its hold will tuck all our frigates and transports into a little corner—we'll be just a small part of the ship's manifest."

"And we won't be able to leave our frigates?"

"That's part of the price you pay for Guild Security. There could be Harkonnen ships right alongside us and we'd have nothing to fear from them. The Harkonnens know better than to endanger their shipping privileges."

"I'm going to watch our screens and try to see a Guildsman."

"You won't. Not even their agents ever see a Guildsman. The Guild's as jealous of its privacy as it is of its monopoly. Don't do anything to endanger our shipping privileges, Paul."

"Do you think they hide because they've mutated and don't look . . . *human* anymore?"

"Who knows?" The Duke shrugged. "It's a mystery we're not likely to solve. We've more immediate problems—among them: you."

"Me?"

"Your mother wanted me to be the one to tell you, Son. You see, you may have Mentat capabilities."

Paul stared at his father, unable to speak for a moment, then: "A Mentat? Me? But I. . . ."

"Hawat agrees, Son. It's true."

"But I thought Mentat training had to start during infancy and the subject couldn't be told because it might inhibit the early. . . ." He broke off, all his past circumstances coming to focus in one flashing computation. "I see," he said.

"A day comes," the Duke said, "when the potential Mentat must learn what's being done. It may no longer be done *to* him. The Mentat has to share in the choice of whether to continue or abandon the training. Some can continue; some are incapable of it. Only the potential Mentat can tell this for sure about himself."

Paul rubbed his chin. All the special training from Hawat and his mother—the mnemonics, the focusing of awareness, the muscle control and sharpening of sensitivities, the study of languages and nuances of voices—all of it clicked into a new kind of understanding in his mind.

"You'll be the Duke someday, Son," his father said. "A Mentat Duke would be formidable indeed. Can you decide now . . . or do you need more time?"

There was no hesitation in his answer. "I'll go on with the training."

"Formidable indeed," the Duke murmured, and Paul saw the proud smile on his father's face. The smile shocked Paul: it had a skull look on the Duke's narrow features. Paul closed his eyes, feeling the terrible purpose reawaken within him. *Perhaps being a Mentat is terrible purpose*, he thought.

But even as he focused on this thought, his new awareness denied it.

With the Lady Jessica and Arrakis, the Bene Gesserit system of sowing implant-legends through the Missionaria Protectiva came to its full fruition. The wisdom of seeding the known universe with a prophecy pattern for the protection of B.G. personnel has long been appreciated, but never have we seen a condition-ut-extremis with more ideal mating of person and preparation. The prophetic legends had taken on Arrakis even to the extent of adopted labels (including Reverend Mother, canto and respondu, and most of the Shari-a panoplia propheticus). And it is generally accepted now that the Lady Jessica's latent abilities were grossly underestimated.

—FROM "ANALYSIS: THE ARRAKEEN CRISIS"
BY THE PRINCESS IRULAN
(PRIVATE CIRCULATION: B.G. FILE NUMBER AR-81088587)

All around the Lady Jessica—piled in corners of the Arrakeen Great Hall, mounded in the open spaces—stood the packaged freight of their lives: boxes, trunks, cartons, cases—some partly unpacked. She could hear the cargo handlers from the Guild shuttle depositing another load in the entry.

Jessica stood in the center of the hall. She moved in a slow turn, looking up and around at shadowed carvings, crannies and deeply recessed windows. This giant anachronism of a room reminded her of the Sisters' Hall at her Bene Gesserit school. But at the school the effect had been of warmth. Here, all was bleak stone.

Some architect had reached far back into history for these buttressed walls and dark hangings, she thought. The arched ceiling stood two stories above her with great crossbeams she felt sure had been shipped here to Arrakis across space at monstrous cost. No planet of this system grew trees to make such beams—unless the beams were imitation wood.

She thought not.

This had been the government mansion in the days of the Old Empire. Costs had been of less importance then. It had been before the Harkonnens and their new megalopolis of Carthag—a cheap and brassy place some two hundred kilometers northeast across the Broken Land. Leto had been wise to choose this place for his seat of government. The name, Arrakeen, had a good sound, filled with tradition. And this was a smaller city, easier to sterilize and defend.

Again there came the clatter of boxes being unloaded in the entry. Jessica sighed.

Against a carton to her right stood the painting of the Duke's father. Wrapping twine hung from it like a frayed decoration. A piece of the twine was still clutched in Jessica's left hand. Beside the painting lay a black bull's head mounted on a polished board. The head was a dark island in a sea of wadded paper. Its plaque lay flat on the floor, and the bull's shiny muzzle pointed at the ceiling as though the beast were ready to bellow a challenge into this echoing room.

Jessica wondered what compulsion had brought her to uncover those two things first—the head and the painting. She knew there was something symbolic in the action. Not since the day when the Duke's buyers had taken her from the school had she felt this frightened and unsure of herself.

The head and the picture.

They heightened her feelings of confusion. She shuddered, glanced at the slit windows high overhead. It was still early afternoon here, and in these latitudes the sky looked black and cold—so much darker than the warm blue of Caladan. A pang of homesickness throbbed through her.

So far away, Caladan.

"Here we are!"

The voice was Duke Leto's.

She whirled, saw him striding from the arched passage to the dining hall. His black working uniform with red armorial hawk crest at the breast looked dusty and rumpled.

"I thought you might have lost yourself in this hideous place," he said.

"It is a cold house," she said. She looked at his tallness, at the dark skin that made her think of olive groves and golden sun on blue waters. There was woodsmoke in the gray of his eyes, but the face was predatory: thin, full of sharp angles and planes.

A sudden fear of him tightened her breast. He had become such a savage, driving person since the decision to bow to the Emperor's command.

"The whole city feels cold," she said.

"It's a dirty, dusty little garrison town," he agreed. "But we'll change that." He looked around the hall. "These are public rooms for state occasions. I've just glanced at some of the family apartments in the south wing. They're much nicer." He stepped closer, touched her arm, admiring her stateliness.

And again, he wondered at her unknown ancestry—a renegade House, perhaps? Some black-barred royalty? She looked more regal than the Emperor's own blood.

Under the pressure of his stare, she turned half away, exposing her profile. And he realized there was no single and precise thing that brought her beauty to focus. The face was oval under a cap of hair the color of polished bronze. Her eyes were set wide, as green and clear as the morning skies of Caladan. The nose was small, the mouth wide and generous. Her figure was good but scant: tall and with its curves gone to slimness.

He remembered that the lay sisters at the school had called her skinny, so his buyers had told him. But that description oversimplified. She had brought a regal beauty back into the Atreides line. He was glad that Paul favored her.

"Where's Paul?" he asked.

"Someplace around the house taking his lessons with Yueh."

"Probably in the south wing," he said. "I thought I heard Yueh's voice, but I couldn't take time to look." He glanced down at her, hesitating. "I came here only to hang the key of Caladan Castle in the dining hall."

She caught her breath, stopped the impulse to reach out to him. Hanging the key—there was finality in that action. But this was not the time or place for comforting. "I saw our banner over the house as we came in," she said.

He glanced at the painting of his father. "Where were you going to hang that?"

"Somewhere in here."

"No." The word rang flat and final, telling her she could use trickery to persuade, but open argument was useless. Still, she had to try, even if the gesture served only to remind herself that she would not trick him.

"My Lord," she said, "if you'd only. . . ."

"The answer remains no. I indulge you shamefully in most things, not in this. I've just come from the dining hall where there are—"

"My Lord! Please."

"The choice is between your digestion and my ancestral dignity, my dear," he said. "They will hang in the dining hall."

She sighed. "Yes, my Lord."

"You may resume your custom of dining in your rooms whenever possible. I shall expect you at your proper position only on formal occasions."

"Thank you, my Lord."

"And don't go all cold and formal on me! Be thankful that I never married you, my dear. Then it'd be your *duty* to join me at table for every meal."

She held her face immobile, nodded.

"Hawat already has our own poison snooper over the dining table," he said. "There's a portable in your room."

"You anticipated this . . . disagreement," she said.

"My dear, I think also of your comfort. I've engaged servants. They're locals, but Hawat has cleared them—they're Fremen all. They'll do until our own people can be released from their other duties."

"Can anyone from this place be truly safe?"

"Anyone who hates Harkonnens. You may even want to keep the head housekeeper: the Shadout Mapes."

"Shadout," Jessica said. "A Fremen title?"

"I'm told it means 'well-dipper,' a meaning with rather important overtones here. She may not strike you as a servant type, although Hawat speaks highly of her on the basis of Duncan's report. They're convinced she wants to serve—specifically that she wants to serve you."

"Me?"

"The Fremen have learned that you're Bene Gesserit," he said. "There are legends here about the Bene Gesserit."

The Missionaria Protectiva, Jessica thought. *No place escapes them.*

"Does this mean Duncan was successful?" she asked. "Will the Fremen be our allies?"

"There's nothing definite," he said. "They wish to observe us for a while, Duncan believes. They did, however, promise to stop raiding our outlying villages during a truce period. That's a more important gain than it might seem. Hawat tells me the Fremen were a deep thorn in the Harkonnen side, that the extent of their ravages was a carefully guarded secret. It wouldn't have helped for the Emperor to learn the ineffectiveness of the Harkonnen military."

"A Fremen housekeeper," Jessica mused, returning to the subject of the Shadout Mapes. "She'll have the all-blue eyes."

"Don't let the appearance of these people deceive you," he said. "There's a deep strength and healthy vitality in them. I think they'll be everything we need."

"It's a dangerous gamble," she said.

"Let's not go into that again," he said.

She forced a smile. "We *are* committed, no doubt of that." She went through the quick regimen of calmness—the two deep breaths, the ritual thought, then: "When I assign rooms, is there anything special I should reserve for you?"

"You must teach me someday how you do that," he said, "the way you thrust your worries aside and turn to practical matters. It must be a Bene Gesserit thing."

"It's a female thing," she said.

He smiled. "Well, assignment of rooms: make certain I have large office space next to my sleeping quarters. There'll be more paper work here than on Caladan. A guard room, of course. That should cover it. Don't worry about security of the house. Hawat's men have been over it in depth."

"I'm sure they have."

He glanced at his wristwatch. "And you might see that all our time-pieces are adjusted for Arrakeen local. I've assigned a tech to take care of it. He'll be along presently." He brushed a strand of her hair back from her forehead. "I must return to the landing field now. The second shuttle's due any minute with my staff reserves."

"Couldn't Hawat meet them, my Lord? You look so tired."

"The good Thufir is even busier than I am. You know this planet's infested with Harkonnen intrigues. Besides, I must try persuading some of the trained spice hunters against leaving. They have the option, you know, with the change of fief—and this planetologist the Emperor and the Landsraad installed as Judge of the Change cannot be bought. He's allowing the opt. About eight hundred trained hands expect to go out on the spice shuttle and there's a Guild cargo ship standing by."

"My Lord. . . ." She broke off, hesitating.

"Yes?"

He will not be persuaded against trying to make this planet secure for us, she thought. *And I cannot use my tricks on him.*

"At what time will you be expecting dinner?" she asked.

That's not what she was going to say, he thought. *Ah-h-h-h, my Jessica, would that we were somewhere else, anywhere away from this terrible place—alone, the two of us, without a care.*

"I'll eat in the officers' mess at the field," he said. "Don't expect me until very late. And . . . ah, I'll be sending a guardcar for Paul. I want him to attend our strategy conference."

He cleared his throat as though to say something else, then, without warning, turned and strode out, headed for the entry where she could hear more boxes being deposited. His voice sounded once from there, commanding and disdainful, the way he always spoke to servants when he was in a hurry: "The Lady Jessica's in the Great Hall. Join her there immediately."

The outer door slammed.

Jessica turned away, faced the painting of Leto's father. It had been done by the famed artist, Albe, during the Old Duke's middle years. He was portrayed in matador costume with a magenta cape flung over his left arm. The face looked young, hardly older than Leto's now, and with the same hawk features, the same gray stare. She clenched her fists at her sides, glared at the painting.

"Damn you! Damn you! Damn you!" she whispered.

"What are your orders, Noble Born?"

It was a woman's voice, thin and stringy.

Jessica whirled, stared down at a knobby, gray-haired woman in a shapeless sack dress of bondsman brown. The woman looked as wrinkled and desiccated as any member of the mob that had greeted them along the way from the landing field that morning. Every native she had seen on this planet, Jessica thought, looked prune dry and undernourished. Yet, Leto had said they were strong and vital. And there were the eyes, of course—that wash of deepest, darkest blue without any white—secretive, mysterious. Jessica forced herself not to stare.

The woman gave a stiff-necked nod, said: "I am called the Shadout Mapes, Noble Born. What are your orders?"

"You may refer to me as 'my Lady,'" Jessica said. "I'm not noble born. I'm the bound concubine of the Duke Leto."

Again that strange nod, and the woman peered upward at Jessica with a sly questioning. "There's a wife, then?"

"There is not, nor has there ever been. I am the Duke's only . . . companion, the mother of his heir-designate."

Even as she spoke, Jessica laughed inwardly at the pride behind her words. *What was it St. Augustine said?* she asked herself. *"The mind commands the body and it obeys. The mind orders itself and meets resistance." Yes—I am meeting more resistance lately. I could use a quiet retreat by myself.*

A weird cry sounded from the road outside the house. It was repeated: "Soo-soo Sook! Soo-soo Sook!" Then: "Ikhut-eigh! Ikhut-eigh!" And again: "Soo-soo Sook!"

"What *is* that?" Jessica asked. "I heard it several times as we drove through the streets this morning."

"Only a water-seller, my Lady. But you've no need to interest yourself in such as they. The cistern here holds fifty thousand liters and it's always kept full." She glanced down at her dress. "Why, you know, my Lady, I don't even have to wear my stillsuit here?" She cackled. "And me not even dead!"

Jessica hesitated, wanting to question this Fremen woman, needing data to guide her. But bringing order of the confusion in the castle was more imperative. Still, she found the thought unsettling that water was a major mark of wealth here.

"My husband told me of your title, Shadout," Jessica said. "I recognized the word. It's a very ancient word."

"You know the ancient tongues then?" Mapes asked, and she waited with an odd intensity.

"Tongues are the Bene Gesserit's first learning," Jessica said. "I know the Bhotani Jib and the Chakobsa, all the hunting languages."

Mapes nodded. "Just as the legend says."

And Jessica wondered: *Why do I play out this sham?* But the Bene Gesserit ways were devious and compelling.

"I know the Dark Things and the ways of the Great Mother," Jessica said. She read the more obvious signs in Mapes' actions and appearance, the petit betrayals. "Miseces prejia," she said in the Chakobsa tongue. "Andral t're pera! Trada cik buscakri miseces perakri—"

Mapes took a backward step, appeared poised to flee.

"I know many things," Jessica said. "I know that you have borne children, that you have lost loved ones, that you have hidden in fear and that you have done violence and will yet do more violence. I know many things."

In a low voice, Mapes said: "I meant no offense, my Lady."

"You speak of the legend and seek answers," Jessica said. "Beware the answers you may find. I know you came prepared for violence with a weapon in your bodice."

"My Lady, I. . . ."

"There's a remote possibility you could draw my life's blood," Jessica said, "but in so doing you'd bring down more ruin than your wildest fears could imagine. There are worse things than dying, you know— even for an entire people."

"My Lady!" Mapes pleaded. She appeared about to fall to her knees. "The weapon was sent as a gift to *you* should you prove to be the One."

"And as the means of my death should I prove otherwise," Jessica said. She waited in the seeming relaxation that made the Bene Gesserit-trained so terrifying in combat.

Now we see which way the decision tips, she thought.

Slowly, Mapes reached into the neck of her dress, brought out a dark sheath. A black handle with deep finger ridges protruded from it. She took sheath in one hand and handle in the other, withdrew a milk-white blade, held it up. The blade seemed to shine and glitter with a light of its own. It was double-edged like a kindjal and the blade was perhaps twenty centimeters long.

"Do you know this, my Lady?" Mapes asked.

It could only be one thing, Jessica knew, the fabled crysknife of Arrakis, the blade that had never been taken off the planet, and was known only by rumor and wild gossip.

"It's a crysknife," she said.

"Say it not lightly," Mapes said. "Do you know its meaning?"

And Jessica thought: *There was an edge to that question. Here's the reason this Fremen has taken service with me, to ask that one question. My answer could precipitate violence or . . . what? She seeks an answer from me: the meaning of a knife. She's called the Shadout in the Cha kobsa tongue. Knife, that's "Death Maker" in Chakobsa. She's getting restive. I must answer now. Delay is as dangerous as the wrong answer.*

Jessica said: "It's a maker—"

"Eighe-e-e-e-e!" Mapes wailed. It was a sound of both grief and elation. She trembled so hard the knife blade sent glittering shards of reflection shooting around the room.

Jessica waited, poised. She had intended to say the knife was a *maker of death* and then add the ancient word, but every sense warned her now, all the deep training of alertness that exposed meaning in the most casual muscle twitch.

The key word was . . . *maker.*

Maker? Maker.

Still, Mapes held the knife as though ready to use it.

Jessica said: "Did you think that I, knowing the mysteries of the Great Mother, would not know the Maker?"

Mapes lowered the knife. "My Lady, when one has lived with prophecy for so long, the moment of revelation is a shock."

Jessica thought about the prophecy—the Shari-a and all the panoplia propheticus, a Bene Gesserit of the Missionaria Protectiva dropped here long centuries ago—long dead, no doubt, but her purpose accomplished: the protective legends implanted in these people against the day of a Bene Gesserit's need.

Well, that day had come.

Mapes returned knife to sheath, said: "This is an unfixed blade, my Lady. Keep it near you. More than a week away from flesh and it begins to disintegrate. It's yours, a tooth of shai-hulud, for as long as you live."

Jessica reached out her right hand, risked a gamble: "Mapes, you've sheathed that blade unblooded."

With a gasp, Mapes dropped the sheathed knife into Jessica's hand, tore open the brown bodice, wailing: "Take the water of my life!"

Jessica withdrew the blade from its sheath. How it glittered! She directed the point toward Mapes, saw a fear greater than death-panic come over the woman. *Poison in the point?* Jessica wondered. She tipped up the point, drew a delicate scratch with the blade's edge above Mapes' left breast. There was a thick welling of blood that stopped almost immediately. *Ultrafast coagulation*, Jessica thought. *A moisture-conserving mutation?*

She sheathed the blade, said: "Button your dress, Mapes."

Mapes obeyed, trembling. The eyes without whites stared at Jessica. "You are ours," she muttered. "You are the One."

There came another sound of unloading in the entry. Swiftly, Mapes grabbed the sheathed knife, concealed it in Jessica's bodice. "Who sees that knife must be cleansed or slain!" she snarled. "You *know* that, my Lady!"

I know it now, Jessica thought.

The cargo handlers left without intruding on the Great Hall.

Mapes composed herself, said: "The uncleansed who have seen a crysknife may not leave Arrakis alive. Never forget that, my Lady. You've been entrusted with a crysknife." She took a deep breath. "Now the thing must take its course. It cannot be hurried." She glanced at the stacked boxes and piled goods around them. "And there's work aplenty to while the time for us here."

Jessica hesitated. "*The thing must take its course.*" That was a specific catchphrase from the Missionaria Protectiva's stock of incantations— *The coming of the Reverend Mother to free you.*

But I'm not a Reverend Mother, Jessica thought. And then: *Great Mother! They planted* that *one here! This must be a hideous place!*

In matter-of-fact tones, Mapes said: "What'll you be wanting me to do first, my Lady?"

Instinct warned Jessica to match that casual tone. She said: "The painting of the Old Duke over there, it must be hung on one side of the dining hall. The bull's head must go on the wall opposite the painting."

Mapes crossed to the bull's head. "What a great beast it must have been to carry such a head," she said. She stooped. "I'll have to be cleaning this first, won't I, my Lady?"

"No."

"But there's dirt caked on its horns."

"That's not dirt, Mapes. That's the blood of our Duke's father. Those horns were sprayed with a transparent fixative within hours after this beast killed the Old Duke."

Mapes stood up. "Ah, now!" she said.

"It's just blood," Jessica said. "Old blood at that. Get some help hanging these now. The beastly things are heavy."

"Did you think the blood bothered me?" Mapes asked. "I'm of the desert and I've seen blood aplenty."

"I . . . see that you have," Jessica said.

"And some of it my own," Mapes said. "More'n you drew with your puny scratch."

"You'd rather I'd cut deeper?"

"Ah, no! The body's water is scant enough 'thout gushing a wasteful lot of it into the air. You did the thing right."

And Jessica, noting the words and manner, caught the deeper implications in the phrase, "the body's water." Again she felt a sense of oppression at the importance of water on Arrakis.

"On which side of the dining hall shall I hang which one of these pretties, my Lady?" Mapes asked.

Ever the practical one, this Mapes, Jessica thought. She said: "Use your own judgment, Mapes. It makes no real difference."

"As you say, my Lady." Mapes stooped, began clearing wrappings and twine from the head. "Killed an old duke, did you?" she crooned.

"Shall I summon a handler to help you?" Jessica asked.

"I'll manage, my Lady."

Yes, she'll manage, Jessica thought. *There's that about this Fremen creature: the drive to manage.*

Jessica felt the cold sheath of the crysknife beneath her bodice, thought of the long chain of Bene Gesserit scheming that had forged another link here. Because of that scheming, she had survived a deadly crisis. "It cannot be hurried," Mapes had said. Yet there was a tempo of headlong rushing to this place that filled Jessica with foreboding. And not all the preparations of the Missionaria Protectiva nor Hawat's suspicious inspection of this castellated pile of rocks could dispel the feeling.

"When you've finished hanging those, start unpacking the boxes," Jessica said. "One of the cargo men at the entry has all the keys and knows where things should go. Get the keys and the list from him. If there are any questions I'll be in the south wing."

"As you will, my Lady," Mapes said.

Jessica turned away, thinking: *Hawat may have passed this residency as safe, but there's something wrong about the place. I can feel it.*

An urgent need to see her son gripped Jessica. She began walking toward the arched doorway that led into the passage to the dining hall and the family wings. Faster and faster she walked until she was almost running.

Behind her, Mapes paused in clearing the wrappings from the bull's head, looked at the retreating back. "She's the One all right," she muttered. "Poor thing."

"Yueh! Yueh! Yueh!" goes the refrain. "A million deaths were not enough for Yueh!"

—FROM "A CHILD'S HISTORY OF MUAD'DIB"
BY THE PRINCESS IRULAN

The door stood ajar, and Jessica stepped through it into a room with yellow walls. To her left stretched a low settee of black hide and two empty bookcases, a hanging waterflask with dust on its bulging sides. To her right, bracketing another door, stood more empty bookcases, a desk from Caladan and three chairs. At the windows directly ahead of her stood Dr. Yueh, his back to her, his attention fixed upon the outside world.

Jessica took another silent step into the room.

She saw that Yueh's coat was wrinkled, a white smudge near the left elbow as though he had leaned against chalk. He looked, from behind, like a fleshless stick figure in overlarge black clothing, a caricature poised for stringy movement at the direction of a puppet master. Only the squarish block of head with long ebony hair caught in its silver Suk School ring at the shoulder seemed alive—turning slightly to follow some movement outside.

Again, she glanced around the room, seeing no sign of her son, but the closed door on her right, she knew, let into a small bedroom for which Paul had expressed a liking.

"Good afternoon, Dr. Yueh," she said. "Where's Paul?"

He nodded as though to something out the window, spoke in an absent manner without turning: "Your son grew tired, Jessica. I sent him into the next room to rest."

Abruptly, he stiffened, whirled with mustache flopping over his purpled lips. "Forgive me, my Lady! My thoughts were far away . . . I . . . did not mean to be familiar."

She smiled, held out her right hand. For a moment, she was afraid he might kneel. "Wellington, please."

"To use your name like that . . . I. . . ."

"We've known each other six years," she said. "It's long past time formalities should've been dropped between us—in private."

Yueh ventured a thin smile, thinking: *I believe it has worked. Now, she'll think anything unusual in my manner is due to embarrassment. She'll not look for deeper reasons when she believes she already knows the answer.*

"I'm afraid I was woolgathering," he said. "Whenever I . . . feel especially sorry for you, I'm afraid I think of you as . . . well, Jessica."

"Sorry for me? Whatever for?"

Yueh shrugged. Long ago, he had realized Jessica was not gifted with the full Truthsay as his Wanna had been. Still, he always used the truth with Jessica whenever possible. It was safest.

"You've seen this place, my . . . Jessica." He stumbled over the name, plunged ahead: "So barren after Caladan. And the people! Those townswomen we passed on the way here wailing beneath their veils. The way they looked at us."

She folded her arms across her breast, hugging herself, feeling the cryknife there, a blade ground from a sandworm's tooth, if the reports were right. "It's just that we're strange to them—different people, different customs. They've known only the Harkonnens." She looked past him out the windows. "What were you staring at out there?"

He turned back to the window. "The people."

Jessica crossed to his side, looked to the left toward the front of the house where Yueh's attention was focused. A line of twenty palm trees grew there, the ground beneath them swept clean, barren. A screen fence separated them from the road upon which robed people were passing. Jessica detected a faint shimmering in the air between her and the people—a house shield—and went on to study the passing throng, wondering why Yueh found them so absorbing.

The pattern emerged and she put a hand to her cheek. The way the passing people looked at the palm trees! She saw envy, some hate . . . even a sense of hope. Each person raked those trees with a fixity of expression.

"Do you know what they're thinking?" Yueh asked.

"You profess to read minds?" she asked.

"Those minds," he said. "They look at those trees and they think: 'There are one hundred of us.' That's what they think."

She turned a puzzled frown on him. "Why?"

"Those are date palms," he said. "One date palm requires forty liters of water a day. A man requires but eight liters. A palm, then, equals five men. There are twenty palms out there—one hundred men."

"But some of those people look at the trees hopefully."

"They but hope some dates will fall, except it's the wrong season."

"We look at this place with too critical an eye," she said. "There's hope as well as danger here. The spice *could* make us rich. With a fat treasury, we can make this world into whatever we wish."

And she laughed silently at herself: *Who am I trying to convince?* The laugh broke through her restraints, emerging brittle, without humor. "But you can't buy security," she said.

Yueh turned away to hide his face from her. *If only it were possible to hate these people instead of love them!* In her manner, in many ways, Jessica was like his Wanna. Yet that thought carried its own rigors, hardening him to his purpose. The ways of the Harkonnen cruelty were devious. Wanna might not be dead. He had to be certain.

"Do not worry for us, Wellington," Jessica said. "The problem's ours, not yours."

She thinks I worry for her! He blinked back tears. *And I do, of course. But I must stand before that black Baron with his deed accomplished, and take my one chance to strike him where he is weakest—in his gloating moment!*

He sighed.

"Would it disturb Paul if I looked in on him?" she asked.

"Not at all. I gave him a sedative."

"He's taking the change well?" she asked.

"Except for getting a bit overtired. He's excited, but what fifteen-year-old wouldn't be under these circumstances?" He crossed to the door, opened it. "He's in here."

Jessica followed, peered into a shadowy room.

Paul lay on a narrow cot, one arm beneath a light cover, the other thrown back over his head. Slatted blinds at a window beside the bed wove a loom of shadows across face and blanket.

Jessica stared at her son, seeing the oval shape of face so like her own. But the hair was the Duke's—coal-colored and tousled. Long lashes concealed the lime-toned eyes. Jessica smiled, feeling her fears retreat. She was suddenly caught by the idea of genetic traces in her son's features—her lines in eyes and facial outline, but sharp touches of the father peering through that outline like maturity emerging from childhood.

She thought of the boy's features as an exquisite distillation out of random patterns—endless queues of happenstance meeting at this nexus. The thought made her want to kneel beside the bed and take her son in her arms, but she was inhibited by Yueh's presence. She stepped back, closed the door softly.

Yueh had returned to the window, unable to bear watching the way Jessica stared at her son. *Why did Wanna never give me children?* he asked himself. *I know as a doctor there was no physical reason against it. Was there some Bene Gesserit reason? Was she, perhaps, instructed to serve a different purpose? What could it have been? She loved me, certainly.*

For the first time, he was caught up in the thought that he might be part of a pattern more involuted and complicated than his mind could grasp.

Jessica stopped beside him, said: "What delicious abandon in the sleep of a child."

He spoke mechanically: "If only adults could relax like that."

"Yes."

"Where do we lose it?" he murmured.

She glanced at him, catching the odd tone, but her mind was still on Paul, thinking of the new rigors in his training here, thinking of the differences in his life now—so very different from the life they once had planned for him.

"We do, indeed, lose something," she said.

She glanced out to the right at a slope humped with a wind-troubled gray-green of bushes—dusty leaves and dry claw branches. The too-dark sky hung over the slope like a blot, and the milky light of the Arrakeen sun gave the scene a silver cast—light like the crysknife concealed in her bodice.

"The sky's so dark," she said.

"That's partly the lack of moisture," he said.

"Water!" she snapped. "Everywhere you turn here, you're involved with the lack of water!"

"It's the precious mystery of Arrakis," he said.

"Why is there so little of it? There's volcanic rock here. There're a dozen power sources I could name. There's polar ice. They say you can't drill in the desert—storms and sandtides destroy equipment faster than it can be installed, if the worms don't get you first. They've never found water traces there, anyway. But the mystery, Wellington, the real mystery is the wells that've been drilled up here in the sinks and basins. Have you read about those?"

"First a trickle, then nothing," he said.

"But, Wellington, that's the mystery. The water was there. It dries up. And never again is there water. Yet another hole nearby produces the same result: a trickle that stops. Has no one ever been curious about this?"

"It is curious," he said. "You suspect some living agency? Wouldn't that have shown in core samples?"

"What would have shown? Alien plant matter . . . or animal? Who could recognize it?" She turned back to the slope. "The water is stopped. Something plugs it. That's my suspicion."

"Perhaps the reason's known," he said. "The Harkonnens sealed off many sources of information about Arrakis. Perhaps there was reason to suppress this."

"What reason?" she asked. "And then there's the atmospheric moisture. Little enough of it, certainly, but there's some. It's the major source of water here, caught in windtraps and precipitators. Where does that come from?"

"The polar caps?"

"Cold air takes up little moisture, Wellington. There are things here behind the Harkonnen veil that bear close investigation, and not all of those things are directly involved with the spice."

"We are indeed behind the Harkonnen veil," he said. "Perhaps we'll. . . ." He broke off, noting the sudden intense way she was looking at him. "Is something wrong?"

"The way you say 'Harkonnen,'" she said. "Even my Duke's voice doesn't carry that weight of venom when he uses the hated name. I didn't know you had personal reasons to hate them, Wellington."

Great Mother! he thought. *I've aroused her suspicions! Now I must use every trick my Wanna taught me. There's only one solution: tell the truth as far as I can.*

He said: "You didn't know that my wife, my Wanna. . . ." He shrugged, unable to speak past a sudden constriction in his throat. Then: "They. . . ." The words would not come out. He felt panic, closed his eyes tightly, experiencing the agony in his chest and little else until a hand touched his arm gently.

"Forgive me," Jessica said. "I did not mean to open an old wound." And she thought: *Those animals! His wife was Bene Gesserit—the signs are all over him. And it's obvious the Harkonnens killed her. Here's another poor victim bound to the Atreides by a cherem of hate.*

"I am sorry," he said. "I'm unable to talk about it." He opened his eyes, giving himself up to the internal awareness of grief. That, at least, was truth.

Jessica studied him, seeing the up-angled cheeks, the dark sequins of almond eyes, the butter complexion, and stringy mustache hanging like a curved frame around purpled lips and narrow chin. The creases of his cheeks and forehead, she saw, were as much lines of sorrow as of age. A deep affection for him came over her.

"Wellington, I'm sorry we brought you into this dangerous place," she said.

"I came willingly," he said. And that, too, was true.

"But this whole planet's a Harkonnen trap. You must know that."

"It will take more than a trap to catch the Duke Leto," he said. And that, too, was true.

"Perhaps I should be more confident of him," she said. "He is a brilliant tactician."

"We've been uprooted," he said. "That's why we're uneasy."

"And how easy it is to kill the uprooted plant," she said. "Especially when you put it down in hostile soil."

"Are we certain the soil's hostile?"

"There were water riots when it was learned how many people the Duke was adding to the population," she said. "They stopped only when the people learned we were installing new windtraps and condensers to take care of the load."

"There is only so much water to support human life here," he said. "The people know if more come to drink a limited amount of water, the price goes up and the very poor die. But the Duke has solved this. It doesn't follow that the riots mean permanent hostility toward him."

"And guards," she said. "Guards everywhere. And shields. You see the blurring of them everywhere you look. We did not live this way on Caladan."

"Give this planet a chance," he said.

But Jessica continued to stare hard-eyed out the window. "I can smell death in this place," she said. "Hawat sent advance agents in here by the battalion. Those guards outside are his men. The cargo handlers are his men. There've been unexplained withdrawals of large sums from the treasury. The amounts mean only one thing: bribes in high places." She shook her head. "Where Thufir Hawat goes, death and deceit follow."

"You malign him."

"Malign? I praise him. Death and deceit are our only hopes now. I just do not fool myself about Thufir's methods."

"You should . . . keep busy," he said. "Give yourself no time for such morbid—"

"Busy! What is it that takes most of my time, Wellington? I am the Duke's secretary—so busy that each day I learn new things to fear . . . things even he doesn't suspect I know." She compressed her lips, spoke thinly: "Sometimes I wonder how much my Bene Gesserit business training figured in his choice of me."

"What do you mean?" He found himself caught by the cynical tone, the bitterness that he had never seen her expose.

"Don't you think, Wellington," she asked, "that a secretary bound to one by love is so much safer?"

"That is not a worthy thought, Jessica."

The rebuke came naturally to his lips. There was no doubt how the Duke felt about his concubine. One had only to watch him as he followed her with his eyes.

She sighed. "You're right. It's not worthy."

Again, she hugged herself, pressing the sheathed crysknife against her flesh and thinking of the unfinished business it represented.

"There'll be much bloodshed soon," she said. "The Harkonnens won't rest until they're dead or my Duke destroyed. The Baron cannot forget that Leto is a cousin of the royal blood—no matter what the distance— while the Harkonnen titles came out of the CHOAM pocketbook. But the poison in him, deep in his mind, is the knowledge that an Atreides had a Harkonnen banished for cowardice after the Battle of Corrin."

"The old feud," Yueh muttered. And for a moment he felt an acid touch of hate. The old feud had trapped him in its web, killed his Wanna or—worse—left her for Harkonnen tortures until her husband did their bidding. The old feud had trapped him and these people were part of that poisonous thing. The irony was that such deadliness should come to flower here on Arrakis, the one source in the universe of melange, the prolonger of life, the giver of health.

"What are you thinking?" she asked.

"I am thinking that the spice brings six hundred and twenty thousand solaris the decagram on the open market right now. That is wealth to buy many things."

"Does greed touch even you, Wellington?"

"Not greed."

"What then?"

He shrugged. "Futility." He glanced at her. "Can you remember your first taste of spice?"

"It tasted like cinnamon."

"But never twice the same," he said. "It's like life—it presents a different face each time you take it. Some hold that the spice produces a learned-flavor reaction. The body, learning a thing is good for it, interprets the flavor as pleasurable—slightly euphoric. And, like life, never to be truly synthesized."

"I think it would've been wiser for us to go renegade, to take ourselves beyond the Imperial reach," she said.

He saw that she hadn't been listening to him, focused on her words, wondering: *Yes—why didn't she make him do this? She could make him do virtually anything.*

He spoke quickly because here was truth and a change of subject: "Would you think it bold of me . . . Jessica, if I asked a personal question?"

She pressed against the window ledge in an unexplainable pang of disquiet. "Of course not. You're . . . my friend."

"Why haven't you made the Duke marry you?"

She whirled, head up, glaring. "Made him marry me? But—"

"I should not have asked," he said.

"No." She shrugged. "There's good political reason—as long as my Duke remains unmarried some of the Great Houses can still hope for alliance. And. . . ." She sighed. ". . . motivating people, forcing them to your will, gives you a cynical attitude toward humanity. It degrades everything it touches. If I made him do . . . this, then it would not be his doing."

"It's a thing my Wanna might have said," he murmured. And this, too, was truth. He put a hand to his mouth, swallowing convulsively. He had never been closer to speaking out, confessing his secret role.

Jessica spoke, shattering the moment. "Besides, Wellington, the Duke is really two men. One of them I love very much. He's charming, witty, considerate . . . tender—everything a woman could desire. But the other man is . . . cold, callous, demanding, selfish—as harsh and cruel as a winter wind. That's the man shaped by the father." Her face contorted. "If only that old man had died when my Duke was born!"

In the silence that came between them, a breeze from a ventilator could be heard fingering the blinds.

Presently, she took a deep breath, said, "Leto's right—these rooms are nicer than the ones in the other sections of the house." She turned, sweeping the room with her gaze. "If you'll excuse me, Wellington, I want another look through this wing before I assign quarters."

He nodded. "Of course." And he thought: *If only there were some way not to do this thing that I must do.*

Jessica dropped her arms, crossed to the hall door and stood there a moment, hesitating, then let herself out. *All the time we talked he was hiding something, holding something back,* she thought. *To save my feelings, no doubt. He's a good man.* Again, she hesitated, almost turned back to confront Yueh and drag the hidden thing from him. *But that would only shame him, frighten him to learn he's so easily read. I should place more trust in my friends.*

Many have remarked the speed with which Muad'Dib learned the necessities of Arrakis. The Bene Gesserit, of course, know the basis of this speed. For the others, we can say that Muad'Dib learned rapidly because his first training was in how to learn. And the first lesson of all was the basic trust that he could learn. It is shocking to find how many people do not believe they can learn, and how many more believe learning to be difficult. Muad'Dib knew that every experience carries its lesson.

—FROM "THE HUMANITY OF MUAD'DIB"
BY THE PRINCESS IRULAN

Paul lay on the bed feigning sleep. It had been easy to palm Dr. Yueh's sleeping tablet, to pretend to swallow it. Paul suppressed a laugh. Even his mother had believed him asleep. He had wanted to jump up and ask her permission to go exploring the house, but had realized she wouldn't approve. Things were too unsettled yet. No. This way was best.

If I slip out without asking I haven't disobeyed orders. And I will stay in the house where it's safe.

He heard his mother and Yueh talking in the other room. Their words were indistinct—something about the spice . . . the Harkonnens. The conversation rose and fell.

Paul's attention went to the carved headboard of his bed—a false headboard attached to the wall and concealing the controls for this room's functions. A leaping fish had been shaped on the wood with thick brown waves beneath it. He knew if he pushed the fish's one visible eye that would turn on the room's suspensor lamps. One of the waves, when twisted, controlled ventilation. Another changed the temperature.

Quietly, Paul sat up in bed. A tall bookcase stood against the wall to his left. It could be swung aside to reveal a closet with drawers along one side. The handle on the door into the hall was patterned on an ornithopter thrust bar.

It was as though the room had been designed to entice him.

The room and this planet.

He thought of the filmbook Yueh had shown him—"Arrakis: His Imperial Majesty's Desert Botanical Testing Station." It was an old filmbook from before discovery of the spice. Names flitted through Paul's mind, each with its picture imprinted by the book's mnemonic pulse: *saguaro, burro bush, date palm, sand verbena, evening primrose, barrel cactus, incense bush, smoke tree, creosote bush . . . kit fox, desert hawk, kangaroo mouse. . . .*

Names and pictures, names and pictures from man's terranic past— and many to be found now nowhere else in the universe except here on Arrakis.

So many new things to learn about—the spice.

And the sandworms.

A door closed in the other room. Paul heard his mother's footsteps retreating down the hall. Dr. Yueh, he knew, would find something to read and remain in the other room.

Now was the moment to go exploring.

Paul slipped out of the bed, headed for the bookcase door that opened into the closet. He stopped at a sound behind him, turned. The carved headboard of the bed was folding down onto the spot where he had been sleeping. Paul froze, and immobility saved his life.

From behind the headboard slipped a tiny hunter-seeker no more than five centimeters long. Paul recognized it at once—a common assassination weapon that every child of royal blood learned about at an early age. It was a ravening sliver of metal guided by some nearby hand and eye. It could burrow into moving flesh and chew its way up nerve channels to the nearest vital organ.

The seeker lifted, swung sideways across the room and back.

Through Paul's mind flashed the related knowledge, the hunter-seeker limitations: Its compressed suspensor field distorted the room to reflect his target, the operator would be relying on motion—anything that moved. A shield could slow a hunter, give time to destroy it, but Paul had put aside his shield on the bed. Lasguns would knock them down, but lasguns were expensive and notoriously cranky of maintenance—and there was always the peril of explosive pyrotechnics if the laser beam intersected a hot shield. The Atreides relied on their body shields and their wits.

Now, Paul held himself in near catatonic immobility, knowing he had only his wits to meet this threat.

The hunter-seeker lifted another half meter. It rippled through the slatted light from the window blinds, back and forth, quartering the room.

I must try to grab it, he thought. *The suspensor field will make it slippery on the bottom. I must grip tightly.*

The thing dropped a half meter, quartered to the left, circled back around the bed. A faint humming could be heard from it.

Who is operating that thing? Paul wondered. *It has to be someone near. I could shout for Yueh, but it would take him the instant the door opened.*

The hall door behind Paul creaked. A rap sounded there. The door opened.

The hunter-seeker arrowed past his head toward the motion.

Paul's right hand shot out and down, gripping the deadly thing. It hummed and twisted in his hand, but his muscles were locked on it in desperation. With a violent turn and thrust, he slammed the thing's nose against the metal doorplate. He felt the crunch of it as the nose eye smashed and the seeker went dead in his hand.

Still, he held it—to be certain.

Paul's eyes came up, met the open stare of total blue from the Shadout Mapes.

"Your father has sent for you," she said. "There are men in the hall to escort you."

Paul nodded, his eyes and awareness focusing on this odd woman in a sacklike dress of bondsman brown. She was looking now at the thing clutched in his hand.

"I've heard of suchlike," she said. "It would've killed me, not so?"

He had to swallow before he could speak. "I . . . was its target."

"But it was coming for me."

"Because you were moving." And he wondered: *Who is this creature?*

"Then you saved my life," she said.

"I saved both our lives."

"Seems like you could've let it have me and made your own escape," she said.

"Who are you?" he asked.

"The Shadout Mapes, housekeeper."

"How did you know where to find me?"

"Your mother told me. I met her at the stairs to the weirding room down the hall." She pointed to her right. "Your father's men are still waiting."

Those will be Hawat's men, he thought. *We must find the operator of this thing.*

"Go to my father's men," he said. "Tell them I've caught a hunter-seeker in the house and they're to spread out and find the operator. Tell them to seal off the house and its grounds immediately. They'll know how to go about it. The operator's sure to be a stranger among us."

And he wondered: *Could it be this creature?* But he knew it wasn't. The seeker had been under control when she entered.

"Before I do your bidding, manling," Mapes said, "I must cleanse the way between us. You've put a water burden on me that I'm not sure I care to support. But we Fremen pay our debts—be they black debts or white debts. And it's known to us that you've a traitor in your midst. Who it is, we cannot say, but we're certain sure of it. Mayhap there's the hand guided that flesh-cutter."

Paul absorbed this in silence: *a traitor*. Before he could speak, the odd woman whirled away and ran back toward the entry.

He thought to call her back, but there was an air about her that told him she would resent it. She'd told him what she knew and now she was going to do his *bidding*. The house would be swarming with Hawat's men in a minute.

His mind went to other parts of that strange conversation: *weirding room*. He looked to his left where she had pointed. *We Fremen*. So that was a Fremen. He paused for the mnemonic blink that would store the pattern of her face in his memory—prune-wrinkled features darkly browned, blue-on-blue eyes without any white in them. He attached the label: *The Shadout Mapes*.

Still gripping the shattered seeker, Paul turned back into his room, scooped up his shield belt from the bed with his left hand, swung it around his waist and buckled it as he ran back out and down the hall to the left.

She'd said his mother was someplace down here—stairs . . . a *weirding room*.

What had the Lady Jessica to sustain her in her time of trial? Think you carefully on this Bene Gesserit proverb and perhaps you will see: "Any road followed precisely to its end leads precisely nowhere. Climb the mountain just a little bit to test that it's a mountain. From the top of the mountain, you cannot see the mountain."

—FROM "MUAD'DIB: FAMILY COMMENTARIES" BY THE PRINCESS IRULAN

At the end of the south wing, Jessica found a metal stair spiraling up to an oval door. She glanced back down the hall, again up at the door.

Oval? she wondered. *What an odd shape for a door in a house.*

Through the windows beneath the spiral stair she could see the great white sun of Arrakis moving on toward evening. Long shadows stabbed down the hall. She returned her attention to the stairs. Harsh sidelighting picked out bits of dried earth on the open metalwork of the steps.

Jessica put a hand on the rail, began to climb. The rail felt cold under her sliding palm. She stopped at the door, saw it had no handle, but there was a faint depression on the surface of it where a handle should have been.

Surely not a palm lock, she told herself. *A palm lock must be keyed to one individual's hand shape and palm lines.* But it looked like a palm lock. And there were ways to open any palm lock—as she had learned at school.

Jessica glanced back to make certain she was unobserved, placed her palm against the depression in the door. The most gentle of pressures to distort the lines—a turn of the wrist, another turn, a sliding twist of the palm across the surface.

She felt the click.

But there were hurrying footsteps in the hall beneath her. Jessica lifted her hand from the door, turned, saw Mapes come to the foot of the stairs.

"There are men in the Great Hall say they've been sent by the Duke to get young Master Paul," Mapes said. "They've the ducal signet and the guard has identified them." She glanced at the door, back to Jessica.

A cautious one, this Mapes, Jessica thought. *That's a good sign.*

"He's in the fifth room from this end of the hall, the small bedroom," Jessica said. "If you have trouble waking him, call on Dr. Yueh in the next room. Paul may require a wakeshot."

Again, Mapes cast a piercing stare at the oval door, and Jessica thought she detected loathing in the expression. Before Jessica could ask about the door and what it concealed, Mapes had turned away, hurrying back down the hall.

Hawat certified this place, Jessica thought. *There can't be anything too terrible in here.*

She pushed the door. It swung inward onto a small room with another oval door opposite. The other door had a wheel handle.

An airlock! Jessica thought. She glanced down, saw a door prop fallen to the floor of the little room. The prop carried Hawat's personal mark. *The door was left propped open,* she thought. *Someone probably knocked the prop down accidentally, not realizing the outer door would close on a palm lock.*

She stepped over the lip into the little room.

Why an airlock in a house? she asked herself. And she thought suddenly of exotic creatures sealed off in special climates.

Special climate!

That would make sense on Arrakis where even the driest of off-planet growing things had to be irrigated.

The door behind her began swinging closed. She caught it and propped it open securely with the stick Hawat had left. Again, she faced the wheel-locked inner door, seeing now a faint inscription etched in the metal above the handle. She recognized Galach words, read:

"O, Man! Here is a lovely portion of God's Creation; then, stand before it and learn to love the perfection of Thy Supreme Friend."

Jessica put her weight on the wheel. It turned left and the inner door opened. A gentle draft feathered her cheek, stirred her hair. She felt change in the air, a richer taste. She swung the door wide, looked through into massed greenery with yellow sunlight pouring across it.

A yellow sun? she asked herself. Then: *Filter glass!*

She stepped over the sill and the door swung closed behind.

"A wet-planet conservatory," she breathed.

Potted plants and low-pruned trees stood all about. She recognized a mimosa, a flowering quince, a sondagi, green-blossomed pleniscenta, green and white striped akarso . . . roses. . . .

Even roses!

She bent to breathe the fragrance of a giant pink blossom, straightened to peer around the room.

Rhythmic noise invaded her senses.

She parted a jungle overlapping of leaves, looked through to the center of the room. A low fountain stood there, small with fluted lips. The rhythmic noise was a peeling, spooling arc of water falling thud-a-gallop onto the metal bowl.

Jessica sent herself through the quick sense-clearing regimen, began a methodical inspection of the room's perimeter. It appeared to be about ten meters square. From its placement above the end of the hall and from subtle differences in construction, she guessed it had been added onto the roof of this wing long after the original building's completion.

She stopped at the south limits of the room in front of the wide reach of filter glass, stared around. Every available space in the room was crowded with exotic wet-climate plants. Something rustled in the greenery. She tensed, then glimpsed a simple clock-set servok with pipe and hose arms. An arm lifted, sent out a fine spray of dampness that misted her cheeks. The arm retracted and she looked at what it had watered: a fern tree.

Water everywhere in this room—on a planet where water was the most precious juice of life. Water being wasted so conspicuously that it shocked her to inner stillness.

She glanced out at the filter-yellowed sun. It hung low on a jagged horizon above cliffs that formed part of the immense rock uplifting known as the Shield Wall.

Filter glass, she thought. *To turn a white sun into something softer and more familiar. Who could have built such a place? Leto? It would be like him to surprise me with such a gift, but there hasn't been time. And he's been busy with more serious problems.*

She recalled the report that many Arrakeen houses were sealed by airlock doors and windows to conserve and reclaim interior moisture. Leto had said it was a deliberate statement of power and wealth for this house to ignore such precautions, its doors and windows being sealed only against the omnipresent dust.

But this room embodied a statement far more significant than the lack of waterseals on outer doors. She estimated that this pleasure room used water enough to support a thousand persons on Arrakis—possibly more.

Jessica moved along the window, continuing to stare into the room. The move brought into view a metallic surface at table height beside the fountain and she glimpsed a white notepad and stylus there partly concealed by an overhanging fan leaf. She crossed to the table, noted Hawat's daysigns on it, studied a message written on the pad:

"TO THE LADY JESSICA—

May this place give you as much pleasure as it has given me. Please permit the room to convey a lesson we learned from the same teachers: the proximity of a desirable thing tempts one to overindulgence. On that path lies danger.

My kindest wishes,
MARGOT LADY FENRING"

Jessica nodded, remembering that Leto had referred to the Emperor's former proxy here as Count Fenring. But the hidden message of the note demanded immediate attention, couched as it was in a way to inform her the writer was another Bene Gesserit. A bitter thought touched Jessica in passing: *The Count married his Lady.*

Even as this thought flicked through her mind, she was bending to seek out the hidden message. It had to be there. The visible note contained the code phrase every Bene Gesserit not bound by a School Injunction was required to give another Bene Gesserit when conditions demanded it: "On that path lies danger."

Jessica felt the back of the note, rubbed the surface for coded dots. Nothing. The edge of the pad came under her seeking fingers. Nothing. She replaced the pad where she had found it, feeling a sense of urgency.

Something in the position of the pad? she wondered.

But Hawat had been over this room, doubtless had moved the pad. She looked at the leaf above the pad. The leaf! She brushed a finger along the under surface, along the edge, along the stem. It was there! Her fingers detected the subtle coded dots, scanned them in a single passage:

"Your son and the Duke are in immediate danger. A bedroom has been designed to attract your son. The H loaded it with death traps to be discovered, leaving one that may escape detection." Jessica put down the urge to run back to Paul; the full message had to be learned. Her fingers sped over the dots: "I do not know the exact nature of the menace, but it has something to do with a bed. The threat to your Duke involves defection of a trusted companion or lieutenant. The H plan to give you as gift to a minion. To the best of my knowledge, this conservatory is safe. Forgive that I cannot tell more. My sources are few as my Count is not in the pay of the H. In haste, MF."

Jessica thrust the leaf aside, whirled to dash back to Paul. In that instant, the airlock door slammed open. Paul jumped through it, holding something in his right hand, slammed the door behind him. He saw his mother, pushed through the leaves to her, glanced at the fountain, thrust his hand and the thing it clutched under the falling water.

"Paul!" She grabbed his shoulder, staring at the hand. "What is that?"

He spoke casually, but she caught the effort behind the tone: "Hunter-seeker. Caught it in my room and smashed its nose, but I want to be sure. Water should short it out."

"Immerse it!" she commanded.

He obeyed.

Presently, she said: "Withdraw your hand. Leave the thing in the water."

He brought out his hand, shook water from it, staring at the quiescent metal in the fountain. Jessica broke off a plant stem, prodded the deadly sliver.

It was dead.

She dropped the stem into the water, looked at Paul. His eyes studied the room with a searching intensity that she recognized—the B.G. Way.

"This place could conceal anything," he said.

"I've reason to believe it's safe," she said.

"My room was supposed to be safe, too. Hawat said—"

"It was a hunter-seeker," she reminded him. "That means someone inside the house to operate it. Seeker control beams have a limited range. The thing could've been spirited in here after Hawat's investigation."

But she thought of the message of the leaf: "... *defection of a trusted companion or lieutenant.*" *Not Hawat, surely. Oh, surely not Hawat.*

"Hawat's men are searching the house right now," he said. "That seeker almost got the old woman who came to wake me."

"The Shadout Mapes," Jessica said, remembering the encounter at the stairs. "A summons from your father to—"

"That can wait," Paul said. "Why do you think this room's safe?"

She pointed to the note, explained about it.

He relaxed slightly.

But Jessica remained inwardly tense, thinking: *A hunter-seeker! Merciful Mother!* It took all her training to prevent a fit of hysterical trembling.

Paul spoke matter-of-factly: "It's the Harkonnens, of course. We shall have to destroy them."

A rapping sounded at the airlock door—the code knock of one of Hawat's corps.

"Come in," Paul called.

The door swung wide and a tall man in Atreides uniform with a Hawat insignia on his cap leaned into the room. "There you are, sir," he said. "The housekeeper said you'd be here." He glanced around the room. "We found a cairn in the cellar and caught a man in it. He had a seeker console."

"I'll want to take part in the interrogation," Jessica said.

"Sorry, my Lady. We messed him up catching him. He died."

"Nothing to identify him?" she asked.

"We've found nothing yet, my Lady."

"Was he an Arrakeen native?" Paul asked.

Jessica nodded at the astuteness of the question.

"He has the native look," the man said. "Put into that cairn more'n a month ago, by the look, and left there to await our coming. Stone and mortar where he came through into the cellar were untouched when we inspected the place yesterday. I'll stake my reputation on it."

"No one questions your thoroughness," Jessica said.

"I question it, my Lady. We should've used sonic probes down there."

"I presume that's what you're doing now," Paul said.

"Yes, sir."

"Send word to my father that we'll be delayed."

"At once, sir." He glanced at Jessica. "It's Hawat's order that under such circumstances as these the young Master be guarded in a safe place." Again, his eyes swept the room. "What of this place?"

"I've reason to believe it safe," she said. "Both Hawat and I have inspected it."

"Then I'll mount guard outside here, m'Lady, until we've been over the house once more." He bowed, touched his cap to Paul, backed out and swung the door closed behind him.

Paul broke the sudden silence, saying: "Had we better go over the house later ourselves? Your eyes might see things others would miss."

"This wing was the only place I hadn't examined," she said. "I put it off to last because. . . ."

"Because Hawat gave it his personal attention," he said.

She darted a quick look at his face, questioning.

"Do you distrust Hawat?" she asked.

"No, but he's getting old . . . he's overworked. We could take some of the load from him."

"That'd only shame him and impair his efficiency," she said. "A stray insect won't be able to wander into this wing after he hears about this. He'll be shamed that. . . ."

"We must take our own measures," he said.

"Hawat has served three generations of Atreides with honor," she said. "He deserves every respect and trust we can pay him . . . many times over."

Paul said: "When my father is bothered by something you've done he says *'Bene Gesserit!'* like a swear word."

"And what is it about me that bothers your father?"

"When you argue with him."

"You are not your father, Paul."

And Paul thought: *It'll worry her, but I must tell her what that Mapes woman said about a traitor among us.*

"What're you holding back?" Jessica asked. "This isn't like you, Paul."

He shrugged, recounted the exchange with Mapes.

And Jessica thought of the message of the leaf. She came to sudden decision, showed Paul the leaf, told him its message.

"My father must learn of this at once," he said. "I'll radiograph it in code and get it off."

"No," she said. "You will wait until you can see him alone. As few as possible must learn about it."

"Do you mean we should trust no one?"

"There's another possibility," she said. "This message may have been meant to get to us. The people who gave it to us may believe it's true, but it may be that the only purpose was to get this message to us."

Paul's face remained sturdily somber. "To sow distrust and suspicion in our ranks, to weaken us that way," he said.

"You must tell your father privately and caution him about this aspect of it," she said.

"I understand."

She turned to the tall reach of filter glass, stared out to the southwest where the sun of Arrakis was sinking—a yellowed ball above the cliffs.

Paul turned with her, said: "I don't think it's Hawat, either. Is it possible it's Yueh?"

"He's not a lieutenant or companion," she said. "And I can assure you he hates the Harkonnens as bitterly as we do."

Paul directed his attention to the cliffs, thinking: *And it couldn't be Gurney . . . or Duncan. Could it be one of the sub-lieutenants? Impossible. They're all from families that've been loyal to us for generations—for good reason.*

Jessica rubbed her forehead, sensing her own fatigue. *So much peril here!* She looked out at the filter-yellowed landscape, studying it. Beyond the ducal grounds stretched a high-fenced storage yard—lines of spice silos in it with stilt-legged watchtowers standing around it like so many startled spiders. She could see at least twenty storage yards of silos reaching out to the cliffs of the Shield Wall—silos repeated, stuttering across the basin.

Slowly, the filtered sun buried itself beneath the horizon. Stars leaped out. She saw one bright star so low on the horizon that it twinkled with a clear, precise rhythm—a trembling of light: blink-blink-blink-blink-blink . . .

Paul stirred beside her in the dusky room.

But Jessica concentrated on that single bright star, realizing that it was *too* low, that it must come from the Shield Wall cliffs.

Someone signaling!

She tried to read the message, but it was in no code she had ever learned.

Other lights had come on down on the plain beneath the cliffs: little yellows spaced out against blue darkness. And one light off to their left grew brighter, began to wink back at the cliff—very fast: blinksquirt, glimmer, blink!

And it was gone.

The false star in the cliff winked out immediately.

Signals . . . and they filled her with premonition.

Why were lights used to signal across the basin? she asked herself. *Why couldn't they use the communications network?*

The answer was obvious: the communinet was certain to be tapped now by agents of the Duke Leto. Light signals could only mean that messages were being sent between his enemies—between Harkonnen agents.

There came a tapping at the door behind them and the voice of Hawat's man: "All clear, sir . . . m'Lady. Time to be getting the young Master to his father."

It is said that the Duke Leto blinded himself to the perils of Arrakis, that he walked heedlessly into the pit. Would it not be more likely to suggest he had lived so long in the presence of extreme danger he misjudged a change in its intensity? Or is it possible he deliberately sacrificed himself that his son might find a better life? All evidence indicates the Duke was a man not easily hoodwinked.

—FROM "MUAD'DIB: FAMILY COMMENTARIES" BY THE PRINCESS IRULAN

The Duke Leto Atreides leaned against a parapet of the landing control tower outside Arrakeen. The night's first moon, an oblate silver coin, hung well above the southern horizon. Beneath it, the jagged cliffs of the Shield Wall shone like parched icing through a dust haze. To his left, the lights of Arrakeen glowed in the haze—yellow . . . white . . . blue.

He thought of the notices posted now above his signature all through the populous places of the planet: "Our Sublime Padishah Emperor has charged me to take possession of this planet and end all dispute."

The ritualistic formality of it touched him with a feeling of loneliness. *Who was fooled by that fatuous legalism? Not the Fremen, certainly. Nor the Houses Minor who controlled the interior trade of Arrakis . . . and were Harkonnen creatures almost to a man.*

They have tried to take the life of my son!

The rage was difficult to suppress.

He saw lights of a moving vehicle coming toward the landing field from Arrakeen. He hoped it was the guard and troop carrier bringing Paul. The delay was galling even though he knew it was prompted by caution on the part of Hawat's lieutenant.

They have tried to take the life of my son!

He shook his head to drive out the angry thoughts, glanced back at the field where five of his own frigates were posted around the rim like monolithic sentries.

Better a cautious delay than . . .

The lieutenant was a good one, he reminded himself. A man marked for advancement, *completely loyal.*

"Our Sublime Padishah Emperor. . . ."

If the people of this decadent garrison city could only see the Emperor's private note to his "Noble Duke"—the disdainful allusions to veiled men and women: ". . . but what else is one to expect of barbarians whose dearest dream is to live outside the ordered security of the faufreluches?"

The Duke felt in this moment that his own dearest dream was to end all class distinctions and never again think of deadly order. He looked up and out of the dust at the unwinking stars, thought: *Around one of those little lights circles Caladan . . . but I'll never again see my home.* The longing for Caladan was a sudden pain in his breast. He felt that it did not come from within himself, but that it reached out to him from Caladan. He could not bring himself to call this dry wasteland of Arrakis his home, and he doubted he ever would.

I must mask my feelings, he thought. *For the boy's sake. If ever he's to have a home, this must be it. I may think of Arrakis as a hell I've reached before death, but he must find here that which will inspire him. There must be something.*

A wave of self-pity, immediately despised and rejected, swept through him, and for some reason he found himself recalling two lines from a poem Gurney Halleck often repeated—

> *"My lungs taste the air of Time*
> *Blown past falling sands. . . ."*

Well, Gurney would find plenty of falling sands here, the Duke thought. The central wastelands beyond those moon-frosted cliffs were desert—barren rock, dunes, and blowing dust, an uncharted dry wilderness with here and there along its rim and perhaps scattered through it, knots of Fremen. If anything could buy a future for the Atreides line, the Fremen just might do it.

Provided the Harkonnens hadn't managed to infect even the Fremen with their poisonous schemes.

They have tried to take the life of my son!

A scraping metal racket vibrated through the tower, shook the parapet beneath his arms. Blast shutters dropped in front of him, blocking the view.

Shuttle's coming in, he thought. *Time to go down and get to work.* He turned to the stairs behind him, headed down to the big assembly room, trying to remain calm as he descended, to prepare his face for the coming encounter.

They have tried to take the life of my son!

The men were already boiling in from the field when he reached the yellow-domed room. They carried their spacebags over their shoulders, shouting and roistering like students returning from vacation.

"Hey! Feel that under your dogs? That's gravity, man!" "How many G's does this place pull? Feels heavy." "Nine-tenths of a G by the book."

The crossfire of thrown words filled the big room.

"Did you get a good look at this hole on the way down? Where's all the loot this place's supposed to have?" "The Harkonnens took it with 'em!" "Me for a hot shower and a soft bed!" "Haven't you heard, stupid? No showers down here. You scrub your ass with sand!" "Hey! Can it! The Duke!"

The Duke stepped out of the stair entry into a suddenly silent room.

Gurney Halleck strode along at the point of the crowd, bag over one shoulder, the neck of his nine-string baliset clutched in the other hand. They were long-fingered hands with big thumbs, full of tiny movements that drew such delicate music from the baliset.

The Duke watched Halleck, admiring the ugly lump of a man, noting the glass-splinter eyes with their gleam of savage understanding. Here was a man who lived outside the faufreluches while obeying their every precept. What was it Paul had called him? *"Gurney, the valorous."*

Halleck's wispy blond hair trailed across barren spots on his head. His wide mouth was twisted into a pleasant sneer, and the scar of the inkvine whip slashed across his jawline seemed to move with a life of its own. His whole air was of casual, shoulder-set capability. He came up to the Duke, bowed.

"Gurney," Leto said.

"My Lord." He gestured with the baliset toward the men in the room. "This is the last of them. I'd have preferred coming in with the first wave, but. . . ."

"There are still some Harkonnens for you," the Duke said. "Step aside with me, Gurney, where we may talk."

"Yours to command, my Lord."

They moved into an alcove beside a coil-slot water machine while the men stirred restlessly in the big room. Halleck dropped his bag into a corner, kept his grip on the baliset.

"How many men can you let Hawat have?" the Duke asked.

"Is Thufir in trouble, Sire?"

"He's lost only two agents, but his advance men gave us an excellent line on the entire Harkonnen setup here. If we move fast we may gain a measure of security, the breathing space we require. He wants as many men as you can spare—men who won't balk at a little knife work."

"I can let him have three hundred of my best," Halleck said. "Where shall I send them?"

"To the main gate. Hawat has an agent there waiting to take them."

"Shall I get about it at once, Sire?"

"In a moment. We have another problem. The field commandant will hold the shuttle here until dawn on a pretext. The Guild Heighliner that brought us is going on about its business, and the shuttle's supposed to make contact with a cargo ship taking up a load of spice."

"Our spice, m'Lord?"

"Our spice. But the shuttle also will carry some of the spice hunters from the old regime. They've opted to leave with the change of fief and the Judge of the Change is allowing it. These are valuable workers, Gurney, about eight hundred of them. Before the shuttle leaves, you must persuade some of those men to enlist with us."

"How strong a persuasion, Sire?"

"I want their willing cooperation, Gurney. Those men have experience and skills we need. The fact that they're leaving suggests they're not part of the Harkonnen machine. Hawat believes there could be some bad ones planted in the group, but he sees assassins in every shadow."

"Thufir has found some very productive shadows in his time, m'Lord."

"And there are some he hasn't found. But I think planting sleepers in this outgoing crowd would show too much imagination for the Harkonnens."

"Possibly, Sire. Where are these men?"

"Down on the lower level, in a waiting room. I suggest you go down and play a tune or two to soften their minds, then turn on the pressure. You may offer positions of authority to those who qualify. Offer twenty per cent higher wages than they received under the Harkonnens."

"No more than that, Sire? I know the Harkonnen pay scales. And to men with their termination pay in their pockets and the wanderlust on them . . . well, Sire, twenty per cent would hardly seem proper inducement to stay."

Leto spoke impatiently: "Then use your own discretion in particular cases. Just remember that the treasury isn't bottomless. Hold it to twenty per cent whenever you can. We particularly need spice drivers, weather scanners, dune men—any with open sand experience."

"I understand, Sire. 'They shall come all for violence: their faces shall sup up as the east wind, and they shall gather the captivity of the sand.'"

"A very moving quotation," the Duke said. "Turn your crew over to a lieutenant. Have him give a short drill on water discipline, then bed the men down for the night in the barracks adjoining the field. Field personnel will direct them. And don't forget the men for Hawat."

"Three hundred of the best, Sire." He took up his spacebag. "Where shall I report to you when I've completed my chores?"

"I've taken over a council room topside here. We'll hold staff there. I want to arrange a new planetary dispersal order with armored squads going out first."

Halleck stopped in the act of turning away, caught Leto's eye. "Are you anticipating *that* kind of trouble, Sire? I thought there was a Judge of the Change here."

"Both open battle and secret," the Duke said. "There'll be blood aplenty spilled here before we're through."

"'And the water which thou takest out of the river shall become blood upon the dry land,'" Halleck quoted.

The Duke sighed. "Hurry back, Gurney."

"Very good, m'Lord." The whipscar rippled to his grin. "'Behold, as a wild ass in the desert, go I forth to my work.'" He turned, strode to the center of the room, paused to relay his orders, hurried on through the men.

Leto shook his head at the retreating back. Halleck was a continual amazement—a head full of songs, quotations, and flowery phrases . . . and the heart of an assassin when it came to dealing with the Harkonnens.

Presently, Leto took a leisurely diagonal course across to the lift, acknowledging salutes with a casual hand wave. He recognized a propaganda corpsman, stopped to give him a message that could be relayed to the men through channels: those who had brought their women would want to know the women were safe and where they could be found. The others would wish to know that the population here appeared to boast more women than men.

The Duke slapped the propaganda man on the arm, a signal that the message had top priority to be put out immediately, then continued across the room. He nodded to the men, smiled, traded pleasantries with a subaltern.

Command must always look confident, he thought. *All that faith riding on your shoulders while you sit in the critical seat and never show it.*

He breathed a sigh of relief when the lift swallowed him and he could turn and face the impersonal doors.

They have tried to take the life of my son!

Over the exit of the Arrakeen landing field, crudely carved as though with a poor instrument, there was an inscription that Muad'Dib was to repeat many times. He saw it that first night on Arrakis, having been brought to the ducal command post to participate in his father's first full staff conference. The words of the inscription were a plea to those leaving Arrakis, but they fell with dark import on the eyes of a boy who had just escaped a close brush with death. They said: "O you who know what we suffer here, do not forget us in your prayers."

—FROM "MANUAL OF MUAD'DIB"
BY THE PRINCESS IRULAN

"The whole theory of warfare is calculated risk," the Duke said, "but when it comes to risking your own family, the element of *calculation* gets submerged in . . . other things."

He knew he wasn't holding in his anger as well as he should, and he turned, strode down the length of the long table and back.

The Duke and Paul were alone in the conference room at the landing field. It was an empty-sounding room, furnished only with the long table, old-fashioned three-legged chairs around it, and a map board and projector at one end. Paul sat at the table near the map board. He had told his father the experience with the hunter-seeker and given the reports that a traitor threatened him.

The Duke stopped across from Paul, pounded the table: "Hawat told me that house was secure!"

Paul spoke hesitantly: "I was angry, too—at first. And I blamed Hawat. But the threat came from outside the house. It was simple, clever, and direct. And it would've succeeded were it not for the training given me by you and many others—including Hawat."

"Are you defending him?" the Duke demanded.

"Yes."

"He's getting old. That's it. He should be—"

"He's wise with much experience," Paul said. "How many of Hawat's mistakes can you recall?"

"I should be the one defending him," the Duke said. "Not you."

Paul smiled.

Leto sat down at the head of the table, put a hand over his son's. "You've . . . matured lately, Son." He lifted his hand. "It gladdens me." He matched his son's smile. "Hawat will punish himself. He'll direct more anger against himself over this than both of us together could pour on him."

Paul glanced toward the darkened windows beyond the map board, looked at the night's blackness. Room lights reflected from a balcony railing out there. He saw movement and recognized the shape of a guard in Atreides uniform. Paul looked back at the white wall behind his father, then down to the shiny surface of the table, seeing his own hands clenched into fists there.

The door opposite the Duke banged open. Thufir Hawat strode through it looking older and more leathery than ever. He paced down the length of the table, stopped at attention facing Leto.

"My Lord," he said, speaking to a point over Leto's head, "I have just learned how I failed you. It becomes necessary that I tender my resig—"

"Oh, sit down and stop acting the fool," the Duke said. He waved to the chair across from Paul. "If you made a mistake, it was in *over*estimating the Harkonnens. Their simple minds came up with a simple trick. We didn't count on simple tricks. And my son has been at great pains to point out to me that he came through this largely because of your training. You didn't fail there!" He tapped the back of the empty chair. "Sit down, I say!"

Hawat sank into the chair. "But—"

"I'll hear no more of it," the Duke said. "The incident is past. We have more pressing business. Where are the others?"

"I asked them to wait outside while I—"

"Call them in."

Hawat looked into Leto's eyes. "Sire, I—"

"I know who my true friends are, Thufir," the Duke said. "Call in the men."

Hawat swallowed. "At once, my Lord." He swiveled in the chair, called to the open door: "Gurney, bring them in."

Halleck led the file of men into the room, the staff officers looking grimly serious followed by the younger aides and specialists, an air of eagerness among them. Brief scuffing sounds echoed around the room as the men took seats. A faint smell of rachag stimulant wafted down the table.

"There's coffee for those who want it," the Duke said.

He looked over his men, thinking: *They're a good crew. A man could do far worse for this kind of war.* He waited while coffee was brought in from the adjoining room and served, noting the tiredness in some of the faces.

Presently, he put on his mask of quiet efficiency, stood up and commanded their attention with a knuckle rap against the table.

"Well, gentlemen," he said, "our civilization appears to've fallen so deeply into the habit of invasion that we cannot even obey a simple order of the Imperium without the old ways cropping up."

Dry chuckles sounded around the table, and Paul realized that his father had said the precisely correct thing in precisely the correct tone to lift the mood here. Even the hint of fatigue in his voice was right.

"I think first we'd better learn if Thufir has anything to add to his report on the Fremen," the Duke said. "Thufir?"

Hawat glanced up. "I've some economic matters to go into after my general report, Sire, but I can say now that the Fremen appear more and more to be the allies we need. They're waiting now to see if they can trust us, but they appear to be dealing openly. They've sent us a gift—stillsuits of their own manufacture ... maps of certain desert areas surrounding strongpoints the Harkonnens left behind. . . ." He glanced down at the table. "Their intelligence reports have proved completely reliable and have helped us considerably in our dealings with the Judge of the Change. They've also sent some incidental things—jewelry for the Lady Jessica, spice liquor, candy, medicinals. My men are processing the lot right now. There appears to be no trickery."

"You like these people, Thufir?" asked a man down the table.

Hawat turned to face his questioner. "Duncan Idaho says they're to be admired."

Paul glanced at his father, back to Hawat, ventured a question: "Have you any new information on how many Fremen there are?"

Hawat looked at Paul. "From food processing and other evidence, Idaho estimates the cave complex he visited consisted of some ten thousand people, all told. Their leader said he ruled a sietch of two thousand hearths. We've reason to believe there are a great many such sietch communities. All seem to give their allegiance to someone called Liet."

"That's something new," Leto said.

"It could be an error on my part, Sire. There are things to suggest this Liet may be a local deity."

Another man down the table cleared his throat, asked: "Is it certain they deal with the smugglers?"

"A smuggler caravan left this sietch while Idaho was there, carrying a heavy load of spice. They used pack beasts and indicated they faced an eighteen-day journey."

"It appears," the Duke said, "that the smugglers have redoubled their operations during this period of unrest. This deserves some careful thought. We shouldn't worry too much about unlicensed frigates working off our planet—it's always done. But to have them completely outside our observation—that's not good."

"You have a plan, Sire," Hawat asked.

The Duke looked at Halleck. "Gurney, I want you to head a delegation, an embassy if you will, to contact these romantic businessmen. Tell them I'll ignore their operations as long as they give me a ducal tithe. Hawat here estimates that graft and extra fighting men heretofore required in their operations have been costing them four times that amount."

"What if the Emperor gets wind of this?" Halleck asked. "He's very jealous of his CHOAM profits, m'Lord."

Leto smiled. "We'll bank the entire tithe openly in the name of Shaddam IV and deduct it legally from our levy support costs. Let the Harkonnens fight that! And we'll be ruining a few more of the locals who grew fat under the Harkonnen system. No more graft!"

A grin twisted Halleck's face. "Ahh, m'Lord, a beautiful low blow. Would that I could see the Baron's face when he learns of this."

The Duke turned to Hawat. "Thufir, did you get those account books you said you could buy?"

"Yes, my Lord. They're being examined in detail even now. I've skimmed them, though, and can give a first approximation."

"Give it, then."

"The Harkonnens took ten billion solaris out of here every three hundred and thirty Standard days."

A muted gasp ran around the table. Even the younger aides, who had been betraying some boredom, sat up straighter and exchanged wide-eyed looks.

Halleck murmured: "'For they shall suck of the abundance of the seas and of the treasure hid in the sand.'"

"You see, gentlemen," Leto said. "Is there anyone here so naive he believes the Harkonnens have quietly packed up and walked away from all this merely because the Emperor ordered it?"

There was a general shaking of heads, murmurous agreement.

"We will have to take it at the point of the sword," Leto said. He turned to Hawat. "This'd be a good point to report on equipment. How many sandcrawlers, harvesters, spice factories, and supporting equipment have they left us?"

"A full complement, as it says in the Imperial inventory audited by the Judge of the Change, my Lord," Hawat said. He gestured for an aide to pass him a folder, opened the folder on the table in front of him. "They neglect to mention that less than half the crawlers are operable, that only about a third have carryalls to fly them to spice sands—that everything the Harkonnens left us is ready to break down and fall apart. We'll be lucky to get half the equipment into operation and luckier yet if a fourth of it's still working six months from now."

"Pretty much as we expected," Leto said. "What's the firm estimate on basic equipment?"

Hawat glanced at his folder. "About nine hundred and thirty harvester factories that can be sent out in a few days. About sixty-two hundred and fifty ornithopters for survey, scouting, and weather observation . . . carryalls, a little under a thousand."

Halleck said: "Wouldn't it be cheaper to reopen negotiations with the Guild for permission to orbit a frigate as a weather satellite?"

The Duke looked at Hawat. "Nothing new there, eh, Thufir?"

"We must pursue other avenues for now," Hawat said. "The Guild agent wasn't really negotiating with us. He was merely making it plain—one Mentat to another—that the price was out of our reach and would remain so no matter how long a reach we develop. Our task is to find out why before we approach him again."

One of Halleck's aides down the table swiveled in his chair, snapped: "There's no justice in this!"

"Justice?" The Duke looked at the man. "Who asks for justice? We make our own justice. We make it here on Arrakis—win or die. Do you regret casting your lot with us, sir?"

The man stared at the Duke, then: "No, Sire. You couldn't turn and I could do nought but follow you. Forgive the outburst, but. . . ." He shrugged. ". . . we must all feel bitter at times."

"Bitterness I understand," the Duke said. "But let us not rail about justice as long as we have arms and the freedom to use them. Do any of the rest of you harbor bitterness? If so, let it out. This is friendly council where any man may speak his mind."

Halleck stirred, said: "I think what rankles, Sire, is that we've had no volunteers from the other Great Houses. They address you as 'Leto the Just' and promise eternal friendship, but only as long as it doesn't cost them anything."

"They don't know yet who's going to win this exchange," the Duke said. "Most of the Houses have grown fat by taking few risks. One cannot truly blame them for this; one can only despise them." He looked at Hawat. "We were discussing equipment. Would you care to project a few examples to familiarize the men with this machinery?"

Hawat nodded, gestured to an aide at the projector.

A solido tri-D projection appeared on the table surface about a third of the way down from the Duke. Some of the men farther along the table stood up to get a better look at it.

Paul leaned forward, staring at the machine.

Scaled against the tiny projected human figures around it, the thing was about one hundred and twenty meters long and about forty meters wide. It was basically a long, buglike body moving on independent sets of wide tracks.

"This is a harvester factory," Hawat said. "We chose one in good repair for this projection. There's one dragline outfit that came in with the first team of Imperial ecologists, though, and it's still running . . . although I don't know how . . . or why."

"If that's the one they call 'Old Maria,' it belongs in a museum," an aide said. "I think the Harkonnens kept it as a punishment job, a threat hanging over their workers' heads. Be good or you'll be assigned to Old Maria."

Chuckles sounded around the table.

Paul held himself apart from the humor, his attention focused on the projection and the question that filled his mind. He pointed to the image on the table, said: "Thufir, are there sandworms big enough to swallow that whole?"

Quick silence settled on the table. The Duke cursed under his breath, then thought: *No—they have to face the realities here.*

"There're worms in the deep desert could take this entire factory in one gulp," Hawat said. "Up here closer to the Shield Wall where most of the spicing's done there are plenty of worms that could cripple this factory and devour it at their leisure."

"Why don't we shield them?" Paul asked.

"According to Idaho's report," Hawat said, "shields are dangerous in the desert. A body-size shield will call every worm for hundreds of meters around. It appears to drive them into a killing frenzy. We've the Fremen word on this and no reason to doubt it. Idaho saw no evidence of shield equipment at the sietch."

"None at all?" Paul asked.

"It'd be pretty hard to conceal that kind of thing among several thousand people," Hawat said. "Idaho had free access to every part of the sietch. He saw no shields or any indication of their use."

"It's a puzzle," the Duke said.

"The Harkonnens certainly used plenty of shields here," Hawat said. "They had repair depots in every garrison village, and their accounts show a heavy expenditure for shield replacements and parts."

"Could the Fremen have a way of nullifying shields?" Paul asked.

"It doesn't seem likely," Hawat said. "It's theoretically possible, of course—a shire-sized static counter charge is supposed to do the trick, but no one's ever been able to put it to the test."

"We'd have heard about it before now," Halleck said. "The smugglers have close contact with the Fremen and would've acquired such a device if it were available. And they'd have had no inhibitions against marketing it off planet."

"I don't like an unanswered question of this importance," Leto said. "Thufir, I want you to give top priority to solution of this problem."

"We're already working on it, my Lord." He cleared his throat. "Ah-h, Idaho did say one thing: he said you couldn't mistake the Fremen attitude toward shields. He said they were mostly amused by them."

The Duke frowned, then: "The subject under discussion is spicing equipment."

Hawat gestured to his aide at the projector.

The solido-image of the harvester factory was replaced by a projection of a winged device that dwarfed the images of human figures around it. "This is a carryall," Hawat said. "It's essentially a large 'thopter, whose sole function is to deliver a factory to spice-rich sands, then to rescue the factory when a sandworm appears. They always appear.

Harvesting the spice is a process of getting in and getting out with as much as possible."

"Admirably suited to Harkonnen morality," the Duke said.

Laughter was abrupt and too loud.

An ornithopter replaced the carryall in the projection focus.

"These 'thopters are fairly conventional," Hawat said. "Major modifications give them extended range. Extra care has been used in sealing essential areas against sand and dust. Only about one in thirty is shielded—possibly discarding the shield generator's weight for greater range."

"I don't like this de-emphasis on shields," the Duke muttered. And he thought: *Is this the Harkonnen secret? Does it mean we won't even be able to escape on shielded frigates if all goes against us?* He shook his head sharply to drive out such thoughts, said: "Let's get to the working estimate. What'll our profit figure be?"

Hawat turned two pages in his notebook. "After assessing the repairs and operable equipment, we've worked out a first estimate on operating costs. It's based naturally on a depreciated figure for a clear safety margin." He closed his eyes in Mentat semitrance, said: "Under the Harkonnens, maintenance and salaries were held to fourteen per cent. We'll be lucky to make it at thirty per cent at first. With reinvestment and growth factors accounted for, including the CHOAM percentage and military costs, our profit margin will be reduced to a very narrow six or seven per cent until we can replace worn-out equipment. We then should be able to boost it up to twelve or fifteen per cent where it belongs." He opened his eyes. "Unless my Lord wishes to adopt Harkonnen methods."

"We're working for a solid and permanent planetary base," the Duke said. "We have to keep a large percentage of the people happy—especially the Fremen."

"Most especially the Fremen," Hawat agreed.

"Our supremacy on Caladan," the Duke said, "depended on sea and air power. Here, we must develop something I choose to call *desert* power. This may include air power, but it's possible it may not. I call your attention to the lack of 'thopter shields." He shook his head. "The Harkonnens relied on turnover from off planet for some of their key personnel. We don't dare. Each new lot would have its quota of provocateurs."

"Then we'll have to be content with far less profit and a reduced harvest," Hawat said. "Our output the first two seasons should be down a third from the Harkonnen average."

"There it is," the Duke said, "exactly as we expected. We'll have to move fast with the Fremen. I'd like five full battalions of Fremen troops before the first CHOAM audit."

"That's not much time, Sire," Hawat said.

"We don't have much time, as you well know. They'll be here with Sardaukar disguised as Harkonnens at the first opportunity. How many do you think they'll ship in, Thufir?"

"Four or five battalions all told, Sire. No more, Guild troop-transport costs being what they are."

"Then five battalions of Fremen plus our own forces ought to do it. Let us have a few captive Sardaukar to parade in front of the Landsraad Council and matters will be much different—profits or no profits."

"We'll do our best, Sire."

Paul looked at his father, back to Hawat, suddenly conscious of the Mentat's great age, aware that the old man had served three generations of Atreides. *Aged.* It showed in the rheumy shine of the brown eyes, in the cheeks cracked and burned by exotic weathers, in the rounded curve of the shoulders and the thin set of his lips with the cranberry-colored stain of sapho juice.

So much depends on one aged man, Paul thought.

"We're presently in a war of assassins," the Duke said, "but it has not achieved full scale. Thufir, what's the condition of the Harkonnen machine here?"

"We've eliminated two hundred and fifty-nine of their key people, my Lord. No more than three Harkonnen cells remain—perhaps a hundred people in all."

"These Harkonnen creatures you eliminated," the Duke said, "were they propertied?"

"Most were well situated, my Lord—in the entrepreneur class."

"I want you to forge certificates of allegiance over the signatures of each of them," the Duke said. "File copies with the Judge of the Change. We'll take the legal position that they stayed under false allegiance. Confiscate their property, take everything, turn out their families, strip them. And make sure the Crown gets its ten per cent. It must be entirely legal."

Thufir smiled, revealing red-stained teeth beneath the carmine lips. "A move worthy of your grandsire, my Lord. It shames me I didn't think of it first."

Halleck frowned across the table, noticing a deep scowl on Paul's face. The others were smiling and nodding.

It's wrong, Paul thought. *This'll only make the others fight all the harder. They've nothing to gain by surrendering.*

He knew the actual no-holds-barred convention that ruled in kanly, but this was the sort of move that could destroy them even as it gave them victory.

"'I have been a stranger in a strange land,'" Halleck quoted.

Paul stared at him, recognizing the quotation from the O.C. Bible, wondering: *Does Gurney, too, wish an end to devious plots?*

The Duke glanced at the darkness out the windows, looked back at Halleck. "Gurney, how many of those sandworkers did you persuade to stay with us?"

"Two hundred eighty-six in all, Sire. I think we should take them and consider ourselves lucky. They're all in useful categories."

"No more?" The Duke pursed his lips, then: "Well, pass the word along to—"

A disturbance at the door interrupted him. Duncan Idaho came through the guard there, hurried down the length of the table and bent over the Duke's ear.

Leto waved him back, said: "Speak out, Duncan. You can see this is strategy staff."

Paul studied Idaho, marking the feline movements, the swiftness of reflex that made him such a difficult weapons teacher to emulate. Idaho's dark round face turned toward Paul, the cave-sitter eyes giving no hint of recognition, but Paul recognized the mask of serenity over excitement.

Idaho looked down the length of the table, said: "We've taken a force of Harkonnen mercenaries disguised as Fremen. The Fremen themselves sent us a courier to warn of the false band. In the attack, however, we found the Harkonnens had waylaid the Fremen courier—badly wounded him. We were bringing him here for treatment by our medics when he died. I'd seen how badly off the man was and stopped to do what I could. I surprised him in the attempt to throw something away." Idaho glanced down at Leto. "A knife, m'Lord, a knife the like of which you've never seen."

"Crysknife?" someone asked.

"No doubt of it," Idaho said. "Milky white and glowing with a light of its own like." He reached into his tunic, brought out a sheath with a black-ridged handle protruding from it.

"Keep that blade in its sheath!"

The voice came from the open door at the end of the room, a vibrant and penetrating voice that brought them all up, staring.

A tall, robed figure stood in the door, barred by the crossed swords of the guard. A light tan robe completely enveloped the man except for a gap in the hood and black veil that exposed eyes of total blue—no white in them at all.

"Let him enter," Idaho whispered.

"Pass that man," the Duke said.

The guards hesitated, then lowered their swords.

The man swept into the room, stood across from the Duke.

"This is Stilgar, chief of the sietch I visited, leader of those who warned us of the false band," Idaho said.

"Welcome, sir," Leto said. "And why shouldn't we unsheath this blade?"

Stilgar glanced at Idaho, said: "You observed the customs of cleanliness and honor among us. I would permit you to see the blade of the man you befriended." His gaze swept the others in the room. "But I do not know these others. Would you have them defile an honorable weapon?"

"I am the Duke Leto," the Duke said. "Would you permit me to see this blade?"

"I'll permit you to earn the right to unsheath it," Stilgar said, and, as a mutter of protest sounded around the table, he raised a thin, darkly veined hand. "I remind you this is the blade of one who befriended you."

In the waiting silence, Paul studied the man, sensing the aura of power that radiated from him. He was a leader—a *Fremen* leader.

A man near the center of the table across from Paul muttered: "Who's he to tell us what rights we have on Arrakis?"

"It is said that the Duke Leto Atreides rules with the consent of the governed," the Fremen said. "Thus I must tell you the way it is with us: a certain responsibility falls on those who have seen a crysknife." He passed a dark glance across Idaho. "They are ours. They may never leave Arrakis without our consent."

Halleck and several of the others started to rise, angry expressions on their faces. Halleck said: "The Duke Leto determines whether—"

"One moment, please," Leto said, and the very mildness of his voice held them. *This must not get out of hand*, he thought. He addressed himself to the Fremen: "Sir, I honor and respect the personal dignity of any man who respects my dignity. I am indeed indebted to you. And I *always* pay my debts. If it is your custom that this knife remain sheathed here, then it is so ordered—by *me*. And if there is any other way we may honor the man who died in our service, you have but to name it."

The Fremen stared at the Duke, then slowly pulled aside his veil, revealing a thin nose and full-lipped mouth in a glistening black beard. Deliberately he bent over the end of the table, spat on its polished surface.

As the men around the table started to surge to their feet, Idaho's voice boomed across the room: "Hold!"

Into the sudden charged stillness, Idaho said: "We thank you, Stilgar, for the gift of your body's moisture. We accept it in the spirit with which it is given." And Idaho spat on the table in front of the Duke.

Aside to the Duke, he said: "Remember how precious water is here, Sire. That was a token of respect."

Leto sank back into his own chair, caught Paul's eye, a rueful grin on his son's face, sensed the slow relaxation of tension around the table as understanding came to his men.

The Fremen looked at Idaho, said: "You measured well in my sietch, Duncan Idaho. Is there a bond on your allegiance to your Duke?"

"He's asking me to enlist with him, Sire," Idaho said.

"Would he accept a dual allegiance?" Leto asked.

"You wish me to go with him, Sire?"

"I wish you to make your own decision in the matter," Leto said, and he could not keep the urgency out of his voice.

Idaho studied the Fremen. "Would you have me under these conditions, Stilgar? There'd be times when I'd have to return to serve my Duke."

"You fight well and you did your best for our friend," Stilgar said. He looked at Leto. "Let it be thus: the man Idaho keeps the crysknife he holds as a mark of his allegiance to us. He must be cleansed, of course, and the rites observed, but this can be done. He will be Fremen and soldier of the Atreides. There is precedent for this: Liet serves two masters."

"Duncan?" Leto asked.

"I understand, Sire," Idaho said.

"It is agreed, then," Leto said.

"Your water is ours, Duncan Idaho," Stilgar said. "The body of our friend remains with your Duke. His water is Atreides water. It is a bond between us."

Leto sighed, glanced at Hawat, catching the old Mentat's eye. Hawat nodded, his expression pleased.

"I will await below," Stilgar said, "while Idaho makes farewell with his friends. Turok was the name of our dead friend. Remember that when it comes time to release his spirit. You are friends of Turok."

Stilgar started to turn away.

"Will you not stay a while?" Leto asked.

The Fremen turned back, whipping his veil into place with a casual gesture, adjusting something beneath it. Paul glimpsed what looked like a thin tube before the veil settled into place.

"Is there reason to stay?" the Fremen asked.

"We would honor you," the Duke said.

"Honor requires that I be elsewhere soon," the Fremen said. He shot another glance at Idaho, whirled, and strode out past the door guards.

"If the other Fremen match him, we'll serve each other well," Leto said.

Idaho spoke in a dry voice: "He's a fair sample, Sire."

"You understand what you're to do, Duncan?"

"I'm your ambassador to the Fremen, Sire."

"Much depends on you, Duncan. We're going to need at least five battalions of those people before the Sardaukar descend on us."

"This is going to take some doing, Sire. The Fremen are a pretty independent bunch." Idaho hesitated, then: "And, Sire, there's one other thing. One of the mercenaries we knocked over was trying to get this blade from our dead Fremen friend. The mercenary says there's a Harkonnen reward of a million solaris for anyone who'll bring in a single crysknife."

Leto's chin came up in a movement of obvious surprise. "Why do they want one of those blades so badly?"

"The knife is ground from a sandworm's tooth; it's the mark of the Fremen, Sire. With it, a blue-eyed man could penetrate any sietch in the land. They'd question me unless I were known. I don't look Fremen. But. . . ."

"Piter de Vries," the Duke said.

"A man of devilish cunning, my Lord," Hawat said.

Idaho slipped the sheathed knife beneath his tunic.

"Guard that knife," the Duke said.

"I understand, m'Lord." He patted the transceiver on his belt kit.

"I'll report soon as possible. Thufir has my call code. Use battle language." He saluted, spun about, and hurried after the Fremen.

They heard his footsteps drumming down the corridor.

A look of understanding passed between Leto and Hawat. They smiled.

"We've much to do, Sire," Halleck said.

"And I keep you from your work," Leto said.

"I have the report on the advance bases," Hawat said. "Shall I give it another time, Sire?"

"Will it take long?"

"Not for a briefing. It's said among the Fremen that there were more than two hundred of these advance bases built here on Arrakis during the Desert Botanical Testing Station period. All supposedly have been abandoned, but there are reports they were sealed off before being abandoned."

"Equipment in them?" the Duke asked.

"According to the reports I have from Duncan."

"Where are they located?" Halleck asked.

"The answer to that question," Hawat said, "is invariably: 'Liet knows.'"

"God knows," Leto muttered.

"Perhaps not, Sire," Hawat said. "You heard this Stilgar use the name. Could he have been referring to a real person?"

"Serving two masters," Halleck said. "It sounds like a religious quotation."

"And you should know," the Duke said. Halleck smiled.

"This Judge of the Change," Leto said, "the Imperial ecologist— Kynes. . . . Wouldn't he know where those bases are?"

"Sire," Hawat cautioned, "this Kynes is an Imperial servant."

"And he's a long way from the Emperor," Leto said. "I want those bases. They'd be loaded with materials we could salvage and use for repair of our working equipment."

"Sire!" Hawat said. "Those bases are still legally His Majesty's fief."

"The weather here's savage enough to destroy anything," the Duke said. "We can always blame the weather. Get this Kynes and at least find out if the bases exist."

"'Twere dangerous to commandeer them," Hawat said. "Duncan was clear on one thing: those bases or the idea of them hold some deep significance for the Fremen. We might alienate the Fremen if we took those bases."

Paul looked at the faces of the men around them, saw the intensity of the way they followed every word. They appeared deeply disturbed by his father's attitude.

"Listen to him, Father," Paul said in a low voice. "He speaks truth."

"Sire," Hawat said, "those bases could give us material to repair every piece of equipment left us, yet be beyond reach for strategic reasons. It'd be rash to move without greater knowledge. This Kynes has arbiter authority from the Imperium. We mustn't forget that. And the Fremen defer to him."

"Do it gently, then," the Duke said. "I wish to know only if those bases exist."

"As you will, Sire." Hawat sat back, lowered his eyes.

"All right, then," the Duke said. "We know what we have ahead of us—work. We've been trained for it. We've some experience in it. We know what the rewards are and the alternatives are clear enough. You all have your assignments." He looked at Halleck. "Gurney, take care of that smuggler situation first."

"'I shall go unto the rebellious that dwell in the dry land,'" Halleck intoned.

"Someday I'll catch that man without a quotation and he'll look undressed," the Duke said.

Chuckles echoed around the table, but Paul heard the effort in them.

The Duke turned to Hawat. "Set up another command post for intelligence and communications on this floor, Thufir. When you have them ready, I'll want to see you."

Hawat arose, glancing around the room as though seeking support.

He turned away, led the procession out of the room. The others moved hurriedly, scraping their chairs on the floor, balling up in little knots of confusion.

It ended up in confusion, Paul thought, staring at the backs of the last men to leave. Always before, Staff had ended on an incisive air. This meeting had just seemed to trickle out, worn down by its own inadequacies, and with an argument to top it off.

For the first time, Paul allowed himself to think about the real possibility of defeat—not thinking about it out of fear or because of warnings such as that of the old Reverend Mother, but facing up to it because of his own assessment of the situation.

My father is desperate, he thought. *Things aren't going well for us at all.*

And Hawat—Paul recalled how the old Mentat had acted during the conference—subtle hesitations, signs of unrest.

Hawat was deeply troubled by something.

"Best you remain here the rest of the night, Son," the Duke said. "It'll be dawn soon, anyway. I'll inform your mother." He got to his feet, slowly, stiffly. "Why don't you pull a few of these chairs together and stretch out on them for some rest."

"I'm not very tired, sir."

"As you will."

The Duke folded his hands behind him, began pacing up and down the length of the table.

Like a caged animal, Paul thought.

"Are you going to discuss the traitor possibility with Hawat?" Paul asked.

The Duke stopped across from his son, spoke to the dark windows. "We've discussed the possibility many times."

"The old woman seemed so sure of herself," Paul said. "And the message Mother—"

"Precautions have been taken," the Duke said. He looked around the room, and Paul marked the hunted wildness in his father's eyes. "Remain here. There are some things about the command posts I want to discuss with Thufir." He turned, strode out of the room, nodding shortly to the door guards.

Paul stared at the place where his father had stood. The space had been empty even before the Duke left the room. And he recalled the old woman's warning: ". . . for the father, nothing."

On that first day when Muad'Dib rode through the streets of Arrakeen with his family, some of the people along the way recalled the legends and the prophecy and they ventured to shout: "Mahdi!" But their shout was more a question than a statement, for as yet they could only hope he was the one foretold as the Lisan al-Gaib, the Voice from the Outer World. Their attention was focused, too, on the mother, because they had heard she was a Bene Gesserit and it was obvious to them that she was like the other Lisan al-Gaib.

—FROM "MANUAL OF MUAD'DIB"
BY THE PRINCESS IRULAN

The Duke found Thufir Hawat alone in the corner room to which a guard directed him. There was the sound of men setting up communications equipment in an adjoining room, but this place was fairly quiet. The Duke glanced around as Hawat arose from a paper-cluttered table. It was a green-walled enclosure with, in addition to the table, three suspensor chairs from which the Harkonnen *"H"* had been hastily removed, leaving an imperfect color patch.

"The chairs are liberated but quite safe," Hawat said. "Where is Paul, Sire?"

"I left him in the conference room. I'm hoping he'll get some rest without me there to distract him."

Hawat nodded, crossed to the door to the adjoining room, closed it, shutting off the noise of static and electronic sparking.

"Thufir," Leto said, "the Imperial and Harkonnen stockpiles of spice attract my attention."

"M'Lord?"

The Duke pursed his lips. "Storehouses are susceptible to destruction." He raised a hand as Hawat started to speak. "Ignore the Emperor's hoard. He'd secretly enjoy it if the Harkonnens were embarrassed. And can the Baron object if something is destroyed which he cannot openly admit that he has?"

Hawat shook his head. "We've few men to spare, Sire."

"Use some of Idaho's men. And perhaps some of the Fremen would enjoy a trip off planet. A raid on Giedi Prime—there are tactical advantages to such a diversion, Thufir."

"As you say, my Lord." Hawat turned away, and the Duke saw evidence of nervousness in the old man, thought: *Perhaps he suspects I distrust him. He must know I've private reports of traitors. Well—best quiet his fears immediately.*

"Thufir," he said, "since you're one of the few I can trust completely, there's another matter bears discussion. We both know how constant a watch we must keep to prevent traitors from infiltrating our forces . . . but I have two new reports."

Hawat turned, stared at him.

And Leto repeated the stories Paul had brought.

Instead of bringing on the intense Mentat concentration, the reports only increased Hawat's agitation.

Leto studied the old man and, presently, said: "You've been holding something back, old friend. I should've suspected when you were so nervous during Staff. What is it that was too hot to dump in front of the full conference?"

Hawat's sapho-stained lips were pulled into a prim, straight line with tiny wrinkles radiating into them. They maintained their wrinkled stiffness as he said: "My Lord, I don't quite know how to broach this."

"We've suffered many a scar for each other, Thufir," the Duke said. "You know you can broach *any* subject with me."

Hawat continued to stare at him, thinking: *This is how I like him best. This is the man of honor who deserves every bit of my loyalty and service. Why must I hurt him?*

"Well?" Leto demanded.

Hawat shrugged. "It's a scrap of a note. We took it from a Harkonnen courier. The note was intended for an agent named Pardee. We've good reason to believe Pardee was top man in the Harkonnen underground here. The note—it's a thing that could have great consequence or no consequence. It's susceptible to various interpretations."

"What's the delicate content of this note?"

"Scrap of a note, my Lord. Incomplete. It was on minimic film with the usual destruction capsule attached. We stopped the acid action just short of full erasure, leaving only a fragment. The fragment, however, is extremely suggestive."

"Yes?"

Hawat rubbed at his lips. "It says: '. . . eto will never suspect, and when the blow falls on him from a beloved hand, its source alone should be enough to destroy him.' The note was under the Baron's own seal and I've authenticated the seal."

"Your suspicion is obvious," the Duke said and his voice was suddenly cold.

"I'd sooner cut off my arms than hurt you," Hawat said. "My Lord, what if . . ."

"The Lady Jessica," Leto said, and he felt anger consuming him. "Couldn't you wring the facts out of this Pardee?"

"Unfortunately, Pardee no longer was among the living when we intercepted the courier. The courier, I'm certain, did not know what he carried."

"I see."

Leto shook his head, thinking: *What a slimy piece of business. There can't be anything in it. I know my woman.*

"My Lord, if—"

"No!" the Duke barked. "There's a mistake here that—"

"We cannot ignore it, my Lord."

"She's been with me for sixteen years! There've been countless opportunities for— You yourself investigated the school and the woman!"

Hawat spoke bitterly: "Things have been known to escape me."

"It's impossible, I tell you! The Harkonnens want to destroy the Atreides *line*—meaning Paul, too. They've already tried once. Could a woman conspire against her own son?"

"Perhaps she doesn't conspire against her son. And yesterday's attempt could've been a clever sham."

"It couldn't have been a sham."

"Sire, she isn't supposed to know her parentage, but what if she does know? What if she were an orphan, say, orphaned by an Atreides?"

"She'd have moved long before now. Poison in my drink . . . a stiletto at night. Who has had better opportunity?"

"The Harkonnens mean to *destroy* you, my Lord. Their intent is not just to kill. There's a range of fine distinctions in kanly. This could be a work of art among vendettas."

The Duke's shoulders slumped. He closed his eyes, looking old and tired. *It cannot be*, he thought. *The woman has opened her heart to me.*

"What better way to destroy me than to sow suspicion of the woman I love?" he asked.

"An interpretation I've considered," Hawat said. "Still. . . ."

The Duke opened his eyes, stared at Hawat, thinking: *Let him be suspicious. Suspicion is his trade, not mine. Perhaps if I appear to believe this, that will make another man careless.*

"What do you suggest?" the Duke whispered.

"For now, constant surveillance, my Lord. She should be watched at all times. I will see it's done unobtrusively. Idaho would be the ideal choice for the job. Perhaps in a week or so we can bring him back. There's a young man we've been training in Idaho's troop who might be ideal to send to the Fremen as a replacement. He's gifted in diplomacy."

"Don't jeopardize our foothold with the Fremen."

"Of course not, Sire."

"And what about Paul?"

"Perhaps we could alert Dr. Yueh."

Leto turned his back on Hawat. "I leave it in your hands."

"I shall use discretion, my Lord."

At least I can count on that, Leto thought. And he said: "I will take a walk. If you need me, I'll be within the perimeter. The guard can—"

"My Lord, before you go, I've a filmclip you should read. It's a first-approximation analysis on the Fremen religion. You'll recall you asked me to report on it."

The Duke paused, spoke without turning. "Will it not wait?"

"Of course, my Lord. You asked what they were shouting, though. It was 'Mahdi!' They directed the term at the young Master. When they—"

"At Paul?"

"Yes, my Lord. They've a legend here, a prophecy, that a leader will come to them, child of a Bene Gesserit, to lead them to true freedom. It follows the familiar messiah pattern."

"They think Paul is this . . . this. . . ."

"They only hope, my Lord." Hawat extended a filmclip capsule.

The Duke accepted it, thrust it into a pocket. "I'll look at it later."

"Certainly, my Lord."

"Right now, I need time to . . . think."

"Yes, my Lord."

The Duke took a deep sighing breath, strode out the door. He turned to his right down the hall, began walking, hands behind his back, paying little attention to where he was. There were corridors and stairs and balconies and halls . . . people who saluted and stood aside for him.

In time he came back to the conference room, found it dark and Paul asleep on the table with a guard's robe thrown over him and a ditty pack for a pillow. The Duke walked softly down the length of the room and onto the balcony overlooking the landing field. A guard at the corner of the balcony, recognizing the Duke by the dim reflection of lights from the field, snapped to attention.

"At ease," the Duke murmured. He leaned against the cold metal of the balcony rail.

A predawn hush had come over the desert basin. He looked up. Straight overhead, the stars were a sequin shawl flung over blue-black. Low on the southern horizon, the night's second moon peered through a thin dust haze—an unbelieving moon that looked at him with a cynical light.

As the Duke watched, the moon dipped beneath the Shield Wall cliffs, frosting them, and in the sudden intensity of darkness, he experienced a chill. He shivered.

Anger shot through him.

The Harkonnens have hindered and hounded and hunted me for the last time, he thought. *They are dung heaps with village provost minds! Here I make my stand!* And he thought with a touch of sadness: *I must rule with eye and claw—as the hawk among lesser birds.* Unconsciously, his hand brushed the hawk emblem on his tunic.

To the east, the night grew a faggot of luminous gray, then seashell opalescence that dimmed the stars. There came the long, bell-tolling movement of dawn striking across a broken horizon.

It was a scene of such beauty it caught all his attention.

Some things beggar likeness, he thought.

He had never imagined anything here could be as beautiful as that shattered red horizon and the purple and ochre cliffs. Beyond the landing field where the night's faint dew had touched life into the hurried seeds of Arrakis, he saw great puddles of red blooms and, running through them, an articulate tread of violet . . . like giant footsteps.

"It's a beautiful morning, Sire," the guard said.

"Yes, it is."

The Duke nodded, thinking: *Perhaps this planet could grow on one. Perhaps it could become a good home for my son.*

Then he saw the human figures moving into the flower fields, sweeping them with strange scythelike devices—dew gatherers. Water so precious here that even the dew must be collected.

And it could be a hideous place, the Duke thought.

There is probably no more terrible instant of enlightenment than the one in which you discover your father is a man— with human flesh.

—FROM "COLLECTED SAYINGS OF MUAD'DIB" BY THE PRINCESS IRULAN

The Duke said: "Paul, I'm doing a hateful thing, but I must." He stood beside the portable poison snooper that had been brought into the conference room for their breakfast. The thing's sensor arms hung limply over the table, reminding Paul of some weird insect newly dead.

The Duke's attention was directed out the windows at the landing field and its roiling of dust against the morning sky.

Paul had a viewer in front of him containing a short filmclip on Fremen religious practices. The clip had been compiled by one of Hawat's experts and Paul found himself disturbed by the references to himself.

"*Mahdi!*"

"*Lisan al-Gaib!*"

He could close his eyes and recall the shouts of the crowds. *So that is what they hope*, he thought. And he remembered what the old Reverend Mother had said: Kwisatz Haderach. The memories touched his feelings of terrible purpose, shading this strange world with sensations of familiarity that he could not understand.

"A hateful thing," the Duke said.

"What do you mean, sir?"

Leto turned, looked down at his son. "Because the Harkonnens think to trick me by making me distrust your mother. They don't know that I'd sooner distrust myself."

"I don't understand, sir."

Again, Leto looked out the windows. The white sun was well up into its morning quadrant. Milky light picked out a boiling of dust clouds that spilled over into the blind canyons interfingering the Shield Wall.

Slowly, speaking in a slow voice to contain his anger, the Duke explained to Paul about the mysterious note.

"You might just as well mistrust me," Paul said.

"They have to think they've succeeded," the Duke said. "They must think me this much of a fool. It must look real. Even your mother may not know the sham."

"But, sir! Why?"

"Your mother's response must not be an act. Oh, she's capable of a supreme act . . . but too much rides on this. I hope to smoke out a traitor. It must seem that I've been completely cozened. She must be hurt this way that she does not suffer greater hurt."

"Why do you tell me, Father? Maybe I'll give it away."

"They'll not watch you in this thing," the Duke said. "You'll keep the secret. You must." He walked to the windows, spoke without turning. "This way, if anything should happen to me, you can tell her the truth—that I never doubted her, not for the smallest instant. I should want her to know this."

Paul recognized the death thoughts in his father's words, spoke quickly: "Nothing's going to happen to you, sir. The—"

"Be silent, Son."

Paul stared at his father's back, seeing the fatigue in the angle of the neck, in the line of the shoulders, in the slow movements.

"You're just tired, Father."

"I *am* tired," the Duke agreed. "I'm morally tired. The melancholy degeneration of the Great Houses has afflicted me at last, perhaps. And we were such strong people once."

Paul spoke in quick anger: "Our House hasn't degenerated!"

"Hasn't it?"

The Duke turned, faced his son, revealing dark circles beneath hard eyes, a cynical twist of mouth. "I should wed your mother, make her my Duchess. Yet . . . my unwedded state gives some Houses hope they may yet ally with me through their marriageable daughters." He shrugged. "So, I. . . ."

"Mother has explained this to me."

"Nothing wins more loyalty for a leader than an air of bravura," the Duke said. "I, therefore, cultivate an air of bravura."

"You lead well," Paul protested. "You govern well. Men follow you willingly and love you."

"My propaganda corps is one of the finest," the Duke said. Again, he turned to stare out at the basin. "There's greater possibility for us here on Arrakis than the Imperium could ever suspect. Yet sometimes I think it'd have been better if we'd run for it, gone renegade. Sometimes I wish we could sink back into anonymity among the people, become less exposed to. . . ."

"Father!"

"Yes, I *am* tired," the Duke said. "Did you know we're using spice residue as raw material and already have our own factory to manufacture filmbase?"

"Sir?"

"We mustn't run short of filmbase," the Duke said. "Else, how could we flood village and city with our information? The people must learn how well I govern them. How would they know if we didn't tell them?"

"You should get some rest," Paul said.

Again, the Duke faced his son. "Arrakis has another advantage I almost forgot to mention. Spice is in everything here. You breathe it and eat it in almost everything. And I find that this imparts a certain natural immunity to some of the most common poisons of the Assassins' Handbook. And the need to watch every drop of water puts all food production—yeast culture, hydroponics, chemavit, everything—under the strictest surveillance. We cannot kill off large segments of our population with poison—and we cannot be attacked this way, either. Arrakis makes us moral and ethical."

Paul started to speak, but the Duke cut him off, saying: "I have to have someone I can say these things to, Son." He sighed, glanced back at the dry landscape where even the flowers were gone now—trampled by the dew gatherers, wilted under the early sun.

"On Caladan, we ruled with sea and air power," the Duke said. "Here, we must scrabble for desert power. This is your inheritance, Paul. What is to become of you if anything happens to me? You'll not be a renegade House, but a guerrilla House—running, hunted."

Paul groped for words, could find nothing to say. He had never seen his father this despondent.

"To hold Arrakis," the Duke said, "one is faced with decisions that may cost one his self-respect." He pointed out the window to the Atreides green and black banner hanging limply from a staff at the edge of the landing field. "That honorable banner could come to mean many evil things."

Paul swallowed in a dry throat. His father's words carried futility, a sense of fatalism that left the boy with an empty feeling in his chest.

The Duke took an antifatigue tablet from a pocket, gulped it dry. "Power and fear," he said. "The tools of statecraft. I must order new emphasis on guerrilla training for you. That filmclip there—they call you 'Mahdi'—'Lisan al-Gaib'—as a last resort, you might capitalize on that."

Paul stared at his father, watching the shoulders straighten as the tablet did its work, but remembering the words of fear and doubt.

"What's keeping that ecologist?" the Duke muttered. "I told Thufir to have him here early."

My father, the Padishah Emperor, took me by the hand one day and I sensed in the ways my mother had taught me that he was disturbed. He led me down the Hall of Portraits to the ego-likeness of the Duke Leto Atreides. I marked the strong resemblance between them—my father and this man in the portrait—both with thin, elegant faces and sharp features dominated by cold eyes. "Princess-daughter," my father said, "I would that you'd been older when it came time for this man to choose a woman." My father was 71 at the time and looking no older than the man in the portrait, and I was but 14, yet I remember deducing in that instant that my father secretly wished the Duke had been his son, and disliked the political necessities that made them enemies.

— FROM "IN MY FATHER'S HOUSE"
BY THE PRINCESS IRULAN

His first encounter with the people he had been ordered to betray left Dr. Kynes shaken. He prided himself on being a scientist to whom legends were merely interesting clues, pointing toward cultural roots. Yet the boy fitted the ancient prophecy so precisely. He had "the questing eyes," and the air of "reserved candor."

Of course, the prophecy left certain latitude as to whether the Mother Goddess would bring the Messiah with her or produce Him on the scene. Still, there was this odd correspondence between prediction and persons.

They met in midmorning outside the Arrakeen landing field's administration building. An unmarked ornithopter squatted nearby, humming softly on standby like a somnolent insect. An Atreides guard stood beside it with bared sword and the faint air-distortion of a shield around him.

Kynes sneered at the shield pattern, thinking: *Arrakis has a surprise for them there!*

The planetologist raised a hand, signaled for his Fremen guard to fall back. He strode on ahead toward the building's entrance—the dark hole in plastic-coated rock. So exposed, that monolithic building, he thought. So much less suitable than a cave.

Movement within the entrance caught his attention. He stopped, taking the moment to adjust his robe and the set of his stillsuit at the left shoulder.

The entrance doors swung wide. Atreides guards emerged swiftly, all of them heavily armed—slow-pellet stunners, swords and shields. Behind them came a tall man, hawk-faced, dark of skin and hair. He wore a jubba cloak with Atreides crest at the breast, and wore it in a way that betrayed his unfamiliarity with the garment. It clung to the legs of his stillsuit on one side. It lacked a free-swinging, striding rhythm.

Beside the man walked a youth with the same dark hair, but rounder in the face. The youth seemed small for the fifteen years Kynes knew him to have. But the young body carried a sense of command, a poised assurance, as though he saw and knew things all around him that were not visible to others. And he wore the same style cloak as his father, yet with casual ease that made one think the boy had always worn such clothing.

"*The Mahdi will be aware of things others cannot see,*" went the prophecy.

Kynes shook his head, telling himself: *They're just people.*

With the two, garbed like them for the desert, came a man Kynes recognized—Gurney Halleck. Kynes took a deep breath to still his resentment against Halleck, who had briefed him on how to *behave* with the Duke and ducal heir.

"*You may call the Duke 'my Lord' or 'Sire.' 'Noble Born' also is cor-*

rect, but usually reserved for more formal occasions. The son may be addressed as 'young Master' or 'my Lord.' The Duke is a man of much leniency, but brooks little familiarity.

And Kynes thought as he watched the group approach: *They'll learn soon enough who's master on Arrakis. Order me questioned half the night by that Mentat, will they? Expect me to guide them on an inspection of spice mining, do they?*

The import of Hawat's questions had not escaped Kynes. They wanted the Imperial bases. And it was obvious they'd learned of the bases from Idaho.

I will have Stilgar send Idaho's head to this Duke, Kynes told himself.

The ducal party was only a few paces away now, their feet in desert boots crunching the sand.

Kynes bowed. "My Lord, Duke."

As he had approached the solitary figure standing near the ornithopter, Leto had studied him: tall, thin, dressed for the desert in loose robe, stillsuit, and low boots. The man's hood was thrown back, its veil hanging to one side, revealing long sandy hair, a sparse beard. The eyes were that fathomless blue-within-blue under thick brows. Remains of dark stains smudged his eye sockets.

"You're the ecologist," the Duke said.

"We prefer the old title here, my Lord," Kynes said. "Planetologist."

"As you wish," the Duke said. He glanced down at Paul. "Son, this is the Judge of the Change, the arbiter of dispute, the man set here to see that the forms are obeyed in our assumption of power over this fief." He glanced at Kynes. "And this is my son."

"My Lord," Kynes said.

"Are you a Fremen?" Paul asked.

Kynes smiled. "I am accepted in both sietch and village, young Master. But I am in His Majesty's service, the Imperial Planetologist."

Paul nodded, impressed by the man's air of strength. Halleck had pointed Kynes out to Paul from an upper window of the administration building: "The man standing there with the Fremen escort—the one moving now toward the ornithopter."

Paul had inspected Kynes briefly with binoculars, noting the prim, straight mouth, the high forehead. Halleck had spoken in Paul's ear: "Odd sort of fellow. Has a precise way of speaking—clipped off, no fuzzy edges—razor-apt."

And the Duke, behind them, had said: "Scientist type."

Now, only a few feet from the man, Paul sensed the power in Kynes, the impact of personality, as though he were blood royal, born to command.

"I understand we have you to thank for our stillsuits and these cloaks," the Duke said.

"I hope they fit well, my Lord," Kynes said. "They're of Fremen make and as near as possible the dimensions given me by your man Halleck here."

"I was concerned that you said you couldn't take us into the desert unless we wore these garments," the Duke said. "We can carry plenty of water. We don't intend to be out long and we'll have air cover—the escort you see overhead right now. It isn't likely we'd be forced down."

Kynes stared at him, seeing the water-fat flesh. He spoke coldly: "You never talk of likelihoods on Arrakis. You speak only of possibilities."

Halleck stiffened. "The Duke is to be addressed as my Lord or Sire!"

Leto gave Halleck their private hand signal to desist, said: "Our ways are new here, Gurney. We must make allowances."

"As you wish, Sire."

"We are indebted to you, Dr. Kynes," Leto said. "These suits and the consideration for our welfare will be remembered."

On impulse, Paul called to mind a quotation from the O.C. Bible, said: "'The gift is the blessing of the giver.'"

The words rang out overloud in the still air. The Fremen escort Kynes had left in the shade of the administration building leaped up from their squatting repose, muttering in open agitation. One cried out: "Lisan al-Gaib!"

Kynes whirled, gave a curt, chopping signal with a hand, waved the guard away. They fell back, grumbling among themselves, trailed away around the building.

"Most interesting," Leto said.

Kynes passed a hard glare over the Duke and Paul, said: "Most of the desert natives here are a superstitious lot. Pay no attention to them. They mean no harm." But he thought of the words of the legend: *"They will greet you with Holy Words and your gifts will be a blessing."*

Leto's assessment of Kynes—based partly on Hawat's brief verbal report (guarded and full of suspicions)—suddenly crystallized: the man was Fremen. Kynes had come with a Fremen escort, which could mean simply that the Fremen were testing their new freedom to enter urban areas—but it had seemed an honor guard. And by his manner, Kynes was a proud man, accustomed to freedom, his tongue and his manner guarded only by his own suspicions. Paul's question had been direct and pertinent.

Kynes had gone native.

"Shouldn't we be going, Sire?" Halleck asked.

The Duke nodded. "I'll fly my own 'thopter. Kynes can sit up front with me to direct me. You and Paul take the rear seats."

"One moment, please," Kynes said. "With your permission, Sire, I must check the security of your suits."

The Duke started to speak, but Kynes pressed on: "I have concern for my own flesh as well as yours . . . my Lord. I'm well aware of whose throat would be slit should harm befall you two while you're in my care."

The Duke frowned, thinking: *How delicate this moment! If I refuse, it may offend him. And this could be a man whose value to me is beyond measure. Yet . . . to let him inside my shield, touching my person when I know so little about him?*

The thoughts flicked through his mind with decision hard on their heels. "We're in your hands," the Duke said. He stepped forward, opening his robe, saw Halleck come up on the balls of his feet, poised and alert, but remaining where he was. "And, if you'd be so kind," the Duke said, "I'd appreciate an explanation of the suit from one who lives so intimately with it."

"Certainly," Kynes said. He felt up under the robe for the shoulder seals, speaking as he examined the suit. "It's basically a micro-sandwich—a high-efficiency filter and heat-exchange system." He adjusted the shoulder seals. "The skin-contact layer's porous. Perspiration passes through it, having cooled the body . . . near-normal evaporation process. The next two layers . . ." Kynes tightened the chest fit. ". . . include heat-exchange filaments and salt precipitators. Salt's reclaimed."

The Duke lifted his arms at a gesture, said: "Most interesting."

"Breathe deeply," Kynes said.

The Duke obeyed.

Kynes studied the underarm seals, adjusted one. "Motions of the body, especially breathing," he said, "and some osmotic action provide the pumping force." He loosened the chest fit slightly. "Reclaimed water circulates to catchpockets from which you draw it through this tube in the clip at your neck."

The Duke twisted his chin in and down to look at the end of the tube. "Efficient and convenient," he said. "Good engineering."

Kynes knelt, examined the leg seals. "Urine and feces are processed in the thigh pads," he said, and stood up, felt the neck fitting, lifted a sectioned flap there. "In the open desert, you wear this filter across your face, this tube in the nostrils with these plugs to insure a tight fit. Breathe in through the mouth filter, out through the nose tube. With a Fremen suit in good working order, you won't lose more than a thimbleful of moisture a day—even if you're caught in the Great Erg."

"A thimbleful a day," the Duke said.

Kynes pressed a finger against the suit's forehead pad, said: "This may rub a little. If it irritates you, please tell me. I could slit-patch it a bit tighter."

"My thanks," the Duke said. He moved his shoulders in the suit as Kynes stepped back, realizing that it did feel better now—tighter and less irritating.

Kynes turned to Paul. "Now, let's have a look at you, lad."

A good man but he'll have to learn to address us properly, the Duke thought.

Paul stood passively as Kynes inspected the suit. It had been an odd sensation putting on the crinkling, slick-surfaced garment. In his fore-consciousness had been the absolute knowledge that he had never before worn a stillsuit. Yet, each motion of adjusting the adhesion tabs under Gurney's inexpert guidance had seemed natural, instinctive. When he had tightened the chest to gain maximum pumping action from the motion of breathing, he had known what he did and why. When he had fitted the neck and forehead tabs tightly, he had known it was to prevent friction blisters.

Kynes straightened, stepped back with a puzzled expression. "You've worn a stillsuit before?" he asked.

"This is the first time."

"Then someone adjusted it for you?"

"No."

"Your desert boots are fitted slip-fashion at the ankles. Who told you to do that?"

"It . . . seemed the right way."

"That it most certainly is."

And Kynes rubbed his cheek, thinking of the legend: *"He shall know your ways as though born to them."*

"We waste time," the Duke said. He gestured to the waiting 'thopter, led the way, accepting the guard's salute with a nod. He climbed in, fastened his safety harness, checked controls and instruments. The craft creaked as the others clambered aboard.

Kynes fastened his harness, focused on the padded comfort of the aircraft—soft luxury of gray-green upholstery, gleaming instruments, the sensation of filtered and washed air in his lungs as doors slammed and vent fans whirred alive.

So soft! he thought.

"All secure, Sire," Halleck said.

Leto fed power to the wings, felt them cup and dip—once, twice. They were airborne in ten meters, wings feathered tightly and afterjets thrusting them upward in a steep, hissing climb.

"Southeast over the Shield Wall," Kynes said. "That's where I told your sandmaster to concentrate his equipment."

"Right."

The Duke banked into his air cover, the other craft taking up their guard positions as they headed southeast.

"The design and manufacture of these stillsuits bespeaks a high degree of sophistication," the Duke said.

"Someday I may show you a sietch factory," Kynes said.

"I would find that interesting," the Duke said. "I note that suits are manufactured also in some of the garrison cities."

"Inferior copies," Kynes said. "Any Dune man who values his skin wears a Fremen suit."

"And it'll hold your water loss to a thimbleful a day?"

"Properly suited, your forehead cap tight, all seals in order, your major water loss is through the palms of your hands," Kynes said. "You can wear suit gloves if you're not using your hands for critical work, but most Fremen in the open desert rub their hands with juice from the leaves of the creosote bush. It inhibits perspiration."

The Duke glanced down to the left at the broken landscape of the Shield Wall—chasms of tortured rock, patches of yellow-brown crossed by black lines of fault shattering. It was as though someone had dropped this ground from space and left it where it smashed.

They crossed a shallow basin with the clear outline of gray sand spreading across it from a canyon opening to the south. The sand fingers ran out into the basin—a dry delta outlined against darker rock.

Kynes sat back, thinking about the water-fat flesh he had felt beneath the stillsuits. They wore shield belts over their robes, slow-pellet stunners at the waist, coin-sized emergency transmitters on cords around their necks. Both the Duke and his son carried knives in wrist sheaths and the sheaths appeared well worn. The people struck Kynes as a strange combination of softness and armed strength. There was a poise to them totally unlike the Harkonnens.

"When you report to the Emperor on the change of government here, will you say we observed the rules?" Leto asked. He glanced at Kynes, back to their course.

"The Harkonnens left; you came," Kynes said.

"And is everything as it should be?" Leto asked.

Momentary tension showed in the tightening of a muscle along Kynes' jaw. "As Planetologist and Judge of the Change, I am a direct subject of the Imperium . . . my Lord."

The Duke smiled grimly. "But we both know the realities."

"I remind you that His Majesty supports my work."

"Indeed? And what is your work?"

In the brief silence, Paul thought: *He's pushing this Kynes too hard.* Paul glanced at Halleck, but the minstrel-warrior was staring out at the barren landscape.

Kynes spoke stiffly: "You, of course, refer to my duties as planetologist."

"Of course."

"It is mostly dry land biology and botany . . . some geological work—core drilling and testing. You never really exhaust the possibilities of an entire planet."

"Do you also investigate the spice?"

Kynes turned, and Paul noted the hard line of the man's cheek. "A curious question, my Lord."

"Bear in mind, Kynes, that this is now my fief. My methods differ from those of the Harkonnens. I don't care if you study the spice as long as I share what you discover." He glanced at the planetologist. "The Harkonnens discouraged investigation of the spice, didn't they?"

Kynes stared back without answering.

"You may speak plainly," the Duke said, "without fear for your skin."

"The Imperial Court is, indeed, a long way off," Kynes muttered.

And he thought: *What does this water-soft invader expect? Does he think me fool enough to enlist with him?*

The Duke chuckled, keeping his attention on their course. "I detect a sour note in your voice, sir. We've waded in here with our mob of tame killers, eh? And we expect you to realize immediately that we're different from the Harkonnens?"

"I've seen the propaganda you've flooded into sietch and village," Kynes said. "'Love the good Duke!' Your corps of—"

"Here now!" Halleck barked. He snapped his attention away from the window, leaned forward.

Paul put a hand on Halleck's arm.

"Gurney!" the Duke said. He glanced back. "This man's been long under the Harkonnens."

Halleck sat back. "Ayah."

"Your man Hawat's subtle," Kynes said, "but his object's plain enough."

"Will you open those bases to us, then?" the Duke asked.

Kynes spoke curtly: "They're His Majesty's property."

"They're not being used."

"They could be used."

"Does His Majesty concur?"

Kynes darted a hard stare at the Duke. "Arrakis could be an Eden if its rulers would look up from grubbing for spice!"

He didn't answer my question, the Duke thought. And he said: "How is a planet to become an Eden without money?"

"What is money," Kynes asked, "if it won't buy the services you need?"

Ah, now! the Duke thought. And he said: "We'll discuss this another time. Right now, I believe we're coming to the edge of the Shield Wall. Do I hold the same course?"

"The same course," Kynes muttered.

Paul looked out his window. Beneath them, the broken ground began to drop away in tumbled creases toward a barren rock plain and a knife-edged shelf. Beyond the shelf, fingernail crescents of dunes marched toward the horizon with here and there in the distance a dull smudge, a darker blotch to tell of something not sand. Rock outcroppings, perhaps. In the heat-addled air, Paul couldn't be sure.

"Are there any plants down there?" Paul asked.

"Some," Kynes said. "This latitude's life-zone has mostly what we call minor water stealers—adapted to raiding each other for moisture, gobbling up the trace-dew. Some parts of the desert teem with life. But all of it has learned how to survive under these rigors. If *you* get caught down there, you imitate that life or you die."

"You mean steal water from each other?" Paul asked. The idea outraged him, and his voice betrayed his emotion.

"It's done," Kynes said, "but that wasn't precisely my meaning. You see, my climate demands a special attitude toward water. You are aware of water at all times. You waste nothing that contains moisture."

And the Duke thought: ". . . *my climate!*"

"Come around two degrees more southerly, my Lord," Kynes said. "There's a blow coming up from the west."

The Duke nodded. He had seen the billowing of tan dust there. He banked the 'thopter around, noting the way the escort's wings reflected milky orange from the dust-refracted light as they turned to keep pace with him.

"This should clear the storm's edge," Kynes said.

"That sand must be dangerous if you fly into it," Paul said. "Will it really cut the strongest metals?"

"At this altitude, it's not sand but dust," Kynes said. "The danger is lack of visibility, turbulence, clogged intakes."

"We'll see actual spice mining today?" Paul asked.

"Very likely," Kynes said.

Paul sat back. He had used the questions and hyperawareness to do what his mother called "registering" the person. He had Kynes now—tone of voice, each detail of face and gesture. An unnatural folding of the left sleeve on the man's robe told of a knife in an arm sheath. The waist bulged strangely. It was said that desert men wore a belted sash into which they tucked small necessities. Perhaps the bulges came from such a sash—certainly not from a concealed shield belt. A copper pin engraved with the likeness of a hare clasped the neck of Kynes' robe. Another smaller pin with similar likeness hung at the corner of the hood which was thrown back over his shoulders.

Halleck twisted in the seat beside Paul, reached back into the rear compartment and brought out his baliset. Kynes looked around as Halleck tuned the instrument, then returned his attention to their course.

"What would you like to hear, young Master?" Halleck asked.

"You choose, Gurney," Paul said.

Halleck bent his ear close to the sounding board, strummed a chord and sang softly:

> *"Our fathers ate manna in the desert,*
> *In the burning places where whirlwinds came.*
> *Lord, save us from that horrible land!*
> *Save us . . . oh-h-h-h, save us*
> *From the dry and thirsty land."*

Kynes glanced at the Duke, said: "You *do* travel with a light complement of guards, my Lord. Are all of them such men of many talents?"

"Gurney?" The Duke chuckled. "Gurney's one of a kind. I like him with me for his eyes. His eyes miss very little."

The planetologist frowned.

Without missing a beat in his tune, Halleck interposed:

> *"For I am like an owl of the desert, o!*
> *Aiyah! am like an owl of the des-ert!"*

The Duke reached down, brought up a microphone from the instrument panel, thumbed it to life, said: "Leader to Escort Gemma. Flying object at nine o'clock, Sector B. Do you identify it?"

"It's merely a bird," Kynes said, and added: "You have sharp eyes."

The panel speaker crackled, then: "Escort Gemma. Object examined under full amplification. It's a large bird."

Paul looked in the indicated direction, saw the distant speck: a dot of intermittent motion, and realized how keyed up his father must be. Every sense was at full alert.

"I'd not realized there were birds that large this far into the desert," the Duke said.

"That's likely an eagle," Kynes said. "Many creatures have adapted to this place."

The ornithopter swept over a bare rock plain. Paul looked down from their two thousand meters' altitude, saw the wrinkled shadow of their craft and escort. The land beneath seemed flat, but shadow wrinkles said otherwise.

"Has anyone ever walked out of the desert?" the Duke asked.

Halleck's music stopped. He leaned forward to catch the answer.

"Not from the deep desert," Kynes said. "Men have walked out of the second zone several times. They've survived by crossing the rock areas where worms seldom go."

The timbre of Kynes' voice held Paul's attention. He felt his senses come alert the way they were trained to do.

"Ah-h, the worms," the Duke said. "I must see one sometime."

"You may see one today," Kynes said. "Wherever there is spice, there are worms."

"Always?" Halleck asked.

"Always."

"Is there a relationship between worm and spice?" the Duke asked.

Kynes turned and Paul saw the pursed lips as the man spoke. "They defend spice *sands*. Each worm has a—territory. As to the spice . . . who knows? Worm specimens we've examined lead us to suspect complicated chemical interchanges within them. We find traces of hydrochloric acid in the ducts, more complicated acid forms elsewhere. I'll give you my monograph on the subject."

"And a shield's no defense?" the Duke asked.

"Shields!" Kynes sneered. "Activate a shield within the worm zone and you seal your fate. Worms ignore territory lines, come from far around to attack a shield. No man wearing a shield has ever survived such attack."

"How are worms taken, then?"

"High voltage electrical shock applied separately to each ring segment is the only known way of killing and preserving an entire worm," Kynes said. "They can be stunned and shattered by explosives, but each ring segment has a life of its own. Barring atomics, I know of no explosive powerful enough to destroy a large worm entirely. They're incredibly tough."

"Why hasn't an effort been made to wipe them out?" Paul asked.

"Too expensive," Kynes said. "Too much area to cover."

Paul leaned back in his corner. His truthsense, awareness of tone shadings, told him that Kynes was lying and telling half-truths. And he thought: *If there's a relationship between spice and worms, killing the worms would destroy the spice.*

"No one will have to walk out of the desert soon," the Duke said. "Trip these little transmitters at our necks and rescue is on its way. All our workers will be wearing them before long. We're setting up a special rescue service."

"Very commendable," Kynes said.

"Your tone says you don't agree," the Duke said.

"Agree? Of course I agree, but it won't be much use. Static electricity from sandstorms masks out many signals. Transmitters short out. They've been tried here before, you know. Arrakis is tough on equipment. And if a worm's hunting you there's not much time. Frequently, you have no more than fifteen or twenty minutes."

"What would you advise?" the Duke asked.

"You ask my advice?"

"As planetologist, yes."

"You'd follow my advice?"

"If I found it sensible."

"Very well, my Lord. Never travel alone."

The Duke turned his attention from the controls. "That's all?"

"That's all. Never travel alone."

"What if you're separated by a storm and forced down?" Halleck asked. "Isn't there anything you could do?"

"*Anything* covers much territory," Kynes said.

"What would *you* do?" Paul asked.

Kynes turned a hard stare at the boy, brought his attention back to the Duke. "I'd remember to protect the integrity of my stillsuit. If I were outside the worm zone or in rock, I'd stay with the ship. If I were down in open sand, I'd get away from the ship as fast as I could. About a thousand meters would be far enough. Then I'd hide beneath my robe. A worm would get the ship, but it might miss me."

"Then what?" Halleck asked.

Kynes shrugged. "Wait for the worm to leave."

"That's all?" Paul asked.

"When the worm has gone, one may try to walk out," Kynes said. "You must walk softly, avoid drum sands, tidal dust basins—head for the nearest rock zone. There are many such zones. You might make it."

"Drum sand?" Halleck asked.

"A condition of sand compaction," Kynes said. "The slightest step sets it drumming. Worms always come to that."

"And a tidal dust basin?" the Duke asked.

"Certain depressions in the desert have filled with dust over the centuries. Some are so vast they have currents and tides. All will swallow the unwary who step into them."

Halleck sat back, resumed strumming the baliset. Presently, he sang:

"*Wild beasts of the desert do hunt there,*
Waiting for the innocents to pass.
Oh-h-h, tempt not the gods of the desert,
Lest you seek a lonely epitaph.
The perils of the—"

He broke off, leaned forward. "Dust cloud ahead, Sire."

"I see it, Gurney."

"That's what we seek," Kynes said.

Paul stretched up in the seat to peer ahead, saw a rolling yellow cloud low on the desert surface some thirty kilometers ahead.

"One of your factory crawlers," Kynes said. "It's on the surface and that means it's on spice. The cloud is vented sand being expelled after the spice has been centrifugally removed. There's no other cloud quite like it."

"Aircraft over it," the Duke said.

"I see two . . . three . . . four spotters," Kynes said. "They're watching for wormsign."

"Wormsign?" the Duke asked.

"A sandwave moving toward the crawler. They'll have seismic probes on the surface, too. Worms sometimes travel too deep for the wave to show." Kynes swung his gaze around the sky. "Should be a carryall wing around, but I don't see it."

"The worm always comes, eh?" Halleck asked.

"Always."

Paul leaned forward, touched Kynes' shoulder. "How big an area does each worm stake out?"

Kynes frowned. The child kept asking adult questions.

"That depends on the size of the worm."

"What's the variation?" the Duke asked.

"Big ones may control three or four hundred square kilometers. Small ones—" He broke off as the Duke kicked on the jet brakes. The ship bucked as its tail pods whispered to silence. Stub wings elongated, cupped the air. The craft became a full 'thopter as the Duke banked it, holding the wings to a gentle beat, pointing with his left hand off to the east beyond the factory crawler.

"Is that wormsign?"

Kynes leaned across the Duke to peer into the distance.

Paul and Halleck were crowded together, looking in the same direction, and Paul noted that their escort, caught by the sudden maneuver, had surged ahead, but now was curving back. The factory crawler lay ahead of them, still some three kilometers away.

Where the Duke pointed, crescent dune tracks spread shadow ripples toward the horizon and, running through them as a level line stretching into the distance, came an elongated mount-in-motion—a cresting of sand. It reminded Paul of the way a big fish disturbed the water when swimming just under the surface.

"Worm," Kynes said. "Big one." He leaned back, grabbed the microphone from the panel, punched out a new frequency selection. Glancing at the grid chart on rollers over their heads, he spoke into the microphone: "Calling crawler at Delta Ajax niner. Wormsign warning. Crawler at Delta Ajax niner. Wormsign warning. Acknowledge, please." He waited.

The panel speaker emitted static crackles, then a voice: "Who calls Delta Ajax niner? Over."

"They seem pretty calm about it," Halleck said.

Kynes spoke into the microphone: "Unlisted flight—north and east of you about three kilometers. Wormsign is on intercept course, your position, estimated contact twenty-five minutes."

Another voice rumbled from the speaker: "This is Spotter Control. Sighting confirmed. Stand by for contact fix." There was a pause, then: "Contact in twenty-six minutes minus. That was a sharp estimate. Who's on that unlisted flight? Over."

Halleck had his harness off and surged forward between Kynes and the Duke. "Is this the regular working frequency, Kynes?"

"Yes. Why?"

"Who'd be listening?"

"Just the work crews in this area. Cuts down interference."

Again, the speaker crackled, then: "This is Delta Ajax niner. Who gets bonus credit for that spot? Over."

Halleck glanced at the Duke.

Kynes said: "There's a bonus based on spice load for whoever gives first worm warning. They want to know—"

"Tell them who had first sight of that worm," Halleck said.

The Duke nodded.

Kynes hesitated, then lifted the microphone: "Spotter credit to the Duke Leto Atreides. The Duke Leto Atreides. Over."

The voice from the speaker was flat and partly distorted by a burst of static: "We read and thank you."

"Now, tell them to divide the bonus among themselves," Halleck ordered. "Tell them it's the Duke's wish."

Kynes took a deep breath, then: "It's the Duke's wish that you divide the bonus among your crew. Do you read? Over."

"Acknowledged and thank you," the speaker said.

The Duke said: "I forgot to mention that Gurney is also very talented in public relations."

Kynes turned a puzzled frown on Halleck.

"This lets the men know their Duke is concerned for their safety," Halleck said. "Word will get around. It was on an area working frequency—not likely Harkonnen agents heard." He glanced out at their air cover. "And we're a pretty strong force. It was a good risk."

The Duke banked their craft toward the sandcloud erupting from the factory crawler. "What happens now?"

"There's a carryall wing somewhere close," Kynes said. "It'll come in and lift off the crawler."

"What if the carryall's wrecked?" Halleck asked.

"Some equipment *is* lost," Kynes said. "Get in close over the crawler, my Lord; you'll find this interesting."

The Duke scowled, busied himself with the controls as they came into turbulent air over the crawler.

Paul looked down, saw sand still spewing out of the metal and plastic monster beneath them. It looked like a great tan and blue beetle with many wide tracks extending on arms around it. He saw a giant inverted funnel snout poked into dark sand in front of it.

"Rich spice bed by the color," Kynes said. "They'll continue working until the last minute."

The Duke fed more power to the wings, stiffened them for a steeper

descent as he settled lower in a circling glide above the crawler. A glance
left and right showed his cover holding altitude and circling overhead.

Paul studied the yellow cloud belching from the crawler's pipe vents,
looked out over the desert at the approaching worm track.

"Shouldn't we be hearing them call in the carryall?" Halleck asked.

"They usually have the wing on a different frequency," Kynes said.

"Shouldn't they have two carryalls standing by for every crawler?"
the Duke asked. "There should be twenty-six men on that machine
down there, not to mention cost of equipment."

Kynes said: "You don't have enough ex—"

He broke off as the speaker erupted with an angry voice: "Any of you
see the wing? He isn't answering."

A garble of noise crackled from the speaker, drowned in an abrupt
override signal, then silence and the first voice: "Report by the numbers! Over."

"This is Spotter Control. Last I saw, the wing was pretty high and
circling off northwest. I don't see him now. Over."

"Spotter one: negative. Over."

"Spotter two: negative. Over."

"Spotter three: negative. Over."

Silence.

The Duke looked down. His own craft's shadow was just passing
over the crawler. "Only four spotters, is that right?"

"Correct," Kynes said.

"There are five in our party," the Duke said. "Our ships are larger.
We can crowd in three extra each. Their spotters ought to be able to lift
off two each."

Paul did the mental arithmetic, said: "That's three short."

"Why don't they have two carryalls to each crawler?" barked the
Duke.

"You don't have enough extra equipment," Kynes said.

"All the more reason we should protect what we have!"

"Where could that carryall go?" Halleck asked.

"Could've been forced down somewhere out of sight," Kynes said.

The Duke grabbed the microphone, hesitated with thumb poised over its switch. "How could they lose sight of a carryall?"

"They keep their attention on the ground looking for wormsign," Kynes said.

The Duke thumbed the switch, spoke into the microphone. "This is your Duke. We are coming down to take off Delta Ajax niner's crew. All spotters are ordered to comply. Spotters will land on the east side. We will take the west. Over." He reached down, punched out his own command frequency, repeated the order for his own air cover, handed the microphone back to Kynes.

Kynes returned to the working frequency and a voice blasted from the speaker: ". . . almost a full load of spice! We have almost a full load! We can't leave that for a damned worm! Over."

"Damn the spice!" the Duke barked. He grabbed back the microphone, said: "We can always get more spice. There are seats in our ships for all but three of you. Draw straws or decide any way you like who's to go. But you're going, and that's an order!" He slammed the microphone back into Kynes' hands, muttered: "Sorry," as Kynes shook an injured finger.

"How much time?" Paul asked.

"Nine minutes," Kynes said.

The Duke said: "This ship has more power than the others. If we took off under jet with three-quarter wings, we could crowd in an additional man."

"That sand's soft," Kynes said.

"With four extra men aboard on a jet takeoff, we could snap the wings, Sire," Halleck said.

"Not on this ship," the Duke said. He hauled back on the controls as the 'thopter glided in beside the crawler. The wings tipped up, braked the 'thopter to a skidding stop within twenty meters of the factory.

The crawler was silent now, no sand spouting from its vents. Only a faint mechanical rumble issued from it, becoming more audible as the Duke opened his door.

Immediately, their nostrils were assailed by the odor of cinnamon—
heavy and pungent.

With a loud flapping, the spotter aircraft glided down to the sand
on the other side of the crawler. The Duke's own escort swooped in to
land in line with him.

Paul, looking out at the factory, saw how all the 'thopters were
dwarfed by it—gnats beside a warrior beetle.

"Gurney, you and Paul toss out that rear seat," the Duke said. He
manually cranked the wings out to three-quarters, set their angle,
checked the jet pod controls. "Why the devil aren't they coming out of
that machine?"

"They're hoping the carryall will show up," Kynes said. "They still
have a few minutes." He glanced off to the east.

All turned to look the same direction, seeing no sign of the worm,
but there was a heavy, charged feeling of anxiety in the air.

The Duke took the microphone, punched for his command frequency, said: "Two of you toss out your shield generators. By the numbers. You can carry one more man that way. We're not leaving any men
for that monster." He keyed back to the working frequency, barked: "All
right, you in Delta Ajax niner! Out! Now! This is a command from your
Duke! On the double or I'll cut that crawler apart with a lasgun!"

A hatch snapped open near the front of the factory, another at the
rear, another at the top. Men came tumbling out, sliding and scrambling down to the sand. A tall man in a patched working robe was the
last to emerge. He jumped down to a track and then to the sand.

The Duke hung the microphone on the panel, swung out onto the
wing step, shouted: "Two men each into your spotters."

The man in the patched robe began tolling off pairs of his crew,
pushing them toward the craft waiting on the other side.

"Four over here!" the Duke shouted. "Four into that ship back
there!" He jabbed a finger at an escort 'thopter directly behind him. The
guards were just wrestling the shield generator out of it. "And four into
that ship over there!" He pointed to the other escort that had shed its
shield generator. "Three each into the others! Run, you sand dogs!"

The tall man finished counting off his crew, came slogging across the sand followed by three of his companions.

"I hear the worm, but I can't see it," Kynes said.

The others heard it then—an abrasive slithering, distant and growing louder.

"Damn sloppy way to operate," the Duke muttered.

Aircraft began flapping off the sand around them. It reminded the Duke of a time in his home planet's jungles, a sudden emergence into a clearing, and carrion birds lifting away from the carcass of a wild ox.

The spice workers slogged up to the side of the 'thopter, started climbing in behind the Duke. Halleck helped, dragging them into the rear.

"In you go, boys!" he snapped. "On the double!"

Paul, crowded into a corner by sweating men, smelled the perspiration of fear, saw that two of the men had poor neck adjustments on their stillsuits. He filed the information in his memory for future action. His father would have to order tighter stillsuit discipline. Men tended to become sloppy if you didn't watch such things.

The last man came gasping into the rear, said, "The worm! It's almost on us! Blast off!"

The Duke slid into his seat, frowning, said: "We still have almost three minutes on the original contact estimate. Is that right, Kynes?" He shut his door, checked it.

"Almost exactly, my Lord," Kynes said, and he thought: *A cool one, this Duke.*

"All secure here, Sire," Halleck said.

The Duke nodded, watched the last of his escort take off. He adjusted the igniter, glanced once more at wings and instruments, punched the jet sequence.

The takeoff pressed the Duke and Kynes deep into their seats, compressed the people in the rear. Kynes watched the way the Duke handled the controls—gently, surely. The 'thopter was fully airborne now, and the Duke studied his instruments, glanced left and right at his wings.

"She's very heavy, Sire," Halleck said.

"Well within the tolerances of this ship," the Duke said. "You didn't really think I'd risk this cargo, did you, Gurney?"

Halleck grinned, said: "Not a bit of it, Sire."

The Duke banked his craft in a long easy curve—climbing over the crawler.

Paul, crushed into a corner beside a window, stared down at the silent machine on the sand. The wormsign had broken off about four hundred meters from the crawler. And now, there appeared to be turbulence in the sand around the factory.

"The worm is now beneath the crawler," Kynes said. "You are about to witness a thing few have seen."

Flecks of dust shadowed the sand around the crawler now. The big machine began to tip down to the right. A gigantic sand whirlpool began forming there to the right of the crawler. It moved faster and faster. Sand and dust filled the air now for hundreds of meters around.

Then they saw it!

A wide hole emerged from the sand. Sunlight flashed from glistening white spokes within it. The hole's diameter was at least twice the length of the crawler, Paul estimated. He watched as the machine slid into that opening in a billow of dust and sand. The hole pulled back.

"Gods, what a monster!" muttered a man beside Paul.

"Got all our floggin' spice!" growled another.

"Someone is going to pay for this," the Duke said. "I promise you that."

By the very flatness of his father's voice, Paul sensed the deep anger. He found that he shared it. This was criminal waste!

In the silence that followed, they heard Kynes.

"Bless the Maker and His water," Kynes murmured. "Bless the coming and going of Him. May His passage cleanse the world. May He keep the world for His people."

"What's that you're saying?" the Duke asked.

But Kynes remained silent.

Paul glanced at the men crowded around him. They were staring fearfully at the back of Kynes' head. One of them whispered: "Liet."

Kynes turned, scowling. The man sank back, abashed.

Another of the rescued men began coughing—dry and rasping. Presently, he gasped: "Curse this hell hole!"

The tall Dune man who had come last out of the crawler said: "Be you still, Coss. You but worsen your cough." He stirred among the men until he could look through them at the back of the Duke's head. "You be the Duke Leto, I warrant," he said. "It's to you we give thanks for our lives. We were ready to end it there until you came along."

"Quiet, man, and let the Duke fly his ship," Halleck muttered.

Paul glanced at Halleck. He, too, had seen the tension wrinkles at the corner of his father's jaw. One walked softly when the Duke was in a rage.

Leto began easing his 'thopter out of its great banking circle, stopped at a new sign of movement on the sand. The worm had withdrawn into the depths and now, near where the crawler had been, two figures could be seen moving north away from the sand depression. They appeared to glide over the surface with hardly a lifting of dust to mark their passage.

"Who's that down there?" the Duke barked.

"Two Johnnies who came along for the ride, Soor," said the tall Dune man.

"Why wasn't something said about them?"

"It was the chance they took, Soor," the Dune man said.

"My Lord," said Kynes, "these men know it's of little use to do anything about men trapped on the desert in worm country."

"We'll send a ship from base for them!" the Duke snapped.

"As you wish, my Lord," Kynes said. "But likely when the ship gets here there'll be no one to rescue."

"We'll send a ship, anyway," the Duke said.

"They were right beside where the worm came up," Paul said. "How'd they escape?"

"The sides of the hole cave in and make the distances deceptive," Kynes said.

"You waste fuel here, Sire," Halleck ventured.

"Aye, Gurney."

The Duke brought his craft around toward the Shield Wall. His escort came down from circling stations, took up positions above and on both sides.

Paul thought about what the Dune man and Kynes had said. He sensed half-truths, outright lies. The men on the sand had glided across the surface so surely, moving in a way obviously calculated to keep from luring the worm back out of its depths.

Fremen! Paul thought. *Who else would be so sure on the sand? Who else might be left out of your worries as a matter of course—because they are in no danger? They know how to live here! They know how to outwit the worm!*

"What were Fremen doing on that crawler?" Paul asked.

Kynes whirled.

The tall Dune man turned wide eyes on Paul—blue within blue within blue. "Who be this lad?" he asked.

Halleck moved to place himself between the man and Paul, said: "This is Paul Atreides, the ducal heir."

"Why says he there were Fremen on our rumbler?" the man asked.

"They fit the description," Paul said.

Kynes snorted. "You can't tell Fremen just by looking at them!" He looked at the Dune man. "You. Who were those men?"

"Friends of one of the others," the Dune man said. "Just friends from a village who wanted to see the spice sands."

Kynes turned away. "Fremen!"

But he was remembering the words of the legend: "*The Lisan al-Gaib shall see through all subterfuge.*"

"They be dead now, most likely, young Soor," the Dune man said. "We should not speak unkindly on them."

But Paul heard the falsehood in their voices, felt the menace that had brought Halleck instinctively into guarding position.

Paul spoke dryly: "A terrible place for them to die."

Without turning, Kynes said: "When God hath ordained a creature to die in a particular place, He causeth that creature's wants to direct him to that place."

Leto turned a hard stare at Kynes.

And Kynes, returning the stare, found himself troubled by a fact he had observed here: *This Duke was concerned more over the men than he was over the spice. He risked his own life and that of his son to save the men. He passed off the loss of a spice crawler with a gesture. The threat to men's lives had him in a rage. A leader such as that would command fanatic loyalty. He would be difficult to defeat.*

Against his own will and all previous judgments, Kynes admitted to himself: *I like this Duke.*

Greatness is a transitory experience. It is never consistent. It depends in part upon the myth-making imagination of humankind. The person who experiences greatness must have a feeling for the myth he is in. He must reflect what is projected upon him. And he must have a strong sense of the sardonic. This is what uncouples him from belief in his own pretensions. The sardonic is all that permits him to move within himself. Without this quality, even occasional greatness will destroy a man.

—FROM "COLLECTED SAYINGS OF MUAD'DIB"
BY THE PRINCESS IRULAN

In the dining hall of the Arrakeen great house, suspensor lamps had been lighted against the early dark. They cast their yellow glows upward onto the black bull's head with its bloody horns, and onto the darkly glistening oil painting of the Old Duke.

Beneath these talismans, white linen shone around the burnished reflections of the Atreides silver, which had been placed in precise arrangements along the great table—little archipelagos of service waiting beside crystal glasses, each setting squared off before a heavy wooden chair. The classic central chandelier remained unlighted, and its chain twisted upward into shadows where the mechanism of the poison snooper had been concealed.

Pausing in the doorway to inspect the arrangements, the Duke thought about the poison snooper and what it signified in his society.

All of a pattern, he thought. *You can plumb us by our language—the precise and delicate delineations for ways to administer treacherous death. Will someone try chaumurky tonight—poison in the drink? Or will it be chaumas—poison in the food?*

He shook his head.

Beside each plate on the long table stood a flagon of water. There was enough water along the table, the Duke estimated, to keep a poor Arrakeen family for more than a year.

Flanking the doorway in which he stood were broad laving basins of ornate yellow and green tile. Each basin had its rack of towels. It was the custom, the housekeeper had explained, for guests as they entered to dip their hands ceremoniously into a basin, slop several cups of water onto the floor, dry their hands on a towel and fling the towel into the growing puddle at the door. After the dinner, beggars gathered outside to get the water squeezings from the towels.

How typical of a Harkonnen fief, the Duke thought. *Every degradation of the spirit that can be conceived.* He took a deep breath, feeling rage tighten his stomach.

"The custom stops here!" he muttered.

He saw a serving woman—one of the old and gnarled ones the housekeeper had recommended—hovering at the doorway from the kitchen across from him. The Duke signaled with upraised hand. She moved out of the shadows, scurried around the table toward him, and he noted the leathery face, the blue-within-blue eyes.

"My Lord wishes?" She kept her head bowed, eyes shielded.

He gestured. "Have these basins and towels removed."

"But . . . Noble Born. . . ." She looked up, mouth gaping.

"I know the custom!" he barked. "Take these basins to the front door. While we're eating and until we've finished, each beggar who calls may have a full cup of water. Understood?"

Her leathery face displayed a twisting of emotions: dismay, anger. . . .

With sudden insight, Leto realized that she must have planned to sell the water squeezings from the foot-trampled towels, wringing a few coppers from the wretches who came to the door. Perhaps that also was a custom.

His face clouded, and he growled: "I'm posting a guard to see that my orders are carried out to the letter."

He whirled, strode back down the passage to the Great Hall. Memories rolled in his mind like the toothless mutterings of old women. He remembered open water and waves—days of grass instead of sand—dazed summers that had whipped past him like windstorm leaves.

All gone.

I'm getting old, he thought. *I've felt the cold hand of my mortality. And in what? An old woman's greed.*

In the Great Hall, the Lady Jessica was the center of a mixed group standing in front of the fireplace. An open blaze crackled there, casting flickers of orange light onto jewels and laces and costly fabrics. He recognized in the group a stillsuit manufacturer down from Carthag, an electronics equipment importer, a water-shipper whose summer mansion was near his polar-cap factory, a representative of the Guild Bank (lean and remote, that one), a dealer in replacement parts for spice mining equipment, a thin and hard-faced woman whose escort service for off-planet visitors reputedly operated as cover for various smuggling, spying, and blackmail operations.

Most of the women in the hall seemed cast from a specific type—decorative, precisely turned out, an odd mingling of untouchable sensuousness.

Even without her position as hostess, Jessica would have dominated the group, he thought. She wore no jewelry and had chosen warm colors—a long dress almost the shade of the open blaze, and an earth-brown band around her bronzed hair.

He realized she had done this to taunt him subtly, a reproof against his recent pose of coldness. She was well aware that he liked her best in these shades—that he saw her as a rustling of warm colors.

Nearby, more an outflanker than a member of the group, stood Duncan Idaho in glittering dress uniform, flat face unreadable, the curling black hair neatly combed. He had been summoned back from the Fremen and had his orders from Hawat—*"Under pretext of guarding her, you will keep the Lady Jessica under constant surveillance."*

The Duke glanced around the room.

There was Paul in the corner surrounded by a fawning group of the younger Arrakeen richece, and, aloof among them, three officers of the House Troop. The Duke took particular note of the young women. What a catch a ducal heir would make. But Paul was treating all equally with an air of reserved nobility.

He'll wear the title well, the Duke thought, and realized with a sudden chill that this was another death thought.

Paul saw his father in the doorway, avoided his eyes. He looked around at the clusterings of guests, the jeweled hands clutching drinks (and the unobtrusive inspections with tiny remote-cast snoopers). Seeing all the chattering faces, Paul was suddenly repelled by them. They were cheap masks locked on festering thoughts—voices gabbling to drown out the loud silence in every breast.

I'm in a sour mood, he thought, and wondered what Gurney would say to that.

He knew his mood's source. He hadn't wanted to attend this function, but his father had been firm. "You have a place—a position to uphold. You're old enough to do this. You're almost a man."

Paul saw his father emerge from the doorway, inspect the room, then cross to the group around the Lady Jessica.

As Leto approached Jessica's group, the water-shipper was asking: "Is it true the Duke will put in weather control?"

From behind the man, the Duke said: "We haven't gone that far in our thinking, sir."

The man turned, exposing a bland round face, darkly tanned. "Ah-h, the Duke," he said. "We missed you."

Leto glanced at Jessica. "A thing needed doing." He returned his attention to the water-shipper, explained what he had ordered for the laving basins, adding: "As far as I'm concerned, the old custom ends now."

"Is this a ducal order, m'Lord?" the man asked.

"I leave that to your own . . . ah . . . conscience," the Duke said. He turned, noting Kynes come up to the group.

One of the women said: "I think it's a very generous gesture—giving water to the—" Someone shushed her.

The Duke looked at Kynes, noting that the planetologist wore an old-style dark brown uniform with epaulets of the Imperial Civil Servant and a tiny gold teardrop of rank at his collar.

The water-shipper asked in an angry voice: "Does the Duke imply criticism of our custom?"

"This custom has been changed," Leto said. He nodded to Kynes, marked the frown on Jessica's face, thought: *A frown does not become her, but it'll increase rumors of friction between us.*

"With the Duke's permission," the water-shipper said, "I'd like to inquire further about customs."

Leto heard the sudden oily tone in the man's voice, noted the watchful silence in this group, the way heads were beginning to turn toward them around the room.

"Isn't it almost time for dinner?" Jessica asked.

"But our guest has some questions," Leto said. And he looked at the water-shipper, seeing a round-faced man with large eyes and thick lips, recalling Hawat's memorandum: *". . . and this water-shipper is a man to watch—Lingar Bewt, remember the name. The Harkonnens used him but never fully controlled him."*

"Water customs are so interesting," Bewt said, and there was a smile on his face. "I'm curious what you intend about the conservatory attached to this house. Do you intend to continue flaunting it in the people's faces . . . m'Lord?"

Leto held anger in check, staring at the man. Thoughts raced through his mind. It had taken bravery to challenge him in his own ducal castle, especially since they now had Bewt's signature over a contract of allegiance. The action had taken, also, a knowledge of personal power. Water was, indeed, power here. If water facilities were mined, for instance, ready to be destroyed at a signal. . . . The man looked capable of such a thing. Destruction of water facilities might well destroy Arrakis. That could well have been the club this Bewt held over the Harkonnens.

"My Lord, the Duke, and I have other plans for our conservatory," Jessica said. She smiled at Leto. "We intend to keep it, certainly, but only to hold it in trust for the people of Arrakis. It is our dream that someday the climate of Arrakis may be changed sufficiently to grow such plants anywhere in the open."

Bless her! Leto thought. *Let our water-shipper chew on that.*

"Your interest in water and weather control is obvious," the Duke said. "I'd advise you to diversify your holdings. One day, water will not be a precious commodity on Arrakis."

And he thought: *Hawat must redouble his efforts at infiltrating this Bewt's organization. And we must start on standby water facilities at once. No man is going to hold a club over my head!*

Bewt nodded, the smile still on his face. "A commendable dream, my Lord." He withdrew a pace.

Leto's attention was caught by the expression on Kynes' face. The man was staring at Jessica. He appeared transfigured—like a man in love . . . or caught in a religious trance.

Kynes' thoughts were overwhelmed at last by the words of prophecy: *"And they shall share your most precious dream."* He spoke directly to Jessica: "Do you bring the shortening of the way?"

"Ah, Dr. Kynes," the water-shipper said. "You've come in from tramping around with your mobs of Fremen. How gracious of you."

Kynes passed an unreadable glance across Bewt, said: "It is said in the desert that possession of water in great amount can inflict a man with fatal carelessness."

"They have many strange sayings in the desert," Bewt said, but his voice betrayed uneasiness.

Jessica crossed to Leto, slipped her hand under his arm to gain a moment in which to calm herself. Kynes had said: ". . . the shortening of the way." In the old tongue, the phrase translated as "Kwisatz Haderach." The planetologist's odd question seemed to have gone unnoticed by the others, and now Kynes was bending over one of the consort women, listening to a low-voiced coquetry.

Kwisatz Haderach, Jessica thought. *Did our Missionaria Protectiva plant that legend here, too?* The thought fanned her secret hope for Paul. *He could be the Kwisatz Haderach. He could be.*

The Guild Bank representative had fallen into conversation with the water-shipper, and Bewt's voice lifted above the renewed hum of conversations: "Many people have sought to change Arrakis."

The Duke saw how the words seemed to pierce Kynes, jerking the planetologist upright and away from the flirting woman.

Into the sudden silence, a house trooper in uniform of a footman cleared his throat behind Leto, said: "Dinner is served, my Lord."

The Duke directed a questioning glance down at Jessica.

"The custom here is for host and hostess to follow their guests to table," she said, and smiled: "Shall we change that one, too, my Lord?"

He spoke coldly: "That seems a goodly custom. We shall let it stand for now."

The illusion that I suspect her of treachery must be maintained, he thought. He glanced at the guests filing past them. *Who among you believes this lie?*

Jessica, sensing his remoteness, wondered at it as she had done frequently the past week. *He acts like a man struggling with himself,* she thought. *Is it because I moved so swiftly setting up this dinner party? Yet, he knows how important it is that we begin to mix our officers and men with the locals on a social plane. We are father and mother surrogate to them all. Nothing impresses that fact more firmly than this sort of social sharing.*

Leto, watching the guests file past, recalled what Thufir Hawat had said when informed of the affair: "Sire! I forbid it!"

A grim smile touched the Duke's mouth. What a scene that had been. And when the Duke had remained adamant about attending the dinner, Hawat had shaken his head. "I have bad feelings about this, my Lord," he'd said. "Things move too swiftly on Arrakis. That's not like the Harkonnens. Not like them at all."

Paul passed his father escorting a young woman half a head taller than himself. He shot a sour glance at his father, nodded at something the young woman said.

"Her father manufactures stillsuits," Jessica said. "I'm told that only a fool would be caught in the deep desert wearing one of the man's suits."

"Who's the man with the scarred face ahead of Paul?" the Duke asked. "I don't place him."

"A late addition to the list," she whispered. "Gurney arranged the invitation. Smuggler."

"Gurney arranged?"

"At my request. It was cleared with Hawat, although I thought Hawat was a little stiff about it. The smuggler's called Tuek, Esmar Tuek. He's a power among his kind. They all know him here. He's dined at many of the houses."

"Why is he here?"

"Everyone here will ask that question," she said. "Tuek will sow doubt and suspicion just by his presence. He'll also serve notice that you're prepared to back up your orders against graft—by enforcement from the smugglers' end as well. This was the point Hawat appeared to like."

"I'm not sure *I* like it." He nodded to a passing couple, saw only a few of their guests remained to precede them. "Why didn't you invite some Fremen?"

"There's Kynes," she said.

"Yes, there's Kynes," he said. "Have you arranged any other little surprises for me?" He led her into step behind the procession.

"All else is most conventional," she said.

And she thought: *My darling, can't you see that this smuggler controls fast ships, that he can be bribed? We must have a way out, a door of escape from Arrakis if all else fails us here.*

As they emerged into the dining hall, she disengaged her arm, allowed Leto to seat her. He strode to his end of the table. A footman held his chair for him. The others settled with a swishing of fabrics, a scraping of chairs, but the Duke remained standing. He gave a hand signal, and the house troopers in footman uniform around the table stepped back, standing at attention.

Uneasy silence settled over the room.

Jessica, looking down the length of the table, saw a faint trembling at the corners of Leto's mouth, noted the dark flush of anger on his cheeks. *What has angered him?* she asked herself. *Surely not my invitation to the smuggler.*

"Some question my changing of the laving basin custom," Leto said. "This is my way of telling you that many things will change."

Embarrassed silence settled over the table.

They think him drunk, Jessica thought.

Leto lifted his water flagon, held it aloft where the suspensor lights shot beams of reflection off it. "As a Chevalier of the Imperium, then," he said, "I give you a toast."

The others grasped their flagons, all eyes focused on the Duke. In the sudden stillness, a suspensor light drifted slightly in an errant breeze from the serving kitchen hallway. Shadows played across the Duke's hawk features.

"Here I am and here I remain!" he barked.

There was an abortive movement of flagons toward mouths— stopped as the Duke remained with arm upraised. "My toast is one of those maxims so dear to our hearts: 'Business makes progress! Fortune passes everywhere!'"

He sipped his water.

The others joined him. Questioning glances passed among them.

"Gurney!" the Duke called.

From an alcove at Leto's end of the room came Halleck's voice. "Here, my Lord."

"Give us a tune, Gurney."

A minor chord from the baliset floated out of the alcove. Servants began putting plates of food on the table at the Duke's gesture releasing them—roast desert hare in sauce cepeda, aplomage sirian, chukka under glass, coffee with melange (a rich cinnamon odor from the spice wafted across the table), a true pot-a-oie served with sparkling Caladan wine.

Still, the Duke remained standing.

As the guests waited, their attention torn between the dishes placed before them and the standing Duke, Leto said: "In olden times, it was the duty of the host to entertain his guests with his own talents." His knuckles turned white, so fiercely did he grip his water flagon. "I cannot sing, but I give you the words of Gurney's song. Consider it another toast—a toast to all who've died bringing us to this station."

An uncomfortable stirring sounded around the table.

Jessica lowered her gaze, glanced at the people seated nearest her—there was the round-faced water-shipper and his woman, the pale and austere Guild Bank representative (he seemed a whistle-faced scarecrow with his eyes fixed on Leto), the rugged and scar-faced Tuek, his blue-within-blue eyes downcast.

"Review, friends—troops long past review," the Duke intoned. "All to fate a weight of pains and dollars. Their spirits wear our silver collars. Review, friends—troops long past review: Each a dot of time without pretense or guile. With them passes the lure of fortune. Review, friends—troops long past review. When our time ends on its rictus smile, we'll pass the lure of fortune."

The Duke allowed his voice to trail off on the last line, took a deep drink from his water flagon, slammed it back onto the table. Water slopped over the brim onto the linen.

The others drank in embarrassed silence.

Again, the Duke lifted his water flagon, and this time emptied its remaining half onto the floor, knowing that the others around the table must do the same.

Jessica was first to follow his example.

There was a frozen moment before the others began emptying their flagons. Jessica saw how Paul, seated near his father, was studying the reactions around him. She found herself also fascinated by what her guests' actions revealed—especially among the women. This was clean, potable water, not something already cast away in a sopping towel. Reluctance to just discard it exposed itself in trembling hands, delayed reactions, nervous laughter . . . and violent obedience to the necessity.

One woman dropped her flagon, looked the other way as her male companion recovered it.

Kynes, though, caught her attention most sharply. The planetologist hesitated, then emptied his flagon into a container beneath his jacket. He smiled at Jessica as he caught her watching him, raised the empty flagon to her in a silent toast. He appeared completely unembarrassed by his action.

Halleck's music still wafted over the room, but it had come out of its minor key, lilting and lively now as though he were trying to lift the mood.

"Let the dinner commence," the Duke said, and sank into his chair.

He's angry and uncertain, Jessica thought. *The loss of that factory crawler hit him more deeply than it should have. It must be something more than that loss. He acts like a desperate man.* She lifted her fork, hoping in the motion to hide her own sudden bitterness. *Why not? He is desperate.*

Slowly at first, then with increasing animation, the dinner got under way. The stillsuit manufacturer complimented Jessica on her chef and wine.

"We brought both from Caladan," she said.

"Superb!" he said, tasting the chukka. "Simply superb! And not a hint of melange in it. One gets so tired of the spice in everything."

The Guild Bank representative looked across at Kynes. "I understand, Doctor Kynes, that another factory crawler has been lost to a worm."

"News travels fast," the Duke said.

"Then it's true?" the banker asked, shifting his attention to Leto.

"Of course, it's true!" the Duke snapped. "The blasted carryall disappeared. It shouldn't be possible for anything that big to disappear!"

"When the worm came, there was nothing to recover the crawler," Kynes said.

"It should *not* be possible!" the Duke repeated.

"No one saw the carryall leave?" the banker asked.

"Spotters customarily keep their eyes on the sand," Kynes said. "They're primarily interested in wormsign. A carryall's complement usually is four men—two pilots and two journeymen attachers. If one— or even two of this crew were in the pay of the Duke's foes—"

"Ah-h-h, I see," the banker said. "And you, as Judge of the Change, do you challenge this?"

"I shall have to consider my position carefully," Kynes said, "and I certainly will not discuss it at table." And he thought: *That pale skeleton of a man! He knows this is the kind of infraction I was instructed to ignore.*

The banker smiled, returned his attention to his food.

Jessica sat remembering a lecture from her Bene Gesserit school days. The subject had been espionage and counter-espionage. A plump, happy-faced Reverend Mother had been the lecturer, her jolly voice contrasting weirdly with the subject matter.

A thing to note about any espionage and/or counter-espionage school is the similar basic reaction pattern of all its graduates. Any enclosed discipline sets its stamp, its pattern, upon its students. That pattern is susceptible to analysis and prediction.

Now, motivational patterns are going to be similar among all espionage agents. That is to say: there will be certain types of motivation that are similar despite differing schools or opposed aims. You will study first how to separate this element for your analysis—in the beginning, through interrogation patterns that betray the inner orientation of the interrogators; secondly, by close observation of language-thought orientation of those under analysis. You will find it fairly simple to determine the root languages of your subjects, of course, both through voice inflection and speech pattern.

Now, sitting at table with her son and her Duke and their guests, hearing that Guild Bank representative, Jessica felt a chill of realization: the man was a Harkonnen agent. He had the Giedi Prime speech pattern—subtly masked, but exposed to her trained awareness as though he had announced himself.

Does this mean the Guild itself has taken sides against House Atre-

ides? she asked herself. The thought shocked her, and she masked her emotion by calling for a new dish, all the while listening for the man to betray his purpose. *He will shift the conversation next to something seemingly innocent, but with ominous overtones,* she told herself. *It's his pattern.*

The banker swallowed, took a sip of wine, smiled at something said to him by the woman on his right. He seemed to listen for a moment to a man down the table who was explaining to the Duke that native Arrakeen plants had no thorns.

"I enjoy watching the flights of birds on Arrakis," the banker said, directing his words at Jessica. "All of our birds, of course, are carrion-eaters, and many exist without water, having become blood-drinkers."

The stillsuit manufacturer's daughter, seated between Paul and his father at the other end of the table, twisted her pretty face into a frown, said: "Oh, Soo-Soo, you say the most disgusting things."

The banker smiled. "They call me Soo-Soo because I'm financial adviser to the Water Peddlers Union." And, as Jessica continued to look at him without comment, he added: "Because of the water-sellers' cry—'Soo-Soo Sook!'" And he imitated the call with such accuracy that many around the table laughed.

Jessica heard the boastful tone of voice, but noted most that the young woman had spoken on cue—a set piece. She had produced the excuse for the banker to say what he had said. She glanced at Lingar Bewt. The water magnate was scowling, concentrating on his dinner. It came to Jessica that the banker had said: *"I, too, control that ultimate source of power on Arrakis—water."*

Paul had marked the falseness in his dinner companion's voice, saw that his mother was following the conversation with Bene Gesserit intensity. On impulse, he decided to play the foil, draw the exchange out. He addressed himself to the banker.

"Do you mean, sir, that these birds are cannibals?"

"That's an odd question, young Master," the banker said. "I merely said the birds drink blood. It doesn't have to be the blood of their own kind, does it?"

"It was *not* an odd question," Paul said, and Jessica noted the brittle riposte quality of her training exposed in his voice. "Most educated people know that the worst potential competition for any young organism can come from its own kind." He deliberately forked a bite of food from his companion's plate, ate it. "They are eating from the same bowl. They have the same basic requirements."

The banker stiffened, scowled at the Duke.

"Do not make the error of considering my son a child," the Duke said. And he smiled.

Jessica glanced around the table, noted that Bewt had brightened, that both Kynes and the smuggler, Tuek, were grinning.

"It's a rule of ecology," Kynes said, "that the young Master appears to understand quite well. The struggle between life elements is the struggle for the free energy of a system. Blood's an efficient energy source."

The banker put down his fork, spoke in an angry voice: "It's said that the Fremen scum drink the blood of their dead."

Kynes shook his head, spoke in a lecturing tone: "Not the blood, sir. But all of a man's water, ultimately, belongs to his people—to his tribe. It's a necessity when you live near the Great Flat. All water's precious there, and the human body is composed of some seventy per cent water by weight. A dead man, surely, no longer requires that water."

The banker put both hands against the table beside his plate, and Jessica thought he was going to push himself back, leave in a rage.

Kynes looked at Jessica. "Forgive me, my Lady, for elaborating on such an ugly subject at table, but you were being told falsehood and it needed clarifying."

"You've associated so long with Fremen that you've lost all sensibilities," the banker rasped.

Kynes looked at him calmly, studied the pale, trembling face. "Are you challenging me, sir?"

The banker froze. He swallowed, spoke stiffly: "Of course not. I'd not so insult our host and hostess."

Jessica heard the fear in the man's voice, saw it in his face, in his

breathing, in the pulse of a vein at his temple. The man was terrified of
Kynes!

"Our host and hostess are quite capable of deciding for themselves
when they've been insulted," Kynes said. "They're brave people who
understand defense of honor. We all may attest to their courage by the
fact that they are here . . . now . . . on Arrakis."

Jessica saw that Leto was enjoying this. Most of the others were not.
People all around the table sat poised for flight, hands out of sight under
the table. Two notable exceptions were Bewt, who was openly smiling
at the banker's discomfiture, and the smuggler, Tuek, who appeared to
be watching Kynes for a cue. Jessica saw that Paul was looking at Kynes
in admiration.

"Well?" Kynes said.

"I meant no offense," the banker muttered. "If offense was taken,
please accept my apologies."

"Freely given, freely accepted," Kynes said. He smiled at Jessica, resumed eating as though nothing had happened.

Jessica saw that the smuggler, too, had relaxed. She marked this: the
man had shown every aspect of an aide ready to leap to Kynes' assis-
tance. There existed an accord of some sort between Kynes and Tuek.

Leto toyed with a fork, looked speculatively at Kynes. The ecologist's
manner indicated a change in attitude toward the House of Atreides.
Kynes had seemed colder on their trip over the desert.

Jessica signaled for another course of food and drink. Servants appeared with *langues de lapins de garenne*—red wine and a sauce of
mushroom-yeast on the side.

Slowly, the dinner conversation resumed, but Jessica heard the agitation in it, the brittle quality, saw that the banker ate in sullen silence.
Kynes would have killed him without hesitating, she thought. And she
realized that there was an offhand attitude toward killing in Kynes'
manner. He was a casual killer, and she guessed that this was a Fremen
quality.

Jessica turned to the stillsuit manufacturer on her left, said: "I find
myself continually amazed by the importance of water on Arrakis."

"Very important," he agreed. "What is this dish? It's delicious."

"Tongues of wild rabbit in a special sauce," she said. "A very old recipe."

"I must have that recipe," the man said.

She nodded. "I'll see that you get it."

Kynes looked at Jessica, said: "The newcomer to Arrakis frequently underestimates the importance of water here. You are dealing, you see, with the Law of the Minimum."

She heard the testing quality in his voice, said, "Growth is limited by that necessity which is present in the least amount. And, naturally, the least favorable condition controls the growth rate."

"It's rare to find members of a Great House aware of planetological problems," Kynes said. "Water is the least favorable condition for life on Arrakis. And remember that *growth* itself can produce unfavorable conditions unless treated with extreme care."

Jessica sensed a hidden message in Kynes' words, but knew she was missing it. "Growth," she said. "Do you mean Arrakis can have an orderly cycle of water to sustain human life under more favorable conditions?"

"Impossible!" the water magnate barked.

Jessica turned her attention to Bewt. "Impossible?"

"Impossible on Arrakis," he said. "Don't listen to this dreamer. All the laboratory evidence is against him."

Kynes looked at Bewt, and Jessica noted that the other conversations around the table had stopped while people concentrated on this new interchange.

"Laboratory evidence tends to blind us to a very simple fact," Kynes said. "That fact is this: we are dealing here with matters that originated and exist out-of-doors where plants and animals carry on their normal existence."

"Normal!" Bewt snorted. "Nothing about Arrakis is normal!"

"Quite the contrary," Kynes said. "Certain harmonies could be set up here along self-sustaining lines. You merely have to understand the limits of the planet and the pressures upon it."

"It'll never be done," Bewt said.

The Duke came to a sudden realization, placing the point where Kynes' attitude had changed—it had been when Jessica had spoken of holding the conservatory plants in trust for Arrakis.

"What would it take to set up the self-sustaining system, Doctor Kynes?" Leto asked.

"If we can get three per cent of the green plant element on Arrakis involved in forming carbon compounds as foodstuffs, we've started the cyclic system," Kynes said.

"Water's the only problem?" the Duke asked. He sensed Kynes' excitement, felt himself caught up in it.

"Water overshadows the other problems," Kynes said. "This planet has much oxygen without its usual concomitants—widespread plant life and large sources of free carbon dioxide from such phenomena as volcanoes. There are unusual chemical interchanges over large surface areas here."

"Do you have pilot projects?" the Duke asked.

"We've had a long time in which to build up the Tansley Effect—small-unit experiments on an amateur basis from which my science may now draw its working facts," Kynes said.

"There isn't enough water," Bewt said. "There just isn't enough water."

"Master Bewt is an expert on water," Kynes said. He smiled, turned back to his dinner.

The Duke gestured sharply down with his right hand, barked: "No! I want an answer! Is there enough water, Doctor Kynes?"

Kynes stared at his plate.

Jessica watched the play of emotion on his face. *He masks himself well*, she thought, but she had him registered now and read that he regretted his words.

"Is there enough water!" the Duke demanded.

"There . . . may be," Kynes said.

He's faking uncertainty! Jessica thought.

With his deeper truthsense, Paul caught the underlying motive, had to use every ounce of his training to mask his excitement. *There is enough water! But Kynes doesn't wish it to be known.*

"Our planetologist has many interesting dreams," Bewt said. "He dreams with the Fremen—of prophecies and messiahs."

Chuckles sounded at odd places around the table. Jessica marked them—the smuggler, the stillsuit manufacturer's daughter, Duncan Idaho, the woman with the mysterious escort service.

Tensions are oddly distributed here tonight, Jessica thought. *There's too much going on of which I'm not aware. I'll have to develop new information sources.*

The Duke passed his gaze from Kynes to Bewt to Jessica. He felt oddly let down, as though something vital had passed him here. "*May*be," he muttered.

Kynes spoke quickly: "Perhaps we should discuss this another time, my Lord. There are so many—"

The planetologist broke off as a uniformed Atreides trooper hurried in through the service door, was passed by the guard and rushed to the Duke's side. The man bent, whispering into Leto's ear.

Jessica recognized the capsign of Hawat's corps, fought down uneasiness. She addressed herself to the stillsuit manufacturer's feminine companion—a tiny, dark-haired woman with a doll face, a touch of epicanthic fold to the eyes.

"You've hardly touched your dinner, my dear," Jessica said. "May I order you something?"

The woman looked at the stillsuit manufacturer before answering, then: "I'm not very hungry."

Abruptly, the Duke stood up beside his trooper, spoke in a harsh tone of command: "Stay seated, everyone. You will have to forgive me, but a matter has arisen that requires my personal attention." He stepped aside. "Paul, take over as host for me, if you please."

Paul stood, wanting to ask why his father had to leave, knowing he had to play this with the grand manner. He moved around to his father's chair, sat down in it.

The Duke turned to the alcove where Halleck sat, said: "Gurney, please take Paul's place at table. We mustn't have an odd number here. When the dinner's over, I may want you to bring Paul to the field C.P. Wait for my call."

Halleck emerged from the alcove in dress uniform, his lumpy ugliness seeming out of place in the glittering finery. He leaned his baliset against the wall, crossed to the chair Paul had occupied, sat down.

"There's no need for alarm," the Duke said, "but I must ask that no one leave until our house guard says it's safe. You will be perfectly secure as long as you remain here, and we'll have this little trouble cleared up very shortly."

Paul caught the code words in his father's message—*guard-safe-secure-shortly*. The problem was security, not violence. He saw that his mother had read the same message. They both relaxed.

The Duke gave a short nod, wheeled and strode through the service door followed by his trooper.

Paul said: "Please go on with your dinner. I believe Doctor Kynes was discussing water."

"May we discuss it another time?" Kynes asked.

"By all means," Paul said.

And Jessica noted with pride her son's dignity, the mature sense of assurance.

The banker picked up his water flagon, gestured with it at Bewt. "None of us here can surpass Master Lingar Bewt in flowery phrases. One might almost assume he aspired to Great House status. Come, Master Bewt, lead us in a toast. Perhaps you've a dollop of wisdom for the boy who must be treated like a man."

Jessica clenched her right hand into a fist beneath the table. She saw a hand signal pass from Halleck to Idaho, saw the house troopers along the walls move into positions of maximum guard.

Bewt cast a venomous glare at the banker.

Paul glanced at Halleck, took in the defensive positions of his guards, looked at the banker until the man lowered the water flagon. He said: "Once, on Caladan, I saw the body of a drowned fisherman recovered. He—"

"Drowned?" It was the stillsuit manufacturer's daughter.

Paul hesitated, then: "Yes. Immersed in water until dead. Drowned."

"What an interesting way to die," she murmured.

Paul's smile became brittle. He returned his attention to the banker. "The interesting thing about this man was the wounds on his shoulders—made by another fisherman's claw-boots. This fisherman was one of several in a boat—a craft for traveling on water—that foundered . . . sank beneath the water. Another fisherman helping recover the body said he'd seen marks like this man's wounds several times. They meant another drowning fisherman had tried to stand on this poor fellow's shoulders in the attempt to reach up to the surface—to reach air."

"Why is this interesting?" the banker asked.

"Because of an observation made by my father at the time. He said the drowning man who climbs on your shoulders to save himself is understandable—except when you see it happen in the drawing room." Paul hesitated just long enough for the banker to see the point coming, then: "And, I should add, except when you see it at the dinner table."

A sudden stillness enfolded the room.

That was rash, Jessica thought. *This banker might have enough rank to call my son out.* She saw that Idaho was poised for instant action. The house troopers were alert. Gurney Halleck had his eyes on the men opposite him.

"Ho-ho-ho-o-o-o!" It was the smuggler, Tuek, head thrown back laughing with complete abandon.

Nervous smiles appeared around the table.

Bewt was grinning.

The banker had pushed his chair back, was glaring at Paul.

Kynes said: "One baits an Atreides at his own risk."

"Is it Atreides custom to insult their guests?" the banker demanded.

Before Paul could answer, Jessica leaned forward, said: "Sir!" And she thought: *We must learn this Harkonnen creature's game. Is he here to try for Paul? Does he have help?*

"My son displays a general garment and you claim it's cut to your fit?" Jessica asked. "What a fascinating revelation." She slid a hand down to her leg to the crysknife she had fastened in a calf-sheath.

The banker turned his glare on Jessica. Eyes shifted away from Paul and she saw him ease himself back from the table, freeing himself for action. He had focused on the code word: *garment. "Prepare for violence."*

Kynes directed a speculative look at Jessica, gave a subtle hand signal to Tuek.

The smuggler lurched to his feet, lifted his flagon. "I'll give you a toast," he said. "To young Paul Atreides, still a lad by his looks, but a man by his actions."

Why do they intrude? Jessica asked herself.

The banker stared now at Kynes, and Jessica saw terror return to the agent's face.

People began responding all around the table.

Where Kynes leads, people follow, Jessica thought. *He has told us he sides with Paul. What's the secret of his power? It can't be because he's Judge of the Change. That's temporary. And certainly not because he's a civil servant.*

She removed her hand from the crysknife hilt, lifted her flagon to Kynes, who responded in kind.

Only Paul and the banker—(*Soo-Soo! What an idiotic nickname!* Jessica thought.)—remained empty-handed. The banker's attention stayed fixed on Kynes. Paul stared at his plate.

I was handling it correctly, Paul thought. *Why do they interfere?* He glanced covertly at the male guests nearest him. Prepare for violence? From whom? Certainly not from that banker fellow.

Halleck stirred, spoke as though to no one in particular, directing his words over the heads of the guests across from him: "In our society, people shouldn't be quick to take offense. It's frequently suicidal." He looked at the stillsuit manufacturer's daughter beside him. "Don't you think so, miss?"

"Oh, yes. Yes. Indeed I do," she said. "There's too much violence. It makes me sick. And lots of times no offense is meant, but people die anyway. It doesn't make sense."

"Indeed it doesn't," Halleck said.

Jessica saw the near perfection of the girl's act, realized: *That empty-headed little female is not an empty-headed little female.* She saw then the pattern of the threat and understood that Halleck, too, had detected it. They had planned to lure Paul with sex. Jessica relaxed. Her son had probably been the first to see it—his training hadn't overlooked that obvious gambit.

Kynes spoke to the banker: "Isn't another apology in order?"

The banker turned a sickly grin toward Jessica, said: "My Lady, I fear I've overindulged in your wines. You serve potent drink at table, and I'm not accustomed to it."

Jessica heard the venom beneath his tone, spoke sweetly: "When strangers meet, great allowance should be made for differences of custom and training."

"Thank you, my Lady," he said.

The dark-haired companion of the stillsuit manufacturer leaned toward Jessica, said: "The Duke spoke of our being secure here. I do hope that doesn't mean more fighting."

She was directed to lead the conversation this way, Jessica thought.

"Likely this will prove unimportant," Jessica said. "But there's so much detail requiring the Duke's personal attention in these times. As long as enmity continues between Atreides and Harkonnen we cannot be too careful. The Duke has sworn kanly. He will leave no Harkonnen agent alive on Arrakis, of course." She glanced at the Guild Bank agent. "And the Conventions, naturally, support him in this." She shifted her attention to Kynes. "Is this not so, Dr. Kynes?"

"Indeed it is," Kynes said.

The stillsuit manufacturer pulled his companion gently back. She looked at him, said: "I do believe I'll eat something now. I'd like some of that bird dish you served earlier."

Jessica signaled a servant, turned to the banker: "And you, sir, were speaking of birds earlier and of their habits. I find so many interesting things about Arrakis. Tell me, where is the spice found? Do the hunters go deep into the desert?"

"Oh, no, my Lady," he said. "Very little's known of the deep desert. And almost nothing of the southern regions."

"There's a tale that a great Mother Lode of spice is to be found in the southern reaches," Kynes said, "but I suspect it was an imaginative invention made solely for purposes of a song. Some daring spice hunters do, on occasion, penetrate into the edge of the central belt, but that's extremely dangerous—navigation is uncertain, storms are frequent. Casualties increase dramatically the farther you operate from Shield Wall bases. It hasn't been found profitable to venture too far south. Perhaps if we had a weather satellite. . . ."

Bewt looked up, spoke around a mouthful of food: "It's said the Fremen travel there, that they go anywhere and have hunted out soaks and sip-wells even in the southern latitudes."

"Soaks and sip-wells?" Jessica asked.

Kynes spoke quickly: "Wild rumors, my Lady. These are known on other planets, not on Arrakis. A soak is a place where water seeps to the surface or near enough to the surface to be found by digging according to certain signs. A sip-well is a form of soak where a person draws water through a straw . . . so it is said."

There's deception in his words, Jessica thought.

Why is he lying? Paul wondered.

"How very interesting," Jessica said. And she thought: *"It is said. . . ." What a curious speech mannerism they have here. If they only knew what it reveals about their dependence on superstitions.*

"I've heard you have a saying," Paul said, "that polish comes from the cities, wisdom from the desert."

"There are many sayings on Arrakis," Kynes said.

Before Jessica could frame a new question, a servant bent over her with a note. She opened it, saw the Duke's handwriting and code signs, scanned it.

"You'll all be delighted to know," she said, "that our Duke sends his reassurances. The matter which called him away has been settled. The missing carryall has been found. A Harkonnen agent in the crew overpowered the others and flew the machine to a smugglers' base, hoping to sell it there. Both man and machine were turned over to our forces." She nodded to Tuek.

The smuggler nodded back.

Jessica refolded the note, tucked it into her sleeve.

"I'm glad it didn't come to open battle," the banker said. "The people have such hopes the Atreides will bring peace and prosperity."

"Especially prosperity," Bewt said.

"Shall we have our dessert now?" Jessica asked. "I've had our chef prepare a Caladan sweet: pongi rice in sauce dolsa."

"It sounds wonderful," the stillsuit manufacturer said. "Would it be possible to get the recipe?"

"Any recipe you desire," Jessica said, *registering* the man for later mention to Hawat. The stillsuit manufacturer was a fearful little climber and could be bought.

Small talk resumed around her: "Such a lovely fabric. . . ." "He is having a setting made to match the jewel. . . ." "We might try for a production increase next quarter. . . ."

Jessica stared down at her plate, thinking of the coded part of Leto's message: *The Harkonnens tried to get in a shipment of lasguns. We captured them. This may mean they've succeeded with other shipments. It certainly means they don't place much store in shields. Take appropriate precautions.*

Jessica focused her mind on lasguns, wondering. The white-hot beams of disruptive light could cut through any known substance, provided that substance was not shielded. The fact that feedback from a shield would explode both lasgun and shield did not bother the Harkonnens. Why? A lasgun-shield explosion was a dangerous variable, could be more powerful than atomics, could kill only the gunner and his shielded target.

The unknowns here filled her with uneasiness.

Paul said: "I never doubted we'd find the carryall. Once my father moves to solve a problem, he solves it. This is a fact the Harkonnens are beginning to discover."

He's boasting, Jessica thought. *He shouldn't boast. No person who'll be sleeping far below ground level this night as a precaution against lasguns has the right to boast.*

There is no escape—we pay for the violence of our ancestors.

—FROM "COLLECTED SAYINGS OF MUAD'DIB"
BY THE PRINCESS IRULAN

Jessica heard the disturbance in the Great Hall, turned on the light beside her bed. The clock there had not been properly adjusted to local time, and she had to subtract twenty-one minutes to determine that it was about 2 A.M.

The disturbance was loud and incoherent.

Is this the Harkonnen attack? she wondered.

She slipped out of bed, checked the screen monitors to see where her family was. The screen showed Paul asleep in the deep cellar room they'd hastily converted to a bedroom for him. The noise obviously wasn't penetrating to his quarters. There was no one in the Duke's room, his bed was unrumpled. Was he still at the field C.P.?

There were no screens yet to the front of the house.

Jessica stood in the middle of her room, listening.

There was one shouting, incoherent voice. She heard someone call for Dr. Yueh. Jessica found a robe, pulled it over her shoulders, pushed her feet into slippers, strapped the crysknife to her leg.

Again, a voice called out for Yueh.

Jessica belted the robe around her, stepped into the hallway. Then the thought struck her: *What if Leto's hurt?*

The hall seemed to stretch out forever under her running feet. She turned through the arch at the end, dashed past the dining hall and down the passage to the Great Hall, finding the place brightly lighted, all the wall suspensors glowing at maximum.

To her right near the front entry, she saw two house guards holding Duncan Idaho between them. His head lolled forward, and there was an abrupt, panting silence to the scene.

One of the house guards spoke accusingly to Idaho: "You see what you did? You woke the Lady Jessica."

The great draperies billowed behind the men, showing that the front door remained open. There was no sign of the Duke or Yueh. Mapes stood to one side staring coldly at Idaho. She wore a long brown robe with serpentine design at the hem. Her feet were pushed into unlaced desert boots.

"So I woke the Lady Jessica," Idaho muttered. He lifted his face toward the ceiling, bellowed: "My sword was firs' blooded on Grumman!"

Great Mother! He's drunk! Jessica thought.

Idaho's dark, round face was drawn into a frown. His hair, curling like the fur of a black goat, was plastered with dirt. A jagged rent in his tunic exposed an expanse of the dress shirt he had worn at the dinner party earlier.

Jessica crossed to him.

One of the guards nodded to her without releasing his hold on Idaho. "We didn't know what to do with him, my Lady. He was creating a disturbance out front, refusing to come inside. We were afraid locals might come along and see him. That wouldn't do at all. Give us a bad name here."

"Where has he been?" Jessica asked.

"He escorted one of the young ladies home from the dinner, my Lady. Hawat's orders."

"Which young lady?"

"One of the escort wenches. You understand, my Lady?" He glanced at Mapes, lowered his voice. "They're always calling on Idaho for special surveillance of the ladies."

And Jessica thought: *So they are. But why is he drunk?*

She frowned, turned to Mapes. "Mapes, bring a stimulant. I'd suggest caffeine. Perhaps there's some of the spice coffee left."

Mapes shrugged, headed for the kitchen. Her unlaced desert boots slap-slapped against the stone floor.

Idaho swung his unsteady head around to peer at an angle toward Jessica. "Killed more'n three hunner' men f'r the Duke," he muttered. "Whadduh wanna know is why'm mere? Can't live unner th' groun' here. Can't live onna groun' here. Wha' kinna place is 'iss, huh?"

A sound from the side hall entry caught Jessica's attention. She turned, saw Yueh crossing to them, his medical kit swinging in his left hand. He was fully dressed, looked pale, exhausted. The diamond tattoo stood out sharply on his forehead.

"Th' good docker!" Idaho shouted. "Whad're you, Doc? Splint 'n' pill man?" He turned blearily toward Jessica. "Makin' uh damn fool uh m'self, huh?"

Jessica frowned, remained silent, wondering: *Why would Idaho get drunk? Was he drugged?*

"Too much spice beer," Idaho said, attempting to straighten.

Mapes returned with a steaming cup in her hands, stopped uncertainly behind Yueh. She looked at Jessica, who shook her head.

Yueh put his kit on the floor, nodded greeting to Jessica, said: "Spice beer, eh?"

"Bes' damn stuff ever tas'ed," Idaho said. He tried to pull himself to attention. "My sword was firs' blooded on Grumman! Killed a Harkon . . . Harkon . . . killed 'im f'r th' Duke."

Yueh turned, looked at the cup in Mapes' hand. "What is that?"

"Caffeine," Jessica said.

Yueh took the cup, held it toward Idaho. "Drink this, lad."

"Don't wan' any more t' drink."

"Drink it, I say!"

Idaho's head wobbled toward Yueh, and he stumbled one step ahead, dragging the guards with him. "I'm almighdy fed up with pleasin' th' 'Mperial Universe, Doc. Jus' once, we're gonna do th' thing my way."

"After you drink this," Yueh said. "It's just caffeine."

"'Sprolly like all res' uh this place! Damn sun 'stoo brighd. Nothin' has uh righd color. Ever'thing's wrong or. . . ."

"Well, it's nighttime now," Yueh said. He spoke reasonably. "Drink this like a good lad. It'll make you feel better."

"Don' wanna feel bedder!"

"We can't argue with him all night," Jessica said. And she thought: *This calls for shock treatment.*

"There's no reason for you to stay, my Lady," Yueh said. "I can take care of this."

Jessica shook her head. She stepped forward, slapped Idaho sharply across the cheek.

He stumbled back with his guards, glaring at her.

"This is no way to act in your Duke's home," she said. She snatched the cup from Yueh's hands, spilling part of it, thrust the cup toward Idaho. "Now drink this! That's an order!"

Idaho jerked himself upright, scowling down at her. He spoke slowly, with careful and precise enunciation: "I do not take orders from a damn Harkonnen spy."

Yueh stiffened, whirled to face Jessica.

Her face had gone pale, but she was nodding. It all became clear to her—the broken stems of meaning she had seen in words and actions around her these past few days could now be translated. She found herself in the grip of anger almost too great to contain. It took the most profound of her Bene Gesserit training to quiet her pulse and smooth her breathing. Even then she could feel the blaze flickering.

They were always calling on Idaho for surveillance of the ladies!

She shot a glance at Yueh. The doctor lowered his eyes.

"You knew this?" she demanded.

"I . . . heard rumors, my Lady. But I didn't want to add to your burdens."

"Hawat!" she snapped. "I want Thufir Hawat brought to me immediately!"

"But, my Lady. . . ."

"Immediately!"

It has to be Hawat, she thought. *Suspicion such as this could come from no other source without being discarded immediately.*

Idaho shook his head, mumbled: "Chuck th' whole damn thing."

Jessica looked down at the cup in her hand, abruptly dashed its contents across Idaho's face. "Lock him in one of the guest rooms of the east wing," she ordered. "Let him *sleep* it off."

The two guards stared at her unhappily. One ventured: "Perhaps we should take him someplace else, m'Lady. We could. . . ."

"He's supposed to be here!" Jessica snapped. "He has a job to do here." Her voice dripped bitterness. "He's so good at watching the ladies."

The guard swallowed.

"Do you know where the Duke is?" she demanded.

"He's at the command post, my Lady."

"Is Hawat with him?"

"Hawat's in the city, my Lady."

"You will bring Hawat to me at once," Jessica said. "I will be in my sitting room when he arrives."

"But, my Lady. . . ."

"If necessary, I will call the Duke," she said. "I hope it will not be necessary. I would not want to disturb him with this."

"Yes, my Lady."

Jessica thrust the empty cup into Mapes' hands, met the questioning stare of the blue-within-blue eyes. "You may return to bed, Mapes."

"You're sure you'll not need me?"

Jessica smiled grimly. "I'm sure."

"Perhaps this could wait until tomorrow," Yueh said. "I could give you a sedative and. . . ."

"You will return to your quarters and leave me to handle this my way," she said. She patted his arm to take the sting out of her command. "This is the only way."

Abruptly, head high, she turned and stalked off through the house to her rooms. Cold walls . . . passages . . . a familiar door. . . . She jerked the door open, strode in, and slammed it behind her. Jessica stood there glaring at the shield-blanked windows of her sitting room. *Hawat! Could he be the one the Harkonnens bought? We shall see.*

Jessica crossed to the deep, old-fashioned armchair with an embroidered cover of schlag skin, moved the chair into position to command the door. She was suddenly very conscious of the crysknife in its sheath on her leg. She removed the sheath and strapped it to her arm, tested the drop of it. Once more, she glanced around the room, placing everything precisely in her mind against any emergency: the chaise near the corner, the straight chairs along the wall, the two low tables, her stand-mounted zither beside the door to her bedroom.

Pale rose light glowed from the suspensor lamps. She dimmed them, sat down in the armchair, patting the upholstery, appreciating the chair's regal heaviness for this occasion.

Now, let him come, she thought. *We shall see what we shall see.* And she prepared herself in the Bene Gesserit fashion for the wait, accumulating patience, saving her strength.

Sooner than she had expected, a rap sounded at the door and Hawat entered at her command.

She watched him without moving from the chair, seeing the crackling sense of drug-induced energy in his movements, seeing the fatigue beneath. Hawat's rheumy old eyes glittered. His leathery skin appeared faintly yellow in the room's light, and there was a wide, wet stain on the sleeve of his knife arm.

She smelled blood there.

Jessica gestured to one of the straight-backed chairs, said: "Bring that chair and sit facing me."

Hawat bowed, obeyed. *That drunken fool of an Idaho!* he thought. He studied Jessica's face, wondering how he could save this situation.

"It's long past time to clear the air between us," Jessica said.

"What troubles my Lady?" He sat down, placed hands on knees.

"Don't play coy with me!" she snapped. "If Yueh didn't tell you why I summoned you, then one of your spies in my household did. Shall we be at least that honest with each other?"

"As you wish, my Lady."

"First, you will answer me one question," she said. "Are you now a Harkonnen agent?"

Hawat surged half out of his chair, his face dark with fury, demanding: "You dare insult me so?"

"Sit down," she said. "You insulted me so."

Slowly, he sank back into the chair.

And Jessica, reading the signs of this face that she knew so well, allowed herself a deep breath. *It isn't Hawat.*

"Now I know you remain loyal to my Duke," she said. "I'm prepared, therefore, to forgive your affront to me."

"Is there something to forgive?"

Jessica scowled, wondering: *Shall I play my trump? Shall I tell him of the Duke's daughter I've carried within me these few weeks? No . . . Leto himself doesn't know. This would only complicate his life, divert him in a time when he must concentrate on our survival. There is yet time to use this.*

"A Truthsayer would solve this," she said, "but we have no Truthsayer qualified by the High Board."

"As you say. We've no Truthsayer."

"Is there a traitor among us?" she asked. "I've studied our people with great care. Who could it be? Not Gurney. Certainly not Duncan. *Their* lieutenants are not strategically enough placed to consider. It's not you, Thufir. It cannot be Paul. I *know* it's not me. Dr. Yueh, then? Shall I call him in and put him to the test?"

"You know that's an empty gesture," Hawat said. "He's conditioned by the High College. *That* I know for certain."

"Not to mention that his wife was a Bene Gesserit slain by the Harkonnens," Jessica said.

"So that's what happened to her," Hawat said.

"Haven't you heard the hate in his voice when he speaks the Harkonnen name?"

"You know I don't have the ear," Hawat said.

"What brought this base suspicion on me?" she asked.

Hawat frowned. "My Lady puts her servant in an impossible posi-tion. My first loyalty is to the Duke."

"I'm prepared to forgive much because of that loyalty," she said.

"And again I must ask: Is there something to forgive?"

"Stalemate?" she asked.

He shrugged.

"Let us discuss something else for a minute, then," she said. "Dun-can Idaho, the admirable fighting man whose abilities at guarding and surveillance are so esteemed. Tonight, he overindulged in something called spice beer. I hear reports that others among our people have been stupefied by this concoction. Is that true?"

"You have your reports, my Lady."

"So I do. Don't you see this drinking as a symptom, Thufir?"

"My Lady speaks riddles."

"Apply your Mentat abilities to it!" she snapped. "What's the prob-lem with Duncan and the others? I can tell you in four words—they have no home."

He jabbed a finger at the floor. "Arrakis, that's their home."

"Arrakis is an unknown! Caladan was their home, but we've uprooted them. They have no home. And they fear the Duke's failing them."

He stiffened. "Such talk from one of the men would be cause for—"

"Oh, stop that, Thufir. Is it defeatist or treacherous for a doctor to diagnose a disease correctly? My only intention is to cure the disease."

"The Duke gives me charge over such matters."

"But you understand I have a certain natural concern over the prog-ress of this disease," she said. "And perhaps you'll grant I have certain abilities along these lines."

Will I have to shock him severely? she wondered. *He needs shaking up—something to break him from routine.*

"There could be many interpretations for your concern," Hawat said. He shrugged.

"Then you've already convicted me?"

"Of course not, my Lady. But I cannot afford to take *any* chances, the situation being what it is."

"A threat to my son got past you right here in this house," she said. "Who took that chance?"

His face darkened. "I offered my resignation to the Duke."

"Did you offer your resignation to me . . . or to Paul?"

Now he was openly angry, betraying it in quickness of breathing, in dilation of nostrils, a steady stare. She saw a pulse beating at his temple.

"I'm the Duke's man," he said, biting off the words.

"There is no traitor," she said. "The threat's something else. Perhaps it has to do with the lasguns. Perhaps they'll risk secreting a few lasguns with timing mechanisms aimed at house shields. Perhaps they'll. . . ."

"And who could tell after the blast if the explosion wasn't atomic?" he asked. "No, my Lady. They'll not risk anything *that* illegal. Radiation lingers. The evidence is hard to erase. No. They'll observe *most* of the forms. It has to be a traitor."

"You're the Duke's man," she sneered. "Would you destroy him in the effort to save him?"

He took a deep breath, then: "If you're innocent, you'll have my most abject apologies."

"Look at you now, Thufir," she said. "Humans live best when each has his own place, when each knows where he belongs in the scheme of things. Destroy the place and destroy the person. You and I, Thufir, of all those who love the Duke, are most ideally situated to destroy the other's place. Could I not whisper suspicions about you into the Duke's ear at night? When would he be most susceptible to such whispering, Thufir? Must I draw it for you more clearly?"

"You threaten me?" he growled.

"Indeed not. I merely point out to you that someone is attacking us through the basic arrangement of our lives. It's clever, diabolical. I propose to negate this attack by so ordering our lives that there'll be no chinks for such barbs to enter."

"You accuse me of whispering baseless suspicions?"

"Baseless, yes."

"You'd meet this with your own whispers?"

"*Your* life is compounded of whispers, not mine, Thufir."

"Then you question my abilities?"

She sighed. "Thufir, I want you to examine your own emotional involvement in this. The *natural* human's an animal without logic. Your projections of logic onto all affairs is *un*natural, but suffered to continue for its usefulness. You're the embodiment of logic—a Mentat. Yet, your problem solutions are concepts that, in a very real sense, are projected outside yourself, there to be studied and rolled around, examined from all sides."

"You think now to teach me my trade?" he asked, and he did not try to hide the disdain in his voice.

"Anything outside yourself, this you can see and apply your logic to it," she said. "But it's a human trait that when we encounter personal problems, those things most deeply personal are the most difficult to bring out for our logic to scan. We tend to flounder around, blaming everything but the actual, deep-seated thing that's really chewing on us."

"You're deliberately attempting to undermine my faith in my abilities as a Mentat," he rasped. "Were I to find one of our people attempting thus to sabotage any other weapon in our arsenal, I should not hesitate to denounce and destroy him."

"The finest Mentats have a healthy respect for the error factor in their computations," she said.

"I've never said otherwise!"

"Then apply yourself to these symptoms we've both seen: drunkenness among the men, quarrels—they gossip and exchange wild rumors about Arrakis; they ignore the most simple—"

"Idleness, no more," he said. "Don't try to divert my attention by trying to make a simple matter appear mysterious."

She stared at him, thinking of the Duke's men rubbing their woes together in the barracks until you could almost smell the charge there, like burnt insulation. *They're becoming like the men of the pre-Guild legend*, she thought: *Like the men of the lost star-searcher, Ampoliros— sick at their guns—forever seeking, forever prepared and forever unready.*

"Why have you never made full use of my abilities in your service to the Duke?" she asked. "Do you fear a rival for *your* position?"

He glared at her, the old eyes blazing. "I know some of the training they give you Bene Gesserit. . . ." He broke off, scowling.

"Go ahead, say it," she said. "Bene Gesserit *witches.*"

"I know something of the *real* training they give you," he said. "I've seen it come out in Paul. I'm not fooled by what your schools tell the public: you exist only to serve."

The shock must be severe and he's almost ready for it, she thought.

"You listen respectfully to me in Council," she said, "yet you seldom heed my advice. Why?"

"I don't trust your Bene Gesserit motives," he said. "You may think you can look through a man; you may *think* you can make a man do exactly what you—"

"You poor *fool*, Thufir!" she raged.

He scowled, pushing himself back in the chair.

"Whatever rumors you've heard about our schools," she said, "the truth is far greater. If I wished to destroy the Duke . . . or you, or any other person within my reach, you could not stop me."

And she thought: *Why do I let pride drive such words out of me? This is not the way I was trained. This is not how I must shock him.*

Hawat slipped a hand beneath his tunic where he kept a tiny projector of poison darts. *She wears no shield*, he thought. *Is this just a brag she makes? I could slay her now . . . but, ah-h-h-h, the consequences if I'm wrong.*

Jessica saw the gesture toward his pocket, said: "Let us pray violence shall never be necessary between us."

"A worthy prayer," he agreed.

"Meanwhile, the sickness spreads among us," she said. "I must ask you again: Isn't it more reasonable to suppose the Harkonnens have planted this suspicion to pit the two of us against each other?"

"We appear to've returned to stalemate," he said.

She sighed, thinking: *He's almost ready for it.*

"The Duke and I are father and mother surrogates to our people," she said. "The position—"

"He hasn't married you," Hawat said.

She forced herself to calmness, thinking: *A good riposte, that.*

"But he'll not marry anyone else," she said. "Not as long as I live. And we are surrogates, as I've said. To break up this natural order in our affairs, to disturb, disrupt, and confuse us—which target offers itself most enticingly to the Harkonnens?"

He sensed the direction she was taking, and his brows drew down in a lowering scowl.

"The Duke?" she asked. "Attractive target, yes, but no one with the possible exception of Paul is better guarded. Me? I tempt them, surely, but they must know the Bene Gesserit make difficult targets. And there's a better target, one whose duties create, necessarily, a monstrous blind spot. One to whom suspicion is as natural as breathing. One who builds his entire life on innuendo and mystery." She darted her right hand toward him. "You!"

Hawat started to leap from his chair.

"I have not dismissed you, Thufir!" she flared.

The old Mentat almost fell back into the chair, so quickly did his muscles betray him.

She smiled without mirth.

"Now you know something of the *real* training they give us," she said.

Hawat tried to swallow in a dry throat. Her command had been regal, peremptory—uttered in a tone and manner he had found completely irresistible. His body had obeyed her before he could think about it. Nothing could have prevented his response—not logic, not passionate anger . . . nothing. To do what she had done spoke of a sensitive, intimate knowledge of the person thus commanded, a depth of control he had not dreamed possible.

"I have said to you before that we should understand each other," she said. "I meant *you* should understand *me.* I already understand you. And I tell you now that your loyalty to the Duke is all that guarantees your safety with me."

He stared at her, wet his lips with his tongue.

"If I desired a puppet, the Duke would marry me," she said. "He might even think he did it of his own free will."

Hawat lowered his head, looked upward through his sparse lashes. Only the most rigid control kept him from calling the guard. Control . . . and the suspicion now that the woman might not permit it. His skin crawled with the memory of how she had controlled him. In the moment of hesitation, she could have drawn a weapon and killed him!

Does every human have this blind spot? he wondered. *Can any of us be ordered into action before he can resist? The idea staggered him. Who could stop a person with such power?*

"You've glimpsed the fist within the Bene Gesserit glove," she said. "Few glimpse it and live. And what I did was a relatively simple thing for us. You've not seen my entire arsenal. Think on that."

"Why aren't you out destroying the Duke's enemies?" he asked.

"What would you have me destroy?" she asked. "Would you have me make a weakling of our Duke, have him forever leaning on me?"

"But, with such power. . . ."

"Power's a two-edged sword, Thufir," she said. "You think: 'How easy for her to shape a human tool to thrust into an enemy's vitals.' True, Thufir; even into your vitals. Yet, what would I accomplish? If enough of us Bene Gesserit did this, wouldn't it make all Bene Gesserit suspect? We don't want that, Thufir. We do not wish to destroy ourselves." She nodded. "We truly exist only to serve."

"I cannot answer you," he said. "You know I cannot answer."

"You'll say nothing about what has happened here to anyone," she said. "I know you, Thufir."

"My Lady. . . ." Again the old man tried to swallow in a dry throat. And he thought: *She has great powers, yes. But would these not make her an even more formidable tool for the Harkonnens?*

"The Duke could be destroyed as quickly by his friends as by his enemies," she said. "I trust now you'll get to the bottom of this suspicion and remove it."

"If it proves baseless," he said.

"*If,*" she sneered.

"If," he said.

"You *are* tenacious," she said.

"Cautious," he said, "and aware of the error factor."

"Then I'll pose another question for you: What does it mean to you that you stand before another human, that you are bound and helpless and the other human holds a knife at your throat—yet this other human refrains from killing you, frees you from your bonds and gives you the knife to use as you will?"

She lifted herself out of the chair, turned her back on him. "You may go now, Thufir."

The old Mentat arose, hesitated, hand creeping toward the deadly weapon beneath his tunic. He was reminded of the bull ring and of the Duke's father (who'd been brave, no matter what his other failings) and one day of the *corrida* long ago: The fierce black beast had stood there, head bowed, immobilized and confused. The Old Duke had turned his back on the horns, cape thrown flamboyantly over one arm, while cheers rained down from the stands.

I am the bull and she the matador, Hawat thought. He withdrew his hand from the weapon, glanced at the sweat glistening in his empty palm.

And he knew that whatever the facts proved to be in the end, he would never forget this moment nor lose this sense of supreme admiration for the Lady Jessica.

Quietly, he turned and left the room.

Jessica lowered her gaze from the reflection in the windows, turned, and stared at the closed door.

"Now we'll see some proper action," she whispered.

Do you wrestle with dreams?
Do you contend with shadows?
Do you move in a kind of sleep?
Time has slipped away.
Your life is stolen.
You tarried with trifles,
Victim of your folly.

—DIRGE FOR JAMIS ON THE FUNERAL PLAIN,
FROM "SONGS OF MUAD'DIB"
BY THE PRINCESS IRULAN

Leto stood in the foyer of his house, studying a note by the light of a single suspensor lamp. Dawn was yet a few hours away, and he felt his tiredness. A Fremen messenger had brought the note to the outer guard just now as the Duke arrived from his command post.

The note read: "A column of smoke by day, a pillar of fire by night." There was no signature.

What does it mean? he wondered.

The messenger had gone without waiting for an answer and before he could be questioned. He had slipped into the night like some smoky shadow.

Leto pushed the paper into a tunic pocket, thinking to show it to Hawat later. He brushed a lock of hair from his forehead, took a sighing breath. The antifatigue pills were beginning to wear thin. It had been a long two days since the dinner party and longer than that since he had slept.

On top of all the military problems, there'd been the disquieting session with Hawat, the report on his meeting with Jessica.

Should I waken Jessica? he wondered. *There's no reason to play the secrecy game with her any longer. Or is there?*

Blast and damn that Duncan Idaho!

He shook his head. *No, not Duncan. I was wrong not to take Jessica into my confidence from the first. I must do it now, before more damage is done.*

The decision made him feel better, and he hurried from the foyer through the Great Hall and down the passages toward the family wing.

At the turn where the passages split to the service area, he paused. A strange mewling came from somewhere down the service passage. Leto put his left hand to the switch on his shield belt, slipped his kindjal into his right hand. The knife conveyed a sense of reassurance. That strange sound had sent a chill through him.

Softly, the Duke moved down the service passage, cursing the inadequate illumination. The smallest of suspensors had been spaced about eight meters apart along here and tuned to their dimmest level. The dark stone walls swallowed the light.

A dull blob stretching across the floor appeared out of the gloom ahead.

Leto hesitated, almost activated his shield, but refrained because that would limit his movements, his hearing . . . and because the captured shipment of lasguns had left him filled with doubts.

Silently, he moved toward the gray blob, saw that it was a human figure, a man face down on the stone. Leto turned him over with a foot, knife poised, bent close in the dim light to see the face. It was the smuggler, Tuek, a wet stain down his chest. The dead eyes stared with empty darkness. Leto touched the stain—warm.

How could this man be dead here? Leto asked himself. *Who killed him?*

The mewling sound was louder here. It came from ahead and down the side passage to the central room where they had installed the main shield generator for the house.

Hand on belt switch, kindjal poised, the Duke skirted the body, slipped down the passage and peered around the corner toward the shield generator room.

Another gray blob lay stretched on the floor a few paces away, and he saw at once this was the source of the noise. The shape crawled toward him with painful slowness, gasping, mumbling.

Leto stilled his sudden constriction of fear, darted down the passage, crouched beside the crawling figure. It was Mapes, the Fremen housekeeper, her hair tumbled around her face, clothing disarrayed. A dull shininess of dark stain spread from her back along her side. He touched her shoulder and she lifted herself on her elbows, head tipped up to peer at him, the eyes black-shadowed emptiness.

"S'you," she gasped. "Killed . . . guard . . . sent . . . get . . . Tuek . . . escape . . . m'Lady . . . you . . . you . . . here . . . no. . . ." She flopped forward, her head thumping against the stone.

Leto felt for pulse at the temples. There was none. He looked at the stain: she'd been stabbed in the back. Who? His mind raced. Did she mean someone had killed a guard? And Tuek—had Jessica sent for him? Why?

He started to stand up. A sixth sense warned him. He flashed a hand toward the shield switch—too late. A numbing shock slammed his arm aside. He felt pain there, saw a dart protruding from the sleeve, sensed paralysis spreading from it up his arm. It took an agonizing effort to lift his head and look down the passage.

Yueh stood in the open door of the generator room. His face reflected yellow from the light of a single, brighter suspensor above the door. There was stillness from the room behind him—no sound of generators.

Yueh! Leto thought. *He's sabotaged the house generators! We're wide open!*

Yueh began walking toward him, pocketing a dartgun.

Leto found he could still speak, gasped: "Yueh! How?" Then the paralysis reached his legs and he slid to the floor with his back propped against the stone wall.

Yueh's face carried a look of sadness as he bent over, touched Leto's forehead. The Duke found he could feel the touch, but it was remote . . . dull.

"The drug on the dart is selective," Yueh said. "You can speak, but I'd advise against it." He glanced down the hall, and again bent over Leto, pulled out the dart, tossed it aside. The sound of the dart clattering on the stones was faint and distant to the Duke's ears.

It can't be Yueh, Leto thought. *He's conditioned.*

"How?" Leto whispered.

"I'm sorry, my dear Duke, but there *are* things which will make greater demands than this." He touched the diamond tattoo on his forehead. "I find it very strange, myself—an override on my pyretic conscience—but I wish to kill a man. Yes, I actually wish it. I will stop at nothing to do it."

He looked down at the Duke. "Oh, not you, my dear Duke. The Baron Harkonnen. I wish to kill the Baron."

"Bar . . . on Har. . . ."

"Be quiet, please, my poor Duke. You haven't much time. That peg tooth I put in your mouth after the tumble at Narcal—that tooth must be replaced. In a moment, I'll render you unconscious and replace that tooth." He opened his hand, stared at something in it. "An exact duplicate, its core shaped most exquisitely like a nerve. It'll escape the usual detectors, even a fast scanning. But if you bite down hard on it, the cover crushes. Then, when you expel your breath sharply, you fill the air around you with a poison gas—most deadly."

Leto stared up at Yueh, seeing madness in the man's eyes, the perspiration along brow and chin.

"You were dead anyway, my poor Duke," Yueh said. "But you will get close to the Baron before you die. He'll believe you're stupefied by drugs beyond any dying effort to attack him. And you will be drugged—and tied. But attack can take strange forms. And *you* will remember the tooth. The *tooth*, Duke Leto Atreides. You will remember the tooth."

The old doctor leaned closer and closer until his face and drooping mustache dominated Leto's narrowing vision.

"The tooth," Yueh muttered.

"Why?" Leto whispered.

Yueh lowered himself to one knee beside the Duke. "I made a shaitan's bargain with the Baron. And I must be certain he has fulfilled his half of it. When I see him, I'll know. When I look at the Baron, then I *will* know. But I'll never enter his presence without the price. You're the price, my poor Duke. And I'll know when I see him. My poor Wanna taught me many things, and one is to see certainty of truth when the stress is great. I cannot do it always, but when I see the Baron—then, I *will* know."

Leto tried to look down at the tooth in Yueh's hand. He felt this was happening in a nightmare—it could not be.

Yueh's purple lips turned up in a grimace. "I'll not get close enough to the Baron, or I'd do this myself. No. I'll be detained at a safe distance. But you . . . ah, now! You, my lovely weapon! He'll want you close to him—to gloat over you, to boast a little."

Leto found himself almost hypnotized by a muscle on the left side of Yueh's jaw. The muscle twisted when the man spoke.

Yueh leaned closer. "And you, my good Duke, my precious Duke, you must remember this tooth." He held it up between thumb and forefinger. "It will be all that remains to you."

Leto's mouth moved without sound, then: "Refuse."

"Ah-h, no! You mustn't refuse. Because, in return for this small service, I'm doing a thing for you. I will save your son and your woman. No other can do it. They can be removed to a place where no Harkonnen can reach them."

"How . . . save . . . them?" Leto whispered.

"By making it appear they're dead, by secreting them among people who draw knife at hearing the Harkonnen name, who hate the Harkonnens so much they'll burn a chair in which a Harkonnen has sat, salt the ground over which a Harkonnen has walked." He touched Leto's jaw. "Can you feel anything in your jaw?"

The Duke found that he could not answer. He sensed distant tugging, saw Yueh's hand come up with the ducal signet ring.

"For Paul," Yueh said. "You'll be unconscious presently. Goodbye, my poor Duke. When next we meet we'll have no time for conversation."

Cool remoteness spread upward from Leto's jaw, across his cheeks. The shadowy hall narrowed to a pinpoint with Yueh's purple lips centered in it.

"Remember the tooth!" Yueh hissed. "The tooth!"

There should be a science of discontent. People need hard times and oppression to develop psychic muscles.

—FROM "COLLECTED SAYINGS OF MUAD'DIB"
BY THE PRINCESS IRULAN

Jessica awoke in the dark, feeling premonition in the stillness around her. She could not understand why her mind and body felt so sluggish. Skin raspings of fear ran along her nerves. She thought of sitting up and turning on a light, but something stayed the decision. Her mouth felt . . . strange.

Lump-lump-lump-lump!

It was a dull sound, directionless in the dark. Somewhere.

The waiting moment was packed with time, with rustling needle-stick movements.

She began to feel her body, grew aware of bindings on wrists and ankles, a gag in her mouth. She was on her side, hands tied behind her. She tested the bindings, realized they were krimskell fiber, would only claw tighter as she pulled.

And now, she remembered.

There had been movement in the darkness of her bedroom, something wet and pungent slapped against her face, filling her mouth, hands grasping for her. She had gasped—one indrawn breath—sensing the narcotic in the wetness. Consciousness had receded, sinking her into a black bin of terror.

It has come, she thought. *How simple it was to subdue the Bene Gesserit. All it took was treachery. Hawat was right.*

She forced herself not to pull on her bindings.

This is not my bedroom, she thought. *They've taken me someplace else.*

Slowly, she marshaled the inner calmness.

She grew aware of the smell of her own stale sweat with its chemical infusion of fear.

Where is Paul? she asked herself. *My son—what have they done to him?*

Calmness.

She forced herself to it, using the ancient routines.

But terror remained so near.

Leto? Where are you, Leto?

She sensed a diminishing in the dark. It began with shadows. Dimensions separated, became new thorns of awareness. White. A line under a door.

I'm on the floor.

People walking. She sensed it through the floor.

Jessica squeezed back the memory of terror. *I must remain calm, alert, and prepared. I may get only one chance.* Again, she forced the inner calmness.

The ungainly thumping of her heartbeats evened, shaping out time. She counted back. *I was unconscious about an hour.* She closed her eyes, focused her awareness onto the approaching footsteps.

Four people.

She counted the differences in their steps.

I must pretend I'm still unconscious. She relaxed against the cold floor, testing her body's readiness, heard a door open, sensed increased light through her eyelids.

Feet approached: someone standing over her.

"You are awake," rumbled a basso voice. "Do not pretend."

She opened her eyes.

The Baron Vladimir Harkonnen stood over her. Around them, she recognized the cellar room where Paul had slept, saw his cot at one side—empty. Suspensor lamps were brought in by guards, distributed near the open door. There was a glare of light in the hallway beyond that hurt her eyes.

She looked up at the Baron. He wore a yellow cape that bulged over his portable suspensors. The fat cheeks were two cherubic mounds beneath spider-black eyes.

"The drug was timed," he rumbled. "We knew to the minute when you'd be coming out of it."

How could that be? she wondered. *They'd have to know my exact weight, my metabolism, my. . . . Yueh!*

"Such a pity you must remain gagged," the Baron said. "We could have such an interesting conversation."

Yueh's the only one it could be, she thought. *How?*

The Baron glanced behind him at the door. "Come in, Piter."

She had never before seen the man who entered to stand beside the Baron, but the face was known—and the man: *Piter de Vries, the Mentat-Assassin.* She studied him—hawk features, blue-ink eyes that suggested he was a native of Arrakis, but subtleties of movement and stance told her he was not. And his flesh was too well firmed with water. He was tall, though slender, and something about him suggested effeminacy.

"Such a pity we cannot have our conversation, my dear Lady Jessica," the Baron said. "However, I'm aware of your abilities." He glanced at the Mentat. "Isn't that true, Piter?"

"As you say, Baron," the man said.

The voice was tenor. It touched her spine with a wash of coldness. She had never heard such a chill voice. To one with the Bene Gesserit training, the voice screamed: *Killer!*

"I have a surprise for Piter," the Baron said. "He thinks he has come here to collect his reward—you, Lady Jessica. But I wish to demonstrate a thing: that he does not really want you."

"You play with me, Baron?" Piter asked, and he smiled.

Seeing that smile, Jessica wondered that the Baron did not leap to defend himself from this Piter. Then she corrected herself. The Baron could not read that smile. He did not have the Training.

"In many ways, Piter is quite naive," the Baron said. "He doesn't admit to himself what a deadly creature you are, Lady Jessica. I'd show him, but it'd be a foolish risk." The Baron smiled at Piter, whose face had become a waiting mask. "I know what Piter really wants. Piter wants power."

"You promised I could have *her*," Piter said. The tenor voice had lost some of its cold reserve.

Jessica heard the clue-tones in the man's voice, allowed herself an inward shudder. *How could the Baron have made such an animal out of a Mentat?*

"I give you a choice, Piter," the Baron said.

"What choice?"

The Baron snapped fat fingers. "This woman and exile from the Imperium, or the Duchy of Atreides on Arrakis to rule as you see fit in my name."

Jessica watched the Baron's spider eyes study Piter.

"You could be Duke here in all but name," the Baron said.

Is my Leto dead, then? Jessica asked herself. She felt a silent wail begin somewhere in her mind.

The Baron kept his attention on the Mentat. "Understand yourself, Piter. You want her because she was a Duke's woman, a symbol of his power—beautiful, useful, exquisitely trained for her role. But an entire duchy, Piter! That's more than a symbol; that's the reality. With it you could have many women . . . and more."

"You do not joke with Piter?"

The Baron turned with that dancing lightness the suspensors gave him. "Joke? I? Remember—*I* am giving up the boy. You heard what the traitor said about the lad's training. They are alike, this mother and son—deadly." The Baron smiled. "I must go now. I will send in the guard I've reserved for this moment. He's stone deaf. His orders will be to convey you on the first leg of your journey into exile. He will subdue this woman if he sees her gain control of you. He'll not permit you to untie her gag until you're off Arrakis. If you choose not to leave . . . he has other orders."

"You don't have to leave," Piter said. "I've chosen."

"Ah, hah!" the Baron chortled. "Such quick decision can mean only one thing."

"I will take the duchy," Piter said.

And Jessica thought: *Doesn't Piter know the Baron's lying to him? But—how could he know? He's a twisted Mentat.*

The Baron glanced down at Jessica. "Is it not wonderful that I know Piter so well? I wagered with my Master at Arms that this would be Piter's choice. Hah! Well, I leave now. This is much better. Ah-h, much better. You understand, Lady Jessica? I had no rancor toward you. It's a necessity. Much better this way. Yes. And I've not *actually* ordered you destroyed. When it's asked of me what happened to you, I can shrug it off in all truth."

"You leave it to me then?" Piter asked.

"The guard I send you will take your orders," the Baron said. "Whatever's done I leave to you." He stared at Piter. "Yes. There will be no blood on my hands here. It's your decision. Yes. I know nothing of it. You will wait until I've gone before doing whatever you must do. Yes. Well . . . ah, yes. Yes. Good."

He fears the questioning of a Truthsayer, Jessica thought. *Who? Ah-h-h, the Reverend Mother Gaius Helen, of course! If he knows he must face her questions, then the Emperor is in on this for sure. Ah-h-h-h, my poor Leto.*

With one last glance at Jessica, the Baron turned, went out the door. She followed him with her eyes, thinking: *It's as the Reverend Mother warned—too potent an adversary.*

Two Harkonnen troopers entered. Another, his face a scarred mask, followed and stood in the doorway with drawn lasgun.

The deaf one, Jessica thought, studying the scarred face. *The Baron knows I could use the Voice on any other man.*

Scarface looked at Piter. "We've the boy on a litter outside. What are your orders?"

Piter spoke to Jessica. "I'd thought of binding you by a threat held over your son, but I begin to see that would not have worked. I let emotion cloud reason. Bad policy for a Mentat." He looked at the first pair of troopers, turning so the deaf one could read his lips: "Take them into the desert as the traitor suggested for the boy. His plan is a good one. The worms will destroy all evidence. Their bodies must never be found."

"You don't wish to dispatch them yourself?" Scarface asked.

He reads lips, Jessica thought.

"I follow my Baron's example," Piter said. "Take them where the traitor said."

Jessica heard the harsh Mentat control in Piter's voice, thought: *He, too, fears the Truthsayer.*

Piter shrugged, turned, and went through the doorway. He hesitated there, and Jessica thought he might turn back for a last look at her, but he went out without turning.

"Me, I wouldn't like the thought of facing that Truthsayer after this night's work," Scarface said.

"You ain't likely ever to run into that old witch," one of the other troopers said. He went around to Jessica's head, bent over her. "It ain't getting our work done standing around here chattering. Take her feet and—"

"Why'n't we kill 'em here?" Scarface asked.

"Too messy," the first one said. "Unless you wants to strangle 'em. Me, I likes a nice straightforward job. Drop 'em on the desert like that traitor said, cut 'em once or twice, leave the evidence for the worms. Nothing to clean up afterwards."

"Yeah . . . well, I guess you're right," Scarface said.

Jessica listened to them, watching, registering. But the gag blocked her Voice, and there was the deaf one to consider.

Scarface holstered his lasgun, took her feet. They lifted her like a sack of grain, maneuvered her through the door and dumped her onto a suspensor-buoyed litter with another bound figure. As they turned her, fitting her to the litter, she saw her companion's face—Paul! He was bound, but not gagged. His face was no more than ten centimeters from hers, eyes closed, his breathing even.

Is he drugged? she wondered.

The troopers lifted the litter, and Paul's eyes opened the smallest fraction—dark slits staring at her.

He mustn't try the Voice! she prayed. *The deaf guard!*

Paul's eyes closed.

He had been practicing the awareness-breathing, calming his mind, listening to their captors. The deaf one posed a problem, but Paul contained his despair. The mind-calming Bene Gesserit regimen his mother had taught him kept him poised, ready to expand any opportunity.

Paul allowed himself another slit-eyed inspection of his mother's face. She appeared unharmed. Gagged, though.

He wondered who could've captured her. His own captivity was plain enough—to bed with a capsule prescribed by Yueh, awaking to find himself bound to this litter. Perhaps a similar thing had befallen her. Logic said the traitor was Yueh, but he held final decision in abeyance. There was no understanding it—a Suk doctor a traitor.

The litter tipped slightly as the Harkonnen troopers maneuvered it through a doorway into starlit night. A suspensor-buoy rasped against the doorway. Then they were on sand, feet grating in it. A 'thopter wing loomed overhead, blotting the stars. The litter settled to the ground.

Paul's eyes adjusted to the faint light. He recognized the deaf trooper as the man who opened the 'thopter door, peered inside at the green gloom illuminated by the instrument panel.

"This the 'thopter we're supposed to use?" he asked, and turned to watch his companion's lips.

"It's the one the traitor said was fixed for desert work," the other said.

Scarface nodded. "But—it's one of them little liaison jobs. Ain't room in there for more'n them an' two of us."

"Two's enough," said the litter-bearer, moving up close and presenting his lips for reading. "We can take care of it from here on, Kinet."

"The Baron, he told me to make sure what happened to them two," Scarface said.

"What you so worried about?" asked another trooper from behind the litter-bearer.

"She is a Bene Gesserit witch," the deaf one said. "They have powers."

"Ah-h-h. . . ." The litter-bearer made the sign of the fist at his ear. "One of them, eh? Know whatcha mean."

The trooper behind him grunted. "She'll be worm meat soon enough. Don't suppose even a Bene Gesserit witch has powers over one of them big worms. Eh, Czigo?" He nudged the litter-bearer.

"Yee-up," the litter-bearer said. He returned to the litter, took Jessica's shoulders. "C'mon, Kinet. You can go along if you wants to make sure what happens."

"It is nice of you to invite me, Czigo," Scarface said.

Jessica felt herself lifted, the wing shadow spinning—stars. She was pushed into the rear of the 'thopter, her *krimskell* fiber bindings examined, and she was strapped down. Paul was jammed in beside her, strapped securely, and she noted his bonds were simple rope.

Scarface, the deaf one they called Kinet, took his place in front. The litter-bearer, the one they called Czigo, came around and took the other front seat.

Kinet closed his door, bent to the controls. The 'thopter took off in a wing-tucked surge, headed south over the Shield Wall. Czigo tapped his companion's shoulder, said: "Whyn't you turn around and keep an eye on them two?"

"Sure you know the way to go?" Kinet watched Czigo's lips.

"I listened to the traitor same's you."

Kinet swiveled his seat. Jessica saw the glint of starlight on a lasgun in his hand. The 'thopter's light-walled interior seemed to collect illumination as her eyes adjusted, but the guard's scarred face remained dim. Jessica tested her seat belt, found it loose. She felt roughness in the strap against her left arm, realized the strap had been almost severed, would snap at a sudden jerk.

Has someone been at this 'thopter, preparing it for us? she wondered. *Who?* Slowly, she twisted her bound feet clear of Paul's.

"Sure do seem a shame to waste a good-looking woman like this," Scarface said. "You ever have any highborn types?" He turned to look at the pilot.

"Bene Gesserit ain't all highborn," the pilot said.

"But they all looks heighty."

He can see me plain enough, Jessica thought. She brought her bound legs up onto the seat, curled into a sinuous ball, staring at Scarface.

"Real pretty, she is," Kinet said. He wet his lips with his tongue. "Sure do seem a shame." He looked at Czigo.

"You thinking what I think you're thinking?" the pilot asked.

"Who'd be to know?" the guard asked. "Afterwards. . . ." He shrugged. "I just never had me no highborns. Might never get a chance like this one again."

"You lay a hand on my mother. . . ." Paul grated. He glared at Scarface.

"Hey!" the pilot laughed. "Cub's got a bark. Ain't got no bite, though."

And Jessica thought: *Paul's pitching his voice too high. It may work, though.*

They flew on in silence.

These poor fools, Jessica thought, studying her guards and reviewing the Baron's words. *They'll be killed as soon as they report success on their mission. The Baron wants no witnesses.*

The 'thopter banked over the southern rim of the Shield Wall, and Jessica saw a moonshadowed expanse of sand beneath them.

"This oughta be far enough," the pilot said. "The traitor said to put 'em on the sand anywhere near the Shield Wall." He dipped the craft toward the dunes in a long, falling stoop, brought it up stiffly over the desert surface.

Jessica saw Paul begin taking the rhythmic breaths of the calming exercise. He closed his eyes, opened them. Jessica stared, helpless to aid him. *He hasn't mastered the Voice yet,* she thought, *if he fails. . . .*

The 'thopter touched sand with a soft lurch, and Jessica, looking north back across the Shield Wall, saw a shadow of wings settle out of sight up there.

Someone's following us! she thought. *Who? Then: The ones the Baron set to watch this pair. And there'll be watchers for the watchers, too.*

Czigo shut off his wing rotors. Silence flooded in upon them.

Jessica turned her head. She could see out the window beyond Scarface a dim glow of light from a rising moon, a frosted rim of rock rising from the desert. Sandblast ridges streaked its sides.

Paul cleared his throat.

The pilot said: "Now, Kinet?"

"I dunno, Czigo."

Czigo turned, said: "Ah-h-h, look." He reached out for Jessica's skirt.

"Remove her gag," Paul commanded.

Jessica felt the words rolling in the air. The tone, the timbre excellent—imperative, very sharp. A slightly lower pitch would have been better, but it could still fall within this man's spectrum.

Czigo shifted his hand up to the band around Jessica's mouth, slipped the knot on the gag.

"Stop that!" Kinet ordered.

"Ah, shut your trap," Czigo said. "Her hands're tied." He freed the knot and the binding dropped. His eyes glittered as he studied Jessica.

Kinet put a hand on the pilot's arm. "Look, Czigo, no need to. . . ."

Jessica twisted her neck, spat out the gag. She pitched her voice in low, intimate tones. "Gentlemen! No need to *fight* over me." At the same time, she writhed sinuously for Kinet's benefit.

She saw them grow tense, knowing that in this instant they were convinced of the need to fight over her. Their disagreement required no other reason. In their minds, they *were* fighting over her.

She held her face high in the instrument glow to be sure Kinet would read her lips, said: "You mustn't disagree." They drew farther apart, glanced warily at each other. "Is any woman worth fighting over?" she asked.

By uttering the words, by being there, she made herself infinitely worth their fighting.

Paul clamped his lips tightly closed, forced himself to be silent. There had been the one chance for him to succeed with the Voice. Now—everything depended on his mother whose experience went so far beyond his own.

"Yeah," Scarface said. "No need to fight over. . . ."

His hand flashed toward the pilot's neck. The blow was met by a splash of metal that caught the arm and in the same motion slammed into Kinet's chest.

Scarface groaned, sagged backward against his door.

"Thought I was some dummy didn't know that trick," Czigo said. He brought back his hand, revealing the knife. It glittered in reflected moonlight.

"Now for the cub," he said and leaned toward Paul.

"No need for that," Jessica murmured.

Czigo hesitated.

"Wouldn't you rather have me cooperative?" Jessica asked. "Give the boy a chance." Her lip curled in a sneer. "Little enough chance he'd have out there in that sand. Give him that and. . . ." She smiled. "You could find yourself well rewarded."

Czigo glanced left, right, returned his attention to Jessica. "I've heard me what can happen to a man in this desert," he said. "Boy might find the knife a kindness."

"Is it so much I ask?" Jessica pleaded.

"You're trying to trick me," Czigo muttered.

"I don't want to see my son die," Jessica said. "Is that a trick?"

Czigo moved back, elbowed the door latch. He grabbed Paul, dragged him across the seat, pushed him half out the door and held the knife posed. "What'll y' do, cub, if I cut y'r bonds?"

"He'll leave here immediately and head for those rocks," Jessica said.

"Is that what y'll do, cub?" Czigo asked.

Paul's voice was properly surly. "Yes."

The knife moved down, slashed the bindings of his legs. Paul felt the hand on his back to hurl him down onto the sand, feigned a lurch against the doorframe for purchase, turned as though to catch himself, lashed out with his right foot.

The toe was aimed with a precision that did credit to his long years of training, as though all of that training focused on this instant. Almost every muscle of his body cooperated in the placement of it. The tip struck the soft part of Czigo's abdomen just below the sternum, slammed upward with terrible force over the liver and through the diaphragm to crush the right ventricle of the man's heart.

With one gurgling scream, the guard jerked backward across the seats. Paul, unable to use his hands, continued his tumble onto the sand, landing with a roll that took up the force and brought him back to his feet in one motion. He dove back into the cabin, found the knife and held it in his teeth while his mother sawed her bonds. She took the blade and freed his hands.

"I could've handled him," she said. "He'd have had to cut my bindings. That was a foolish risk."

"I saw the opening and used it," he said.

She heard the harsh control in his voice, said: "Yueh's house sign is scrawled on the ceiling of this cabin."

He looked up, saw the curling symbol.

"Get out and let us study this craft," she said. "There's a bundle under the pilot's seat. I felt it when we got in."

"Bomb?"

"Doubt it. There's something peculiar here."

Paul leaped out to the sand and Jessica followed. She turned, reached under the seat for the strange bundle, seeing Czigo's feet close to her face, feeling dampness on the bundle as she removed it, realizing the dampness was the pilot's blood.

Waste of moisture, she thought, knowing that this was Arrakeen thinking.

Paul stared around them, saw the rock scarp lifting out of the desert like a beach rising from the sea, wind-carved palisades beyond. He turned back as his mother lifted the bundle from the 'thopter, saw her stare across the dunes toward the Shield Wall. He looked to see what drew her attention, saw another 'thopter swooping toward them, realized they'd not have time to clear the bodies out of this 'thopter and escape.

"Run, Paul!" Jessica shouted. "It's Harkonnens!"

Arrakis teaches the attitude of the knife—chopping off what's incomplete and saying: "Now, it's complete because it's ended here."

—FROM "COLLECTED SAYINGS OF MUAD'DIB"
BY THE PRINCESS IRULAN

A man in Harkonnen uniform skidded to a stop at the end of the hall, stared in at Yueh, taking in at a single glance Mapes' body, the sprawled form of the Duke, Yueh standing there. The man held a lasgun in his right hand. There was a casual air of brutality about him, a sense of toughness and poise that sent a shiver through Yueh.

Sardaukar, Yueh thought. *A Bashar by the look of him. Probably one of the Emperor's own sent here to keep an eye on things. No matter what the uniform, there's no disguising them.*

"You're Yueh," the man said. He looked speculatively at the Suk School ring on the Doctor's hair, stared once at the diamond tattoo and then met Yueh's eyes.

"I am Yueh," the Doctor said.

"You can relax, Yueh," the man said. "When you dropped the house shields we came right in. Everything's under control here. Is this the Duke?"

"This is the Duke."

"Dead?"

"Merely unconscious. I suggest you tie him."

"Did you do for these others?" He glanced back down the hall where Mapes' body lay.

"More's the pity," Yueh muttered.

"Pity!" the Sardaukar sneered. He advanced, looked down at Leto. "So that's the great Red Duke."

If I had doubts about what this man is, that would end them, Yueh thought. *Only the Emperor calls the Atreides the Red Dukes.*

The Sardaukar reached down, cut the red hawk insignia from Leto's uniform. "Little souvenir," he said. "Where's the ducal signet ring?"

"He doesn't have it on him," Yueh said.

"I can see that!" the Sardaukar snapped.

Yueh stiffened, swallowed. *If they press me, bring in a Truthsayer, they'll find out about the ring, about the 'thopter I prepared—all will fail.*

"Sometimes the Duke sent the ring with a messenger as surety that an order came directly from him," Yueh said.

"Must be damned trusted messengers," the Sardaukar muttered.

"Aren't you going to tie him?" Yueh ventured.

"How long'll he be unconscious?"

"Two hours or so. I wasn't as precise with his dosage as I was for the woman and boy."

The Sardaukar spurned the Duke with his toe. "This was nothing to fear even when awake. When will the woman and boy awaken?"

"About ten minutes."

"So soon?"

"I was told the Baron would arrive immediately behind his men."

"So he will. You'll wait outside, Yueh." He shot a hard glance at Yueh. "Now!"

Yueh glanced at Leto. "What about. . . ."

"He'll be delivered to the Baron all properly trussed like a roast for the oven." Again, the Sardaukar looked at the diamond tattoo on Yueh's forehead. "You're known; you'll be safe enough in the halls. We've no more time for chit-chat, traitor. I hear the others coming."

Traitor, Yueh thought. He lowered his gaze, pressed past the Sardaukar, knowing this as a foretaste of how history would remember him: *Yueh the traitor.*

He passed more bodies on his way to the front entrance and glanced at them, fearful that one might be Paul or Jessica. All were house troopers or wore Harkonnen uniform.

Harkonnen guards came alert, staring at him as he emerged from the front entrance into flame-lighted night. The palms along the road had been fired to illuminate the house. Black smoke from the flammables used to ignite the trees poured upward through orange flames.

"It's the traitor," someone said.

"The Baron will want to see you soon," another said.

I must get to the 'thopter, Yueh thought. *I must put the ducal signet where Paul will find it.* And fear struck him: *If Idaho suspects me or grows impatient—if he doesn't wait and go exactly where I told him—Jessica and Paul will not be saved from the carnage. I'll be denied even the smallest relief from my act.*

The Harkonnen guard released his arm, said, "Wait over there out of the way."

Abruptly, Yueh saw himself as cast away in this place of destruction, spared nothing, given not the smallest pity. *Idaho must not fail!*

Another guard bumped into him, barked: "Stay out of the way, you!"

Even when they've profited by me they despise me, Yueh thought. He straightened himself as he was pushed aside, regained some of his dignity.

"Wait for the Baron!" a guard officer snarled.

Yueh nodded, walked with controlled casualness along the front of the house, turned the corner into shadows out of sight of the burning palms. Quickly, every step betraying his anxiety, Yueh made for the rear yard beneath the conservatory where the 'thopter waited—the craft they had placed there to carry away Paul and his mother.

A guard stood at the open rear door of the house, his attention focused on the lighted hall and men banging through there, searching from room to room.

How confident they were!

Yueh hugged the shadows, worked his way around the 'thopter, eased open the door on the side away from the guard. He felt under the front seats for the Fremkit he had hidden there, lifted a flap and slipped in the ducal signet. He felt the crinkling of the spice paper there, the note he had written, pressed the ring into the paper. He removed his hand, resealed the pack.

Softly, Yueh closed the 'thopter door, worked his way back to the corner of the house and around toward the flaming trees.

Now, it is done, he thought.

Once more, he emerged into the light of the blazing palms. He pulled his cloak around him, stared at the flames. *Soon I will know. Soon I will see the Baron and I will know. And the Baron—he will encounter a small tooth.*

There is a legend that the instant the Duke Leto Atreides died a meteor streaked across the skies above his ancestral palace on Caladan.

—FROM "INTRODUCTION TO A CHILD'S HISTORY
OF MUAD'DIB"
BY THE PRINCESS IRULAN

The Baron Vladimir Harkonnen stood at a viewport of the grounded lighter he was using as a command post. Out the port he saw the flame-lighted night of Arrakeen. His attention focused on the distant Shield Wall where his secret weapon was doing its work.

Explosive artillery.

The guns nibbled at the caves where the Duke's fighting men had retreated for a last-ditch stand. Slowly measured bites of orange glare, showers of rock and dust in the brief illumination—and the Duke's men were being sealed off to die by starvation, caught like animals in their burrows.

The Baron could feel the distant chomping—a drumbeat carried to him through the ship's metal: *broomp . . . broomp.* Then: *BROOMP-broomp!*

Who would think of reviving artillery in this day of shields? The thought was a chuckle in his mind. *But it was predictable the Duke's men would run for those caves. And the Emperor will appreciate my cleverness in preserving the lives of our mutual force.*

He adjusted one of the little suspensors that guarded his fat body against the pull of gravity. A smile creased his mouth, pulled at the lines of his jowls.

A pity to waste such fighting men as the Duke's, he thought. He smiled more broadly, laughing at himself. *Pity should be cruel!* He nodded. Failure was, by definition, expendable. The whole universe sat there, open to the man who could make the right decisions. The uncertain rabbits had to be exposed, made to run for their burrows. Else how could you control them and breed them? He pictured his fighting men as bees routing the rabbits. And he thought: *The day hums sweetly when you have enough bees working for you.*

A door opened behind him. The Baron studied the reflection in the night-blackened viewport before turning.

Piter de Vries advanced into the chamber followed by Umman Kudu, the captain of the Baron's personal guard. There was a motion of men just outside the door, the mutton faces of his guard, their expressions carefully sheeplike in his presence.

The Baron turned.

Piter touched finger to forelock in his mocking salute. "Good news, m'Lord. The Sardaukar have brought in the Duke."

"Of course they have," the Baron rumbled.

He studied the somber mask of villainy on Piter's effeminate face. And the eyes: those shaded slits of bluest blue-in-blue.

Soon I must remove him, the Baron thought. *He has almost outlasted his usefulness, almost reached the point of positive danger to my person. First, though, he must make the people of Arrakis hate him. Then—they will welcome my darling Feyd-Rautha as a savior.*

The Baron shifted his attention to the guard captain—Umman Kudu: scissors-line of jaw muscles, chin like a boot toe—a man to be trusted because the captain's vices were known.

"First, where is the traitor who gave me the Duke?" the Baron asked. "I must give the traitor his reward."

Piter turned on one toe, motioned to the guard outside.

A bit of black movement there and Yueh walked through. His motions were stiff and stringy. The mustache drooped beside his purple lips. Only the old eyes seemed alive. Yueh came to a stop three paces into the room, obeying a motion from Piter, and stood there staring across the open space at the Baron.

"Ah-h-h, Dr. Yueh."

"M'Lord Harkonnen."

"You've given us the Duke, I hear."

"My half of the bargain, m'Lord."

The Baron looked at Piter.

Piter nodded.

The Baron looked back at Yueh. "The letter of the bargain, eh? And I. . . ." He spat the words out: "What was I to do in return?"

"You remember quite well, m'Lord Harkonnen."

And Yueh allowed himself to think now, hearing the loud silence of clocks in his mind. He had seen the subtle betrayals in the Baron's manner. Wanna was indeed dead—gone far beyond their reach. Otherwise, there'd still be a hold on the weak doctor. The Baron's manner showed there was no hold; it was ended.

"Do I?" the Baron asked.

"You promised to deliver my Wanna from her agony."

The Baron nodded. "Oh, yes. Now, I remember. So I did. That was my promise. That was how we bent the Imperial Conditioning. You couldn't endure seeing your Bene Gesserit witch grovel in Piter's pain amplifiers. Well, the Baron Vladimir Harkonnen always keeps his promises. I told you I'd free her from the agony and permit you to join her. So be it." He waved a hand at Piter.

Piter's blue eyes took a glazed look. His movement was catlike in its sudden fluidity. The knife in his hand glistened like a claw as it flashed into Yueh's back.

The old man stiffened, never taking his attention from the Baron.

"So join her!" the Baron spat.

Yueh stood, swaying. His lips moved with careful precision, and his voice came in oddly measured cadence: "You . . . think . . . you . . . de . . . feated . . . me. You . . . think . . . I . . . did . . . not . . . know . . . what . . . I . . . bought . . . for . . . my . . . Wanna."

He toppled. No bending or softening. It was like a tree falling.

"So join her," the Baron repeated. But his words were like a weak echo.

Yueh had filled him with a sense of foreboding. He whipped his attention to Piter, watched the man wipe the blade on a scrap of cloth, watched the creamy look of satisfaction in the blue eyes.

So that's how he kills by his own hand, the Baron thought. *It's well to know.*

"He *did* give us the Duke?" the Baron asked.

"Of a certainty, my Lord," Piter said.

"Then get him in here!"

Piter glanced at the guard captain, who whirled to obey.

The Baron looked down at Yueh. From the way the man had fallen, you could suspect oak in him instead of bones.

"I never could bring myself to trust a traitor," the Baron said. "Not even a traitor I created."

He glanced at the night-shrouded viewport. That black bag of stillness out there was his, the Baron knew. There was no more crump of artillery against the Shield Wall caves; the burrow traps were sealed off. Quite suddenly, the Baron's mind could conceive of nothing more beautiful than that utter emptiness of black. Unless it were white on the black. Plated white on the black. Porcelain white.

But there was still the feeling of doubt.

What had the old fool of a doctor meant? Of course, he'd probably known what would happen to him in the end. But that bit about thinking he'd been defeated: *"You think you defeated me."*

What had he meant?

The Duke Leto Atreides came through the door. His arms were bound in chains, the eagle face streaked with dirt. His uniform was torn where someone had ripped off his insignia. There were tatters at his waist where the shield belt had been removed without first freeing the uniform ties. The Duke's eyes held a glazed, insane look.

"Wel-l-l-l," the Baron said. He hesitated, drawing in a deep breath.

He knew he had spoken too loudly. This moment, long-envisioned, had lost some of its savor.

Damn that cursed doctor through all eternity!

"I believe the good Duke is drugged," Piter said. "That's how Yueh caught him for us." Piter turned to the Duke. "Aren't you drugged, my dear Duke?"

The voice was far away. Leto could feel the chains, the ache of muscles, his cracked lips, his burning cheeks, the dry taste of thirst whispering its grit in his mouth. But sounds were dull, hidden by a cottony blanket. And he saw only dim shapes through the blanket.

"What of the woman and the boy, Piter?" the Baron asked. "Any word yet?"

Piter's tongue darted over his lips.

"You've heard something!" the Baron snapped. "What?"

Piter glanced at the guard captain, back to the Baron. "The men who were sent to do the job, m'Lord—they've . . . ah . . . been . . . ah . . . found."

"Well, they report everything satisfactory?"

"They're dead, m'Lord."

"Of course they are! What I want to know is—"

"They were dead when found, m'Lord."

The Baron's face went livid. "And the woman and boy?"

"No sign, m'Lord, but there was a worm. It came while the scene was being investigated. Perhaps it's as we wished—an accident. Possibly—"

"We do not deal in possibilities, Piter. What of the missing 'thopter? Does that suggest anything to my Mentat?"

"One of the Duke's men obviously escaped in it, m'Lord. Killed our pilot and escaped."

"Which of the Duke's men?"

"It was a clean, silent killing, m'Lord. Hawat, perhaps, or that Halleck one. Possibly Idaho. Or any top lieutenant."

"Possibilities," the Baron muttered. He glanced at the swaying, drugged figure of the Duke.

"The situation is in hand, m'Lord," Piter said.

"No, it isn't! Where is that stupid planetologist? Where is this man Kynes?"

"We've word where to find him and he's been sent for, m'Lord."

"I don't like the way the Emperor's servant is helping us," the Baron muttered.

They were words through a cottony blanket, but some of them burned in Leto's mind. *Woman and boy—no sign.* Paul and Jessica had escaped. And the fate of Hawat, Halleck, and Idaho remained an unknown. There was still hope.

"Where is the ducal signet ring?" the Baron demanded. "His finger is bare."

"The Sardaukar say it was not on him when he was taken, my Lord," the guard captain said.

"You killed the doctor too soon," the Baron said. "That was a mistake. You should've warned me, Piter. You moved too precipitately for the good of our enterprise." He scowled. "Possibilities!"

The thought hung like a sine wave in Leto's mind: *Paul and Jessica have escaped!* And there was something else in his memory: a bargain. He could almost remember it.

The tooth!

He remembered part of it now: *a pill of poison gas shaped into a false tooth.*

Someone had told him to remember the tooth. The tooth was in his mouth. He could feel its shape with his tongue. All he had to do was bite sharply on it.

Not yet!

The someone had told him to wait until he was near the Baron. Who had told him? He couldn't remember.

"How long will he remain drugged like this?" the Baron asked.

"Perhaps another hour, m'Lord."

"Perhaps," the Baron muttered. Again, he turned to the night-blackened window. "I am hungry."

That's the Baron, that fuzzy gray shape there, Leto thought. The shape danced back and forth, swaying with the movement of the room. And the room expanded and contracted. It grew brighter and darker. It folded into blackness and faded.

Time became a sequence of layers for the Duke. He drifted up through them. *I must wait.*

There was a table. Leto saw the table quite clearly. And a gross, fat man on the other side of the table, the remains of a meal in front of him. Leto felt himself sitting in a chair across from the fat man, felt the chains, the straps that held his tingling body in the chair. He was aware there had been a passage of time, but its length escaped him.

"I believe he's coming around, Baron."

A silky voice, that one. That was Piter.

"So I see, Piter."

A rumbling basso: the Baron.

Leto sensed increasing definition in his surroundings. The chair beneath him took on firmness, the bindings were sharper.

And he saw the Baron clearly now. Leto watched the movements of the man's hands: compulsive touchings—the edge of a plate, the handle of a spoon, a finger tracing the fold of a jowl.

Leto watched the moving hand, fascinated by it.

"You can hear me, Duke Leto," the Baron said. "I know you can hear me. We want to know from you where to find your concubine and the child you sired on her."

No sign escaped Leto, but the words were a wash of calmness through him. *It's true, then: they don't have Paul and Jessica.*

"This is not a child's game we play," the Baron rumbled. "You must know that." He leaned toward Leto, studying the face. It pained the Baron that this could not be handled privately, just between the two of them. To have others see royalty in such straits—it set a bad precedent.

Leto could feel strength returning. And now, the memory of the false tooth stood out in his mind like a steeple in a flat landscape. The nerve-shaped capsule within that tooth—the poison gas—he remembered who had put the deadly weapon in his mouth.

Yueh.

Drug-fogged memory of seeing a limp corpse dragged past him in this room hung like a vapor in Leto's mind. He knew it had been Yueh.

"Do you hear that noise, Duke Leto?" the Baron asked.

Leto grew conscious of a frog sound, the burred mewling of someone's agony.

"We caught one of your men disguised as a Fremen," the Baron said. "We penetrated the disguise quite easily: the eyes, you know. He insists he was sent among the Fremen to spy on them. I've lived for a time on this planet, cher cousin. One does not spy on those ragged scum of the desert. Tell me, did you buy their help? Did you send your woman and son to them?"

Leto felt fear tighten his chest. *If Yueh sent them to the desert fold . . . the search won't stop until they're found.*

"Come, come," the Baron said. "We don't have much time and pain is quick. Please don't bring it to this, my dear Duke." The Baron looked up at Piter who stood at Leto's shoulder. "Piter doesn't have all his tools here, but I'm sure he could improvise."

"Improvisation is sometimes the best, Baron."

That silky, insinuating voice! Leto heard it at his ear.

"You had an emergency plan," the Baron said. "Where have your woman and the boy been sent?" He looked at Leto's hand. "Your ring is missing. Does the boy have it?"

The Baron looked up, stared into Leto's eyes.

"You don't answer," he said. "Will you force me to do a thing I do not want to do? Piter will use simple, direct methods. I agree they're sometimes the best, but it's not good that *you* should be subjected to such things."

"Hot tallow on the back, perhaps, or on the eyelids," Piter said. "Perhaps on other portions of the body. It's especially effective when the subject doesn't know where the tallow will fall next. It's a good method and there's a sort of beauty in the pattern of pus-white blisters on naked skin, eh, Baron?"

"Exquisite," the Baron said, and his voice sounded sour.

Those touching fingers! Leto watched the fat hands, the glittering jewels on baby-fat hands—their compulsive wandering.

The sounds of agony coming through the door behind him gnawed at the Duke's nerves. *Who is it they caught?* he wondered. *Could it have been Idaho?*

"Believe me, cher cousin," the Baron said. "I do not want it to come to this."

"You think of nerve couriers racing to summon help that cannot come," Piter said. "There's an artistry in this, you know."

"You're a superb artist," the Baron growled. "Now, have the decency to be silent."

Leto suddenly recalled a thing Gurney Halleck had said once, seeing a picture of the Baron: *"And I stood upon the sand of the sea and saw a beast rise up out of the sea . . . and upon his heads the name of blasphemy."*

"We waste time, Baron," Piter said.

"Perhaps."

The Baron nodded. "You know, my dear Leto, you'll tell us in the end where they are. There's a level of pain that'll buy you."

He's most likely correct, Leto thought. *Were it not for the tooth . . . and the fact that I truly don't know where they are.*

The Baron picked up a sliver of meat, pressed the morsel into his mouth, chewed slowly, swallowed. *We must try a new tack,* he thought.

"Observe this prize person who denies he's for hire," the Baron said. "Observe him, Piter."

And the Baron thought: *Yes! See him there, this man who believes he cannot be bought. See him detained there by a million shares of himself sold in dribbles every second of his life! If you took him up now and shook him, he'd rattle inside. Emptied! Sold out! What difference how he dies now?*

The frog sounds in the background stopped.

The Baron saw Umman Kudu, the guard captain, appear in the doorway across the room, shake his head. The captive hadn't produced the needed information. Another failure. Time to quit stalling with this fool Duke, this stupid soft fool who didn't realize how much hell there was so near him—only a nerve's thickness away.

This thought calmed the Baron, overcoming his reluctance to have a royal person subject to pain. He saw himself suddenly as a surgeon exercising endless supple scissor dissections—cutting away the masks from fools, exposing the hell beneath.

Rabbits, all of them!

And how they cowered when they saw the carnivore!

Leto stared across the table, wondering why he waited. The tooth would end it all quickly. Still—it had been good, much of this life. He found himself remembering an antenna kite updangling in the shell-blue sky of Caladan, and Paul laughing with joy at the sight of it. And he remembered sunrise here on Arrakis—colored strata of the Shield Wall mellowed by dust haze.

"Too bad," the Baron muttered. He pushed himself back from the table, stood up lightly in his suspensors and hesitated, seeing a change come over the Duke. He saw the man draw in a deep breath, the jawline stiffen, the ripple of a muscle there as the Duke clamped his mouth shut.

How he fears me! the Baron thought.

Shocked by fear that the Baron might escape him, Leto bit sharply on the capsule tooth, felt it break. He opened his mouth, expelled the biting vapor he could taste as it formed on his tongue. The Baron grew smaller, a figure seen in a tightening tunnel. Leto heard a gasp beside his ear—the silky-voiced one: Piter.

It got him, too!

"Piter! What's wrong?"

The rumbling voice was far away.

Leto sensed memories rolling in his mind—the old toothless mutterings of hags. The room, the table, the Baron, a pair of terrified eyes—blue within blue, the eyes—all compressed around him in ruined symmetry.

There was a man with a boot-toe chin, a toy man falling. The toy man had a broken nose slanted to the left: an offbeat metronome caught forever at the start of an upward stroke. Leto heard the crash of crockery—so distant—a roaring in his ears. His mind was a bin without end, catching everything. Everything that had ever been: every shout, every whisper, every . . . silence.

One thought remained to him. Leto saw it in formless light on rays of black: *The day the flesh shapes and the flesh the day shapes.* The thought struck him with a sense of fullness he knew he could never explain.

Silence.

The Baron stood with his back against his private door, his own bolt hole behind the table. He had slammed it on a room full of dead men. His senses took in guards swarming around him. *Did I breathe it?* he asked himself. *Whatever it was in there, did it get me, too?*

Sounds returned to him . . . and reason. He heard someone shouting orders—gas masks . . . keep a door closed . . . get blowers going.

The others fell quickly, he thought. *I'm still standing. I'm still breathing. Merciless hell! That was close!*

He could analyze it now. His shield had been activated, set low but still enough to slow molecular interchange across the field barrier. And he had been pushing himself away from the table . . . that and Piter's shocked gasp which had brought the guard captain darting forward into his own doom.

Chance and the warning in a dying man's gasp—these had saved him.

The Baron felt no gratitude to Piter. The fool had got himself killed. And that stupid guard captain! He'd said he scoped everyone before bringing them into the Baron's presence! How had it been possible for the Duke . . . ? No warning. Not even from the poison snooper over the table—until it was too late. How?

Well, no matter now, the Baron thought, his mind firming. *The next guard captain will begin by finding answers to these questions.*

He grew aware of more activity down the hall—around the corner at the other door to that room of death. The Baron pushed himself away from his own door, studied the lackeys around him. They stood there staring, silent, waiting for the Baron's reaction.

Would the Baron be angry?

And the Baron realized only a few seconds had passed since his flight from that terrible room.

Some of the guards had weapons leveled at the door. Some were directing their ferocity toward the empty hall that stretched away toward the noises around the corner to their right.

A man came striding around that corner, gas mask dangling by its straps at his neck, his eyes intent on the overhead poison snoopers that lined this corridor. He was yellow-haired, flat of face with green eyes. Crisp lines radiated from his thick-lipped mouth. He looked like some water creature misplaced among those who walked the land.

The Baron stared at the approaching man, recalling the name: Nefud. Iakin Nefud. Guard corporal. Nefud was addicted to semuta, the drug-music combination that played itself in the deepest consciousness. A useful item of information, that.

The man stopped in front of the Baron, saluted. "Corridor's clear, m'Lord. I was outside watching and saw that it must be poison gas. Ventilators in your room were pulling air in from these corridors." He glanced up at the snooper over the Baron's head. "None of the stuff escaped. We have the room cleaned out now. What are your orders?"

The Baron recognized the man's voice—the one who'd been shouting orders. *Efficient, this corporal*, he thought.

"They're all dead in there?" the Baron asked.

"Yes, m'Lord."

Well, we must adjust, the Baron thought.

"First," he said, "let me congratulate you, Nefud. You're the new captain of my guard. And I hope you'll take to heart the lesson to be learned from the fate of your predecessor."

The Baron watched the awareness grow in his newly promoted guardsman. Nefud knew he'd never again be without his semuta.

Nefud nodded. "My Lord knows I'll devote myself entirely to his safety."

"Yes. Well, to business. I suspect the Duke had something in his mouth. You will find out what that something was, how it was used, who helped him put it there. You'll take every precaution—"

He broke off, his chain of thought shattered by a disturbance in the corridor behind him—guards at the door to the lift from the lower levels of the frigate trying to hold back a tall colonel bashar who had just emerged from the lift.

The Baron couldn't place the colonel bashar's face: thin with mouth like a slash in leather, twin ink spots for eyes.

"Get your hands off me, you pack of carrion-eaters!" the man roared, and he dashed the guards aside.

Ah-h-h, one of the Sardaukar, the Baron thought.

The colonel bashar came striding toward the Baron, whose eyes went to slits of apprehension. The Sardaukar officers filled him with unease. They all seemed to look like relatives of the Duke . . . the late Duke. And their manners with the Baron!

The colonel bashar planted himself half a pace in front of the Baron, hands on hips. The guard hovered behind him in twitching uncertainty.

The Baron noted the absence of salute, the disdain in the Sardaukar's manner, and his unease grew. There was only the one legion of them locally—ten brigades—reinforcing the Harkonnen legions, but the Baron did not fool himself. That one legion was perfectly capable of turning on the Harkonnens and overcoming them.

"Tell your men they are not to prevent me from seeing you, Baron," the Sardaukar growled. "My men brought you the Atreides Duke before I could discuss his fate with you. We will discuss it now."

I must not lose face before my men, the Baron thought.

"So?" It was a coldly controlled word, and the Baron felt proud of it.

"My Emperor has charged me to make certain his royal cousin dies cleanly without agony," the colonel bashar said.

"Such were the Imperial orders to me," the Baron lied. "Did you think I'd disobey?"

"I'm to report to my Emperor what I see with my own eyes," the Sardaukar said.

"The Duke's already dead," the Baron snapped, and he waved a hand to dismiss the fellow.

The colonel bashar remained planted facing the Baron. Not by flicker of eye or muscle did he acknowledge he had been dismissed. "How?" he growled.

Really! the Baron thought. *This is too much.*

"By his own hand, if you must know," the Baron said. "He took poison."

"I will see the body now," the colonel bashar said.

The Baron raised his gaze to the ceiling in feigned exasperation while his thoughts raced. *Damnation! This sharp-eyed Sardaukar will see the room before a thing's been changed!*

"Now," the Sardaukar growled. "I'll see it with my own eyes."

There was no preventing it, the Baron realized. The Sardaukar would see all. He'd know the Duke had killed Harkonnen men . . . that the Baron most likely had escaped by a narrow margin. There was the evidence of the dinner remnants on the table, and the dead Duke across from it with destruction around him.

No preventing it at all.

"I'll not be put off," the colonel bashar snarled.

"You're not being put off," the Baron said, and he stared into the Sardaukar's obsidian eyes. "I hide nothing from my Emperor." He nodded to Nefud. "The colonel bashar is to see everything, at once. Take him in by the door where you stood, Nefud."

"This way, sir," Nefud said.

Slowly, insolently, the Sardaukar moved around the Baron, shouldered a way through the guardsmen.

Insufferable, the Baron thought. *Now, the Emperor will know how I slipped up. He'll recognize it as a sign of weakness.*

And it was agonizing to realize that the Emperor and his Sardaukar were alike in their disdain for weakness. The Baron chewed at his lower lip, consoling himself that the Emperor, at least, had not learned of the Atreides raid on Giedi Prime, the destruction of the Harkonnen spice stores there.

Damn that slippery Duke!

The Baron watched the retreating backs—the arrogant Sardaukar and the stocky, efficient Nefud.

We must adjust, the Baron thought. *I'll have to put Rabban over this damnable planet once more. Without restraint. I must spend my own Harkonnen blood to put Arrakis into a proper condition for accepting Feyd-Rautha. Damn that Piter! He would get himself killed before I was through with him.*

The Baron sighed.

And I must send at once to Tleilax for a new Mentat. They undoubtedly have the new one ready for me by now.

One of the guardsmen beside him coughed.

The Baron turned toward the man. "I am hungry."

"Yes, m'Lord."

"And I wish to be diverted while you're clearing out that room and studying its secrets for me," the Baron rumbled.

The guardsman lowered his eyes. "What diversion does m'Lord wish?"

"I'll be in my sleeping chambers," the Baron said. "Bring me that young fellow we bought on Gamont, the one with the lovely eyes. Drug him well. I don't feel like wrestling."

"Yes, m'Lord."

The Baron turned away, began moving with his bouncing, suspensor-buoyed pace toward his chambers. *Yes*, he thought. *The one with the lovely eyes, the one who looks so much like the young Paul Atreides.*

O Seas of Caladan,
O people of Duke Leto—
Citadel of Leto fallen,
Fallen forever . . .

—FROM "SONGS OF MUAD'DIB"
BY THE PRINCESS IRULAN

Paul felt that all his past, every experience before this night, had become sand curling in an hourglass. He sat near his mother hugging his knees within a small fabric and plastic hutment—a stilltent—that had come, like the Fremen clothing they now wore, from the pack left in the 'thopter.

There was no doubt in Paul's mind who had put the Fremkit there, who had directed the course of the 'thopter carrying them captive.

Yueh.

The traitor doctor had sent them directly into the hands of Duncan Idaho.

Paul stared out the transparent end of the stilltent at the moon-shadowed rocks that ringed this place where Idaho had hidden them.

Hiding like a child when I'm now the Duke, Paul thought. He felt the thought gall him, but could not deny the wisdom in what they did.

Something had happened to his awareness this night—he saw with sharpened clarity every circumstance and occurrence around him. He felt unable to stop the inflow of data or the cold precision with which each new item was added to his knowledge and the computation was centered in his awareness. It was Mentat power and more.

Paul thought back to the moment of impotent rage as the strange 'thopter dived out of the night onto them, stooping like a giant hawk above the desert with wind screaming through its wings. The thing in Paul's mind had happened then. The 'thopter had skidded and slewed across a sand ridge toward the running figures—his mother and himself. Paul remembered how the smell of burned sulfur from abrasion of 'thopter skids against sand had drifted across them.

His mother, he knew, had turned, expected to meet a lasgun in the hands of Harkonnen mercenaries, and had recognized Duncan Idaho leaning out the 'thopter's open door shouting: "Hurry! There's wormsign south of you!"

But Paul had known as he turned who piloted the 'thopter. An accumulation of minutiae in the way it was flown, the dash of the landing—clues so small even his mother hadn't detected them—had told Paul *precisely* who sat at those controls.

Across the stilltent from Paul, Jessica stirred, said: "There can be only one explanation. The Harkonnens held Yueh's wife. He hated the Harkonnens! I cannot be wrong about that. You read his note. But why has he saved us from the carnage?"

She is only now seeing it and that poorly, Paul thought. The thought was a shock. He had known this fact as a by-the-way thing while reading the note that had accompanied the ducal signet in the pack.

"Do not try to forgive me," Yueh had written. "I do not want your forgiveness. I already have enough burdens. What I have done was done without malice or hope of another's understanding. It is my own tahaddi al-burhan, my ultimate test. I give you the Atreides ducal signet as token that I write truly. By the time you read this, Duke Leto will be dead. Take consolation from my assurance that he did not die alone, that one we hate above all others died with him."

It had not been addressed or signed, but there'd been no mistaking the familiar scrawl—Yueh's.

Remembering the letter, Paul re-experienced the distress of that moment—a thing sharp and strange that seemed to happen outside his new mental alertness. He had read that his father was dead, known the truth of the words, but had felt them as no more than another datum to be entered in his mind and used.

I loved my father, Paul thought, and knew this for truth. *I should mourn him. I should feel something.*

But he felt nothing except: *Here's an important fact.*

It was one with all the other facts.

All the while his mind was adding sense impressions, extrapolating, computing.

Halleck's words came back to Paul: *"Mood's a thing for cattle or for making love. You fight when the necessity arises, no matter your mood."*

Perhaps that's it, Paul thought. *I'll mourn my father later . . . when there's time.*

But he felt no letup in the cold precision of his being. He sensed that his new awareness was only a beginning, that it was growing. The sense of terrible purpose he'd first experienced in his ordeal with the Reverend Mother Gaius Helen Mohiam pervaded him. His right hand—the hand of remembered pain—tingled and throbbed.

Is this what it is to be their Kwisatz Haderach? he wondered.

"For a while, I thought Hawat had failed us again," Jessica said. "I thought perhaps Yueh wasn't a Suk doctor."

"He was everything we thought him . . . and more," Paul said. And he thought: *Why is she so slow seeing these things?* He said, "If Idaho doesn't get through to Kynes, we'll be—"

"He's not our only hope," she said.

"Such was not my suggestion," he said.

She heard the steel in his voice, the sense of command, and stared across the gray darkness of the stilltent at him. Paul was a silhouette against moon-frosted rocks seen through the tent's transparent end.

"Others among your father's men will have escaped," she said. "We must regather them, find—"

"We will depend upon ourselves," he said. "Our immediate concern is our family atomics. We must get them before the Harkonnens can search them out."

"Not likely they'll be found," she said, "the way they were hidden."

"It must not be left to chance."

And she thought: *Blackmail with the family atomics as a threat to the planet and its spice—that's what he has in mind. But all he can hope for then is escape into renegade anonymity.*

His mother's words had provoked another train of thought in Paul—a duke's concern for all the people they'd lost this night. *People are the true strength of a Great House,* Paul thought. And he remembered Hawat's words: *"Parting with people is a sadness; a place is only a place."*

"They're using Sardaukar," Jessica said. "We must wait until the Sardaukar have been withdrawn."

"They think us caught between the desert and the Sardaukar," Paul said. "They intend that there be no Atreides survivors—total extermination. Do not count on any of our people escaping."

"They cannot go on indefinitely risking exposure of the Emperor's part in this."

"Can't they?"

"Some of our people are bound to escape."

"Are they?"

Jessica turned away, frightened of the bitter strength in her son's voice, hearing the precise assessment of chances. She sensed that his mind had leaped ahead of her, that it now saw more in some respects than she did. She had helped train the intelligence which did this, but now she found herself fearful of it. Her thoughts turned, seeking toward the lost sanctuary of her Duke, and tears burned her eyes.

This is the way it had to be, Leto, she thought. *"A time of love and a time of grief."* She rested her hand on her abdomen, awareness focused on the embryo there. *I have the Atreides daughter I was ordered to produce, but the Reverend Mother was wrong: a daughter wouldn't have saved my Leto. This child is only life reaching for the future in the midst of death. I conceived out of instinct and not out of obedience.*

"Try the communinet receiver again," Paul said.

The mind goes on working no matter how we try to hold it back, she thought.

Jessica found the tiny receiver Idaho had left for them, flipped its switch. A green light glowed on the instrument's face. Tinny screeching came from its speaker. She reduced the volume, hunted across the bands. A voice speaking Atreides battle language came into the tent.

"... back and regroup at the ridge. Fedor reports no survivors in Carthag and the Guild Bank has been sacked."

Carthag! Jessica thought. *That was a Harkonnen hotbed.*

"They're Sardaukar," the voice said. "Watch out for Sardaukar in Atreides uniforms. They're...."

A roaring filled the speaker, then silence.

"Try the other bands," Paul said.

"Do you realize what that means?" Jessica asked.

"I expected it. They want the Guild to blame us for destruction of their bank. With the Guild against us, we're trapped on Arrakis. Try the other bands."

She weighed his words: *I expected it.* What had happened to him? Slowly, Jessica returned to the instrument. As she moved the bandslide, they caught glimpses of violence in the few voices calling out in Atreides battle language: "...fall back...." "...try to regroup at...." "...trapped in a cave at...."

And there was no mistaking the victorious exultation in the Harkonnen gibberish that poured from the other bands. Sharp commands, battle reports. There wasn't enough of it for Jessica to register and break the language, but the tone was obvious.

Harkonnen victory.

Paul shook the pack beside him, hearing the two literjons of water gurgle there. He took a deep breath, looked up through the transparent end of the tent at the rock escarpment outlined against the stars. His left hand felt the sphincter-seal of the tent's entrance. "It'll be dawn soon," he said. "We can wait through the day for Idaho, but not through another night. In the desert, you must travel by night and rest in shade through the day."

Remembered lore insinuated itself into Jessica's mind: *Without a stillsuit, a man sitting in shade on the desert needs five liters of water a day to maintain body weight.* She felt the slick-soft skin of the stillsuit against her body, thinking how their lives depended on these garments.

"If we leave here, Idaho can't find us," she said.

"There are ways to make any man talk," he said. "If Idaho hasn't returned by dawn, we must consider the possibility he has been captured. How long do you think he could hold out?"

The question required no answer, and she sat in silence.

Paul lifted the seal on the pack, pulled out a tiny micromanual with glowtab and magnifier. Green and orange letters leaped up at him from the pages: "literjons, stilltent, energy caps, recaths, sandsnork, binoculars, stillsuit repkit, baradye pistol, sinkchart, filt-plugs, paracompass, maker hooks, thumpers, Fremkit, fire pillar. . . ."

So many things for survival on the desert.

Presently, he put the manual aside on the tent floor.

"Where can we possibly go?" Jessica asked.

"My father spoke of *desert power*," Paul said. "The Harkonnens cannot rule this planet without it. They've never ruled this planet, nor shall they. Not even with ten thousand legions of Sardaukar."

"Paul, you can't think that—"

"We've all the evidence in our hands," he said. "Right here in this tent—the tent itself, this pack and its contents, these stillsuits. We know the Guild wants a prohibitive price for weather satellites. We know that—"

"What've weather satellites to do with it?" she asked. "They couldn't possibly. . . ." She broke off.

Paul sensed the hyperalertness of his mind reading her reactions, computing on minutiae. "You see it now," he said. "Satellites watch the terrain below. There are things in the deep desert that will not bear frequent inspection."

"You're suggesting the Guild itself controls this planet?"

She was so slow.

"No!" he said. "The Fremen! They're paying the Guild for privacy, paying in a coin that's freely available to anyone with desert power—spice. This is more than a second-approximation answer; it's the straight-line computation. Depend on it."

"Paul," Jessica said, "you're not a Mentat yet; you can't know for sure how—"

"I'll never be a Mentat," he said. "I'm something else . . . a freak."

"Paul! How can you say such—"

"Leave me alone!"

He turned away from her, looking out into the night. *Why can't I mourn?* he wondered. He felt that every fiber of his being craved this release, but it would be denied him forever.

Jessica had never heard such distress in her son's voice. She wanted to reach out to him, hold him, comfort him, help him—but she sensed there was nothing she could do. He had to solve this problem by himself.

The glowing tab of the Fremkit manual between them on the tent floor caught her eye. She lifted it, glanced at the flyleaf, reading: "Manual of 'The Friendly Desert,' the place full of life. Here are the ayat and burhan of Life. Believe, and al-Lat shall never burn you."

It reads like the Azhar Book, she thought, recalling her studies of the Great Secrets. *Has a Manipulator of Religions been on Arrakis?*

Paul lifted the paracompass from the pack, returned it, said: "Think of all these special-application Fremen machines. They show unrivaled sophistication. Admit it. The culture that made these things betrays depths no one suspected."

Hesitating, still worried by the harshness in his voice, Jessica returned to the book, studied an illustrated constellation from the Arrakeen sky: "Muad'Dib: The Mouse," and noted that the tail pointed north.

Paul stared into the tent's darkness at the dimly discerned movements of his mother revealed by the manual's glowtab. *Now is the time to carry out my father's wish*, he thought. *I must give her his message now while she has time for grief. Grief would inconvenience us later.* And he found himself shocked by precise logic.

"Mother," he said.

"Yes?"

She heard the change in his voice, felt coldness in her entrails at the sound. Never had she heard such harsh control.

"My father is dead," he said.

She searched within herself for the coupling of fact and fact and fact—the Bene Gesserit way of assessing data—and it came to her: the sensation of terrifying loss.

Jessica nodded, unable to speak.

"My father charged me once," Paul said, "to give you a message if anything happened to him. He feared you might believe he distrusted you."

That useless suspicion, she thought.

"He wanted you to know he never suspected you," Paul said, and explained the deception, adding: "He wanted you to know he always trusted you completely, always loved you and cherished you. He said he would sooner have mistrusted himself and he had but one regret—that he never made you his Duchess."

She brushed the tears coursing down her cheeks, thought: *What a stupid waste of the body's water!* But she knew this thought for what it was—the attempt to retreat from grief into anger. *Leto, my Leto*, she thought. *What terrible things we do to those we love!* With a violent motion, she extinguished the little manual's glowtab.

Sobs shook her.

Paul heard his mother's grief and felt the emptiness within himself. *I have no grief*, he thought. *Why? Why?* He felt the inability to grieve as a terrible flaw.

"A time to get and time to lose," Jessica thought, quoting to herself from the O.C. Bible. *"A time to keep and a time to cast away; a time for love and a time to hate; a time of war and a time of peace."*

Paul's mind had gone on in its chilling precision. He saw the avenues ahead of them on this hostile planet. Without even the safety valve of dreaming, he focused his prescient awareness, seeing it as a computation of most probable futures, but with something more, an edge of mystery—as though his mind dipped into some timeless stratum and sampled the winds of the future.

Abruptly, as though he had found a necessary key, Paul's mind climbed another notch in awareness. He felt himself clinging to this new level, clutching at a precarious hold and peering about. It was as though he existed within a globe with avenues radiating away in all directions . . . yet this only approximated the sensation.

He remembered once seeing a gauze kerchief blowing in the wind and now he sensed the future as though it twisted across some surface as undulant and impermanent as that of the windblown kerchief.

He saw people.

He felt the heat and cold of uncounted probabilities.

He knew names and places, experienced emotions without number, reviewed data of innumerable unexplored crannies. There was time to probe and test and taste, but no time to shape.

The thing was a spectrum of possibilities from the most remote past to the most remote future—from the most probable to the most improbable. He saw his own death in countless ways. He saw new planets, new cultures.

People.

People.

He saw them in such swarms they could not be listed, yet his mind catalogued them.

Even the Guildsmen.

And he thought: *The Guild—there'd be a way for us, my strangeness accepted as a familiar thing of high value, always with an assured supply of the now-necessary spice.*

But the idea of living out his life in the mind-groping-ahead-through-possible-futures that guided hurtling spaceships appalled him. It *was* a way, though. And in meeting the *possible future* that contained Guildsmen he recognized his own strangeness.

I have another kind of sight. I see another kind of terrain: the available paths.

The awareness conveyed both reassurance and alarm—so many places on that other kind of terrain dipped or turned out of his sight.

As swiftly as it had come, the sensation slipped away from him, and he realized the entire experience had taken the space of a heartbeat.

Yet, his own personal awareness had been turned over, illuminated in a terrifying way. He stared around him.

Night still covered the stilltent within its rock-enclosed hideaway. His mother's grief could still be heard.

His own lack of grief could still be felt . . . that hollow place somewhere separated from his mind, which went on in its steady pace—dealing with data, evaluating, computing, submitting answers in something like the Mentat way.

And now he saw that he had a wealth of data few such minds ever before had encompassed. But this made the empty place within him no easier to bear. He felt that something must shatter. It was as though a clockwork control for a bomb had been set to ticking within him. It went on about its business no matter what he wanted. It recorded minuscule shadings of difference around him—a slight change in moisture, a fractional fall in temperature, the progress of an insect across their stilltent roof, the solemn approach of dawn in the starlighted patch of sky he could see out the tent's transparent end.

The emptiness was unbearable. Knowing how the clockwork had been set in motion made no difference. He could look to his own past and see the start of it—the training, the sharpening of talents, the refined pressures of sophisticated disciplines, even exposure to the O.C. Bible at a critical moment . . . and, lastly, the heavy intake of spice. And he could look ahead—the most terrifying direction—to see where it all pointed.

I'm a monster! he thought. *A freak!*

"No," he said. Then: "No. No! NO!"

He found that he was pounding the tent floor with his fists. (The implacable part of him recorded this as an interesting emotional datum and fed it into computation.)

"Paul!"

His mother was beside him, holding his hands, her face a gray blob peering at him. "Paul, what's wrong?"

"You!" he said.

"I'm here, Paul," she said. "It's all right."

"What have you done to me?" he demanded.

In a burst of clarity, she sensed some of the roots in the question, said: "I gave birth to you."

It was, from instinct as much as her own subtle knowledge, the precisely correct answer to calm him. He felt her hands holding him, focused on the dim outline of her face. (Certain gene traces in her facial structure were noted in the new way by his onflowing mind, the clues added to other data, and a final-summation answer put forward.)

"Let go of me," he said.

She heard the iron in his voice, obeyed. "Do you want to tell me what's wrong, Paul?"

"Did you know what you were doing when you trained me?" he asked.

There's no more childhood in his voice, she thought. And she said: "I hoped the thing any parent hopes—that you'd be . . . superior, different."

"Different?"

She heard the bitterness in his tone, said: "Paul, I—"

"You didn't want a son!" he said. "You wanted a Kwisatz Haderach! You wanted a male Bene Gesserit!"

She recoiled from his bitterness. "But Paul. . . ."

"Did you ever consult my father in this?"

She spoke gently out of the freshness of her grief: "Whatever you are, Paul, the heredity is as much your father as me."

"But not the training," he said. "Not the things that . . . awakened . . . the sleeper."

"Sleeper?"

"It's here." He put a hand to his head and then to his breast. "In me. It goes on and on and on and on and—"

"Paul!"

She had heard the hysteria edging his voice.

"Listen to me," he said. "You wanted the Reverend Mother to hear about my dreams: You listen in her place now. I've just had a *waking* dream. Do you know why?"

"You must calm yourself," she said. "If there's—"

"The spice," he said. "It's in everything here—the air, the soil, the food, the *geriatric* spice. It's like the Truthsayer drug. It's a poison!"

She stiffened.

His voice lowered and he repeated: "A poison—so subtle, so insidious . . . so irreversible. It won't even kill you unless you stop taking it. We can't leave Arrakis unless we take part of Arrakis with us."

The terrifying *presence* of his voice brooked no dispute.

"You and the spice," Paul said. "The spice changes anyone who gets this much of it, but thanks to *you*, I could bring the change to consciousness. I don't get to leave it in the unconscious where its disturbance can be blanked out. I can *see* it."

"Paul, you—"

"I *see* it!" he repeated.

She heard madness in his voice, didn't know what to do.

But he spoke again, and she heard the iron control return to him: "We're trapped here."

We're trapped here, she agreed.

And she accepted the truth of his words. No pressure of the Bene Gesserit, no trickery or artifice could pry them completely free from Arrakis: the spice was addictive. Her body had known the fact long before her mind awakened to it.

So here we live out our lives, she thought, *on this hell planet. The place is prepared for us, if we can evade the Harkonnens. And there's no doubt of my course: a broodmare preserving an important bloodline for the Bene Gesserit Plan.*

"I must tell you about my waking dream," Paul said. (Now there was fury in his voice.) "To be sure you accept what I say, I'll tell you first I know you'll bear a daughter, my sister, here on Arrakis."

Jessica placed her hands against the tent floor, pressed back against the curving fabric wall to still a pang of fear. She knew her pregnancy could not show yet. Only her own Bene Gesserit training had allowed her to read the first faint signals of her body, to know of the embryo only a few weeks old.

"Only to serve," Jessica whispered, clinging to the Bene Gesserit motto. "We exist only to serve."

"We'll find a home among the Fremen," Paul said, "where your Missionaria Protectiva has bought us a bolt hole."

They've prepared a way for us in the desert, Jessica told herself. *But how can he know of the Missionaria Protectiva?* She found it increasingly difficult to subdue her terror at the overpowering strangeness in Paul.

He studied the dark shadow of her, seeing her fear and every reaction with his new awareness as though she were outlined in blinding light. A beginning of compassion for her crept over him.

"The things that can happen here, I cannot begin to tell you," he said. "I cannot even begin to tell myself, although I've seen them. This *sense* of the future—I seem to have no control over it. The thing just happens. The immediate future—say, a year—I can see some of that . . . a *road* as broad as our Central Avenue on Caladan. Some places I don't see . . . shadowed places . . . as though it went behind a hill" (and again he thought of the surface of a blowing kerchief) ". . . and there are branchings. . . ."

He fell silent as memory of that *seeing* filled him. No prescient dream, no experience of his life had quite prepared him for the totality with which the veils had been ripped away to reveal naked time.

Recalling the experience, he recognized his own terrible purpose—the pressure of his life spreading outward like an expanding bubble . . . time retreating before it. . . .

Jessica found the tent's glowtab control, activated it.

Dim green light drove back the shadows, easing her fear. She looked at Paul's face, his eyes—the inward stare. And she knew where she had seen such a look before: pictured in records of disasters—on the faces of children who experienced starvation or terrible injury. The eyes were like pits, mouth a straight line, cheeks indrawn.

It's the look of terrible awareness, she thought, *of someone forced to the knowledge of his own mortality.*

He was, indeed, no longer a child.

The underlying import of his words began to take over in her mind, pushing all else aside. Paul could see ahead, a way of escape for them.

"There's a way to evade the Harkonnens," she said.

"The Harkonnens!" he sneered. "Put those twisted humans out of your mind." He stared at his mother, studying the lines of her face in the light of the glowtab. The lines betrayed her.

She said: "You shouldn't refer to people as humans without—"

"Don't be so sure you know where to draw the line," he said. "We carry our past with us. And, mother mine, there's a thing you don't know and should—*we* are Harkonnens."

Her mind did a terrifying thing: it blanked out as though it needed to shut off all sensation. But Paul's voice went on at that implacable pace, dragging her with it.

"When next you find a mirror, study your face—study mine now. The traces are there if you don't blind yourself. Look at my hands, the set of my bones. And if none of this convinces you, then take my word for it. I've walked the future, I've looked at a record, I've seen a place, I have all the data. We're Harkonnens."

"A . . . renegade branch of the family," she said. "That's it, isn't it? Some Harkonnen cousin who—"

"You're the Baron's own daughter," he said, and watched the way she pressed her hands to her mouth. "The Baron sampled many pleasures in his youth, and once permitted himself to be seduced. But it was for the genetic purposes of the Bene Gesserit, by one of *you.*"

The way he said *you* struck her like a slap. But it set her mind to working and she could not deny his words. So many blank ends of meaning in her past reached out now and linked. The daughter the Bene

Gesserit wanted—it wasn't to end the old Atreides-Harkonnen feud, but to fix some genetic factor in their lines. *What?* She groped for an answer.

As though he saw inside her mind, Paul said: "They thought they were reaching for me. But I'm not what they expected, and I've arrived before my time. And *they* don't know it."

Jessica pressed her hands to her mouth.

Great Mother! He's the Kwisatz Haderach!

She felt exposed and naked before him, realizing then that he saw her with eyes from which little could be hidden. And *that,* she knew, was the basis of her fear.

"You're thinking I'm the Kwisatz Haderach," he said. "Put that out of your mind. I'm something unexpected."

I must get word out to one of the schools, she thought. *The mating index may show what has happened.*

"They won't learn about me until it's too late," he said.

She sought to divert him, lowered her hands and said: "We'll find a place among the Fremen?"

"The Fremen have a saying they credit to Shai-hulud, Old Father Eternity," he said. "They say: 'Be prepared to appreciate what you meet.'"

And he thought: *Yes, mother mine—among the Fremen. You'll acquire the blue eyes and a callus beside your lovely nose from the filter tube to your stillsuit . . . and you'll bear my sister: St. Alia of the Knife.*

"If you're not the Kwisatz Haderach," Jessica said, "what—"

"You couldn't possibly know," he said. "You won't believe it until you see it."

And he thought: *I'm a seed.*

He suddenly saw how fertile was the ground into which he had fallen, and with this realization, the terrible purpose filled him, creeping through the empty place within, threatening to choke him with grief.

He had seen two main branchings along the way ahead—in one he confronted an evil old Baron and said: "Hello, Grandfather." The thought of that path and what lay along it sickened him.

The other path held long patches of gray obscurity except for peaks of violence. He had seen a warrior religion there, a fire spreading across the universe with the Atreides green and black banner waving at the head of fanatic legions drunk on spice liquor. Gurney Halleck and a few others of his father's men—a pitiful few—were among them, all marked by the hawk symbol from the shrine of his father's skull.

"I can't go that way," he muttered. "That's what the old witches of your schools really want."

"I don't understand you, Paul," his mother said.

He remained silent, thinking like the seed he was, thinking with the race consciousness he had first experienced as terrible purpose. He found that he no longer could hate the Bene Gesserit or the Emperor or even the Harkonnens. They were all caught up in the need of their race to renew its scattered inheritance, to cross and mingle and infuse their bloodlines in a great new pooling of genes. And the race knew only one sure way for this—the ancient way, the tried and certain way that rolled over everything in its path: jihad.

Surely, I cannot choose that way, he thought.

But he saw again in his mind's eye the shrine of his father's skull and the violence with the green and black banner waving in its midst.

Jessica cleared her throat, worried by his silence. "Then . . . the Fremen will give us sanctuary?"

He looked up, staring across the green-lighted tent at the inbred, patrician lines of her face. "Yes," he said. "That's one of the ways." He nodded. "Yes. They'll call me . . . Muad'Dib, 'The One Who Points the Way.' Yes . . . that's what they'll call me."

And he closed his eyes, thinking: *Now, my father, I can mourn you.* And he felt the tears coursing down his cheeks.

BOOK TWO

MUAD'DIB

When my father, the Padishah Emperor, heard of Duke Leto's death and the manner of it, he went into such a rage as we had never before seen. He blamed my mother and the compact forced on him to place a Bene Gesserit on the throne. He blamed the Guild and the evil old Baron. He blamed everyone in sight, not excepting even me, for he said I was a witch like all the others. And when I sought to comfort him, saying it was done according to an older law of self-preservation to which even the most ancient rulers gave allegiance, he sneered at me and asked if I thought him a weakling. I saw then that he had been aroused to this passion not by concern over the dead Duke but by what that death implied for all royalty. As I look back on it, I think there may have been some prescience in my father, too, for it is certain that his line and Muad'Dib's shared common ancestry.

—FROM "IN MY FATHER'S HOUSE"
BY THE PRINCESS IRULAN

"Now Harkonnen shall kill Harkonnen," Paul whispered.

He had awakened shortly before nightfall, sitting up in the sealed and darkened stilltent. As he spoke, he heard the vague stirrings of his mother where she slept against the tent's opposite wall.

Paul glanced at the proximity detector on the floor, studying the dials illuminated in the blackness by phosphor tubes.

"It should be night soon," his mother said. "Why don't you lift the tent shades?"

Paul realized then that her breathing had been different for some time, that she had lain silent in the darkness until certain he was awake.

"Lifting the shades wouldn't help," he said. "There's been a storm. The tent's covered by sand. I'll dig us out soon."

"No sign of Duncan yet?"

"None."

Paul rubbed absently at the ducal signet on his thumb, and a sudden rage against the very substance of this planet which had helped kill his father set him trembling.

"I heard the storm begin," Jessica said.

The undemanding emptiness of her words helped restore some of his calm. His mind focused on the storm as he had seen it begin through the transparent end of their stilltent—cold dribbles of sand crossing the basin, then runnels and tails furrowing the sky. He had looked up to a rock spire, seen it change shape under the blast, becoming a low, cheddar-colored wedge. Sand funneled into their basin had shadowed the sky with dull curry, then blotted out all light as the tent was covered.

Tent bows had creaked once as they accepted the pressure, then— silence broken only by the dim bellows wheezing of their sand snorkel pumping air from the surface.

"Try the receiver again," Jessica said.

"No use," he said.

He found his stillsuit's watertube in its clip at his neck, drew a warm swallow into his mouth, and he thought that here he truly began an Arrakeen existence—living on reclaimed moisture from his own breath and body. It was flat and tasteless water, but it soothed his throat.

Jessica heard Paul drinking, felt the slickness of her own stillsuit clinging to her body, but she refused to accept her thirst. To accept it would require awakening fully into the terrible necessities of Arrakis where they must guard even fractional traces of moisture, hoarding the few drops in the tent's catchpockets, begrudging a breath wasted on the open air.

So much easier to drift back down into sleep.

But there had been a dream in this day's sleep, and she shivered at the memory of it. She had held dreaming hands beneath sandflow where a name had been written: *Duke Leto Atreides.* The name had blurred with the sand and she had moved to restore it, but the first letter filled before the last was begun.

The sand would not stop.

Her dream became wailing: louder and louder. That ridiculous wailing—part of her mind had realized the sound was her own voice as a tiny child, little more than a baby. A woman not quite visible to memory was going away.

My unknown mother, Jessica thought. *The Bene Gesserit who bore me and gave me to the Sisters because that's what she was commanded to do. Was she glad to rid herself of a Harkonnen child?*

"The place to hit them is in the spice," Paul said.

How can he think of attack at a time like this? she asked herself.

"An entire planet full of spice," she said. "How can you hit them there?"

She heard him stirring, the sound of their pack being dragged across the tent floor.

"It was sea power and air power on Caladan," he said. "Here, it's *desert power.* The Fremen are the key."

His voice came from the vicinity of the tent's sphincter. Her Bene Gesserit training sensed in his tone an unresolved bitterness toward her.

All his life he has been trained to hate Harkonnens, she thought. *Now, he finds he is Harkonnen . . . because of me. How little he knows me! I was my Duke's only woman. I accepted his life and his values even to defying my Bene Gesserit orders.*

The tent's glowtab came alight under Paul's hand, filled the domed area with green radiance. Paul crouched at the sphincter, his stillsuit hood adjusted for the open desert—forehead capped, mouth filter in place, nose plugs adjusted. Only his dark eyes were visible: a narrow band of face that turned once toward her and away.

"Secure yourself for the open," he said, and his voice was blurred behind the filter.

Jessica pulled the filter across her mouth, began adjusting her hood as she watched Paul break the tent seal.

Sand rasped as he opened the sphincter and a burred fizzle of grains ran into the tent before he could immobilize it with a static compaction tool. A hole grew in the sandwall as the tool realigned the grains. He slipped out and her ears followed his progress to the surface.

What will we find out there? she wondered. *Harkonnen troops and the Sardaukar, those are dangers we can expect. But what of the dangers we don't know?*

She thought of the compaction tool and the other strange instruments in the pack. Each of these tools suddenly stood in her mind as a sign of mysterious dangers.

She felt then a hot breeze from surface sand touch her cheeks where they were exposed above the filter.

"Pass up the pack." It was Paul's voice, low and guarded.

She moved to obey, heard the water literjons gurgle as she shoved the pack across the floor. She peered upward, saw Paul framed against stars.

"Here," he said and reached down, pulled the pack to the surface.

Now she saw only the circle of stars. They were like the luminous tips of weapons aimed down at her. A shower of meteors crossed her patch of night. The meteors seemed to her like a warning, like tiger stripes, like luminous grave slats clabbering her blood. And she felt the chill of the price on their heads.

"Hurry up," Paul said. "I want to collapse the tent."

A shower of sand from the surface brushed her left hand. *How much sand will the hand hold?* she asked herself.

"Shall I help you?" Paul asked.

"No."

She swallowed in a dry throat, slipped into the hole, felt static-packed sand rasp under her hands. Paul reached down, took her arm. She stood beside him on a smooth patch of starlit desert, stared around. Sand almost brimmed their basin, leaving only a dim lip of surrounding rock. She probed the farther darkness with her trained senses.

Noise of small animals.

Birds.

A fall of dislodged sand and faint creature sounds within it.

Paul collapsing their tent, recovering it up the hole.

Starlight displaced just enough of the night to charge each shadow with menace. She looked at patches of blackness.

Black is a blind remembering, she thought. *You listen for pack sounds, for the cries of those who hunted your ancestors in a past so ancient only your most primitive cells remember. The ears see. The nostrils see.*

Presently, Paul stood beside her, said: "Duncan told me that if he was captured, he could hold out . . . this long. We must leave here now." He shouldered the pack, crossed to the shallow lip of the basin, climbed to a ledge that looked down on open desert.

Jessica followed automatically, noting how she now lived in her son's orbit.

For now is my grief heavier than the sands of the seas, she thought. *This world has emptied me of all but the oldest purpose: tomorrow's life. I live now for my young Duke and the daughter yet to be.*

She felt the sand drag her feet as she climbed to Paul's side.

He looked north across a line of rocks, studying a distant escarpment.

The faraway rock profile was like an ancient battleship of the seas outlined by stars. The long swish of it lifted on an invisible wave with syllables of boomerang antennae, funnels arcing back, a pi-shaped upthrusting at the stern.

An orange glare burst above the silhouette and a line of brilliant purple cut downward toward the glare.

Another line of purple!

And another upthrusting orange glare!

It was like an ancient naval battle, remembered shellfire, and the sight held them staring.

"Pillars of fire," Paul whispered.

A ring of red eyes lifted over the distant rock. Lines of purple laced the sky.

"Jetflares and lasguns," Jessica said.

The dust-reddened first moon of Arrakis lifted above the horizon to their left and they saw a storm trail there—a ribbon of movement over the desert.

"It must be Harkonnen 'thopters hunting us," Paul said. "The way they're cutting up the desert . . . it's as though they were making certain they stamped out whatever's there . . . the way you'd stamp out a nest of insects."

"Or a nest of Atreides," Jessica said.

"We must seek cover," Paul said. "We'll head south and keep to the rocks. If they caught us in the open. . . ." He turned, adjusting the pack to his shoulders. "They're killing anything that moves."

He took one step along the ledge and, in that instant, heard the low hiss of gliding aircraft, saw the dark shapes of ornithopters above them.

My father once told me that respect for the truth comes close to being the basis for all morality. "Something cannot emerge from nothing," he said. This is profound thinking if you understand how unstable "the truth" can be.

—FROM "CONVERSATIONS WITH MUAD'DIB"
BY THE PRINCESS IRULAN

"I've always prided myself on seeing things the way they truly are," Thufir Hawat said. "That's the curse of being a Mentat. You can't stop analyzing your data."

The leathered old face appeared composed in the predawn dimness as he spoke. His sapho-stained lips were drawn into a straight line with radial creases spreading upward.

A robed man squatted silently on sand across from Hawat, apparently unmoved by the words.

The two crouched beneath a rock overhang that looked down on a wide, shallow sink. Dawn was spreading over the shattered outline of cliffs across the basin, touching everything with pink. It was cold under the overhang, a dry and penetrating chill left over from the night. There had been a warm wind just before dawn, but now it was cold. Hawat could hear teeth chattering behind him among the few troopers remaining in his force.

The man squatting across from Hawat was a Fremen who had come across the sink in the first light of false dawn, skittering over the sand, blending into the dunes, his movements barely discernible.

The Fremen extended a finger to the sand between them, drew a figure there. It looked like a bowl with an arrow spilling out of it. "There are many Harkonnen patrols," he said. He lifted his finger, pointed upward across the cliffs that Hawat and his men had descended.

Hawat nodded.

Many patrols. Yes.

But still he did not know what this Fremen wanted and this rankled. Mentat training was supposed to give a man the power to see motives.

This had been the worst night of Hawat's life. He had been at Tsimpo, a garrison village, buffer outpost for the former capital city, Carthag, when the reports of attack began arriving. At first, he'd thought: *It's a raid. The Harkonnens are testing.*

But report followed report—faster and faster.

Two legions landed at Carthag.

Five legions—fifty brigades!—attacking the Duke's main base at Arrakeen.

A legion at Arsunt.

Two battle groups at Splintered Rock.

Then the reports became more detailed—there were Imperial Sardaukar among the attackers—possibly two legions of them. And it became clear that the invaders knew precisely which weight of arms to send where. Precisely! Superb Intelligence.

Hawat's shocked fury had mounted until it threatened the smooth functioning of his Mentat capabilities. The size of the attack struck his mind like a physical blow.

Now, hiding beneath a bit of desert rock, he nodded to himself, pulled his torn and slashed tunic around him as though warding off the cold shadows.

The size of the attack.

He had always expected their enemy to hire an occasional lighter from the Guild for probing raids. That was an ordinary enough gambit in this kind of House-to-House warfare. Lighters landed and took off on Arrakis regularly to transport the spice for House Atreides. Hawat had taken precautions against random raids by false spice lighters. For a full attack they'd expected no more than ten brigades.

But there were more than two thousand ships down on Arrakis at the last count—not just lighters, but frigates, scouts, monitors, crushers, troop carriers, dump-boxes. . . .

More than a hundred brigades—ten legions!

The entire spice income of Arrakis for fifty years might just cover the cost of such a venture.

It might.

I underestimated what the Baron was willing to spend in attacking us, Hawat thought. *I failed my Duke.*

Then there was the matter of the traitor.

I will live long enough to see her strangled! he thought. *I should've killed that Bene Gesserit witch when I had the chance.* There was no doubt in his mind who had betrayed them—the Lady Jessica. She fitted all the facts available.

"Your man Gurney Halleck and part of his force are safe with our smuggler friends," the Fremen said.

"Good."

So Gurney will get off this hell planet. We're not all gone.

Hawat glanced back at the huddle of his men. He had started the night just past with three hundred of his finest. Of those, an even twenty remained and half of them were wounded. Some of them slept now, standing up, leaning against the rock, sprawled on the sand beneath the rock. Their last 'thopter, the one they'd been using as a ground-effect machine to carry their wounded, had given out just before dawn. They had cut it up with lasguns and hidden the pieces, then worked their way down into this hiding place at the edge of the basin.

Hawat had only a rough idea of their location—some two hundred kilometers southeast of Arrakeen. The main traveled ways between the Shield Wall sietch communities were somewhere south of them.

The Fremen across from Hawat threw back his hood and stillsuit cap to reveal sandy hair and beard. The hair was combed straight back from a high, thin forehead. He had the unreadable total blue eyes of the spice diet. Beard and mustache were stained at one side of the mouth, his hair matted there by pressure of the looping catchtube from his nose plugs.

The man removed his plugs, readjusted them. He rubbed at a scar beside his nose.

"If you cross the sink here this night," the Fremen said, "you must not use shields. There is a break in the wall. . . ." He turned on his heels, pointed south. ". . . there, and it is open sand down to the erg. Shields will attract a. . . ." He hesitated. ". . . worm. They don't often come in here, but a shield will bring one every time."

He said worm, Hawat thought. *He was going to say something else. What? And what does he want of us?*

Hawat sighed.

He could not recall ever before being this tired. It was a muscle weariness that energy pills were unable to ease.

Those damnable Sardaukar!

With a self-accusing bitterness, he faced the thought of the soldier-fanatics and the Imperial treachery they represented. His own Mentat assessment of the data told him how little chance he had ever to present evidence of this treachery before the High Council of the Landsraad where justice might be done.

"Do you wish to go to the smugglers?" the Fremen asked.

"Is it possible?"

"The way is long."

"Fremen don't like to say no," Idaho had told him once.

Hawat said: "You haven't yet told me whether your people can help my wounded."

"They are wounded."

The same damned answer every time!

"We know they're wounded!" Hawat snapped. "That's not the—"

"Peace, friend," the Fremen cautioned. "What do your wounded say? Are there those among them who can see the water need of your tribe?"

"We haven't talked about water," Hawat said. "We—"

"I can understand your reluctance," the Fremen said. "They are your friends, your tribesmen. Do you have water?"

"Not enough."

The Fremen gestured to Hawat's tunic, the skin exposed beneath it. "You were caught in-sietch, without your suits. You must make a water decision, friend."

"Can we hire your help?"

The Fremen shrugged. "You have no water." He glanced at the group behind Hawat. "How many of your wounded would you spend?"

Hawat fell silent, staring at the man. He could see as a Mentat that their communication was out of phase. Word-sounds were not being linked up here in the normal manner.

"I am Thufir Hawat," he said. "I can speak for my Duke. I will make promissory commitment now for your help. I wish a limited form of help, preserving my force long enough only to kill a traitor who thinks herself beyond vengeance."

"You wish our siding in a vendetta?"

"The vendetta I'll handle myself. I wish to be freed of responsibility for my wounded that I may get about it."

The Fremen scowled. "How can you be responsible for your wounded? They are their own responsibility. The water's at issue, Thufir Hawat. Would you have me take that decision away from you?"

The man put a hand to a weapon concealed beneath his robe.

Hawat tensed, wondering: *Is there betrayal here?*

"What do you fear?" the Fremen demanded.

These people and their disconcerting directness! Hawat spoke cautiously. "There's a price on my head."

"Ah-h-h-h." The Fremen removed his hand from his weapon. "You think we have the Byzantine corruption. You don't know us. The Harkonnens have not water enough to buy the smallest child among us."

But they had the price of Guild passage for more than two thousand fighting ships, Hawat thought. And the size of that price still staggered him.

"We both fight Harkonnens," Hawat said. "Should we not share the problems and ways of meeting the battle issue?"

"We are sharing," the Fremen said. "I have seen you fight Harkonnens. You are good. There've been times I'd have appreciated your arm beside me."

"Say where my arm may help you," Hawat said.

"Who knows?" the Fremen asked. "There are Harkonnen forces everywhere. But you still have not made the water decision or put it to your wounded."

I must be cautious, Hawat told himself. *There's a thing here that's not understood.*

He said: "Will you show me your way, the Arrakeen way?"

"Stranger-thinking," the Fremen said, and there was a sneer in his tone. He pointed to the northwest across the clifftop. "We watched you come across the sand last night." He lowered his arm. "You keep your force on the slipface of the dunes. Bad. You have no stillsuits, no water. You will not last long."

"The ways of Arrakis don't come easily," Hawat said.

"Truth. But we've killed Harkonnens."

"What do you do with your own wounded?" Hawat demanded.

"Does a man not know when he is worth saving?" the Fremen asked. "Your wounded know you have no water." He tilted his head, looking sideways up at Hawat. "This is clearly a time for water decision. Both wounded and unwounded must look to the tribe's future."

The tribe's future, Hawat thought. *The tribe of Atreides. There's sense in that.* He forced himself to the question he had been avoiding.

"Have you word of my Duke or his son?"

Unreadable blue eyes stared upward into Hawat's. "Word?"

"Their fate!" Hawat snapped.

"Fate is the same for everyone," the Fremen said. "Your Duke, it is said, has met his fate. As to the Lisan al-Gaib, his son, that is in Liet's hands. Liet has not said."

I knew the answer without asking, Hawat thought.

He glanced back at his men. They were all awake now. They had heard. They were staring out across the sand, the realization in their expressions: there was no returning to Caladan for them, and now Arrakis was lost.

Hawat turned back to the Fremen. "Have you heard of Duncan Idaho?"

"He was in the great house when the shield went down," the Fremen said. "This I've heard . . . no more."

She dropped the shield and let in the Harkonnens, he thought. *I was the one who sat with my back to a door. How could she do this when it meant turning also against her own son? But . . . who knows how a Bene Gesserit witch thinks . . . if you can call it thinking?*

Hawat tried to swallow in a dry throat. "When will you hear about the boy?"

"We know little of what happens in Arrakeen," the Fremen said. He shrugged. "Who knows?"

"You have ways of finding out?"

"Perhaps." The Fremen rubbed at the scar beside his nose. "Tell me, Thufir Hawat, do you have knowledge of the big weapons the Harkonnens used?"

The artillery, Hawat thought bitterly. *Who could have guessed they'd use artillery in this day of shields?*

"You refer to the artillery they used to trap our people in the caves," he said. "I've . . . theoretical knowledge of such explosive weapons."

"Any man who retreats into a cave which has only one opening deserves to die," the Fremen said.

"Why do you ask about these weapons?"

"Liet wishes it."

Is that what he wants from us? Hawat wondered. He said: "Did you come here seeking information about the big guns?"

"Liet wished to see one of the weapons for himself."

"Then you should just go take one," Hawat sneered.

"Yes," the Fremen said. "We took one. We have it hidden where Stilgar can study it for Liet and where Liet can see it for himself if he wishes. But I doubt he'll want to: the weapon is not a very good one. Poor design for Arrakis."

"You . . . took one?" Hawat asked.

"It was a good fight," the Fremen said. "We lost only two men and spilled the water from more than a hundred of theirs."

There were Sardaukar at every gun, Hawat thought. *This desert madman speaks casually of losing only two men against Sardaukar!*

"We would not have lost the two except for those others fighting beside the Harkonnens," the Fremen said. "Some of those are good fighters."

One of Hawat's men limped forward, looked down at the squatting Fremen. "Are you talking about Sardaukar?"

"He's talking about Sardaukar," Hawat said.

"Sardaukar!" the Fremen said, and there appeared to be glee in his voice. "Ah-h-h, so that's what they are! This was a good night indeed. Sardaukar. Which legion? Do you know?"

"We . . . don't know," Hawat said.

"Sardaukar," the Fremen mused. "Yet they wear Harkonnen clothing. Is that not strange?"

"The Emperor does not wish it known he fights against a Great House," Hawat said.

"But *you* know they are Sardaukar."

"Who am I?" Hawat asked bitterly.

"You are Thufir Hawat," the man said matter-of-factly. "Well, we would have learned it in time. We've sent three of them captive to be questioned by Liet's men."

Hawat's aide spoke slowly, disbelief in every word: "You . . . *captured* Sardaukar?"

"Only three of them," the Fremen said. "They fought well."

If only we'd had the time to link up with these Fremen, Hawat thought. It was a sour lament in his mind. *If only we could've trained them and armed them. Great Mother, what a fighting force we'd have had!*

"Perhaps you delay because of worry over the Lisan al-Gaib," the Fremen said. "If he is truly the Lisan al-Gaib, harm cannot touch him. Do not spend thoughts on a matter which has not been proved."

"I serve the . . . Lisan al-Gaib," Hawat said. "His welfare is my concern. I've pledged myself to this."

"You are pledged to his water?"

Hawat glanced at his aide, who was still staring at the Fremen, returned his attention to the squatting figure. "To his water, yes."

"You wish to return to Arrakeen, to the place of his water?"

"To . . . yes, to the place of his water."

"Why did you not say at first it was a water matter?" The Fremen stood up, seated his nose plugs firmly.

Hawat motioned with his head for his aide to return to the others. With a tired shrug, the man obeyed. Hawat heard a low-voiced conversation arise among the men.

The Fremen said: "There is always a way to water."

Behind Hawat, a man cursed. Hawat's aide called: "Thufir! Arkie just died."

The Fremen put a fist to his ear. "The bond of water! It's a sign!" He stared at Hawat. "We have a place nearby for accepting the water. Shall I call my men?"

The aide returned to Hawat's side, said: "Thufir, a couple of the men left wives in Arrakeen. They're . . . well, you know how it is at a time like this."

The Fremen still held his fist to his ear. "Is it the bond of water, Thufir Hawat?" he demanded.

Hawat's mind was racing. He sensed now the direction of the Fremen's words, but feared the reaction of the tired men under the rock overhang when they understood it.

"The bond of water," Hawat said.

"Let our tribes be joined," the Fremen said, and he lowered his fist.

As though that were the signal, four men slid and dropped down from the rocks above them. They darted back under the overhang, rolled the dead man in a loose robe, lifted him and began running with him along the cliff wall to the right. Spurts of dust lifted around their running feet.

It was over before Hawat's tired men could gather their wits. The group with the body hanging like a sack in its enfolding robe was gone around a turn in the cliff.

One of Hawat's men shouted: "Where they going with Arkie? He was—"

"They're taking him to . . . bury him," Hawat said.

"Fremen don't bury their dead!" the man barked. "Don't you try any tricks on us, Thufir. We know what they do. Arkie was one of—"

"Paradise were sure for a man who died in the service of Lisan al-Gaib," the Fremen said. "If it is the Lisan al-Gaib you serve, as you have said it, why raise mourning cries? The memory of one who died in this fashion will live as long as the memory of man endures."

But Hawat's men advanced, angry looks on their faces. One had captured a lasgun. He started to draw it.

"Stop right where you are!" Hawat barked. He fought down the sick fatigue that gripped his muscles. "These people respect our dead. Customs differ, but the meaning's the same."

"They're going to render Arkie down for his water," the man with the lasgun snarled.

"Is it that your men wish to attend the ceremony?" the Fremen asked.

He doesn't even see the problem, Hawat thought. The naïveté of the Fremen was frightening.

"They're concerned for a respected comrade," Hawat said.

"We will treat your comrade with the same reverence we treat our own," the Fremen said. "This is the bond of water. We know the rites. A man's flesh is his own; the water belongs to the tribe."

Hawat spoke quickly as the man with the lasgun advanced another step. "Will you now help our wounded?"

"One does not question the bond," the Fremen said. "We will do for you what a tribe does for its own. First, we must get all of you suited and see to the necessities."

The man with the lasgun hesitated.

Hawat's aide said: "Are we buying help with Arkie's . . . water?"

"Not buying," Hawat said. "We've joined these people."

"Customs differ," one of his men muttered.

Hawat began to relax.

"And they'll help us get to Arrakeen?"

"We will kill Harkonnens," the Fremen said. He grinned. "And Sardaukar." He stepped backward, cupped his hands beside his ears and tipped his head back, listening. Presently, he lowered his hands, said: "An aircraft comes. Conceal yourselves beneath the rock and remain motionless."

At a gesture from Hawat, his men obeyed.

The Fremen took Hawat's arm, pressed him back with the others. "We will fight in the time of fighting," the man said. He reached beneath his robes, brought out a small cage, lifted a creature from it.

Hawat recognized a tiny bat. The bat turned its head and Hawat saw its blue-within-blue eyes.

The Fremen stroked the bat, soothing it, crooning to it. He bent over the animal's head, allowed a drop of saliva to fall from his tongue into the bat's upturned mouth. The bat stretched its wings, but remained on the Fremen's opened hand. The man took a tiny tube, held it beside the bat's head and chattered into the tube; then, lifting the creature high, he threw it upward.

The bat swooped away beside the cliff and was lost to sight.

The Fremen folded the cage, thrust it beneath his robe. Again, he bent his head, listening. "They quarter the high country," he said. "One wonders who they seek up there."

"It's known that we retreated in this direction," Hawat said.

"One should never presume one is the sole object of a hunt," the Fremen said. "Watch the other side of the basin. You will see a thing."

Time passed.

Some of Hawat's men stirred, whispering.

"Remain silent as frightened animals," the Fremen hissed.

Hawat discerned movement near the opposite cliff—flitting blurs of tan on tan.

"My little friend carried his message," the Fremen said. "He is a good messenger—day or night. I'll be unhappy to lose that one."

The movement across the sink faded away. On the entire four to five kilometer expanse of sand nothing remained but the growing pressure of the day's heat—blurred columns of rising air.

"Be most silent now," the Fremen whispered.

A file of plodding figures emerged from a break in the opposite cliff, headed directly across the sink. To Hawat, they appeared to be Fremen, but a curiously inept band. He counted six men making heavy going of it over the dunes.

A "thwok-thwok" of ornithopter wings sounded high to the right behind Hawat's group. The craft came over the cliff wall above them— an Atreides 'thopter with Harkonnen battle colors splashed on it. The 'thopter swooped toward the men crossing the sink.

The group there stopped on a dune crest, waved.

The 'thopter circled once over them in a tight curve, came back for a dust-shrouded landing in front of the Fremen. Five men swarmed from the 'thopter and Hawat saw the dust-repellent shimmering of shields and, in their motions, the hard competence of Sardaukar.

"Aiihh! They use their stupid shields," the Fremen beside Hawat hissed. He glanced toward the open south wall of the sink.

"They are Sardaukar," Hawat whispered.

"Good."

The Sardaukar approached the waiting group of Fremen in an enclosing half-circle. Sun glinted on blades held ready. The Fremen stood in a compact group, apparently indifferent.

Abruptly, the sand around the two groups sprouted Fremen. They were at the ornithopter, then in it. Where the two groups had met at the dune crest, a dust cloud partly obscured violent motion.

Presently, dust settled. Only Fremen remained standing.

"They left only three men in their 'thopter," the Fremen beside Hawat said. "That was fortunate. I don't believe we had to damage the craft in taking it."

Behind Hawat, one of his men whispered: "Those were Sardaukar!"

"Did you notice how well they fought?" the Fremen asked.

Hawat took a deep breath. He smelled the burned dust around him, felt the heat, the dryness. In a voice to match that dryness, he said: "Yes, they fought well, indeed."

The captured 'thopter took off with a lurching flap of wings, angled upward to the south in a steep, wing-tucked climb.

So these Fremen can handle 'thopters, too, Hawat thought.

On the distant dune, a Fremen waved a square of green cloth: once . . . twice.

"More come!" the Fremen beside Hawat barked. "Be ready. I'd hoped to have us away without more inconvenience."

Inconvenience! Hawat thought.

He saw two more 'thopters swooping from high in the west onto an area of sand suddenly devoid of visible Fremen. Only eight splotches of blue—the bodies of the Sardaukar in Harkonnen uniforms—remained at the scene of violence.

Another 'thopter glided in over the cliff wall above Hawat. He drew in a sharp breath as he saw it—a big troop carrier. It flew with the slow, spread-wing heaviness of a full load—like a giant bird coming to its nest.

In the distance, the purple finger of a lasgun beam flicked from one of the diving 'thopters. It laced across the sand, raising a sharp trail of dust.

"The cowards!" the Fremen beside Hawat rasped.

The troop carrier settled toward the patch of blue-clad bodies. Its wings crept out to full reach, began the cupping action of a quick stop.

Hawat's attention was caught by a flash of sun on metal to the south, a 'thopter plummeting there in a power dive, wings folded flat against its sides, its jets a golden flare against the dark silvered gray of the sky. It plunged like an arrow toward the troop carrier which was unshielded because of the lasgun activity around it. Straight into the carrier the diving 'thopter plunged.

A flaming roar shook the basin. Rocks tumbled from the cliff walls all around. A geyser of red-orange shot skyward from the sand where the carrier and its companion 'thopters had been—everything there caught in the flame.

It was the Fremen who took off in that captured 'thopter, Hawat thought. *He deliberately sacrificed himself to get that carrier. Great Mother! What are these Fremen?*

"A reasonable exchange," said the Fremen beside Hawat. "There must've been three hundred men in that carrier. Now, we must see to their water and make plans to get another aircraft." He started to step out of their rock-shadowed concealment.

A rain of blue uniforms came over the cliff wall in front of him, falling in low-suspensor slowness. In the flashing instant, Hawat had time to see that they were Sardaukar, hard faces set in battle frenzy, that they were unshielded and each carried a knife in one hand, a stunner in the other.

A thrown knife caught Hawat's Fremen companion in the throat, hurling him backward, twisting face down. Hawat had only time to draw his own knife before blackness of a stunner projectile felled him.

Muad'Dib could indeed see the Future, but you must understand the limits of this power. Think of sight. You have eyes, yet cannot see without light. If you are on the floor of a valley, you cannot see beyond your valley. Just so, Muad'Dib could not always choose to look across the mysterious terrain. He tells us that a single obscure decision of prophecy, perhaps the choice of one word over another, could change the entire aspect of the future. He tells us "The vision of time is broad, but when you pass through it, time becomes a narrow door." And always, he fought the temptation to choose a clear, safe course, warning "That path leads ever down into stagnation."

—FROM "ARRAKIS AWAKENING"
BY THE PRINCESS IRULAN

As the ornithopters glided out of the night above them, Paul grabbed his mother's arm, snapped: "Don't move!"

Then he saw the lead craft in the moonlight, the way its wings cupped to brake for landing, the reckless dash of the hands at the controls.

"It's Idaho," he breathed.

The craft and its companions settled into the basin like a covey of birds coming to nest. Idaho was out of his 'thopter and running toward them before the dust settled. Two figures in Fremen robes followed him. Paul recognized one: the tall, sandy-bearded Kynes.

"This way!" Kynes called and he veered left.

Behind Kynes, other Fremen were throwing fabric covers over their ornithopters. The craft became a row of shallow dunes.

Idaho skidded to a stop in front of Paul, saluted. "M'Lord, the Fremen have a temporary hiding place nearby where we—"

"What about that back there?"

Paul pointed to the violence above the distant cliff—the jetflares, the purple beams of lasguns lacing the desert.

A rare smile touched Idaho's round, placid face. "M'Lord . . . Sire, I've left them a little sur—"

Glaring white light filled the desert—bright as a sun, etching their shadows onto the rock floor of the ledge. In one sweeping motion, Idaho had Paul's arm in one hand, Jessica's shoulder in the other, hurling them down off the ledge into the basin. They sprawled together in the sand as the roar of an explosion thundered over them. Its shock wave tumbled chips off the rock ledge they had vacated.

Idaho sat up, brushed sand from himself.

"Not the family atomics!" Jessica said. "I thought—"

"You planted a shield back there," Paul said.

"A big one turned to full force," Idaho said. "A lasgun beam touched it and. . . ." He shrugged.

"Subatomic fusion," Jessica said. "That's a dangerous weapon."

"Not weapon, m'Lady, defense. That scum will think twice before using lasguns another time."

The Fremen from the ornithopters stopped above them. One called in a low voice: "We should get under cover, friends."

Paul got to his feet as Idaho helped Jessica up.

"That blast *will* attract considerable attention, Sire," Idaho said.

Sire, Paul thought.

The word had such a strange sound when directed at him. Sire had always been his father.

He felt himself touched briefly by his powers of prescience, seeing himself infected by the wild race consciousness that was moving the human universe toward chaos. The vision left him shaken, and he al-

lowed Idaho to guide him along the edge of the basin to a rock projection. Fremen there were opening a way down into the sand with their
compaction tools.

"May I take your pack, Sire?" Idaho asked.

"It's not heavy, Duncan," Paul said.

"You have no body shield," Idaho said. "Do you wish mine?" He
glanced at the distant cliff. "Not likely there'll be any more lasgun activity about."

"Keep your shield, Duncan. Your right arm is shield enough for me."

Jessica saw the way the praise took effect, how Idaho moved closer
to Paul, and she thought: *Such a sure hand my son has with his people.*

The Fremen removed a rock plug that opened a passage down into
the native basement complex of the desert. A camouflage cover was
rigged for the opening.

"This way," one of the Fremen said, and he led them down rock steps
into darkness.

Behind them, the cover blotted out the moonlight. A dim green
glow came alive ahead, revealing the steps and rock walls, a turn to the
left. Robed Fremen were all around them now, pressing downward.
They rounded the corner, found another down-slanting passage. It
opened into a rough cave chamber.

Kynes stood before them, jubba hood thrown back. The neck of his
stillsuit glistening in the green light. His long hair and beard were
mussed. The blue eyes without whites were a darkness under heavy
brows.

In the moment of encounter, Kynes wondered at himself: *Why am I
helping these people? It's the most dangerous thing I've ever done. It could
doom me with them.*

Then he looked squarely at Paul, seeing the boy who had taken on
the mantle of manhood, masking grief, suppressing all except the position that now must be assumed—the dukedom. And Kynes realized in
that moment the dukedom still existed and solely because of this
youth—and this was not a thing to be taken lightly.

Jessica glanced once around the chamber, registering it on her senses in the Bene Gesserit way—a laboratory, a civil place full of angles and squares in the ancient manner.

"This is one of the Imperial Ecological Testing Stations my father wanted as advance bases," Paul said.

His father wanted! Kynes thought.

And again Kynes wondered at himself: *Am I foolish to aid these fugitives? Why am I doing it? It'd be so easy to take them now, to buy the Harkonnen trust with them.*

Paul followed his mother's example, gestalting the room, seeing the workbench down one side, the walls of featureless rock. Instruments lined the bench—dials glowing, wire gridex planes with fluting glass emerging from them. An ozone smell permeated the place.

Some of the Fremen moved on around a concealing angle in the chamber and new sounds started there—machine coughs, the whinnies of spinning belts and multidrives.

Paul looked to the end of the room, saw cages with small animals in them stacked against the wall.

"You've recognized this place correctly," Kynes said. "For what would you use such a place, Paul Atreides?"

"To make this planet a fit place for humans," Paul said.

Perhaps that's why I help them, Kynes thought.

The machine sounds abruptly hummed away to silence. Into this void there came a thin animal squeak from the cages. It was cut off abruptly as though in embarrassment.

Paul returned his attention to the cages, saw that the animals were brown-winged bats. An automatic feeder extended from the side wall across the cages.

A Fremen emerged from the hidden area of the chamber, spoke to Kynes: "Liet, the field-generator equipment is not working. I am unable to mask us from proximity detectors."

"Can you repair it?" Kynes asked.

"Not quickly. The parts. . . ." The man shrugged.

"Yes," Kynes said. "Then we'll do without machinery. Get a hand pump for air out to the surface."

"Immediately." The man hurried away.

Kynes turned back to Paul. "You gave a good answer."

Jessica marked the easy rumble of the man's voice. It was a *royal* voice, accustomed to command. And she had not missed the reference to him as Liet. Liet was the Fremen alter ego, the other face of the tame planetologist.

"We're most grateful for your help, Doctor Kynes," she said.

"Mm-m-m, we'll see," Kynes said. He nodded to one of his men. "Spice coffee in my quarters, Shamir."

"At once, Liet," the man said.

Kynes indicated an arched opening in the side wall of the chamber. "If you please?"

Jessica allowed herself a regal nod before accepting. She saw Paul give a hand signal to Idaho, telling him to mount guard here.

The passage, two paces deep, opened through a heavy door into a square office lighted by golden glowglobes. Jessica passed her hand across the door as she entered, was startled to identify plasteel.

Paul stepped three paces into the room, dropped his pack to the floor. He heard the door close behind him, studied the place—about eight meters to a side, walls of natural rock, curry-colored, broken by metal filing cabinets on their right. A low desk with a milk glass top shot full of yellow bubbles occupied the room's center. Four suspensor chairs ringed the desk.

Kynes moved around Paul, held a chair for Jessica. She sat down, noting the way her son examined the room.

Paul remained standing for another eyeblink. A faint anomaly in the room's air currents told him there was a secret exit to their right behind the filing cabinets.

"Will you sit down, Paul Atreides?" Kynes asked.

How carefully he avoids my title, Paul thought. But he accepted the chair, remained silent while Kynes sat down.

"You sense that Arrakis could be a paradise," Kynes said. "Yet, as you see, the Imperium sends here only its trained hatchetmen, its seekers after the spice!"

Paul held up his thumb with its ducal signet. "Do you see this ring?"

"Yes."

"Do you know its significance?"

Jessica turned sharply to stare at her son.

"Your father lies dead in the ruins of Arrakeen," Kynes said. "You are technically the Duke."

"I'm a soldier of the Imperium," Paul said, "*technically* a hatchetman."

Kynes' face darkened. "Even with the Emperor's Sardaukar standing over your father's body?"

"The Sardaukar are one thing, the legal source of my authority is another," Paul said.

"Arrakis has its own way of determining who wears the mantle of authority," Kynes said.

And Jessica, turning back to look at him, thought: *There's steel in this man that no one has taken the temper out of . . . and we've need of steel. Paul's doing a dangerous thing.*

Paul said: "The Sardaukar on Arrakis are a measure of how much our beloved Emperor feared my father. Now, *I* will give the Padishah Emperor reasons to fear the—"

"Lad," Kynes said, "there are things you don't—"

"You will address me as Sire or my Lord," Paul said.

Gently, Jessica thought.

Kynes stared at Paul, and Jessica noted the glint of admiration in the planetologist's face, the touch of humor there.

"Sire," Kynes said.

"I am an embarrassment to the Emperor," Paul said. "I am an embarrassment to all who would divide Arrakis as their spoil. As I live, I shall continue to be such an embarrassment that I stick in their throats and choke them to death!"

"Words," Kynes said.

Paul stared at him. Presently, Paul said: "You have a legend of the Lisan al-Gaib here, the Voice from the Outer World, the one who will lead the Fremen to paradise. Your men have—"

"Superstition!" Kynes said.

"Perhaps," Paul agreed. "Yet perhaps not. Superstitions sometimes have strange roots and stranger branchings."

"You have a plan," Kynes said. "This much is obvious . . . *Sire.*"

"Could your Fremen provide me with proof positive that the Sardaukar are here in Harkonnen uniform?"

"Quite likely."

"The Emperor will put a Harkonnen back in power here," Paul said. "Perhaps even Beast Rabban. Let him. Once he has involved himself beyond escaping his guilt, let the Emperor face the possibility of a Bill of Particulars laid before the Landsraad. Let him answer there where—"

"Paul!" Jessica said.

"Granted that the Landsraad High Council accepts your case," Kynes said, "there could be only one outcome: general warfare between the Imperium and the Great Houses."

"Chaos," Jessica said.

"But I'd present my case to the Emperor," Paul said, "and give him an alternative to chaos."

Jessica spoke in a dry tone: "Blackmail?"

"One of the tools of statecraft, as you've said yourself," Paul said, and Jessica heard the bitterness in his voice. "The Emperor has no sons, only daughters."

"You'd aim for the throne?" Jessica asked.

"The Emperor will not risk having the Imperium shattered by total war," Paul said. "Planets blasted, disorder everywhere—he'll not risk that."

"This is a desperate gamble you propose," Kynes said.

"What do the Great Houses of the Landsraad fear most?" Paul asked. "They fear most what is happening here right now on Arrakis—the Sardaukar picking them off one by one. That's why there *is* a Landsraad. This is the glue of the Great Convention. Only in union do they match the Imperial forces."

"But they're—"

"This is what they fear," Paul said. "Arrakis would become a rallying cry. Each of them would see himself in my father—cut out of the herd and killed."

Kynes spoke to Jessica: "Would his plan work?"

"I'm no Mentat," Jessica said.

"But you are Bene Gesserit."

She shot a probing stare at him, said: "His plan has good points and bad points . . . as any plan would at this stage. A plan depends as much upon execution as it does upon concept."

"'Law is the ultimate science,'" Paul quoted. "Thus it reads above the Emperor's door. I propose to show him law."

"And I'm not sure I could trust the person who conceived this plan," Kynes said. "Arrakis has its own plan that we—"

"From the throne," Paul said, "I could make a paradise of Arrakis with the wave of a hand. This is the coin I offer for your support."

Kynes stiffened. "My loyalty's not for sale, *Sire*."

Paul stared across the desk at him, meeting the cold glare of those blue-within-blue eyes, studying the bearded face, the commanding appearance. A harsh smile touched Paul's lips and he said: "Well spoken. I apologize."

Kynes met Paul's stare and, presently, said: "No Harkonnen ever admitted error. Perhaps you're not like them, Atreides."

"It could be a fault in their education," Paul said. "You say you're not for sale, but I believe I've the coin you'll accept. For your loyalty I offer *my* loyalty to you . . . totally."

My son has the Atreides sincerity, Jessica thought. *He has that tremendous, almost naive honor—and what a powerful force that truly is.*

She saw that Paul's words had shaken Kynes.

"This is nonsense," Kynes said. "You're just a boy and—"

"I'm the Duke," Paul said. "I'm an Atreides. No Atreides has ever broken such a bond."

Kynes swallowed.

"When I say totally," Paul said, "I mean without reservation. I would give my life for you."

"Sire!" Kynes said, and the word was torn from him, but Jessica saw that he was not now speaking to a boy of fifteen, but to a man, to a superior. Now Kynes meant the word.

In this moment he'd give his life for Paul, she thought. *How do the Atreides accomplish this thing so quickly, so easily?*

"I know you mean this," Kynes said. "Yet the Harkon—"

The door behind Paul slammed open. He whirled to see reeling violence—shouting, the clash of steel, wax-image faces grimacing in the passage.

With his mother beside him, Paul leaped for the door, seeing Idaho blocking the passage, his blood-pitted eyes there visible through a shield blur, claw hands beyond him, arcs of steel chopping futilely at the shield. There was the orange fire-mouth of a stunner repelled by the shield. Idaho's blades were through it all, flick-flicking, red dripping from them.

Then Kynes was beside Paul and they threw their weight against the door.

Paul had one last glimpse of Idaho standing against a swarm of Harkonnen uniforms—his jerking, controlled staggers, the black goat hair with a red blossom of death in it. Then the door was closed and there came a snick as Kynes threw the bolts.

"I appear to've decided," Kynes said.

"Someone detected your machinery before it was shut down," Paul said. He pulled his mother away from the door, met the despair in her eyes.

"I should've suspected trouble when the coffee failed to arrive," Kynes said.

"You've a bolt hole out of here," Paul said. "Shall we use it?"

Kynes took a deep breath, said: "This door should hold for at least twenty minutes against all but a lasgun."

"They'll not use a lasgun for fear we've shields on this side," Paul said.

"Those were Sardaukar in Harkonnen uniform," Jessica whispered.

They could hear pounding on the door now, rhythmic blows.

Kynes indicated the cabinets against the right-hand wall, said: "This way." He crossed to the first cabinet, opened a drawer, manipulated a handle within it. The entire wall of cabinets swung open to expose the black mouth of a tunnel. "This door also is plasteel," Kynes said.

"You were well prepared," Jessica said.

"We lived under the Harkonnens for eighty years," Kynes said. He herded them into the darkness, closed the door.

In the sudden blackness, Jessica saw a luminous arrow on the floor ahead of her.

Kynes' voice came from behind them: "We'll separate here. This wall is tougher. It'll stand for at least an hour. Follow the arrows like that one on the floor. They'll be extinguished by your passage. They lead through a maze to another exit where I've secreted a 'thopter. There's a storm across the desert tonight. Your only hope is to run for that storm, dive into the top of it, ride with it. My people have done this in stealing 'thopters. If you stay high in the storm you'll survive."

"What of you?" Paul asked.

"I'll try to escape another way. If I'm captured . . . well, I'm still Imperial Planetologist. I can say I was your captive."

Running like cowards, Paul thought. *But how else can I live to avenge my father?* He turned to face the door.

Jessica heard him move, said, "Duncan's dead, Paul. You saw the wound. You can do nothing for him."

"I'll take full payment for them all one day," Paul said.

"Not unless you hurry now," Kynes said.

Paul felt the man's hand on his shoulder.

"Where will we meet, Kynes?" Paul asked.

"I'll send Fremen searching for you. The storm's path is known. Hurry now, and the Great Mother give you speed and luck."

They heard him go, a scrambling in the blackness.

Jessica found Paul's hand, pulled him gently. "We must not get separated," she said.

"Yes."

He followed her across the first arrow, seeing it go black as they touched it. Another arrow beckoned ahead.

They crossed it, saw it extinguish itself, saw another arrow ahead.

They were running now.

Plans within plans within plans within plans, Jessica thought. *Have we become part of someone else's plan now?*

The arrows led them around turnings, past side openings only dimly sensed in the faint luminescence. Their way slanted downward for a time, then up, ever up. They came finally to steps, rounded a corner and were brought short by a glowing wall with a dark handle visible in its center.

Paul pressed the handle.

The wall swung away from them. Light flared to reveal a rock-hewn cavern with an ornithopter squatting in its center. A flat gray wall with a doorsign on it loomed beyond the aircraft.

"Where did Kynes go?" Jessica asked.

"He did what any good guerrilla leader would," Paul said. "He separated us into two parties and arranged that he couldn't reveal where we are if he's captured. He won't really know."

Paul drew her into the room, noting how their feet kicked up dust on the floor.

"No one's been here for a long time," he said.

"He seemed confident the Fremen could find us," she said.

"I share that confidence."

Paul released her hand, crossed to the ornithopter's left door, opened it, and secured his pack in the rear. "This ship's proximity masked," he said. "Instrument panel has remote door control, light control. Eighty years under the Harkonnens taught them to be thorough."

Jessica leaned against the craft's other side, catching her breath.

"The Harkonnens will have a covering force over this area," she said. "They're not stupid." She considered her direction sense, pointed right. "The storm we saw is that way."

Paul nodded, fighting an abrupt reluctance to move. He knew its cause, but found no help in the knowledge. Somewhere this night he had passed a decision-nexus into the deep unknown. He knew the time-area surrounding them, but the here-and-now existed as a place of mystery. It was as though he had seen himself from a distance go out of sight down into a valley. Of the countless paths up out of that valley, some might carry a Paul Atreides back into sight, but many would not.

"The longer we wait the better prepared they'll be," Jessica said.

"Get in and strap yourself down," he said.

He joined her in the ornithopter, still wrestling with the thought that this was *blind* ground, unseen in any prescient vision. And he realized with an abrupt sense of shock that he had been giving more and more reliance to prescient memory and it had weakened him for this particular emergency.

"If you rely only on your eyes, your other senses weaken." It was a Bene Gesserit axiom. He took it to himself now, promising never again to fall into that trap . . . if he lived through this.

Paul fastened his safety harness, saw that his mother was secure, checked the aircraft. The wings were at full spread-rest, their delicate metal interleavings extended. He touched the retractor bar, watched the wings shorten for jet-boost takeoff the way Gurney Halleck had taught him. The starter switch moved easily. Dials on the instrument panel came alive as the jetpods were armed. Turbines began their low hissing.

"Ready?" he asked.

"Yes."

He touched the remote control for lights.

Darkness blanketed them.

His hand was a shadow against the luminous dials as he tripped the remote door control. Grating sounded ahead of them. A cascade of sand swished away to silence. A dusty breeze touched Paul's cheeks. He closed his door, feeling the sudden pressure.

A wide patch of dust-blurred stars framed in angular darkness appeared where the door-wall had been. Starlight defined a shelf beyond, a suggestion of sand ripples.

Paul depressed the glowing action-sequence switch on his panel.

The wings snapped back and down, hurling the 'thopter out of its nest. Power surged from the jetpods as the wings locked into lift attitude.

Jessica let her hands ride lightly on the dual controls, feeling the sureness of her son's movements. She was frightened, yet exhilarated. *Now, Paul's training is our only hope,* she thought. *His youth and swiftness.*

Paul fed more power to the jetpods. The 'thopter banked, sinking them into their seats as a dark wall lifted against the stars ahead. He gave the craft more wing, more power. Another burst of lifting wingbeats and they came out over rocks, silver-frosted angles and outcroppings in the starlight. The dust-reddened second moon showed itself above the horizon to their right, defining the ribbon trail of the storm.

Paul's hands danced over the controls. Wings snicked in to beetle stubs. G-force pulled at their flesh as the craft came around in a tight bank.

"Jetflares behind us!" Jessica said.

"I saw them."

He slammed the power arm forward.

Their 'thopter leaped like a frightened animal, surged southwest toward the storm and the great curve of desert. In the near distance, Paul saw scattered shadows telling where the line of rocks ended, the basement complex sinking beneath the dunes. Beyond stretched moonlit fingernail shadows—dunes diminishing one into another.

And above the horizon climbed the flat immensity of the storm like a wall against the stars.

Something jarred the 'thopter.

"Shellburst!" Jessica gasped. "They're using some kind of projectile weapon."

She saw a sudden animal grin on Paul's face. "They seem to be avoiding their lasguns," he said.

"But we've no shields!"

"Do they know that?"

Again the 'thopter shuddered.

Paul twisted to peer back. "Only one of them appears to be fast enough to keep up with us."

He returned his attention to their course, watching the storm wall grow high in front of them. It loomed like a tangible solid.

"Projectile launchers, rockets, all the ancient weaponry—that's one thing we'll give the Fremen," Paul whispered.

"The storm," Jessica said. "Hadn't you better turn?"

"What about the ship behind us?"

"He's pulling up."

"Now!"

Paul stubbed the wings, banked hard left into the deceptively slow boiling of the storm wall, felt his cheeks pull in the G-force.

They appeared to glide into a slow clouding of dust that grew heavier and heavier until it blotted out the desert and the moon. The aircraft became a long, horizontal whisper of darkness lighted only by the green luminosity of the instrument panel.

Through Jessica's mind flashed all the warnings about such storms—that they cut metal like butter, etched flesh to bone and ate away the bones. She felt the buffeting of dust-blanketed wind. It twisted them as Paul fought the controls. She saw him chop the power, felt the ship buck. The metal around them hissed and trembled.

"Sand!" Jessica shouted.

She saw the negative shake of his head in the light from the panel. "Not much sand this high."

But she could feel them sinking deeper into the maelstrom.

Paul sent the wings to their full soaring length, heard them creak with the strain. He kept his eyes fixed on the instruments, gliding by instinct, fighting for altitude.

The sound of their passage diminished.

The 'thopter began rolling off to the left. Paul focused on the glowing globe within the attitude curve, fought his craft back to level flight.

Jessica had the eerie feeling that they were standing still, that all motion was external. A vague tan flowing against the windows, a rumbling hiss reminded her of the powers around them.

Winds to seven or eight hundred kilometers an hour, she thought.

Adrenaline edginess gnawed at her. *I must not fear,* she told herself, mouthing the words of the Bene Gesserit litany. *Fear is the mind-killer.*

Slowly her long years of training prevailed.

Calmness returned.

"We have the tiger by the tail," Paul whispered. "We can't go down, can't land . . . and I don't think I can lift us out of this. We'll have to ride it out."

Calmness drained out of her. Jessica felt her teeth chattering, clamped them together. Then she heard Paul's voice, low and controlled, reciting the litany:

"Fear is the mind-killer. Fear is the little-death that brings total obliteration. I will face my fear. I will permit it to pass over me and through me. And when it has gone past me I will turn to see fear's path. Where the fear has gone there will be nothing. Only I will remain."

What do you despise? By this are you truly known.

—FROM "MANUAL OF MUAD'DIB"
BY THE PRINCESS IRULAN

"They are dead, Baron," said Iakin Nefud, the guard captain. "Both the woman and the boy are certainly dead."

The Baron Vladimir Harkonnen sat up in the sleep suspensors of his private quarters. Beyond these quarters and enclosing him like a multi-shelled egg stretched the space frigate he had grounded on Arrakis. Here in his quarters, though, the ship's harsh metal was disguised with draperies, with fabric paddings and rare art objects.

"It is a certainty," the guard captain said. "They are dead."

The Baron shifted his gross body in the suspensors, focused his attention on an ebaline statue of a leaping boy in a niche across the room. Sleep faded from him. He straightened the padded suspensor beneath the fat folds of his neck, stared across the single glowglobe of his bedchamber to the doorway where Captain Nefud stood blocked by the pentashield.

"They're certainly dead, Baron," the man repeated.

The Baron noted the trace of semuta dullness in Nefud's eyes. It was obvious the man had been deep within the drug's rapture when he received this report, and had stopped only to take the antidote before rushing here.

"I have a full report," Nefud said.

Let him sweat a little, the Baron thought. *One must always keep the tools of statecraft sharp and ready. Power and fear—sharp and ready.*

"Have you seen their bodies?" the Baron rumbled.

Nefud hesitated.

"Well?"

"M'Lord . . . they were seen to dive into a sandstorm . . . winds over eight hundred kilometers. Nothing survives such a storm, m'Lord. Nothing! One of our own craft was destroyed in the pursuit."

The Baron stared at Nefud, noting the nervous twitch in the scissorsline of the man's jaw muscles, the way the chin moved as Nefud swallowed.

"You have seen the bodies?" the Baron asked.

"M'Lord—"

"For what purpose do you come here rattling your armor?" the Baron roared. "To tell me a thing is certain when it is not? Do you think I'll praise you for such stupidity, give you another promotion?"

Nefud's face went bone pale.

Look at the chicken, the Baron thought. *I am surrounded by such useless clods. If I scattered sand before this creature and told him it was grain, he'd peck at it.*

"The man Idaho led us to them, then?" the Baron asked.

"Yes, m'Lord!"

Look how he blurts out his answer, the Baron thought. He said: "They were attempting to flee to the Fremen, eh?"

"Yes, m'Lord."

"Is there more to this . . . report?"

"The Imperial Planetologist, Kynes, is involved, m'Lord. Idaho joined this Kynes under mysterious circumstances . . . I might even say *suspicious* circumstances."

"So?"

"They . . . ah, fled together to a place in the desert where it's apparent the boy and his mother were hiding. In the excitement of the chase, several of our groups were caught in a lasgun-shield explosion."

"How many did we lose?"

"I'm . . . ah, not sure yet, m'Lord."

He's lying, the Baron thought. *It must've been pretty bad.*

"The Imperial lackey, this Kynes," the Baron said. "He was playing a double game, eh?"

"I'd stake my reputation on it, m'Lord."

His reputation!

"Have the man killed," the Baron said.

"M'Lord! Kynes is the *Imperial* Planetologist, His Majesty's own serv—"

"Make it look like an accident, then!"

"M'Lord, there were Sardaukar with our forces in the subjugation of this Fremen nest. They have Kynes in custody now."

"Get him away from them. Say I wish to question him."

"If they demur?"

"They will not if you handle it correctly."

Nefud swallowed. "Yes, m'Lord."

"The man must die," the Baron rumbled. "He tried to help my enemies."

Nefud shifted from one foot to the other.

"Well?"

"M'Lord, the Sardaukar have . . . two persons in custody who might be of interest to you. They've caught the Duke's Master of Assassins."

"Hawat? Thufir Hawat?"

"I've seen the captive myself, m'Lord. 'Tis Hawat."

"I'd not've believed it possible!"

"They say he was knocked out by a stunner, m'Lord. In the desert where he couldn't use his shield. He's virtually unharmed. If we can get our hands on him, he'll provide great sport."

"This is a Mentat you speak of," the Baron growled. "One doesn't waste a Mentat. Has he spoken? What does he say of his defeat? Could he know the extent of . . . but no."

"He has spoken only enough, m'Lord, to reveal his belief that the Lady Jessica was his betrayer."

"Ah-h-h-h-h."

The Baron sank back, thinking; then: "You're sure? It's the Lady Jessica who attracts his anger?"

"He said it in my presence, m'Lord."

"Let him think she's alive, then."

"But, m'Lord—"

"Be quiet. I wish Hawat treated kindly. He must be told nothing of the late Doctor Yueh, his true betrayer. Let it be said that Doctor Yueh died defending his Duke. In a way, this may even be true. We will, instead, feed his suspicions against the Lady Jessica."

"M'Lord, I don't—"

"The way to control and direct a Mentat, Nefud, is through his information. False information—false results."

"Yes, m'Lord, but . . ."

"Is Hawat hungry? Thirsty?"

"M'Lord, Hawat's still in the hands of the Sardaukar!"

"Yes. Indeed, yes. But the Sardaukar will be as anxious to get information from Hawat as I am. I've noticed a thing about our allies, Nefud. They're not very devious . . . politically. I do believe this is a deliberate thing; the Emperor wants it that way. Yes. I do believe it. You will remind the Sardaukar commander of my renown at obtaining information from reluctant subjects."

Nefud looked unhappy. "Yes, m'Lord."

"You will tell the Sardaukar commander that I wish to question both Hawat and this Kynes at the same time, playing one off against the other. He can understand that much, I think."

"Yes, m'Lord."

"And once we have them in our hands. . . ." The Baron nodded.

"M'Lord, the Sardaukar will want an observer with you during any . . . questioning."

"I'm sure we can produce an emergency to draw off any unwanted observers, Nefud."

"I understand, m'Lord. That's when Kynes can have his accident."

"Both Kynes and Hawat will have accidents then, Nefud. But only Kynes will have a real accident. It's Hawat I want. Yes. Ah, yes."

Nefud blinked, swallowed. He appeared about to ask a question, but remained silent.

"Hawat will be given both food and drink," the Baron said. "Treated with kindness, with sympathy. In his water you will administer the residual poison developed by the late Piter de Vries. *And* you will see that the antidote becomes a regular part of Hawat's diet from this point on . . . unless I say otherwise."

"The antidote, yes." Nefud shook his head. "But—"

"Don't be dense, Nefud. The Duke almost killed me with that poison-capsule tooth. The gas he exhaled into my presence deprived me of my most valuable Mentat, Piter. I need a replacement."

"Hawat?"

"Hawat."

"But—"

"You're going to say Hawat's completely loyal to the Atreides. True, but the Atreides are dead. We will woo him. He must be convinced he's not to blame for the Duke's demise. It was all the doing of that Bene Gesserit witch. He had an inferior master, one whose reason was clouded by emotion. Mentats admire the ability to calculate without emotion, Nefud. We will woo the formidable Thufir Hawat."

"Woo him. Yes, m'Lord."

"Hawat, unfortunately, had a master whose resources were poor, one who could not elevate a Mentat to the sublime peaks of reasoning that are a Mentat's right. Hawat will see a certain element of truth in this. The Duke couldn't afford the most efficient spies to provide his Mentat with the required information." The Baron stared at Nefud. "Let us never deceive ourselves, Nefud. The truth is a powerful weapon. We know how we overwhelmed the Atreides. Hawat knows, too. We did it with wealth."

"With wealth. Yes, m'Lord."

"We will woo Hawat," the Baron said. "We will hide him from the Sardaukar. And we will hold in reserve . . . the withdrawal of the antidote for the poison. There's no way of removing the residual poison. And, Nefud, Hawat need never suspect. The antidote will not betray itself to a poison snooper. Hawat can scan his food as he pleases and detect no trace of poison."

Nefud's eyes opened wide with understanding.

"The absence of a thing," the Baron said, "this can be as deadly as the *presence*. The absence of air, eh? The absence of water? The absence of anything else we're addicted to." The Baron nodded. "You understand me, Nefud?"

Nefud swallowed. "Yes, m'Lord."

"Then get busy. Find the Sardaukar commander and set things in motion."

"At once, m'Lord." Nefud bowed, turned, and hurried away.

Hawat by my side! the Baron thought. *The Sardaukar will give him to me. If they suspect anything at all it's that I wish to destroy the Mentat. And this suspicion I'll confirm! The fools! One of the most formidable Mentats in all history, a Mentat trained to kill, and they'll toss him to me like some silly toy to be broken. I will show them what use can be made of such a toy.*

The Baron reached beneath a drapery beside his suspensor bed, pressed a button to summon his older nephew, Rabban. He sat back, smiling.

And all the Atreides dead!

The stupid guard captain had been right, of course. Certainly, nothing survived in the path of a sandblast storm on Arrakis. Not an ornithopter . . . or its occupants. The woman and the boy were dead. The bribes in the right places, the *unthinkable* expenditure to bring overwhelming military force down onto one planet . . . all the sly reports tailored for the Emperor's ears alone, all the careful scheming were here at last coming to full fruition.

Power and fear—fear and power!

The Baron could see the path ahead of him. One day, a Harkonnen would be Emperor. Not himself, and no spawn of his loins. But a Harkonnen. Not this Rabban he'd summoned, of course. But Rabban's younger brother, young Feyd-Rautha. There was a sharpness to the boy that the Baron enjoyed . . . a ferocity.

A lovely boy, the Baron thought. *A year or two more—say, by the time he's seventeen, I'll know for certain whether he's the tool that House Harkonnen requires to gain the throne.*

"M'Lord Baron."

The man who stood outside the doorfield of the Baron's bedchamber was low built, gross of face and body, with the Harkonnen paternal line's narrow-set eyes and bulge of shoulders. There was yet some rigidity in his fat, but it was obvious to the eye that he'd come one day to the portable suspensors for carrying his excess weight.

A muscle-minded tank-brain, the Baron thought. *No Mentat, my nephew . . . not a Piter de Vries, but perhaps something more precisely devised for the task at hand. If I give him freedom to do it, he'll grind over everything in his path. Oh, how he'll be hated here on Arrakis!*

"My dear Rabban," the Baron said. He released the doorfield, but pointedly kept his body shield at full strength, knowing that the shimmer of it would be visible above the bedside glowglobe.

"You summoned me," Rabban said. He stepped into the room, flicked a glance past the air disturbance of the body shield, searched for a suspensor chair, found none.

"Stand closer where I can see you easily," the Baron said.

Rabban advanced another step, thinking that the damnable old man had deliberately removed all chairs, forcing a visitor to stand.

"The Atreides are dead," the Baron said. "The last of them. That's why I summoned you here to Arrakis. This planet is again yours."

Rabban blinked. "But I thought you were going to advance Piter de Vries to the—"

"Piter, too, is dead."

"Piter?"

"Piter."

The Baron reactivated the doorfield, blanked it against all energy penetration.

"You finally tired of him, eh?" Rabban asked.

His voice fell flat and lifeless in the energy-blanketed room.

"I will say a thing to you just this once," the Baron rumbled. "You insinuate that I obliterated Piter as one obliterates a trifle." He snapped fat fingers. "Just like that, eh? I am not so stupid, Nephew. I will take it unkindly if ever again you suggest by word or action that I am so stupid."

Fear showed in the squinting of Rabban's eyes. He knew within certain limits how far the old Baron would go against family. Seldom to the point of death unless there were outrageous profit or provocation in it. But family punishments could be painful.

"Forgive me, m'Lord Baron," Rabban said. He lowered his eyes as much to hide his own anger as to show subservience.

"You do not fool me, Rabban," the Baron said.

Rabban kept his eyes lowered, swallowed.

"I make a point," the Baron said. "Never obliterate a man unthinkingly, the way an entire fief might do it through some *due process of law.* Always do it for an overriding purpose—and *know your purpose!*"

Anger spoke in Rabban: "But you obliterated the traitor, Yueh! I saw his body being carried out as I arrived last night."

Rabban stared at his uncle, suddenly frightened by the sound of those words.

But the Baron smiled. "I'm very careful about dangerous weapons," he said. "Doctor Yueh was a traitor. He gave me the Duke." Strength poured into the Baron's voice. "*I* suborned a doctor of the Suk School! The *Inner* School! You hear, boy? But that's a wild sort of weapon to leave lying about. I didn't obliterate him casually."

"Does the Emperor know you suborned a Suk doctor?"

This was a penetrating question, the Baron thought. *Have I misjudged this nephew?*

"The Emperor doesn't know it yet," the Baron said. "But his Sardaukar are sure to report it to him. Before that happens, though, I'll have my own report in his hands through CHOAM Company channels. I will explain that I *luckily* discovered a doctor who pretended to the conditioning. A false doctor, you understand? Since everyone *knows* you cannot counter the conditioning of a Suk School, this will be accepted."

"Ah-h-h, I see," Rabban murmured.

And the Baron thought: *Indeed, I hope you do see. I hope you do see how vital it is that this remain secret.* The Baron suddenly wondered at himself. *Why did I do that? Why did I boast to this fool nephew of mine—the nephew I must use and discard?* The Baron felt anger at himself. He felt betrayed.

"It must be kept secret," Rabban said. "I understand."

The Baron sighed. "I give you different instructions about Arrakis this time, Nephew. When last you ruled this place, I held you in strong rein. This time, I have only one requirement."

"M'Lord?"

"Income."

"Income?"

"Have you any idea, Rabban, how much we spent to bring such military force to bear on the Atreides? Do you have even the first inkling of how much the Guild charges for military transport?"

"Expensive, eh?"

"Expensive!"

The Baron shot a fat arm toward Rabban. "If you squeeze Arrakis for every cent it can give us for sixty years, you'll just barely repay us!"

Rabban opened his mouth, closed it without speaking.

"Expensive," the Baron sneered. "The damnable Guild monopoly on space would've ruined us if I hadn't planned for this expense long ago. You should know, Rabban, that *we* bore the entire brunt of it. We even paid for transport of the Sardaukar."

And not for the first time, the Baron wondered if there ever would come a day when the Guild might be circumvented. They were insidious—bleeding off just enough to keep the host from objecting until they had you in their fist where they could force you to pay and pay and pay.

Always, the exorbitant demands rode upon military ventures. "Hazard rates," the oily Guild agents explained. And for every agent you managed to insert as a watchdog in the Guild Bank structure, they put two agents into your system.

Insufferable!

"Income then," Rabban said.

The Baron lowered his arm, made a fist. "You must squeeze."

"And I may do anything I wish as long as I squeeze?"

"Anything."

"The cannons you brought," Rabban said. "Could I—"

"I'm removing them," the Baron said.

"But you—"

"You won't need such toys. They were a special innovation and are now useless. We need the metal. They cannot go against a shield, Rabban. They were merely the unexpected. It was predictable that the Duke's men would retreat into cliff caves on this abominable planet. Our cannon merely sealed them in."

"The Fremen don't use shields."

"You may keep some lasguns if you wish."

"Yes, m'Lord. And I have a free hand."

"As long as you squeeze."

Rabban's smile was gloating. "I understand perfectly, m'Lord."

"You understand nothing perfectly," the Baron growled. "Let us have that clear at the outset. What you *do* understand is how to carry out my orders. Has it occurred to you, Nephew, that there are at least five million persons on this planet?"

"Does m'Lord forget that I was his regent-siridar here before? And if m'Lord will forgive me, his estimate may be low. It's difficult to count a population scattered among sinks and pans the way they are here. And when you consider the Fremen of—"

"The Fremen aren't worth considering!"

"Forgive me, m'Lord, but the Sardaukar believe otherwise."

The Baron hesitated, staring at his nephew. "You know something?"

"M'Lord had retired when I arrived last night. I . . . ah, took the liberty of contacting some of my lieutenants from . . . ah, before. They've been acting as guides to the Sardaukar. They report that a Fremen band ambushed a Sardaukar force somewhere southeast of here and wiped it out."

"Wiped out a Sardaukar force?"

"Yes, m'Lord."

"Impossible!"

Rabban shrugged.

"Fremen defeating Sardaukar," the Baron sneered.

"I repeat only what was reported to me," Rabban said. "It is said this Fremen force already had captured the Duke's redoubtable Thufir Hawat."

"Ah-h-h-h-h-h."

The Baron nodded, smiling.

"I believe the report," Rabban said. "You've no idea what a problem the Fremen were."

"Perhaps, but these weren't Fremen your lieutenants saw. They must've been Atreides men trained by Hawat and disguised as Fremen. It's the only possible answer."

Again, Rabban shrugged. "Well, the Sardaukar think they were Fremen. The Sardaukar already have launched a program to wipe out all Fremen."

"Good!"

"But—"

"It'll keep the Sardaukar occupied. And we'll soon have Hawat. I know it! I can feel it! Ah, this has been a day! The Sardaukar off hunting a few useless desert bands while we get the real prize!"

"M'Lord. . . ." Rabban hesitated, frowning. "I've always felt that we underestimated the Fremen, both in numbers and in—"

"Ignore them, boy! They're rabble. It's the populous towns, cities, and villages that concern us. A great many people there, eh?"

"A great many, m'Lord."

"They worry me, Rabban."

"Worry you?"

"Oh . . . ninety per cent of them are of no concern. But there are always a few . . . Houses Minor and so on, people of ambition who might try a dangerous thing. If one of them should get off Arrakis with an unpleasant story about what happened here, I'd be most displeased. Have you any idea how displeased I'd be?"

Rabban swallowed.

"You must take immediate measures to hold a hostage from each House Minor," the Baron said. "As far as anyone off Arrakis must learn, this was straightforward House-to-House battle. The Sardaukar had no part in it, you understand? The Duke was offered the usual quarter and exile, but he died in an unfortunate accident before he could accept. He was about to accept, though. That is the story. And any rumor that there were Sardaukar here, it must be laughed at."

"As the Emperor wishes it," Rabban said.

"As the Emperor wishes it."

"What about the smugglers?"

"No one believes smugglers, Rabban. They are tolerated, but not believed. At any rate, you'll be spreading some bribes in that quarter . . . and taking other measures which I'm sure you can think of."

"Yes, m'Lord."

"Two things from Arrakis, then, Rabban: income and a merciless fist. You must show no mercy here. Think of these clods as what they are—slaves envious of their masters and awaiting only the opportunity to rebel. Not the slightest vestige of pity or mercy must you show them."

"Can one exterminate an entire planet?" Rabban asked.

"Exterminate?" Surprise showed in the swift turning of the Baron's head. "Who said anything about exterminating?"

"Well, I presumed you were going to bring in new stock and—"

"I said *squeeze*, Nephew, not exterminate. Don't waste the population, merely drive them into utter submission. You must be the carnivore, my boy." He smiled, a baby's expression in the dimple-fat face. "A carnivore never stops. Show no mercy. Never stop. Mercy is a chimera. It can be defeated by the stomach rumbling its hunger, by the throat crying its thirst. You must be always hungry and thirsty." The Baron caressed his bulges beneath the suspensors. "Like me."

"I see, m'Lord."

Rabban swung his gaze left and right.

"It's all clear then, Nephew?"

"Except for one thing, Uncle: the planetologist, Kynes."

"Ah, yes, Kynes."

"He's the Emperor's man, m'Lord. He can come and go as he pleases. And he's very close to the Fremen . . . married one."

"Kynes will be dead by tomorrow's nightfall."

"That's dangerous work, Uncle, killing an Imperial servant."

"How do you think I've come this far this quickly?" the Baron demanded. His voice was low, charged with unspeakable adjectives. "Besides, you need never have feared Kynes would leave Arrakis. You're forgetting that he's addicted to the spice."

"Of course!"

"Those who know will do nothing to endanger their supply," the Baron said. "Kynes certainly must know."

"I forgot," Rabban said.

They stared at each other in silence.

Presently, the Baron said: "Incidentally, you will make my own supply one of your first concerns. I've quite a stockpile of private stuff, but that suicide raid by the Duke's men got most of what we'd stored for sale."

Rabban nodded. "Yes, m'Lord."

The Baron brightened. "Now, tomorrow morning, you will assemble what remains of organization here and you'll say to them: 'Our Sublime Padishah Emperor has charged me to take possession of this planet and end all dispute.'"

"I understand, m'Lord."

"This time, I'm sure you do. We will discuss it in more detail tomorrow. Now, leave me to finish my sleep."

The Baron deactivated his doorfield, watched his nephew out of sight.

A tank-brain, the Baron thought. *Muscle-minded tank-brain. They will be bloody pulp here when he's through with them. Then, when I send in Feyd-Rautha to take the load off them, they'll cheer their rescuer. Beloved Feyd-Rautha, Benign Feyd-Rautha, the compassionate one who saves them from a beast. Feyd-Rautha, a man to follow and die for. The boy will know by that time how to oppress with impunity. I'm sure he's the one we need. He'll learn. And such a lovely body. Really a lovely boy.*

At the age of fifteen, he had already learned silence.

—FROM "A CHILD'S HISTORY OF MUAD'DIB"
BY THE PRINCESS IRULAN

As Paul fought the 'thopter's controls, he grew aware that he was sorting out the interwoven storm forces, his more than Mentat awareness computing on the basis of fractional minutiae. He felt dust fronts, billowings, mixings of turbulence, an occasional vortex.

The cabin interior was an angry box lighted by the green radiance of instrument dials. The tan flow of dust outside appeared featureless, but his inner sense began to *see* through the curtain.

I must find the right vortex, he thought.

For a long time now he had sensed the storm's power diminishing, but still it shook them. He waited out another turbulence.

The vortex began as an abrupt billowing that rattled the entire ship. Paul defied all fear to bank the 'thopter left.

Jessica saw the maneuver on the attitude globe.

"Paul!" she screamed.

The vortex turned them, twisting, tipping. It lifted the 'thopter like a chip on a geyser, spewed them up and out—a winged speck within a core of winding dust lighted by the second moon.

Paul looked down, saw the dust-defined pillar of hot wind that had disgorged them, saw the dying storm trailing away like a dry river into the desert—moon-gray motion growing smaller and smaller below as they rode the updraft.

"We're out of it," Jessica whispered.

Paul turned their craft away from the dust in swooping rhythm while he scanned the night sky.

"We've given them the slip," he said.

Jessica felt her heart pounding. She forced herself to calmness, looked at the diminishing storm. Her time sense said they had ridden within that compounding of elemental forces almost four hours, but part of her mind computed the passage as a lifetime. She felt reborn.

It was like the litany, she thought. *We faced it and did not resist. The storm passed through us and around us. It's gone, but we remain.*

"I don't like the sound of our wing motion," Paul said. "We suffered some damage in there."

He felt the grating, injured flight through his hands on the controls. They were out of the storm, but still not out into the full view of his prescient vision. Yet, they had escaped, and Paul sensed himself trembling on the verge of a revelation.

He shivered.

The sensation was magnetic and terrifying, and he found himself caught on the question of what caused this trembling awareness. Part of it, he felt, was the spice-saturated diet of Arrakis. But he thought part of it could be the litany, as though the words had a power of their own.

"I shall not fear . . ."

Cause and effect: he was alive despite malignant forces, and he felt himself poised on a brink of self-awareness that could not have been without the litany's magic.

Words from the Orange Catholic Bible rang through his memory: *"What senses do we lack that we cannot see or hear another world all around us?"*

"There's rock all around," Jessica said.

Paul focused on the 'thopter's launching, shook his head to clear it. He looked where his mother pointed, saw uplifting rock shapes black on the sand ahead and to the right. He felt wind around his ankles, a stirring of dust in the cabin. There was a hole somewhere, more of the storm's doing.

"Better set us down on sand," Jessica said. "The wings might not take full brake."

He nodded toward a place ahead where sandblasted ridges lifted into moonlight above the dunes. "I'll set us down near those rocks. Check your safety harness."

She obeyed, thinking: *We've water and stillsuits. If we can find food, we can survive a long time on this desert. Fremen live here. What they can do we can do.*

"Run for those rocks the instant we're stopped," Paul said. "I'll take the pack."

"Run for. . . ." She fell silent, nodded. "Worms."

"Our friends, the worms," he corrected her. "They'll get this 'thopter. There'll be no evidence of where we landed."

How direct his thinking, she thought.

They glided lower . . . lower . . .

There came a rushing sense of motion to their passage—blurred shadows of dunes, rocks lifting like islands. The 'thopter touched a dune top with a soft lurch, skipped a sand valley, touched another dune.

He's killing our speed against the sand, Jessica thought, and permitted herself to admire his competence.

"Brace yourself!" Paul warned.

He pulled back on the wing brakes, gently at first, then harder and harder. He felt them cup the air, their aspect ratio dropping faster and faster. Wind screamed through the lapped coverts and primaries of the wings' leaves.

Abruptly, with only the faintest lurch of warning, the left wing, weakened by the storm, twisted upward and in, slamming across the side of the 'thopter. The craft skidded across a dune top, twisting to the left. It tumbled down the opposite face to bury its nose in the next dune amid a cascade of sand. They lay stopped on the broken wing side, the right wing pointing toward the stars.

Paul jerked off his safety harness, hurled himself upward across his mother, wrenching the door open. Sand poured around them into the cabin, bringing a dry smell of burned flint. He grabbed the pack from the rear, saw that his mother was free of her harness. She stepped up onto the side of the right-hand seat and out onto the 'thopter's metal skin. Paul followed, dragging the pack by its straps.

"Run!" he ordered.

He pointed up the dune face and beyond it where they could see a rock tower undercut by sandblast winds.

Jessica leaped off the 'thopter and ran, scrambling and sliding up the dune. She heard Paul's panting progress behind. They came out onto a sand ridge that curved away toward the rocks.

"Follow the ridge," Paul ordered. "It'll be faster."

They slogged toward the rocks, sand gripping their feet.

A new sound began to impress itself on them: a muted whisper, a hissing, an abrasive slithering.

"Worm," Paul said.

It grew louder.

"Faster!" Paul gasped.

The first rock shingle, like a beach slanting from the sand, lay no more than ten meters ahead when they heard metal crunch and shatter behind them.

Paul shifted his pack to his right arm, holding it by the straps. It slapped his side as he ran. He took his mother's arm with his other hand. They scrambled onto the lifting rock, up a pebble-littered surface through a twisted, wind-carved channel. Breath came dry and gasping in their throats.

"I can't run any farther," Jessica panted.

Paul stopped, pressed her into a gut of rock, turned and looked down onto the desert. A mound-in-motion ran parallel to their rock island—moonlit ripples, sand waves, a cresting burrow almost level with Paul's eyes at a distance of about a kilometer. The flattened dunes of its track curved once—a short loop crossing the patch of desert where they had abandoned their wrecked ornithopter.

Where the worm had been there was no sign of the aircraft.

The burrow mound moved outward into the desert, coursed back across its own path, questing.

"It's bigger than a Guild spaceship," Paul whispered. "I was told worms grew large in the deep desert, but I didn't realize . . . how big."

"Nor I," Jessica breathed.

Again, the thing turned out away from the rocks, sped now with a curbing track toward the horizon. They listened until the sound of its passage was lost in gentle sand stirrings around them.

Paul took a deep breath, looked up at the moon-frosted escarpment, and quoted from the Kitab al-Ibar: "Travel by night and rest in black shade through the day." He looked at his mother. "We still have a few hours of night. Can you go on?"

"In a moment."

Paul stepped out onto the rock shingle, shouldered the pack and adjusted its straps. He stood a moment with a paracompass in his hands.

"Whenever you're ready," he said.

She pushed herself away from the rock, feeling her strength return. "Which direction?"

"Where this ridge leads." He pointed.

"Deep into the desert," she said.

"The Fremen desert," Paul whispered.

And he paused, shaken by the remembered high relief imagery of a prescient vision he had experienced on Caladan. He had seen this desert. But the *set* of the vision had been subtly different, like an optical image that had disappeared into his consciousness, been absorbed by memory, and now failed of perfect registry when projected onto the real scene. The vision appeared to have shifted and approached him from a different angle while he remained motionless.

Idaho was with us in the vision, he remembered. *But now Idaho is dead.*

"Do you see a way to go?" Jessica asked, mistaking his hesitation.

"No," he said. "But we'll go anyway."

He settled his shoulders more firmly in the pack, struck out up a sand-carved channel in the rock. The channel opened onto a moonlit floor of rock with benched ledges climbing away to the south.

Paul headed for the first ledge, clambered onto it. Jessica followed.

She noted presently how their passage became a matter of the immediate and particular—the sand pockets between rocks where their
steps were slowed, the wind-carved ridge that cut their hands, the obstruction that forced a choice: Go over or go around? The terrain
enforced its own rhythms. They spoke only when necessary and then
with the hoarse voices of their exertion.

"Careful here—this ledge is slippery with sand."

"Watch you don't hit your head against this overhang."

"Stay below this ridge; the moon's at our backs and it'd show our
movement to anyone out there."

Paul stopped in a bight of rock, leaned the pack against a narrow
ledge.

Jessica leaned beside him, thankful for the moment of rest. She
heard Paul pulling at his stillsuit tube, sipped her own reclaimed water.
It tasted brackish, and she remembered the waters of Caladan—a tall
fountain enclosing a curve of sky, such a richness of moisture that it
hadn't been noticed for itself . . . only for its shape, or its reflection, or
its sound as she stopped beside it.

To stop, she thought. *To rest . . . truly rest.*

It occurred to her that mercy was the ability to stop, if only for a
moment. There was no mercy where there could be no stopping.

Paul pushed away from the rock ledge, turned, and climbed over a
sloping surface. Jessica followed with a sigh.

They slid down onto a wide shelf that led around a sheer rock face.
Again, they fell into the disjointed rhythm of movement across this
broken land.

Jessica felt that the night was dominated by degrees of smallness in
substances beneath their feet and hands—boulders or pea gravel or
flaked rock or pea sand or sand itself or grit or dust or gossamer powder.

The powder clogged nose filters and had to be blown out. Pea sand
and pea gravel rolled on a hard surface and could spill the unwary. Rock
flakes cut.

And the omnipresent sand patches dragged against their feet.

Paul stopped abruptly on a rock shelf, steadied his mother as she stumbled into him.

He was pointing left and she looked along his arm to see that they stood atop a cliff with the desert stretched out like a static ocean some two hundred meters below. It lay there full of moon-silvered waves— shadows of angles that lapsed into curves and, in the distance, lifted to the misted gray blur of another escarpment.

"Open desert," she said.

"A wide place to cross," Paul said, and his voice was muffled by the filter trap across his face.

Jessica glanced left and right—nothing but sand below.

Paul stared straight ahead across the open dunes, watching the movement of shadows in the moon's passage. "About three or four kilometers across," he said.

"Worms," she said.

"Sure to be."

She focused on her weariness, the muscle ache that dulled her senses. "Shall we rest and eat?"

Paul slipped out of the pack, sat down and leaned against it. Jessica supported herself by a hand on his shoulder as she sank to the rock beside him. She felt Paul turn as she settled herself, heard him scrabbling in the pack.

"Here," he said.

His hand felt dry against hers as he pressed two energy capsules into her palm.

She swallowed them with a grudging spit of water from her stillsuit tube.

"Drink all your water," Paul said. "Axiom: the best place to conserve your water is in your body. It keeps your energy up. You're stronger. Trust your stillsuit."

She obeyed, drained her catchpockets, feeling energy return. She thought then how peaceful it was here in this moment of their tiredness, and she recalled once hearing the minstrel-warrior Gurney Halleck say, "Better a dry morsel and quietness therewith than a house full of sacrifice and strife."

Jessica repeated the words to Paul.

"That was Gurney," he said.

She caught the tone of his voice, the way he spoke as of someone dead, thought: *And well poor Gurney might be dead.* The Atreides forces were either dead or captive or lost like themselves in this waterless void.

"Gurney always had the right quotation," Paul said. "I can hear him now: 'And I will make the rivers dry, and sell the land into the hand of the wicked: and I will make the land waste, and all that is therein, by the hand of strangers.'"

Jessica closed her eyes, found herself moved close to tears by the pathos in her son's voice.

Presently, Paul said: "How do you . . . feel?"

She recognized that his question was directed at her pregnancy, said: "Your sister won't be born for many months yet. I still feel . . . physically adequate."

And she thought: *How stiffly formal I speak to my own son!* Then, because it was the Bene Gesserit way to seek within for the answer to such an oddity, she searched and found the source of her formality: *I'm afraid of my son; I fear his strangeness; I fear what he may see ahead of us, what he may tell me.*

Paul pulled his hood down over his eyes, listened to the bug-hustling sounds of the night. His lungs were charged with his own silence. His nose itched. He rubbed it, removed the filter and grew conscious of the rich smell of cinnamon.

"There's melange spice nearby," he said.

An eider wind feathered Paul's cheeks, ruffled the folds of his burnoose. But this wind carried no threat of storm; already he could sense the difference.

"Dawn soon," he said.

Jessica nodded.

"There's a way to get safely across that open sand," Paul said. "The Fremen do it."

"The worms?"

"If we were to plant a thumper from our Fremkit back in the rocks here," Paul said. "It'd keep a worm occupied for a time."

She glanced at the stretch of moonlighted desert between them and the other escarpment. "Four kilometers' worth of time?"

"Perhaps. And if we crossed there making only *natural* sounds, the kind that don't attract the worms. . . ."

Paul studied the open desert, questing in his prescient memory, probing the mysterious allusions to thumpers and maker hooks in the Fremkit manual that had come with their escape pack. He found it odd that all he sensed was pervasive terror at thought of the worms. He knew as though it lay just at the edge of his awareness that the worms were to be respected and not feared . . . if . . . if. . . .

He shook his head.

"It'd have to be sounds without rhythm," Jessica said.

"What? Oh. Yes. If we broke our steps . . . the sand itself must shift down at times. Worms can't investigate every little sound. We should be fully rested before we try it, though."

He looked across at that other rock wall, seeing the passage of time in the vertical moonshadows there. "It'll be dawn within the hour."

"Where'll we spend the day?" she asked.

Paul turned left, pointed. "The cliff curves back north over there. You can see by the way it's wind-cut that's the windward face. There'll be crevasses there, deep ones."

"Had we better get started?" she asked.

He stood, helped her to her feet. "Are you rested enough for a climb down? I want to get as close as possible to the desert floor before we camp."

"Enough." She nodded for him to lead the way.

He hesitated, then lifted the pack, settled it onto his shoulders and turned along the cliff.

If only we had suspensors, Jessica thought. *It'd be such a simple matter to jump down there. But perhaps suspensors are another thing to avoid in the open desert. Maybe they attract the worms the way a shield does.*

They came to a series of shelves dropping down and, beyond them, saw a fissure with its ledge outlined by moonshadow leading along the vestibule.

Paul led the way down, moving cautiously but hurrying because it was obvious the moonlight could not last much longer. They wound down into a world of deeper and deeper shadows. Hints of rock shape climbed to the stars around them. The fissure narrowed to some ten meters' width at the brink of a dim gray sandslope that slanted downward into darkness.

"Can we go down?" Jessica whispered.

"I think so."

He tested the surface with one foot.

"We can slide down," he said. "I'll go first. Wait until you hear me stop."

"Careful," she said.

He stepped onto the slope and slid and slipped down its soft surface onto an almost level floor of packed sand. The place was deep within the rock walls.

There came the sound of sand sliding behind him. He tried to see up the slope in the darkness, was almost knocked over by the cascade. It trailed away to silence.

"Mother?" he said.

There was no answer.

"Mother?"

He dropped the pack, hurled himself up the slope, scrambling, digging, throwing sand like a wild man. "Mother!" he gasped. "Mother, where are you?"

Another cascade of sand swept down on him, burying him to the hips. He wrenched himself out of it.

She's been caught in the sandslide, he thought. *Buried in it. I must be calm and work this out carefully. She won't smother immediately. She'll*

*compose herself in bindu suspension to reduce her oxygen needs. She
knows I'll dig for her.*

In the Bene Gesserit Way she had taught him, Paul stilled the savage
beating of his heart, set his mind as a blank slate upon which the past
few moments could write themselves. Every partial shift and twist of
the slide replayed itself in his memory, moving with an interior stateliness that contrasted with the fractional second of real time required for
the total recall.

Presently, Paul moved slantwise up the slope, probing cautiously
until he found the wall of the fissure, an outcurve of rock there. He
began to dig, moving the sand with care not to dislodge another slide.
A piece of fabric came under his hands. He followed it, found an arm.
Gently, he traced the arm, exposed her face.

"Do you hear me?" he whispered.

No answer.

He dug faster, freed her shoulders. She was limp beneath his hands,
but he detected a slow heartbeat.

Bindu suspension, he told himself.

He cleared the sand away to her waist, draped her arms over his
shoulders and pulled downslope, slowly at first, then dragging her as
fast as he could, feeling the sand give way above. Faster and faster he
pulled her, gasping with the effort, fighting to keep his balance. He was
out on the hard-packed floor of the fissure then, swinging her to his
shoulder and breaking into a staggering run as the entire sandslope
came down with a loud hiss that echoed and was magnified within the
rock walls.

He stopped at the end of the fissure where it looked out on the desert's marching dunes some thirty meters below. Gently, he lowered her
to the sand, uttered the word to bring her out of the catalepsis.

She awakened slowly, taking deeper and deeper breaths.

"I knew you'd find me," she whispered.

He looked back up the fissure. "It might have been kinder if I
hadn't."

"Paul!"

"I lost the pack," he said. "It's buried under a hundred tons of sand . . . at least."

"Everything?"

"The spare water, the stilltent—everything that counts." He touched a pocket. "I still have the paracompass." He fumbled at the waist sash. "Knife and binoculars. We can get a good look around the place where we'll die."

In that instant, the sun lifted above the horizon somewhere to the left beyond the end of the fissure. Colors blinked in the sand out on the open desert. A chorus of birds held forth their songs from hidden places among the rocks.

But Jessica had eyes only for the despair in Paul's face. She edged her voice with scorn, said: "Is this the way you were taught?"

"Don't you understand?" he asked. "Everything we need to survive in this place is under that sand."

"You found me," she said, and now her voice was soft, reasonable.

Paul squatted back on his heels.

Presently, he looked up the fissure at the new slope, studying it, marking the looseness of the sand.

"If we could immobilize a small area of that slope and the upper face of a hole dug into the sand, we might be able to put down a shaft to the pack. Water might do it, but we don't have enough water for. . . ." He broke off, then: "Foam."

Jessica held herself to stillness lest she disturb the hyperfunctioning of his mind.

Paul looked out at the open dunes, searching with his nostrils as well as his eyes, finding the direction and then centering his attention on a darkened patch of sand below them.

"Spice," he said. "Its essence—highly alkaline. And I have the paracompass. Its power pack is acid-base."

Jessica sat up straight against the rock.

Paul ignored her, leaped to his feet, and was off down the wind-compacted surface that spilled from the end of the fissure to the desert's floor.

She watched the way he walked, breaking his stride—step . . . pause, step-step . . . slide . . . pause . . .

There was no rhythm to it that might tell a marauding worm something not of the desert moved here.

Paul reached the spice patch, shoveled a mound of it into a fold of his robe, returned to the fissure. He spilled the spice onto the sand in front of Jessica, squatted and began dismantling the paracompass, using the point of his knife. The compass face came off. He removed his sash, spread the compass parts on it, lifted out the power pack. The dial mechanism came out next, leaving an empty dished compartment in the instrument.

"You'll need water," Jessica said.

Paul took the catchtube from his neck, sucked up a mouthful, expelled it into the dished compartment.

If this fails, that's water wasted, Jessica thought. *But it won't matter then, anyway.*

With his knife, Paul cut open the power pack, spilled its crystals into the water. They foamed slightly, subsided.

Jessica's eyes caught motion above them. She looked up to see a line of hawks along the rim of the fissure. They perched there staring down at the open water.

Great Mother! she thought. *They can sense water even at that distance!*

Paul had the cover back on the paracompass, leaving off the reset button which gave a small hole into the liquid. Taking the reworked instrument in one hand, a handful of spice in the other, Paul went back up the fissure, studying the lay of the slope. His robe billowed gently without the sash to hold it. He waded part way up the slope, kicking off the sand rivulets, spurts of dust.

Presently, he stopped, pressed a pinch of the spice into the paracompass, shook the instrument case.

Green foam boiled out of the hole where the reset button had been. Paul aimed it at the slope, spread a low dike there, began kicking away the sand beneath it, immobilizing the opened face with more foam.

Jessica moved to a position below him, called out: "May I help?"

"Come up and dig," he said. "We've about three meters to go. It's going to be a near thing." As he spoke, the foam stopped billowing from the instrument.

"Quickly," Paul said. "No telling how long this foam will hold the sand."

Jessica scrambled up beside Paul as he sifted another pinch of spice into the hole, shook the paracompass case. Again, foam boiled from it.

As Paul directed the foam barrier, Jessica dug with her hands, hurling the sand down the slope. "How deep?" she panted.

"About three meters," he said. "And I can only approximate the position. We may have to widen this hole." He moved a step aside, slipping in loose sand. "Slant your digging backward. Don't go straight down."

Jessica obeyed.

Slowly, the hole went down, reaching a level even with the floor of the basin and still no sign of the pack.

Could I have miscalculated? Paul asked himself. *I'm the one that panicked originally and caused this mistake. Has that warped my ability?*

He looked at the paracompass. Less than two ounces of the acid infusion remained.

Jessica straightened in the hole, rubbed a foam-stained hand across her cheek. Her eyes met Paul's.

"The upper face," Paul said. "Gently, now." He added another pinch of spice to the container, sent the foam boiling around Jessica's hands as she began cutting a vertical face in the upper slant of the hole. On the second pass, her hands encountered something hard. Slowly, she worked out a length of strap with a plastic buckle.

"Don't move any more of it," Paul said and his voice was almost a whisper.

"We're out of foam."

Jessica held the strap in one hand, looked up at him.

Paul threw the empty paracompass down onto the floor of the basin, said: "Give me your other hand. Now listen carefully. I'm going to pull you to the side and downhill. Don't let go of that strap. We won't get much more spill from the top. This slope has stabilized itself. All I'm going to aim for is to keep your head free of the sand. Once that hole's filled, we can dig you out and pull up the pack."

"I understand," she said.

"Ready?"

"Ready." She tensed her fingers on the strap.

With one surge, Paul had her half out of the hole, holding her head up as the foam barrier gave way and sand spilled down. When it had subsided, Jessica remained buried to the waist, her left arm and shoulder still under the sand, her chin protected on a fold of Paul's robe. Her shoulder ached from the strain put on it.

"I still have the strap," she said.

Slowly, Paul worked his hand into the sand beside her, found the strap. "Together," he said. "Steady pressure. We mustn't break it."

More sand spilled down as they worked the pack up. When the strap cleared the surface, Paul stopped, freed his mother from the sand. Together then they pulled the pack downslope and out of its trap.

In a few minutes they stood on the floor of the fissure holding the pack between them.

Paul looked at his mother. Foam stained her face, her robe. Sand was caked to her where the foam had dried. She looked as though she had been a target for balls of wet, green sand.

"You look a mess," he said.

"You're not so pretty yourself," she said.

They started to laugh, then sobered.

"That shouldn't have happened," Paul said. "I was careless."

She shrugged, feeling caked sand fall away from her robe.

"I'll put up the tent," he said. "Better slip off that robe and shake it out." He turned away, taking the pack.

Jessica nodded, suddenly too tired to answer.

"There's anchor holes in the rock," Paul said. "Someone's tented here before."

Why not? she thought as she brushed at her robe. This was a likely place—deep in rock walls and facing another cliff some four kilometers away—far enough above the desert to avoid worms but close enough for easy access before a crossing.

She turned, seeing that Paul had the tent up, its rib-domed hemisphere blending with the rock walls of the fissure. Paul stepped past her, lifting his binoculars. He adjusted their internal pressure with a quick twist, focused the oil lenses on the other cliff, lifting golden tan in morning light across open sand.

Jessica watched as he studied that apocalyptic landscape, his eyes probing into sand rivers and canyons.

"There are growing things over there," he said.

Jessica found the spare binoculars in the pack beside the tent, moved up beside Paul.

"There," he said, holding the binoculars with one hand and pointing with the other.

She looked where he pointed.

"Saguaro," she said. "Scrawny stuff."

"There may be people nearby," Paul said.

"That could be the remains of a botanical testing station," she warned.

"This is pretty far south into the desert," he said. He lowered his binoculars, rubbed beneath his filter baffle, feeling how dry and chapped his lips were, sensing the dusty taste of thirst in his mouth. "This has the feeling of a Fremen place," he said.

"Are we certain the Fremen will be friendly?" she asked.

"Kynes promised their help."

But there's desperation in the people of this desert, she thought. *I felt some of it myself today. Desperate people might kill us for our water.*

She closed her eyes and, against this wasteland, conjured in her mind a scene from Caladan. There had been a vacation trip once on Caladan—she and the Duke Leto, before Paul's birth. They'd flown over the southern jungles, above the weed-wild shouting leaves and rice paddies of the deltas. And they had seen the ant lines in the greenery—man-gangs carrying their loads on suspensor-buoyed shoulder poles. And in the sea reaches there'd been the white petals of trimaran dhows.

All of it gone.

Jessica opened her eyes to the desert stillness, to the mounting warmth of the day. Restless heat devils were beginning to set the air aquiver out on the open sand. The other rock face across from them was like a thing seen through cheap glass.

A spill of sand spread its brief curtain across the open end of the fissure. The sand hissed down, loosed by puffs of morning breeze, by the hawks that were beginning to lift away from the clifftop. When the sand-fall was gone, she still heard it hissing. It grew louder, a sound that once heard, was never forgotten.

"Worm," Paul whispered.

It came from their right with an uncaring majesty that could not be ignored. A twisting burrow-mound of sand cut through the dunes within their field of vision. The mound lifted in front, dusting away like a bow wave in water. Then it was gone, coursing off to the left.

The sound diminished, died.

"I've seen space frigates that were smaller," Paul whispered.

She nodded, continuing to stare across the desert. Where the worm had passed there remained that tantalizing gap. It flowed bitterly endless before them, beckoning beneath its horizontal collapse of skyline.

"When we've rested," Jessica said, "we should continue with your lessons."

He suppressed a sudden anger, said: "Mother, don't you think we could do without. . . ."

"Today you panicked," she said. "You know your mind and bindu-nervature perhaps better than I do, but you've much yet to learn about your body's prana-musculature. The body does things of itself some-times, Paul, and I can teach you about this. You must learn to control every muscle, every fiber of your body. You need review of the hands. We'll start with finger muscles, palm tendons, and tip sensitivity." She turned away. "Come, into the tent, now."

He flexed the fingers of his left hand, watching her crawl through the sphincter valve, knowing that he could not deflect her from this determination . . . that he must agree.

Whatever has been done to me, I've been a party to it, he thought.

Review of the hand!

He looked at his hand. How inadequate it appeared when measured against such creatures as that worm.

We came from Caladan—a paradise world for our form of life.
There existed no need on Caladan to build a physical paradise or a paradise of the mind—we could see the actuality all
around us. And the price we paid was the price men have always paid for achieving a paradise in this life—we went soft,
we lost our edge.

—FROM "MUAD'DIB: CONVERSATIONS"
BY THE PRINCESS IRULAN

"So you're the great Gurney Halleck," the man said.

Halleck stood staring across the round cavern office at the smuggler
seated behind a metal desk. The man wore Fremen robes and had the
half-tint blue eyes that told of off-planet foods in his diet. The office
duplicated a space frigate's master control center—communications
and viewscreens along a thirty-degree arc of wall, remote arming and
firing banks adjoining, and the desk formed as a wall projection—part
of the remaining curve.

"I am Staban Tuek, son of Esmar Tuek," the smuggler said.

"Then you're the one I owe thanks for the help we've received," Halleck said.

"Ah-h-h, gratitude," the smuggler said. "Sit down."

A ship-type bucket seat emerged from the wall beside the screens
and Halleck sank onto it with a sigh, feeling his weariness. He could see
his own reflection now in a dark surface beside the smuggler and

scowled at the lines of fatigue in his lumpy face. The inkvine scar along his jaw writhed with the scowl.

Halleck turned from his reflection, stared at Tuek. He saw the family resemblance in the smuggler now—the father's heavy, overhanging eyebrows and rock planes of cheeks and nose.

"Your men tell me your father is dead, killed by the Harkonnens," Halleck said.

"By the Harkonnens or by a traitor among your people," Tuek said.

Anger overcame part of Halleck's fatigue. He straightened, said: "Can you name the traitor?"

"We are not sure."

"Thufir Hawat suspected the Lady Jessica."

"Ah-h-h, the Bene Gesserit witch . . . perhaps. But Hawat is now a Harkonnen captive."

"I heard." Halleck took a deep breath. "It appears we've a deal more killing ahead of us."

"We will do nothing to attract attention to us," Tuek said.

Halleck stiffened. "But—"

"You and those of your men we've saved are welcome to sanctuary among us," Tuek said. "You speak of gratitude. Very well; work off your debt to us. We can always use good men. We'll destroy you out of hand, though, if you make the slightest open move against the Harkonnens."

"But they killed your father, man!"

"Perhaps. And if so, I'll give you my father's answer to those who act without thinking: 'A stone is heavy and the sand is weighty; but a fool's wrath is heavier than them both.'"

"You mean to do nothing about it, then?" Halleck sneered.

"You did not hear me say that. I merely say I will protect our contract with the Guild. The Guild requires that we play a circumspect game. There are other ways of destroying a foe."

"Ah-h-h-h-h."

"Ah, indeed. If you've a mind to seek out the witch, have at it. But I warn you that you're probably too late . . . and we doubt she's the one you want, anyway."

"Hawat made few mistakes."

"He allowed himself to fall into Harkonnen hands."

"You think *he's* the traitor?"

Tuek shrugged. "This is academic. We think the witch is dead. At least the Harkonnens believe it."

"You seem to know a great deal about the Harkonnens."

"Hints and suggestions . . . rumors and hunches."

"We are seventy-four men," Halleck said. "If you seriously wish us to enlist with you, you must believe our Duke is dead."

"His body has been seen."

"And the boy, too—young Master Paul?" Halleck tried to swallow, found a lump in his throat.

"According to the last word we had, he was lost with his mother in a desert storm. Likely not even their bones will ever be found."

"So the witch is dead then . . . all dead."

Tuek nodded. "And Beast Rabban, so they say, will sit once more in the seat of power here on Dune."

"The Count Rabban of Lankiveil?"

"Yes."

It took Halleck a moment to put down the upsurge of rage that threatened to overcome him. He spoke with panting breath: "I've a score of my own against Rabban. I owe him for the lives of my family. . . ." He rubbed at the scar along his jaw. ". . . and for this. . . ."

"One does not risk everything to settle a score prematurely," Tuek said. He frowned, watching the play of muscles along Halleck's jaw, the sudden withdrawal in the man's shed-lidded eyes.

"I know . . . I know." Halleck took a deep breath.

"You and your men can work out your passage off Arrakis by serving with us. There are many places to—"

"I release my men from any bond to me; they can choose for themselves. With Rabban here—I stay."

"In your mood, I'm not sure we want you to stay."

Halleck stared at the smuggler. "You doubt my word?"

"No-o-o. . . ."

"You've saved me from the Harkonnens. I gave loyalty to the Duke Leto for no greater reason. I'll stay on Arrakis—with you . . . or with the Fremen."

"Whether a thought is spoken or not it is a real thing and it has power," Tuek said. "You might find the line between life and death among the Fremen to be too sharp and quick."

Halleck closed his eyes briefly, feeling the weariness surge up in him. "Where is the Lord who led us through the land of deserts and of pits?" he murmured.

"Move slowly and the day of your revenge will come," Tuek said. "Speed is a device of Shaitan. Cool your sorrow—we've the diversions for it; three things there are that ease the heart—water, green grass, and the beauty of woman."

Halleck opened his eyes. "I would prefer the blood of Rabban Harkonnen flowing about my feet." He stared at Tuek. "You think that day will come?"

"I have little to do with how you'll meet tomorrow, Gurney Halleck. I can only help you meet today."

"Then I'll accept that help and stay until the day you tell me to revenge your father and all the others who—"

"Listen to me, *fighting man*," Tuek said. He leaned forward over his desk, his shoulders level with his ears, eyes intent. The smuggler's face was suddenly like weathered stone. "My father's water—I'll buy that back myself, with my own blade."

Halleck stared back at Tuek. In that moment, the smuggler reminded him of Duke Leto: a leader of men, courageous, secure in his own position and his own course. He was like the Duke . . . before Arrakis.

"Do you wish my blade beside you?" Halleck asked.

Tuek sat back, relaxed, studying Halleck silently.

"Do you think of me as *fighting man?*" Halleck pressed.

"You're the only one of the Duke's lieutenants to escape," Tuek said.

"Your enemy was overwhelming, yet you rolled with him. . . . You defeated him the way we defeat Arrakis."

"Eh?"

"We live on sufferance down here, Gurney Halleck," Tuek said. "Arrakis is our enemy."

"One enemy at a time, is that it?"

"That's it."

"Is that the way the Fremen make out?"

"Perhaps."

"You said I might find life with the Fremen too tough. They live in the desert, in the open, is that why?"

"Who knows where the Fremen live? For us, the Central Plateau is a no-man's land. But I wish to talk more about—"

"I'm told that the Guild seldom routes spice lighters in over the desert," Halleck said. "But there are rumors that you can see bits of greenery here and there if you know where to look."

"Rumors!" Tuek sneered. "Do you wish to choose now between me and the Fremen? We have a measure of security, our own sietch carved out of the rock, our own hidden basins. We live the lives of civilized men. The Fremen are a few ragged bands that *we* use as spice-hunters."

"But they can kill Harkonnens."

"And do you wish to know the result? Even now they are being hunted down like animals—with lasguns, because they have no shields. They are being exterminated. Why? Because they killed Harkonnens."

"Was it Harkonnens they killed?" Halleck asked.

"What do you mean?"

"Haven't you heard that there may've been Sardaukar with the Harkonnens?"

"More rumors."

"But a pogrom—that isn't like the Harkonnens. A pogrom is wasteful."

"I believe what I see with my own eyes," Tuek said. "Make your choice, fighting man. Me or the Fremen. I will promise you sanctuary and a chance to draw the blood we both want. Be sure of that. The Fremen will offer you only the life of the hunted."

Halleck hesitated, sensing wisdom and sympathy in Tuek's words, yet troubled for no reason he could explain.

"Trust your own abilities," Tuek said. "Whose decisions brought your force through the battle? Yours. Decide."

"It must be," Halleck said. "The Duke and his son are dead?"

"The Harkonnens believe it. Where such things are concerned, I incline to trust the Harkonnens." A grim smile touched Tuek's mouth. "But it's about the only trust I give them."

"Then it must be," Halleck repeated. He held out his right hand, palm up and thumb folded flat against it in the traditional gesture. "I give you my sword."

"Accepted."

"Do you wish me to persuade my men?"

"You'd let them make their own decision?"

"They've followed me this far, but most are Caladan-born. Arrakis isn't what they thought it'd be. Here, they've lost everything except their lives. I'd prefer they decided for themselves now."

"Now is no time for you to falter," Tuek said. "They've followed you this far."

"You need them, is that it?"

"We can always use experienced fighting men . . . in these times more than ever."

"You've accepted my sword. Do you wish me to persuade them?"

"I think they'll follow you, Gurney Halleck."

"'Tis to be hoped."

"Indeed."

"I may make my own decision in this, then?"

"Your own decision."

Halleck pushed himself up from the bucket seat, feeling how much of his reserve strength even that small effort required. "For now, I'll see to their quarters and well-being," he said.

"Consult my quartermaster," Tuek said. "Drisq is his name. Tell him it's my wish that you receive every courtesy. I'll join you myself presently. I've some off-shipments of spice to see to first."

"Fortune passes everywhere," Halleck said.

"Everywhere," Tuek said. "A time of upset is a rare opportunity for our business."

Halleck nodded, heard the faint susurration and felt the air shift as a lockport swung open beside him. He turned, ducked through it and out of the office.

He found himself in the assembly hall through which he and his men had been led by Tuek's aides. It was a long, fairly narrow area chewed out of the native rock, its smooth surface betraying the use of cutteray burners for the job. The ceiling stretched away high enough to continue the natural supporting curve of the rock and to permit internal air-convection currents. Weapons racks and lockers lined the walls.

Halleck noted with a touch of pride that those of his men still able to stand were standing—no relaxation in weariness and defeat for them. Smuggler medics were moving among them tending the wounded. Litter cases were assembled in one area down to the left, each wounded man with an Atreides companion.

The Atreides training—*"We care for our own!"*—it held like a core of native rock in them, Halleck noted.

One of his lieutenants stepped forward carrying Halleck's ninestring baliset out of its case. The man snapped a salute, said: "Sir, the medics here say there's no hope for Mattai. They have no bone and organ banks here—only outpost medicine. Mattai can't last, they say, and he has a request of you."

"What is it?"

The lieutenant thrust the baliset forward. "Mattai wants a song to ease his going, sir. He says you'll know the one . . . he's asked it of you often enough." The lieutenant swallowed. "It's the one called 'My Woman,' sir. If you—"

"I know." Halleck took the baliset, flicked the multipick out of its catch on the fingerboard. He drew a soft chord from the instrument, found that someone had already tuned it. There was a burning in his eyes, but he drove that out of his thoughts as he strolled forward, strumming the tune, forcing himself to smile casually.

Several of his men and a smuggler medic were bent over one of the litters. One of the men began singing softly as Halleck approached, catching the counter-beat with the ease of long familiarity:

> "My woman stands at her window,
> Curved lines 'gainst square glass.
> Uprais'd arms . . . bent . . . downfolded.
> 'Gainst sunset red and golded—
> Come to me . . .
> Come to me, warm arms of my lass.
> For me . . .
> For me, the warm arms of my lass."

The singer stopped, reached out a bandaged arm and closed the eyelids of the man on the litter.

Halleck drew a final soft chord from the baliset, thinking: *Now we are seventy-three.*

Family life of the Royal Creche is difficult for many people to understand, but I shall try to give you a capsule view of it. My father had only one real friend, I think. That was Count Hasimir Fenring, the genetic-eunuch and one of the deadliest fighters in the Imperium. The Count, a dapper and ugly little man, brought a new slave-concubine to my father one day and I was dispatched by my mother to spy on the proceedings. All of us spied on my father as a matter of self-protection. One of the slave-concubines permitted my father under the Bene Gesserit-Guild agreement could not, of course, bear a Royal Successor, but the intrigues were constant and oppressive in their similarity. We became adept, my mother and sisters and I, at avoiding subtle instruments of death. It may seem a dreadful thing to say, but I'm not at all sure my father was innocent in all these attempts. A Royal Family is not like other families. Here was a new slave-concubine, then, red-haired like my father, willowy and graceful. She had a dancer's muscles, and her training obviously had included neuro-enticement. My father looked at her for a long time as she postured unclothed before him. Finally he said: "She is too beautiful. We will save her as a gift." You have no idea how much consternation this restraint created in the Royal Creche. Subtlety and self-control were, after all, the most deadly threats to us all.

—FROM "IN MY FATHER'S HOUSE"
BY THE PRINCESS IRULAN

Paul stood outside the stilltent in the late afternoon. The crevasse where he had pitched their camp lay in deep shadow. He stared out across the open sand at the distant cliff, wondering if he should waken his mother, who lay asleep in the tent.

Folds upon folds of dunes spread beyond their shelter. Away from the setting sun, the dunes exposed greased shadows so black they were like bits of night.

And the flatness.

His mind searched for something tall in that landscape. But there was no persuading tallness out of heat-addled air and that horizon—no bloom or gently shaken thing to mark the passage of a breeze . . . only dunes and that distant cliff beneath a sky of burnished silver-blue.

What if there isn't one of the abandoned testing stations across there? he wondered. *What if there are no Fremen, either, and the plants we see are only an accident?*

Within the tent, Jessica awakened, turned onto her back and peered sidelong out the transparent end at Paul. He stood with his back to her and something about his stance reminded her of his father. She sensed the well of grief rising within her and turned away.

Presently she adjusted her stillsuit, refreshed herself with water from the tent's catchpocket, and slipped out to stand and stretch the sleep from her muscles.

Paul spoke without turning: "I find myself enjoying the quiet here."

How the mind gears itself for its environment, she thought. And she recalled a Bene Gesserit axiom: *"The mind can go either direction under stress—toward positive or toward negative: on or off. Think of it as a spectrum whose extremes are unconsciousness at the negative end and hyperconsciousness at the positive end. The way the mind will lean under stress is strongly influenced by training."*

"It could be a good life here," Paul said.

She tried to see the desert through his eyes, seeking to encompass all the rigors this planet accepted as commonplace, wondering at the possible futures Paul had glimpsed. *One could be alone out here,* she thought, *without fear of someone behind you, without fear of the hunter.*

She stepped past Paul, lifted her binoculars, adjusted the oil lenses and studied the escarpment across from them. Yes, saguaro in the arroyos and other spiny growth . . . and a matting of low grasses, yellow-green in the shadows.

"I'll strike camp," Paul said.

Jessica nodded, walked to the fissure's mouth where she could get a sweep of the desert, and swung her binoculars to the left. A salt pan glared white there with a blending of dirty tan at its edges—a field of white out here where white was death. But the pan said another thing: *water*. At some time water had flowed across that glaring white. She lowered her binoculars, adjusted her burnoose, listened for a moment to the sound of Paul's movements.

The sun dipped lower. Shadows stretched across the salt pan. Lines of wild color spread over the sunset horizon. Color streamed into a toe of darkness testing the sand. Coal-colored shadows spread, and the thick collapse of night blotted the desert.

Stars!

She stared up at them, sensing Paul's movements as he came up beside her. The desert night focused upward with a feeling of lift toward the stars. The weight of the day receded. There came a brief flurry of breeze across her face.

"The first moon will be up soon," Paul said. "The pack's ready. I've planted the thumper."

We could be lost forever in this hellplace, she thought. *And no one to know.*

The night wind spread sand runnels that grated across her face, bringing the smell of cinnamon: a shower of odors in the dark.

"Smell that," Paul said.

"I can smell it even through the filter," she said. "Riches. But will it buy water?" She pointed across the basin. "There are no artificial lights across there."

"Fremen would be hidden in a sietch behind those rocks," he said.

A sill of silver pushed above the horizon to their right: the first moon. It lifted into view, the hand pattern plain on its face. Jessica studied the white-silver of sand exposed in the light.

"I planted the thumper in the deepest part of the crevasse," Paul said. "Whenever I light its candle it'll give us about thirty minutes."

"Thirty minutes?"

"Before it starts calling . . . a . . . worm."

"Oh. I'm ready to go."

He slipped away from her side and she heard his progress back up their fissure.

The night is a tunnel, she thought, *a hole into tomorrow . . . if we're to have a tomorrow.* She shook her head. *Why must I be so morbid? I was trained better than that!*

Paul returned, took up the pack, led the way down to the first spreading dune where he stopped and listened as his mother came up behind him. He heard her soft progress and the cold single-grain dribbles of sound—the desert's own code spelling out its measure of safety.

"We must walk without rhythm," Paul said and he called up memory of men walking the sand . . . both prescient memory and real memory.

"Watch how I do it," he said. "This is how Fremen walk the sand."

He stepped out onto the windward face of the dune, following the curve of it, moved with a dragging pace.

Jessica studied his progress for ten steps, followed, imitating him. She saw the sense of it: they must sound like the natural shifting of sand . . . like the wind. But muscles protested this unnatural, broken pattern: Step . . . drag . . . drag . . . step . . . step . . . wait . . . drag . . . step. . . .

Time stretched out around them. The rock face ahead seemed to grow no nearer. The one behind still towered high.

"Lump! Lump! Lump! Lump!"

It was a drumming from the cliff behind.

"The thumper," Paul hissed.

Its pounding continued and they found difficulty avoiding the rhythm of it in their stride.

"Lump . . . lump . . . lump . . . lump. . . ."

They moved in a moonlit bowl punctured by that hollowed thumping. Down and up through spilling dunes: step . . . drag . . . wait . . . step. . . . Across pea sand that rolled under their feet: drag . . . wait . . . step. . . .

And all the while their ears searched for a special hissing.

The sound, when it came, started so low that their own dragging passage masked it. But it grew . . . louder and louder . . . out of the west.

"Lump . . . lump . . . lump . . . lump. . . ." drummed the thumper.

The hissing approach spread across the night behind them. They turned their heads as they walked, saw the mound of the coursing worm.

"Keep moving," Paul whispered. "Don't look back."

A grating sound of fury exploded from the rock shadows they had left. It was a flailing avalanche of noise.

"Keep moving," Paul repeated.

He saw that they had reached an unmarked point where the two rock faces—the one ahead and the one behind—appeared equally remote.

And still behind them, that whipping, frenzied tearing of rocks dominated the night.

They moved on and on and on. . . . Muscles reached a stage of mechanical aching that seemed to stretch out indefinitely, but Paul saw that the beckoning escarpment ahead of them had climbed higher.

Jessica moved in a void of concentration, aware that the pressure of her will alone kept her walking. Dryness ached in her mouth, but the sounds behind drove away all hope of stopping for a sip from her stillsuit's catchpockets.

"Lump . . . lump. . . ."

Renewed frenzy erupted from the distant cliff, drowning out the thumper.

Silence!

"Faster," Paul whispered.

She nodded, knowing he did not see the gesture, but needing the action to tell herself that it was necessary to demand even more from muscles that already were being taxed to their limits—the unnatural movement. . . .

The rock face of safety ahead of them climbed into the stars, and Paul saw a plane of flat sand stretching out at the base. He stepped onto it, stumbled in his fatigue, righted himself with an involuntary out-thrusting of a foot.

Resonant booming shook the sand around them.

Paul lurched sideways two steps.

"Boom! Boom!"

"Drum sand!" Jessica hissed.

Paul recovered his balance. A sweeping glance took in the sand around them, the rock escarpment perhaps two hundred meters away.

Behind them, he heard a hissing—like the wind, like a riptide where there was no water.

"Run!" Jessica screamed. "Paul, run!"

They ran.

Drum sound boomed beneath their feet. Then they were out of it and into pea gravel. For a time, the running was a relief to muscles that ached from unfamiliar, rhythmless use. Here was action that could be understood. Here was rhythm. But sand and gravel dragged at their feet. And the hissing approach of the worm was storm sound that grew around them.

Jessica stumbled to her knees. All she could think of was the fatigue and the sound and the terror.

Paul dragged her up.

They ran on, hand in hand.

A thin pole jutted from the sand ahead of them. They passed it, saw another.

Jessica's mind failed to register on the poles until they were past.

There was another—wind-etched surface thrust up from a crack in rock.

Another.

Rock!

She felt it through her feet, the shock of unresisting surface, gained new strength from the firmer footing.

A deep crack stretched its vertical shadow upward into the cliff ahead of them. They sprinted for it, crowded into the narrow hole.

Behind them, the sound of the worm's passage stopped.

Jessica and Paul turned, peered out onto the desert.

Where the dunes began, perhaps fifty meters away at the foot of a rock beach, a silver-gray curve broached from the desert, sending rivers of sand and dust cascading all around. It lifted higher, resolved into a giant, questing mouth. It was a round, black hole with edges glistening in the moonlight.

The mouth snaked toward the narrow crack where Paul and Jessica huddled. Cinnamon yelled in their nostrils. Moonlight flashed from crystal teeth.

Back and forth the great mouth wove.

Paul stilled his breathing.

Jessica crouched staring.

It took intense concentration of her Bene Gesserit training to put down the primal terrors, subduing a race-memory fear that threatened to fill her mind.

Paul felt a kind of elation. In some recent instant, he had crossed a time barrier into more unknown territory. He could sense the darkness ahead, nothing revealed to his inner eye. It was as though some step he had taken had plunged him into a well . . . or into the trough of a wave where the future was invisible. The landscape had undergone a profound shifting.

Instead of frightening him, the sensation of time-darkness forced a hyper-acceleration of his other senses. He found himself registering every available aspect of the thing that lifted from the sand there seeking him. Its mouth was some eighty meters in diameter . . . crystal teeth with the curved shape of crysknives glinting around the rim . . . the bellows breath of cinnamon, subtle aldehydes . . . Acids. . . .

The worm blotted out the moonlight as it brushed the rocks above them. A shower of small stones and sand cascaded into the narrow hiding place.

Paul crowded his mother farther back.

Cinnamon!

The smell of it flooded across him.

What has the worm to do with the spice, melange? he asked himself. And he remembered Liet-Kynes betraying a veiled reference to some association between worm and spice.

"Barrrroooom!"

It was like a peal of dry thunder coming from far off to their right.

Again: "Barrrroooom!"

The worm drew back onto the sand, lay there momentarily, its crystal teeth weaving moonflashes.

"Lump! Lump! Lump! Lump!"

Another thumper! Paul thought.

Again it sounded off to their right.

A shudder passed through the worm. It drew farther away into the sand. Only a mounded upper curve remained like half a bell mouth, the curve of a tunnel rearing above the dunes.

Sand rasped.

The creature sank farther, retreating, turning. It became a mound of cresting sand that curved away through a saddle in the dunes.

Paul stepped out of the crack, watched the sand wave recede across the waste toward the new thumper summons.

Jessica followed, listening: "Lump . . . lump . . . lump . . . lump . . . lump. . . ."

Presently the sound stopped.

Paul found the tube into his stillsuit, sipped at the reclaimed water.

Jessica focused on his action, but her mind felt blank with fatigue and the aftermath of terror. "Has it gone for sure?" she whispered.

"Somebody called it," Paul said. "Fremen."

She felt herself recovering. "It was so big!"

"Not as big as the one that got our 'thopter."

"Are you sure it was Fremen?"

"They used a thumper."

"Why would they help us?"

"Maybe they weren't helping us. Maybe they were just calling a worm."

"Why?"

An answer lay poised at the edge of his awareness, but refused to come. He had a vision in his mind of something to do with the telescoping barbed sticks in their packs—the "maker hooks."

"Why would they call a worm?" Jessica asked.

A breath of fear touched his mind, and he forced himself to turn away from his mother, to look up the cliff. "We'd better find a way up there before daylight." He pointed. "Those poles we passed—there are more of them."

She looked, following the line of his hand, saw the poles— wind-scratched markers—made out the shadow of a narrow ledge that twisted into a crevasse high above them.

"They mark a way up the cliff," Paul said. He settled his shoulders into the pack, crossed to the foot of the ledge and began the climb upward.

Jessica waited a moment, resting, restoring her strength; then she followed.

Up they climbed, following the guide poles until the ledge dwindled to a narrow lip at the mouth of a dark crevasse.

Paul tipped his head to peer into the shadowed place. He could feel the precarious hold his feet had on the slender ledge, but forced himself to slow caution. He saw only darkness within the crevasse. It stretched away upward, open to the stars at the top. His ears searched, found only sounds he could expect—a tiny spill of sand, an insect *brrr*, the patter of a small running creature. He tested the darkness in the crevasse with one foot, found rock beneath a gritting surface. Slowly, he inched around the corner, signaled for his mother to follow. He grasped a loose edge of her robe, helped her around.

They looked upward at starlight framed by two rock lips. Paul saw his mother beside him as a cloudy gray movement. "If we could only risk a light," he whispered.

"We have other senses than eyes," she said.

Paul slid a foot forward, shifted his weight, and probed with the other foot, met an obstruction. He lifted his foot, found a step, pulled himself up onto it. He reached back, felt his mother's arm, tugged at her robe for her to follow.

Another step.

"It goes on up to the top, I think," he whispered.

Shallow and even steps, Jessica thought. *Man-carved beyond a doubt.*

She followed the shadowy movement of Paul's progress, feeling out the steps. Rock walls narrowed until her shoulders almost brushed them. The steps ended in a slitted defile about twenty meters long, its floor level, and this opened onto a shallow, moonlit basin.

Paul stepped out into the rim of the basin, whispered: "What a beautiful place."

Jessica could only stare in silent agreement from her position a step behind him.

In spite of weariness, the irritation of recaths and nose plugs and the confinement of the stillsuit, in spite of fear and the aching desire for rest, this basin's beauty filled her senses, forcing her to stop and admire it.

"Like a fairyland," Paul whispered.

Jessica nodded.

Spreading away in front of her stretched desert growth—bushes, cacti, tiny clumps of leaves—all trembling in the moonlight. The ring-walls were dark to her left, moon-frosted on her right.

"This must be a Fremen place," Paul said.

"There would have to be people for this many plants to survive," she agreed. She uncapped the tube to her stillsuit's catchpockets, sipped at it. Warm, faintly acrid wetness slipped down her throat. She marked how it refreshed her. The tube's cap grated against flakes of sand as she replaced it.

Movement caught Paul's attention—to his right and down on the basin floor curving out beneath them. He stared down through smoke bushes and weeds into a wedged slab sand-surface of moonlight inhabited by an *up-hop, jump, pop-hop* of tiny motion.

"Mice!" he hissed.

Pop-hop-hop! they went, into shadows and out.

Something fell soundlessly past their eyes into the mice. There came a thin screech, a flapping of wings, and a ghostly gray bird lifted away across the basin with a small, dark shadow in its talons.

We needed that reminder, Jessica thought.

Paul continued to stare across the basin. He inhaled, sensed the softly cutting contralto smell of sage climbing the night. The predatory bird—he thought of it as the way of this desert. It had brought a stillness to the basin so unuttered that the blue-milk moonlight could almost be heard flowing across sentinel saguaro and spiked paintbush. There was a low humming of light here more basic in its harmony than any other music in his universe.

"We'd better find a place to pitch the tent," he said. "Tomorrow we can try to find the Fremen who—"

"Most intruders here regret finding the Fremen!"

It was a heavy masculine voice chopping across his words, shattering the moment. The voice came from above them and to their right.

"Please do not run, intruders," the voice said as Paul made to withdraw into the defile. "If you run you'll only waste your body's water."

They want us for the water of our flesh! Jessica thought. Her muscles overrode all fatigue, flowed into maximum readiness without external betrayal. She pinpointed the location of the voice, thinking: *Such stealth! I didn't hear him.* And she realized that the owner of that voice had permitted himself only the small sounds, the natural sounds of the desert.

Another voice called from the basin's rim to their left. "Make it quick, Stil. Get their water and let's be on our way. We've little enough time before dawn."

Paul, less conditioned to emergency response than his mother, felt chagrin that he had stiffened and tried to withdraw, that he had clouded his abilities by a momentary panic. He forced himself now to obey her teachings: relax, then fall into the semblance of relaxation, then into the arrested whipsnap of muscles that can slash in any direction.

Still, he felt the edge of fear within him and knew its source. This was blind time, no future he had seen . . . and they were caught between wild Fremen whose only interest was the water carried in the flesh of two unshielded bodies.

This Fremen religious adaptation, then, is the source of what we now recognize as "The Pillars of the Universe," whose Qizara Tafwid are among us all with signs and proofs and prophecy. They bring us the Arrakeen mystical fusion whose profound beauty is typified by the stirring music built on the old forms, but stamped with the new awakening. Who has not heard and been deeply moved by "The Old Man's Hymn"?

> I drove my feet through a desert
> Whose mirage fluttered like a host.
> Voracious for glory, greedy for danger,
> I roamed the horizons of al-Kulab.
> Watching time level mountains
> In its search and its hunger for me.
> And I saw the sparrows swiftly approach,
> Bolder than the onrushing wolf.
> They spread in the tree of my youth.
> I heard the flock in my branches
> And was caught on their beaks and claws!

—FROM "ARRAKIS AWAKENING"
BY THE PRINCESS IRULAN

The man crawled across a dune top. He was a mote caught in the glare of the noon sun. He was dressed only in torn remnants of a jubba cloak, his skin bare to the heat through the tatters. The hood had been ripped from the cloak, but the man had fashioned a turban from a torn strip of cloth. Wisps of sandy hair protruded from it, matched by a sparse beard and thick brows. Beneath the blue-within-blue eyes, remains of a dark stain spread down to his cheeks. A matted depression across mustache and beard showed where a stillsuit tube had marked out its path from nose to catchpockets.

The man stopped half across the dune crest, arms stretched down the slipface. Blood had clotted on his back and on his arms and legs. Patches of yellow-gray sand clung to the wounds. Slowly, he brought his hands under him, pushed himself to his feet, stood there swaying. And even in this almost-random action there remained a trace of once-precise movement.

"I am Liet-Kynes," he said, addressing himself to the empty horizon, and his voice was a hoarse caricature of the strength it had known. "I am His Imperial Majesty's Planetologist," he whispered, "planetary ecologist for Arrakis. I am steward of this land."

He stumbled, fell sideways along the crusty surface of the windward face. His hands dug feebly into the sand.

I am steward of this sand, he thought.

He realized that he was semidelirious, that he should dig himself into the sand, find the relatively cool underlayer and cover himself with it. But he could still smell the rank, semisweet esthers of a pre-spice pocket somewhere underneath this sand. He knew the peril within this fact more certainly than any other Fremen. If he could smell the pre-spice mass, that meant the gasses deep under the sand were nearing explosive pressure. He had to get away from here.

His hands made weak scrabbling motions along the dune face.

A thought spread across his mind—clear, distinct: *The real wealth of a planet is in its landscape, how we take part in that basic source of civilization—agriculture.*

And he thought how strange it was that the mind, long fixed on a single track, could not get off that track. The Harkonnen troopers had left him here without water or stillsuit, thinking a worm would get him if the desert didn't. They had thought it amusing to leave him alive to die by inches at the impersonal hands of his planet.

The Harkonnens always did find it difficult to kill Fremen, he thought.

We don't die easily. I should be dead now . . . I will be dead soon . . . but I can't stop being an ecologist.

"The highest function of ecology is understanding consequences."

The voice shocked him because he recognized it and knew the owner of it was dead. It was the voice of his father who had been planetologist here before him—his father long dead, killed in the cave-in at Plaster Basin.

"Got yourself into quite a fix here, Son," his father said. "You should've known the consequences of trying to help the child of that Duke."

I'm delirious, Kynes thought.

The voice seemed to come from his right. Kynes scraped his face through sand, turning to look in that direction—nothing except a curving stretch of dune dancing with heat devils in the full glare of the sun.

"The more life there is within a system, the more niches there are for life," his father said. And the voice came now from his left, from behind him.

Why does he keep moving around? Kynes asked himself. *Doesn't he want me to see him?*

"Life improves the capacity of the environment to sustain life," his father said. "Life makes needed nutrients more readily available. It binds more energy into the system through the tremendous chemical interplay from organism to organism."

Why does he keep harping on the same subject? Kynes asked himself. *I knew that before I was ten.*

Desert hawks, carrion-eaters in this land as were most wild creatures, began to circle over him. Kynes saw a shadow pass near his hand, forced his head farther around to look upward. The birds were a blurred patch on silver-blue sky—distant flecks of soot floating above him.

"We are generalists," his father said. "You can't draw neat lines around planet-wide problems. Planetology is a cut-and-fit science."

What's he trying to tell me? Kynes wondered. *Is there some consequence I failed to see?*

His cheek slumped back against the hot sand, and he smelled the burned rock odor beneath the pre-spice gasses. From some corner of logic in his mind, a thought formed: *Those are carrion-eater birds over me. Perhaps some of my Fremen will see them and come to investigate.*

"To the working planetologist, his most important tool is human beings," his father said. "You must cultivate ecological literacy among the people. That's why I've created this entirely new form of ecological notation."

He's repeating things he said to me when I was a child, Kynes thought.

He began to feel cool, but that corner of logic in his mind told him: *The sun is overhead. You have no stillsuit and you're hot; the sun is burning the moisture out of your body.*

His fingers clawed feebly at the sand.

They couldn't even leave me a stillsuit!

"The presence of moisture in the air helps prevent too-rapid evaporation from living bodies," his father said.

Why does he keep repeating the obvious? Kynes wondered.

He tried to think of moisture in the air—grass covering this dune . . . open water somewhere beneath him, a long qanat flowing with water open to the sky except in text illustrations. Open water . . . irrigation water . . . it took five thousand cubic meters of water to irrigate one hectare of land per growing season, he remembered.

"Our first goal on Arrakis," his father said, "is grassland provinces. We will start with these mutated poverty grasses. When we have moisture locked in grasslands, we'll move on to start upland forests, then a few open bodies of water—small at first—and situated along lines of prevailing winds with windtrap moisture precipitators spaced in the lines to recapture what the wind steals. We must create a true sirocco— a moist wind—but we will never get away from the necessity for windtraps."

Always lecturing me, Kynes thought. *Why doesn't he shut up? Can't he see I'm dying?*

"You will die, too," his father said, "if you don't get off the bubble that's forming right now deep underneath you. It's there and you know it. You can smell the pre-spice gasses. You know the little makers are beginning to lose some of their water into the mass."

The thought of that water beneath him was maddening. He imagined it now—sealed off in strata of porous rock by the leathery half-plant, half-animal little makers—and the thin rupture that was pouring a cool stream of clearest, pure, liquid, soothing water into. . . .

A pre-spice mass!

He inhaled, smelling the rank sweetness. The odor was much richer around him than it had been.

Kynes pushed himself to his knees, heard a bird screech, the hurried flapping of wings.

This is spice desert, he thought. *There must be Fremen about even in the day sun. Surely they can see the birds and will investigate.*

"Movement across the landscape is a necessity for animal life," his father said. "Nomad peoples follow the same necessity. Lines of movement adjust to physical needs for water, food, minerals. We must control this movement now, align it for our purposes."

"Shut up, old man," Kynes muttered.

"We must do a thing on Arrakis never before attempted for an entire planet," his father said. "We must use man as a constructive ecological force—inserting adapted terraform life: a plant here, an animal there, a man in that place—to transform the water cycle, to build a new kind of landscape."

"Shut up!" Kynes croaked.

"It was lines of movement that gave us the first clue to the relationship between worms and spice," his father said.

A worm, Kynes thought with a surge of hope. *A maker's sure to come when this bubble bursts. But I have no hooks. How can I mount a big maker without hooks?*

He could feel frustration sapping what little strength remained to him. Water so near—only a hundred meters or so beneath him; a worm sure to come, but no way to trap it on the surface and use it.

Kynes pitched forward onto the sand, returning to the shallow depression his movements had defined. He felt sand hot against his left cheek, but the sensation was remote.

"The Arrakeen environment built itself into the evolutionary pattern of native life forms," his father said. "How strange that so few people ever looked up from the spice long enough to wonder at the near-ideal nitrogen-oxygen-CO_2 balance being maintained here in the absence of large areas of plant cover. The energy sphere of the planet is there to see and understand—a relentless process, but a process nonetheless. There is a gap in it? Then something occupies that gap. Science is made up of so many things that appear obvious after they are explained. I knew the little maker was there, deep in the sand, long before I ever saw it."

"Please stop lecturing me, Father," Kynes whispered.

A hawk landed on the sand near his outstretched hand. Kynes saw it fold its wings, tip its head to stare at him. He summoned the energy to croak at it. The bird hopped away two steps, but continued to stare at him.

"Men and their works have been a disease on the surface of their planets before now," his father said. "Nature tends to compensate for diseases, to remove or encapsulate them, to incorporate them into the system in her own way."

The hawk lowered its head, stretched its wings, refolded them. It transferred its attention to his outstretched hand.

Kynes found that he no longer had the strength to croak at it.

"The historical system of mutual pillage and extortion stops here on Arrakis," his father said. "You cannot go on forever stealing what you need without regard to those who come after. The physical qualities of a planet are written into its economic and political record. We have the record in front of us and our course is obvious."

He never could stop lecturing, Kynes thought. *Lecturing, lecturing, lecturing—always lecturing.*

The hawk hopped one step closer to Kynes' outstretched hand, turned its head first one way and then the other to study the exposed flesh.

"Arrakis is a one-crop planet," his father said. "One crop. It supports a ruling class that lives as ruling classes have lived in all times while, beneath them, a semihuman mass of semislaves exists on the leavings. It's the masses and the leavings that occupy our attention. These are far more valuable than has ever been suspected."

"I'm ignoring you, Father," Kynes whispered. "Go away."

And he thought: *Surely there must be some of my Fremen near. They cannot help but see the birds over me. They will investigate if only to see if there's moisture available.*

"The masses of Arrakis will know that we work to make the land flow with water," his father said. "Most of them, of course, will have only a semimystical understanding of how we intend to do this. Many, not understanding the prohibitive mass-ratio problem, may even think we'll bring water from some other planet rich in it. Let them think anything they wish as long as they believe in us."

In a minute I'll get up and tell him what I think of him, Kynes thought. *Standing there lecturing me when he should be helping me.*

The bird took another hop closer to Kynes' outstretched hand. Two more hawks drifted down to the sand behind it.

"Religion and law among our masses must be one and the same," his father said. "An act of disobedience must be a sin and require religious penalties. This will have the dual benefit of bringing both greater obedience and greater bravery. We must depend not so much on the bravery of individuals, you see, as upon the bravery of a whole population."

Where is my population now when I need it most? Kynes thought. He summoned all his strength, moved his hand a finger's width toward the nearest hawk. It hopped backward among its companions and all stood poised for flight.

"Our timetable will achieve the stature of a natural phenomenon," his father said. "A planet's life is a vast, tightly interwoven fabric. Vegetation and animal changes will be determined at first by the raw physical forces we manipulate. As they establish themselves, though, our changes will become controlling influences in their own right—and we will have to deal with them, too. Keep in mind, though, that we need control only three per cent of the energy surface—only three per cent— to tip the entire structure over into our self-sustaining system."

Why aren't you helping me? Kynes wondered. *Always the same: when I need you most, you fail me.* He wanted to turn his head, to stare in the direction of his father's voice, stare the old man down. Muscles refused to answer his demand.

Kynes saw the hawk move. It approached his hand, a cautious step at a time while its companions waited in mock indifference. The hawk stopped only a hop away from his hand.

A profound clarity filled Kynes' mind. He saw quite suddenly a potential for Arrakis that his father had never seen. The possibilities along that different path flooded through him.

"No more terrible disaster could befall your people than for them to fall into the hands of a Hero," his father said.

Reading my mind! Kynes thought. *Well . . . let him.*

The messages already have been sent to my sietch villages, he thought. *Nothing can stop them. If the Duke's son is alive they'll find him and protect him as I have commanded. They may discard the woman, his mother, but they'll save the boy.*

The hawk took one hop that brought it within slashing distance of his hand. It tipped its head to examine the supine flesh. Abruptly, it straightened, stretched its head upward and with a single screech, leaped into the air and banked away overhead with its companions behind it.

They've come! Kynes thought. *My Fremen have found me!*

Then he heard the sand rumbling.

Every Fremen knew the sound, could distinguish it immediately from the noises of worms or other desert life. Somewhere beneath him, the pre-spice mass had accumulated enough water and organic matter from the little makers, had reached the critical stage of wild growth. A gigantic bubble of carbon dioxide was forming deep in the sand, heaving upward in an enormous "blow" with a dust whirlpool at its center. It would exchange what had been formed deep in the sand for whatever lay on the surface.

The hawks circled overhead screeching their frustration. They knew what was happening. Any desert creature would know.

And I am a desert creature, Kynes thought. *You see me, Father? I am a desert creature.*

He felt the bubble lift him, felt it break and the dust whirlpool engulf him, dragging him down into cool darkness. For a moment, the sensation of coolness and the moisture were blessed relief. Then, as his planet killed him, it occurred to Kynes that his father and all the other scientists were wrong, that the most persistent principles of the universe were accident and error.

Even the hawks could appreciate these facts.

Prophecy and prescience—How can they be put to the test in the face of the unanswered question? Consider: How much is actual prediction of the "wave form" (as Muad'Dib referred to his vision-image) and how much is the prophet shaping the future to fit the prophecy? What of the harmonics inherent in the act of prophecy? Does the prophet see the future or does he see a line of weakness, a fault or cleavage that he may shatter with words or decisions as a diamond-cutter shatters his gem with a blow of a knife?

—FROM "PRIVATE REFLECTIONS ON MUAD'DIB"
BY THE PRINCESS IRULAN

"*Get their water*," the man calling out of the night had said. And Paul fought down his fear, glanced at his mother. His trained eyes saw her readiness for battle, the waiting whipsnap of her muscles.

"It would be regrettable should we have to destroy you out of hand," the voice above them said.

That's the one who spoke to us first, Jessica thought. *There are at least two of them—one to our right and one on our left.*

"Cignoro hrobosa sukares hin mange la pchagavas doi me kamavas na beslas lele pal hrobas!"

It was the man to their right calling out across the basin.

To Paul, the words were gibberish, but out of her Bene Gesserit training, Jessica recognized the speech. It was Chakobsa, one of the ancient hunting languages, and the man above them was saying that perhaps these were the strangers they sought.

In the sudden silence that followed the calling voice, the hoopwheel face of the second moon—faintly ivory blue—rolled over the rocks across the basin, bright and peering.

Scrambling sounds came from the rocks—above and to both sides . . . dark motions in the moonlight. Many figures flowed through the shadows.

A whole troop! Paul thought with a sudden pang.

A tall man in a mottled burnoose stepped in front of Jessica. His mouth baffle was thrown aside for clear speech, revealing a heavy beard in the sidelight of the moon, but face and eyes were hidden in the overhang of his hood.

"What have we here—jinn or human?" he asked.

When Jessica heard the true-banter in his voice, she allowed herself a faint hope. This was the voice of command, the voice that had first shocked them with its intrusion from the night.

"Human, I warrant," the man said.

Jessica sensed rather than saw the knife hidden in a fold of the man's robe. She permitted herself one bitter regret that she and Paul had no shields.

"Do you also speak?" the man asked.

Jessica put all the royal arrogance at her command into her manner and voice. Reply was urgent, but she had not heard enough of this man to be certain she had a register on his culture and weaknesses.

"Who comes on us like criminals out of the night?" she demanded.

The burnoose-hooded head showed tension in a sudden twist, then slow relaxation that revealed much. The man had good control.

Paul shifted away from his mother to separate them as targets and give each of them a clearer arena of action.

The hooded head turned at Paul's movement, opening a wedge of face to moonlight. Jessica saw a sharp nose, one glinting eye—*dark, so dark the eye, without any white in it*—a heavy brown and upturned mustache.

"A likely cub," the man said. "If you're fugitives from the Harkonnens, it may be you're welcome among us. What is it, boy?"

The possibilities flashed through Paul's mind: *A trick? A fact?* Immediate decision was needed.

"Why should you welcome fugitives?" he demanded.

"A child who thinks and speaks like a man," the tall man said. "Well, now, to answer your question, my young wali, I am one who does not pay the fai, the water tribute, to the Harkonnens. That is why I might welcome a fugitive."

He knows who we are, Paul thought. *There's concealment in his voice.*

"I am Stilgar, the Fremen," the tall man said. "Does that speed your tongue, boy?"

It is the same voice, Paul thought. And he remembered the Council with this man seeking the body of a friend slain by the Harkonnens.

"I know you, Stilgar," Paul said. "I was with my father in Council when you came for the water of your friend. You took away with you my father's man, Duncan Idaho—an exchange of friends."

"And Idaho abandoned us to return to his Duke," Stilgar said.

Jessica heard the shading of disgust in his voice, held herself prepared for attack.

The voice from the rocks above them called: "We waste time here, Stil."

"This is the Duke's son," Stilgar barked. "He's certainly the one Liet told us to seek."

"But . . . a child, Stil."

"The Duke was a man and this lad used a thumper," Stilgar said. "That was a brave crossing he made in the path of *shai-hulud.*"

And Jessica heard him excluding her from his thoughts. Had he already passed sentence?

"We haven't time for the test," the voice above them protested.

"Yet he could be the Lisan al-Gaib," Stilgar said.

He's looking for an omen! Jessica thought.

"But the woman," the voice above them said.

Jessica readied herself anew. There had been death in that voice.

"Yes, the woman," Stilgar said. "And her water."

"You know the law," said the voice from the rocks. "Ones who cannot live with the desert—"

"Be quiet," Stilgar said. "Times change."

"Did Liet *command* this?" asked the voice from the rocks.

"You heard the voice of the cielago, Jamis," Stilgar said. "Why do you press me?"

And Jessica thought: *Cielago!* The clue of the tongue opened wide avenues of understanding: this was the language of Ilm and Fiqh, and cielago meant *bat*, a small flying mammal. *Voice of the cielago*: they had received a distrans message to seek Paul and herself.

"I but remind you of your duties, friend Stilgar," said the voice above them.

"My duty is the strength of the tribe," Stilgar said. "That is my only duty. I need no one to remind me of it. This child-man interests me. He is full-fleshed. He has lived on much water. He has lived away from the father sun. He has not the eyes of the Ibad. Yet he does not speak or act like a weakling of the pans. Nor did his father. How can this be?"

"We cannot stay out here all night arguing," said the voice from the rocks. "If a patrol—"

"I will not tell you again, Jamis, to be quiet," Stilgar said.

The man above them remained silent, but Jessica heard him moving, crossing by a leap over a defile and working his way down to the basin floor on their left.

"The voice of the cielago suggested there'd be value to us in saving you two," Stilgar said. "I can see possibility in this strong boy-man: he is young and can learn. But what of yourself, woman?" He stared at Jessica.

I have his voice and pattern registered now, Jessica thought. *I could control him with a word, but he's a strong man . . . worth much more to us unblunted and with full freedom of action. We shall see.*

"I am the mother of this boy," Jessica said. "In part, his strength which you admire is the product of my training."

"The strength of a woman can be boundless," Stilgar said. "Certain it is in a Reverend Mother. Are you a Reverend Mother?"

For the moment, Jessica put aside the implications of the question, answered truthfully, "No."

"Are you trained in the ways of the desert?"

"No, but many consider my training valuable."

"We make our own judgments on value," Stilgar said.

"Every man has the right to his own judgments," she said.

"It is well that you see the reason," Stilgar said. "We cannot dally here to test you, woman. Do you understand? We'd not want your shade to plague us. I will take the boy-man, your son, and he shall have my countenance, sanctuary in my tribe. But for you, woman—you understand there is nothing personal in this? It is the rule, Istislah, in the general interest. Is that not enough?"

Paul took a half-step forward. "What are you talking about?"

Stilgar flicked a glance across Paul, but kept his attention on Jessica. "Unless you've been deep-trained from childhood to live here, you could bring destruction onto an entire tribe. It is the law, and we cannot carry useless. . . ."

Jessica's motion started as a slumping, deceptive faint to the ground. It was the obvious thing for a weak outworlder to do, and the obvious slows an opponent's reactions. It takes an instant to interpret a known thing when that thing is exposed as something unknown. She shifted as she saw his right shoulder drop to bring a weapon within the folds of his robe to bear on her new position. A turn, a slash of her arm, a whirling of mingled robes, and she was against the rocks with the man helpless in front of her.

At his mother's first movement, Paul backed two steps. As she attacked, he dove for shadows. A bearded man rose up in his path, half-crouched, lunging forward with a weapon in one hand. Paul took the man beneath the sternum with a straight-hand jab, sidestepped and chopped the base of his neck, relieving him of the weapon as he fell.

Then Paul was into the shadows, scrambling upward among the rocks, the weapon tucked into his waist sash. He had recognized it in spite of its unfamiliar shape—a projectile weapon, and that said many things about this place, another clue that shields were not used here.

They will concentrate on my mother and that Stilgar fellow. She can handle him. I must get to a safe vantage point where I can threaten them and give her time to escape.

There came a chorus of sharp spring-clicks from the basin. Projectiles whined off the rocks around him. One of them flicked his robe. He squeezed around a corner in the rocks, found himself in a narrow vertical crack, began inching upward—his back against one side, his feet against the other—slowly, as silently as he could.

The roar of Stilgar's voice echoed up to him: "Get back, you worm-headed lice! She'll break my neck if you come near!"

A voice out of the basin said: "The boy got away, Stil. What are we—"

"Of course he got away, you sand-brained . . . Ugh-h-h! Easy, woman!"

"Tell them to stop hunting my son," Jessica said.

"They've stopped, woman. He got away as you intended him to. Great gods below! Why didn't you say you were a weirding woman and a fighter?"

"Tell your men to fall back," Jessica said. "Tell them to go out into the basin where I can see them . . . and you'd better believe that I know how many of them there are."

And she thought: *This is the delicate moment, but if this man is as sharp-minded as I think him, we have a chance.*

Paul inched his way upward, found a narrow ledge on which he could rest and look down into the basin. Stilgar's voice came up to him.

"And if I refuse? How can you . . . ugh-h-h! Leave be, woman! We mean no harm to you, now. Great gods! If you can do this to the strongest of us, you're worth ten times your weight of water."

Now, the test of reason, Jessica thought. She said: "You ask after the Lisan al-Gaib."

"You could be the folk of the legend," he said, "but I'll believe that when it's been tested. All I know now is that you came here with that stupid Duke who. . . . Aiee-e-e! Woman! I care not if you kill me! He was honorable and brave, but it was stupid to put himself in the way of the Harkonnen fist!"

Silence.

Presently, Jessica said: "He had no choice, but we'll not argue it. Now, tell that man of yours behind the bush over there to stop trying to bring his weapon to bear on me, or I'll rid the universe of you and take him next."

"You there!" Stilgar roared. "Do as she says!"

"But, Stil—"

"Do as she says, you wormfaced, crawling, sand-brained piece of lizard turd! Do it or I'll help her dismember you! Can't you see the worth of this woman?"

The man at the bush straightened from his partial concealment, lowered his weapon.

"He has obeyed," Stilgar said.

"Now," Jessica said, "explain clearly to your people what it is you wish of me. I want no young hothead to make a foolish mistake."

"When we slip into the villages and towns we must mask our origin, blend with the pan and graben folk," Stilgar said. "We carry no weapons, for the crysknife is sacred. But you, woman, you have the weirding ability of battle. We'd only heard of it and many doubted, but one cannot doubt what he sees with his own eyes. You mastered an armed Fremen. *This* is a weapon no search could expose."

There was a stirring in the basin as Stilgar's words sank home.

"And if I agree to teach you the . . . weirding way?"

"My countenance for you as well as your son."

"How can we be sure of the truth in your promise?"

Stilgar's voice lost some of its subtle undertone of reasoning, took on an edge of bitterness. "Out here, woman, we carry no paper for contracts. We make no evening promises to be broken at dawn. When a man says a thing, that's the contract. As leader of my people, I've put them in bond to my word. Teach us this weirding way and you have sanctuary with us as long as you wish. Your water shall mingle with our water."

"Can you speak for all Fremen?" Jessica asked.

"In time, that may be. But only my brother, Liet, speaks for all

Fremen. Here, I promise only secrecy. My people will not speak of you to any other sietch. The Harkonnens have returned to Dune in force and your Duke is dead. It is said that you two died in a Mother storm. The hunter does not seek dead game."

There's a safety in that, Jessica thought. *But these people have good communications and a message could be sent.*

"I presume there was a reward offered for us," she said.

Stilgar remained silent, and she could almost see the thoughts turning over in his head, sensing the shifts of his muscles beneath her hands.

Presently, he said: "I will say it once more: I've given the tribe's word-bond. My people know your worth to us now. What could the Harkonnens give us? Our freedom? Hah! No, you are the taqwa, that which buys us more than all the spice in the Harkonnen coffers."

"Then I shall teach you my way of battle," Jessica said, and she sensed the unconscious ritual-intensity of her own words.

"Now, will you release me?"

"So be it," Jessica said. She released her hold on him, stepped aside in full view of the bank in the basin. *This is the test-mashad,* she thought. *But Paul must know about them even if I die for his knowledge.*

In the waiting silence, Paul inched forward to get a better view of where his mother stood. As he moved, he heard heavy breathing, suddenly stilled, above him in the vertical crack of the rock, and sensed a faint shadow there outlined against the stars.

Stilgar's voice came up from the basin: "You, up there! Stop hunting the boy. He'll come down presently."

The voice of a young boy or a girl sounded from the darkness above Paul: "But, Stil, he can't be far from—"

"I said leave him be, Chani! You spawn of a lizard!"

There came a whispered imprecation from above Paul and a low voice: "Call *me* spawn of a lizard!" But the shadow pulled back out of view.

Paul returned his attention to the basin, picking out the gray-shadowed movement of Stilgar beside his mother.

"Come in, all of you," Stilgar called. He turned to Jessica. "And now I'll ask you how *we* may be certain you'll fulfill your half of our bargain? You're the ones lived with papers and empty contracts and such as—"

"We of the Bene Gesserit don't break our vows any more than you do," Jessica said.

There was a protracted silence, then a multiple hissing of voices: "A Bene Gesserit witch!"

Paul brought his captured weapon from his sash, trained it on the dark figure of Stilgar, but the man and his companions remained immobile, staring at Jessica.

"It *is* the legend," someone said.

"It was said that the Shadout Mapes gave this report on you," Stilgar said. "But a thing so important must be tested. If you are the Bene Gesserit of the legend whose son will lead us to paradise. . . ." He shrugged.

Jessica sighed, thinking: *So our Missionaria Protectiva even planted religious safety valves all through this hell hole. Ah, well . . . it'll help, and that's what it was meant to do.*

She said: "The seeress who brought you the legend, she gave it under the binding of karama and ijaz, the miracle and the inimitability of the prophecy—this I know. Do you wish a sign?"

His nostrils flared in the moonlight. "We cannot tarry for the rites," he whispered.

Jessica recalled a chart Kynes had shown her while arranging emergency escape routes. How long ago it seemed. There had been a place called "Sietch Tabr" on the chart and beside it the notation: "Stilgar."

"Perhaps when we get to Sietch Tabr," she said.

The revelation shook him, and Jessica thought: *If only he knew the tricks we use! She must've been good, that Bene Gesserit of the Missionaria Protectiva. These Fremen are beautifully prepared to believe in us.*

Stilgar shifted uneasily. "We must go now."

She nodded, letting him know that they left with her permission.

He looked up at the cliff almost directly at the rock ledge where Paul crouched. "You there, lad: you may come down now." He returned his attention to Jessica, spoke with an apologetic tone: "Your son made an incredible amount of noise climbing. He has much to learn lest he endanger us all, but he's young."

"No doubt we have much to teach each other," Jessica said. "Meanwhile, you'd best see to your companion out there. My noisy son was a bit rough in disarming him."

Stilgar whirled, his hood flapping. "Where?"

"Beyond those bushes." She pointed.

Stilgar touched two of his men. "See to it." He glanced at his companions, identifying them. "Jamis is missing." He turned to Jessica. "Even your cub knows the weirding way."

"And you'll notice that my son hasn't stirred from up there as you ordered," Jessica said.

The two men Stilgar had sent returned supporting a third who stumbled and gasped between them. Stilgar gave them a flicking glance, returned his attention to Jessica. "The son will take only your orders, eh? Good. He knows discipline."

"Paul, you may come down now," Jessica said.

Paul stood up, emerging into moonlight above his concealing cleft, slipped the Fremen weapon back into his sash. As he turned, another figure arose from the rocks to face him.

In the moonlight and reflection off gray stone, Paul saw a small figure in Fremen robes, a shadowed face peering out at him from the hood, and the muzzle of one of the projectile weapons aimed at him from a fold of robe.

"I am Chani, daughter of Liet."

The voice was lilting, half filled with laughter.

"I would not have permitted you to harm my companions," she said.

Paul swallowed. The figure in front of him turned into the moon's path and he saw an elfin face, black pits of eyes. The familiarity of that face, the features out of numberless visions in his earliest prescience, shocked Paul to stillness. He remembered the angry bravado with which he had once described this face-from-a-dream, telling the Reverend Mother Gaius Helen Mohiam: "I will meet her."

And here was the face, but in no meeting he had ever dreamed.

"You were as noisy as shai-hulud in a rage," she said. "And you took the most difficult way up here. Follow me; I'll show you an easier way down."

He scrambled out of the cleft, followed the swirling of her robe across a tumbled landscape. She moved like a gazelle, dancing over the rocks. Paul felt hot blood in his face, was thankful for the darkness.

That girl! She was like a touch of destiny. He felt caught up on a wave, in tune with a motion that lifted all his spirits.

They stood presently amidst the Fremen on the basin floor.

Jessica turned a wry smile on Paul, but spoke to Stilgar: "This will be a good exchange of teachings. I hope you and your people feel no anger at our violence. It seemed . . . necessary. You were about to . . . make a mistake."

"To save one from a mistake is a gift of paradise," Stilgar said. He touched his lips with his left hand, lifted the weapon from Paul's waist with the other, tossed it to a companion. "You will have your own maula pistol, lad, when you've earned it."

Paul started to speak, hesitated, remembering his mother's teaching: *"Beginnings are such delicate times."*

"My son has what weapons he needs," Jessica said. She stared at Stilgar, forcing him to think of how Paul had acquired the pistol.

Stilgar glanced at the man Paul had subdued—Jamis. The man stood at one side, head lowered, breathing heavily. "You are a difficult woman," Stilgar said. He held out his left hand to a companion, snapped his fingers. "Kushti bakka te."

More Chakobsa, Jessica thought.

The companion pressed two squares of gauze into Stilgar's hand. Stilgar ran them through his fingers, fixed one around Jessica's neck beneath her hood, fitted the other around Paul's neck in the same way.

"Now you wear the kerchief of the bakka," he said. "If we become separated, you will be recognized as belonging to Stilgar's sietch. We will talk of weapons another time."

He moved out through his band now, inspecting them, giving Paul's Fremkit pack to one of his men to carry.

Bakka, Jessica thought, recognizing the religious term: *bakka—the weeper.* She sensed how the symbolism of the kerchiefs united this band. *Why should weeping unite them?* she asked herself.

Stilgar came to the young girl who had embarrassed Paul, said: "Chani, take the child-man under your wing. Keep him out of trouble."

Chani touched Paul's arm. "Come along, child-man."

Paul hid the anger in his voice, said: "My name is Paul. It were well you—"

"We'll give you a name, manling," Stilgar said, "in the time of the mihna, at the test of aql."

The test of reason, Jessica translated. The sudden need of Paul's ascendancy overrode all other consideration, and she barked, "My son's been tested with the gom jabbar!"

In the stillness that followed, she knew she had struck to the heart of them.

"There's much we don't know of each other," Stilgar said. "But we tarry overlong. Day-sun mustn't find us in the open." He crossed to the man Paul had struck down, said, "Jamis, can you travel?"

A grunt answered him. "Surprised me, he did. 'Twas an accident. I can travel."

"No accident," Stilgar said. "I'll hold you responsible with Chani for the lad's safety, Jamis. These people have my countenance."

Jessica stared at the man, Jamis. His was the voice that had argued with Stilgar from the rocks. His was the voice with death in it. And Stilgar had seen fit to reinforce his order with this Jamis.

Stilgar flicked a testing glance across the group, motioned two men out. "Larus and Farrukh, you are to hide our tracks. See that we leave no trace. Extra care—we have two with us who've not been trained." He turned, hand upheld and aimed across the basin. "In squad line with flankers—move out. We must be at Cave of the Ridges before dawn."

Jessica fell into step beside Stilgar, counting heads. There were forty

Fremen—she and Paul made it forty-two. And she thought: *They travel as a military company—even the girl, Chani.*

Paul took a place in the line behind Chani. He had put down the black feeling at being caught by the girl. In his mind now was the memory called up by his mother's barked reminder: "My son's been tested with the gom jabbar!" He found that his hand tingled with remembered pain.

"Watch where you go," Chani hissed. "Do not brush against a bush lest you leave a thread to show our passage."

Paul swallowed, nodded.

Jessica listened to the sounds of the troop, hearing her own footsteps and Paul's, marveling at the way the Fremen moved. They were forty people crossing the basin with only the sounds natural to the place—ghostly feluccas, their robes flitting through the shadows. Their destination was Sietch Tabr—Stilgar's sietch.

She turned the word over in her mind: sietch. It was a Chakobsa word, unchanged from the old hunting language out of countless centuries. Sietch: a meeting place in time of danger. The profound implications of the word and the language were just beginning to register with her after the tension of their encounter.

"We move well," Stilgar said. "With Shai-hulud's favor, we'll reach Cave of the Ridges before dawn."

Jessica nodded, conserving her strength, sensing the terrible fatigue she held at bay by force of will . . . and, she admitted it: by the force of elation. Her mind focused on the value of this troop, seeing what was revealed here about the Fremen culture.

All of them, she thought, *an entire culture trained to military order. What a priceless thing is here for an outcast Duke!*

The Fremen were supreme in that quality the ancients called "spannungsbogen"—which is the self-imposed delay between desire for a thing and the act of reaching out to grasp that thing.

—FROM "THE WISDOM OF MUAD'DIB"
BY THE PRINCESS IRULAN

They approached Cave of the Ridges at dawnbreak, moving through a split in the basin wall so narrow they had to turn sideways to negotiate it. Jessica saw Stilgar detach guards in the thin dawnlight, saw them for a moment as they began their scrambling climb up the cliff.

Paul turned his head upward as he walked, seeing the tapestry of this planet cut in cross section where the narrow cleft gaped toward gray-blue sky.

Chani pulled at his robe to hurry him, said: "Quickly. It is already light."

"The men who climbed above us, where are they going?" Paul whispered.

"The first daywatch," she said. "Hurry now!"

A guard left outside, Paul thought. *Wise. But it would've been wiser still for us to approach this place in separate bands. Less chance of losing the whole troop.* He paused in the thought, realizing that this was guerrilla thinking, and he remembered his father's fear that the Atreides might become a guerrilla house.

"Faster," Chani whispered.

Paul sped his steps, hearing the swish of robes behind. And he thought of the words of the sirat from Yueh's tiny O.C. Bible.

"Paradise on my right, Hell on my left, and the Angel of Death behind." He rolled the quotation in his mind.

They rounded a corner where the passage widened. Stilgar stood at one side motioning them into a low hole that opened at right angles.

"Quickly!" he hissed. "We're like rabbits in a cage if a patrol catches us here."

Paul bent for the opening, followed Chani into a cave illuminated by thin gray light from somewhere ahead.

"You can stand up," she said.

He straightened, studied the place: a deep and wide area with domed ceiling that curved away just out of a man's handreach. The troop spread out through shadows. Paul saw his mother come up on one side, saw her examine their companions. And he noted how she failed to blend with the Fremen even though her garb was identical. The way she moved—such a sense of power and grace.

"Find a place to rest and stay out of the way, child-man," Chani said. "Here's food." She pressed two leaf-wrapped morsels into his hand. They reeked of spice.

Stilgar came up behind Jessica, called an order to a group on the left. "Get the doorseal in place and see to moisture security." He turned to another Fremen: "Lemil, get glowglobes." He took Jessica's arm. "I wish to show you something, weirding woman." He led her around a curve of rock toward the light source.

Jessica found herself looking out across the wide lip of another opening to the cave, an opening high in a cliff wall—looking out across another basin about ten or twelve kilometers wide. The basin was shielded by high rock walls. Sparse clumps of plant growth were scattered around it.

As she looked at the dawn-gray basin, the sun lifted over the far escarpment illuminating a biscuit-colored landscape of rocks and sand. And she noted how the sun of Arrakis appeared to leap over the horizon.

It's because we want to hold it back, she thought. *Night is safer than day*. There came over her then a longing for a rainbow in this place that would never see rain. *I must suppress such longings*, she thought. *They're a weakness. I no longer can afford weaknesses.*

Stilgar gripped her arm, pointed across the basin. "There! There you see proper Druses."

She looked where he pointed, saw movement: people on the basin floor scattering at the daylight into the shadows of the opposite cliff wall. In spite of the distance, their movements were plain in the clear air. She lifted her binoculars from beneath her robe, focused the oil lenses on the distant people. Kerchiefs fluttered like a flight of multicolored butterflies.

"That is home," Stilgar said. "We will be there this night." He stared across the basin, tugging at his mustache. "My people stayed out overlate working. That means there are no patrols about. I'll signal them later and they'll prepare for us."

"Your people show good discipline," Jessica said. She lowered the binoculars, saw that Stilgar was looking at them.

"They obey the preservation of the tribe," he said. "It is the way we choose among us for a leader. The leader is the one who is strongest, the one who brings water and security." He lifted his attention to her face.

She returned his stare, noted the whiteless eyes, the stained eyepits, the dust-rimmed beard and mustache, the line of the catchtube curving down from his nostrils into his stillsuit.

"Have I compromised your leadership by besting you, Stilgar?" she asked.

"You did not call me out," he said.

"It's important that a leader keep the respect of his troop," she said.

"Isn't a one of those sandlice I cannot handle," Stilgar said. "When you bested me, you bested us all. Now, they hope to learn from you . . . the weirding way . . . and some are curious to see if you intend to call me out."

She weighed the implications. "By besting you in formal battle?"

He nodded. "I'd advise you against this because they'd not follow you. You're not of the sand. They saw this in our night's passage."

"Practical people," she said.

"True enough." He glanced at the basin. "We know our needs. But not many are thinking deep thoughts now this close to home. We've been out overlong arranging to deliver our spice quota to the free traders for the cursed Guild . . . may their faces be forever black."

Jessica stopped in the act of turning away from him, looked back up into his face. "The Guild? What has the Guild to do with your spice?"

"It's Liet's command," Stilgar said. "We know the reason, but the taste of it sours us. We bribe the Guild with a monstrous payment in spice to keep our skies clear of satellites and such that none may spy what we do to the face of Arrakis."

She weighed out her words, remembering that Paul had said this must be the reason Arrakeen skies were clear of satellites. "And what is it you do to the face of Arrakis that must not be seen?"

"We change it . . . slowly but with certainty . . . to make it fit for human life. Our generation will not see it, nor our children nor our children's children nor the grandchildren of their children . . . but it will come." He stared with veiled eyes out over the basin. "Open water and tall green plants and people walking freely without stillsuits."

So that's the dream of this Liet-Kynes, she thought. And she said: "Bribes are dangerous; they have a way of growing larger and larger."

"They grow," he said, "but the slow way is the safe way."

Jessica turned, looked out over the basin, trying to see it the way Stilgar was seeing it in his imagination. She saw only the grayed mustard stain of distant rocks and a sudden hazy motion in the sky above the cliffs.

"Ah-h-h-h," Stilgar said.

She thought at first it must be a patrol vehicle, then realized it was a mirage—another landscape hovering over the desert-sand and a distant wavering of greenery and in the middle distance a long worm traveling the surface with what looked like Fremen robes fluttering on its back.

The mirage faded.

"It would be better to ride," Stilgar said, "but we cannot permit a maker into this basin. Thus, we must walk again tonight."

Maker—their word for worm, she thought.

She measured the import of his words, the statement that they could not *permit* a worm into this basin. She knew what she had seen in the mirage—Fremen riding on the back of a giant worm. It took heavy control not to betray her shock at the implications.

"We must be getting back to the others," Stilgar said. "Else my people may suspect I dally with you. Some already are jealous that my hands tasted your loveliness when we struggled last night in Tuono Basin."

"That will be enough of that!" Jessica snapped.

"No offense," Stilgar said, and his voice was mild. "Women among us are not taken against their will . . . and with you. . . ." He shrugged. ". . . even that convention isn't required."

"You will keep in mind that I was a duke's lady," she said, but her voice was calmer.

"As you wish," he said. "It's time to seal off this opening, to permit relaxation of stillsuit discipline. My people need to rest in comfort this day. Their families will give them little rest on the morrow."

Silence fell between them.

Jessica stared out into the sunlight. She had heard what she had heard in Stilgar's voice—the unspoken offer of more than his *countenance*. Did he need a wife? She realized she could step into that place with him. It would be one way to end conflict over tribal leadership—female properly aligned with male.

But what of Paul then? Who could tell yet what rules of parenthood prevailed here? And what of the unborn daughter she had carried these few weeks? What of a dead Duke's daughter? And she permitted herself to face fully the significance of this other child growing within her, to see her own motives in permitting the conception. She knew what it was—she had succumbed to that profound drive shared by all creatures who are faced with death—the drive to seek immortality through progeny. The fertility drive of the species had overpowered them.

Jessica glanced at Stilgar, saw that he was studying her, waiting. *A daughter born here to a woman wed to such a one as this man—what would be the fate of such a daughter?* she asked herself. *Would he try to limit the necessities that a Bene Gesserit must follow?*

Stilgar cleared his throat and revealed then that he understood some of the questions in her mind. "What is important for a leader is that which makes him a leader. It is the needs of his people. If you teach me your powers, there may come a day when one of us must challenge the other. I would prefer some alternative."

"There are several alternatives?" she asked.

"The Sayyadina," he said. "Our Reverend Mother is old."

Their Reverend Mother!

Before she could probe this, he said: "I do not necessarily offer myself as mate. This is nothing personal, for you are beautiful and desirable. But should you become one of my women, that might lead some of my young men to believe that I'm too much concerned with pleasures of the flesh and not enough concerned with the tribe's needs. Even now they listen to us and watch us."

A man who weighs his decisions, who thinks of consequences, she thought.

"There are those among my young men who have reached the age of wild spirits," he said. "They must be eased through this period. I must leave no great reasons around for them to challenge me. Because I would have to maim and kill among them. This is not the proper course for a leader if it can be avoided with honor. A leader, you see, is one of the things that distinguishes a mob from a people. He maintains the level of individuals. Too few individuals, and a people reverts to a mob."

His words, the depth of their awareness, the fact that he spoke as much to her as to those who secretly listened, forced her to reevaluate him.

He has stature, she thought. *Where did he learn such inner balance?*

"The law that demands our form of choosing a leader is a just law," Stilgar said. "But it does not follow that justice is always the thing a people needs. What we truly need now is time to grow and prosper, to spread our force over more land."

What is his ancestry? she wondered. *Whence comes such breeding?* She said: "Stilgar, I underestimated you."

"Such was my suspicion," he said.

"Each of us apparently underestimated the other," she said.

"I should like an end to this," he said. "I should like friendship with you . . . and trust. I should like that respect for each other which grows in the breast without demand for the huddlings of sex."

"I understand," she said.

"Do you trust me?"

"I hear your sincerity."

"Among us," he said, "the Sayyadina, when they are not the formal leaders, hold a special place of honor. They teach. They maintain the strength of God here." He touched his breast.

Now I must probe this Reverend Mother mystery, she thought. And she said: "You spoke of your Reverend Mother . . . and I've heard words of legend and prophecy."

"It is said that a Bene Gesserit and her offspring hold the key to our future," he said.

"Do you believe I am that one?"

She watched his face, thinking: *The young reed dies so easily. Beginnings are times of such great peril.*

"We do not know," he said.

She nodded, thinking: *He's an honorable man. He wants a sign from me, but he'll not tip fate by telling me the sign.*

Jessica turned her head, stared down into the basin at the golden shadows, the purple shadows, the vibrations of dust-mote air across the lip of their cave. Her mind was filled suddenly with feline prudence. She knew the cant of the Missionaria Protectiva, knew how to adapt the techniques of legend and fear and hope to her emergency needs, but she sensed wild changes here . . . as though someone had been in among these Fremen and capitalized on the Missionaria Protectiva's imprint.

Stilgar cleared his throat.

She sensed his impatience, knew that the day moved ahead and men waited to seal off this opening. This was a time for boldness on her part, and she realized what she needed: some dar al-hikman, some school of translation that would give her. . . .

"Adab," she whispered.

Her mind felt as though it had rolled over within her. She recognized the sensation with a quickening of pulse. Nothing in all the Bene Gesserit training carried such a signal of recognition. It could be only the adab, the demanding memory that comes upon you of itself. She gave herself up to it, allowing the words to flow from her.

"Ibn qirtaiba," she said, "as far as the spot where the dust ends." She stretched out an arm from her robe, seeing Stilgar's eyes go wide. She heard a rustling of many robes in the background. "I see a . . . Fremen with the book of examples," she intoned. "He reads to al-Lat, the sun whom he defied and subjugated. He reads to the Sadus of the Trial and this is what he reads:

> "Mine enemies are like green blades eaten down
> That did stand in the path of the tempest.
> Hast thou not seen what our Lord did?
> He sent the pestilence among them
> That did lay schemes against us.
> They are like birds scattered by the huntsman.
> Their schemes are like pellets of poison
> That every mouth rejects."

A trembling passed through her. She dropped her arm.

Back to her from the inner cave's shadows came a whispered response of many voices: "Their works have been overturned."

"The fire of God mount over thy heart," she said. And she thought: *Now, it goes in the proper channel.*

"The fire of God set alight," came the response.

She nodded. "Thine enemies shall fall," she said.

"Bi-la kaifa," they answered.

In the sudden hush, Stilgar bowed to her. "Sayyadina," he said. "If the Shai-hulud grant, then you may yet pass within to become a Reverend Mother."

Pass within, she thought. *An odd way of putting it. But the rest of it fitted into the cant well enough.* And she felt a cynical bitterness at what she had done. *Our Missionaria Protectiva seldom fails. A place was prepared for us in this wilderness. The prayer of the salat has carved out our hiding place. Now . . . I must play the part of Auliya, the Friend of God . . . Sayyadina to rogue peoples who've been so heavily imprinted with our Bene Gesserit soothsay they even call their chief priestesses Reverend Mothers.*

Paul stood beside Chani in the shadows of the inner cave. He could still taste the morsel she had fed him—bird flesh and grain bound with spice honey and encased in a leaf. In tasting it he had realized he never before had eaten such a concentration of spice essence and there had been a moment of fear. He knew what this essence could do to him—the *spice change* that pushed his mind into prescient awareness.

"Bi-la kaifa," Chani whispered.

He looked at her, seeing the awe with which the Fremen appeared to accept his mother's words. Only the man called Jamis seemed to stand aloof from the ceremony, holding himself apart with arms folded across his breast.

"Duy yakha hin mange," Chani whispered. "Duy punra hin mange. I have two eyes. I have two feet."

And she stared at Paul with a look of wonder.

Paul took a deep breath, trying to still the tempest within him. His mother's words had locked onto the working of the spice essence, and he had felt her voice rise and fall within him like the shadows of an open fire. Through it all, he had sensed the edge of cynicism in her—he knew her so well!—but nothing could stop this thing that had begun with a morsel of food.

Terrible purpose!

He sensed it, the race consciousness that he could not escape. There was the sharpened clarity, the inflow of data, the cold precision of his awareness. He sank to the floor, sitting with his back against rock, giving himself up to it. Awareness flowed into that timeless stratum where he could view time, sensing the available paths, the winds of the future . . . the winds of the past: the one-eyed vision of the past, the one-eyed vision of the present and the one-eyed vision of the future—all combined in a trinocular vision that permitted him to see time-become-space.

There was danger, he felt, of overrunning himself, and he had to hold onto his awareness of the present, sensing the blurred deflection of experience, the flowing moment, the continual solidification of that-which-is into the perpetual-was.

In grasping the present, he felt for the first time the massive steadiness of time's movement everywhere complicated by shifting currents, waves, surges, and countersurges, like surf against rocky cliffs. It gave him a new understanding of his prescience, and he saw the source of blind time, the source of error in it, with an immediate sensation of fear.

The prescience, he realized, was an illumination that incorporated the limits of what it revealed—at once a source of accuracy and meaningful error. A kind of Heisenberg indeterminacy intervened: the expenditure of energy that revealed what he saw, changed what he saw.

And what he saw was a time nexus within this cave, a boiling of possibilities focused here, wherein the most minute action—the wink of an eye, a careless word, a misplaced grain of sand—moved a gigantic lever across the known universe. He saw violence with the outcome subject to so many variables that his slightest movement created vast shiftings in the pattern.

The vision made him want to freeze into immobility, but this, too, was action with its consequences.

The countless consequences—lines fanned out from this cave, and along most of these consequence-lines he saw his own dead body with blood flowing from a gaping knife wound.

My father, the Padishah Emperor, was 72 yet looked no more than 35 the year he encompassed the death of Duke Leto and gave Arrakis back to the Harkonnens. He seldom appeared in public wearing other than a Sardaukar uniform and a Burseg's black helmet with the Imperial lion in gold upon its crest. The uniform was an open reminder of where his power lay. He was not always that blatant, though. When he wanted, he could radiate charm and sincerity, but I often wonder in these later days if anything about him was as it seemed. I think now he was a man fighting constantly to escape the bars of an invisible cage. You must remember that he was an emperor, father-head of a dynasty that reached back into the dimmest history. But we denied him a legal son. Was this not the most terrible defeat a ruler ever suffered? My mother obeyed her Sister Superiors where the Lady Jessica disobeyed. Which of them was the stronger? History already has answered.

—FROM "IN MY FATHER'S HOUSE"
BY THE PRINCESS IRULAN

Jessica awakened in cave darkness, sensing the stir of Fremen around her, smelling the acrid stillsuit odor. Her inner time sense told her it would soon be night outside, but the cave remained in blackness, shielded from the desert by the plastic hoods that trapped their body moisture within this space.

She realized that she had permitted herself the utterly relaxing sleep of great fatigue, and this suggested something of her own unconscious assessment on personal security within Stilgar's troop. She turned in the hammock that had been fashioned of her robe, slipped her feet to the rock floor and into her desert boots.

I must remember to fasten the boots slip-fashion to help my stillsuit's pumping action, she thought. *There are so many things to remember.*

She could still taste their morning meal—the morsel of bird flesh and grain bound within a leaf with spice honey—and it came to her that the use of time was turned around here: night was the day of activity and day was the time of rest.

Night conceals; night is safest.

She unhooked her robe from its hammock pegs in a rock alcove, fumbled with the fabric in the dark until she found the top, slipped into it.

How to get a message out to the Bene Gesserit? she wondered. They would have to be told of the two strays in Arrakeen sanctuary.

Glowglobes came alight farther into the cave. She saw people moving there, Paul among them already dressed and with his hood thrown back to reveal the aquiline Atreides profile.

He had acted so strangely before they retired, she thought. *Withdrawn.* He was like one come back from the dead, not yet fully aware of his return, his eyes half shut and glassy with the inward stare. It made her think of his warning about the spice-impregnated diet: *addictive.*

Are there side effects? she wondered. *He said it had something to do with his prescient faculty, but he has been strangely silent about what he sees.*

Stilgar came from shadows to her right, crossed to the group beneath the glowglobes. She marked how he fingered his beard and the watchful, cat-stalking look of him.

Abrupt fear shot through Jessica as her senses awakened to the tensions visible in the people gathered around Paul—the stiff movements, the ritual positions.

"They have my countenance!" Stilgar rumbled.

Jessica recognized the man Stilgar confronted—Jamis! She saw then the rage in Jamis—the tight set of his shoulders.

Jamis, the man Paul bested! she thought.

"You know the rule, Stilgar," Jamis said.

"Who knows it better?" Stilgar asked, and she heard the tone of placation in his voice, the attempt to smooth something over.

"I choose the combat," Jamis growled.

Jessica sped across the cave, grasped Stilgar's arm. "What is this?" she asked.

"It is the amtal rule," Stilgar said. "Jamis is demanding the right to test your part in the legend."

"She must be championed," Jamis said. "If her champion wins, that's the truth in it. But it's said. . . ." He glanced across the press of people. ". . . that she'd need no champion from the Fremen—which can mean only that she brings her own champion."

He's talking of single combat with Paul! Jessica thought.

She released Stilgar's arm, took a half-step forward. "I'm always my own champion," she said. "The meaning's simple enough for. . . ."

"You'll not tell us our ways!" Jamis snapped. "Not without more proof than I've seen. Stilgar could've told you what to say last morning. He could've filled your mind full of the coddle and you could've bird-talked it to us, hoping to make a false way among us."

I can take him, Jessica thought, *but that might conflict with the way they interpret the legend.* And again she wondered at the way the Missionaria Protectiva's work had been twisted on this planet.

Stilgar looked at Jessica, spoke in a low voice but one designed to carry to the crowd's fringe. "Jamis is one to hold a grudge, Sayyadina. Your son bested him and—"

"It was an accident!" Jamis roared. "There was witch-force at Tuono Basin and I'll prove it now!"

". . . and I've bested him myself," Stilgar continued. "He seeks by this tahaddi challenge to get back at me as well. There's too much of violence in Jamis for him ever to make a good leader—too much ghafla, the distraction. He gives his mouth to the rules and his heart to the sarfa, the turning away. No, he could never make a good leader. I've preserved him this long because he's useful in a fight as such, but when he gets this carving anger on him he's dangerous to his own society."

"Stilgar-r-r-r!" Jamis rumbled.

And Jessica saw what Stilgar was doing, trying to enrage Jamis, to take the challenge away from Paul.

Stilgar faced Jamis, and again Jessica heard the soothing in the rumbling voice. "Jamis, he's but a boy. He's—"

"You named him a man," Jamis said. "His mother *says* he's been through the gom jabbar. He's full-fleshed and with a surfeit of water. The ones who carried their pack say there's literjons of water in it. Literjons! And us sipping our catchpockets the instant they show dewsparkle."

Stilgar glanced at Jessica. "Is this true? Is there water in your pack?"

"Yes."

"Literjons of it?"

"Two literjons."

"What was intended with this wealth?"

Wealth? she thought. She shook her head, feeling the coldness in his voice.

"Where I was born, water fell from the sky and ran over the land in wide rivers," she said. "There were oceans of it so broad you could not see the other shore. I've not been trained to your water discipline. I never before had to think of it this way."

A sighing gasp arose from the people around them: "Water fell from the sky . . . it ran *over* the land."

"Did you know there're those among us who've lost from their catchpockets by accident and will be in sore trouble before we reach Tabr this night?"

"How could I know?" Jessica shook her head. "If they're in need, give them water from our pack."

"Is that what you intended with this wealth?"

"I intended it to save life," she said.

"Then we accept your blessing, Sayyadina."

"You'll not buy us off with water," Jamis growled. "Nor will you anger me against yourself, Stilgar. I see you trying to make me call you out before I've proved my words."

Stilgar faced Jamis. "Are you determined to press this fight against a child, Jamis?" His voice was low, venomous.

"She must be championed."

"Even though she has my countenance?"

"I invoke the amtal rule," Jamis said. "It's my right."

Stilgar nodded. "Then, if the boy does not carve you down, you'll answer to my knife afterward. And this time I'll not hold back the blade as I've done before."

"You cannot do this thing," Jessica said. "Paul's just—"

"You must not interfere, Sayyadina," Stilgar said. "Oh, I know you can take me and, therefore, can take anyone among us, but you cannot best us all united. This must be; it is the amtal rule."

Jessica fell silent, staring at him in the green light of the glowglobes, seeing the demoniacal stiffness that had taken over his expression. She shifted her attention to Jamis, saw the brooding look to his brows and thought: *I should've seen that before. He broods. He's the silent kind, one who works himself up inside. I should've been prepared.*

"If you harm my son," she said, "you'll have me to meet. I call you out now. I'll carve you into a joint of—"

"Mother." Paul stepped forward, touched her sleeve. "Perhaps if I explain to Jamis how—"

"Explain!" Jamis sneered.

Paul fell silent, staring at the man. He felt no fear of him. Jamis appeared clumsy in his movements and he had fallen so easily in their night encounter on the sand. But Paul still felt the nexus-boiling of this cave, still remembered the prescient visions of himself dead under a knife. There had been so few avenues of escape for him in that vision....

Stilgar said: "Sayyadina, you must step back now where—"

"Stop calling her Sayyadina!" Jamis said. "That's yet to be proved. So she knows the prayer! What's that? Every child among us knows it."

He has talked enough, Jessica thought. *I've the key to him. I could immobilize him with a word.* She hesitated. *But I cannot stop them all.*

"You will answer to me then," Jessica said, and she pitched her voice in a twisting tone with a little whine in it and a catch at the end.

Jamis stared at her, fright visible on his face.

"I'll teach you agony," she said in the same tone. "Remember *that* as you fight. You'll have agony such as will make the gom jabbar a happy memory by comparison. You will writhe with your entire—"

"She tries a spell on me!" Jamis gasped. He put his clenched right fist beside his ear. "I invoke the silence on her!"

"So be it then," Stilgar said. He cast a warning glance at Jessica. "If you speak again, Sayyadina, we'll know it's your witchcraft and you'll be forfeit." He nodded for her to step back.

Jessica felt hands pulling her, helping her back, and she sensed they were not unkindly. She saw Paul being separated from the throng, the elfin-faced Chani whispering in his ear as she nodded toward Jamis.

A ring formed within the troop. More glowglobes were brought and all of them tuned to the yellow band.

Jamis stepped into the ring, slipped out of his robe and tossed it to someone in the crowd. He stood there in a cloudy gray slickness of stillsuit that was patched and marked by tucks and gathers. For a moment, he bent with his mouth to his shoulder, drinking from a catch-pocket tube. Presently he straightened, peeled off and detached the suit, handed it carefully into the crowd. He stood waiting, clad in loincloth and some tight fabric over his feet, a crysknife in his right hand.

Jessica saw the girl-child Chani helping Paul, saw her press a crysknife handle into his palm, saw him heft it, testing the weight and balance. And it came to Jessica that Paul had been trained in prana and bindu, the nerve and the fiber—that he had been taught fighting in a deadly school, his teachers men like Duncan Idaho and Gurney Halleck, men who were legends in their own lifetimes. The boy knew the devious ways of the Bene Gesserit and he looked supple and confident.

But he's only fifteen, she thought. *And he has no shield. I must stop this. Somehow, there must be a way to. . . .* She looked up, saw Stilgar watching her.

"You cannot stop it," he said. "You must not speak."

She put a hand over her mouth, thinking: *I've planted fear in Jamis' mind. It'll slow him some . . . perhaps. If I could only pray—truly pray.*

Paul stood alone now just into the ring, clad in the fighting trunks he'd worn under his stillsuit. He held a crysknife in his right hand; his feet were bare against the sand-gritted rock. Idaho had warned him time and again: "*When in doubt of your surface, bare feet are best.*" And there were Chani's words of instruction still in the front of his consciousness: "*Jamis turns to the right with his knife after a parry. It's a habit in him we've all seen. And he'll aim for the eyes to catch a blink in which to slash you. And he can fight either hand; look out for a knife shift.*"

But strongest in Paul so that he felt it with his entire body was training and the instinctual reaction mechanism that had been hammered into him day after day, hour after hour on the practice floor.

Gurney Halleck's words were there to remember: "*The good knife fighter thinks on point and blade and shearing-guard simultaneously. The point can also cut; the blade can also stab; the shearing-guard can also trap your opponent's blade.*"

Paul glanced at the crysknife. There was no shearing-guard; only the slim round ring of the handle with its raised lips to protect the hand. And even so, he realized that he did not know the breaking tension of this blade, did not even know if it *could* be broken.

Jamis began sidling to the right along the edge of the ring opposite Paul.

Paul crouched, realizing then that he had no shield, but was trained to fighting with its subtle field around him, trained to react on defense with utmost speed while his attack would be timed to the controlled slowness necessary for penetrating the enemy's shield. In spite of constant warning from his trainers not to depend on the shield's mindless blunting of attack speed, he knew that shield-awareness was part of him.

Jamis called out in ritual challenge: "May thy knife chip and shatter!"

This knife will break then, Paul thought.

He cautioned himself that Jamis also was without shield, but the man wasn't trained to its use, had no shield-fighter inhibitions.

Paul stared across the ring at Jamis. The man's body looked like knotted whipcord on a dried skeleton. His crysknife shone milky yellow in the light of the glowglobes.

Fear coursed through Paul. He felt suddenly alone and naked standing in dull yellow light within this ring of people. Prescience had fed his knowledge with countless experiences, hinted at the strongest currents of the future and the strings of decision that guided them, but this was the *real-now*. This was death hanging on an infinite number of minuscule mischances.

Anything could tip the future here, he realized. Someone coughing in the troop of watchers, a distraction. A variation in a glowglobe's brilliance, a deceptive shadow.

I'm afraid, Paul told himself.

And he circled warily opposite Jamis, repeating silently to himself the Bene Gesserit Litany Against Fear. *"Fear is the mind-killer. . . ."* It was a cool bath washing over him. He felt muscles untie themselves, become poised and ready.

"I'll sheath my knife in your blood," Jamis snarled. And in the middle of the last word he pounced.

Jessica saw the motion, stifled an outcry.

Where the man struck there was only empty air and Paul stood now behind Jamis with a clear shot at the exposed back.

Now, Paul! Now! Jessica screamed it in her mind.

Paul's motion was slowly timed, beautifully fluid, but so slow it gave Jamis the margin to twist away, backing and turning to the right.

Paul withdrew, crouching low. "First, you must find my blood," he said.

Jessica recognized the shield-fighter timing in her son, and it came over her what a two-edged thing that was. The boy's reactions were those of youth and trained to a peak these people had never seen. But the attack was trained, too, and conditioned by the necessities of penetrating a shield barrier. A shield would repel too fast a blow, admit only the slowly deceptive counter. It needed control and trickery to get through a shield.

Does Paul see it? she asked herself. *He must!*

Again Jamis attacked, ink-dark eyes glaring, his body a yellow blur under the glowglobes.

And again Paul slipped away to return too slowly on the attack.

And again.

And again.

Each time, Paul's counterblow came an instant late.

And Jessica saw a thing she hoped Jamis did not see. Paul's defensive reactions were blindingly fast, but they moved each time at the precisely correct angle they would take if a shield were helping deflect part of Jamis' blow.

"Is your son playing with that poor fool?" Stilgar asked. He waved her to silence before she could respond. "Sorry; you must remain silent."

Now the two figures on the rock floor circled each other: Jamis with knife hand held far forward and tipped up slightly; Paul crouched with knife held low.

Again, Jamis pounced, and this time he twisted to the right where Paul had been dodging.

Instead of faking back and out, Paul met the man's knife hand on the point of his own blade. Then the boy was gone, twisting away to the left and thankful for Chani's warning.

Jamis backed into the center of the circle, rubbing his knife hand. Blood dripped from the injury for a moment, stopped. His eyes were wide and staring—two blue-black holes—studying Paul with a new wariness in the dull light of the glowglobes.

"Ah, that one hurt," Stilgar murmured.

Paul crouched at the ready and, as he had been trained to do after first blood, called out: "Do you yield?"

"Hah!" Jamis cried.

An angry murmur arose from the troop.

"Hold!" Stilgar called out. "The lad doesn't know our rule." Then, to Paul: "There can be no yielding in the tahaddi challenge. Death is the test of it."

Jessica saw Paul swallow hard. And she thought: *He's never killed a man like this . . . in the hot blood of a knife fight. Can he do it?*

Paul circled slowly right, forced by Jamis' movement. The prescient knowledge of the time-boiling variables in this cave came back to plague him now. His new understanding told him there were too many swiftly compressed decisions in this fight for any clear channel ahead to show itself.

Variable piled on variable—that was why this cave lay as a blurred nexus in his path. It was like a gigantic rock in the flood, creating maelstroms in the current around it.

"Have an end to it, lad," Stilgar muttered. "Don't play with him."

Paul crept farther into the ring, relying on his own edge in speed.

Jamis backed now that the realization swept over him—that this was no soft offworlder in the tahaddi ring, easy prey for a Fremen crysknife.

Jessica saw the shadow of desperation in the man's face. *Now is when he's most dangerous,* she thought. *Now he's desperate and can do anything. He sees that this is not like a child of his own people, but a fighting machine born and trained to it from infancy. Now the fear I planted in him has come to bloom.*

And she found in herself a sense of pity for Jamis—an emotion tempered by awareness of the immediate peril to her son.

Jamis could do anything . . . any unpredictable thing, she told herself. She wondered then if Paul had glimpsed this future, if he were reliving this experience. But she saw the way her son moved, the beads of perspiration on his face and shoulders, the careful wariness visible in the flow of muscles. And for the first time she sensed, without understanding it, the uncertainty factor in Paul's gift.

Paul pressed the fight now, circling but not attacking. He had seen the fear in his opponent. Memory of Duncan Idaho's voice flowed through Paul's awareness: *"When your opponent fears you, then's the moment when you give the fear its own rein, give it the time to work on him. Let it become terror. The terrified man fights himself. Eventually, he attacks in desperation. That is the most dangerous moment, but the ter-*

rified man can be trusted usually to make a fatal mistake. You are being trained here to detect these mistakes and use them."

The crowd in the cavern began to mutter.

They think Paul's toying with Jamis, Jessica thought. *They think Paul's being needlessly cruel.*

But she sensed also the undercurrent of crowd excitement, their enjoyment of the spectacle. And she could see the pressure building up in Jamis. The moment when it became too much for him to contain was as apparent to her as it was to Jamis . . . or to Paul.

Jamis leaped high, feinting and striking down with his right hand, but the hand was empty. The crysknife had been shifted to his left hand.

Jessica gasped.

But Paul had been warned by Chani: *"Jamis fights with either hand."* And the depth of his training had taken in that trick *en passant*. *"Keep the mind on the knife and not on the hand that holds it,"* Gurney Halleck had told him time and again. *"The knife is more dangerous than the hand and the knife can be in either hand."*

And Paul had seen Jamis' mistake: bad footwork so that it took the man a heartbeat longer to recover from his leap, which had been intended to confuse Paul and hide the knife shift.

Except for the low yellow light of the glowglobes and the inky eyes of the staring troop, it was similar to a session on the practice floor. Shields didn't count where the body's own movement could be used against it. Paul shifted his own knife in a blurred motion, slipped sideways and thrust upward where Jamis' chest was descending—then away to watch the man crumble.

Jamis fell like a limp rag, face down, gasped once and turned his face toward Paul, then lay still on the rock floor. His dead eyes stared out like beads of dark glass.

"Killing with the point lacks artistry," Idaho had once told Paul, *"but don't let that hold your hand when the opening presents itself."*

The troop rushed forward, filling the ring, pushing Paul aside. They hid Jamis in a frenzy of huddling activity. Presently a group of them hurried back into the depths of the cavern carrying a burden wrapped in a robe.

And there was no body on the rock floor.

Jessica pressed through toward her son. She felt that she swam in a sea of robed and stinking backs, a throng strangely silent.

Now is the terrible moment, she thought. *He has killed a man in clear superiority of mind and muscle. He must not grow to enjoy such a victory.*

She forced herself through the last of the troop and into a small open space where two bearded Fremen were helping Paul into his stillsuit.

Jessica stared at her son. Paul's eyes were bright. He breathed heavily, permitting the ministrations to his body rather than helping them.

"Him against Jamis and not a mark on him," one of the men muttered.

Chani stood at one side, her eyes focused on Paul. Jessica saw the girl's excitement, the admiration in the elfin face.

It must be done now and swiftly, Jessica thought.

She compressed ultimate scorn into her voice and manner, said: "Well-l-l, now—how does it feel to be a killer?"

Paul stiffened as though he had been struck. He met his mother's cold glare and his face darkened with a rush of blood. Involuntarily he glanced toward the place on the cavern floor where Jamis had lain.

Stilgar pressed through to Jessica's side, returning from the cave depths where the body of Jamis had been taken. He spoke to Paul in a bitter, controlled tone: "When the time comes for you to call me out and try for my burda, do not think you will play with me the way you played with Jamis."

Jessica sensed the way her own words and Stilgar's sank into Paul, doing their harsh work on the boy. The mistake these people made—it served a purpose now. She searched the faces around them as Paul was doing, seeing what he saw. Admiration, yes, and fear . . . and in some—loathing. She looked at Stilgar, saw his fatalism, knew how the fight had seemed to him.

Paul looked at his mother. "You know what it was," he said.

She heard the return to sanity, the remorse in his voice. Jessica swept her glance across the troop, said: "Paul has never before killed a man with a naked blade."

Stilgar faced her, disbelief in his face.

"I wasn't playing with him," Paul said. He pressed in front of his mother, straightening his robe, glanced at the dark place of Jamis' blood on the cavern floor. "I did not want to kill him."

Jessica saw belief come slowly to Stilgar, saw the relief in him as he tugged at his beard with a deeply veined hand. She heard muttering awareness spread through the troop.

"That's why y' asked him to yield," Stilgar said. "I see. Our ways are different, but you'll see the sense in them. I thought we'd admitted a scorpion into our midst." He hesitated, then: "And I shall not call you lad the more."

A voice from the troop called out: "Needs a naming, Stil."

Stilgar nodded, tugging at his beard. "I see strength in you . . . like the strength beneath a pillar." Again he paused, then: "You shall be known among us as Usul, the base of the pillar. This is your secret name, your troop name. We of Sietch Tabr may use it, but none other may so presume . . . Usul."

Murmuring went through the troop: "Good choice, that . . . strong . . . bring us luck." And Jessica sensed the acceptance, knowing she was included in it with her champion. She was indeed Sayyadina.

"Now, what name of manhood do *you* choose for us to call you openly?" Stilgar asked.

Paul glanced at his mother, back to Stilgar. Bits and pieces of this moment registered on his prescient *memory*, but he felt the differences as though they were physical, a pressure forcing him through the narrow door of the present.

"How do you call among you the little mouse, the mouse that jumps?" Paul asked, remembering the *pop-hop* of motion at Tuono Basin. He illustrated with one hand.

A chuckle sounded through the troop.

"We call that one muad'dib," Stilgar said.

Jessica gasped. It was the name Paul had told her, saying that the Fremen would accept them and call him thus. She felt a sudden fear *of* her son and *for* him.

Paul swallowed. He felt that he played a part already played over countless times in his mind . . . yet . . . there were differences. He could see himself perched on a dizzying summit, having experienced much and possessed of a profound store of knowledge, but all around him was abyss.

And again he remembered the vision of fanatic legions following the green and black banner of the Atreides, pillaging and burning across the universe in the name of their prophet Muad'Dib. *That must not happen,* he told himself.

"Is that the name you wish, Muad'Dib?" Stilgar asked.

"I am an Atreides," Paul whispered, and then louder: "It's not right that I give up entirely the name my father gave me. Could I be known among you as Paul-Muad'Dib?"

"You are Paul-Muad'Dib," Stilgar said.

And Paul thought: *That was in no vision of mine. I did a different thing.*

But he felt that the abyss remained all around him.

Again a murmuring response went through the troop as man turned to man: "Wisdom with strength . . . Couldn't ask more . . . It's the legend for sure . . . Lisan al-Gaib . . . Lisan al-Gaib. . . ."

"I will tell you a thing about your new name," Stilgar said. "The choice pleases us. Muad'Dib is wise in the ways of the desert. Muad'Dib creates his own water. Muad'Dib hides from the sun and travels in the cool night. Muad'Dib is fruitful and multiplies over the land. Muad'Dib we call 'instructor-of-boys.' That is a powerful base on which to build your life, Paul-Muad'Dib, who is Usul among us. We welcome you."

Stilgar touched Paul's forehead with one palm, withdrew his hand, embraced Paul and murmured, "Usul."

As Stilgar released him, another member of the troop embraced Paul, repeating his new troop name. And Paul was passed from embrace to embrace through the troop, hearing the voices, the shadings of tone: "Usul . . . Usul . . . Usul." Already, he could place some of them by name. And there was Chani who pressed her cheek against his as she held him and said his name.

Presently Paul stood again before Stilgar, who said: "Now, you are of the Ichwan Bedwine, our brother." His face hardened, and he spoke with command in his voice. "And now, Paul-Muad'Dib, tighten up that stillsuit." He glanced at Chani. "Chani! Paul-Muad'Dib's nose plugs are as poor a fit I've ever seen! I thought I ordered you to see after him!"

"I hadn't the makings, Stil," she said. "There's Jamis', of course, but—"

"Enough of that!"

"Then I'll share one of mine," she said. "I can make do with one until—"

"You will not," Stilgar said. "I know there are spares among us. Where are the spares? Are we a troop together or a band of savages?"

Hands reached out from the troop offering hard, fibrous objects. Stilgar selected four, handed them to Chani. "Fit these to Usul and the Sayyadina."

A voice lifted from the back of the troop: "What of the water, Stil? What of the literjons in their pack?"

"I know your need, Farok," Stilgar said. He glanced at Jessica. She nodded.

"Broach one for those that need it," Stilgar said. "Watermaster . . . where is a watermaster? Ah, Shimoom, care for the measuring of what is needed. The necessity and no more. This water is the dower property of the Sayyadina and will be repaid in the sietch at field rates less pack fees."

"What is the repayment at field rates?" Jessica asked.

"Ten for one," Stilgar said.

"But—"

"It's a wise rule as you'll come to see," Stilgar said.

A rustling of robes marked movement at the back of the troop as men turned to get the water.

DUNE 391

Stilgar held up a hand, and there was silence. "As to Jamis," he said, "I order the full ceremony. Jamis was our companion and brother of the Ichwan Bedwine. There shall be no turning away without the respect due one who proved our fortune by his tahaddi challenge. I invoke the rite . . . at sunset when the dark shall cover him."

Paul, hearing these words, realized that he had plunged once more into the abyss . . . blind time. There was no past occupying the future in his mind . . . except . . . except . . . he could still sense the green and black Atreides banner waving . . . somewhere ahead . . . still see the jihad's bloody swords and fanatic legions.

It will not be, he told himself. *I cannot let it be.*

God created Arrakis to train the faithful.

—FROM "THE WISDOM OF MUAD'DIB"
BY THE PRINCESS IRULAN

In the stillness of the cavern, Jessica heard the scrape of sand on rock as people moved, the distant bird calls that Stilgar had said were the signals of his watchmen.

The great plastic hood-seals had been removed from the cave's opening. She could see the march of evening shadows across the lip of rock in front of her and the open basin beyond. She sensed the daylight leaving them, sensed it in the dry heat as well as the shadows. She knew her trained awareness soon would give her what these Fremen obviously had—the ability to sense even the slightest change in the air's moisture.

How they had scurried to tighten their stillsuits when the cave was opened! Deep within the cave, someone began chanting:

> "Ima trava okolo!
> I korenja okolo!"

Jessica translated silently: *These are ashes! And these are roots!*

The funeral ceremony for Jamis was beginning.

She looked out at the Arrakeen sunset, at the banked decks of color in the sky. Night was beginning to utter its shadows along the distant rocks and the dunes.

Yet the heat persisted.

Heat forced her thoughts onto water and the observed fact that this whole people could be trained to be thirsty only at given times.

Thirst.

She could remember moonlit waves on Caladan throwing white robes over rocks . . . and the wind heavy with dampness. Now the breeze that fingered her robes seared the patches of exposed skin at cheeks and forehead. The new nose plugs irritated her, and she found herself overly conscious of the tube that trailed down across her face into the suit, recovering her breath's moisture.

The suit itself was a sweatbox.

"Your suit will be more comfortable when you've adjusted to a lower water content in your body," Stilgar had said.

She knew he was right, but the knowledge made this moment no more comfortable. The unconscious preoccupation with water here weighed on her mind. *No,* she corrected herself: *it was preoccupation with* moisture.

And that was a more subtle and profound matter.

She heard approaching footsteps, turned to see Paul come out of the cave's depths trailed by the elfin-faced Chani.

There's another thing, Jessica thought. *Paul must be cautioned about their women. One of these desert women would not do as wife to a Duke. As concubine, yes, but not as wife.*

Then she wondered at herself, thinking: *Have I been infected with his schemes?* And she saw how well she had been conditioned. *I can think of the marital needs of royalty without once weighing my own concubinage. Yet . . . I was more than concubine.*

"Mother."

Paul stopped in front of her. Chani stood at his elbow.

"Mother, do you know what they're doing back there?"

Jessica looked at the dark patch of his eyes staring out from the hood. "I think so."

"Chani showed me . . . because I'm supposed to see it and give my . . . permission for the weighing of the water."

Jessica looked at Chani.

"They're recovering Jamis' water," Chani said, and her thin voice came out nasal past the nose plugs. "It's the rule. The flesh belongs to the person, but his water belongs to the tribe . . . except in the combat."

"They say the water's mine," Paul said.

Jessica wondered why this should make her suddenly alert and cautious.

"Combat water belongs to the winner," Chani said. "It's because you have to fight in the open without stillsuits. The winner has to get his water back that he loses while fighting."

"I don't want his water," Paul muttered. He felt that he was a part of many images moving simultaneously in a fragmenting way that was disconcerting to the inner eye. He could not be certain what he would do, but of one thing he was positive: he did not want the water distilled out of Jamis' flesh.

"It's . . . water," Chani said.

Jessica marveled at the way she said it. *"Water."* So much meaning in a simple sound. A Bene Gesserit axiom came to Jessica's mind: *"Survival is the ability to swim in strange water."* And Jessica thought: *Paul and I, we must find the currents and patterns in these strange waters . . . if we're to survive.*

"You will accept the water," Jessica said.

She recognized the tone in her voice. She had used that same tone once with Leto, telling her lost Duke that he would accept a large sum offered for his support in a questionable venture—because money maintained power for the Atreides.

On Arrakis, water was money. She saw that clearly.

Paul remained silent, knowing then that he would do as she ordered—not because she ordered it, but because her tone of voice had forced him to reevaluate. To refuse the water would be to break with accepted Fremen practice.

Presently Paul recalled the words of 467 Kalima in Yueh's O.C. Bible. He said: "From water does all life begin."

Jessica stared at him. *Where did he learn that quotation?* she asked herself. *He hasn't studied the mysteries.*

"Thus it is spoken," Chani said. "Giudichar mantene: It is written in the Shah-Nama that water was the first of all things created."

For no reason she could explain (and *this* bothered her more than the sensation), Jessica suddenly shuddered. She turned away to hide her confusion and was just in time to see the sunset. A violent calamity of color spilled over the sky as the sun dipped beneath the horizon.

"It is time!"

The voice was Stilgar's ringing in the cavern. "Jamis' weapon has been killed. Jamis has been called by Him, by Shai-hulud, who has ordained the phases for the moons that daily wane and—in the end—appear as bent and withered twigs." Stilgar's voice lowered. "Thus it is with Jamis."

Silence fell like a blanket on the cavern.

Jessica saw the gray-shadow movement of Stilgar like a ghost figure within the dark inner reaches. She glanced back at the basin, sensing the coolness.

"The friends of Jamis will approach," Stilgar said.

Men moved behind Jessica, dropping a curtain across the opening. A single glowglobe was lighted overhead far back in the cave. Its yellow glow picked out an inflowing of human figures. Jessica heard the rustling of the robes.

Chani took a step away as though pulled by the light.

Jessica bent close to Paul's ear, speaking in the family code: "Follow their lead; do as they do. It will be a simple ceremony to placate the shade of Jamis."

It will be more than that, Paul thought. And he felt a wrenching sensation within his awareness as though he were trying to grasp something in motion and render it motionless.

Chani glided back to Jessica's side, took her hand. "Come, Sayyadina. We must sit apart."

Paul watched them move off into the shadows, leaving him alone. He felt abandoned.

The men who had fixed the curtain came up beside him.

"Come, Usul."

He allowed himself to be guided forward, to be pushed into a circle of people being formed around Stilgar, who stood beneath the glow-globe and beside a bundled, curving, and angular shape gathered beneath a robe on the rock floor.

The troop crouched down at a gesture from Stilgar, their robes hissing with the movement. Paul settled with them, watching Stilgar, noting the way the overhead globe made pits of his eyes and brightened the touch of green fabric at his neck. Paul shifted his attention to the robe-covered mound at Stilgar's feet, recognized the handle of a baliset protruding from the fabric.

"The spirit leaves the body's water when the first moon rises," Stilgar intoned. "Thus it is spoken. When we see the first moon rise this night, whom will it summon?"

"Jamis," the troop responded.

Stilgar turned full circle on one heel, passing his gaze across the ring of faces. "I was a friend of Jamis," he said. "When the hawk plane stooped upon us at Hole-in-the-Rock, it was Jamis pulled me to safety."

He bent over the pile beside him, lifted away the robe. "I take this robe as a friend of Jamis—leader's right." He draped the robe over a shoulder, straightening.

Now, Paul saw the contents of the mound exposed: the pale glistening gray of a stillsuit, a battered literjon, a kerchief with a small book in its center, the bladeless handle of a crysknife, an empty sheath, a folded pack, a paracompass, a distrans, a thumper, a pile of fist-sized metallic hooks, an assortment of what looked like small rocks within a fold of cloth, a clump of bundled feathers . . . and the baliset exposed beside the folded pack.

So Jamis played the baliset, Paul thought. The instrument reminded him of Gurney Halleck and all that was lost. Paul knew with his memory of the future in the past that some chance-lines could produce a meeting with Halleck, but the reunions were few and shadowed. They puzzled him. The uncertainty factor touched him with wonder. *Does it mean that something I will do . . . that I may do, could destroy Gurney . . . or bring him back to life . . . or. . . .*

Paul swallowed, shook his head.

Again, Stilgar bent over the mound.

"For Jamis' woman and for the guards," he said. The small rocks and the book were taken into the folds of his robe.

"Leader's right," the troop intoned.

"The marker for Jamis' coffee service," Stilgar said, and he lifted a flat disc of green metal. "That it shall be given to Usul in suitable ceremony when we return to the sietch."

"Leader's right," the troop intoned.

Lastly, he took the crysknife handle and stood with it. "For the Funeral Plain," he said.

"For the Funeral Plain," the troop responded.

At her place in the circle across from Paul, Jessica nodded, recognizing the ancient source of the rite, and she thought: *The meeting between ignorance and knowledge, between brutality and culture—it begins in the dignity with which we treat our dead.* She looked across at Paul, wondering: *Will he see it? Will he know what to do?*

"We are friends of Jamis," Stilgar said. "We are not wailing for our dead like a pack of garvarg."

A gray-bearded man to Paul's left stood up. "I was a friend of Jamis," he said. He crossed to the mound, lifted the distrans. "When our water went below minim at the siege at Two Brids, Jamis shared." The man returned to his place in the circle.

Am I supposed to say I was a friend of Jamis? Paul wondered. *Do they expect me to take something from that pile?* He saw faces turn toward him, turn away. *They do expect it!*

Another man across from Paul arose, went to the pack and removed the paracompass. "I was a friend of Jamis," he said. "When the patrol caught us at Bight-of-the-Cliff and I was wounded, Jamis drew them off so the wounded could be saved." He returned to his place in the circle.

Again, the faces turned toward Paul, and he saw the expectancy in them, lowered his eyes. An elbow nudged him and a voice hissed: "Would you bring the destruction on us?"

How can I say I was his friend? Paul wondered.

Another figure arose from the circle opposite Paul and, as the hooded face came into the light, he recognized his mother. She removed a kerchief from the mount. "I was a friend of Jamis," she said. "When the spirit of spirits within him saw the needs of truth, that spirit withdrew and spared my son." She returned to her place.

And Paul recalled the scorn in his mother's voice as she had confronted him after the fight. *"How does it feel to be a killer?"*

Again, he saw the faces turned toward him, felt the anger and fear in the troop. A passage his mother had once filmbooked for him on "The Cult of the Dead" flickered through Paul's mind. He knew what he had to do.

Slowly, Paul got to his feet.

A sigh passed around the circle.

Paul felt the diminishment of his *self* as he advanced into the center of the circle. It was as though he lost a fragment of himself and sought it here. He bent over the mound of belongings, lifted out the baliset. A string twanged softly as it struck against something in the pile.

"I was a friend of Jamis," Paul whispered.

He felt tears burning his eyes, forced more volume into his voice. "Jamis taught me . . . that . . . when you kill . . . you pay for it. I wish I'd known Jamis better."

Blindly, he groped his way back to his place in the circle, sank to the rock floor.

A voice hissed: "He sheds tears!"

It was taken up around the ring: "Usul gives moisture to the dead!"

He felt fingers touch his damp cheek, heard the awed whispers.

Jessica, hearing the voices, felt the depth of the experience, realized what terrible inhibitions there must be against shedding tears. She focused on the words: *"He gives moisture to the dead."* It was a gift to the shadow world—tears. They would be sacred beyond a doubt.

Nothing on this planet had so forcefully hammered into her the ultimate value of water. Not the water-sellers, not the dried skins of the natives, not stillsuits or the rules of water discipline. Here there was a substance more precious than all others—it was life itself and entwined all around with symbolism and ritual.

Water.

"I touched his cheek," someone whispered. "I felt the gift."

At first, the fingers touching his face frightened Paul. He clutched the cold handle of the baliset, feeling the strings bite his palm. Then he saw the faces beyond the groping hands—the eyes wide and wondering.

Presently, the hands withdrew. The funeral ceremony resumed. But now there was a subtle space around Paul, a drawing back as the troop honored him by a respectful isolation.

The ceremony ended with a low chant:

> *"Full moon calls thee—*
> *Shai-hulud shalt thou see;*
> *Red the night, dusky sky,*
> *Bloody death didst thou die.*
> *We pray to a moon: she is round—*
> *Luck with us will then abound,*
> *What we seek for shall be found*
> *In the land of solid ground."*

A bulging sack remained at Stilgar's feet. He crouched, placed his palms against it. Someone came up beside him, crouched at his elbow, and Paul recognized Chani's face in the hood shadow.

"Jamis carried thirty-three liters and seven and three-thirty-seconds drachms of the tribe's water," Chani said. "I bless it now in the presence of a Sayyadina. Ekkeri-akairi, this is the water, fillissin-follasy of Paul-Muad'Dib! Kivi a-kavi, never the more, nakalas! Nakelas! to be measured and counted, ukair-an! by the heartbeats jan-jan-jan of our friend . . . Jamis."

In an abrupt and profound silence, Chani turned, stared at Paul.

Presently she said: "Where I am flame be thou the coals. Where I am dew be thou the water."

"Bi-lal kaifa," intoned the troop.

"To Paul-Muad'Dib goes this portion," Chani said. "May he guard it for the tribe, preserving it against careless loss. May he be generous with it in time of need. May he pass it on in his time for the good of the tribe."

"Bi-lal kaifa," intoned the troop.

I must accept that water, Paul thought. Slowly, he arose, made his way to Chani's side. Stilgar stepped back to make room for him, took the baliset gently from his hand.

"Kneel," Chani said.

Paul knelt.

She guided his hands to the waterbag, held them against the resilient surface. "With this water the tribe entrusts thee," she said. "Jamis is gone from it. Take it in peace." She stood, pulling Paul up with her.

Stilgar returned the baliset, extended a small pile of metal rings in one palm. Paul looked at them, seeing the different sizes, the way the light of the glowglobe reflected off them.

Chani took the largest ring, held it on a finger. "Thirty liters," she said. One by one, she took the others, showing each to Paul, counting them. "Two liters; one liter; seven watercounters of one drachm each; one watercounter of three-thirty-seconds drachms. In all—thirty-three liters and seven and three-thirty-seconds drachms."

She held them up on her finger for Paul to see.

"Do you accept them?" Stilgar asked.

Paul swallowed, nodded. "Yes."

"Later," Chani said, "I will show you how to tie them in a kerchief so they won't rattle and give you away when you need silence." She extended her hand.

"Will you . . . hold them for me?" Paul asked.

Chani turned a startled glance on Stilgar.

He smiled, said, "Paul-Muad'Dib who is Usul does not yet know our ways, Chani. Hold his watercounters without commitment until it's time to show him the manner of carrying them."

She nodded, whipped a ribbon of cloth from beneath her robe, linked the rings onto it with an intricate over and under weaving, hesitated, then stuffed them into the sash beneath her robe.

I missed something there, Paul thought. He sensed the feeling of humor around him, something bantering in it, and his mind linked up a prescient memory: *watercounters offered to a woman—courtship ritual.*

"Watermasters," Stilgar said.

The troop arose in a hissing of robes. Two men stepped out, lifted the waterbag. Stilgar took down the glowglobe, led the way with it into the depths of the cave.

Paul was pressed in behind Chani, noted the buttery glow of light over rock walls, the way the shadows danced, and he felt the troop's lift of spirits contained in a hushed air of expectancy.

Jessica, pulled into the end of the troop by eager hands, hemmed around by jostling bodies, suppressed a moment of panic. She had recognized fragments of the ritual, identified the shards of Chakobsa and Bhotani Jib in the words, and she knew the wild violence that could explode out of these seemingly simple moments.

Jan-jan-jan, she thought. *Go-go-go.*

It was like a child's game that had lost all inhibition in adult hands.

Stilgar stopped at a yellow rock wall. He pressed an outcropping and the wall swung silently away from him, opening along an irregular crack. He led the way through past a dark honeycomb lattice that directed a cool wash of air across Paul when he passed it.

Paul turned a questioning stare on Chani, tugged her arm. "That air felt damp," he said.

"Sh-h-h-h," she whispered.

But a man behind them said: "Plenty of moisture in the trap tonight. Jamis' way of telling us he's satisfied."

Jessica passed through the secret door, heard it close behind. She saw how the Fremen slowed while passing the honeycomb lattice, felt the dampness of the air as she came opposite it.

Windtrap! she thought. *They've a concealed windtrap somewhere on the surface to funnel air down here into cooler regions and precipitate the moisture from it.*

They passed through another rock door with latticework above it, and the door closed behind them. The draft of air at their backs carried a sensation of moisture clearly perceptible to both Jessica and Paul.

At the head of the troop, the glowglobe in Stilgar's hands dropped below the level of the heads in front of Paul. Presently he felt steps beneath his feet, curving down to the left. Light reflected back up across hooded heads and a winding movement of people spiraling down the steps.

Jessica sensed mounting tension in the people around her, a pressure of silence that rasped her nerves with its urgency.

The steps ended and the troop passed through another low door. The light of the glowglobe was swallowed in a great open space with a high curved ceiling.

Paul felt Chani's hand on his arm, heard a faint dripping sound in the chill air, felt an utter stillness come over the Fremen in the cathedral presence of water.

I have seen this place in a dream, he thought.

The thought was both reassuring and frustrating. Somewhere ahead of him on this path, the fanatic hordes cut their gory path across the universe in his name. The green and black Atreides banner would become a symbol of terror. Wild legions would charge into battle screaming their war cry: "Muad'Dib!"

It must not be, he thought. *I cannot let it happen.*

But he could feel the demanding race consciousness within him, his own terrible purpose, and he knew that no small thing could deflect the juggernaut. It was gathering weight and momentum. If he died this instant, the thing would go on through his mother and his unborn sister. Nothing less than the deaths of all the troop gathered here and now—himself and his mother included—could stop the thing.

Paul stared around him, saw the troop spread out in a line. They pressed him forward against a low barrier carved from native rock. Beyond the barrier in the glow of Stilgar's globe, Paul saw an unruffled dark surface of water. It stretched away into shadows—deep and black— the far wall only faintly visible, perhaps a hundred meters away.

Jessica felt the dry pulling of skin on her cheeks and forehead relaxing in the presence of moisture. The water pool was deep; she could sense its deepness, and resisted a desire to dip her hands into it.

A splashing sounded on her left. She looked down the shadowy line of Fremen, saw Stilgar with Paul standing beside him and the watermasters emptying their load into the pool through a flowmeter. The meter was a round gray eye above the pool's rim. She saw its glowing pointer move as the water flowed through it, saw the pointer stop at thirty-three liters, seven and three-thirty-seconds drachms.

Superb accuracy in water measurement, Jessica thought. And she noted that the walls of the meter trough held no trace of moisture after the water's passage. The water flowed off those walls without binding tension. She saw a profound clue to Fremen technology in the simple fact: they were perfectionists.

Jessica worked her way down the barrier to Stilgar's side. Way was made for her with casual courtesy. She noted the withdrawn look in Paul's eyes, but the mystery of this great pool of water dominated her thoughts.

Stilgar looked at her. "There were those among us in need of water," he said, "yet they would come here and not touch this water. Do you know that?"

"I believe it," she said.

He looked at the pool. "We have more than thirty-eight million decaliters here," he said. "Walled off from the little makers, hidden and preserved."

"A treasure trove," she said.

Stilgar lifted the globe to look into her eyes. "It is greater than treasure. We have thousands of such caches. Only a few of us know them all." He cocked his head to one side. The globe cast a yellow-shadowed glow across face and beard. "Hear that?"

They listened.

The dripping of water precipitated from the windtrap filled the room with its presence. Jessica saw that the entire troop was caught up in a rapture of listening. Only Paul seemed to stand remote from it.

To Paul, the sound was like moments ticking away. He could feel time flowing through him, the instants never to be recaptured. He sensed a need for decision, but felt powerless to move.

"It has been calculated with precision," Stilgar whispered. "We know to within a million decaliters how much we need. When we have it, we shall change the face of Arrakis."

A hushed whisper of response lifted from the troop: "Bi-lal kaifa."

"We will trap the dunes beneath grass plantings," Stilgar said, his voice growing stronger. "We will tie the water into the soil with trees and undergrowth."

"Bi-lal kaifa," intoned the troop.

"Each year the polar ice retreats," Stilgar said.

"Bi-lal kaifa," they chanted.

"We shall make a homeworld of Arrakis—with melting lenses at the poles, with lakes in the temperate zones, and only the deep desert for the maker and his spice."

"Bi-lal kaifa."

"And no man ever again shall want for water. It shall be his for dipping from well or pond or lake or canal. It shall run down through the qanats to feed our plants. It shall be there for any man to take. It shall be his for holding out his hand."

"Bi-lal kaifa."

Jessica felt the religious ritual in the words, noted her own instinctively awed response. *They're in league with the future*, she thought. *They have their mountain to climb. This is the scientist's dream . . . and these simple people, these peasants, are filled with it.*

Her thoughts turned to Liet-Kynes, the Emperor's planetary ecologist, the man who had gone native—and she wondered at him. This was a dream to capture men's souls, and she could sense the hand of the ecologist in it. This was a dream for which men would die willingly. It was another of the essential ingredients that she felt her son needed: people with a goal. Such people would be easy to imbue with fervor and fanaticism. They could be wielded like a sword to win back Paul's place for him.

"We leave now," Stilgar said, "and wait for the first moon's rising. When Jamis is safely on his way, we will go home."

Whispering their reluctance, the troop fell in behind him, turned back along the water barrier and up the stairs.

And Paul, walking behind Chani, felt that a vital moment had passed him, that he had missed an essential decision and was now caught up in his own myth. He knew he had seen this place before, experienced it in a fragment of prescient dream on faraway Caladan, but details of the place were being filled in now that he had not seen. He felt a new sense of wonder at the limits of his gift. It was as though he rode within the wave of time, sometimes in its trough, sometimes on a crest—and all around him the other waves lifted and fell, revealing and then hiding what they bore on their surface.

Through it all, the wild jihad still loomed ahead of him, the violence and the slaughter. It was like a promontory above the surf.

The troop filed through the last door into the main cavern. The door was sealed. Lights were extinguished, hoods removed from the cavern openings, revealing the night and the stars that had come over the desert.

Jessica moved to the dry lip of the cavern's edge, looked up at the stars. They were sharp and near. She felt the stirring of the troop around her, heard the sound of a baliset being tuned somewhere behind her, and Paul's voice humming the pitch. There was a melancholy in his tone that she did not like.

Chani's voice intruded from the deep cave darkness: "Tell me about the waters of your birthworld, Paul-Muad'Dib."

And Paul: "Another time, Chani. I promise."

Such sadness.

"It's a good baliset," Chani said.

"Very good," Paul said. "Do you think Jamis'll mind my using it?"

He speaks of the dead in the present tense, Jessica thought. The implications disturbed her.

A man's voice intruded: "He liked music betimes, Jamis did."

"Then sing me one of your songs," Chani pleaded.

Such feminine allure in that girl-child's voice, Jessica thought. *I must caution Paul about their women . . . and soon.*

"This was a song of a friend of mine," Paul said. "I expect he's dead now, Gurney is. He called it his evensong."

The troop grew still, listening as Paul's voice lifted in a sweet boy tenor with the baliset tinkling and strumming beneath it:

> *"This clear time of seeing embers—*
> *A gold-bright sun's lost in first dusk.*
> *What frenzied senses, desp'rate musk*
> *Are consort of rememb'ring."*

Jessica felt the verbal music in her breast—pagan and charged with sounds that made her suddenly and intensely aware of herself, feeling her own body and its needs. She listened with a tense stillness.

> *"Night's pearl-censered requi-em . . .*
> *'Tis for us!*
> *What joys run, then—*
> *Bright in your eyes—*
> *What flower-spangled amores*
> *Pull at our hearts . . .*
> *What flower-spangled amores*
> *Fill our desires."*

And Jessica heard the after-stillness that hummed in the air with the last note. *Why does my son sing a love song to that girl-child?* she asked herself. She felt an abrupt fear. She could sense life flowing around her and she had no grasp on its reins. *Why did he choose that song?* she wondered. *The instincts are true sometimes. Why did he do this?*

Paul sat silently in the darkness, a single stark thought dominating his awareness: *My mother is my enemy. She does not know it, but she is. She is bringing the jihad. She bore me; she trained me. She is my enemy.*

The concept of progress acts as a protective mechanism to shield us from the terrors of the future.

—FROM "COLLECTED SAYINGS OF MUAD'DIB"
BY THE PRINCESS IRULAN

On his seventeenth birthday, Feyd-Rautha Harkonnen killed his one hundredth slave-gladiator in the family games. Visiting observers from the Imperial Court—a Count and Lady Fenring—were on the Harkonnen homeworld of Giedi Prime for the event, invited to sit that afternoon with the immediate family in the golden box above the triangular arena.

In honor of the na-Baron's nativity and to remind all Harkonnens and subjects that Feyd-Rautha was heir-designate, it was holiday on Giedi Prime. The old Baron had decreed a meridian-to-meridian rest from labors, and effort had been spent in the family city of Harko to create the illusion of gaiety: banners flew from buildings, new paint had been splashed on the walls along Court Way.

But off the main way, Count Fenring and his lady noted the rubbish heaps, the scabrous brown walls reflected in the dark puddles of the streets, and the furtive scurrying of the people.

In the Baron's blue-walled keep, there was fearful perfection, but the Count and his lady saw the price being paid—guards everywhere and weapons with that special sheen that told a trained eye they were in regular use. There were checkpoints for routine passage from area to area even within the keep. The servants revealed their military training in the way they walked, in the set of their shoulders . . . in the way their eyes watched and watched and watched.

"The pressure's on," the Count hummed to his lady in their secret language. "The Baron is just beginning to see the price he really paid to rid himself of the Duke Leto."

"Sometime I must recount for you the legend of the phoenix," she said.

They were in the reception hall of the keep waiting to go to the family games. It was not a large hall—perhaps forty meters long and half that in width—but false pillars along the sides had been shaped with an abrupt taper, and the ceiling had a subtle arch, all giving the illusion of much greater space.

"Ah-h-h, here comes the Baron," the Count said.

The Baron moved down the length of the hall with that peculiar waddling-glide imparted by the necessities of guiding suspensor-hung weight. His jowls bobbed up and down; the suspensors jiggled and shifted beneath his orange robe. Rings glittered on his hands and opafires shone where they had been woven into the robe.

At the Baron's elbow walked Feyd-Rautha. His dark hair was dressed in close ringlets that seemed incongruously gay above sullen eyes. He wore a tight-fitting black tunic and snug trousers with a suggestion of bell at the bottom. Soft-soled slippers covered his small feet.

Lady Fenring, noting the young man's poise and the sure flow of muscles beneath the tunic, thought: *Here's one who won't let himself go to fat.*

The Baron stopped in front of them, took Feyd-Rautha's arm in a possessive grip, said, "My nephew, the na-Baron, Feyd-Rautha Harkonnen." And, turning his baby-fat face toward Feyd-Rautha, he said, "The Count and Lady Fenring of whom I've spoken."

Feyd-Rautha dipped his head with the required courtesy. He stared at the Lady Fenring. She was golden-haired and willowy, her perfection of figure clothed in a flowing gown of ecru—simple fitness of form without ornament. Gray-green eyes stared back at him. She had that Bene Gesserit serene repose about her that the young man found subtly disturbing.

"Um-m-m-m-ah-hm-m-m-m," said the Count. He studied Feyd-Rautha. "The, hm-m-m-m, *precise* young man, ah, my . . . hm-m-m-m . . . dear?" The Count glanced at the Baron. "My dear Baron, you say you've spoken of us to this *precise* young man? What did you say?"

"I told my nephew of the great esteem our Emperor holds for you, Count Fenring," the Baron said. And he thought: *Mark him well, Feyd! A killer with the manners of a rabbit—this is the most dangerous kind.*

"Of course!" said the Count, and he smiled at his lady.

Feyd-Rautha found the man's actions and words almost insulting. They stopped just short of something overt that would require notice. The young man focused his attention on the Count: a small man, weak-looking. The face was weaselish with overlarge dark eyes. There was gray at the temples. And his movements—he moved a hand or turned his head one way, then he spoke another way. It was difficult to follow.

"Um-m-m-m-m-ah-h-h-hm-m-m, you come upon such, mm-m-m, preciseness so rarely," the Count said, addressing the Baron's shoulder. "I . . . ah, congratulate you on the hm-m-m perfection of your ah-h-h heir. In the light of the hm-m-m elder, one might say."

"You are too kind," the Baron said. He bowed, but Feyd-Rautha noted that his uncle's eyes did not agree with the courtesy.

"When you're mm-m-m ironic, that ah-h-h suggests you're hm-mm-m thinking deep thoughts," the Count said.

There he goes again, Feyd-Rautha thought. *It sounds like he's being insulting, but there's nothing you can call out for satisfaction.*

Listening to the man gave Feyd-Rautha the feeling his head was being pushed through mush . . . *um-m-m-ah-h-h-hm-m-m-m!* Feyd-Rautha turned his attention back to the Lady Fenring.

"We're ah-h-h taking up too much of this young man's time," she said. "I understand he's to appear in the arena today."

By the houris of the Imperial hareem, she's a lovely one! Feyd-Rautha thought. He said: "I shall make a kill for you this day, my Lady. I shall make the dedication in the arena, with your permission."

She returned his stare serenely, but her voice carried whiplash as she said: "You do *not* have my permission."

"Feyd!" the Baron said. And he thought: *That imp! Does he want this deadly Count to call him out?*

But the Count only smiled and said: "Hm-m-m-m-um-m-m."

"You really *must* be getting ready for the arena, Feyd," the Baron said. "You must be rested and not take any foolish risks."

Feyd-Rautha bowed, his face dark with resentment. "I'm sure everything will be as you wish, Uncle." He nodded to Count Fenring. "Sir." To the lady: "My Lady." And he turned, strode out of the hall, barely glancing at the knot of Families Minor near the double doors.

"He's so young," the Baron sighed.

"Um-m-m-m-ah indeed hmmm," the Count said.

And the Lady Fenring thought: *Can that be the young man the Reverend Mother meant? Is that a bloodline we must preserve?*

"We've more than an hour before going to the arena," the Baron said. "Perhaps we could have our little talk now, Count Fenring." He tipped his gross head to the right. "There's a considerable amount of progress to be discussed."

And the Baron thought: *Let us see now how the Emperor's errand boy gets across whatever message he carries without ever being so crass as to speak it right out.*

The Count spoke to his lady: "Um-m-m-m-ah-h-h-hm-m-m, you mm-m will ah-h-h excuse us, my dear?"

"Each day, some time each hour, brings change," she said. "Mmm-mm." And she smiled sweetly at the Baron before turning away. Her long skirts swished and she walked with a straight-backed regal stride toward the double doors at the end of the hall.

The Baron noted how all conversation among the Houses Minor there stopped at her approach, how the eyes followed her. *Bene Gesserit!* the Baron thought. *The universe would be better rid of them all!*

"There's a cone of silence between two of the pillars over here on our left," the Baron said. "We can talk there without fear of being overheard." He led the way with his waddling gait into the sound-deadening field, feeling the noises of the keep become dull and distant.

The Count moved up beside the Baron, and they turned, facing the wall so their lips could not be read.

"We're not satisfied with the way you ordered the Sardaukar off Arrakis," the Count said.

Straight talk! the Baron thought.

"The Sardaukar could not stay longer without risking that *others* would find out how the Emperor helped me," the Baron said.

"But your nephew Rabban does not appear to be pressing strongly enough toward a solution of the Fremen problem."

"What does the Emperor wish?" the Baron asked. "There cannot be more than a handful of Fremen left on Arrakis. The southern desert is uninhabitable. The northern desert is swept regularly by our patrols."

"Who says the southern desert is uninhabitable?"

"Your own planetologist said it, my dear Count."

"But Doctor Kynes is dead."

"Ah, yes . . . unfortunate, that."

"We've word from an overflight across the southern reaches," the Count said. "There's evidence of plant life."

"Has the Guild then agreed to a watch from space?"

"You know better than that, Baron. The Emperor cannot legally post a watch on Arrakis."

"And *I* cannot afford it," the Baron said. "Who made this overflight?"

"A . . . smuggler."

"Someone has lied to you, Count," the Baron said. "Smugglers cannot navigate the southern reaches any better than can Rabban's men. Storms, sand-static, and all that, you know. Navigation markers are knocked out faster than they can be installed."

"We'll discuss various types of static another time," the Count said.

Ah-h-h-h, the Baron thought. "Have you found some mistake in my accounting then?" he demanded.

"When you imagine mistakes there can be no self-defense," the Count said.

He's deliberately trying to arouse my anger, the Baron thought. He took two deep breaths to calm himself. He could smell his own sweat, and the harness of the suspensors beneath his robe felt suddenly itchy and galling.

"The Emperor cannot be unhappy about the death of the concubine and the boy," the Baron said. "They fled into the desert. There was a storm."

"Yes, there were so many convenient accidents," the Count agreed.

"I do not like your tone, Count," the Baron said.

"Anger is one thing, violence another," the Count said. "Let me caution you: Should an unfortunate accident occur to me here the Great Houses all would learn what you did on Arrakis. They've long suspected how you do business."

"The only recent business I can recall," the Baron said, "was transportation of several legions of Sardaukar to Arrakis."

"You think you could hold that over the Emperor's head?"

"I wouldn't think of it!"

The Count smiled. "Sardaukar commanders could be found who'd confess they acted without orders because they wanted a battle with your Fremen scum."

"Many might doubt such a confession," the Baron said, but the threat staggered him. *Are Sardaukar truly that disciplined?* he wondered.

"The Emperor does wish to audit your books," the Count said.

"Anytime."

"You . . . ah . . . have no objections?"

"None. My CHOAM Company directorship will bear the closest scrutiny." And he thought: *Let him bring a false accusation against me and have it exposed. I shall stand there, promethean, saying: "Behold me, I am wronged." Then let him bring any other accusation against me, even a true one. The Great Houses will not believe a second attack from an accuser once proved wrong.*

"No doubt your books will bear the closest scrutiny," the Count muttered.

"Why is the Emperor so interested in exterminating the Fremen?" the Baron asked.

"You wish the subject to be changed, eh?" The Count shrugged. "It is the Sardaukar who wish it, not the Emperor. They needed practice in killing . . . and they hate to see a task left undone."

Does he think to frighten me by reminding me that he is supported by bloodthirsty killers? the Baron wondered.

"A certain amount of killing has always been an arm of business," the Baron said, "but a line has to be drawn somewhere. Someone must be left to work the spice."

The Count emitted a short, barking laugh. "You think you can harness the Fremen?"

"There never were enough of them for that," the Baron said. "But the killing has made the rest of my population uneasy. It's reaching the point where I'm considering another solution to the Arrakeen problem, my dear Fenring. And I must confess the Emperor deserves credit for the inspiration."

"Ah-h-h?"

"You see, Count, I have the Emperor's prison planet, Salusa Secundus, to inspire me."

The Count stared at him with glittering intensity. "What possible connection is there between Arrakis and Salusa Secundus?"

The Baron felt the alertness in Fenring's eyes, said: "No connection yet."

"Yet?"

"You must admit it'd be a way to develop a substantial work force on Arrakis—use the place as a prison planet."

"You anticipate an increase in prisoners?"

"There has been unrest," the Baron admitted. "I've had to squeeze rather severely, Fenring. After all, you know the price I paid that damnable Guild to transport our mutual force to Arrakis. That money has to come from *somewhere*."

"I suggest you not use Arrakis as a prison planet without the Emperor's permission, Baron."

"Of course not," the Baron said, and he wondered at the sudden chill in Fenring's voice.

"Another matter," the Count said. "We learn that Duke Leto's Mentat, Thufir Hawat, is not dead but in your employ."

"I could not bring myself to waste him," the Baron said.

"You lied to our Sardaukar commander when you said Hawat was dead."

"Only a white lie, my dear Count. I hadn't the stomach for a long argument with the man."

"Was Hawat the real traitor?"

"Oh, goodness, no! It was the false doctor." The Baron wiped at perspiration on his neck. "You must understand, Fenring, I was without a Mentat. You know that. I've never been without a Mentat. It was most unsettling."

"How could you get Hawat to shift allegiance?"

"His Duke was dead." The Baron forced a smile. "There's nothing to fear from Hawat, my dear Count. The Mentat's flesh has been impregnated with a latent poison. We administer an antidote in his meals. Without the antidote, the poison is triggered—he'd die in a few days."

"Withdraw the antidote," the Count said.

"But he's useful!"

"And he knows too many things no living man should know."

"You said the Emperor doesn't fear exposure."

"Don't play games with me, Baron!"

"When I see such an order above the Imperial seal I'll obey it," the Baron said. "But I'll not submit to your whim."

"You think it whim?"

"What else can it be? The Emperor has obligations to me, too, Fenring. I rid him of the troublesome Duke."

"With the help of a few Sardaukar."

"Where else would the Emperor have found a House to provide the disguising uniforms to hide his hand in this matter?"

"He has asked himself the same question, Baron, but with a slightly different emphasis."

The Baron studied Fenring, noting the stiffness of jaw muscles, the careful control. "Ah-h-h, now," the Baron said. "I hope the Emperor doesn't believe he can move against *me* in total secrecy."

"He hopes it won't become necessary."

"The Emperor cannot believe I threaten him!" The Baron permitted anger and grief to edge his voice, thinking: *Let him wrong me in that! I could place myself on the throne while still beating my breast over how I'd been wronged.*

The Count's voice went dry and remote as he said: "The Emperor believes what his senses tell him."

"Dare the Emperor charge me with treason before a full Landsraad Council?" And the Baron held his breath with the hope of it.

"The Emperor need *dare* nothing."

The Baron whirled away in his suspensors to hide his expression. *It could happen in my lifetime!* he thought. *Emperor! Let him wrong me! Then—the bribes and coercion, the rallying of the Great Houses: they'd flock to my banner like peasants running for shelter. The thing they fear above all else is the Emperor's Sardaukar loosed upon them one House at a time.*

"It's the Emperor's sincere hope he'll never have to charge you with treason," the Count said.

The Baron found it difficult to keep irony out of his voice and permit only the expression of hurt, but he managed. "I've been a most loyal subject. These words hurt me beyond my capacity to express."

"Um-m-m-m-ah-hm-m-m," said the Count.

The Baron kept his back to the Count, nodding. Presently he said, "It's time to go to the arena."

"Indeed," said the Count.

They moved out of the cone of silence and, side by side, walked toward the clumps of Houses Minor at the end of the hall. A bell began a slow tolling somewhere in the keep—twenty-minute warning for the arena gathering.

"The Houses Minor wait for you to lead them," the Count said, nodding toward the people they approached.

Double meaning . . . double meaning, the Baron thought.

He looked up at the new talismans flanking the exit to his hall—the mounted bull's head and the oil painting of the Old Duke Atreides, the late Duke Leto's father. They filled the Baron with an odd sense of foreboding, and he wondered what thoughts these talismans had inspired in the Duke Leto as they hung in the halls of Caladan and then on Arrakis—the bravura father and the head of the bull that had killed him.

"Mankind has ah only one mm-m-m science," the Count said as they picked up their parade of followers and emerged from the hall into the waiting room—a narrow space with high windows and floor of patterned white and purple tile.

"And what science is that?" the Baron asked.

"It's the um-m-m-ah-h science of ah-h-h discontent," the Count said.

The Houses Minor behind them, sheep-faced and responsive, laughed with just the right tone of appreciation, but the sound carried a note of discord as it collided with the sudden blast of motors that came to them when pages threw open the outer doors, revealing the line of ground cars, their guidon pennants whipping in a breeze.

The Baron raised his voice to surmount the sudden noise, said, "I hope you'll not be discontented with the performance of my nephew today, Count Fenring."

"I ah-h-h am filled um-m-m only with a hm-m-m sense of anticipation, yes," the Count said. "Always in the ah-h-h proces verbal, one um-m-m ah-h-h must consider the ah-h-h office of origin."

The Baron hid his sudden stiffening of surprise by stumbling on the first step down from the exit. *Proces verbal! That was a report of a crime against the Imperium!*

But the Count chuckled to make it seem a joke, and patted the Baron's arm.

All the way to the arena, though, the Baron sat back among the armored cushions of his car, casting covert glances at the Count beside him, wondering why the Emperor's *errand boy* had thought it necessary to make that particular kind of joke in front of the Houses Minor. It was obvious that Fenring seldom did anything he felt to be unnecessary, or used two words where one would do, or held himself to a single meaning in a single phrase.

They were seated in the golden box above the triangular arena— horns blaring, the tiers above and around them jammed with a hubbub of people and waving pennants—when the answer came to the Baron.

"My dear Baron," the Count said, leaning close to his ear, "you know, don't you, that the Emperor has not given official sanction to your choice of heir?"

The Baron felt himself to be within a sudden personal cone of silence produced by his own shock. He stared at Fenring, barely seeing the Count's lady come through the guards beyond to join the party in the golden box.

"That's really why I'm here today," the Count said. "The Emperor wishes me to report on whether you've chosen a worthy successor. There's nothing like the arena to expose the true person from beneath the mask, eh?"

"The Emperor promised me free choice of heir!" the Baron grated.

"We shall see," Fenring said, and turned away to greet his lady. She sat down, smiling at the Baron, then giving her attention to the sand floor beneath them where Feyd-Rautha was emerging in giles and tights—the black glove and the long knife in his right hand, the white glove and the short knife in his left hand.

"White for poison, black for purity," the Lady Fenring said. "A curious custom, isn't it, my love?"

"Um-m-m-m," the Count said.

The greeting cheer lifted from the family galleries, and Feyd-Rautha paused to accept it, looking up and scanning the faces—seeing his cousines and cousins, the demibrothers, the concubines and out-freyn relations. They were so many pink trumpet mouths yammering amidst a flutter of colorful clothing and banners.

It came to Feyd-Rautha then that the packed ranks of faces would look just as avidly at his blood as at that of the slave-gladiator. There was not a doubt of the outcome in this fight, of course. Here was only the form of danger without its substance—yet. . . .

Feyd-Rautha held up his knives to the sun, saluted the three corners of the arena in the ancient manner. The short knife in white-gloved hand (white, the sign of poison) went first into its sheath. Then the long blade in the black-gloved hand—the pure blade that now was unpure, his secret weapon to turn this day into a purely personal victory: poison on the black blade.

The adjustment of his body shield took only a moment, and he paused to sense the skin-tightening at his forehead assuring him he was properly guarded.

This moment carried its own suspense, and Feyd-Rautha dragged it out with the sure hand of a showman, nodding to his handlers and distractors, checking their equipment with a measuring stare—gyves in place with their prickles sharp and glistening, the barbs and hooks waving with their blue streamers.

Feyd-Rautha signaled the musicians.

The slow march began, sonorous with its ancient pomp, and Feyd-Rautha led his troupe across the arena for obeisance at the foot of his uncle's box. He caught the ceremonial key as it was thrown.

The music stopped.

Into the abrupt silence, he stepped back two paces, raised the key and shouted. "I dedicate this truth to. . . ." And he paused, knowing his uncle would think: *The young fool's going to dedicate to Lady Fenring after all and cause a ruckus!*

". . . to my uncle and patron, the Baron Vladimir Harkonnen!" Feyd-Rautha shouted.

And he was delighted to see his uncle sigh.

The music resumed at the quick-march, and Feyd-Rautha led his men scampering back across the arena to the prudence door that admitted only those wearing the proper identification band. Feyd-Rautha prided himself that he never used the pru-door and seldom needed distractors. But it was good to know they were available this day—special plans sometimes involved special dangers.

Again, silence settled over the arena.

Feyd-Rautha turned, faced the big red door across from him through which the gladiator would emerge.

The special gladiator.

The plan Thufir Hawat had devised was admirably simple and direct, Feyd-Rautha thought. The slave would not be drugged—that was the danger. Instead, a key word had been drummed into the man's unconscious to immobilize his muscles at a critical instant. Feyd-Rautha rolled the vital word in his mind, mouthing it without sound: "Scum!" To the audience, it would appear that an undrugged slave had been slipped into the arena to kill the na-Baron. And all the carefully arranged evidence would point to the slavemaster.

A low humming arose from the red door's servo-motors as they were armed for opening.

Feyd-Rautha focused all his awareness on the door. This first moment was the critical one. The appearance of the gladiator as he emerged told the trained eye much it needed to know. All gladiators were supposed to be hyped on elacca drug to come out kill-ready in fighting stance—but you had to watch how they hefted the knife, which way they turned in defense, whether they were actually aware of the audience in the stands. The way a slave cocked his head could give the most vital clue to counter and feint.

The red door slammed open.

Out charged a tall, muscular man with shaved head and darkly pitted eyes. His skin was carrot-colored as it should be from the elacca drug, but Feyd-Rautha knew the color was paint. The slave wore green leotards and the red belt of a semishield—the belt's arrow pointing left to indicate the slave's left side was shielded. He held his knife sword-fashion, cocked slightly outward in the stance of a trained fighter. Slowly, he advanced into the arena, turning his shielded side toward Feyd-Rautha and the group at the pru-door.

"I like not the look of this one," said one of Feyd-Rautha's barbmen. "Are you sure he's drugged, m'Lord?"

"He has the color," Feyd-Rautha said.

"Yet he stands like a fighter," said another helper.

Feyd-Rautha advanced two steps onto the sand, studied this slave.

"What has he done to his arm?" asked one of the distractors.

Feyd-Rautha's attention went to a bloody scratch on the man's left forearm, followed the arm down to the hand as it pointed to a design drawn in blood on the left hip of the green leotards—a wet shape there: the formalized outline of a hawk.

Hawk!

Feyd-Rautha looked up into the darkly pitted eyes, saw them glaring at him with uncommon alertness.

It's one of Duke Leto's fighting men we took on Arrakis! Feyd-Rautha thought. *No simple gladiator this!* A chill ran through him, and he wondered if Hawat had another plan for this arena—a feint within a feint within a feint. And only the slavemaster prepared to take the blame!

Feyd-Rautha's chief handler spoke at his ear: "I like not the look on that one, m'Lord. Let me set a barb or two in his knife arm to try him."

"I'll set my own barbs," Feyd-Rautha said. He took a pair of the long, hooked shafts from the handler, hefted them, testing the balance. These barbs, too, were supposed to be drugged—but not this time, and the chief handler might die because of that. But it was all part of the plan.

"You'll come out of this a hero," Hawat had said. *"Killed your gladiator man to man and in spite of treachery. The slavemaster will be executed and your man will step into his spot."*

Feyd-Rautha advanced another five paces into the arena, playing out the moment, studying the slave. Already, he knew, the experts in the stands above him were aware that something was wrong. The gladiator had the correct skin color for a drugged man, but he stood his ground and did not tremble. The aficionados would be whispering among themselves now: "See how he stands. He should be agitated—attacking or retreating. See how he conserves his strength, how he waits. He should not wait."

Feyd-Rautha felt his own excitement kindle. *Let there be treachery in Hawat's mind,* he thought. *I can handle this slave. And it's my long knife that carries the poison this time, not the short one. Even Hawat doesn't know that.*

"Hai, Harkonnen!" the slave called. "Are you prepared to die?"

Deathly stillness gripped the arena. *Slaves did not issue the challenge!*

Now, Feyd-Rautha had a clear view of the gladiator's eyes, saw the cold ferocity of despair in them. He marked the way the man stood, loose and ready, muscles prepared for victory. The slave grapevine had carried Hawat's message to this one: *"You'll get a true chance to kill the na-Baron."* That much of the scheme was as they'd planned it, then.

A tight smile crossed Feyd-Rautha's mouth. He lifted the barbs, seeing success for his plans in the way the gladiator stood.

"Hai! Hai!" the slave challenged, and crept forward two steps.

No one in the galleries can mistake it now, Feyd-Rautha thought.

This slave should have been partly crippled by drug-induced terror. Every movement should have betrayed his inner knowledge that there was no hope for him—he could not win. He should have been filled with the stories of the poisons the na-Baron chose for the blade in his white-gloved hand. The na-Baron never gave quick death; he delighted in demonstrating rare poisons, could stand in the arena pointing out interesting side effects on a writhing victim. There was fear in the slave, yes—but not terror.

Feyd-Rautha lifted the barbs high, nodded in an almost-greeting.

The gladiator pounced.

His feint and defensive counter were as good as any Feyd-Rautha had ever seen. A timed side blow missed by the barest fraction from severing the tendons of the na-Baron's left leg.

Feyd-Rautha danced away, leaving a barbed shaft in the slave's right forearm, the hooks completely buried in flesh where the man could not withdraw them without ripping tendons.

A concerted gasp lifted from the galleries.

The sound filled Feyd-Rautha with elation.

He knew now what his uncle was experiencing, sitting up there with the Fenrings, the observers from the Imperial Court, beside him. There could be no interference with this fight. The forms must be observed in front of witnesses. And the Baron would interpret the events in the arena only one way—threat to himself.

The slave backed, holding knife in teeth and lashing the barbed shaft to his arm with the pennant. "I do not feel your needle!" he shouted. Again he crept forward, knife ready, left side presented, his body bent backward to give it the greatest surface of protection from the half-shield.

That action, too, didn't escape the galleries. Sharp cries came from the family boxes. Feyd-Rautha's handlers were calling out to ask if he needed them.

He waved them back to the pru-door.

I'll give them a show such as they've never had before, Feyd-Rautha thought. *No tame killing where they can sit back and admire the style. This'll be something to take them by the guts and twist them. When I'm Baron they'll remember this day and won't be a one of them can escape fear of me because of this day.*

Feyd-Rautha gave ground slowly before the gladiator's crablike advance. Arena sand grated underfoot. He heard the slave's panting, smelled his own sweat and a faint odor of blood on the air.

Steadily, the na-Baron moved backward, turning to the right, his second barb ready. The slave danced sideways. Feyd-Rautha appeared to stumble, heard the scream from the galleries.

Again, the slave pounced.

Gods, what a fighting man! Feyd-Rautha thought as he leaped aside. Only youth's quickness saved him, but he left the second barb buried in the deltoid muscle of the slave's right arm.

Shrill cheers rained from the galleries.

They cheer me now, Feyd-Rautha thought. He heard the wildness in the voices just as Hawat had said he would. They'd never cheered a family fighter that way before. And he thought with an edge of grimness on a thing Hawat had told him: *"It's easier to be terrified by an enemy you admire."*

Swiftly, Feyd-Rautha retreated to the center of the arena where all could see clearly. He drew his long blade, crouched and waited for the advancing slave.

The man took only the time to lash the second barb tight to his arm, then sped in pursuit.

Let the family see me do this thing, Feyd-Rautha thought. *I am their enemy: let them think of me as they see me now.*

He drew his short blade.

"I do not fear you, Harkonnen swine," the gladiator said. "Your tortures cannot hurt a dead man. I can be dead on my own blade before a handler lays finger to my flesh. And I'll have you dead beside me!"

Feyd-Rautha grinned, offered now the long blade, the one with the poison. "Try this on," he said, and feinted with the short blade in his other hand.

The slave shifted knife hands, turned inside both parry and feint to grapple the na-Baron's short blade—the one in the white-gloved hand that tradition said should carry the poison.

"You will die, Harkonnen," the gladiator gasped.

They struggled sideways across the sand. Where Feyd-Rautha's shield met the slave's halfshield, a blue glow marked the contact. The air around them filled with ozone from the field.

"Die on your own poison!" the slave grated.

He began forcing the white-gloved hand inward, turning the blade he thought carried the poison.

Let them see this! Feyd-Rautha thought. He brought down the long blade, felt it clang uselessly against the barbed shaft lashed to the slave's arm.

Feyd-Rautha felt a moment of desperation. He had not thought the barbed shafts would be an advantage for the slave. But they gave the man another shield. And the strength of this gladiator! The short blade was being forced inward inexorably, and Feyd-Rautha focused on the fact that a man could also die on an unpoisoned blade.

"Scum!" Feyd-Rautha gasped.

At the key word, the gladiator's muscles obeyed with a momentary slackness. It was enough for Feyd-Rautha. He opened a space between them sufficient for the long blade. Its poisoned tip flicked out, drew a red line down the slave's chest. There was instant agony in the poison. The man disengaged himself, staggered backward.

Now, let my dear family watch, Feyd-Rautha thought. *Let them think on this slave who tried to turn the knife he thought poisoned and use it against me. Let them wonder how a gladiator could come into this arena ready for such an attempt. And let them always be aware they cannot know for sure which of my hands carries the poison.*

Feyd-Rautha stood in silence, watching the slowed motions of the slave. The man moved within a hesitation-awareness. There was an orthographic thing on his face now for every watcher to recognize. The death was written there. The slave knew it had been done to him and he knew how it had been done. The wrong blade had carried the poison.

"You!" the man moaned.

Feyd-Rautha drew back to give death its space. The paralyzing drug in the poison had yet to take full effect, but the man's slowness told of its advance.

The slave staggered forward as though drawn by a string—one dragging step at a time. Each step was the only step in his universe. He still clutched his knife, but its point wavered.

"One day . . . one . . . of us . . . will . . . get . . . you," he gasped.

A sad little moue contorted his mouth. He sat, sagged, then stiffened and rolled away from Feyd-Rautha, face down.

Feyd-Rautha advanced in the silent arena, put a toe under the gladiator and rolled him onto his back to give the galleries a clear view of the face when the poison began its twisting, wrenching work on the muscles. But the gladiator came over with his own knife, protruding from his breast.

In spite of frustration, there was for Feyd-Rautha a measure of admiration for the effort this slave had managed in overcoming the paralysis to do this thing to himself. With the admiration came the realization that here was *truly* a thing to fear.

That which makes a man superhuman is terrifying.

As he focused on this thought, Feyd-Rautha became conscious of the eruption of noise from the stands and galleries around him. They were cheering with utter abandon.

Feyd-Rautha turned, looking up at them.

All were cheering except the Baron, who sat with hand to chin in deep contemplation—and the Count and his lady, both of whom were staring down at him, their faces masked by smiles.

Count Fenring turned to his lady, said: "Ah-h-h-um-m-m, a resourceful um-m-m-m young man. Eh, mm-m-m-ah, my dear?"

"His ah-h-h synaptic responses are very swift," she said.

The Baron looked at her, at the Count, returned his attention to the arena, thinking: *If someone could get that close to one of mine!* Rage began to replace his fear. *I'll have the slavemaster dead over a slow fire this night . . . and if this Count and his lady had a hand in it. . . .*

The conversation in the Baron's box was remote movement to Feyd-Rautha, the voices drowned in the foot-stamping chant that came now from all around:

"Head! Head! Head! Head!"

The Baron scowled, seeing the way Feyd-Rautha turned to him. Languidly, controlling his rage with difficulty, the Baron waved his hand toward the young man standing in the arena beside the sprawled body of the slave. *Give the boy a head. He earned it by exposing the slavemaster.*

Feyd-Rautha saw the signal of agreement, thought: *They think they honor me. Let them see what I think!*

He saw his handlers approaching with a saw-knife to do the honors, waved them back, repeated the gesture as they hesitated. *They think they honor me with just a head!* he thought. He bent and crossed the gladiator's hands around the protruding knife handle, then removed the knife and placed it in the limp hands.

It was done in an instant, and he straightened, beckoned his handlers. "Bury this slave intact with his knife in his hands," he said. "The man earned it."

In the golden box, Count Fenring leaned close to the Baron, said: "A grand gesture, that—true bravura. Your nephew has style as well as courage."

"He insults the crowd by refusing the head," the Baron muttered.

"Not at all," Lady Fenring said. She turned, looking up at the tiers around them.

And the Baron noted the line of her neck—a truly lovely flowing of muscles—like a young boy's.

"They like what your nephew did," she said.

As the import of Feyd-Rautha's gesture penetrated to the most distant seats, as the people saw the handlers carrying off the dead gladiator intact, the Baron watched them and realized she had interpreted the reaction correctly. The people were going wild, beating on each other, screaming and stamping.

The Baron spoke wearily. "I shall have to order a fete. You cannot send people home like this, their energies unspent. They must see that I share their elation." He gave a hand signal to his guard, and a servant above them dipped the Harkonnen orange pennant over the box—once, twice, three times—signal for a fete.

Feyd-Rautha crossed the arena to stand beneath the golden box, his weapons sheathed, arms hanging at his sides. Above the undiminished frenzy of the crowd, he called: "A fete, Uncle?"

The noise began to subside as people saw the conversation and waited.

"In your honor, Feyd!" the Baron called down. And again, he caused the pennant to be dipped in signal.

Across the arena, the pru-barriers had been dropped and young men were leaping down into the arena, racing toward Feyd-Rautha.

"You ordered the pru-shields dropped, Baron?" the Count asked.

"No one will harm the lad," the Baron said. "He's a hero."

The first of the charging mass reached Feyd-Rautha, lifted him on their shoulders, began parading around the arena.

"He could walk unarmed and unshielded through the poorest quarters of Harko tonight," the Baron said. "They'd give him the last of their food and drink just for his company."

The Baron pushed himself from his chair, settled his weight into his suspensors. "You will forgive me, please. There are matters that require my immediate attention. The guard will see you to the keep."

The Count arose, bowed. "Certainly, Baron. We're looking forward to the fete. I've ah-h-h-mm-m-m never seen a Harkonnen fete."

"Yes," the Baron said. "The fete." He turned, was enveloped by guards as he stepped into the private exit from the box.

A guard captain bowed to Count Fenring. "Your orders, my Lord?"

"We will ah-h-h wait for the worst mm-m-m crush to um-m-m pass," the Count said.

"Yes, m'Lord." The man bowed himself back three paces.

Count Fenring faced his lady, spoke again in their personal humming-code tongue: "You saw it, of course?"

In the same humming tongue, she said: "The lad knew the gladiator wouldn't be drugged. There was a moment of fear, yes, but no surprise."

"It was planned," he said. "The entire performance."

"Without a doubt."

"It stinks of Hawat."

"Indeed," she said.

"I demanded earlier that the Baron eliminate Hawat."

"That was an error, my dear."

"I see that now."

"The Harkonnens may have a new Baron ere long."

"If that's Hawat's plan."

"That will bear examination, true," she said.

"The young one will be more amenable to control."

"For us . . . after tonight," she said.

"You don't anticipate difficulty seducing him, my little broodmother?"

"No, my love. You saw how he looked at me."

"Yes, and I can see now why we must have that bloodline."

"Indeed, and it's obvious we must have a hold on him. I'll plant deep in his deepest self the necessary prana-bindu phrases to bend him."

"We'll leave as soon as possible—as soon as you're sure," he said.

She shuddered. "By all means. I should not want to bear a child in this terrible place."

"The things we do in the name of humanity," he said.

"Yours is the easy part," she said.

"There *are* some ancient prejudices I overcome," he said. "They're quite primordial, you know."

"My poor dear," she said, and patted his cheek. "You know this is the only way to be sure of saving that bloodline."

He spoke in a dry voice: "I quite understand what we do."

"We won't fail," she said.

"Guilt starts as a feeling of failure," he reminded.

"There'll be no guilt," she said. "Hypno-ligation of that Feyd-Rautha's psyche and his child in my womb—then we go."

"That uncle," he said. "Have you ever seen such distortion?"

"He's pretty fierce," she said, "but the nephew could well grow to be worse."

"Thanks to that uncle. You know, when you think what this lad could've been with some other upbringing—with the Atreides code to guide him, for example."

"It's sad," she said.

"Would that we could've saved both the Atreides youth and this one. From what I heard of that young Paul—a most admirable lad, good union of breeding and training." He shook his head. "But we shouldn't waste sorrow over the aristocracy of misfortune."

"There's a Bene Gesserit saying," she said.

"You have sayings for everything!" he protested.

"You'll like this one," she said. "It goes: 'Do not count a human dead until you've seen his body. And even then you can make a mistake.'"

Muad'Dib tells us in "A Time of Reflection" that his first colli-
sions with Arrakeen necessities were the true beginnings of
his education. He learned then how to pole the sand for its
weather, learned the language of the wind's needles stinging
his skin, learned how the nose can buzz with sand-itch and
how to gather his body's precious moisture around him to
guard it and preserve it. As his eyes assumed the blue of the
Ibad, he learned the Chakobsa way.

—STILGAR'S PREFACE TO "MUAD'DIB, THE MAN"
BY THE PRINCESS IRULAN

Stilgar's troop returning to the sietch with its two strays from the desert
climbed out of the basin in the waning light of the first moon. The
robed figures hurried with the smell of home in their nostrils. Dawn's
gray line behind them was brightest at the notch in their horizon-
calendar that marked the middle of autumn, the month of Caprock.

Wind-raked dead leaves strewed the cliffbase where the sietch children had been gathering them, but the sounds of the troop's passage
(except for occasional blunderings by Paul and his mother) could not be
distinguished from the natural sounds of the night.

Paul wiped sweat-caked dust from his forehead, felt a tug at his arm,
heard Chani's voice hissing. "Do as I told you: bring the fold of your
hood down over your forehead! Leave only the eyes exposed. You waste
moisture."

A whispered command behind them demanded silence: "The desert hears you!"

A bird chirruped from the rocks high above them.

The troop stopped, and Paul sensed abrupt tension.

There came a faint thumping from the rocks, a sound no louder than mice jumping in the sand.

Again, the bird chirruped.

A stir passed through the troop's ranks. And again, the mouse-thumping pecked its way across the sand.

Once more, the bird chirruped.

The troop resumed its climb up into a crack in the rocks, but there was a stillness of breath about the Fremen now that filled Paul with caution, and he noted covert glances toward Chani, the way she seemed to withdraw, pulling in upon herself.

There was rock underfoot now, a faint gray swishing of robes around them, and Paul sensed a relaxing of discipline, but still that quiet-of-the-person about Chani and the others. He followed a shadow shape—up steps, a turn, more steps, into a tunnel, past two moisture-sealed doors and into a globelighted narrow passage with yellow rock walls and ceiling.

All around him, Paul saw the Fremen throwing back their hoods, removing nose plugs, breathing deeply. Someone sighed. Paul looked for Chani, found that she had left his side. He was hemmed in by a press of robed bodies. Someone jostled him, said, "Excuse me, Usul. What a crush! It's always this way."

On his left, the narrow bearded face of the one called Farok turned toward Paul. The stained eyepits and blue darkness of eyes appeared even darker under the yellow globes. "Throw off your hood, Usul," Farok said. "You're home." And he helped Paul, releasing the hood catch, elbowing a space around them.

Paul slipped out his nose plugs, swung the mouth baffle aside. The odor of the place assailed him: unwashed bodies, distillate esthers of reclaimed wastes, everywhere the sour effluvia of humanity with, over it all, a turbulence of spice and spicelike harmonics.

"Why are we waiting, Farok?" Paul asked.

"For the Reverend Mother, I think. You heard the message—poor Chani."

Poor Chani? Paul asked himself. He looked around, wondering where she was, where his mother had got to in all this crush.

Farok took a deep breath. "The smells of home," he said.

Paul saw that the man was enjoying the stink of this air, that there was no irony in his tone. He heard his mother cough then, and her voice came back to him through the press of the troop: "How rich the odors of your sietch, Stilgar. I see you do much working with the spice . . . you make paper . . . plastics . . . and isn't that chemical explosives?"

"You know this from what you smell?" It was another man's voice.

And Paul realized she was speaking for his benefit, that she wanted him to make a quick acceptance of this assault on his nostrils.

There came a buzz of activity at the head of the troop and a prolonged indrawn breath that seemed to pass through the Fremen, and Paul heard hushed voices back down the line: "It's true then—Liet is dead."

Liet, Paul thought. Then: *Chani, daughter of Liet.* The pieces fell together in his mind. Liet was the Fremen name of the planetologist.

Paul looked at Farok, asked: "Is it the Liet known as Kynes?"

"There is only one Liet," Farok said.

Paul turned, stared at the robed back of a Fremen in front of him. *Then Liet-Kynes is dead,* he thought.

"It was Harkonnen treachery," someone hissed. "They made it seem an accident . . . lost in the desert . . . a 'thopter crash. . . ."

Paul felt a burst of anger. The man who had befriended them, helped save them from the Harkonnen hunters, the man who had sent his Fremen cohorts searching for two strays in the desert . . . another victim of the Harkonnens.

"Does Usul hunger yet for revenge?" Farok asked.

Before Paul could answer, there came a low call and the troop swept forward into a wider chamber, carrying Paul with them. He found himself in an open space confronted by Stilgar and a strange woman wearing a flowing wraparound garment of brilliant orange and green. Her arms were bare to the shoulders, and he could see she wore no stillsuit. Her skin was a pale olive. Dark hair swept back from her high forehead, throwing emphasis on sharp cheekbones and aquiline nose between the dense darkness of her eyes.

She turned toward him, and Paul saw golden rings threaded with water tallies dangling from her ears.

"*This* bested my Jamis?" she demanded.

"Be silent, Harah," Stilgar said. "It was Jamis' doing—*he* invoked the tahaddi al-burhan."

"He's not but a boy!" she said. She gave her head a sharp shake from side to side, setting the water tallies to jingling. "My children made fatherless by another child? Surely, 'twas an accident!"

"Usul, how many years have you?" Stilgar asked.

"Fifteen Standard," Paul said.

Stilgar swept his eyes over the troop. "Is there one among you cares to challenge me?"

Silence.

Stilgar looked at the woman. "Until I've learned his weirding ways, I'd not challenge him."

She returned his stare. "But—"

"You saw the stranger woman who went with Chani to the Reverend Mother?" Stilgar asked. "She's an out-freyn Sayyadina, mother to this lad. The mother and son are masters of the weirding ways of battle."

"Lisan al-Gaib," the woman whispered. Her eyes held awe as she turned them back toward Paul.

The legend again, Paul thought.

"Perhaps," Stilgar said. "It hasn't been tested, though." He returned his attention to Paul. "Usul, it's our way that you've now the responsibility for Jamis' woman here and for his two sons. His yali . . . his quarters, are yours. His coffee service is yours . . . and this, his woman."

Paul studied the woman, wondering: *Why isn't she mourning her man? Why does she show no hate for me?* Abruptly, he saw that the Fremen were staring at him, waiting.

Someone whispered: "There's work to do. Say how you accept her."

Stilgar said: "Do you accept Harah as woman or servant?"

Harah lifted her arms, turning slowly on one heel. "I am still young, Usul. It's said I still look as young as when I was with Geoff . . . before Jamis bested him."

Jamis killed another to win her, Paul thought.

Paul said: "If I accept her as servant, may I yet change my mind at a later time?"

"You'd have a year to change your decision," Stilgar said. "After that, she's a free woman to choose as she wishes . . . or you could free her to choose for herself at any time. But she's your responsibility, no matter what, for one year . . . and you'll always share some responsibility for the sons of Jamis."

"I accept her as servant," Paul said.

Harah stamped a foot, shook her shoulders with anger. "But I'm young!"

Stilgar looked at Paul, said: "Caution's a worthy trait in a man who'd lead."

"But I'm young!" Harah repeated.

"Be silent," Stilgar commanded. "If a thing has merit, it'll be. Show Usul to his quarters and see he has fresh clothing and a place to rest."

"Oh-h-h-h!" she said.

Paul had registered enough of her to have a first approximation. He felt the impatience of the troop, knew many things were being delayed here. He wondered if he dared ask the whereabouts of his mother and Chani, saw from Stilgar's nervous stance that it would be a mistake.

He faced Harah, pitched his voice with tone and tremolo to accent her fear and awe, said: "Show me my quarters, Harah! We will discuss your youth another time."

She backed away two steps, cast a frightened glance at Stilgar. "He has the weirding voice," she husked.

"Stilgar," Paul said. "Chani's father put heavy obligation on me. If there's anything. . . ."

"It'll be decided in council," Stilgar said. "You can speak then." He nodded in dismissal, turned away with the rest of the troop following him.

Paul took Harah's arm, noting how cool her flesh seemed, feeling her tremble. "I'll not harm you, Harah," he said. "Show me our quarters." And he smoothed his voice with relaxants.

"You'll not cast me out when the year's gone?" she said. "I know for true I'm not as young as once I was."

"As long as I live you'll have a place with me," he said. He released her arm. "Come now, where are our quarters?"

She turned, led the way down the passage, turning right into a wide cross tunnel lighted by evenly spaced yellow overhead globes. The stone floor was smooth, swept clean of sand.

Paul moved up beside her, studied the aquiline profile as they walked. "You do not hate me, Harah?"

"Why should I hate you?"

She nodded to a cluster of children who stared at them from the raised ledge of a side passage. Paul glimpsed adult shapes behind the children partly hidden by filmy hangings.

"I . . . bested Jamis."

"Stilgar said the ceremony was held and you're a friend of Jamis." She glanced sidelong at him. "Stilgar said you gave moisture to the dead. Is that truth?"

"Yes."

"It's more than I'll do . . . can do."

"Don't you mourn him?"

"In the time of mourning, I'll mourn him."

They passed an arched opening. Paul looked through it at men and women working with stand-mounted machinery in a large, bright chamber. There seemed an extra tempo of urgency to them.

"What're they doing in there?" Paul asked.

She glanced back as they passed beyond the arch, said: "They hurry to finish the quota in the plastics shop before we flee. We need many dew collectors for the planting."

"Flee?"

"Until the butchers stop hunting us or are driven from our land."

Paul caught himself in a stumble, sensing an arrested instant of time, remembering a fragment, a visual projection of prescience—but it was displaced, like a montage in motion. The bits of his prescient memory were not quite as he remembered them.

"The Sardaukar hunt us," he said.

"They'll not find much excepting an empty sietch or two," she said. "And they'll find their share of death in the sand."

"They'll find this place?" he asked.

"Likely."

"Yet we take the time to. . . ." He motioned with his head toward the arch now far behind them. ". . . make . . . dew collectors?"

"The planting goes on."

"What're dew collectors?" he asked.

The glance she turned on him was full of surprise. "Don't they teach you anything in the . . . wherever it is you come from?"

"Not about dew collectors."

"Hai!" she said, and there was a whole conversation in the one word.

"Well, what are they?"

"Each bush, each weed you see out there in the erg," she said, "how do you suppose it lives when we leave it? Each is planted most tenderly in its own little pit. The pits are filled with smooth ovals of chromoplastic. Light turns them white. You can see them glistening in the dawn if you look down from a high place. White reflects. But when Old Father Sun departs, the chromoplastic reverts to transparency in the dark. It cools with extreme rapidity. The surface condenses moisture out of the air. That moisture trickles down to keep our plants alive."

"Dew collectors," he muttered, enchanted by the simple beauty of such a scheme.

"I'll mourn Jamis in the proper time for it," she said, as though her mind had not left his other question. "He was a good man, Jamis, but quick to anger. A good provider, Jamis, and a wonder with the children. He made no separation between Geoff's boy, my firstborn, and his own true son. They were equal in his eyes." She turned a questing stare on Paul. "Would it be that way with you, Usul?"

"We don't have that problem."

"But if—"

"Harah!"

She recoiled at the harsh edge in his voice.

They passed another brightly lighted room visible through an arch on their left. "What's made there?" he asked.

"They repair the weaving machinery," she said. "But it must be dismantled by tonight." She gestured at a tunnel branching to their left. "Through there and beyond, that's food processing and stillsuit maintenance." She looked at Paul. "Your suit looks new. But if it needs work, I'm good with suits. I work in the factory in season."

They began coming on knots of people now and thicker clusterings of openings in the tunnel's sides. A file of men and women passed them carrying packs that gurgled heavily, the smell of spice strong about them.

"They'll not get our water," Harah said. "Or our spice. You can be sure of that."

Paul glanced at the openings in the tunnel walls, seeing the heavy carpets on the raised ledge, glimpses of rooms with bright fabrics on the walls, piled cushions. People in the openings fell silent at their approach, followed Paul with untamed stares.

"The people find it strange you bested Jamis," Harah said. "Likely you'll have some proving to do when we're settled in a new sietch."

"I don't like killing," he said.

"Thus Stilgar tells it," she said, but her voice betrayed her disbelief.

A shrill chanting grew louder ahead of them. They came to another side opening wider than any of the others Paul had seen. He slowed his pace, staring in at a room crowded with children sitting cross-legged on a maroon-carpeted floor.

At a chalkboard against the far wall stood a woman in a yellow wraparound, a projecto-stylus in one hand. The board was filled with designs—circles, wedges and curves, snake tracks and squares, flowing arcs split by parallel lines. The woman pointed to the designs one after the other as fast as she could move the stylus, and the children chanted in rhythm with her moving hand.

Paul listened, hearing the voices grow dimmer behind as he moved deeper into the sietch with Harah.

"Tree," the children chanted. "Tree, grass, dune, wind, mountain, hill, fire, lightning, rock, rocks, dust, sand, heat, shelter, full, winter, cold, empty, erosion, summer, cavern, day, tension, moon, night, caprock, sandtide, slope, planting, binder. . . ."

"You conduct classes at a time like this?" Paul asked.

Her face went somber and grief edged her voice: "What Liet taught us, we cannot pause an instant in that. Liet who is dead must not be forgotten. It's the Chakobsa way."

She crossed the tunnel to the left, stepped up onto a ledge, parted gauzy orange hangings and stood aside: "Your yali is ready for you, Usul."

Paul hesitated before joining her on the ledge. He felt a sudden reluctance to be alone with this woman. It came to him that he was surrounded by a way of life that could only be understood by postulating an ecology of ideas and values. He felt that this Fremen world was fishing for him, trying to snare him in its ways. And he knew what lay in that snare—the wild jihad, the religious war he felt he should avoid at any cost.

"This is your yali," Harah said. "Why do you hesitate?"

Paul nodded, joined her on the ledge. He lifted the hangings across from her, feeling metal fibers in the fabric, followed her into a short entrance way and then into a larger room, square, about six meters to a side—thick blue carpets on the floor, blue and green fabrics hiding the rock walls, glowglobes tuned to yellow overhead bobbing against draped yellow ceiling fabrics.

The effect was that of an ancient tent.

Harah stood in front of him, left hand on hip, her eyes studying his face. "The children are with a friend," she said. "They will present themselves later."

Paul masked his unease beneath a quick scanning of the room. Thin hangings to the right, he saw, partly concealed a larger room with cushions piled around the walls. He felt a soft breeze from an air duct, saw the outlet cunningly hidden in a pattern of hangings directly ahead of him.

"Do you wish me to help you remove your stillsuit?" Harah asked.

"No . . . thank you."

"Shall I bring food?"

"Yes."

"There is a reclamation chamber off the other room." She gestured. "For your comfort and convenience when you're out of your stillsuit."

"You said we have to leave this sietch," Paul said. "Shouldn't we be packing or something?"

"It will be done in its time," she said. "The butchers have yet to penetrate to our region."

Still she hesitated, staring at him.

"What is it?" he demanded.

"You've not the eyes of the Ibad," she said. "It's strange but not entirely unattractive."

"Get the food," he said. "I'm hungry."

She smiled at him—a knowing, woman's smile that he found disquieting. "I am your servant," she said, and whirled away in one lithe motion, ducking behind a heavy wall hanging that revealed another passage before falling back into place.

Feeling angry with himself, Paul brushed through the thin hanging on the right and into the larger room. He stood there a moment caught by uncertainty. And he wondered where Chani was . . . Chani who had just lost her father.

We're alike in that, he thought.

A wailing cry sounded from the outer corridors, its volume muffled by the intervening hangings. It was repeated, a bit more distant. And again. Paul realized someone was calling the time. He focused on the fact that he had seen no clocks.

The faint smell of burning creosote bush came to his nostrils, riding on the omnipresent stink of the sietch. Paul saw that he had already suppressed the odorous assault on his senses.

And he wondered again about his mother, how the moving montage of the future would incorporate her . . . and the daughter she bore. Mutable time-awareness danced around him. He shook his head sharply, focusing his attention on the evidences that spoke of profound depth and breadth in this Fremen culture that had swallowed them.

With its subtle oddities.

He had seen a thing about the caverns and this room, a thing that suggested far greater differences than anything he had yet encountered.

There was no sign of a poison snooper here, no indication of their use anywhere in the cave warren. Yet he could smell poisons in the sietch stench—strong ones, common ones.

He heard a rustle of hangings, thought it was Harah returning with food, and turned to watch her. Instead, from beneath a displaced pattern of hangings, he saw two young boys—perhaps aged nine and ten—staring out at him with greedy eyes. Each wore a small kindjal-type of crysknife, rested a hand on the hilt.

And Paul recalled the stories of the Fremen—that their children fought as ferociously as the adults.

The hands move, the lips move—
Ideas gush from his words,
And his eyes devour!
He is an island of Selfdom.

—DESCRIPTION FROM "A MANUAL OF MUAD'DIB"
BY THE PRINCESS IRULAN

Phosphor tubes in the faraway upper reaches of the cavern cast a dim light onto the thronged interior, hinting at the great size of this rock-enclosed space . . . larger, Jessica saw, than even the Gathering Hall of her Bene Gesserit school. She estimated there were more than five thousand people gathered out there beneath the ledge where she stood with Stilgar.

And more were coming.

The air was murmurous with people.

"Your son has been summoned from his rest, Sayyadina," Stilgar said. "Do you wish him to share in your decision?"

"Could he change my decision?"

"Certainly, the air with which you speak comes from your own lungs, but—"

"The decision stands," she said.

But she felt misgivings, wondering if she should use Paul as an excuse for backing out of a dangerous course. There was an unborn daughter to think of as well. What endangered the flesh of the mother endangered the flesh of the daughter.

Men came with rolled carpets, grunting under the weight of them, stirring up dust as the loads were dropped onto the ledge.

Stilgar took her arm, led her back into the acoustical horn that formed the rear limits of the ledge. He indicated a rock bench within the horn. "The Reverend Mother will sit here, but you may rest yourself until she comes."

"I prefer to stand," Jessica said.

She watched the men unroll the carpets, covering the ledge, looked out at the crowd. There were at least ten thousand people on the rock floor now.

And still they came.

Out on the desert, she knew, it already was red nightfall, but here in the cavern hall was perpetual twilight, a gray vastness thronged with people come to see her risk her life.

A way was opened through the crowd to her right, and she saw Paul approaching flanked by two small boys. There was a swaggering air of self-importance about the children. They kept hands on knives, scowled at the wall of people on either side.

"The sons of Jamis who are now the sons of Usul," Stilgar said. "They take their escort duties seriously." He ventured a smile at Jessica.

Jessica recognized the effort to lighten her mood and was grateful for it, but could not take her mind from the danger that confronted her.

I had no choice but to do this, she thought. *We must move swiftly if we're to secure our place among these Fremen.*

Paul climbed to the ledge, leaving the children below. He stopped in front of his mother, glanced at Stilgar, back to Jessica. "What is happening? I thought I was being summoned to council."

Stilgar raised a hand for silence, gestured to his left where another way had been opened in the throng. Chani came down the lane opened there, her elfin face set in lines of grief. She had removed her stillsuit and wore a graceful blue wraparound that exposed her thin arms. Near the shoulder on her left arm, a green kerchief had been tied.

Green for mourning, Paul thought.

It was one of the customs the two sons of Jamis had explained to him by indirection, telling him they wore no green because they accepted him as guardian-father.

"Are you the Lisan al-Gaib?" they had asked. And Paul had sensed the jihad in their words, shrugged off the question with one of his own—learning then that Kaleff, the elder of the two, was ten, and the natural son of Geoff. Orlop, the younger, was eight, the natural son of Jamis.

It had been a strange day with these two standing guard over him because he asked it, keeping away the curious, allowing him the time to nurse his thoughts and prescient memories, to plan a way to prevent the jihad.

Now, standing beside his mother on the cavern ledge and looking out at the throng, he wondered if any plan could prevent the wild outpouring of fanatic legions.

Chani, nearing the ledge, was followed at a distance by four women carrying another woman in a litter.

Jessica ignored Chani's approach, focusing all her attention on the woman in the litter—a crone, a wrinkled and shriveled ancient thing in a black gown with hood thrown back to reveal the tight knot of gray hair and the stringy neck.

The litter-carriers deposited their burden gently on the ledge from below, and Chani helped the old woman to her feet.

So this is their Reverend Mother, Jessica thought.

The old woman leaned heavily on Chani as she hobbled toward Jessica, looking like a collection of sticks draped in the black robe. She stopped in front of Jessica, peered upward for a long moment before speaking in a husky whisper.

"So you're the one." The old head nodded once precariously on the thin neck. "The Shadout Mapes was right to pity you."

Jessica spoke quickly, scornfully: "I need no one's pity."

"That remains to be seen," husked the old woman. She turned with surprising quickness and faced the throng. "Tell them, Stilgar."

"Must I?" he asked.

"We are the people of Misr," the old woman rasped. "Since our

Sunni ancestors fled from Nilotic al-Ourouba, we have known flight and death. The young go on that our people shall not die."

Stilgar took a deep breath, stepped forward two paces.

Jessica felt the hush come over the crowded cavern—some twenty thousand people now, standing silently, almost without movement. It made her feel suddenly small and filled with caution.

"Tonight we must leave this sietch that has sheltered us for so long and go south into the desert," Stilgar said. His voice boomed out across the uplifted faces, reverberating with the force given it by the acoustical horn behind the ledge.

Still the throng remained silent.

"The Reverend Mother tells me she cannot survive another hajra," Stilgar said. "We have lived before without a Reverend Mother, but it is not good for people to seek a new home in such straits."

Now, the throng stirred, rippling with whispers and currents of disquiet.

"That this may not come to pass," Stilgar said, "our new Sayyadina Jessica of the Weirding, has consented to enter the rite at this time. She will attempt to pass within that we not lose the strength of our Reverend Mother."

Jessica of the Weirding, Jessica thought. She saw Paul staring at her, his eyes filled with questions, but his mouth held silent by all the strangeness around them.

If I die in the attempt, what will become of him? Jessica asked herself. Again she felt the misgivings fill her mind.

Chani led the old Reverend Mother to a rock bench deep in the acoustical horn, returned to stand beside Stilgar.

"That we may not lose all if Jessica of the Weirding should fail," Stilgar said, "Chani, daughter of Liet, will be consecrated in the Sayyadina at this time." He stepped one pace to the side.

From deep in the acoustical horn, the old woman's voice came out to them, an amplified whisper, harsh and penetrating: "Chani has returned from her hajra—Chani has seen the waters."

A susurrant response arose from the crowd: "She has seen the waters."

"I consecrate the daughter of Liet in the Sayyadina," husked the old woman.

"She is accepted," the crowd responded.

Paul barely heard the ceremony, his attention still centered on what had been said of his mother.

If she should fail?

He turned and looked back at the one they called Reverend Mother, studying the dried crone features, the fathomless blue fixation of her eyes. She looked as though a breeze would blow her away, yet there was that about her which suggested she might stand untouched in the path of a coriolis storm. She carried the same aura of power that he remembered from the Reverend Mother Gaius Helen Mohiam who had tested him with agony in the way of the gom jabbar.

"I, the Reverend Mother Ramallo, whose voice speaks as a multitude, say this to you," the old woman said. "It is fitting that Chani enter the Sayyadina."

"It is fitting," the crowd responded.

The old woman nodded, whispered: "I give her the silver skies, the golden desert and its shining rocks, the green fields that will be. I give these to Sayyadina Chani. And lest she forget that she's servant of us all, to her fall the menial tasks in this Ceremony of the Seed. Let it be as Shai-hulud will have it." She lifted a brown-stick arm, dropped it.

Jessica, feeling the ceremony close around her with a current that swept her beyond all turning back, glanced once at Paul's question-filled face, then prepared herself for the ordeal.

"Let the watermasters come forward," Chani said with only the slightest quaver of uncertainty in her girl-child voice.

Now, Jessica felt herself at the focus of danger, knowing its presence in the watchfulness of the throng, in the silence.

A band of men made its way through a serpentine path opened in the crowd, moving up from the back in pairs. Each pair carried a small skin sack, perhaps twice the size of a human head. The sacks sloshed heavily.

The two leaders deposited their load at Chani's feet on the ledge and stepped back.

Jessica looked at the sack, then at the men. They had their hoods thrown back, exposing long hair tied in a roll at the base of the neck. The black pits of their eyes stared back at her without wavering.

A furry redolence of cinnamon arose from the sack, wafted across Jessica. *The spice?* she wondered.

"Is there water?" Chani asked.

The watermaster on the left, a man with a purple scar line across the bridge of his nose, nodded once. "There is water, Sayyadina," he said, "but we cannot drink of it."

"Is there seed?" Chani asked.

"There is seed," the man said.

Chani knelt and put her hands to the sloshing sack. "Blessed is the water and its seed."

There was familiarity to the rite, and Jessica looked back at the Reverend Mother Ramallo. The old woman's eyes were closed and she sat hunched over as though asleep.

"Sayyadina Jessica," Chani said.

Jessica turned to see the girl staring up at her.

"Have you tasted the blessed water?" Chani asked.

Before Jessica could answer, Chani said: "It is not possible that you have tasted the blessed water. You are outworlder and unprivileged."

A sigh passed through the crowd, a susurration of robes that made the nape hairs creep on Jessica's neck.

"The crop was large and the maker has been destroyed," Chani said. She began unfastening a coiled spout fixed to the top of the sloshing sack.

Now, Jessica felt the sense of danger boiling around her. She glanced at Paul, saw that he was caught up in the mystery of the ritual and had eyes only for Chani.

Has he seen this moment in time? Jessica wondered. She rested a hand on her abdomen, thinking of the unborn daughter there, asking herself: *Do I have the right to risk us both?*

Chani lifted the spout toward Jessica, said: "Here is the Water of Life, the water that is greater than water—Kan, the water that frees the soul. If you be a Reverend Mother, it opens the universe to you. Let Shai-hulud judge now."

Jessica felt herself torn between duty to her unborn child and duty to Paul. For Paul, she knew, she should take that spout and drink of the sack's contents, but as she bent to the proffered spout, her senses told her its peril.

The stuff in the sack had a bitter smell subtly akin to many poisons that she knew, but unlike them, too.

"You must drink it now," Chani said.

There's no turning back, Jessica reminded herself. But nothing in all her Bene Gesserit training came into her mind to help her through this instant.

What is it? Jessica asked herself. *Liquor? A drug?*

She bent over the spout, smelled the esthers of cinnamon, remembering then the drunkenness of Duncan Idaho. *Spice liquor?* she asked herself. She took the siphon tube in her mouth, pulled up only the most minuscule sip. It tasted of the spice, a faint bite acrid on the tongue.

Chani pressed down on the skin bag. A great gulp of the stuff surged into Jessica's mouth and before she could help herself, she swallowed it, fighting to retain her calmness and dignity.

"To accept a little-death is worse than death itself," Chani said. She stared at Jessica, waiting.

And Jessica stared back, still holding the spout in her mouth. She tasted the sack's contents in her nostrils, in the roof of her mouth, in her cheeks, in her eyes—a biting sweetness, now.

Cool.

Again, Chani sent the liquid gushing into Jessica's mouth.

Delicate.

Jessica studied Chani's face—elfin features—seeing the traces of Liet-Kynes there as yet unfixed by time.

This is a drug they feed me, Jessica told herself.

But it was unlike any other drug of her experience, and Bene Gesserit training included the taste of many drugs.

Chani's features were so clear, as though outlined in light.

A drug.

Whirling silence settled around Jessica. Every fiber of her body accepted the fact that something profound had happened to it. She felt that she was a conscious mote, smaller than any subatomic particle, yet capable of motion and of sensing her surroundings. Like an abrupt revelation—the curtains whipped away—she realized she had become aware of a psychokinesthetic extension of herself. She was the mote, yet not the mote.

The cavern remained around her—the people. She sensed them: Paul, Chani, Stilgar, the Reverend Mother Ramallo.

Reverend Mother!

At the school there had been rumors that some did not survive the Reverend Mother ordeal, that the drug took them.

Jessica focused her attention on the Reverend Mother Ramallo, aware now that all this was happening in a frozen instant of time—suspended time for her alone.

Why is time suspended? she asked herself. She stared at the frozen expressions around her, seeing a dust mote above Chani's head, stopped there.

Waiting.

The answer to this instant came like an explosion in her consciousness: her personal time was suspended to save her life.

She focused on the psychokinesthetic extension of herself, looking within, and was confronted immediately with a cellular core, a pit of blackness from which she recoiled.

That is the place where we cannot look, she thought. *There is the place the Reverend Mothers are so reluctant to mention—the place where only a Kwisatz Haderach may look.*

This realization returned a small measure of confidence, and again she ventured to focus on the psychokinesthetic extension, becoming a mote-self that searched within her for danger.

She found it within the drug she had swallowed.

The stuff was dancing particles within her, its motions so rapid that even frozen time could not stop them. Dancing particles. She began recognizing familiar structures, atomic linkages: a carbon atom here, helical wavering . . . a glucose molecule. An entire chain of molecules confronted her, and she recognized a protein . . . a methyl-protein configuration.

Ah-h-h!

It was a soundless mental sigh within her as she saw the nature of the poison.

With her psychokinesthetic probing, she moved into it, shifted an oxygen mote, allowed another carbon mote to link, reattached a linkage of oxygen . . . hydrogen.

The change spread . . . faster and faster as the catalyzed reaction opened its surface of contact.

The suspension of time relaxed its hold upon her, and she sensed motion. The tube spout from the sack was touched to her mouth—gently, collecting a drop of moisture.

Chani's taking the catalyst from my body to change the poison in that sack, Jessica thought. *Why?*

Someone eased her to a sitting position. She saw the old Reverend Mother Ramallo being brought to sit beside her on the carpeted ledge. A dry hand touched her neck.

And there was another psychokinesthetic mote within her awareness! Jessica tried to reject it, but the mote swept closer . . . closer.

They touched!

It was like an ultimate *simpatico,* being two people at once: not telepathy, but mutual awareness.

With the old Reverend Mother!

But Jessica saw that the Reverend Mother didn't think of herself as old. An image unfolded before the mutual mind's eye: a young girl with a dancing spirit and tender humor.

Within the mutual awareness, the young girl said, "Yes, that is how I am."

Jessica could only accept the words, not respond to them.

"You'll have it all soon, Jessica," the inward image said.

This is hallucination, Jessica told herself.

"You know better than that," the inward image said. "Swiftly now, do not fight me. There isn't much time. We. . . ." There came a long pause, then: "You should've told us you were pregnant!"

Jessica found the voice that talked within the mutual awareness. "Why?"

"This changes both of you! Holy Mother, what have we done?"

Jessica sensed a forced shift in the mutual awareness, saw another mote-presence with the inward eye. The other mote darted wildly here, there, circling. It radiated pure terror.

"You'll have to be strong," the old Reverend Mother's image-presence said. "Be thankful it's a daughter you carry. This would've killed a male fetus. Now . . . carefully, gently . . . touch your daughter-presence. Be your daughter-presence. Absorb the fear . . . soothe . . . use your courage and your strength . . . gently now . . . gently. . . ."

The other whirling mote swept near, and Jessica compelled herself to touch it.

Terror threatened to overwhelm her.

She fought it the only way she knew: *"I shall not fear. Fear is the mind-killer. . . ."*

The litany brought a semblance of calm. The other mote lay quiescent against her.

Words won't work, Jessica told herself.

She reduced herself to basic emotional reactions, radiated love, comfort, a warm snuggling of protection.

The terror receded.

Again, the presence of the old Reverend Mother asserted itself, but now there was a tripling of mutual awareness—two active and one that lay quietly absorbing.

"Time compels me," the Reverend Mother said within the awareness. "I have much to give you. And I do not know if your daughter can accept all this while remaining sane. But it must be: the needs of the tribe are paramount."

"What—"

"Remain silent and accept!"

Experiences began to unroll before Jessica. It was like a lecture strip in a subliminal training projector at the Bene Gesserit school . . . but faster . . . blindingly faster.

Yet . . . distinct.

She knew each experience as it happened: there was a lover—virile, bearded, with the Fremen eyes, and Jessica saw his strength and tenderness, all of him in one blink-moment, through the Reverend Mother's memory.

There was no time now to think of what this might be doing to the daughter fetus, only time to accept and record. The experiences poured in on Jessica—birth, life, death—important matters and unimportant, an outpouring of single-view time.

Why should a fall of sand from a clifftop stick in the memory? she asked herself.

Too late, Jessica saw what was happening: the old woman was dying and, in dying, pouring her experiences into Jessica's awareness as water is poured into a cup. The other mote faded back into pre-birth awareness as Jessica watched it. And, dying-in-conception, the old Reverend Mother left her life in Jessica's memory with one last sighing blur of words.

"I've been a long time waiting for you," she said. "Here is my life."

There it was, encapsuled, all of it.

Even the moment of death.

I am now a Reverend Mother, Jessica realized.

And she knew with a generalized awareness that she had become, in truth, precisely what was meant by a Bene Gesserit Reverend Mother. The poison drug had transformed her.

This wasn't exactly how they did it at the Bene Gesserit school, she knew. No one had ever introduced her to the mysteries of it, but she knew.

The end result was the same.

Jessica sensed the daughter-mote still touching her inner awareness, probed it without response.

A terrible sense of loneliness crept through Jessica in the realization of what had happened to her. She saw her own life as a pattern that had slowed and all life around her speeded up so that the dancing interplay became clearer.

The sensation of mote-awareness faded slightly, its intensity easing as her body relaxed from the threat of the poison, but still she felt that *other* mote, touching it with a sense of guilt at what she had allowed to happen to it.

I did it, my poor, unformed, dear little daughter, I brought you into this universe and exposed your awareness to all its varieties without any defenses.

A tiny outflowing of love-comfort, like a reflection of what she had poured into it, came from the other mote.

Before Jessica could respond, she felt the adab presence of demanding memory. There was something that needed doing. She groped for it, realizing she was being impeded by a muzziness of the changed drug permeating her senses.

I could change that, she thought. *I could take away the drug action and make it harmless.* But she sensed this would be an error. *I'm within a rite of joining.*

Then she knew what she had to do.

Jessica opened her eyes, gestured to the watersack now being held above her by Chani.

"It has been blessed," Jessica said. "Mingle the waters, let the change come to all, that the people may partake and share in the blessing."

Let the catalyst do its work, she thought. *Let the people drink of it and have their awareness of each other heightened for a while. The drug is safe now . . . now that a Reverend Mother has changed it.*

Still, the demanding memory worked on her, thrusting. There was another thing she had to do, she realized, but the drug made it difficult to focus.

Ah-h-h-h-h . . . the old Reverend Mother.

"I have met the Reverend Mother Ramallo," Jessica said. "She is gone, but she remains. Let her memory be honored in the rite."

Now, where did I get those words? Jessica wondered.

And she realized they came from another memory, the *life* that had been given to her and now was part of herself. Something about that gift felt incomplete, though.

"Let them have their orgy," the other-memory said within her. "They've little enough pleasure out of living. Yes, and you and I need this little time to become acquainted before I recede and pour out through your memories. Already, I feel myself being tied to bits of you. Ah-h-h, you've a mind filled with interesting things. So many things I'd never imagined."

And the memory-mind encapsulated within her opened itself to Jessica, permitting a view down a wide corridor to other Reverend Mothers until there seemed no end to them.

Jessica recoiled, fearing she would become lost in an ocean of oneness. Still, the corridor remained, revealing to Jessica that the Fremen culture was far older than she had suspected.

There had been Fremen on Poritrin, she saw, a people grown soft with an easy planet, fair game for Imperial raiders to harvest and plant human colonies on Bela Tegeuse and Salusa Secundus.

Oh, the wailing Jessica sensed in *that* parting.

Far down the corridor, an image-voice screamed: "They denied us the Hajj!"

Jessica saw the slave cribs on Bela Tegeuse down that inner corridor, saw the weeding out and the selecting that spread men to Rossak and Harmonthep. Scenes of brutal ferocity opened to her like the petals of a terrible flower. And she saw the thread of the past carried by Sayyadina after Sayyadina—first by word of mouth, hidden in the sand chanteys, then refined through their own Reverend Mothers with the discovery of the poison drug on Rossak . . . and now developed to subtle strength on Arrakis in the discovery of the Water of Life.

Far down the inner corridor, another voice screamed: "Never to forgive! Never to forget!"

But Jessica's attention was focused on the revelation of the Water of Life, seeing its source: the liquid exhalation of a dying sandworm, a maker. And as she saw the killing of it in her new memory, she suppressed a gasp.

The creature was drowned!

"Mother, are you all right?"

Paul's voice intruded on her, and Jessica struggled out of the inner awareness to stare up at him, conscious of duty to him, but resenting his presence.

I'm like a person whose hands were kept numb, without sensation from the first moment of awareness—until one day the ability to feel is forced into them.

The thought hung in her mind, an enclosing awareness.

And I say: "Look! I have no hands!" But the people all around me say: "What are hands?"

"Are you all right?" Paul repeated.

"Yes."

"Is this all right for me to drink?" He gestured to the sack in Chani's hands. "They want me to drink it."

She heard the hidden meaning in his words, realized he had detected the poison in the original, unchanged substance, that he was concerned for her. It occurred to Jessica then to wonder about the limits of Paul's prescience. His question revealed much to her.

"You may drink it," she said. "It has been changed." And she looked beyond him to see Stilgar staring down at her, the dark-dark eyes studying.

"Now, we know you cannot be false," he said.

She sensed hidden meaning here, too, but the muzziness of the drug was overpowering her senses. How warm it was and soothing. How beneficent these Fremen to bring her into the fold of such companionship.

Paul saw the drug take hold of his mother.

He searched his memory—the fixed past, the flux-lines of the possible futures. It was like scanning through arrested instants of time, disconcerting to the lens of the inner eye. The fragments were difficult to understand when snatched out of the flux.

This drug—he could assemble knowledge about it, understand what it was doing to his mother, but the knowledge lacked a natural rhythm, lacked a system of mutual reflection.

He realized suddenly that it was one thing to see the past occupying the present, but the true test of prescience was to see the past in the future.

Things persisted in not being what they seemed.

"Drink it," Chani said. She waved the hornspout of a watersack under his nose.

Paul straightened, staring at Chani. He felt carnival excitement in the air. He knew what would happen if he drank this spice drug with its quintessence of the substance that brought the change onto him. He would return to the vision of pure time, of time-become-space. It would perch him on the dizzying summit and defy him to understand.

From behind Chani, Stilgar said: "Drink it, lad. You delay the rite."

Paul listened to the crowd then, hearing the wildness in their voices—"Lisan al-Gaib," they said. "Muad'Dib!" He looked down at his mother. She appeared peacefully asleep in a sitting position—her breathing even and deep. A phrase out of the future that was his lonely past came into his mind: *"She sleeps in the Waters of Life."*

Chani tugged at his sleeve.

Paul took the hornspout into his mouth, hearing the people shout. He felt the liquid gush into his throat as Chani pressed the sack, sensed giddiness in the fumes. Chani removed the spout, handed the sack into hands that reached for it from the floor of the cavern. His eyes focused on her arm, the green band of mourning there.

As she straightened, Chani saw the direction of his gaze, said: "I can mourn him even in the happiness of the waters. This was something he gave us." She put her hand into his, pulling him along the ledge. "We are alike in a thing, Usul: We have each lost a father to the Harkonnens."

Paul followed her. He felt that his head had been separated from his body and restored with odd connections. His legs were remote and rubbery.

They entered a narrow side passage, its walls dimly lighted by spaced-out glowglobes. Paul felt the drug beginning to have its unique effect on him, opening time like a flower. He found need to steady himself against Chani as they turned through another shadowed tunnel. The mixture of whipcord and softness he felt beneath her robe stirred his blood. The sensation mingled with the work of the drug, folding future and past into the present, leaving him the thinnest margin of trinocular focus.

"I know you, Chani," he whispered. "We've sat upon a ledge above the sand while I soothed your fears. We've caressed in the dark of the sietch. We've. . . ." He found himself losing focus, tried to shake his head, stumbled.

Chani steadied him, led him through thick hangings into the yellow warmth of a private apartment—low tables, cushions, a sleeping pad beneath an orange spread.

Paul grew aware that they had stopped, that Chani stood facing him, and that her eyes betrayed a look of quiet terror.

"You must tell me," she whispered.

"You are Sihaya," he said, "the desert spring."

"When the tribe shares the Water," she said, "we're together—all of us. We . . . share. I can . . . sense the others with me, but I'm afraid to share with you."

"Why?"

He tried to focus on her, but past and future were merging into the present, blurring her image. He saw her in countless ways and positions and settings.

"There's something frightening in you," she said. "When I took you away from the others . . . I did it because I could feel what the others wanted. You . . . press on people. You . . . make us *see* things!"

He forced himself to speak distinctly: "What do you see?"

She looked down at her hands. "I see a child . . . in my arms. It's our child, yours and mine." She put a hand to her mouth. "How can I know every feature of you?"

They've a little of the talent, his mind told him. *But they suppress it because it terrifies.*

In a moment of clarity, he saw how Chani was trembling.

"What is it you want to say?" he asked.

"Usul," she whispered, and still she trembled.

"You cannot back into the future," he said.

A profound compassion for her swept through him. He pulled her against him, stroked her head. "Chani, Chani, don't fear."

"Usul, help me," she cried.

As she spoke, he felt the drug complete its work within him, ripping away the curtains to let him see the distant gray turmoil of his future.

"You're so quiet," Chani said.

He held himself poised in the awareness, seeing time stretch out in its weird dimension, delicately balanced yet whirling, narrow yet spread like a net gathering countless worlds and forces, a tightwire that he must walk, yet a teeter-totter on which he balanced.

On one side he could see the Imperium, a Harkonnen called Feyd-Rautha who flashed toward him like a deadly blade, the Sardaukar raging off their planet to spread pogrom on Arrakis, the Guild conniving and plotting, the Bene Gesserit with their scheme of selective breeding. They lay massed like a thunderhead on his horizon, held back by no more than the Fremen and their Muad'Dib, the sleeping giant Fremen poised for their wild crusade across the universe.

Paul felt himself at the center, at the pivot where the whole structure turned, walking a thin wire of peace with a measure of happiness, Chani at his side. He could see it stretching ahead of him, a time of relative quiet in a hidden sietch, a moment of peace between periods of violence.

"There's no other place for peace," he said.

"Usul, you're crying," Chani murmured. "Usul, my strength, do you give moisture to the dead? To whose dead?"

"To ones not yet dead," he said.

"Then let them have their time of life," she said.

He sensed through the drug fog how right she was, pulled her against him with savage pressure. "Sihaya!" he said.

She put a palm against his cheek. "I'm no longer afraid, Usul. Look at me. I see what you see when you hold me thus."

"What do you see?" he demanded.

"I see us giving love to each other in a time of quiet between storms. It's what we were meant to do."

The drug had him again and he thought: *So many times you've given me comfort and forgetfulness.* He felt anew the hyperillumination with its high-relief imagery of time, sensed his future becoming memories— the tender indignities of physical love, the sharing and communion of selves, the softness and the violence.

"You're the strong one, Chani," he muttered. "Stay with me."

"Always," she said, and kissed his cheek.

BOOK THREE

THE PROPHET

No woman, no man, no child ever was deeply intimate with my father. The closest anyone ever came to casual camaraderie with the Padishah Emperor was the relationship offered by Count Hasimir Fenring, a companion from childhood. The measure of Count Fenring's friendship may be seen first in a positive thing: he allayed the Landsraad's suspicions after the Arrakis Affair. It cost more than a billion solaris in spice bribes, so my mother said, and there were other gifts as well: slave women, royal honors, and tokens of rank. The second major evidence of the Count's friendship was negative. He refused to kill a man even though it was within his capabilities and my father commanded it. I will relate this presently.

—FROM "COUNT FENRING: A PROFILE"
BY THE PRINCESS IRULAN

The Baron Vladimir Harkonnen raged down the corridor from his private apartments, flitting through patches of late afternoon sunlight that poured down from high windows. He bobbed and twisted in his suspensors with violent movements.

Past the private kitchen he stormed—past the library, past the small reception room and into the servants' antechamber where the evening relaxation already had set in.

The guard captain, Iakin Nefud, squatted on a divan across the chamber, the stupor of semuta dullness in his flat face, the eerie wailing of semuta music around him. His own court sat near to do his bidding.

"Nefud!" the Baron roared.

Men scrambled.

Nefud stood, his face composed by the narcotic but with an overlay of paleness that told of his fear. The semuta music had stopped.

"My Lord Baron," Nefud said. Only the drug kept the trembling out of his voice.

The Baron scanned the faces around him, seeing the looks of frantic quiet in them. He returned his attention to Nefud, and spoke in a silken tone:

"How long have you been my guard captain, Nefud?"

Nefud swallowed. "Since Arrakis, my Lord. Almost two years."

"And have you always anticipated dangers to my person?"

"Such has been my only desire, my Lord."

"Then where is Feyd-Rautha?" the Baron roared.

Nefud recoiled. "M'Lord?"

"You do not consider Feyd-Rautha a danger to my person?" Again, the voice was silken.

Nefud wet his lips with his tongue. Some of the semuta dullness left his eyes. "Feyd-Rautha's in the slave quarters, my Lord."

"With the women again, eh?" The Baron trembled with the effort of suppressing anger.

"Sire, it could be he's—"

"Silence!"

The Baron advanced another step into the antechamber, noting how the men moved back, clearing a subtle space around Nefud, dissociating themselves from the object of wrath.

"Did I not command you to know precisely where the na-Baron was at all times?" the Baron asked. He moved a step closer. "Did I not say to you that you were to know *precisely* what the na-Baron was saying at all times—and to whom?" Another step. "Did I not say to you that you were to tell me whenever he went into the quarters of the slave women?"

Nefud swallowed. Perspiration stood out on his forehead.

The Baron held his voice flat, almost devoid of emphasis: "Did I not say these things to you?"

Nefud nodded.

"And did I not say that you were to check all slave boys sent to me and that you were to do this yourself . . . *personally*?"

Again, Nefud nodded.

"Did you, perchance, not see the blemish on the thigh of the one sent me this evening?" the Baron asked. "Is it possible you—"

"Uncle."

The Baron whirled, stared at Feyd-Rautha standing in the doorway. The presence of his nephew here, now—the look of hurry that the young man could not quite conceal—all revealed much. Feyd-Rautha had his own spy system focused on the Baron.

"There is a body in my chambers that I wish removed," the Baron said, and he kept his hand at the projectile weapon beneath his robes, thankful that his shield was the best.

Feyd-Rautha glanced at two guardsmen against the right wall, nodded. The two detached themselves, scurried out the door and down the hall toward the Baron's apartments.

Those two, eh? the Baron thought. *Ah, this young monster has much to learn yet about conspiracy!*

"I presume you left matters peaceful in the slave quarters, Feyd," the Baron said.

"I've been playing cheops with the slavemaster," Feyd-Rautha said, and he thought: *What has gone wrong? The boy we sent to my uncle has obviously been killed. But he was perfect for the job. Even Hawat couldn't have made a better choice. The boy was perfect!*

"Playing pyramid chess," the Baron said. "How nice. Did you win?"

"I . . . ah, yes, Uncle." And Feyd-Rautha strove to contain his disquiet.

The Baron snapped his fingers. "Nefud, you wish to be restored to my good graces?"

"Sire, what have I done?" Nefud quavered.

"That's unimportant now," the Baron said. "Feyd has beaten the slavemaster at cheops. Did you hear that?"

"Yes . . . Sire."

"I wish you to take three men and go to the slavemaster," the Baron said. "Garrote the slavemaster. Bring his body to me when you've finished that I may see it was done properly. We cannot have such inept chess players in our employ."

Feyd-Rautha went pale, took a step forward. "But, Uncle, I—"

"Later, Feyd," the Baron said, and waved a hand. "Later."

The two guards who had gone to the Baron's quarters for the slave boy's body staggered past the antechamber door with their load sagging between them, arms trailing. The Baron watched until they were out of sight.

Nefud stepped up beside the Baron. "You wish me to kill the slavemaster, now, my Lord?"

"Now," the Baron said. "And when you've finished, add those two who just passed to your list. I don't like the way they carried that body. One should do such things neatly. I'll wish to see their carcasses, too."

Nefud said, "My Lord, is it anything that I've—"

"Do as your master has ordered," Feyd-Rautha said. And he thought: *All I can hope for now is to save my own skin.*

Good! the Baron thought. *He yet knows how to cut his losses.* And the Baron smiled inwardly at himself, thinking: *The lad knows, too, what will please me and be most apt to stay my wrath from falling on him. He knows I must preserve him. Who else do I have who could take the reins I must leave someday? I have no other as capable. But he must learn! And I must preserve myself while he's learning.*

Nefud signaled men to assist him, led them out the door.

"Would you accompany me to my chambers, Feyd?" the Baron asked.

"I am yours to command," Feyd-Rautha said. He bowed, thinking: *I'm caught.*

"After you," the Baron said, and he gestured to the door.

Feyd-Rautha indicated his fear by only the barest hesitation. *Have I failed utterly?* he asked himself. *Will he slip a poisoned blade into my back . . . slowly, through the shield? Does he have an alternative successor?*

Let him experience this moment of terror, the Baron thought as he walked along behind his nephew. *He will succeed me, but at a time of my choosing. I'll not have him throwing away what I've built!*

Feyd-Rautha tried not to walk too swiftly. He felt the skin crawling on his back as though his body itself wondered when the blow could come. His muscles alternately tensed and relaxed.

"Have you heard the latest word from Arrakis?" the Baron asked.

"No, Uncle."

Feyd-Rautha forced himself not to look back. He turned down the hall out of the servants' wing.

"They've a new prophet or religious leader of some kind among the Fremen," the Baron said. "They call him Muad'Dib. Very funny, really. It means 'the Mouse.' I've told Rabban to let them have their religion. It'll keep them occupied."

"That's very interesting, Uncle," Feyd-Rautha said. He turned into the private corridor to his uncle's quarters, wondering: *Why does he talk about religion? Is it some subtle hint to me?*

"Yes, isn't it?" the Baron said.

They came into the Baron's apartments through the reception salon to the bedchamber. Subtle signs of a struggle greeted them here—a suspensor lamp displaced, a bedcushion on the floor, a soother-reel spilled open across a bedstand.

"It was a clever plan," the Baron said. He kept his body shield tuned to maximum, stopped, facing his nephew. "But not clever enough. Tell me, Feyd, why didn't you strike me down yourself? You've had opportunity enough."

Feyd-Rautha found a suspensor chair, accomplished a mental shrug as he sat down in it without being asked.

I must be bold now, he thought.

"You taught me that my own hands must remain clean," he said.

"Ah, yes," the Baron said. "When you face the Emperor, you must be able to say truthfully that you did not do the deed. The witch at the Emperor's elbow will hear your words and know their truth or falsehood. Yes. I warned you about that."

"Why haven't you ever bought a Bene Gesserit, Uncle?" Feyd-Rautha asked. "With a Truthsayer at your side—"

"You know my tastes!" the Baron snapped.

Feyd-Rautha studied his uncle, said: "Still, one would be valuable for—"

"I trust them not!" the Baron snarled. "And stop trying to change the subject!"

Feyd-Rautha spoke mildly: "As you wish, Uncle."

"I remember a time in the arena several years ago," the Baron said. "It seemed there that day a slave had been set to kill you. Is that truly how it was?"

"It's been so long ago, Uncle. After all, I—"

"No evasions, please," the Baron said, and the tightness of his voice exposed the rein on his anger.

Feyd-Rautha looked at his uncle, thinking: *He knows, else he wouldn't ask.*

"It was a sham, Uncle. I arranged it to discredit your slavemaster."

"Very clever," the Baron said. "Brave, too. That slave-gladiator almost took you, didn't he?"

"Yes."

"If you had finesse and subtlety to match such courage, you'd be truly formidable." The Baron shook his head from side to side. And as he had done many times since that terrible day on Arrakis, he found himself regretting the loss of Piter, the Mentat. There'd been a man of delicate, devilish subtlety. It hadn't saved him, though. Again, the Baron shook his head. Fate was sometimes inscrutable.

Feyd-Rautha glanced around the bedchamber, studying the signs of the struggle, wondering how his uncle had overcome the slave they'd prepared so carefully.

"How did I best him?" the Baron asked. "Ah-h-h, now, Feyd—let me keep some weapons to preserve me in my old age. It's better we use this time to strike a bargain."

Feyd-Rautha stared at him. *A bargain! He means to keep me as his heir for certain, then. Else why bargain? One bargains with equals or near equals!*

"What bargain, Uncle?" And Feyd-Rautha felt proud that his voice remained calm and reasonable, betraying none of the elation that filled him.

The Baron, too, noted the control. He nodded. "You're good material, Feyd. I don't waste good material. You persist, however, in refusing to learn my true value to you. You are obstinate. You do not see why I should be preserved as someone of the utmost value to you. This. . . ." He gestured at the evidence of the struggle in the bedchamber. "This was foolishness. I do not reward foolishness."

Get to the point, you old fool! Feyd-Rautha thought.

"You think of me as an old fool," the Baron said. "I must dissuade you of that."

"You speak of a bargain."

"Ah, the impatience of youth," the Baron said. "Well, this is the substance of it, then: You will cease these foolish attempts on my life. And I, when you are ready for it, will step aside in your favor. I will retire to an advisory position, leaving you in the seat of power."

"Retire, Uncle?"

"You still think me the fool," the Baron said, "and this but confirms it, eh? You think I'm begging you! Step cautiously, Feyd. This old fool saw through the shielded needle you'd planted in that slave boy's thigh. Right where I'd put my hand on it, eh? The smallest pressure and— snick! A poison needle in the old fool's palm! Ah-h-h, Feyd. . . ."

The Baron shook his head, thinking: *It would've worked, too, if Hawat hadn't warned me. Well, let the lad believe I saw the plot on my own. In a way, I did. I was the one who saved Hawat from the wreckage of Arrakis. And this lad needs greater respect for my prowess.*

Feyd-Rautha remained silent, struggling with himself. *Is he being truthful? Does he really mean to retire? Why not? I'm sure to succeed him one day if I move carefully. He can't live forever. Perhaps it was foolish to try hurrying the process.*

"You speak of a bargain," Feyd-Rautha said. "What pledge do we give to bind it?"

"How can we trust each other, eh?" the Baron asked. "Well, Feyd, as for you: I'm setting Thufir Hawat to watch over you. I trust Hawat's Mentat capabilities in this. Do you understand me? And as for me, you'll have to take me on faith. But I can't live forever, can I, Feyd? And perhaps you should begin to suspect now that there're things I know which you *should* know."

"I give you my pledge and what do you give me?" Feyd-Rautha asked.

"I let you go on living," the Baron said.

Again, Feyd-Rautha studied his uncle. *He sets Hawat over me! What would he say if I told him Hawat planned the trick with the gladiator that cost him his slavemaster? He'd likely say I was lying in the attempt to discredit Hawat. No, the good Thufir is a Mentat and has anticipated this moment.*

"Well, what do you say?" the Baron asked.

"What can I say? I accept, of course."

And Feyd-Rautha thought: *Hawat! He plays both ends against the middle . . . is that it? Has he moved to my uncle's camp because I didn't counsel with him over the slave boy attempt?*

"You haven't said anything about my setting Hawat to watch you," the Baron said.

Feyd-Rautha betrayed anger by a flaring of nostrils. The name of Hawat had been a danger signal in the Harkonnen family for so many years . . . and now it had a new meaning: still dangerous.

"Hawat's a dangerous toy," Feyd-Rautha said.

"Toy! Don't be stupid. I know what I have in Hawat and how to control it. Hawat has deep emotions, Feyd. The man without emotions is the one to fear. But deep emotions . . . ah, now, those can be bent to your needs."

"Uncle, I don't understand you."

"Yes, that's plain enough."

Only a flicker of eyelids betrayed the passage of resentment through Feyd-Rautha.

"And you do not understand Hawat," the Baron said.

Nor do you! Feyd-Rautha thought.

"Who does Hawat blame for his present circumstances?" the Baron asked. "Me? Certainly. But he was an Atreides tool and bested me for years until the Imperium took a hand. That's how he sees it. His hate for me is a casual thing now. He believes he can best me anytime. Believing this, he is bested. For I direct his attention where I want it—against the Imperium."

Tensions of a new understanding drew tight lines across Feyd-Rautha's forehead, thinned his mouth. "Against the Emperor?"

Let my dear nephew try the taste of that, the Baron thought. *Let him say to himself: "The Emperor Feyd-Rautha Harkonnen!" Let him ask himself how much that's worth. Surely it must be worth the life of one old uncle who could make that dream come to pass!*

Slowly, Feyd-Rautha wet his lips with his tongue. Could it be true what the old fool was saying? There was more here than there seemed to be.

"And what has Hawat to do with this?" Feyd-Rautha asked.

"He thinks he uses us to wreak his revenge upon the Emperor."

"And when that's accomplished?"

"He does not think beyond his revenge. Hawat's a man who must serve others, and doesn't even know this about himself."

"I've learned much from Hawat," Feyd-Rautha agreed, and felt the truth of the words as he spoke them. "But the more I learn, the more I feel we should dispose of him . . . and soon."

"You don't like the idea of his watching you?"

"Hawat watches everybody."

"And he may put you on a throne. Hawat is subtle. He is dangerous, devious. But I'll not yet withhold the antidote from him. A sword is dangerous, too, Feyd. We have the scabbard for this one, though. The poison's in him. When we withdraw the antidote, death will sheathe him."

"In a way, it's like the arena," Feyd-Rautha said. "Feints within feints within feints. You watch to see which way the gladiator leans, which way he looks, how he holds his knife."

He nodded to himself, seeing that these words pleased his uncle, but thinking: *Yes! Like the arena! And the cutting edge is the mind!*

"Now you see how you need me," the Baron said. "I'm yet of use, Feyd."

A sword to be wielded until he's too blunt for use, Feyd-Rautha thought.

"Yes, Uncle," he said.

"And now," the Baron said, "we will go down to the slave quarters, we two. And I will watch while you, with your own hands, kill all the women in the pleasure wing."

"Uncle!"

"There will be other women, Feyd. But I have said that you do not make a mistake casually with me."

Feyd-Rautha's face darkened. "Uncle, you—"

"You will accept your punishment and learn something from it," the Baron said.

Feyd-Rautha met the gloating stare in his uncle's eyes. *And I must remember this night,* he thought. *And remembering it, I must remember other nights.*

"You will not refuse," the Baron said.

What could you do if I refused, old man? Feyd-Rautha asked himself. But he knew there might be some other punishment, perhaps a more subtle one, a more brutal lever to bend him.

"I know you, Feyd," the Baron said. "You will not refuse."

All right, Feyd-Rautha thought. *I need you now. I see that. The bargain's made. But I'll not always need you. And . . . someday . . .*

Deep in the human unconscious is a pervasive need for a logical universe that makes sense. But the real universe is always one step beyond logic.

—FROM "THE SAYINGS OF MUAD'DIB"
BY THE PRINCESS IRULAN

I've sat across from many rulers of Great Houses, but never seen a more gross and dangerous pig than this one, Thufir Hawat told himself.

"You may speak plainly with me, Hawat," the Baron rumbled. He leaned back in his suspensor chair, the eyes in their folds of fat boring into Hawat.

The old Mentat looked down at the table between him and the Baron Vladimir Harkonnen, noting the opulence of its grain. Even this was a factor to consider in assessing the Baron, as were the red walls of this private conference room and the faint sweet herb scent that hung on the air, masking a deeper musk.

"You didn't have me send that warning to Rabban as an idle whim," the Baron said.

Hawat's leathery old face remained impassive, betraying none of the loathing he felt. "I suspect many things, my Lord," he said.

"Yes. Well, I wish to know how Arrakis figures in your suspicions about Salusa Secundus. It is not enough that you say to me the Emperor is in a ferment about some association between Arrakis and his mysterious prison planet. Now, I rushed the warning out to Rabban only because the courier had to leave on that Heighliner. You said there could be no delay. Well and good. But now I will have an explanation."

He babbles too much, Hawat thought. *He's not like Leto who could tell me a thing with the lift of an eyebrow or the wave of a hand. Nor like the Old Duke who could express an entire sentence in the way he accented a single word. This is a clod! Destroying him will be a service to mankind.*

"You will not leave here until I've had a full and complete explanation," the Baron said.

"You speak too casually of Salusa Secundus," Hawat said.

"It's a penal colony," the Baron said. "The worst riff-raff in the galaxy are sent to Salusa Secundus. What else do we need to know?"

"That conditions on the prison planet are more oppressive than anywhere else," Hawat said. "You hear that the mortality rate among new prisoners is higher than sixty per cent. You hear that the Emperor practices every form of oppression there. You hear all this and do not ask questions?"

"The Emperor doesn't permit the Great Houses to inspect his prison," the Baron growled. "But he hasn't seen into my dungeons, either."

"And curiosity about Salusa Secundus is . . . ah. . . ." Hawat put a bony finger to his lips. ". . . discouraged."

"So he's not proud of some of the things he must do there!"

Hawat allowed the faintest of smiles to touch his dark lips. His eyes glinted in the glowtube light as he stared at the Baron. "And you've never wondered where the Emperor gets his Sardaukar?"

The Baron pursed his fat lips. This gave his features the look of a pouting baby, and his voice carried a tone of petulance as he said: "Why . . . he recruits . . . that is to say, there are the levies and he enlists from—"

"Faaa!" Hawat snapped. "The stories you hear about the exploits of the Sardaukar, they're not rumors, are they? Those are first-hand accounts from the limited number of survivors who've fought against the Sardaukar, eh?"

"The Sardaukar are excellent fighting men, no doubt of it," the Baron said. "But I think my own legions—"

"A pack of holiday excursionists by comparison!" Hawat snarled. "You think I don't know why the Emperor turned against House Atreides?"

"This is not a realm open to your speculation," the Baron warned.

Is it possible that even he doesn't know what motivated the Emperor in this? Hawat asked himself.

"Any area is open to my speculation if it does what you've hired me to do," Hawat said. "I am a Mentat. You do not withhold information or computation lines from a Mentat."

For a long minute, the Baron stared at him, then: "Say what you must say, Mentat."

"The Padishah Emperor turned against House Atreides because the Duke's Warmasters Gurney Halleck and Duncan Idaho had trained a fighting force—a *small* fighting force—to within a hair as good as the Sardaukar. Some of them were even better. And the Duke was in a position to enlarge his force, to make it every bit as strong as the Emperor's."

The Baron weighed this disclosure, then: "What has Arrakis to do with this?"

"It provides a pool of recruits already conditioned to the bitterest survival training."

The Baron shook his head. "You cannot mean the Fremen?"

"I mean the Fremen."

"Hah! Then why warn Rabban? There cannot be more than a handful of Fremen left after the Sardaukar pogrom and Rabban's oppression."

Hawat continued to stare at him silently.

"Not more than a handful!" the Baron repeated. "Rabban killed six thousand of them last year alone!"

Still, Hawat stared at him.

"And the year before it was nine thousand," the Baron said. "And before they left, the Sardaukar must've accounted for at least twenty thousand."

"What are Rabban's troop losses for the past two years?" Hawat asked.

The Baron rubbed his jowls. "Well, he has been recruiting rather heavily, to be sure. His agents make rather extravagant promises and—"

"Shall we say thirty thousand in round numbers?" Hawat asked.

"That would seem a little high," the Baron said.

"Quite the contrary," Hawat said. "I can read between the lines of Rabban's reports as well as you can. And you certainly must've understood my reports from our agents."

"Arrakis is a fierce planet," the Baron said. "Storm losses can—"

"We both know the figure for storm accretion," Hawat said.

"What if he has lost thirty thousand?" the Baron demanded, and blood darkened his face.

"By your own count," Hawat said, "he killed fifteen thousand over two years while losing twice that number. You say the Sardaukar accounted for another twenty thousand, possibly a few more. And I've seen the transportation manifests for their return from Arrakis. If they killed twenty thousand, they lost almost five for one. Why won't you face these figures, Baron, and understand what they mean?"

The Baron spoke in a coldly measured cadence: "This is your job, Mentat. What do they mean?"

"I gave you Duncan Idaho's head count on the sietch he visited," Hawat said. "It all fits. If they had just two hundred and fifty such sietch communities, their population would be about five million. My best estimate is that they had at least twice that many communities. You scatter your population on such a planet."

"Ten million?"

The Baron's jowls quivered with amazement.

"At least."

The Baron pursed his fat lips. The beady eyes stared without wavering at Hawat. *Is this true Mentat computation?* he wondered. *How could this be and no one suspect?*

"We haven't even cut heavily into their birth-rate-growth figure," Hawat said. "We've just weeded out some of their less successful specimens, leaving the strong to grow stronger—just like on Salusa Secundus."

"Salusa Secundus!" the Baron barked. "What has this to do with the Emperor's prison planet?"

"A man who survives Salusa Secundus starts out being tougher than most others," Hawat said. "When you add the very best of military training—"

"Nonsense! By your argument, *I* could recruit from among the Fremen after the way they've been oppressed by my nephew."

Hawat spoke in a mild voice: "Don't you oppress any of your troops?"

"Well . . . I . . . but—"

"Oppression is a relative thing," Hawat said. "Your fighting men are much better off than those around them, heh? They see unpleasant alternative to being soldiers of the Baron, heh?"

The Baron fell silent, eyes unfocused. The possibilities—had Rabban unwittingly given House Harkonnen its ultimate weapon?

Presently he said: "How could you be sure of the loyalty of such recruits?"

"I would take them in small groups, not larger than platoon strength," Hawat said. "I'd remove them from their oppressive situation and isolate them with a training cadre of people who understood their background, preferably people who had preceded them from the same oppressive situation. Then I'd fill them with the mystique that their planet had really been a secret training ground to produce just such superior beings as themselves. And all the while, I'd show them what such superior beings could earn: rich living, beautiful women, fine mansions . . . whatever they desired."

The Baron began to nod. "The way the Sardaukar live at home."

"The recruits come to believe in time that such a place as Salusa Secundus is justified because it produced them—the elite. The commonest Sardaukar trooper lives a life, in many respects, as exalted as that of any member of a Great House."

"Such an idea!" the Baron whispered.

"You begin to share my suspicions," Hawat said.

"Where did such a thing start?" the Baron asked.

"Ah, yes: Where did House Corrino originate? Were there people on Salusa Secundus before the Emperor sent his first contingents of prisoners there? Even the Duke Leto, a cousin on the distaff side, never knew for sure. Such questions are not encouraged."

The Baron's eyes glazed with thought. "Yes, a very carefully kept secret. They'd use every device of—"

"Besides, what's there to conceal?" Hawat asked. "That the Padishah Emperor has a prison planet? Everyone knows this. That he has—"

"Count Fenring!" the Baron blurted.

Hawat broke off, studied the Baron with a puzzled frown. "What of Count Fenring?"

"At my nephew's birthday several years ago," the Baron said. "This Imperial popinjay, Count Fenring, came as official observer and to . . . ah, conclude a business arrangement between the Emperor and myself."

"So?"

"I . . . ah, during one of our conversations, I believe I said something about making a prison planet of Arrakis. Fenring—"

"What did you say exactly?" Hawat asked.

"Exactly? That was quite a while ago and—"

"My Lord Baron, if you wish to make the best use of my services, you must give me adequate information. Wasn't this conversation recorded?"

The Baron's face darkened with anger. "You're as bad as Piter! I don't like these—"

"Piter is no longer with you, my Lord," Hawat said. "As to that, whatever *did* happen to Piter?"

"He became too familiar, too demanding of me," the Baron said.

"You assure me you don't waste a useful man," Hawat said. "Will you waste me by threats and quibbling? We were discussing what you said to Count Fenring."

Slowly, the Baron composed his features. *When the time comes,* he thought, *I'll remember his manner with me. Yes. I will remember.*

"One moment," the Baron said, and he thought back to the meeting in his Great Hall. It helped to visualize the cone of silence in which they had stood. "I said something like this," the Baron said. "'The Emperor knows a certain amount of killing has always been an arm of business.' I was referring to our work force losses. Then I said something about considering another solution to the Arrakeen problem and I said the Emperor's prison planet inspired me to emulate him."

"Witch blood!" Hawat snapped. "What did Fenring say?"

"That's when he began questioning me about you."

Hawat sat back, closed his eyes in thought. "So that's why they started looking into Arrakis," he said. "Well, the thing's done." He opened his eyes. "They must have spies all over Arrakis by now. Two years!"

"But certainly my innocent suggestion that—"

"Nothing is innocent in an Emperor's eyes! What were your instructions to Rabban?"

"Merely that he should teach Arrakis to fear us."

Hawat shook his head. "You now have two alternatives, Baron. You can kill off the natives, wipe them out entirely, or—"

"Waste an entire work force?"

"Would you prefer to have the Emperor and those Great Houses he can still swing behind him come in here and perform a curettement, scrape out Giedi Prime like a hollow gourd?"

The Baron studied his Mentat, then: "He wouldn't dare!"

"Wouldn't he?"

The Baron's lips quivered. "What is your alternative?"

"Abandon your dear nephew, Rabban."

"Aband. . . ." The Baron broke off, stared at Hawat.

"Send him no more troops, no aid of any kind. Don't answer his messages other than to say you've heard of the terrible way he's handled things on Arrakis and you intend to take corrective measures as soon as you're able. I'll arrange to have some of your messages intercepted by Imperial spies."

"But what of the spice, the revenues, the—"

"Demand your baronial profits, but be careful how you make your demands. Require fixed sums of Rabban. We can—"

The Baron turned his hands palms up. "But how can I be certain that my weasel nephew isn't—"

"We still have our spies on Arrakis. Tell Rabban he either meets the spice quotas you set him or he'll be replaced."

"I know my nephew," the Baron said. "This would only make him oppress the population even more."

"Of course he will!" Hawat snapped. "You don't want that stopped now! You merely want your own hands clean. Let Rabban make your Salusa Secundus for you. There's no need even to send him any prisoners. He has all the population required. If Rabban is driving his people to meet your spice quotas, then the Emperor need suspect no other motive. That's reason enough for putting the planet on the rack. And you, Baron, will not show by word or action that there's any other reason for this."

The Baron could not keep the sly tone of admiration out of his voice. "Ah, Hawat, you are a devious one. Now, how do we move into Arrakis and make use of what Rabban prepares?"

"That's the simplest thing of all, Baron. If you set each year's quota a bit higher than the one before, matters will soon reach a head there. Production will drop off. You can remove Rabban and take over yourself . . . to correct the mess."

"It fits," the Baron said. "But I can feel myself tiring of all this. I'm preparing another to take over Arrakis for me."

Hawat studied the fat round face across from him. Slowly the old soldier-spy began to nod his head. "Feyd-Rautha," he said. "So that's the reason for the oppression now. You're very devious yourself, Baron. Perhaps we can incorporate these two schemes. Yes. Your Feyd-Rautha can go to Arrakis as their savior. He can win the populace. Yes."

The Baron smiled. And behind his smile, he asked himself: *Now, how does this fit in with Hawat's personal scheming?*

And Hawat, seeing that he was dismissed, arose and left the red-walled room. As he walked, he could not put down the disturbing unknowns that cropped into every computation about Arrakis. This new religious leader that Gurney Halleck hinted at from his hiding place among the smugglers, this Muad'Dib.

Perhaps I should not have told the Baron to let this religion flourish where it will, even among the folk of pan and graben, he told himself. *But it's well known that repression makes a religion flourish.*

And he thought about Halleck's reports on Fremen battle tactics. The tactics smacked of Halleck himself . . . and Idaho . . . and even of Hawat.

Did Idaho survive? he asked himself.

But this was a futile question. He did not yet ask himself if it was possible that Paul had survived. He knew the Baron was convinced that all Atreides were dead. The Bene Gesserit witch had been his weapon, the Baron admitted. And that could only mean an end to all—even to the woman's own son.

What a poisonous hate she must've had for the Atreides, he thought. *Something like the hate I hold for this Baron. Will my blow be as final and complete as hers?*

There is in all things a pattern that is part of our universe. It has symmetry, elegance, and grace—those qualities you find always in that which the true artist captures. You can find it in the turning of the seasons, in the way sand trails along a ridge, in the branch clusters of the creosote bush or the pattern of its leaves. We try to copy these patterns in our lives and our society, seeking the rhythms, the dances, the forms that comfort. Yet, it is possible to see peril in the finding of ultimate perfection. It is clear that the ultimate pattern contains its own fixity. In such perfection, all things move toward death.

—FROM "COLLECTED SAYINGS OF MUAD'DIB"
BY THE PRINCESS IRULAN

Paul-Muad'Dib remembered that there had been a meal heavy with spice essence. He clung to this memory because it was an anchor point and he could tell himself from this vantage that his immediate experience must be a dream.

I am a theater of processes, he told himself. *I am a prey to the imperfect vision, to the race consciousness and its terrible purpose.*

Yet, he could not escape the fear that he had somehow overrun himself, lost his position in time, so that past and future and present mingled without distinction. It was a kind of visual fatigue and it came, he knew, from the constant necessity of holding the prescient future as a kind of memory that was in itself a thing intrinsically of the past.

Chani prepared the meal for me, he told himself.

Yet Chani was deep in the south—in the cold country where the sun was hot—secreted in one of the new sietch strongholds, safe with their son, Leto II.

Or, was that a thing yet to happen?

No, he reassured himself, for Alia-the-Strange-One, his sister, had gone there with his mother and with Chani—a twenty-thumper trip into the south, riding a Reverend Mother's palanquin fixed to the back of a wild maker.

He shied away from the thought of riding the giant worms, asking himself: *Or is Alia yet to be born?*

I was on razzia, Paul recalled. *We went raiding to recover the water of our dead in Arrakeen. And I found the remains of my father in the funeral pyre. I enshrined the skull of my father in a Fremen rock mound overlooking Harg Pass.*

Or was that a thing yet to be?

My wounds are real, Paul told himself. *My scars are real. The shrine of my father's skull is real.*

Still in the dreamlike state, Paul remembered that Harah, Jamis' wife, had intruded on him once to say there'd been a fight in the sietch corridor. That had been the interim sietch before the women and children had been sent into the deep south. Harah had stood there in the entrance to the inner chamber, the black wings of her hair tied back by water rings on a chain. She had held aside the chamber's hangings and told him that Chani had just killed someone.

This happened, Paul told himself. *This was real, not born out of its time and subject to change.*

Paul remembered he had rushed out to find Chani standing beneath the yellow globes of the corridor, clad in a brilliant blue wraparound robe with hood thrown back, a flush of exertion on her elfin features. She had been sheathing her crysknife. A huddled group had been hurrying away down the corridor with a burden.

And Paul remembered telling himself: You always know when they're carrying a body.

Chani's water rings, worn openly in sietch on a cord around her neck, tinkled as she turned toward him.

"Chani, what is this?" he asked.

"I dispatched one who came to challenge you in single combat, Usul."

"*You* killed him?"

"Yes. But perhaps I should've left him for Harah."

(And Paul recalled how the faces of the people around them had showed appreciation for these words. Even Harah had laughed.)

"But he came to challenge *me!*"

"You trained me yourself in the weirding way, Usul."

"Certainly! But you shouldn't—"

"I was born in the desert, Usul. I know how to use a crysknife."

He suppressed his anger, tried to talk reasonably. "This may all be true, Chani, but—"

"I am no longer a child hunting scorpions in the sietch by the light of a handglobe, Usul. I do not play games."

Paul glared at her, caught by the odd ferocity beneath her casual attitude.

"He was not worthy, Usul," Chani said. "I'd not disturb your meditations with the likes of him." She moved closer, looking at him out of the corners of her eyes, dropping her voice so that only he might hear. "And, beloved, when it's learned that a challenger may face *me* and be brought to shameful death by Muad'Dib's woman, there'll be fewer challengers."

Yes, Paul told himself, *that had certainly happened. It was true-past. And the number of challengers testing the new blade of Muad'Dib did drop dramatically.*

Somewhere, in a world not-of-the-dream, there was a hint of motion, the cry of a nightbird.

I dream, Paul reassured himself. *It's the spice meal.*

Still, there was about him a feeling of abandonment. He wondered if it might be possible that his ruh-spirit had slipped over somehow into the world where the Fremen believed he had his true existence—into the alam al-mithal, the world of similitudes, that metaphysical realm where all physical limitations were removed. And he knew fear at the thought of such a place, because removal of all limitations meant removal of all points of reference. In the landscape of a myth he could not orient himself and say: "I am I because I am here."

His mother had said once: "The people are divided, some of them, in how they think of you."

I must be waking from the dream, Paul told himself. For this had happened—these words from his mother, the Lady Jessica who was now a Reverend Mother of the Fremen, these words had passed through reality.

Jessica was fearful of the religious relationship between himself and the Fremen, Paul knew. She didn't like the fact that people of both sietch and graben referred to Muad'Dib as *Him*. And she went questioning among the tribes, sending out her Sayyadina spies, collecting their answers and brooding on them.

She had quoted a Bene Gesserit proverb to him: "When religion and politics travel in the same cart, the riders believe nothing can stand in their way. Their movement becomes headlong—faster and faster and faster. They put aside all thought of obstacles and forget that a precipice does not show itself to the man in a blind rush until it's too late."

Paul recalled that he had sat there in his mother's quarters, in the inner chamber shrouded by dark hangings with their surfaces covered by woven patterns out of Fremen mythology. He had sat there, hearing her out, noting the way she was always observing—even when her eyes were lowered. Her oval face had new lines in it at the corners of the mouth, but the hair was still like polished bronze. The wide-set green eyes, though, hid beneath their overcasting of spice-imbued blue.

"The Fremen have a simple, practical religion," he said.

"Nothing about religion is simple," she warned.

But Paul, seeing the clouded future that still hung over them, found himself swayed by anger. He could only say: "Religion unifies our forces. It's our mystique."

"You deliberately cultivate this air, this bravura," she charged. "You never cease indoctrinating."

"Thus you yourself taught me," he said.

But she had been full of contentions and arguments that day. It had been the day of the circumcision ceremony for little Leto. Paul had understood some of the reasons for her upset. She had never accepted his liaison—the "marriage of youth"—with Chani. But Chani had produced an Atreides son, and Jessica had found herself unable to reject the child with the mother.

Jessica had stirred finally under his stare, said: "You think me an unnatural mother."

"Of course not."

"I see the way you watch me when I'm with your sister. You don't understand about your sister."

"I know why Alia is different," he said. "She was unborn, part of you, when you changed the Water of Life. She—"

"You know nothing of it!"

And Paul, suddenly unable to express the knowledge gained out of its time, said only: "I don't think you unnatural."

She saw his distress, said: "There is a thing, Son."

"Yes?"

"I do love your Chani. I accept her."

This was real, Paul told himself. This wasn't the imperfect vision to be changed by the twistings out of time's own birth.

The reassurance gave him a new hold on his world. Bits of solid reality began to dip through the dream state into his awareness. He knew suddenly that he was in a hiereg, a desert camp. Chani had planted their stilltent on flour sand for its softness. That could only mean Chani was nearby—Chani, his soul, Chani his sihaya, sweet as the desert spring, Chani up from the palmaries of the deep south.

Now, he remembered her singing a sand chanty to him in the time for sleep.

"O my soul,
Have no taste for Paradise this night,
And I swear by Shai-hulud

You will go there,
Obedient to my love."

And she had sung the walking song lovers shared on the sand, its rhythm like the drag of the dunes against the feet:

"Tell me of thine eyes
And I will tell thee of thy heart.
Tell me of thy feet
And I will tell thee of thy hands.
Tell me of thy sleeping
And I will tell thee of thy waking.
Tell me of thy desires
And I will tell thee of thy need."

He had heard someone strumming a baliset in another tent. And he'd thought then of Gurney Halleck. Reminded by the familiar instrument, he had thought of Gurney whose face he had seen in a smuggler band, but who had not seen him, could not see him or know of him lest that inadvertently lead the Harkonnens to the son of the Duke they had killed.

But the style of the player in the night, the distinctiveness of the fingers on the baliset's strings, brought the real musician back to Paul's memory. It had been Chatt the Leaper, captain of the Fedaykin, leader of the death commandos who guarded Muad'Dib.

We are in the desert, Paul remembered. *We are in the central erg beyond the Harkonnen patrols. I am here to walk the sand, to lure a maker and mount him by my own cunning that I may be a Fremen entire.*

He felt now the maula pistol at his belt, the crysknife. He felt the silence surrounding him.

It was that special pre-morning silence when the nightbirds had gone and the day creatures had not yet signaled their alertness to their enemy, the sun.

"You must ride the sand in the light of day that Shai-hulud shall see and know you have no fear," Stilgar had said. "Thus we turn our time around and set ourselves to sleep this night."

Quietly, Paul sat up, feeling the looseness of a slacked stillsuit around his body, the shadowed stilltent beyond. So softly he moved, yet Chani heard him.

She spoke from the tent's gloom, another shadow there: "It's not yet full light, beloved."

"Sihaya," he said, speaking with half a laugh in his voice.

"You call me your desert spring," she said, "but this day I'm thy goad. I am the Sayyadina who watches that the rites be obeyed."

He began tightening his stillsuit. "You told me once the words of the Kitab al-Ibar," he said. "You told me: 'Woman is thy field; go then to thy field and till it.'"

"I am the mother of thy firstborn," she agreed.

He saw her in the grayness matching him movement for movement, securing her stillsuit for the open desert. "You should get all the rest you can," she said.

He recognized her love for him speaking then and chided her gently: "The Sayyadina of the Watch does not caution or warn the candidate."

She slid across to his side, touched his cheek with her palm. "Today, I am both the watcher and the woman."

"You should've left this duty to another," he said.

"Waiting is bad enough at best," she said. "I'd sooner be at thy side."

He kissed her palm before securing the faceflap of his suit, then turned and cracked the seal of the tent. The air that came in to them held the chill not-quite-dryness that would precipitate trace-dew in the dawn. With it came the smell of a pre-spice mass, the mass they had detected off to the northeast, and that told them there would be a maker nearby.

Paul crawled through the sphincter opening, stood on the sand and stretched the sleep from his muscles. A faint green-pearl luminescence etched the eastern horizon. The tents of his troop were small false dunes around him in the gloom. He saw movement off to the left—the guard, and knew they had seen him.

They knew the peril he faced this day. Each Fremen had faced it. They gave him this last few moments of isolation now that he might prepare himself.

It must be done today, he told himself.

He thought of the power he wielded in the face of the pogrom—the old men who sent their sons to him to be trained in the weirding way of battle, the old men who listened to him now in council and followed his plans, the men who returned to pay him that highest Fremen compliment: "Your plan worked, Muad'Dib."

Yet the meanest and smallest of the Fremen warriors could do a thing that he had never done. And Paul knew his leadership suffered from the omnipresent knowledge of this difference between them.

He had not ridden the maker.

Oh, he'd gone up with the others for training trips and raids, but he had not made his own voyage. Until he did, his world was bounded by the abilities of others. No true Fremen could permit this. Until he did this thing himself, even the great southlands—the area some twenty thumpers beyond the erg—were denied him unless he ordered a palanquin and rode like a Reverend Mother or one of the sick and wounded.

Memory returned to him of his wrestling with his inner awareness during the night. He saw a strange parallel here—if he mastered the maker, his rule was strengthened; if he mastered the inward eye, this carried its own measure of command. But beyond them both lay the clouded area, the Great Unrest where all the universe seemed embroiled.

The differences in the ways he comprehended the universe haunted him—accuracy matched with inaccuracy. He saw it in situ. Yet, when it was born, when it came into the pressures of reality, the *now* had its own life and grew with its own subtle differences. Terrible purpose remained. Race consciousness remained. And over all loomed the jihad, bloody and wild.

Chani joined him outside the tent, hugging her elbows, looking up at him from the corners of her eyes the way she did when she studied his mood.

"Tell me again about the waters of thy birthworld, Usul," she said.

He saw that she was trying to distract him, ease his mind of tensions before the deadly test. It was growing lighter, and he noted that some of his Fedaykin were already striking their tents.

"I'd rather you told me about the sietch and about our son," he said. "Does our Leto yet hold my mother in his palm?"

"It's Alia he holds as well," she said. "And he grows rapidly. He'll be a big man."

"What's it like in the south?" he asked.

"When you ride the maker you'll see for yourself," she said.

"But I wish to see it first through your eyes."

"It's powerfully lonely," she said.

He touched the nezhoni scarf at her forehead where it protruded from her stillsuit cap. "Why will you not talk about the sietch?"

"I have talked about it. The sietch is a lonely place without our men. It's a place of work. We labor in the factories and the potting rooms. There are weapons to be made, poles to plant that we may forecast the weather, spice to collect for the bribes. There are dunes to be planted to make them grow and to anchor them. There are fabrics and rugs to make, fuel cells to charge. There are children to train that the tribe's strength may never be lost."

"Is nothing then pleasant in the sietch?" he asked.

"The children are pleasant. We observe the rites. We have sufficient food. Sometimes one of us may come north to be with her man. Life must go on."

"My sister, Alia—is she accepted yet by the people?"

Chani turned toward him in the growing dawnlight. Her eyes bored into him. "It's a thing to be discussed another time, beloved."

"Let us discuss it now."

"You should conserve your energies for the test," she said.

He saw that he had touched something sensitive, hearing the withdrawal in her voice. "The unknown brings its own worries," he said.

Presently she nodded, said, "There is yet . . . misunderstanding because of Alia's strangeness. The women are fearful because a child little more than an infant talks . . . of things that only an adult should know. They do not understand the . . . change in the womb that made Alia . . . different."

"There is trouble?" he asked. And he thought: *I've seen visions of trouble over Alia.*

Chani looked toward the growing line of the sunrise. "Some of the women banded to appeal to the Reverend Mother. They demanded she exorcise the demon in her daughter. They quoted the scripture: 'Suffer not a witch to live among us.'"

"And what did my mother say to them?"

"She recited the law and sent the women away abashed. She said: 'If Alia incites trouble, it is the fault of authority for not foreseeing and preventing the trouble.' And she tried to explain how the change had worked on Alia in the womb. But the women were angry because they had been embarrassed. They went away muttering."

There will be trouble because of Alia, he thought.

A crystal blowing of sand touched the exposed portions of his face, bringing the scent of the pre-spice mass. "El-Sayal, the rain of sand that brings the morning," he said.

He looked out across the gray light of the desert landscape, the landscape beyond pity, the sand that was form absorbed in itself. Dry lightning streaked a dark corner to the south—sign that a storm had built up its static charge there. The roll of thunder boomed long after.

"The voice that beautifies the land," Chani said.

More of his men were stirring out of their tents. Guards were coming in from the rims. Everything around him moved smoothly in the ancient routine that required no orders.

"Give as few orders as possible," his father had told him . . . once . . . long ago. "Once you've given orders on a subject, you must always give orders on that subject."

The Fremen knew this rule instinctively.

The troop's watermaster began the morning chanty, adding to it now the call for the rite to initiate a sandrider.

"The world is a carcass," the man chanted, his voice wailing across the dunes. "Who can turn away the Angel of Death? What Shai-hulud has decreed must be."

Paul listened, recognizing that these were the words that also began the death chant of his Fedaykin, the words the death commandos recited as they hurled themselves into battle.

Will there be a rock shrine here this day to mark the passing of another soul? Paul asked himself. *Will Fremen stop here in the future, each to add another stone and think on Muad'Dib who died in this place?*

He knew this was among the alternatives today, a *fact* along lines of the future radiating from this position in time-space. The imperfect vision plagued him. The more he resisted his terrible purpose and fought against the coming of the jihad, the greater the turmoil that wove through his prescience. His entire future was becoming like a river hurtling toward a chasm—the violent nexus beyond which all was fog and clouds.

"Stilgar approaches," Chani said. "I must stand apart now, beloved. Now, I must be Sayyadina and observe the rite that it may be reported truly in the Chronicles." She looked up at him and, for a moment, her reserve slipped, then she had herself under control. "When this is past, I shall prepare thy breakfast with my own hands," she said. She turned away.

Stilgar moved toward him across the flour sand, stirring up little dust puddles. The dark niches of his eyes remained steady on Paul with their untamed stare. The glimpse of black beard above the stillsuit mask, the lines of craggy cheeks, could have been wind-etched from the native rock for all their movement.

The man carried Paul's banner on its staff—the green and black banner with a water tube in the staff—that already was a legend in the land. Half pridefully, Paul thought: *I cannot do the simplest thing without its becoming a legend. They will mark how I parted from Chani, how I greet Stilgar—every move I make this day. Live or die, it is a legend. I must not die. Then it will be only legend and nothing to stop the jihad.*

Stilgar planted the staff in the sand beside Paul, dropped his hands to his sides. The blue-within-blue eyes remained level and intent. And

Paul thought how his own eyes already were assuming this mask of color from the spice.

"They denied us the Hajj," Stilgar said with ritual solemnity.

As Chani had taught him, Paul responded: "Who can deny a Fremen the right to walk or ride where he wills?"

"I am a Naib," Stilgar said, "never to be taken alive. I am a leg of the death tripod that will destroy our foes."

Silence settled over them.

Paul glanced at the other Fremen scattered over the sand beyond Stilgar, the way they stood without moving for this moment of personal prayer. And he thought of how the Fremen were a people whose living consisted of killing, an entire people who had lived with rage and grief all of their days, never once considering what might take the place of either—except for a dream with which Liet-Kynes had infused them before his death.

"Where is the Lord who led us through the land of desert and of pits?" Stilgar asked.

"He is ever with us," the Fremen chanted.

Stilgar squared his shoulders, stepped closer to Paul and lowered his voice. "Now, remember what I told you. Do it simply and directly—nothing fancy. Among our people, we ride the maker at the age of twelve. You are more than six years beyond that age and not born to this life. You don't have to impress anyone with your courage. We know you are brave. All you must do is call the maker and ride him."

"I will remember," Paul said.

"See that you do. I'll not have you shame my teaching."

Stilgar pulled a plastic rod about a meter long from beneath his robe. The thing was pointed at one end, had a spring-wound clapper at the other end. "I prepared this thumper myself. It's a good one. Take it."

Paul felt the warm smoothness of the plastic as he accepted the thumper.

"Shishakli has your hooks," Stilgar said. "He'll hand them to you as you step out onto that dune over there." He pointed to his right. "Call a big maker, Usul. Show us the way."

Paul marked the tone of Stilgar's voice—half ritual and half that of a worried friend.

In that instant, the sun seemed to bound above the horizon. The sky took on the silvered gray-blue that warned this would be a day of extreme heat and dryness even for Arrakis.

"It is the time of the scalding day," Stilgar said, and now his voice was entirely ritual. "Go, Usul, and ride the maker, travel the sand as a leader of men."

Paul saluted his banner, noting how the green and black flag hung limply now that the dawn wind had died. He turned toward the dune Stilgar had indicated—a dirty tan slope with an S-track crest. Already, most of the troop was moving out in the opposite direction, climbing the other dune that had sheltered their camp.

One robed figure remained in Paul's path: Shishakli, a squad leader of the Fedaykin, only his slope-lidded eyes visible between stillsuit cap and mask.

Shishakli presented two thin, whiplike shafts as Paul approached. The shafts were about a meter and a half long with glistening plasteel hooks at one end, roughened at the other end for a firm grip.

Paul accepted them both in his left hand as required by the ritual.

"They are my own hooks," Shishakli said in a husky voice. "They never have failed."

Paul nodded, maintaining the necessary silence, moved past the man and up the dune slope. At the crest, he glanced back, saw the troop scattering like a flight of insects, their robes fluttering. He stood alone now on the sandy ridge with only the horizon in front of him, the flat and unmoving horizon. This was a good dune Stilgar had chosen, higher than its companions for the viewpoint vantage.

Stooping, Paul planted the thumper deep into the windward face where the sand was compacted and would give maximum transmission to the drumming. Then he hesitated, reviewing the lessons, reviewing the life-and-death necessities that faced him.

When he threw the latch, the thumper would begin its summons. Across the sand, a giant worm—a maker—would hear and come to the drumming. With the whiplike hook-staffs, Paul knew, he could mount the maker's high curving back. For as long as a forward edge of a worm's ring segment was held open by a hook, open to admit abrasive sand into the more sensitive interior, the creature would not retreat beneath the desert. It would, in fact, roll its gigantic body to bring the opened segment as far away from the desert surface as possible.

I am a sandrider, Paul told himself.

He glanced down at the hooks in his left hand, thinking that he had only to shift those hooks down the curve of a maker's immense side to make the creature roll and turn, guiding it where he willed. He had seen it done. He had been helped up the side of a worm for a short ride in training. The captive worm could be ridden until it lay exhausted and quiescent upon the desert surface and a new maker must be summoned.

Once he was past this test, Paul knew, he was qualified to make the twenty-thumper journey into the southland—to rest and restore himself—into the south where the women and the families had been hidden from the pogrom among the new palmaries and sietch warrens.

He lifted his head and looked to the south, reminding himself that the maker summoned wild from the erg was an unknown quantity, and the one who summoned it was equally unknown to this test.

"You must gauge the approaching maker carefully," Stilgar had explained. "You must stand close enough that you can mount it as it passes, yet not so close that it engulfs you."

With abrupt decision, Paul released the thumper's latch. The clapper began revolving and the summons drummed through the sand, a measured "lump . . . lump . . . lump. . . ."

He straightened, scanning the horizon, remembering Stilgar's words: "Judge the line of approach carefully. Remember, a worm seldom makes an unseen approach to a thumper. Listen all the same. You may often hear it before you see it."

And Chani's words of caution, whispered at night when her fear for him overcame her, filled his mind: "When you take your stand along the maker's path, you must remain utterly still. You must think like a patch of sand. Hide beneath your cloak and become a little dune in your very essence."

Slowly, he scanned the horizon, listening, watching for the signs he had been taught.

It came from the southeast, a distant hissing, a sand-whisper. Presently he saw the faraway outline of the creature's track against the dawnlight and realized he had never before seen a maker this large, never heard of one this size. It appeared to be more than half a league long, and the rise of the sandwave at its cresting head was like the approach of a mountain.

This is nothing I have seen by vision or in life, Paul cautioned himself. He hurried across the path of the thing to take his stand, caught up entirely by the rushing needs of this moment.

"Control the coinage and the courts—let the rabble have the rest." Thus the Padishah Emperor advised you. And he tells you: "If you want profits, you must rule." There is truth in these words, but I ask myself: "Who are the rabble and who are the ruled?"

—MUAD'DIB'S SECRET MESSAGE TO THE LANDSRAAD
FROM "ARRAKIS AWAKENING"
BY THE PRINCESS IRULAN

A thought came unbidden to Jessica's mind: *Paul will be undergoing his sandrider test at any moment now. They try to conceal this fact from me, but it's obvious.*

And Chani has gone on some mysterious errand.

Jessica sat in her resting chamber, catching a moment of quiet between the night's classes. It was a pleasant chamber, but not as large as the one she had enjoyed in Sietch Tabr before their flight from the pogrom. Still, this place had thick rugs on the floor, soft cushions, a low coffee table near at hand, multicolored hangings on the walls, and soft yellow glowglobes overhead. The room was permeated with the distinctive acrid furry odor of a Fremen sietch that she had come to associate with a sense of security.

Yet she knew she would never overcome a feeling of being in an alien place. It was the harshness that the rugs and hangings attempted to conceal.

A faint tinkling-drumming-slapping penetrated to the resting chamber. Jessica knew it for a birth celebration, probably Subiay's. Her time was near. And Jessica knew she'd see the baby soon enough—a blue-eyed cherub brought to the Reverend Mother for blessing. She knew also that her daughter, Alia, would be at the celebration and would report on it.

It was not yet time for the nightly prayer of parting. They wouldn't have started a birth celebration near the time of ceremony that mourned the slave raids of Poritrin, Bela Tegeuse, Rossak, and Harmonthep.

Jessica sighed. She knew she was trying to keep her thoughts off her son and the dangers he faced—the pit traps with their poisoned barbs, the Harkonnen raids (although these were growing fewer as the Fremen took their toll of aircraft and raiders with the new weapons Paul had given them), and the natural dangers of the desert—makers and thirst and dust chasms.

She thought of calling for coffee and with the thought came that ever-present awareness of paradox in the Fremen way of life: how well they lived in these sietch caverns compared to the graben pyons; yet, how much more they endured in the open hajr of the desert than anything the Harkonnen bondsmen endured.

A dark hand inserted itself through the hangings beside her, deposited a cup upon the table and withdrew. From the cup arose the aroma of spiced coffee.

An offering from the birth celebration, Jessica thought.

She took the coffee and sipped it, smiling at herself. *In what other society of our universe,* she asked herself, *could a person of my station accept an anonymous drink and quaff that drink without fear? I could alter any poison now before it did me harm, of course, but the donor doesn't realize this.*

She drained the cup, feeling the energy and lift of its contents—hot and delicious.

And she wondered what other society would have such a natural regard for her privacy and comfort that the giver would intrude only enough to deposit the gift and not inflict her with the donor? Respect and love had sent the gift—with only a slight tinge of fear.

Another element of the incident forced itself into her awareness: she had thought of coffee and it had appeared. There was nothing of telepathy here, she knew. It was the tau, the oneness of the sietch community, a compensation from the subtle poison of the spice diet they shared. The great mass of the people could never hope to attain the enlightenment the spice seed brought to her; they had not been trained and prepared for it. Their minds rejected what they could not understand or encompass. Still they felt and reacted sometimes like a single organism.

And the thought of coincidence never entered their minds.

Has Paul passed his test on the sand? Jessica asked herself. *He's capable, but accident can strike down even the most capable.*

The waiting.

It's the dreariness, she thought. *You can wait just so long. Then the dreariness of the waiting overcomes you.*

There was all manner of waiting in their lives.

More than two years we've been here, she thought, *and twice that number at least to go before we can even hope to think of trying to wrest Arrakis from the Harkonnen governor, the Mudir Nahya, the Beast Rabban.*

"Reverend Mother?"

The voice from outside the hangings at her door was that of Harah, the other woman in Paul's menage.

"Yes, Harah."

The hangings parted and Harah seemed to glide through them. She wore sietch sandals, a red-yellow wraparound that exposed her arms almost to the shoulders. Her black hair was parted in the middle and swept back like the wings of an insect, flat and oily against her head. The jutting, predatory features were drawn into an intense frown.

Behind Harah came Alia, a girl-child of about two years.

Seeing her daughter, Jessica was caught as she frequently was by Alia's resemblance to Paul at that age—the same wide-eyed solemnity to her questing look, the dark hair and firmness of mouth. But there were subtle differences, too, and it was in these that most adults found Alia disquieting. The child—little more than a toddler—carried herself

with a calmness and awareness beyond her years. Adults were shocked
to find her laughing at a subtle play of words between the sexes. Or
they'd catch themselves listening to her half-lisping voice, still blurred
as it was by an unformed soft palate, and discover in her words sly remarks that could only be based on experiences no two-year-old had
ever encountered.

Harah sank to a cushion with an exasperated sigh, frowned at the
child.

"Alia." Jessica motioned to her daughter.

The child crossed to a cushion beside her mother, sank to it and
clasped her mother's hand. The contact of flesh restored that mutual
awareness they had shared since before Alia's birth. It wasn't a matter
of shared thoughts—although there were bursts of that if they touched
while Jessica was changing the spice poison for a ceremony. It was
something larger, an immediate awareness of another living spark, a
sharp and poignant thing, a nerve-*simpatico* that made them emotion-
ally one.

In the formal manner that befitted a member of her son's household,
Jessica said: "Subakh ul kuhar, Harah. This night finds you well?"

With the same traditional formality, she said: "Subakh un nar. I am
well." The words were almost toneless. Again, she sighed.

Jessica sensed amusement from Alia.

"My brother's ghanima is annoyed with me," Alia said in her half-
lisp.

Jessica marked the term Alia used to refer to Harah—ghanima. In
the subtleties of the Fremen tongue, the word meant "something acquired in battle" and with the added overtone that the something no
longer was used for its original purpose. An ornament, a spearhead
used as a curtain weight.

Harah scowled at the child. "Don't try to insult me, child. I know
my place."

"What have you done this time, Alia?" Jessica asked.

Harah answered: "Not only has she refused to play with the other
children today, but she intruded where. . . ."

"I hid behind the hangings and watched Subiay's child being born," Alia said. "It's a boy. He cried and cried. What a set of lungs! When he'd cried long enough—"

"She came out and touched him," Harah said, "and he stopped crying. Everyone knows a Fremen baby must get his crying done at birth, if he's in sietch because he can never cry again lest he betray us on hajr."

"He'd cried enough," Alia said. "I just wanted to feel his spark, his life. That's all. And when he felt me he didn't want to cry anymore."

"It's just made more talk among the people," Harah said.

"Subiay's boy is healthy?" Jessica asked. She saw that something was troubling Harah deeply and wondered at it.

"Healthy as any mother could ask," Harah said. "They know Alia didn't hurt him. They didn't so much mind her touching him. He settled down right away and was happy. I was. . . ." Harah shrugged.

"It's the strangeness of my daughter, is that it?" Jessica asked. "It's the way she speaks of things beyond her years and of things no child her age could know—things of the past."

"How could she know what a child looked like on Bela Tegeuse?" Harah demanded.

"But he does!" Alia said. "Subiay's boy looks just like the son of Mitha born before the parting."

"Alia!" Jessica said. "I warned you."

"But, Mother, I saw it and it was true and. . . ."

Jessica shook her head, seeing the signs of disturbance in Harah's face. *What have I borne?* Jessica asked herself. *A daughter who knew at birth everything that I knew . . . and more: everything revealed to her out of the corridors of the past by the Reverend Mothers within me.*

"It's not just the things she says," Harah said. "It's the exercises, too: the way she sits and stares at a rock, moving only one muscle beside her nose, or a muscle on the back of a finger, or—"

"Those are the Bene Gesserit training," Jessica said. "You know that, Harah. Would you deny my daughter her inheritance?"

"Reverend Mother, you know these things don't matter to me," Harah said. "It's the people and the way they mutter. I feel danger in it.

They say your daughter's a demon, that other children refuse to play with her, that she's—"

"She has so little in common with the other children," Jessica said. "She's no demon. It's just the—"

"Of course she's not!"

Jessica found herself surprised at the vehemence in Harah's tone, glanced down at Alia. The child appeared lost in thought, radiating a sense of . . . waiting. Jessica returned her attention to Harah.

"I respect the fact that you're a member of my son's household," Jessica said. (Alia stirred against her hand.) "You may speak openly with me of whatever's troubling you."

"I will not be a member of your son's household much longer," Harah said. "I've waited this long for the sake of my sons, the special training *they* receive as the children of Usul. It's little enough I could give them since it's known I don't share your son's bed."

Again Alia stirred beside her, half-sleeping, warm.

"You'd have made a good companion for my son, though," Jessica said. And she added to herself because such thoughts were ever with her: *Companion . . . not a wife.* Jessica's thoughts went then straight to the center, to the pang that came from the common talk in the sietch that her son's companionship with Chani had become a permanent thing, the marriage.

I love Chani, Jessica thought, but she reminded herself that love might have to step aside for royal necessity. Royal marriages had other reasons than love.

"You think I don't know what you plan for your son?" Harah asked.

"What do you mean?" Jessica demanded.

"You plan to unite the tribes under *Him*," Harah said.

"Is that bad?"

"I see danger for him . . . and Alia is part of that danger."

Alia nestled closer to her mother, eyes opened now and studying Harah.

"I've watched you two together," Harah said, "the way you touch. And Alia is like my own flesh because she's sister to one who is like my brother. I've watched over her and guarded her from the time she was a mere baby, from the time of the razzia when we fled here. I've seen many things about her."

Jessica nodded, feeling disquiet begin to grow in Alia beside her.

"You know what I mean," Harah said. "The way she knew from the first what we were saying to her. When has there been another baby who knew the water discipline so young? What other baby's first words to her nurse were: 'I love you, Harah'?"

Harah stared at Alia. "Why do you think I accept her insults? I know there's no malice in them."

Alia looked up at her mother.

"Yes, I have reasoning powers, Reverend Mother," Harah said. "I could have been of the Sayyadina. I have seen what I have seen."

"Harah. . . ." Jessica shrugged. "I don't know what to say." And she felt surprise at herself, because this literally was true.

Alia straightened, squared her shoulders. Jessica felt the sense of waiting ended, an emotion compounded of decision and sadness.

"We made a mistake," Alia said. "Now we need Harah."

"It was the ceremony of the seed," Harah said, "when you changed the Water of Life, Reverend Mother, when Alia was yet unborn within you."

Need Harah? Jessica asked herself.

"Who else can talk among the people and make them begin to understand me?" Alia asked.

"What would you have her do?" Jessica asked.

"She already knows what to do," Alia said.

"I will tell them the truth," Harah said. Her face seemed suddenly old and sad with its olive skin drawn into frown wrinkles, a witchery in the sharp features. "I will tell them that Alia only pretends to be a little girl, that she has never been a little girl."

Alia shook her head. Tears ran down her cheeks, and Jessica felt the wave of sadness from her daughter as though the emotion were her own.

"I know I'm a freak," Alia whispered. The adult summation coming from the child mouth was like a bitter confirmation.

"You're not a freak!" Harah snapped. "Who dared say you're a freak?"

Again, Jessica marveled at the fierce note of protectiveness in Harah's voice. Jessica saw then that Alia had judged correctly—they did need Harah. The tribe would understand Harah—both her words and her emotions—for it was obvious she loved Alia as though this were her own child.

"Who said it?" Harah repeated.

"Nobody."

Alia used a corner of Jessica's aba to wipe the tears from her face. She smoothed the robe where she had dampened and crumpled it.

"Then don't you say it," Harah ordered.

"Yes, Harah."

"Now," Harah said, "you may tell me what it was like so that I may tell the others. Tell me what it is that happened to you."

Alia swallowed, looked up at her mother.

Jessica nodded.

"One day I woke up," Alia said. "It was like waking from sleep except that I could not remember going to sleep. I was in a warm, dark place. And I was frightened."

Listening to the half-lisping voice of her daughter, Jessica remembered that day in the big cavern.

"When I was frightened," Alia said, "I tried to escape, but there was no way to escape. Then I saw a spark . . . but it wasn't exactly like seeing it. The spark was just there with me and I felt the spark's emotions . . . soothing me, comforting me, telling me that way that everything would be all right. That was my mother."

Harah rubbed at her eyes, smiled reassuringly at Alia. Yet there was a look of wildness in the eyes of the Fremen woman, an intensity as though they, too, were trying to hear Alia's words.

And Jessica thought: *What do we really know of how such a one thinks . . . out of her unique experiences and training and ancestry?*

"Just when I felt safe and reassured," Alia said, "there was another spark with us . . . and everything was happening at once. The other spark was the old Reverend Mother. She was . . . trading lives with my mother . . . everything . . . and I was there with them, seeing it all . . . everything. And it was over, and I was them and all the others and myself . . . only it took me a long time to find myself again. There were so many others."

"It was a cruel thing," Jessica said. "No being should wake into consciousness thus. The wonder of it is you could accept all that happened to you."

"I couldn't do anything else!" Alia said. "I didn't know how to reject or hide my consciousness . . . or shut it off . . . everything just happened . . . everything. . . ."

"We didn't know," Harah murmured. "When we gave your mother the Water to change, we didn't know you existed within her."

"Don't be sad about it, Harah," Alia said. "I shouldn't feel sorry for myself. After all, there's cause for happiness here: I'm a Reverend Mother. The tribe has two Rev. . . ."

She broke off, tipping her head to listen.

Harah rocked back on her heels against the sitting cushion, stared at Alia, bringing her attention then up to Jessica's face.

"Didn't you suspect?" Jessica asked.

"Sh-h-h-h," Alia said.

A distant rhythmic chanting came to them through the hangings that separated them from the sietch corridors. It grew louder, carrying distinct sounds now: "Ya! Ya! Yawm! Ya! Ya! Yawm! Mu zein, wallah! Ya! Ya! Yawm! Mu zein, Wallah!"

The chanters passed the outer entrance, and their voices boomed through to the inner apartments. Slowly the sound receded.

When the sound had dimmed sufficiently, Jessica began the ritual, the sadness in her voice: "It was Ramadhan and April on Bela Tegeuse."

"My family sat in their pool courtyard," Harah said, "in air bathed by the moisture that arose from the spray of a fountain. There was a tree of portyguls, round and deep in color, near at hand. There was a basket with mish-mish and baklawa and mugs of liban—all manner of good things to eat. In our gardens and in our flocks, there was peace . . . peace in all the land."

"Life was full with happiness until the raiders came," Alia said.

"Blood ran cold at the scream of friends," Jessica said. And she felt the memories rushing through her out of all those other pasts she shared.

"La, la, la, the women cried," said Harah.

"The raiders came through the mushtamal, rushing at us with their knives dripping red from the lives of our men," Jessica said.

Silence came over the three of them as it was in all the apartments of the sietch, the silence while they remembered and kept their grief thus fresh.

Presently, Harah uttered the ritual ending to the ceremony, giving the words a harshness that Jessica had never before heard in them.

"We will never forgive and we will never forget," Harah said.

In the thoughtful quiet that followed her words, they heard a muttering of people, the swish of many robes. Jessica sensed someone standing beyond the hangings that shielded her chamber.

"Reverend Mother?"

A woman's voice, and Jessica recognized it: the voice of Tharthar, one of Stilgar's wives.

"What is it, Tharthar?"

"There is trouble, Reverend Mother."

Jessica felt a constriction at her heart, an abrupt fear for Paul. "Paul . . ." she gasped.

Tharthar spread the hangings, stepped into the chamber. Jessica glimpsed a press of people in the outer room before the hangings fell. She looked up at Tharthar—a small, dark woman in a red-figured robe of black, the total blue of her eyes trained fixedly on Jessica, the nostrils of her tiny nose dilated to reveal the plug scars.

"What is it?" Jessica demanded.

"There is word from the sand," Tharthar said. "Usul meets the maker for his test . . . it is today. The young men say he cannot fail, he will be a sandrider by nightfall. The young men are banding for a razzia. They will raid in the north and meet Usul there. They say they will raise the cry then. They say they will force him to call out Stilgar and assume command of the tribes."

Gathering water, planting the dunes, changing their world slowly but surely—these are no longer enough, Jessica thought. *The little raids, the certain raids—these are no longer enough now that Paul and I have trained them. They feel their power. They want to fight.*

Tharthar shifted from one foot to the other, cleared her throat.

We know the need for cautious waiting, Jessica thought, *but there's the core of our frustration. We know also the harm that waiting extended too long can do us. We lose our senses of purpose if the waiting's prolonged.*

"The young men say if Usul does not call out Stilgar, then he must be afraid," Tharthar said.

She lowered her gaze.

"So that's the way of it," Jessica muttered. And she thought: *Well I saw it coming. As did Stilgar.*

Again, Tharthar cleared her throat. "Even my brother, Shoab, says it," she said. "They will leave Usul no choice."

Then it has come, Jessica thought. *And Paul will have to handle it himself. The Reverend Mother dare not become involved in the succession.*

Alia freed her hand from her mother's, said: "I will go with Tharthar and listen to the young men. Perhaps there is a way."

Jessica met Tharthar's gaze, but spoke to Alia: "Go, then. And report to me as soon as you can."

"We do not want this thing to happen, Reverend Mother," Tharthar said.

"We do not want it," Jessica agreed. "The tribe needs *all* its strength." She glanced at Harah. "Will you go with them?"

Harah answered the unspoken part of the question: "Tharthar will allow no harm to befall Alia. She knows we will soon be wives together, she and I, to share the same man. We have talked, Tharthar and I." Harah looked up at Tharthar, back to Jessica. "We have an understanding."

Tharthar held out a hand for Alia, said: "We must hurry. The young men are leaving."

They pressed through the hangings, the child's hand in the small woman's hand, but the child seemed to be leading.

"If Paul-Muad'Dib slays Stilgar, this will not serve the tribe," Harah said. "Always before, it has been the way of succession, but times have changed."

"Times have changed for you, as well," Jessica said.

"You cannot think I doubt the outcome of such a battle," Harah said. "Usul could not but win."

"That was my meaning," Jessica said.

"And you think my personal feelings enter into my judgment," Harah said. She shook her head, her water rings tinkling at her neck. "How wrong you are. Perhaps you think, as well, that I regret not being the chosen of Usul, that I am jealous of Chani?"

"You make your own choice as you are able," Jessica said.

"I pity Chani," Harah said.

Jessica stiffened. "What do you mean?"

"I know what you think of Chani," Harah said. "You think she is not the wife for your son."

Jessica settled back, relaxed on her cushions. She shrugged. "Perhaps."

"You could be right," Harah said. "If you are, you may find a surprising ally—Chani herself. She wants whatever is best for *Him*."

Jessica swallowed past a sudden tightening in her throat. "Chani's very dear to me," she said. "She could be no—"

"Your rugs are very dirty in here," Harah said. She swept her gaze around the floor, avoiding Jessica's eyes. "So many people tramping through here all the time. You really should have them cleaned more often."

You cannot avoid the interplay of politics within an orthodox religion. This power struggle permeates the training, educating and disciplining of the orthodox community. Because of this pressure, the leaders of such a community inevitably must face that ultimate internal question: to succumb to complete opportunism as the price of maintaining their rule, or risk sacrificing themselves for the sake of the orthodox ethic.

—FROM "MUAD'DIB: THE RELIGIOUS ISSUES"
BY THE PRINCESS IRULAN

Paul waited on the sand outside the gigantic maker's line of approach. *I must not wait like a smuggler—impatient and jittering,* he reminded himself. *I must be part of the desert.*

The thing was only minutes away now, filling the morning with the friction-hissing of its passage. Its great teeth within the cavern-circle of its mouth spread like some enormous flower. The spice odor from it dominated the air.

Paul's stillsuit rode easily on his body and he was only distantly aware of his nose plugs, the breathing mask. Stilgar's teaching, the painstaking hours on the sand, overshadowed all else.

"How far outside the maker's radius must you stand in pea sand?" Stilgar had asked him.

And he had answered correctly: "Half a meter for every meter of the maker's diameter."

"Why?"

"To avoid the vortex of its passage and still have time to run in and mount it."

"You've ridden the little ones bred for the seed and the Water of Life," Stilgar had said. "But what you'll summon for your test is a wild maker, an old man of the desert. You must have proper respect for such a one."

Now the thumper's deep drumming blended with the hiss of the approaching worm. Paul breathed deeply, smelling mineral bitterness of sand even through his filters. The wild maker, the old man of the desert, loomed almost on him. Its cresting front segments threw a sandwave that would sweep across his knees.

Come up, you lovely monster, he thought. *Up. You hear me calling. Come up. Come up.*

The wave lifted his feet. Surface dust swept across him. He steadied himself, his world dominated by the passage of that sand-clouded curving wall, that segmented cliff, the ring lines sharply defined in it.

Paul lifted his hooks, sighted along them, leaned in. He felt them bite and pull. He leaped upward, planting his feet against that wall, leaning out against the clinging barbs. This was the true instant of the testing: if he had planted the hooks correctly at the leading edge of a ring segment, opening the segment, the worm would not roll down and crush him.

The worm slowed. It glided across the thumper, silencing it. Slowly, it began to roll—up, up—bringing those irritant barbs as high as possible, away from the sand that threatened the soft inner lapping of its ring segment.

Paul found himself riding upright atop the worm. He felt exultant, like an emperor surveying his world. He suppressed a sudden urge to cavort there, to turn the worm, to show off his mastery of this creature.

Suddenly he understood why Stilgar had warned him once about brash young men who danced and played with these monsters, doing handstands on their backs, removing both hooks and replanting them before the worm could spill them.

Leaving one hook in place, Paul released the other and planted it lower down the side. When the second hook was firm and tested, he brought down the first one, thus worked his way down the side. The maker rolled, and as it rolled, it turned, coming around the sweep of flour sand where the others waited.

Paul saw them come up, using their hooks to climb, but avoiding the sensitive ring edges until they were on top. They rode at last in a triple line behind him, steadied against their hooks.

Stilgar moved up through the ranks, checked the positioning of Paul's hooks, glanced up at Paul's smiling face.

"You did it, eh?" Stilgar asked, raising his voice above the hiss of their passage. "That's what you think? You did it?" He straightened. "Now I tell you that was a very sloppy job. We have twelve-year-olds who do better. There was drumsand to your left where you waited. You could not retreat there if the worm turned that way."

The smile slipped from Paul's face. "I saw the drumsand."

"Then why did you not signal for one of us to take up position secondary to you? It was a thing you could do even in the test."

Paul swallowed, faced into the wind of their passage.

"You think it bad of me to say this now," Stilgar said. "It is my duty. I think of your worth to the troop. If you had stumbled into that drumsand, the maker would've turned toward you."

In spite of a surge of anger, Paul knew that Stilgar spoke the truth. It took a long minute and the full effort of the training he had received from his mother for Paul to recapture a feeling of calm. "I apologize," he said. "It will not happen again."

"In a tight position, always leave yourself a secondary, someone to take the maker if you cannot," Stilgar said. "Remember that we work together. That way, we're certain. We work together, eh?"

He slapped Paul's shoulder.

"We work together," Paul agreed.

"Now," Stilgar said, and his voice was harsh, "show me you know how to handle a maker. Which side are we on?"

Paul glanced down at the scaled ring surface on which they stood, noted the character and size of the scales, the way they grew larger off to his right, smaller to his left. Every worm, he knew, moved characteristically with one side up more frequently. As it grew older, the characteristic up-side became an almost constant thing. Bottom scales grew larger, heavier, smoother. Top scales could be told by size alone on a big worm.

Shifting his hooks, Paul moved to the left. He motioned flankers down to open segments along the side and keep the worm on a straight course as it rolled. When he had it turned, he motioned two steersmen out of the line and into positions ahead.

"Ach, haiiiii-yoh!" he shouted in the traditional call. The left-side steersman opened a ring segment there.

In a majestic circle, the maker turned to protect its opened segment. Full around it came and when it was headed back to the south, Paul shouted: "Geyrat!"

The steersman released his hook. The maker lined out in a straight course.

Stilgar said, "Very good, Paul-Muad'Dib. With plenty of practice, you may yet become a sandrider."

Paul frowned, thinking: *Was I not first up?*

From behind him there came sudden laughter. The troop began chanting, flinging his name against the sky.

"Muad'Dib! Muad'Dib! Muad'Dib! Muad'Dib!"

And far to the rear along the worm's surface, Paul heard the beat of the goaders pounding the tail segments. The worm began picking up speed. Their robes flapped in the wind. The abrasive sound of their passage increased.

Paul looked back through the troop, found Chani's face among them. He looked at her as he spoke to Stilgar. "Then I am a sandrider, Stil?"

"Hal yawm! You are a sandrider this day."

"Then I may choose our destination?"

"That's the way of it."

"And I am a Fremen born this day here in the Habbanya erg. I have had no life before this day. I was as a child until this day."

"Not quite a child," Stilgar said. He fastened a corner of his hood where the wind was whipping it.

"But there was a cork sealing off my world, and that cork has been pulled."

"There is no cork."

"I would go south, Stilgar—twenty thumpers. I would see this land we make, this land that I've only seen through the eyes of others."

And I would see my son and my family, he thought. *I need time now to consider the future that is a past within my mind. The turmoil comes and if I'm not where I can unravel it, the thing will run wild.*

Stilgar looked at him with a steady, measuring gaze. Paul kept his attention on Chani, seeing the interest quicken in her face, noting also the excitement his words had kindled in the troop.

"The men are eager to raid with you in the Harkonnen sinks," Stilgar said. "The sinks are only a thumper away."

"The Fedaykin have raided with me," Paul said. "They'll raid with me again until no Harkonnen breathes Arrakeen air."

Stilgar studied him as they rode, and Paul realized the man was seeing this moment through the memory of how he had risen to command of the Tabr sietch and to leadership of the Council of Leaders now that Liet-Kynes was dead.

He has heard the reports of unrest among the young Fremen, Paul thought.

"Do you wish a gathering of the leaders?" Stilgar asked.

Eyes blazed among the young men of the troop. They swayed as they rode, and they watched. And Paul saw the look of unrest in Chani's glance, the way she looked from Stilgar, who was her uncle, to Paul-Muad'Dib, who was her mate.

"You cannot guess what I want," Paul said.

And he thought: *I cannot back down. I must hold control over these people.*

"You are mudir of the sandride this day," Stilgar said. Cold formality rang in his voice: "How do you use this power?"

We need time to relax, time for cool reflection, Paul thought.

"We shall go south," Paul said.

"Even if I say we shall turn back to the north when this day is over?"

"We shall go south," Paul repeated.

A sense of inevitable dignity enfolded Stilgar as he pulled his robe tightly around him. "There will be a Gathering," he said. "I will send the messages."

He thinks I will call him out, Paul thought. *And he knows he cannot stand against me.*

Paul faced south, feeling the wind against his exposed cheeks, thinking of the necessities that went into his decisions.

They do not know how it is, he thought.

But he knew he could not let any consideration deflect him. He had to remain on the central line of the time storm he could see in the future. There would come an instant when it could be unraveled, but only if he were where he could cut the central knot of it.

I will not call him out if it can be helped, he thought. *If there's another way to prevent the jihad. . . .*

"We'll camp for the evening meal and prayer at Cave of Birds beneath Habbanya Ridge," Stilgar said. He steadied himself with one hook against the swaying of the maker, gestured ahead at a low rock barrier rising out of the desert.

Paul studied the cliff, the great streaks of rock crossing it like waves. No green, no blossom softened that rigid horizon. Beyond it stretched the way to the southern desert—a course of at least ten days and nights, as fast as they could goad the makers.

Twenty thumpers.

The way led far beyond the Harkonnen patrols. He knew how it would be. The dreams had shown him. One day, as they went, there'd be a faint change of color on the far horizon—such a slight change that he might feel he was imagining it out of his hopes—and there would be the new sietch.

"Does my decision suit Muad'Dib?" Stilgar asked. Only the faintest touch of sarcasm tinged his voice, but Fremen ears around them, alert to every tone in a bird's cry or a cielago's piping message, heard the sarcasm and watched Paul to see what he would do.

"Stilgar heard me swear my loyalty to him when we consecrated the Fedaykin," Paul said. "My death commandos know I spoke with honor. Does Stilgar doubt it?"

Real pain exposed itself in Paul's voice. Stilgar heard it and lowered his gaze.

"Usul, the companion of my sietch, him I would never doubt," Stilgar said. "But you are Paul-Muad'Dib, the Atreides Duke, and you are the Lisan al-Gaib, the Voice from the Outer World. These men I don't even know."

Paul turned away to watch the Habbanya Ridge climb out of the desert. The maker beneath them still felt strong and willing. It could carry them almost twice the distance of any other in Fremen experience. He knew it. There was nothing outside the stories told to children that could match this old man of the desert. It was the stuff of a new legend, Paul realized.

A hand gripped his shoulder.

Paul looked at it, followed the arm to the face beyond it—the dark eyes of Stilgar exposed between filter mask and stillsuit hood.

"The one who led Tabr sietch before me," Stilgar said, "he was my friend. We shared dangers. He owed me his life many a time . . . and I owed him mine."

"I am your friend, Stilgar," Paul said.

"No man doubts it," Stilgar said. He removed his hand, shrugged. "It's the way."

Paul saw that Stilgar was too immersed in the Fremen way to consider the possibility of any other. Here a leader took the reins from the dead hands of his predecessor, or slew among the strongest of his tribe if a leader died in the desert. Stilgar had risen to be a naib in that way.

"We should leave this maker in deep sand," Paul said.

"Yes," Stilgar agreed. "We could walk to the cave from here."

"We've ridden him far enough that he'll bury himself and sulk for a day or so," Paul said.

"You're the mudir of the sandride," Stilgar said. "Say when we . . ." He broke off, stared at the eastern sky.

Paul whirled. The spice-blue overcast on his eyes made the sky appear dark, a richly filtered azure against which a distant rhythmic flashing stood out in sharp contrast.

Ornithopter!

"One small 'thopter," Stilgar said.

"Could be a scout," Paul said. "Do you think they've seen us?"

"At this distance we're just a worm on the surface," Stilgar said. He motioned with his left hand. "Off. Scatter on the sand."

The troop began working down the worm's sides, dropping off, blending with the sand beneath their cloaks. Paul marked where Chani dropped. Presently, only he and Stilgar remained.

"First up, last off," Paul said.

Stilgar nodded, dropped down the side on his hooks, leaped onto the sand. Paul waited until the maker was safely clear of the scatter area, then released his hooks. This was the tricky moment with a worm not completely exhausted.

Freed of its goads and hooks, the big worm began burrowing into the sand. Paul ran lightly back along its broad surface, judged his moment carefully and leaped off. He landed running, lunged against the slipface of a dune the way he had been taught, and hid himself beneath the cascade of sand over his robe.

Now, the waiting. . . .

Paul turned, gently, exposed a crack of sky beneath a crease in his robe. He imagined the others back along their path doing the same.

He heard the beat of the 'thopter's wings before he saw it. There was a whisper of jetpods and it came over his patch of desert, turned in a broad arc toward the ridge.

An unmarked 'thopter, Paul noted.

It flew out of sight beyond Habbanya Ridge.

A bird cry sounded over the desert. Another.

Paul shook himself free of sand, climbed to the dune top. Other figures stood out in a line trailing away from the ridge. He recognized Chani and Stilgar among them.

Stilgar signaled toward the ridge.

They gathered and began the sandwalk, gliding over the surface in a broken rhythm that would disturb no maker. Stilgar paced himself beside Paul along the windpacked crest of a dune.

"It was a smuggler craft," Stilgar said.

"So it seemed," Paul said. "But this is deep into the desert for smugglers."

"They've their difficulties with patrols, too," Stilgar said.

"If they come this deep, they may go deeper," Paul said.

"True."

"It wouldn't be well for them to see what they could see if they ventured too deep into the south. Smugglers sell information, too."

"They were hunting spice, don't you think?" Stilgar asked.

"There will be a wing and a crawler waiting somewhere for that one," Paul said. "We've spice. Let's bait a patch of sand and catch us some smugglers. They should be taught that this is our land and our men need practice with the new weapons."

"Now, Usul speaks," Stilgar said. "Usul thinks Fremen."

But Usul must give way to decisions that match a terrible purpose, Paul thought.

And the storm was gathering.

When law and duty are one, united by religion, you never become fully conscious, fully aware of yourself. You are always a little less than an individual.

—FROM "MUAD'DIB: THE NINETY-NINE
WONDERS OF THE UNIVERSE"
BY THE PRINCESS IRULAN

The smuggler's spice factory with its parent carrier and ring of drone ornithopters came over a lifting of dunes like a swarm of insects following its queen. Ahead of the swarm lay one of the low rock ridges that lifted from the desert floor like small imitations of the Shield Wall. The dry beaches of the ridge were swept clean by a recent storm.

In the con-bubble of the factory, Gurney Halleck leaned forward, adjusted the oil lenses of his binoculars and examined the landscape. Beyond the ridge, he could see a dark patch that might be a spiceblow, and he gave the signal to a hovering ornithopter that sent it to investigate.

The 'thopter waggled its wings to indicate it had the signal. It broke away from the swarm, sped down toward the darkened sand, circled the area with its detectors dangling close to the surface.

Almost immediately, it went through the wing-tucked dip and circle that told the waiting factory that spice had been found.

Gurney sheathed his binoculars, knowing the others had seen the signal. He liked this spot. The ridge offered some shielding and protection. This was deep in the desert, an unlikely place for an ambush . . .

still. . . . Gurney signaled for a crew to hover over the ridge, to scan it, sent reserves to take up station in pattern around the area—not too high because then they could be seen from afar by Harkonnen detectors.

He doubted, though, that Harkonnen patrols would be this far south. This was still Fremen country.

Gurney checked his weapons, damning the fate that made shields useless out here. Anything that summoned a worm had to be avoided at all costs. He rubbed the inkvine scar along his jaw, studying the scene, decided it would be safest to lead a ground party through the ridge. Inspection on foot was still the most certain. You couldn't be too careful when Fremen and Harkonnen were at each other's throats.

It was Fremen that worried him here. They didn't mind trading for all the spice you could afford, but they were devils on the warpath if you stepped foot where they forbade you to go. And they were so devilishly cunning of late.

It annoyed Gurney, the cunning and adroitness in battle of these natives. They displayed a sophistication in warfare as good as anything he had ever encountered, and he had been trained by the best fighters in the universe then seasoned in battles where only the superior few survived.

Again Gurney scanned the landscape, wondering why he felt uneasy. Perhaps it was the worm they had seen . . . but that was on the other side of the ridge.

A head popped up into the con-bubble beside Gurney—the factory commander, a one-eyed old pirate with full beard, the blue eyes and milky teeth of a spice diet.

"Looks like a rich patch, sir," the factory commander said. "Shall I take 'er in?"

"Come down at the edge of that ridge," Gurney ordered. "Let me disembark with my men. You can tractor out to the spice from there. We'll have a look at that rock."

"Aye."

"In case of trouble," Gurney said, "save the factory. We'll lift in the 'thopters."

The factory commander saluted. "Aye, sir." He popped back down through the hatch.

Again Gurney scanned the horizon. He had to respect the possibility that there were Fremen here and he was trespassing. Fremen worried him, their toughness and unpredictability. Many things about this business worried him, but the rewards were great. The fact that he couldn't send spotters high overhead worried him, too. The necessity of radio silence added to his uneasiness.

The factory crawler turned, began to descend. Gently it glided down to the dry beach at the foot of the ridge. Treads touched sand.

Gurney opened the bubble dome, released his safety straps. The instant the factory stopped, he was out, slamming the bubble closed behind him, scrambling out over the tread guards to swing down to the sand beyond the emergency netting. The five men of his personal guard were out with him, emerging from the nose hatch. Others released the factory's carrier wing. It detached, lifted away to fly in a parking circle low overhead.

Immediately the big factory crawler lurched off, swinging away from the ridge toward the dark patch of spice out on the sand.

A 'thopter swooped down nearby, skidded to a stop. Another followed and another. They disgorged Gurney's platoon and lifted to hoverflight.

Gurney tested his muscles in his stillsuit, stretching. He left the filter mask off his face, losing moisture for the sake of a greater need—the carrying power of his voice if he had to shout commands. He began climbing up into the rocks, checking the terrain—pebbles and pea sand underfoot, the smell of spice.

Good site for an emergency base, he thought. Might be sensible to bury a few supplies here.

He glanced back, watching his men spread out as they followed him. Good men, even the new ones he hadn't had time to test. Good men. Didn't have to be told every time what to do. Not a shield glimmer showed on any of them. No cowards in this bunch, carrying shields into the desert where a worm could sense the field and come to rob them of the spice they found.

From this slight elevation in the rocks, Gurney could see the spice patch about half a kilometer away and the crawler just reaching the near edge. He glanced up at the coverflight, noting the altitude—not too high. He nodded to himself, turned to resume his climb up the ridge.

In that instant, the ridge erupted.

Twelve roaring paths of flame streaked upward to the hovering 'thopters and carrier wing. There came a blasting of metal from the factory crawler, and the rocks around Gurney were full of hooded fighting men.

Gurney had time to think: *By the horns of the Great Mother! Rockets! They dare to use rockets!*

Then he was face to face with a hooded figure who crouched low, crysknife at the ready. Two more men stood waiting on the rocks above to left and right. Only the eyes of the fighting man ahead of him were visible to Gurney between hood and veil of a sand-colored burnoose, but the crouch and readiness warned him that here was a trained fighting man. The eyes were the blue-in-blue of the deep-desert Fremen.

Gurney moved one hand toward his own knife, kept his eyes fixed on the other's knife. If they dared use rockets, they'd have other projectile weapons. This moment argued extreme caution. He could tell by sound alone that at least part of his skycover had been knocked out. There were gruntings, too, the noise of several struggles behind him.

The eyes of the fighting man ahead of Gurney followed the motion of hand toward knife, came back to glare into Gurney's eyes.

"Leave the knife in its sheath, Gurney Halleck," the man said.

Gurney hesitated. That voice sounded oddly familiar even through a stillsuit filter.

"You know my name?" he said.

"You've no need of a knife with me, Gurney," the man said. He straightened, slipped his crysknife into its sheath back beneath his robe. "Tell your men to stop their useless resistance."

The man threw his hood back, swung the filter aside.

The shock of what he saw froze Gurney's muscles. He thought at first he was looking at a ghost image of Duke Leto Atreides. Full recognition came slowly.

"Paul," he whispered. Then louder: "Is it truly Paul?"

"Don't you trust your own eyes?" Paul asked.

"They said you were dead," Gurney rasped. He took a half-step forward.

"Tell your men to submit," Paul commanded. He waved toward the lower reaches of the ridge.

Gurney turned, reluctant to take his eyes off Paul. He saw only a few knots of struggle. Hooded desert men seemed to be everywhere around. The factory crawler lay silent with Fremen standing atop it. There were no aircraft overhead.

"Stop the fighting," Gurney bellowed. He took a deep breath, cupped his hands for a megaphone. "This is Gurney Halleck! Stop the fight!"

Slowly, warily, the struggling figures separated. Eyes turned toward him, questioning.

"These are friends," Gurney called.

"Fine friends!" someone shouted back. "Half our people murdered."

"It's a mistake," Gurney said. "Don't add to it."

He turned back to Paul, stared into the youth's blue-blue Fremen eyes.

A smile touched Paul's mouth, but there was a hardness in the expression that reminded Gurney of the Old Duke, Paul's grandfather. Gurney saw then the sinewy harshness in Paul that had never before been seen in an Atreides—a leathery look to the skin, a squint to the eyes and calculation in the glance that seemed to weigh everything in sight.

"They said you were dead," Gurney repeated.

"And it seemed the best protection to let them think so," Paul said.

Gurney realized that was all the apology he'd ever get for having been abandoned to his own resources, left to believe his young Duke . . . his friend, was dead. He wondered then if there were anything left here of the boy he had known and trained in the ways of fighting men.

Paul took a step closer to Gurney, found that his eyes were smarting. "Gurney. . . ."

It seemed to happen of itself, and they were embracing, pounding each other on the back, feeling the reassurance of solid flesh.

"You young pup! You young pup!" Gurney kept saying.

And Paul: "Gurney, man! Gurney, man!"

Presently, they stepped apart, looked at each other. Gurney took a deep breath. "So you're why the Fremen have grown so wise in battle tactics. I might've known. They keep doing things I could've planned myself. If I'd only known. . . ." He shook his head. "If you'd only got word to me, lad. Nothing would've stopped me. I'd have come arunning and. . . ."

A look in Paul's eyes stopped him . . . the hard, weighing stare.

Gurney sighed. "Sure, and there'd have been those who wondered why Gurney Halleck went arunning, and some would've done more than question. They'd have gone hunting for answers."

Paul nodded, glanced to the waiting Fremen around them—the looks of curious appraisal on the faces of the Fedaykin. He turned from the death commandos back to Gurney. Finding his former swordmaster filled him with elation. He saw it as a good omen, a sign that he was on the course of the future where all was well.

With Gurney at my side. . . .

Paul glanced down the ridge past the Fedaykin, studied the smuggler crew who had come with Halleck.

"How do your men stand, Gurney?" he asked.

"They're smugglers all," Gurney said. "They stand where the profit is."

"Little enough profit in our venture," Paul said, and he noted the subtle finger signal flashed to him by Gurney's right hand—the old hand code out of their past. There were men to fear and distrust in the smuggler crew.

Paul pulled at his lip to indicate he understood, looked up at the men standing guard above them on the rocks. He saw Stilgar there. Memory of the unsolved problem with Stilgar cooled some of Paul's elation.

"Stilgar," he said, "this is Gurney Halleck of whom you've heard me speak. My father's master-of-arms, one of the swordmasters who instructed me, an old friend. He can be trusted in any venture."

"I hear," Stilgar said. "You are his Duke."

Paul stared at the dark visage above him, wondering at the reasons which had impelled Stilgar to say just that. *His Duke.* There had been a strange subtle intonation in Stilgar's voice, as though he would rather have said something else. And that wasn't like Stilgar, who was a leader of Fremen, a man who spoke his mind.

My Duke! Gurney thought. He looked anew at Paul. *Yes, with Leto dead, the title fell on Paul's shoulders.*

The pattern of the Fremen war on Arrakis began to take on new shape in Gurney's mind. *My Duke!* A place that had been dead within him began coming alive. Only part of his awareness focused on Paul's ordering the smuggler crew disarmed until they could be questioned.

Gurney's mind returned to the command when he heard some of his men protesting. He shook his head, whirled. "Are you men deaf?" he barked. "This is the rightful Duke of Arrakis. Do as he commands."

Grumbling, the smugglers submitted.

Paul moved up beside Gurney, spoke in a low voice. "I'd not have expected you to walk into this trap, Gurney."

"I'm properly chastened," Gurney said. "I'll wager yon patch of spice is little more than a sand grain's thickness, a bait to lure us."

"That's a wager you'd win," Paul said. He looked down at the men being disarmed. "Are there any more of my father's men among your crew?"

"None. We're spread thin. There're a few among the free traders. Most have spent their profits to leave this place."

"But you stayed."

"I stayed."

"Because Rabban is here," Paul said.

"I thought I had nothing left but revenge," Gurney said.

An oddly chopped cry sounded from the ridgetop. Gurney looked up to see a Fremen waving his kerchief.

"A maker comes," Paul said. He moved out to a point of rock with Gurney following, looked off to the southwest. The burrow mound of a worm could be seen in the middle distance, a dust-crowned track that cut directly through the dunes on a course toward the ridge.

"He's big enough," Paul said.

A clattering sound lifted from the factory crawler below them. It turned on its treads like a giant insect, lumbered toward the rocks.

"Too bad we couldn't have saved the carryall," Paul said.

Gurney glanced at him, looked back to the patches of smoke and debris out on the desert where carryall and ornithopters had been brought down by Fremen rockets. He felt a sudden pang for the men lost there—his men, and he said: "Your father would've been more concerned for the men he couldn't save."

Paul shot a hard stare at him, lowered his gaze. Presently, he said: "They were your friends, Gurney. I understand. To us, though, they were trespassers who might see things they shouldn't see. You must understand that."

"I understand it well enough," Gurney said. "Now, I'm curious to see what I shouldn't."

Paul looked up to see the old and well-remembered wolfish grin on Halleck's face, the ripple of the inkvine scar along the man's jaw.

Gurney nodded toward the desert below them. Fremen were going about their business all over the landscape. It struck him that none of them appeared worried by the approach of the worm.

A thumping sounded from the open dunes beyond the baited patch of spice—a deep drumming that seemed to be heard through their feet. Gurney saw Fremen spread out across the sand there in the path of the worm.

The worm came on like some great sandfish, cresting the surface, its rings rippling and twisting. In a moment, from his vantage point above the desert, Gurney saw the taking of a worm—the daring leap of the first hookman, the turning of the creature, the way an entire band of men went up the scaly, glistening curve of the worm's side.

"There's one of the things you shouldn't have seen," Paul said.

"There's been stories and rumors," Gurney said. "But it's not a thing easy to believe without seeing it." He shook his head. "The creature all men on Arrakis fear, you treat it like a riding animal."

"You heard my father speak of desert power," Paul said. "There it is. The surface of this planet is ours. No storm nor creature nor condition can stop us."

Us, Gurney thought. *He means the Fremen. He speaks of himself as one of them.* Again, Gurney looked at the spice blue in Paul's eyes. His own eyes, he knew, had a touch of the color, but smugglers could get offworld foods and there was a subtle caste implication in the tone of the eyes among them. They spoke of "the touch of the spicebrush" to mean a man had gone too native. And there was always a hint of distrust in the idea.

"There was a time when we did not ride the maker in the light of day in these latitudes," Paul said. "But Rabban has little enough air cover left that he can waste it looking for a few specks in the sand." He looked at Gurney. "Your aircraft were a shock to us here."

To us . . . to us. . . .

Gurney shook his head to drive out such thoughts. "We weren't the shock to you that you were to us," he said.

"What's the talk of Rabban in the sinks and villages?" Paul asked.

"They say they've fortified the graben villages to the point where you cannot harm them. They say they need only sit inside their defenses while you wear yourselves out in futile attack."

"In a word," Paul said, "they're immobilized."

"While you can go where you will," Gurney said.

"It's a tactic I learned from you," Paul said. "They've lost the initiative, which means they've lost the war."

Gurney smiled, a slow, knowing expression.

"Our enemy is exactly where I want him to be," Paul said. He glanced at Gurney. "Well, Gurney, do you enlist with me for the finish of this campaign?"

"Enlist?" Gurney stared at him. "My Lord, I've never left your service. You're the only one left me . . . to think you dead. And I, being cast adrift, made what shrift I could, waiting for the moment I might sell my life for what it's worth—the death of Rabban."

An embarrassed silence settled over Paul.

A woman came climbing up the rocks toward them, her eyes between stillsuit hood and face mask flicking between Paul and his companion. She stopped in front of Paul. Gurney noted the possessive air about her, the way she stood close to Paul.

"Chani," Paul said, "this is Gurney Halleck. You've heard me speak of him."

She looked at Halleck, back to Paul. "I have heard."

"Where did the men go on the maker?" Paul asked.

"They but diverted it to give us time to save the equipment."

"Well then. . . ." Paul broke off, sniffed the air.

"There's wind coming," Chani said.

A voice called out from the ridgetop above them: "Ho, there—the wind!"

Gurney saw a quickening of motion among the Fremen now—a rushing about and sense of hurry. A thing the worm had not ignited was brought about by fear of the wind. The factory crawler lumbered up onto the dry beach below them and a way was opened for it among the rocks . . . and the rocks closed behind it so neatly that the passage escaped his eyes.

"Have you many such hiding places?" Gurney asked.

"Many times many," Paul said. He looked at Chani. "Find Korba. Tell him that Gurney has warned me there are men among this smuggler crew who're not to be trusted."

She looked once at Gurney, back to Paul, nodded, and was off down the rocks, leaping with a gazelle-like agility.

"She is your woman," Gurney said.

"The mother of my firstborn," Paul said. "There's another Leto among the Atreides."

Gurney accepted this with only a widening of the eyes.

Paul watched the action around them with a critical eye. A curry color dominated the southern sky now and there came fitful bursts and gusts of wind that whipped dust around their heads.

"Seal your suit," Paul said. And he fastened the mask and hood about his face.

Gurney obeyed, thankful for the filters.

Paul spoke, his voice muffled by the filter: "Which of your crew don't you trust, Gurney?"

"There're some new recruits," Gurney said. "Offworlders. . . ." He hesitated, wondering at himself suddenly. *Offworlders.* The word had come so easily to his tongue.

"Yes?" Paul said.

"They're not like the usual fortune-hunting lot we get," Gurney said. "They're tougher."

"Harkonnen spies?" Paul asked.

"I think, m'Lord, that they report to no Harkonnen. I suspect they're men of the Imperial service. They have a hint of Salusa Secundus about them."

Paul shot a sharp glance at him. "Sardaukar?"

Gurney shrugged. "They could be, but it's well masked."

Paul nodded, thinking how easily Gurney had fallen back into the pattern of Atreides retainer . . . but with subtle reservations . . . differences. Arrakis had changed him, too.

Two hooded Fremen emerged from the broken rock below them, began climbing upward. One of them carried a large black bundle over one shoulder.

"Where are my crew now?" Gurney asked.

"Secure in the rocks below us," Paul said. "We've a cave here—Cave of Birds. We'll decide what to do with them after the storm."

A voice called from above them: "Muad'Dib!"

Paul turned at the call, saw a Fremen guard motioning them down to the cave. Paul signaled he had heard.

Gurney studied him with a new expression. "You're Muad'Dib?" he asked. "You're the will-o'-the-sand?"

"It's my Fremen name," Paul said.

Gurney turned away, feeling an oppressive sense of foreboding. Half his own crew dead on the sand, the others captive. He did not care about the new recruits, the suspicious ones, but among the others were good men, friends, people for whom he felt responsible. *"We'll decide what to do with them after the storm."* That's what Paul had said, Muad'Dib had said. And Gurney recalled the stories told of Muad'Dib, the Lisan al-Gaib—how he had taken the skin of a Harkonnen officer to make his drumheads, how he was surrounded by death commandos, Fedaykin who leaped into battle with their death chants on their lips.

Him.

The two Fremen climbing up the rocks leaped lightly to a shelf in front of Paul. The dark-faced one said: "All secure, Muad'Dib. We best get below now."

"Right."

Gurney noted the tone of the man's voice—half command and half request. This was the man called Stilgar, another figure of the new Fremen legends.

Paul looked at the bundle the other man carried, said: "Korba, what's in the bundle?"

Stilgar answered: "'Twas in the crawler. It had the initial of your friend here and it contains a baliset. Many times have I heard you speak of the prowess of Gurney Halleck on the baliset."

Gurney studied the speaker, seeing the edge of black beard above the stillsuit mask, the hawk stare, the chiseled nose.

"You've a companion who thinks, m'Lord," Gurney said. "Thank you, Stilgar."

Stilgar signaled for his companion to pass the bundle to Gurney, said: "Thank your Lord Duke. His countenance earns your admittance here."

Gurney accepted the bundle, puzzled by the hard undertones in this conversation. There was an air of challenge about the man, and Gurney wondered if it could be a feeling of jealousy in the Fremen. Here was someone called Gurney Halleck who'd known Paul even in the times before Arrakis, a man who shared a camaraderie that Stilgar could never invade.

"You are two I'd have be friends," Paul said.

"Stilgar, the Fremen, is a name of renown," Gurney said. "Any killer of Harkonnens I'd feel honored to count among my friends."

"Will you touch hands with my friend Gurney Halleck, Stilgar?" Paul asked.

Slowly, Stilgar extended his hand, gripped the heavy calluses of Gurney's swordhand. "There're few who haven't heard the name of Gurney Halleck," he said, and released his grip. He turned to Paul. "The storm comes rushing."

"At once," Paul said.

Stilgar turned away, led them down through the rocks, a twisting and turning path into a shadowed cleft that admitted them to the low entrance of a cave. Men hurried to fasten a doorseal behind them. Glowglobes showed a broad, dome-ceilinged space with a raised ledge on one side and a passage leading off from it.

Paul leaped to the ledge with Gurney right behind him, led the way into the passage. The others headed for another passage opposite the entrance. Paul led the way through an anteroom and into a chamber with dark, wine-colored hangings on its walls.

"We can have some privacy here for a while," Paul said. "The others will respect my—"

An alarm cymbal clanged from the outer chamber, was followed by shouting and clashing of weapons. Paul whirled, ran back through the anteroom and out onto the atrium lip above the outer chamber. Gurney was right behind, weapon drawn.

Beneath them on the floor of the cave swirled a melee of struggling figures. Paul stood an instant assessing the scene, separating the Fremen robes and bourkas from the costumes of those they opposed. Senses that his mother had trained to detect the most subtle clues picked out a significant face—the Fremen fought against men wearing smuggler robes, but the smugglers were crouched in trios, backed into triangles where pressed.

That habit of close fighting was a trademark of the Imperial Sardaukar.

A Fedaykin in the crowd saw Paul, and his battle cry was lifted to echo in the chamber: "Muad'Dib! Muad'Dib! Muad'Dib!"

Another eye had also picked Paul out. A black knife came hurtling toward him. Paul dodged, heard the knife clatter against stone behind him, glanced to see Gurney retrieve it.

The triangular knots were being pressed back now.

Gurney held the knife up in front of Paul's eyes, pointed to the hair-line yellow coil of Imperial color, the golden lion crest, multifaceted eyes at the pommel.

Sardaukar for certain.

Paul stepped out to the lip of the ledge. Only three of the Sardaukar remained. Bloody rag mounds of Sardaukar and Fremen lay in a twisted pattern across the chamber.

"Hold!" Paul shouted. "The Duke Paul Atreides commands you to hold!"

The fighting wavered, hesitated.

"You Sardaukar!" Paul called to the remaining group. "By whose orders do you threaten a ruling Duke?" And, quickly, as his men started to press in around the Sardaukar: "Hold, I say!"

One of the cornered trio straightened. "Who says we're Sardaukar?" he demanded.

Paul took the knife from Gurney, held it aloft. "This says you're Sardaukar."

"Then who says you're a ruling Duke?" the man demanded.

Paul gestured to the Fedaykin. "These men say I'm a ruling Duke. Your own emperor bestowed Arrakis on House Atreides. *I* am House Atreides."

The Sardaukar stood silent, fidgeting.

Paul studied the man—tall, flat-featured, with a pale scar across half his left cheek. Anger and confusion were betrayed in his manner, but still there was that pride about him without which a Sardaukar appeared undressed—and with which he could appear fully clothed though naked.

Paul glanced to one of his Fedaykin lieutenants, said: "Korba, how came they to have weapons?"

"They held back knives concealed in cunning pockets within their stillsuits," the lieutenant said.

Paul surveyed the dead and wounded across the chamber, brought his attention back to the lieutenant. There was no need for words. The lieutenant lowered his eyes.

"Where is Chani?" Paul asked and waited, breath held, for the answer.

"Stilgar spirited her aside." He nodded toward the other passage, glanced at the dead and wounded. "I hold myself responsible for this mistake, Muad'Dib."

"How many of these Sardaukar were there, Gurney?" Paul asked.

"Ten."

Paul leaped lightly to the floor of the chamber, strode across to stand within striking distance of the Sardaukar spokesman.

A tense air came over the Fedaykin. They did not like him thus exposed to danger. This was the thing they were pledged to prevent because the Fremen wished to preserve the wisdom of Muad'Dib.

Without turning, Paul spoke to his lieutenant: "How many are our casualties?"

"Four wounded, two dead, Muad'Dib."

Paul saw motion beyond the Sardaukar; Chani and Stilgar were standing in the other passage. He returned his attention to the Sardaukar, staring into the offworld whites of the spokesman's eyes. "You, what is your name?" Paul demanded.

The man stiffened, glanced left and right.

"Don't try it," Paul said. "It's obvious to me that you were ordered to seek out and destroy Muad'Dib. I'll warrant you were the ones suggested seeking spice in the deep desert."

A gasp from Gurney behind him brought a thin smile to Paul's lips. Blood suffused the Sardaukar's face.

"What you see before you is more than Muad'Dib," Paul said. "Seven of you are dead for two of us. Three for one. Pretty good against Sardau-kar, eh?"

The man came up on his toes, sank back as the Fedaykin pressed forward.

"I asked your name," Paul said, and he called up the subtleties of Voice: "Tell me your name!"

"Captain Aramsham, Imperial Sardaukar!" the man snapped. His jaw dropped. He stared at Paul in confusion. The manner about him that had dismissed this cavern as a barbarian warren melted away.

"Well, Captain Aramsham," Paul said, "the Harkonnens would pay dearly to learn what you now know. And the Emperor—what he wouldn't give to learn an Atreides still lives despite his treachery."

The captain glanced left and right at the two men remaining to him. Paul could almost see the thoughts turning over in the man's head. Sardaukar did not submit, but the Emperor *had* to learn of this threat.

Still using the Voice, Paul said: "Submit, Captain."

The man at the captain's left leaped without warning toward Paul, met the flashing impact of his own captain's knife in his chest. The attacker hit the floor in a sodden heap with the knife still in him.

The captain faced his sole remaining companion. "I decide what best serves His Majesty," he said. "Understood?"

The other Sardaukar's shoulders slumped.

"Drop your weapon," the captain said.

The Sardaukar obeyed.

The captain returned his attention to Paul. "I have killed a friend for you," he said. "Let us always remember that."

"You're my prisoners," Paul said. "You submitted to me. Whether you live or die is of no importance." He motioned to his guard to take the two Sardaukar, signaled the lieutenant who had searched the prisoners.

The guard moved in, hustled the Sardaukar away.

Paul bent toward his lieutenant.

"Muad'Dib," the man said. "I failed you in. . . ."

"The failure was mine, Korba," Paul said. "I should've warned you what to seek. In the future, when searching Sardaukar, remember this. Remember, too, that each has a false toenail or two that can be combined with other items secreted about their bodies to make an effective transmitter. They'll have more than one false tooth. They carry coils of shigawire in their hair—so fine you can barely detect it, yet strong enough to garrote a man and cut off his head in the process. With Sardaukar, you must scan them, scope them—both reflex and hard ray—cut off every scrap of body hair. And when you're through, be certain you haven't discovered everything."

He looked up at Gurney, who had moved close to listen.

"Then we best kill them," the lieutenant said.

Paul shook his head, still looking at Gurney. "No. I want them to escape."

Gurney stared at him. "Sire. . . ." he breathed.

"Yes?"

"Your man here is right. Kill those prisoners at once. Destroy all evidence of them. You've shamed Imperial Sardaukar! When the Emperor learns that he'll not rest until he has you over a slow fire."

"The Emperor's not likely to have that power over me," Paul said. He spoke slowly, coldly. Something had happened inside him while he faced the Sardaukar. A sum of decisions had accumulated in his awareness. "Gurney," he said, "are there many Guildsmen around Rabban?"

Gurney straightened, eyes narrowed. "Your question makes no. . . ."

"Are there?" Paul barked.

"Arrakis is crawling with Guild agents. They're buying spice as though it were the most precious thing in the universe. Why else do you think we ventured this far into. . . ."

"It is the most precious thing in the universe," Paul said. "To them."

He looked toward Stilgar and Chani who were now crossing the chamber toward him. "And we control it, Gurney."

"The Harkonnens control it!" Gurney protested.

"The people who can destroy a thing, they control it," Paul said. He waved a hand to silence further remarks from Gurney, nodded to Stilgar who stopped in front of Paul, Chani beside him.

Paul took the Sardaukar knife in his left hand, presented it to Stilgar. "You live for the good of the tribe," Paul said. "Could you draw my life's blood with that knife?"

"For the good of the tribe," Stilgar growled.

"Then use that knife," Paul said.

"Are you calling me out?" Stilgar demanded.

"If I do," Paul said, "I shall stand there without weapon and let you slay me."

Stilgar drew in a quick, sharp breath.

Chani said, "Usul!" then glanced at Gurney, back to Paul.

While Stilgar was still weighing his words, Paul said: "You are Stilgar, a fighting man. When the Sardaukar began fighting here, you were not in the front of battle. Your first thought was to protect Chani."

"She's my niece," Stilgar said. "If there'd been any doubt of your Fedaykin handling those scum. . . ."

"Why was your first thought of Chani?" Paul demanded.

"It wasn't!"

"Oh?"

"It was of you," Stilgar admitted.

"Do you think you could lift your hand against me?" Paul asked.

Stilgar began to tremble. "It's the way," he muttered.

"It's the way to kill offworld strangers found in the desert and take their water as a gift from Shai-hulud," Paul said. "Yet you permitted two such to live one night, my mother and myself."

As Stilgar remained silent, trembling, staring at him, Paul said: "Ways change, Stil. You have changed them yourself."

Stilgar looked down at the yellow emblem on the knife he held.

"When I am Duke in Arrakeen with Chani by my side, do you think I'll have time to concern myself with every detail of governing Tabr sietch?" Paul asked. "Do you concern yourself with the internal problems of every family?"

Stilgar continued staring at the knife.

"Do you think I wish to cut off my right arm?" Paul demanded.

Slowly, Stilgar looked up at him.

"You!" Paul said. "Do you think I wish to deprive myself or the tribe of your wisdom and strength?"

In a low voice, Stilgar said: "The young man of my tribe whose name is known to me, this young man I could kill on the challenge floor, Shai-hulud willing. The Lisan al-Gaib, him I could not harm. You knew this when you handed me this knife."

"I knew it," Paul agreed.

Stilgar opened his hand. The knife clattered against the stone of the floor. "Ways change," he said.

"Chani," Paul said, "go to my mother, send her here that her counsel will be available into—"

"But you said we would go to the south!" she protested.

"I was wrong," he said. "The Harkonnens are not there. The war is not there."

She took a deep breath, accepting this as a desert woman accepted all necessities in the midst of a life involved with death.

"You will give my mother a message for her ears alone," Paul said. "Tell her that Stilgar acknowledges me Duke of Arrakis, but a way must be found to make the young men accept this without combat."

Chani glanced at Stilgar.

"Do as he says," Stilgar growled. "We both know he could overcome me . . . and I could not raise my hand against him . . . for the good of the tribe."

"I shall return with your mother," Chani said.

"Send her," Paul said. "Stilgar's instinct was right. I am stronger when you are safe. You will remain in the sietch."

She started to protest, swallowed it.

"Sihaya," Paul said, using his intimate name for her. He whirled away to the right, met Gurney's glaring eyes.

The interchange between Paul and the older Fremen had passed as though in a cloud around Gurney since Paul's reference to his mother.

"Your mother," Gurney said.

"Idaho saved us the night of the raid," Paul said, distracted by the parting with Chani. "Right now we've—"

"What of Duncan Idaho, m'Lord?" Gurney asked.

"He's dead—buying us a bit of time to escape."

The she-witch alive! Gurney thought. *The one I swore vengeance against, alive! And it's obvious Duke Paul doesn't know what manner of creature gave him birth. The evil one: Betrayed his own father to the Harkonnens!*

Paul pressed past him, jumped up to the ledge. He glanced back, noted that the wounded and dead had been removed, and he thought bitterly that here was another chapter in the legend of Paul-Muad'Dib. *I didn't even draw my knife, but it'll be said of this day that I slew twenty Sardaukar by my own hand.*

Gurney followed with Stilgar, stepping on ground that he did not even feel. The cavern with its yellow light of glowglobes was forced out of his thoughts by rage. *The she-witch alive while those she betrayed are bones in lonesome graves. I must contrive it that Paul learns the truth about her before I slay her.*

How often it is that the angry man rages denial of what his inner self is telling him.

—FROM "COLLECTED SAYINGS OF MUAD'DIB"
BY THE PRINCESS IRULAN

The crowd in the cavern assembly chamber radiated that pack feeling Jessica had sensed the day Paul killed Jamis. There was murmuring nervousness in the voices. Little cliques gathered like knots among the robes.

Jessica tucked a message cylinder beneath her robe as she emerged to the ledge from Paul's private quarters. She felt rested after the long journey up from the south, but still rankled that Paul would not yet permit them to use the captured ornithopters.

"We do not have full control of the air," he had said. "And we must not become dependent upon offworld fuel. Both fuel and aircraft must be gathered and saved for the day of maximum effort."

Paul stood with a group of the younger men near the ledge. The pale light of glowglobes gave the scene a tinge of unreality. It was like a tableau, but with the added dimension of warren smells, the whispers, the sounds of shuffling feet.

She studied her son, wondering why he had not yet trotted out his surprise—Gurney Halleck. The thought of Gurney disturbed her with its memories of an easier past—days of love and beauty with Paul's father.

Stilgar waited with a small group of his own at the other end of the ledge. There was a feeling of inevitable dignity about him, the way he stood without talking.

We must not lose that man, Jessica thought. *Paul's plan must work. Anything else would be the highest tragedy.*

She strode down the ledge, passing Stilgar without a glance, stepped down into the crowd. A way was made for her as she headed toward Paul. And silence followed her.

She knew the meaning of the silence—the unspoken questions of the people, awe of the Reverend Mother.

The young men drew back from Paul as she came up to him, and she found herself momentarily dismayed by the new deference they paid him. *"All men beneath your position covet your station,"* went the Bene Gesserit axiom. But she found no covetousness in these faces. They were held at a distance by the religious ferment around Paul's leadership. And she recalled another Bene Gesserit saying: *"Prophets have a way of dying by violence."*

Paul looked at her.

"It's time," she said, and passed the message cylinder to him.

One of Paul's companions, bolder than the others, glanced across at Stilgar, said: "Are you going to call him out, Muad'Dib? Now's the time for sure. They'll think you a coward if you—"

"Who dares call me coward?" Paul demanded. His hand flashed to his crysknife hilt.

Bated silence came over the group, spreading out into the crowd.

"There's work to do," Paul said as the man drew back from him. Paul turned away, shouldered through the crowd to the ledge, leaped lightly up to it and faced the people.

"Do it!" someone shrieked.

Murmurs and whispers arose behind the shriek.

Paul waited for silence. It came slowly amidst scattered shufflings and coughs. When it was quiet in the cavern, Paul lifted his chin, spoke in a voice that carried to the farthest corners.

"You are tired of waiting," Paul said.

Again, he waited while the cries of response died out.

Indeed, they are tired of waiting, Paul thought. He hefted the message cylinder, thinking of what it contained. His mother had showed it to him, explaining how it had been taken from a Harkonnen courier.

The message was explicit: Rabban was being abandoned to his own resources here on Arrakis! He could not call for help or reinforcements!

Again, Paul raised his voice: "You think it's time I called out Stilgar and changed the leadership of the troops!" Before they could respond, Paul hurled his voice at them in anger: "Do you think the Lisan al-Gaib that stupid?"

There was stunned silence.

He's accepting the religious mantle, Jessica thought. *He must not do it!*

"It's the way!" someone shouted.

Paul spoke dryly, probing the emotional undercurrents. "Ways change."

An angry voice lifted from a corner of the cavern: "We'll say what's to change!"

There were scattered shouts of agreement through the throng.

"As you wish," Paul said.

And Jessica heard the subtle intonations as he used the powers of Voice she had taught him.

"You will say," he agreed. "But first you will hear my say."

Stilgar moved along the ledge, his bearded face impassive. "That is the way, too," he said. "The voice of any Fremen may be heard in Council. Paul-Muad'Dib is a Fremen."

"The good of the tribe, that is the most important thing, eh?" Paul asked.

Still with that flat-voiced dignity, Stilgar said: "Thus our steps are guided."

"All right," Paul said. "Then, who rules this troop of our tribe—and who rules all the tribes and troops through the fighting instructors we've trained in the weirding way?"

Paul waited, looking over the heads of the throng. No answer came.

Presently, he said: "Does Stilgar rule all this? He says himself that he does not. Do I rule? Even Stilgar does my bidding on occasion, and the sages, the wisest of the wise, listen to me and honor me in Council."

There was shuffling silence among the crowd.

"So," Paul said. "Does my mother rule?" He pointed down to Jessica in her black robes of office among them. "Stilgar and all the other troop leaders ask her advice in almost every major decision. You know this. But does a Reverend Mother walk the sand or lead a razzia against the Harkonnens?"

Frowns creased the foreheads of those Paul could see, but still there were angry murmurs.

This is a dangerous way to do it, Jessica thought, but she remembered the message cylinder and what it implied. And she saw Paul's intent: Go right to the depth of their uncertainty, dispose of that, and all the rest must follow.

"No man recognizes leadership without the challenge and the combat, eh?" Paul asked.

"That's the way!" someone shouted.

"What's our goal?" Paul asked. "To unseat Rabban, the Harkonnen beast, and remake our world into a place where we may raise our families in happiness amidst an abundance of water—is this our goal?"

"Hard tasks need hard ways," someone shouted.

"Do you smash your knife before a battle?" Paul demanded. "I say this as fact, not meaning it as boast or challenge: there isn't a man here, Stilgar included, who could stand against me in single combat. This is Stilgar's own admission. He knows it, so do you all."

Again, the angry mutters lifted from the crowd.

"Many of you have been with me on the practice floor," Paul said. "You know this isn't idle boast. I say it because it's fact known to us all, and I'd be foolish not to see it for myself. I began training in these ways earlier than you did and my teachers were tougher than any you've ever seen. How else do you think I bested Jamis at an age when your boys are still fighting only mock battles?"

He's using the Voice well, Jessica thought, *but that's not enough with these people. They've good insulation against vocal control. He must catch them also with logic.*

"So," Paul said, "we come to this." He lifted the message cylinder, removed its scrap of tape. "This was taken from a Harkonnen courier. Its authenticity is beyond question. It is addressed to Rabban. It tells him that his request for new troops is denied, that his spice harvest is far below quota, that he must wring more spice from Arrakis with the people he has."

Stilgar moved up beside Paul.

"How many of you see what this means?" Paul asked. "Stilgar saw it immediately."

"They're cut off!" someone shouted.

Paul pushed message and cylinder into his sash. From his neck he took a braided shigawire cord and removed a ring from the cord, holding the ring aloft.

"This was my father's ducal signet," he said. "I swore never to wear it again until I was ready to lead my troops over all of Arrakis and claim it as my rightful fief." He put the ring on his finger, clenched his fist.

Utter stillness gripped the cavern.

"Who rules here?" Paul asked. He raised his fist. "I rule here! I rule on every square inch of Arrakis! This is my ducal fief whether the Emperor says yea or nay! He gave it to my father and it comes to me through my father!"

Paul lifted himself onto his toes, settled back to his heels. He studied the crowd, feeling their temper.

Almost, he thought.

"There are men here who will hold positions of importance on Arrakis when I claim those Imperial rights which are mine," Paul said. "Stilgar is one of those men. Not because I wish to bribe him! Not out of gratitude, though I'm one of many here who owe him life for life. No! But because he's wise and strong. Because he governs this troop by his own intelligence and not just by rules. Do you think me stupid? Do you think I'll cut off my right arm and leave it bloody on the floor of this cavern just to provide you with a circus?"

Paul swept a hard gaze across the throng. "Who is there here to say I'm not the rightful ruler on Arrakis? Must I prove it by leaving every Fremen tribe in the erg without a leader?"

Beside Paul, Stilgar stirred, looked at him questioningly.

"Will I subtract from our strength when we need it most?" Paul asked. "I am your ruler, and I say to you that it is time we stopped killing off our best men and started killing our real enemies—the Harkonnens!"

In one blurred motion, Stilgar had his crysknife out and pointed over the heads of the throng. "Long live Duke Paul-Muad'Dib!" he shouted.

A deafening roar filled the cavern, echoed and re-echoed. They were cheering and chanting: "Ya hya chouhada! Muad'Dib! Muad'Dib! Muad'Dib! Ya hya chouhada!"

Jessica translated it to herself: *"Long live the fighters of Muad'Dib!"* The scene she and Paul and Stilgar had cooked up between them had worked as they'd planned.

The tumult died slowly.

When silence was restored, Paul faced Stilgar, said: "Kneel, Stilgar."

Stilgar dropped to his knees on the ledge.

"Hand me your crysknife," Paul said.

Stilgar obeyed.

This was not as we planned it, Jessica thought.

"Repeat after me, Stilgar," Paul said, and he called up the words of investiture as he had heard his own father use them. "I, Stilgar, take this knife from the hands of my Duke."

"I, Stilgar, take this knife from the hands of my Duke," Stilgar said, and accepted the milky blade from Paul.

"Where my Duke commands, there shall I place this blade," Paul said.

Stilgar repeated the words, speaking slowly and solemnly.

Remembering the source of the rite, Jessica blinked back tears, shook her head. *I know the reasons for this,* she thought. *I shouldn't let it stir me.*

"I dedicate this blade to the cause of my Duke and the death of his enemies for as long as our blood shall flow," Paul said.

Stilgar repeated it after him.

"Kiss the blade," Paul ordered.

Stilgar obeyed, then, in the Fremen manner, kissed Paul's knife arm. At a nod from Paul, he sheathed the blade, got to his feet.

A sighing whisper of awe passed through the crowd, and Jessica heard the words: "The prophecy—A Bene Gesserit shall show the way and a Reverend Mother shall see it." And, from farther away: "She shows us through her son!"

"Stilgar leads this tribe," Paul said. "Let no man mistake that. He commands with my voice. What he tells you, it is as though I told you."

Wise, Jessica thought. *The tribal commander must lose no face among those who should obey him.*

Paul lowered his voice, said: "Stilgar, I want sandwalkers out this night and cielagos sent to summon a Council Gathering. When you've sent them, bring Chatt, Korba and Otheym and two other lieutenants of your own choosing. Bring them to my quarters for battle planning. We must have a victory to show the Council of Leaders when they arrive."

Paul nodded for his mother to accompany him, led the way down off the ledge and through the throng toward the central passage and the living chambers that had been prepared there. As Paul pressed through the crowd, hands reached out to touch him. Voices called out to him.

"My knife goes where Stilgar commands it, Paul-Muad'Dib! Let us fight soon, Paul-Muad'Dib! Let us wet our world with the blood of Harkonnens!"

Feeling the emotions of the throng, Jessica sensed the fighting edge of these people. They could not be more ready. *We are taking them at the crest*, she thought.

In the inner chamber, Paul motioned his mother to be seated, said: "Wait here." And he ducked through the hangings to the side passage.

It was quiet in the chamber after Paul had gone, so quiet behind the hangings that not even the faint soughing of the wind pumps that circulated air in the sietch penetrated to where she sat.

He is going to bring Gurney Halleck here, she thought. And she wondered at the strange mingling of emotions that filled her. Gurney and his music had been a part of so many pleasant times on Caladan before the move to Arrakis. She felt that Caladan had happened to some other person. In the nearly three years since then, she had *become* another person. Having to confront Gurney forced a reassessment of the changes.

Paul's coffee service, the fluted alloy of silver and jasmium that he had inherited from Jamis, rested on a low table to her right. She stared at it, thinking of how many hands had touched that metal. Chani had served Paul from it within the month.

What can his desert woman do for a Duke except serve him coffee? she asked herself. *She brings him no power, no family. Paul has only one major chance—to ally himself with a powerful Great House, perhaps even with the Imperial family. There are marriagable princesses, after all, and every one of them Bene Gesserit-trained.*

Jessica imagined herself leaving the rigors of Arrakis for the life of power and security she could know as mother of a royal consort. She glanced at the thick hangings that obscured the rock of this cavern cell, thinking of how she had come here—riding amidst a host of worms, the palanquins and pack platforms piled high with necessities for the coming campaign.

As long as Chani lives, Paul will not see his duty, Jessica thought. *She has given him a son and that is enough.*

A sudden longing to see her grandson, the child whose likeness carried so much of the grandfather's features—so like Leto, swept through her. Jessica placed her palms against her cheeks, began the ritual breathing that stilled emotion and clarified the mind, then bent forward from the waist in the devotional exercise that prepared the body for the mind's demands.

Paul's choice of this Cave of Birds as his command post could not be questioned, she knew. It was ideal. And to the north lay Wind Pass opening onto a protected village in a cliff-walled sink. It was a key village, home of artisans and technicians, maintenance center for an entire Harkonnen defensive sector.

A cough sounded outside the chamber hangings. Jessica straightened, took a deep breath, exhaled slowly.

"Enter," she said.

Draperies were flung aside and Gurney Halleck bounded into the room. She had only time for a glimpse of his face with its odd grimace, then he was behind her, lifting her to her feet with one brawny arm beneath her chin.

"Gurney, you fool, what are you doing?" she demanded.

Then she felt the touch of the knife tip against her back. Chill awareness spread out from that knife tip. She knew in that instant that Gurney meant to kill her. *Why?* She could think of no reason, for he wasn't the kind to turn traitor. But she felt certain of his intention. Knowing it, her mind churned. Here was no man to be overcome easily. Here was a killer wary of the Voice, wary of every combat stratagem, wary of every trick of death and violence. Here was an instrument she herself had helped train with subtle hints and suggestions.

"You thought you had escaped, eh, witch?" Gurney snarled.

Before she could turn the question over in her mind or try to answer, the curtains parted and Paul entered.

"Here he is, Moth—" Paul broke off, taking in the tensions of the scene.

"You will stand where you are, m'Lord," Gurney said.

"What. . . ." Paul shook his head.

Jessica started to speak, felt the arm tighten against her throat.

"You will speak only when I permit it, witch," Gurney said. "I want only one thing from you for your son to hear it, and I am prepared to send this knife into your heart by reflex at the first sign of a counter against me. Your voice will remain in a monotone. Certain muscles you will not tense or move. You will act with the most extreme caution to gain yourself a few more seconds of life. And I assure you, these are all you have."

Paul took a step forward. "Gurney, man, what is—"

"Stop right where you are!" Gurney snapped. "One more step and ʼead."

Paul's hand slipped to his knife hilt. He spoke in a deadly quiet: "You had best explain yourself, Gurney."

"I swore an oath to slay the betrayer of your father," Gurney said. "Do you think I can forget the man who rescued me from a Harkonnen slave pit, gave me freedom, life, and honor . . . gave me friendship, a thing I prized above all else? I have his betrayer under my knife. No one can stop me from—"

"You couldn't be more wrong, Gurney," Paul said.

And Jessica thought: *So that's it! What irony!*

"Wrong, am I?" Gurney demanded. "Let us hear it from the woman herself. And let her remember that I have bribed and spied and cheated to confirm this charge. I've even pushed semuta on a Harkonnen guard captain to get part of the story."

Jessica felt the arm at her throat ease slightly, but before she could speak, Paul said: "The betrayer was Yueh. I tell you this once, Gurney. The evidence is complete, cannot be controverted. It was Yueh. I do not care how you came by your suspicion—for it can be nothing else—but if you harm my mother. . . ." Paul lifted his crysknife from its scabbard, held the blade in front of him. ". . . I'll have your blood."

"Yueh was a conditioned medic, fit for a royal house," Gurney snarled. "He could not turn traitor!"

"I know a way to remove that conditioning," Paul said.

"Evidence," Gurney insisted.

"The evidence is not here," Paul said. "It's in Tabr sietch, far to the south, but if—"

"This is a trick," Gurney snarled, and his arm tightened on Jessica's throat.

"No trick, Gurney," Paul said, and his voice carried such a note of terrible sadness that the sound tore at Jessica's heart.

"I saw the message captured from the Harkonnen agent," Gurney said. "The note pointed directly at—"

"I saw it, too," Paul said. "My father showed it to me the night he explained why it had to be a Harkonnen trick aimed at making him suspect the woman he loved."

"Ayah!" Gurney said. "You've not—"

"Be quiet," Paul said, and the monotone stillness of his words carried more command than Jessica had ever heard in another voice.

He has the Great Control, she thought.

Gurney's arm trembled against her neck. The point of the knife at her back moved with uncertainty.

"What you have not done," Paul said, "is heard my mother sobbing in the night over her lost Duke. You have not seen her eyes stab flame when she speaks of killing Harkonnens."

So he has listened, she thought. Tears blinded her eyes.

"What you have not done," Paul went on, "is remembered the lessons you learned in a Harkonnen slave pit. You speak of pride in my father's friendship! Didn't you learn the difference between Harkonnen and Atreides so that you could smell a Harkonnen trick by the stink they left on it? Didn't you learn that Atreides loyalty is bought with love while the Harkonnen coin is hate? Couldn't you see through to the very nature of this betrayal?"

"But Yueh?" Gurney muttered.

"The evidence we have is Yueh's own message to us admitting his treachery," Paul said. "I swear this to you by the love I hold for you, a love I will still hold even after I leave you dead on this floor."

Hearing her son, Jessica marveled at the awareness in him, the penetrating insight of his intelligence.

"My father had an instinct for his friends," Paul said. "He gave his love sparingly, but with never an error. His weakness lay in misunderstanding hatred. He thought anyone who hated Harkonnens could not betray him." He glanced at his mother. "She knows this. I've given her my father's message that he never distrusted her."

Jessica felt herself losing control, bit at her lower lip. Seeing the stiff formality in Paul, she realized what these words were costing him. She wanted to run to him, cradle his head against her breast as she never ad done. But the arm against her throat had ceased its trembling; the point at her back pressed still and sharp.

e of the most terrible moments in a boy's life," Paul said, "is when he discovers his father and mother are human beings who share a love that he can never quite taste. It's a loss, an awakening to the fact that the world is *there* and *here* and we are in it alone. The moment carries its own truth; you can't evade it. I *heard* my father when he spoke of my mother. She's not the betrayer, Gurney."

Jessica found her voice, said: "Gurney, release me." There was no special command in the words, no trick to play on his weaknesses, but Gurney's hand fell away. She crossed to Paul, stood in front of him, not touching him.

"Paul," she said, "there are other awakenings in this universe. I suddenly see how I've used you and twisted you and manipulated you to set you on a course of my choosing . . . a course I had to choose—if that's any excuse—because of my own training." She swallowed past a lump in her throat, looked up into her son's eyes. "Paul . . . I want you to do something for me: choose the course of happiness. Your desert woman, marry her if that's your wish. Defy everyone and everything to do this. But choose your own course. I. . . ."

She broke off, stopped by the low sound of muttering behind her.

Gurney!

She saw Paul's eyes directed beyond her, turned.

Gurney stood in the same spot, but had sheathed his knife, pulled the robe away from his breast to expose the slick grayness of an issue stillsuit, the type the smugglers traded for among the sietch warrens.

"Put your knife right here in my breast," Gurney muttered. "I say kill me and have done with it. I've besmirched my name. I've betrayed my own Duke! The finest—"

"Be still!" Paul said.

Gurney stared at him.

"Close that robe and stop acting like a fool," Paul said. "I've had enough foolishness for one day."

"Kill me, I say!" Gurney raged.

"You know me better than that," Paul said. "How many kinds of an idiot do you think I am? Must I go through this with every man I need?"

Gurney looked at Jessica, spoke in a forlorn, pleading note so unlike him. "Then you, my Lady, please . . . you kill me."

Jessica crossed to him, put her hands on his shoulders. "Gurney, why do you insist the Atreides must kill those they love?" Gently, she pulled the spread robe out of his fingers, closed and fastened the fabric over his chest.

Gurney spoke brokenly: "But . . . I. . . ."

"You thought you were doing a thing for Leto," she said, "and for this I honor you."

"My Lady," Gurney said. He dropped his chin to his chest, squeezed his eyelids closed against the tears.

"Let us think of this as a misunderstanding among old friends," she said, and Paul heard the soothers, the adjusting tones in her voice. "It's over and we can be thankful we'll never again have that sort of misunderstanding between us."

Gurney opened eyes bright with moisture, looked down at her.

"The Gurney Halleck I knew was a man adept with both blade and baliset," Jessica said. "It was the man of the baliset I most admired. Doesn't that Gurney Halleck remember how I used to enjoy listening by the hour while he played for me? Do you still have a baliset, Gurney?"

"I've a new one," Gurney said. "Brought from Chusuk, a sweet instrument. Plays like a genuine Varota, though there's no signature on it. I think myself it was made by a student of Varota's who. . . ." He broke off. "What can I say to you, my Lady? Here we prattle about—"

"Not prattle, Gurney," Paul said. He crossed to stand beside his mother, eye to eye with Gurney. "Not prattle, but a thing that brings happiness between friends. I'd take it a kindness if you'd play for her now. Battle planning can wait a little while. We'll not be going into the fight till tomorrow at any rate."

"I . . . I'll get my baliset," Gurney said. "It's in the passage." He stepped around them and through the hangings.

Paul put a hand on his mother's arm, found that she was trembling.

"It's over, Mother," he said.

Without turning her head, she looked up at him from the corners of her eyes. "Over?"

"Of course. Gurney's. . . ."

"Gurney? Oh . . . yes." She lowered her gaze.

The hangings rustled as Gurney returned with his baliset. He began tuning it, avoiding their eyes. The hangings on the walls dulled the echoes, making the instrument sound small and intimate.

Paul led his mother to a cushion, seated her there with her back to the thick draperies of the wall. He was suddenly struck by how old she seemed to him with the beginnings of desert-dried lines in her face, the stretching at the corners of her blue-veiled eyes.

She's tired, he thought. *We must find some way to ease her burdens.*

Gurney strummed a chord.

Paul glanced at him, said: "I've . . . things that need my attention. Wait here for me."

Gurney nodded. His mind seemed far away, as though he dwelled for this moment beneath the open skies of Caladan with cloud fleece on the horizon promising rain.

Paul forced himself to turn away, let himself out through the heavy hangings over the side passage. He heard Gurney take up a tune behind him, and paused a moment outside the room to listen to the muted music.

> *"Orchards and vineyards,*
> *And full-breasted houris,*
> *And a cup overflowing before me.*
> *Why do I babble of battles,*
> *And mountains reduced to dust?*
> *Why do I feel these tears?*
>
> *Heavens stand open*
> *And scatter their riches;*
> *My hands need but gather their wealth.*
> *Why do I think of an ambush,*

And poison in molten cup?
Why do I feel my years?

Love's arms beckon
With their naked delights,
And Eden's promise of ecstasies.
Why do I remember the scars,
Dream of old transgressions . . .
And why do I sleep with fears?"

A robed Fedaykin courier appeared from a corner of the passage ahead of Paul. The man had hood thrown back and fastenings of his stillsuit hanging loose about his neck, proof that he had come just now from the open desert.

Paul motioned for him to stop, left the hangings of the door and moved down the passage to the courier.

The man bowed, hands clasped in front of him the way he might greet a Reverend Mother or Sayyadina of the rites. He said: "Muad'Dib, leaders are beginning to arrive for the Council."

"So soon?"

"These are the ones Stilgar sent for earlier when it was thought. . . ." He shrugged.

"I see." Paul glanced back toward the faint sound of the baliset, thinking of the old song that his mother favored—an odd stretching of happy tune and sad words. "Stilgar will come here soon with others. Show them where my mother waits."

"I will wait here, Muad'Dib," the courier said.

"Yes . . . yes, do that."

Paul pressed past the man toward the depths of the cavern, headed for the place that each such cavern had—a place near its water-holding basin. There would be a small shai-hulud in this place, a creature no more than nine meters long, kept stunted and trapped by surrounding water ditches. The maker, after emerging from its little maker vector, avoided water for the poison it was. And the drowning of a maker was the greatest Fremen secret because it produced the substance of their union—the Water of Life, the poison that could only be changed by a Reverend Mother.

The decision had come to Paul while he faced the tension of danger to his mother. No line of the future he had ever seen carried that moment of peril from Gurney Halleck. The future—the gray-cloud-future—with its feeling that the entire universe rolled toward a boiling nexus hung around him like a phantom world.

I must see it, he thought.

His body had slowly acquired a certain spice tolerance that made prescient visions fewer and fewer . . . dimmer and dimmer. The solution appeared obvious to him.

I will drown the maker. We will see now whether I'm the Kwisatz Haderach who can survive the test that the Reverend Mothers have survived.

And it came to pass in the third year of the Desert War that Paul-Muad'Dib lay alone in the Cave of Birds beneath the kiswa hangings of an inner cell. And he lay as one dead, caught up in the revelation of the Water of Life, his being translated beyond the boundaries of time by the poison that gives life. Thus was the prophecy made true that the Lisan al-Gaib might be both dead and alive.

—FROM "COLLECTED LEGENDS OF ARRAKIS"
BY THE PRINCESS IRULAN

Chani came up out of the Habbanya basin in the predawn darkness, hearing the 'thopter that had brought her from the south go whir-whirring off to a hiding place in the vastness. Around her, the escort kept its distance, fanning out into the rocks of the ridge to probe for dangers—and giving the mate of Muad'Dib, the mother of his firstborn, the thing she had requested: a moment to walk alone.

Why did he summon me? she asked herself. *He told me before that I must remain in the south with little Leto and Alia.*

She gathered her robe and leaped lightly up across a barrier rock and onto the climbing path that only the desert-trained could recognize in the darkness. Pebbles slithered underfoot and she danced across them without considering the nimbleness required.

The climb was exhilarating, easing the fears that had fermented in her because of her escort's silent withdrawal and the fact that a precious 'thopter had been sent for her. She felt the inner leaping at the nearness of reunion with Paul-Muad'Dib, her Usul. His name might be a battle cry over all the land: *"Muad'Dib! Muad'Dib! Muad'Dib!"* But she knew a different man by a different name—the father of her son, the tender lover.

A great figure loomed out of the rocks above her, beckoning for speed. She quickened her pace. Dawn birds already were calling and lifting into the sky. A dim spread of light grew across the eastern horizon.

The figure above was not one of her own escort. *Otheym?* she wondered, marking a familiarity of movement and manner. She came up to him, recognized in the growing light the broad, flat features of the Fedaykin lieutenant, his hood open and mouth filter loosely fastened the way one did sometimes when venturing out on the desert for only a moment.

"Hurry," he hissed, and led her down the secret crevasse into the hidden cave. "It will be light soon," he whispered as he held a doorseal open for her. "The Harkonnens have been making desperation patrols over some of this region. We dare not chance discovery now."

They emerged into the narrow side-passage entrance to the Cave of Birds. Glowglobes came alight. Otheym pressed past her, said: "Follow me. Quickly, now."

They sped down the passage, through another valve door, another passage and through hangings into what had been the Sayyadina's alcove in the days when this was an overday rest cave. Rugs and cushions now covered the floor. Woven hangings with the red figure of a hawk hid the rock walls. A low field desk at one side was strewn with papers from which lifted the aroma of their spice origin.

The Reverend Mother sat alone directly opposite the entrance. She looked up with the inward stare that made the uninitiated tremble.

Otheym pressed palms together, said: "I have brought Chani." He bowed, retreated through the hangings.

And Jessica thought: *How do I tell Chani?*

"How is my grandson?" Jessica asked.

So it's to be the ritual greeting, Chani thought, and her fears returned. *Where is Muad'Dib? Why isn't he here to greet me?*

"He is healthy and happy, my mother," Chani said. "I left him with Alia in the care of Harah."

My mother, Jessica thought. *Yes, she has the right to call me that in the formal greeting. She has given me a grandson.*

"I hear a gift of cloth has been sent from Coanua sietch," Jessica said.

"It is lovely cloth," Chani said.

"Does Alia send a message?"

"No message. But the sietch moves more smoothly now that the people are beginning to accept the miracle of her status."

Why does she drag this out so? Chani wondered. *Something was so urgent that they sent a 'thopter for me. Now, we drag through the formalities!*

"We must have some of the new cloth cut into garments for little Leto," Jessica said.

"Whatever you wish, my mother," Chani said. She lowered her gaze. "Is there news of battles?" She held her face expressionless that Jessica might not see the betrayal—that this was a question about Paul-Muad'Dib.

"New victories," Jessica said. "Rabban has sent cautious overtures about a truce. His messengers have been returned without their water. Rabban has even lightened the burdens of the people in some of the sink villages. But he is too late. The people know he does it out of fear of us."

"Thus it goes as Muad'Dib said," Chani said. She stared at Jessica, trying to keep her fears to herself. *I have spoken his name, but she has not responded. One cannot see emotion in that glazed stone she calls a face . . . but she is too frozen. Why is she so still? What has happened to my Usul?*

"I wish we were in the south," Jessica said. "The oases were so beautiful when we left. Do you not long for the day when the whole land may blossom thus?"

"The land is beautiful, true," Chani said. "But there is much grief in it."

"Grief is the price of victory," Jessica said.

Is she preparing me for grief? Chani asked herself. She said: "There are so many women without men. There was jealousy when it was learned that I'd been summoned north."

"I summoned you," Jessica said.

Chani felt her heart hammering. She wanted to clap her hands to her ears, fearful of what they might hear. Still, she kept her voice even: "The message was signed Muad'Dib."

"I signed it thus in the presence of his lieutenants," Jessica said. "It was a subterfuge of necessity." And Jessica thought: *This is a brave woman, my Paul's. She holds to the niceties even when fear is almost overwhelming her. Yes. She may be the one we need now.*

Only the slightest tone of resignation crept into Chani's voice as she said: "Now you may say the thing that must be said."

"You were needed here to help me revive Paul," Jessica said. And she thought: *There! I said it in the precisely correct way. Revive. Thus she knows Paul is alive and knows there is peril, all in the same word.*

Chani took only a moment to calm herself, then: "What is it I may do?" She wanted to leap at Jessica, shake her and scream: *"Take me to him!"* But she waited silently for the answer.

"I suspect," Jessica said, "that the Harkonnens have managed to send an agent among us to poison Paul. It's the only explanation that seems to fit. A most unusual poison. I've examined his blood in the most subtle ways without detecting it."

Chani thrust herself forward onto her knees. "Poison? Is he in pain? Could I. . . ."

"He is unconscious," Jessica said. "The processes of his life are so low that they can be detected only with the most refined techniques. I shudder to think what could have happened had I not been the one to discover him. He appears dead to the untrained eye."

"You have reasons other than courtesy for summoning me," Chani said. "I know you, Reverend Mother. What is it you think I may do that you cannot do?"

She is brave, lovely and, ah-h-h, so perceptive, Jessica thought. *She'd have made a fine Bene Gesserit.*

"Chani," Jessica said, "you may find this difficult to believe, but I do not know precisely why I sent for you. It was an instinct . . . a basic intuition. The thought came unbidden: 'Send for Chani.'"

For the first time, Chani saw the sadness in Jessica's expression, the unveiled pain modifying the inward stare.

"I've done all I know to do," Jessica said. "That *all* . . . it is so far beyond what is usually supposed as *all* that you would find difficulty imagining it. Yet . . . I failed."

"The old companion, Halleck," Chani asked, "is it possible he's a traitor?"

"Not Gurney," Jessica said.

The two words carried an entire conversation, and Chani saw the searching, the tests . . . the memories of old failures that went into this flat denial.

Chani rocked back onto her feet, stood up, smoothed her desert-stained robe. "Take me to him," she said.

Jessica arose, turned through hangings on the left wall.

Chani followed, found herself in what had been a storeroom, its rock walls concealed now beneath heavy draperies. Paul lay on a field pad against the far wall. A single glowglobe above him illuminated his face. A black robe covered him to the chest, leaving his arms outside it stretched along his sides. He appeared to be unclothed under the robe. The skin exposed looked waxen, rigid. There was no visible movement to him.

Chani suppressed the desire to dash forward, throw herself across him. She found her thoughts, instead, going to her son—Leto. And she realized in this instant that Jessica once had faced such a moment—her man threatened by death, forced in her own mind to consider what might be done to save a young son. The realization formed a sudden bond with the older woman so that Chani reached out and clasped Jessica's hand. The answering grip was painful in its intensity.

"He lives," Jessica said. "I assure you he lives. But the thread of his life is so thin it could easily escape detection. There are some among the leaders already muttering that the mother speaks and not the Reverend

Mother, that my son is truly dead and I do not want to give up his water to the tribe."

"How long has he been this way?" Chani asked. She disengaged her hand from Jessica's, moved farther into the room.

"Three weeks," Jessica said. "I spent almost a week trying to revive him. There were meetings, arguments . . . investigations. Then I sent for you. The Fedaykin obey my orders, else I might not have been able to delay the. . . ." She wet her lips with her tongue, watching Chani cross to Paul.

Chani stood over him now, looking down on the soft beard of youth that framed his face, tracing with her eyes the high browline, the strong nose, the shuttered eyes—the features so peaceful in this rigid repose.

"How does he take nourishment?" Chani asked.

"The demands of his flesh are so slight he does not yet need food," Jessica said.

"How many know of what has happened?" Chani asked.

"Only his closest advisers, a few of the leaders, the Fedaykin and, of course, whoever administered the poison."

"There is no clue to the poisoner?"

"And it's not for want of investigating," Jessica said.

"What do the Fedaykin say?" Chani asked.

"They believe Paul is in a sacred trance, gathering his holy powers before the final battles. This is a thought I've cultivated."

Chani lowered herself to her knees beside the pad, bent close to Paul's face. She sensed an immediate difference in the air about his face . . . but it was only the spice, the ubiquitous spice whose odor permeated everything in Fremen life. Still. . . .

"You were not born to the spice as we were," Chani said. "Have you investigated the possibility that his body has rebelled against too much spice in his diet?"

"Allergy reactions are all negative," Jessica said.

She closed her eyes, as much to blot out this scene as because of sudden realization of fatigue. *How long have I been without sleep?* she asked herself. *Too long.*

"When you change the Water of Life," Chani said, "you do it within yourself by the inward awareness. Have you used this awareness to test his blood?"

"Normal Fremen blood," Jessica said. "Completely adapted to the diet and the life here."

Chani sat back on her heels, submerging her fears in thought as she studied Paul's face. This was a trick she had learned from watching the Reverend Mothers. Time could be made to serve the mind. One concentrated the entire attention.

Presently, Chani said: "Is there a maker here?"

"There are several," Jessica said with a touch of weariness. "We are never without them these days. Each victory requires its blessing. Each ceremony before a raid—"

"But Paul-Muad'Dib has held himself aloof from these ceremonies," Chani said.

Jessica nodded to herself, remembering her son's ambivalent feelings toward the spice drug and the prescient awareness it precipitated.

"How did you know this?" Jessica asked.

"It is spoken."

"Too much is spoken," Jessica said bitterly.

"Get me the raw Water of the maker," Chani said.

Jessica stiffened at the tone of command in Chani's voice, then observed the intense concentration in the younger woman and said: "At once." She went out through the hangings to send a waterman.

Chani sat staring at Paul. *If he has tried to do this*, she thought. *And it's the sort of thing he might try. . . .*

Jessica knelt beside Chani, holding out a plain camp ewer. The charged odor of the poison was sharp in Chani's nostrils. She dipped a finger in the fluid, held the finger close to Paul's nose.

The skin along the bridge of his nose wrinkled slightly. Slowly, the nostrils flared.

Jessica gasped.

Chani touched the dampened finger to Paul's upper lip.

He drew in a long, sobbing breath.

"What is this?" Jessica demanded.

"Be still," Chani said. "You must convert a small amount of the sacred water. Quickly!"

Without questioning, because she recognized the tone of awareness in Chani's voice, Jessica lifted the ewer to her mouth, drew in a small sip.

Paul's eyes flew open. He stared upward at Chani.

"It is not necessary for her to change the Water," he said. His voice was weak, but steady.

Jessica, a sip of the fluid on her tongue, found her body rallying, converting the poison almost automatically. In the light elevation the ceremony always imparted, she sensed the life-glow from Paul—a radiation there registering on her senses.

In that instant, she knew.

"You drank the sacred water!" she blurted.

"One drop of it," Paul said. "So small . . . one drop."

"How could you do such a foolish thing?" she demanded.

"He is your son," Chani said.

Jessica glared at her.

A rare smile, warm and full of understanding, touched Paul's lips. "Hear my beloved," he said. "Listen to her, Mother. She knows."

"A thing that others can do, he must do," Chani said.

"When I had the drop in my mouth, when I felt it and smelled it, when I knew what it was doing to me, then I knew I could do the thing that you have done," he said. "Your Bene Gesserit proctors speak of the Kwisatz Haderach, but they cannot begin to guess the many places I have been. In the few minutes I. . . ." He broke off, looking at Chani with a puzzled frown. "Chani? How did you get here? You're supposed to be. . . . Why are you here?"

He tried to push himself onto his elbows. Chani pressed him back gently.

"Please, my Usul," she said.

"I feel so weak," he said. His gaze darted around the room. "How long have I been here?"

"You've been three weeks in a coma so deep that the spark of life seemed to have fled," Jessica said.

"But it was. . . . I took it just a moment ago and. . . ."

"A moment for you, three weeks of fear for me," Jessica said.

"It was only one drop, but I converted it," Paul said. "I changed the Water of Life." And before Chani or Jessica could stop him, he dipped his hand into the ewer they had placed on the floor beside him, and he brought the dripping hand to his mouth, swallowed the palm-cupped liquid.

"Paul!" Jessica screamed.

He grabbed her hand, faced her with a death's head grin, and he sent his awareness surging over her.

The rapport was not as tender, not as sharing, not as encompassing as it had been with Alia and with the Old Reverend Mother in the cavern . . . but it was a rapport: a sense-sharing of the entire being. It shook her, weakened her, and she cowered in her mind, fearful of him.

Aloud, he said: "You speak of a place where you cannot enter? This place which the Reverend Mother cannot face, show it to me."

She shook her head, terrified by the very thought.

"Show it to me!" he commanded.

"No!"

But she could not escape him. Bludgeoned by the terrible force of him, she closed her eyes and focused inward—the-direction-that-is-dark.

Paul's consciousness flowed through and around her and into the darkness. She glimpsed the place dimly before her mind blanked itself away from the terror. Without knowing why, her whole being trembled at what she had seen—a region where a wind blew and sparks glared, where rings of light expanded and contracted, where rows of tumescent white shapes flowed over and under and around the lights, driven by darkness and a wind out of nowhere.

Presently, she opened her eyes, saw Paul staring up at her. He still held her hand, but the terrible rapport was gone. She quieted her trembling. Paul released her hand. It was as though some crutch had been removed. She staggered up and back, would have fallen had not Chani jumped to support her.

"Reverend Mother!" Chani said. "What is wrong?"

"Tired," Jessica whispered. "So . . . tired."

"Here," Chani said. "Sit here." She helped Jessica to a cushion against the wall.

The strong young arms felt so good to Jessica. She clung to Chani.

"He has, in truth, seen the Water of Life?" Chani asked. She disengaged herself from Jessica's grip.

"He has seen," Jessica whispered. Her mind still rolled and surged from the contact. It was like stepping to solid land after weeks on a heaving sea. She sensed the old Reverend Mother within her . . . and all the others awakened and questioning: *What was that? What happened? Where was that place?*

Through it all threaded the realization that her son was the Kwisatz Haderach, the one who could be many places at once. He was the fact out of the Bene Gesserit dream. And the fact gave her no peace.

"What happened?" Chani demanded.

Jessica shook her head.

Paul said: "There is in each of us an ancient force that takes and an ancient force that gives. A man finds little difficulty facing that place within himself where the taking force dwells, but it's almost impossible for him to see into the giving force without changing into something other than man. For a woman, the situation is reversed."

Jessica looked up, found Chani was staring at her while listening to Paul.

"Do you understand me, Mother?" Paul asked.

She could only nod.

"These things are so ancient within us," Paul said, "that they're ground into each separate cell of our bodies. We're shaped by such forces. You can say to yourself, 'Yes, I see how such a thing may be.' But when you look inward and confront the raw force of your own life unshielded, you see your peril. You see that this could overwhelm you. The greatest peril to the Giver is the force that takes. The greatest peril to the Taker is the force that gives. It's as easy to be overwhelmed by giving as by taking."

"And you, my son," Jessica asked, "are you one who gives or one who takes?"

"I'm at the fulcrum," he said. "I cannot give without taking and I cannot take without. . . ." He broke off, looking to the wall at his right.

Chani felt a draft against her cheek, turned to see the hangings close.

"It was Otheym," Paul said. "He was listening."

Accepting the words, Chani was touched by some of the prescience that haunted Paul, and she knew a thing-yet-to-be as though it already had occurred. Otheym would speak of what he had seen and heard. Others would spread the story until it was a fire over the land. Paul-Muad'Dib is not as other men, they would say. There can be no more doubt. He is a man, yet he sees through to the Water of Life in the way of a Reverend Mother. He is indeed the Lisan al-Gaib.

"You have seen the future, Paul," Jessica said. "Will you say what you've seen?"

"Not the future," he said. "I've seen the Now." He forced himself to a sitting position, waved Chani aside as she moved to help him. "The Space above Arrakis is filled with the ships of the Guild."

Jessica trembled at the certainty in his voice.

"The Padishah Emperor himself is there," Paul said. He looked at the rock ceiling of his cell. "With his favorite Truthsayer and five legions of Sardaukar. The old Baron Vladimir Harkonnen is there with Thufir Hawat beside him and seven ships jammed with every conscript he could muster. Every Great House has its raiders above us . . . waiting."

Chani shook her head, unable to look away from Paul. His strangeness, the flat tone of voice, the way he looked through her, filled her with awe.

Jessica tried to swallow in a dry throat, said: "For what are they waiting?"

Paul looked at her. "For the Guild's permission to land. The Guild will strand on Arrakis any force that lands without permission."

"The Guild's protecting us?" Jessica asked.

"Protecting us! The Guild itself caused this by spreading tales about what we do here and by reducing troop transport fares to a point where even the poorest Houses are up there now waiting to loot us."

Jessica noted the lack of bitterness in his tone, wondered at it. She couldn't doubt his words—they had that same intensity she'd seen in him the night he'd revealed the path of the future that'd taken them among the Fremen.

Paul took a deep breath, said: "Mother, you must change a quantity of the Water for us. We need the catalyst. Chani, have a scout force sent out . . . to find a pre-spice mass. If we plant a quantity of the Water of Life above a pre-spice mass, do you know what will happen?"

Jessica weighed his words, suddenly saw through to his meaning. "Paul!" she gasped.

"The Water of Death," he said. "It'd be a chain reaction." He pointed to the floor. "Spreading death among the little makers, killing a vector of the life cycle that includes the spice and the makers. Arrakis will become a true desolation—without spice or maker."

Chani put a hand to her mouth, shocked to numb silence by the blasphemy pouring from Paul's lips.

"He who can destroy a thing has the real control of it," Paul said. "We can destroy the spice."

"What stays the Guild's hand?" Jessica whispered.

"They're searching for me," Paul said. "Think of that! The finest Guild navigators, men who can quest ahead through time to find the safest course for the fastest Heighliners, all of them seeking me . . . and unable to find me. How they tremble! They know I have their secret here!" Paul held out his cupped hand. "Without the spice they're blind!"

Chani found her voice. "You said you see the *now*!"

Paul lay back, searching the spread-out *present*, its limits extended into the future and into the past, holding onto the awareness with difficulty as the spice illumination began to fade.

"Go do as I commanded," he said. "The future's becoming as muddled for the Guild as it is for me. The lines of vision are narrowing. Everything focuses here where the spice is . . . where they've dared not interfere before . . . because to interfere was to lose what they must have. But now they're desperate. All paths lead into darkness."

And that day dawned when Arrakis lay at the hub of the universe with the wheel poised to spin.

—FROM "ARRAKIS AWAKENING"
BY THE PRINCESS IRULAN

"Will you look at that thing!" Stilgar whispered.

Paul lay beside him in a slit of rock high on the Shield Wall rim, eye fixed to the collector of a Fremen telescope. The oil lens was focused on a starship lighter exposed by dawn in the basin below them. The tall eastern face of the ship glistened in the flat light of the sun, but the shadow side still showed yellow portholes from glowglobes of the night. Beyond the ship, the city of Arrakeen lay cold and gleaming in the light of the northern sun.

It wasn't the lighter that excited Stilgar's awe, Paul knew, but the construction for which the lighter was only the centerpost. A single metal hutment, many stories tall, reached out in a thousand-meter circle from the base of the lighter—a tent composed of interlocking metal leaves—the temporary lodging place for five legions of Sardaukar and His Imperial Majesty, the Padishah Emperor Shaddam IV.

From his position squatting at Paul's left, Gurney Halleck said: "I count nine levels to it. Must be quite a few Sardaukar in there."

"Five legions," Paul said.

"It grows light," Stilgar hissed. "We like it not, your exposing yourself, Muad'Dib. Let us go back into the rocks now."

"I'm perfectly safe here," Paul said.

"That ship mounts projectile weapons," Gurney said.

"They believe us protected by shields," Paul said. "They wouldn't waste a shot on an unidentified trio even if they saw us."

Paul swung the telescope to scan the far wall of the basin, seeing the pockmarked cliffs, the slides that marked the tombs of so many of his father's troopers. And he had a momentary sense of the fitness of things that the shades of those men should look down on this moment. The Harkonnen forts and towns across the shielded lands lay in Fremen hands or cut away from their source like stalks severed from a plant and left to wither. Only this basin and its city remained to the enemy.

"They might try a sortie by 'thopter," Stilgar said. "If they see us."

"Let them," Paul said. "We've 'thopters to burn today . . . and we know a storm is coming."

He swung the telescope to the far side of the Arrakeen landing field now, to the Harkonnen frigates lined up there with a CHOAM Company banner waving gently from its staff on the ground beneath them. And he thought of the desperation that had forced the Guild to permit these two groups to land while all the others were held in reserve. The Guild was like a man testing the sand with his toe to gauge its temperature before erecting a tent.

"Is there anything new to see from here?" Gurney asked. "We should be getting under cover. The storm *is* coming."

Paul returned his attention on the giant hutment. "They've even brought their women," he said. "And lackeys and servants. Ah-h-h, my dear Emperor, how confident you are."

"Men are coming up the secret way," Stilgar said. "It may be Otheym and Korba returning."

"All right, Stil," Paul said. "We'll go back."

But he took one final look around through the telescope—studying the plain with its tall ships, the gleaming metal hutment, the silent city, the frigates of the Harkonnen mercenaries. Then he slid backward around a scarp of rock. His place at the telescope was taken by a Fedaykin guardsman.

Paul emerged into a shallow depression in the Shield Wall's surface. It was a place about thirty meters in diameter and some three meters deep, a natural feature of the rock that the Fremen had hidden beneath a translucent camouflage cover. Communications equipment was clustered around a hole in the wall to the right. Fedaykin guards deployed through the depression waited for Muad'Dib's command to attack.

Two men emerged from the hole by the communications equipment, spoke to the guards there.

Paul glanced at Stilgar, nodded in the direction of the two men. "Get their report, Stil."

Stilgar moved to obey.

Paul crouched with his back to the rock, stretching his muscles, straightened. He saw Stilgar sending the two men back into that dark hole in the rock, thought about the long climb down that narrow man-made tunnel to the floor of the basin.

Stilgar crossed to Paul.

"What was so important that they couldn't send a cielago with the message?" Paul asked.

"They're saving their birds for the battle," Stilgar said. He glanced at the communications equipment, back to Paul. "Even with a tight beam, it is wrong to use those things, Muad'Dib. They can find you by taking a bearing on its emission."

"They'll soon be too busy to find me," Paul said. "What did the men report?"

"Our pet Sardaukar have been released near Old Gap low on the rim and are on their way to their master. The rocket launchers and other projectile weapons are in place. The people are deployed as you ordered. It was all routine."

Paul glanced across the shallow bowl, studying his men in the filtered light admitted by the camouflage cover. He felt time creeping like an insect working its way across an exposed rock.

"It'll take our Sardaukar a little time afoot before they can signal a troop carrier," Paul said. "They are being watched?"

"They are being watched," Stilgar said.

Beside Paul, Gurney Halleck cleared his throat. "Hadn't we best be getting to a place of safety?"

"There is no such place," Paul said. "Is the weather report still favorable?"

"A great grandmother of a storm coming," Stilgar said. "Can you not feel it, Muad'Dib?"

"The air does feel chancy," Paul agreed. "But I like the certainty of poling the weather."

"The storm'll be here in the hour," Stilgar said. He nodded toward the gap that looked out on the Emperor's hutment and the Harkonnen frigates. "They know it there, too. Not a 'thopter in the sky. Everything pulled in and tied down. They've had a report on the weather from their friends in space."

"Any more probing sorties?" Paul asked.

"Nothing since the landing last night," Stilgar said. "They know we're here. I think now they wait to choose their own time."

"We choose the time," Paul said.

Gurney glanced upward, growled: "If *they* let us."

"That fleet'll stay in space," Paul said.

Gurney shook his head.

"They have no choice," Paul said. "We can destroy the spice. The Guild dares not risk that."

"Desperate people are the most dangerous," Gurney said.

"Are we not desperate?" Stilgar asked.

Gurney scowled at him.

"You haven't lived with the Fremen dream," Paul cautioned. "Stil is thinking of all the water we've spent on bribes, the years of waiting we've added before Arrakis can bloom. He's not—"

"Arrrgh," Gurney scowled.

"Why's he so gloomy?" Stilgar asked.

"He's always gloomy before a battle," Paul said. "It's the only form of good humor Gurney allows himself."

A slow, wolfish grin spread across Gurney's face, the teeth showing white above the chip cut of his stillsuit. "It glooms me much to think on all the poor Harkonnen souls we'll dispatch unshriven," he said.

Stilgar chuckled. "He talks like a Fedaykin."

"Gurney was born a death commando," Paul said. And he thought: *Yes, let them occupy their minds with small talk before we test ourselves against that force on the plain.* He looked to the gap in the rock wall and back to Gurney, found that the troubadour-warrior had resumed a brooding scowl.

"Worry saps the strength," Paul murmured. "You told me that once, Gurney."

"My Duke," Gurney said, "my chief worry is the atomics. If you use them to blast a hole in the Shield Wall. . . ."

"Those people up there won't use atomics against us," Paul said. "They don't dare . . . and for the same reason that they cannot risk our destroying the source of the spice."

"But the injunction against—"

"The injunction!" Paul barked. "It's fear, not the injunction that keeps the Houses from hurling atomics against each other. The language of the Great Convention is clear enough: 'Use of atomics against humans shall be cause for planetary obliteration.' We're going to blast the Shield Wall, not humans."

"It's too fine a point," Gurney said.

"The hair-splitters up there will welcome any point," Paul said. "Let's talk no more about it."

He turned away, wishing he actually felt that confident. Presently, he said: "What about the city people? Are they in position yet?"

"Yes," Stilgar muttered.

Paul looked at him. "What's eating you?"

"I never knew the city man could be trusted completely," Stilgar said.

"I was a city man myself once," Paul said.

Stilgar stiffened. His face grew dark with blood. "Muad'Dib knows I did not mean—"

"I know what you meant, Stil. But the test of a man isn't what you think he'll do. It's what he actually does. These city people have Fremen blood. It's just that they haven't yet learned how to escape their bondage. We'll teach them."

Stilgar nodded, spoke in a rueful tone: "The habits of a lifetime, Muad'Dib. On the Funeral Plain we learned to despise the men of the communities."

Paul glanced at Gurney, saw him studying Stilgar. "Tell us, Gurney, why were the cityfolk down there driven from their homes by the Sardaukar?"

"An old trick, my Duke. They thought to burden us with refugees."

"It's been so long since guerrillas were effective that the mighty have forgotten how to fight them," Paul said. "The Sardaukar have played into our hands. They grabbed some city women for their sport, decorated their battle standards with the heads of the men who objected. And they've built up a fever of hate among people who otherwise would've looked on the coming battle as no more than a great inconvenience . . . and the possibility of exchanging one set of masters for another. The Sardaukar recruit for us, Stilgar."

"The city people do seem eager," Stilgar said.

"Their hate is fresh and clear," Paul said. "That's why we use them as shock troops."

"The slaughter among them will be fearful," Gurney said. Stilgar nodded agreement.

"They were told the odds," Paul said. "They know every Sardaukar they kill will be one less for us. You see, gentlemen, they have something to die for. They've discovered they're a people. They're awakening."

A muttered exclamation came from the watcher at the telescope. Paul moved to the rock slit, asked: "What is it out there?"

"A great commotion, Muad'Dib," the watcher hissed. "At that monstrous metal tent. A surface car came from Rimwall West and it was like a hawk into a nest of rock partridge."

"Our captive Sardaukar have arrived," Paul said.

"They've a shield around the entire landing field now," the watcher said. "I can see the air dancing even to the edge of the storage yard where they kept the spice."

"Now they know who it is they fight," Gurney said. "Let the Harkonnen beasts tremble and fret themselves that an Atreides yet lives!"

Paul spoke to the Fedaykin at the telescope. "Watch the flagpole atop the Emperor's ship. If my flag is raised there—"

"It will not be," Gurney said.

Paul saw the puzzled frown on Stilgar's face, said: "If the Emperor recognized my claim, he'll signal by restoring the Atreides flag to Arrakis. We'll use the second plan then, move only against the Harkonnens. The Sardaukar will stand aside and let us settle the issue between ourselves."

"I've no experience with these offworld things," Stilgar said. "I've heard of them, but it seems unlikely the—"

"You don't need experience to know what they'll do," Gurney said.

"They're sending a new flag up on the tall ship," the watcher said. "The flag is yellow . . . with a black and red circle in the center."

"There's a subtle piece of business," Paul said. "The CHOAM Company flag."

"It's the same as the flag at the other ships," the Fedaykin guard said.

"I don't understand," Stilgar said.

"A subtle piece of business indeed," Gurney said. "Had he sent up the Atreides banner, he'd have had to live by what that meant. Too many observers about. He could've signaled with the Harkonnen flag on his staff—a flat declaration that'd have been. But, no—he sends up the CHOAM rag. He's telling the people up there. . . ." Gurney pointed toward space. ". . . where the profit is. He's saying he doesn't care if it's an Atreides here or not."

"How long till the storm strikes the Shield Wall?" Paul asked.

Stilgar turned away, consulted one of the Fedaykin in the bowl. Presently, he returned, said: "Very soon, Muad'Dib. Sooner than we expected. It's a great-great grandmother of a storm . . . perhaps even more than you wished."

"It's my storm," Paul said, and saw the silent awe on the faces of the Fedaykin who heard him. "Though it shook the entire world it could not be more than I wished. Will it strike the Shield Wall full on?"

"Close enough to make no difference," Stilgar said.

A courier crossed from the hole that led down into the basin, said: "The Sardaukar and Harkonnen patrols are pulling back, Muad'Dib."

"They expect the storm to spill too much sand into the basin for good visibility," Stilgar said. "They think we'll be in the same fix."

"Tell our gunners to set their sights well before visibility drops," Paul said. "They must knock the nose off every one of those ships as soon as the storm has destroyed the shields." He stepped to the wall of the bowl, pulled back a fold of the camouflage cover and looked up at the sky. The horsetail twistings of blow sand could be seen against the dark of the sky. Paul restored the cover, said: "Start sending our men down, Stil."

"Will you not go with us?" Stilgar asked.

"I'll wait here a bit with the Fedaykin," Paul said.

Stilgar gave a knowing shrug toward Gurney, moved to the hole in the rock wall, was lost in its shadows.

"The trigger that blasts the Shield Wall aside, that I leave in your hands, Gurney," Paul said. "You will do it?"

"I'll do it."

Paul gestured to a Fedaykin lieutenant, said: "Otheym, start moving the check patrols out of the blast area. They must be out of there before the storm strikes."

The man bowed, followed Stilgar.

Gurney leaned in to the rock slit, spoke to the man at the telescope: "Keep your attention on the south wall. It'll be completely undefended until we blow it."

"Dispatch a cielago with a time signal," Paul ordered.

"Some ground cars are moving toward the south wall," the man at the telescope said. "Some are using projectile weapons, testing. Our people are using body shields as you commanded. The ground cars have stopped."

In the abrupt silence, Paul heard the wind devils playing overhead—the front of the storm. Sand began to drift down into their bowl through gaps in the cover. A burst of wind caught the cover, whipped it away.

Paul motioned his Fedaykin to take shelter, crossed to the men at the communications equipment near the tunnel mouth. Gurney stayed beside him. Paul crouched over the signalmen.

One said: "A great-great-*great* grandmother of a storm, Muad'Dib."

Paul glanced up at the darkening sky, said: "Gurney, have the south wall observers pulled out." He had to repeat his order, shouting above the growing noise of the storm.

Gurney turned to obey.

Paul fastened his face filter, tightened the stillsuit hood.

Gurney returned.

Paul touched his shoulder, pointed to the blast trigger set into the tunnel mouth beyond the signalmen. Gurney went into the tunnel, stopped there, one hand at the trigger, his gaze on Paul.

"We are getting no messages," the signalman beside Paul said. "Much static."

Paul nodded, kept his eye on the time-standard dial in front of the signalman. Presently, Paul looked at Gurney, raised a hand, returned his attention to the dial. The time counter crawled around its final circuit.

"Now!" Paul shouted, and dropped his hand.

Gurney depressed the blast trigger.

It seemed that a full second passed before they felt the ground beneath them ripple and shake. A rumbling sound was added to the storm's roar.

The Fedaykin watcher from the telescope appeared beside Paul, the telescope clutched under one arm. "The Shield Wall is breached, Muad'Dib!" he shouted. "The storm is on them and our gunners already are firing."

Paul thought of the storm sweeping across the basin, the static charge within the wall of sand that destroyed every shield barrier in the enemy camp.

"The storm!" someone shouted. "We must get under cover, Muad'Dib!"

Paul came to his senses, feeling the sand needles sting his exposed cheeks. *We are committed,* he thought. He put an arm around the signalman's shoulder, said: "Leave the equipment! There's more in the tunnel." He felt himself being pulled away, Fedaykin pressed around him to protect him. They squeezed into the tunnel mouth, feeling its comparative silence, turned a corner into a small chamber with glowglobes overhead and another tunnel opening beyond.

Another signalman sat there at his equipment.

"Much static," the man said.

A swirl of sand filled the air around them.

"Seal off this tunnel!" Paul shouted. A sudden pressure of stillness showed that his command had been obeyed. "Is the way down to the basin still open?" Paul asked.

A Fedaykin went to look, returned, said: "The explosion caused a little rock to fall, but the engineers say it is still open. They're cleaning up with lasbeams."

"Tell them to use their hands!" Paul barked. "There are shields active down there!"

"They are being careful, Muad'Dib," the man said, but he turned to obey.

The signalmen from outside pressed past them carrying their equipment.

"I told those men to leave their equipment!" Paul said.

"Fremen do not like to abandon equipment, Muad'Dib," one of his Fedaykin chided.

"Men are more important than equipment now," Paul said. "We'll have more equipment than we can use soon or have no need for any equipment."

Gurney Halleck came up beside him, said: "I heard them say the way down is open. We're very close to the surface here, m'Lord, should the Harkonnens try to retaliate in kind."

"They're in no position to retaliate," Paul said. "They're just now finding out that they have no shields and are unable to get off Arrakis."

"The new command post is all prepared, though, m'Lord," Gurney said.

"They've no need of me in the command post yet," Paul said. "The plan would go ahead without me. We must wait for the—"

"I'm getting a message, Muad'Dib," said the signalman at the communications equipment. The man shook his head, pressed a receiver phone against his ear. "Much static!" He began scribbling on a pad in front of him, shaking his head waiting, writing . . . waiting.

Paul crossed to the signalman's side. The Fedaykin stepped back, giving him room. He looked down at what the man had written, read:

"Raid . . . on Sietch Tabr . . . captives . . . Alia (blank) families of (blank) dead are . . . they (blank) son of Muad'Dib. . . ."

Again, the signalman shook his head.

Paul looked up to see Gurney staring at him.

"The message is garbled," Gurney said. "The static. You don't know that. . . ."

"My son is dead," Paul said, and knew as he spoke that it was true. "My son is dead . . . and Alia is a captive . . . hostage." He felt emptied, a shell without emotions. Everything he touched brought death and grief. And it was like a disease that could spread across the universe.

He could feel the old-man wisdom, the accumulation out of the experiences from countless possible lives. Something seemed to chuckle and rub its hands within him.

And Paul thought: *How little the universe knows about the nature of real cruelty!*

And Muad'Dib stood before them, and he said: "Though we deem the captive dead, yet does she live. For her seed is my seed and her voice is my voice. And she sees unto the farthest reaches of possibility. Yea, unto the vale of the unknowable does she see because of me."

—FROM "ARRAKIS AWAKENING"
BY THE PRINCESS IRULAN

The Baron Vladimir Harkonnen stood with eyes downcast in the Imperial audience chamber, the oval selamlik within the Padishah Emperor's hutment. With covert glances, the Baron had studied the metal-walled room and its occupants—the noukkers, the pages, the guards, the troop of House Sardaukar drawn up around the walls, standing at ease there beneath the bloody and tattered captured battle flags that were the room's only decoration.

Voices sounded from the right of the chamber, echoing out of a high passage: "Make way! Make way for the Royal Person!"

The Padishah Emperor Shaddam IV came out of the passage into the audience chamber followed by his suite. He stood waiting while his throne was brought, ignoring the Baron, seemingly ignoring every person in the room.

The Baron found that he could not ignore the Royal Person, and studied the Emperor for a sign, any clue to the purpose of this audience. The Emperor stood poised, waiting—a slim, elegant figure in a gray Sardaukar uniform with silver and gold trim. His thin face and cold eyes reminded the Baron of the Duke Leto long dead. There was that same look of the predatory bird. But the Emperor's hair was red, not black, and most of that hair was concealed by a Burseg's ebon helmet with the Imperial crest in gold upon its crown.

Pages brought the throne. It was a massive chair carved from a single piece of Hagal quartz—blue-green translucency shot through with streaks of yellow fire. They placed it on the dais and the Emperor mounted, seated himself.

An old woman in a black aba robe with hood drawn down over her forehead detached herself from the Emperor's suite, took up station behind the throne, one scrawny hand resting on the quartz back. Her face peered out of the hood like a witch caricature—sunken cheeks and eyes, an overlong nose, skin mottled and with protruding veins.

The Baron stilled his trembling at sight of her. The presence of the Reverend Mother Gaius Helen Mohiam, the Emperor's Truthsayer, betrayed the importance of this audience. The Baron looked away from her, studied the suite for a clue. There were two of the Guild agents, one tall and fat, one short and fat, both with bland gray eyes. And among the lackeys stood one of the Emperor's daughters, the Princess Irulan, a woman they said was being trained in the deepest of the Bene Gesserit ways, destined to be a Reverend Mother. She was tall, blonde, face of chiseled beauty, green eyes that looked past and through him.

"My dear Baron."

The Emperor had deigned to notice him. The voice was baritone and with exquisite control. It managed to dismiss him while greeting him.

The Baron bowed low, advanced to the required position ten paces from the dais. "I came at your summons, Majesty."

"Summons!" the old witch cackled.

"Now, Reverend Mother," the Emperor chided, but he smiled at the Baron's discomfiture, said: "First, you will tell me where you've sent your minion, Thufir Hawat."

The Baron darted his gaze left and right, reviled himself for coming here without his own guards, not that they'd be much use against Sardaukar. Still. . . .

"Well?" the Emperor said.

"He has been gone these five days, Majesty." The Baron shot a glance at the Guild agents, back to the Emperor. "He was to land at a smuggler base and attempt infiltrating the camp of the Fremen fanatic, this Muad'Dib."

"Incredible!" the Emperor said.

One of the witch's clawlike hands tapped the Emperor's shoulder. She leaned forward, whispered in his ear.

The Emperor nodded, said: "Five days, Baron. Tell me, why aren't you worried about his absence?"

"But I *am* worried, Majesty!"

The Emperor continued to stare at him, waiting. The Reverend Mother emitted a cackling laugh.

"What I mean, Majesty," the Baron said, "is that Hawat will be dead within another few hours, anyway." And he explained about the latent poison and need for an antidote.

"How clever of you, Baron," the Emperor said. "And where are your nephews, Rabban and the young Feyd-Rautha?"

"The storm comes, Majesty. I sent them to inspect our perimeter lest the Fremen attack under cover of the sand."

"Perimeter," the Emperor said. The word came out as though it puckered his mouth. "The storm won't be much here in the basin, and that Fremen rabble won't attack while I'm here with five legions of Sardaukar."

"Surely not, Majesty," the Baron said. "But error on the side of caution cannot be censured."

"Ah-h-h-h," the Emperor said. "Censure. Then I'm not to speak of how much time this Arrakis nonsense has taken from me? Nor the CHOAM Company profits pouring down this rat hole? Nor the court functions and affairs of state I've had to delay—even cancel—because of this stupid affair?"

The Baron lowered his gaze, frightened by the Imperial anger. The delicacy of his position here, alone and dependent upon the Convention and the dictum familia of the Great Houses, fretted him. *Does he mean to kill me?* the Baron asked himself. *He couldn't! Not with the other Great Houses waiting up there, aching for any excuse to gain from this upset on Arrakis.*

"Have you taken hostages?" the Emperor asked.

"It's useless, Majesty," the Baron said. "These mad Fremen hold a burial ceremony for every captive and act as though such a one were already dead."

"So?" the Emperor said.

And the Baron waited, glancing left and right at the metal walls of the selamlik, thinking of the monstrous fanmetal tent around him. Such unlimited wealth it represented that even the Baron was awed. *He brings pages*, the Baron thought, *and useless court lackeys, his women and their companions—hair-dressers, designers, everything . . . all the fringe parasites of the Court. All here—fawning, slyly plotting, "roughing it" with the Emperor . . . here to watch him put an end to this affair, to make epigrams over the battles and idolize the wounded.*

"Perhaps you've never sought the right kind of hostages," the Emperor said.

He knows something, the Baron thought. Fear sat like a stone in his stomach until he could hardly bear the thought of eating. Yet, the feeling was like hunger, and he poised himself several times in his suspensors on the point of ordering food brought to him. But there was no one here to obey his summons.

"Do you have any idea who this Muad'Dib could be?" the Emperor asked.

"One of the Umma, surely," the Baron said. "A Fremen fanatic, a religious adventurer. They crop up regularly on the fringes of civilization. Your Majesty knows this."

The Emperor glanced at his Truthsayer, turned back to scowl at the Baron. "And you have no other knowledge of this Muad'Dib?"

"A madman," the Baron said. "But all Fremen are a little mad."

"Mad?"

"His people scream his name as they leap into battle. The women throw their babies at us and hurl themselves onto our knives to open a wedge for their men to attack us. They have no . . . no . . . decency!"

"As bad as that," the Emperor murmured, and his tone of derision did not escape the Baron. "Tell me, my dear Baron, have you investigated the southern polar regions of Arrakis?"

The Baron stared up at the Emperor, shocked by the change of subject. "But . . . well, you know, Your Majesty, the entire region is uninhabitable, open to wind and worm. There's not even any spice in those latitudes."

"You've had no reports from spice lighters that patches of greenery appear there?"

"There've always been such reports. Some were investigated—long ago. A few plants were seen. Many 'thopters were lost. Much too costly, Your Majesty. It's a place where men cannot survive for long."

"So," the Emperor said. He snapped his fingers and a door opened at his left behind the throne. Through the door came two Sardaukar herding a girl-child who appeared to be about four years old. She wore a black aba, the hood thrown back to reveal the attachments of a stillsuit hanging free at her throat. Her eyes were Fremen blue, staring out of a soft, round face. She appeared completely unafraid and there was a look to her stare that made the Baron feel uneasy for no reason he could explain.

Even the old Bene Gesserit Truthsayer drew back as the child passed and made a warding sign in her direction. The old witch obviously was shaken by the child's presence.

The Emperor cleared his throat to speak, but the child spoke first—a thin voice with traces of a soft-palate lisp, but clear nonetheless. "So here he is," she said. She advanced to the edge of the dais. "He doesn't appear much, does he—one frightened old fat man too weak to support his own flesh without the help of suspensors."

It was such a totally unexpected statement from the mouth of a child that the Baron stared at her, speechless in spite of his anger. *Is it a midget?* he asked himself.

"My dear Baron," the Emperor said, "become acquainted with the sister of Muad'Dib."

"The sist. . . ." The Baron shifted his attention to the Emperor. "I do not understand."

"I, too, sometimes err on the side of caution," the Emperor said. "It has been reported to me that your *uninhabited* south polar regions exhibit evidence of human activity."

"But that's impossible!" the Baron protested. "The worms . . . there's sand clear to the. . . ."

"These people seem able to avoid the worms," the Emperor said.

The child sat down on the dais beside the throne, dangled her feet over the edge, kicking them. There was such an air of sureness in the way she appraised her surroundings.

The Baron stared at the kicking feet, the way they moved the black robe, the wink of sandals beneath the fabric.

"Unfortunately," the Emperor said, "I only sent in five troop carriers with a light attack force to pick up prisoners for questioning. We barely got away with three prisoners and one carrier. Mind you, Baron, my Sardaukar were almost overwhelmed by a force composed mostly of women, children, and old men. This child here was in command of one of the attacking groups."

"You see, Your Majesty!" the Baron said. "You see how they are!"

"I allowed myself to be captured," the child said. "I did not want to face my brother and have to tell him that his son had been killed."

"Only a handful of our men got away," the Emperor said. "Got away! You hear that?"

"We'd have had them, too," the child said, "except for the flames."

"My Sardaukar used the attitudinal jets on their carrier as flame-throwers," the Emperor said. "A move of desperation and the only thing that got them away with their three prisoners. Mark that, my dear Baron: Sardaukar forced to retreat in confusion from women and children and old men!"

"We must attack in force," the Baron rasped. "We must destroy every last vestige of—"

"Silence!" the Emperor roared. He pushed himself forward on his throne. "Do not abuse my intelligence any longer. You stand there in your foolish innocence and—"

"Majesty," the old Truthsayer said.

He waved her to silence. "You say you don't know about the activity we found, nor the fighting qualities of these superb people!" The Emperor lifted himself half off his throne. "What do you take me for, Baron?"

The Baron took two backward steps, thinking: *It was Rabban. He has done this to me. Rabban has. . . .*

"And this fake dispute with Duke Leto," the Emperor purred, sinking back into his throne. "How beautifully you maneuvered it."

"Majesty," the Baron pleaded. "What are you—"

"Silence!"

The old Bene Gesserit put a hand on the Emperor's shoulder, leaned close to whisper in his ear.

The child seated on the dais stopped kicking her feet, said: "Make him afraid some more, Shaddam. I shouldn't enjoy this, but I find the pleasure impossible to suppress."

"Quiet, child," the Emperor said. He leaned forward, put a hand on her head, stared at the Baron. "Is it possible, Baron? Could you be as simpleminded as my Truthsayer suggests? Do you not recognize this child, daughter of your ally, Duke Leto?"

"My father was never his ally," the child said. "My father is dead and this old Harkonnen beast has never seen me before."

The Baron was reduced to stupefied glaring. When he found his voice it was only to rasp: "Who?"

"I am Alia, daughter of Duke Leto and the Lady Jessica, sister of Duke Paul-Muad'Dib," the child said. She pushed herself off the dais, dropped to the floor of the audience chamber. "My brother has promised to have your head atop his battle standard and I think he shall."

"Be hush, child," the Emperor said, and he sank back into his throne, hand to chin, studying the Baron.

"I do not take the Emperor's orders," Alia said. She turned, looked up at the old Reverend Mother. "She knows."

The Emperor glanced up at his Truthsayer. "What does she mean?"

"That child is an abomination!" the old woman said. "Her mother deserves a punishment greater than anything in history. Death! It cannot come too quickly for that *child* or for the one who spawned her!" The old woman pointed a finger at Alia. "Get out of my mind!"

"T-P?" the Emperor whispered. He snapped his attention back to Alia. "By the Great Mother!"

"You don't understand, Majesty," the old woman said. "Not telepathy. She's in my mind. She's like the ones before me, the ones who gave me their memories. She stands in my mind! She cannot be there, but she is!"

"What others?" the Emperor demanded. "What's this nonsense?"

The old woman straightened, lowered her pointing hand. "I've said too much, but the fact remains that this *child* who is not a child must be destroyed. Long were we warned against such a one and how to prevent such a birth, but one of our own has betrayed us."

"You babble, old woman," Alia said. "You don't know how it was, yet you rattle on like a purblind fool." Alia closed her eyes, took a deep breath, and held it.

The old Reverend Mother groaned and staggered.

Alia opened her eyes. "That is how it was," she said. "A cosmic accident . . . and you played your part in it."

The Reverend Mother held out both hands, palms pushing the air toward Alia.

"What is happening here?" the Emperor demanded. "Child, can you truly project your thoughts into the mind of another?"

"That's not how it is at all," Alia said. "Unless I'm born as you, I cannot think as you."

"Kill her," the old woman muttered, and clutched the back of the throne for support. "Kill her!" The sunken old eyes glared at Alia.

"Silence," the Emperor said, and he studied Alia. "Child, can you communicate with your brother?"

"My brother knows I'm here," Alia said.

"Can you tell him to surrender as the price of your life?"

Alia smiled up at him with clear innocence. "I shall not do that," she said.

The Baron stumbled forward to stand beside Alia. "Majesty," he pleaded, "I knew nothing of—"

"Interrupt me once more, Baron," the Emperor said, "and you will lose the powers of interruption . . . forever." He kept his attention focused on Alia, studying her through slitted lids. "You will not, eh? Can you read in my mind what I'll do if you disobey me?"

"I've already said I cannot read minds," she said, "but one doesn't need telepathy to read your intentions."

The Emperor scowled. "Child, your cause is hopeless. I have but to rally my forces and reduce this planet to—"

"It's not that simple," Alia said. She looked at the two Guildsmen. "Ask them."

"It is not wise to go against my desires," the Emperor said. "You should not deny me the least thing."

"My brother comes now," Alia said. "Even an Emperor may tremble before Muad'Dib, for he has the strength of righteousness and heaven smiles upon him."

The Emperor surged to his feet. "This play has gone far enough. I will take your brother and this planet and grind them to—"

The room rumbled and shook around them. There came a sudden cascade of sand behind the throne where the hutment was coupled to the Emperor's ship. The abrupt flicker-tightening of skin pressure told of a wide-area shield being activated.

"I told you," Alia said. "My brother comes."

The Emperor stood in front of his throne, right hand pressed to right ear, the servo-receiver there chattering its report on the situation. The Baron moved two steps behind Alia. Sardaukar were leaping to positions at the doors.

"We will fall back into space and re-form," the Emperor said. "Baron, my apologies. These madmen *are* attacking under cover of the storm. We will show them an Emperor's wrath, then." He pointed at Alia. "Give her body to the storm."

As he spoke, Alia fled backward, feigning terror. "Let the storm have what it can take!" she screamed. And she backed into the Baron's arms.

"I have her, Majesty!" the Baron shouted. "Shall I dispatch her now-eeeeeeeeeeeh!" He hurled her to the floor, clutched his left arm.

"I'm sorry, Grandfather," Alia said. "You've met the Atreides gom jabbar." She got to her feet, dropped a dark needle from her hand.

The Baron fell back. His eyes bulged as he stared at a red slash on his left palm. "You . . . you. . . ." He rolled sideways in his suspensors, a sagging mass of flesh supported inches off the floor with head lolling and mouth hanging open.

"These people are insane," the Emperor snarled. "Quick! Into the ship. We'll purge this planet of every. . . ."

Something sparkled to his left. A roll of ball lightning bounced away from the wall there, crackled as it touched the metal floor. The smell of burned insulation swept through the selamlik.

"The shield!" one of the Sardaukar officers shouted. "The outer shield is down! They. . . ."

His words were drowned in a metallic roaring as the shipwall behind the Emperor trembled and rocked.

"They've shot the nose off our ship!" someone called.

Dust boiled through the room. Under its cover, Alia leaped up, ran toward the outer door.

The Emperor whirled, motioned his people into an emergency door that swung open in the ship's side behind the throne. He flashed a hand signal to a Sardaukar officer leaping through the dust haze. "We will make our stand here!" the Emperor ordered.

Another crash shook the hutment. The double doors banged open at the far side of the chamber admitting windblown sand and the sound of shouting. A small, black-robed figure could be seen momentarily against the light—Alia darting out to find a knife and, as befitted her Fremen training, to kill Harkonnen and Sardaukar wounded. House Sardaukar charged through a greened yellow haze toward the opening, weapons ready, forming an arc there to protect the Emperor's retreat.

"Save yourself, Sire!" a Sardaukar officer shouted. "Into the ship!"

But the Emperor stood alone now on his dais pointing toward the doors. A forty-meter section of the hutment had been blasted away there and the selamlik's doors opened now onto drifting sand. A dust cloud hung low over the outside world blowing from pastel distances. Static lightning crackled from the cloud and the spark flashes of shields being shorted out by the storm's charge could be seen through the haze. The plain surged with figures in combat—Sardaukar and leaping gyrating robed men who seemed to come down out of the storm.

All this was as a frame for the target of the Emperor's pointing hand.

Out of the sand haze came an orderly mass of flashing shapes—great rising curves with crystal spokes that resolved into the gaping mouths of sandworms, a massed wall of them, each with troops of Fremen riding to the attack. They came in a hissing wedge, robes whipping in the wind as they cut through the melee on the plain.

Onward toward the Emperor's hutment they came while the House Sardaukar stood awed for the first time in their history by an onslaught their minds found difficult to accept.

But the figures leaping from the worm backs were men, and the blades flashing in that ominous yellow light were a thing the Sardaukar had been trained to face. They threw themselves into combat. And it was man to man on the plain of Arrakeen while a picked Sardaukar bodyguard pressed the Emperor back into the ship, sealed the door on him, and prepared to die at the door as part of his shield.

In the shock of comparative silence within the ship, the Emperor stared at the wide-eyed faces of his suite, seeing his oldest daughter with the flush of exertion on her cheeks, the old Truthsayer standing like a black shadow with her hood pulled about her face, finding at last the faces he sought—the two Guildsmen. They wore the Guild gray, unadorned, and it seemed to fit the calm they maintained despite the high emotions around them.

The taller of the two, though, held a hand to his left eye. As the Emperor watched, someone jostled the Guildsman's arm, the hand moved, and the eye was revealed. The man had lost one of his masking contact lenses, and the eye stared out a total blue so dark as to be almost black.

The smaller of the pair elbowed his way a step nearer the Emperor, said: "We cannot know how it will go." And the taller companion, hand restored to eye, added in a cold voice: "But this Muad'Dib cannot know, either."

The words shocked the Emperor out of his daze. He checked the scorn on his tongue by a visible effort because it did not take a Guild navigator's single-minded focus on the main chance to see the immediate future out on that plain. Were these two so dependent upon their *faculty* that they had lost the use of their eyes and their reason? he wondered.

"Reverend Mother," he said, "we must devise a plan."

She pulled the hood from her face, met his gaze with an unblinking stare. The look that passed between them carried complete understanding. They had one weapon left and both knew it: treachery.

"Summon Count Fenring from his quarters," the Reverend Mother said.

The Padishah Emperor nodded, waved for one of his aides to obey that command.

He was warrior and mystic, ogre and saint, the fox and the innocent, chivalrous, ruthless, less than a god, more than a man. There is no measuring Muad'Dib's motives by ordinary standards. In the moment of his triumph, he saw the death prepared for him, yet he accepted the treachery. Can you say he did this out of a sense of justice? Whose justice, then? Remember, we speak now of the Muad'Dib who ordered battle drums made from his enemies' skins, the Muad'Dib who denied the conventions of his ducal past with a wave of the hand, saying merely: "I am the Kwisatz Haderach. That is reason enough."

—FROM "ARRAKIS AWAKENING"
BY THE PRINCESS IRULAN

It was to the Arrakeen governor's mansion, the old Residency the Atreides had first occupied on Dune, that they escorted Paul-Muad'Dib on the evening of his victory. The building stood as Rabban had restored it, virtually untouched by the fighting although there had been looting by townspeople. Some of the furnishings in the main hall had been overturned or smashed.

Paul strode through the main entrance with Gurney Halleck and Stilgar a pace behind. Their escort fanned out into the Great Hall, straightening the place and clearing an area for Muad'Dib. One squad began investigating that no sly trap had been planted here.

"I remember the day we first came here with your father," Gurney said. He glanced around at the beams and the high, slitted windows. "I didn't like this place then and I like it less now. One of our caves would be safer."

"Spoken like a true Fremen," Stilgar said, and he marked the cold smile that his words brought to Muad'Dib's lips. "Will you reconsider, Muad'Dib?"

"This place is a symbol," Paul said. "Rabban lived here. By occupying this place I seal my victory for all to understand. Send men through the building. Touch nothing. Just be certain no Harkonnen people or toys remain."

"As you command," Stilgar said, and reluctance was heavy in his tone as he turned to obey.

Communications men hurried into the room with their equipment, began setting up near the massive fireplace. The Fremen guard that augmented the surviving Fedaykin took up stations around the room. There was muttering among them, much darting of suspicious glances. This had been too long a place of the enemy for them to accept their presence in it casually.

"Gurney, have an escort bring my mother and Chani," Paul said. "Does Chani know yet about our son?"

"The message was sent, m'Lord."

"Are the makers being taken out of the basin yet?"

"Yes, m'Lord. The storm's almost spent."

"What's the extent of the storm damage?" Paul asked.

"In the direct path—on the landing field and across the spice storage yards of the plain—extensive damage," Gurney said. "As much from battle as from the storm."

"Nothing money won't repair, I presume," Paul said.

"Except for the lives, m'Lord," Gurney said, and there was a tone of reproach in his voice as though to say: *When did an Atreides worry first about things when people were at stake?*

But Paul could only focus his attention on the inner eye and the gaps visible to him in the time-wall that still lay across his path. Through each gap the jihad raged away down the corridors of the future.

He sighed, crossed the hall, seeing a chair against the wall. The chair had once stood in the dining hall and might even have held his own father. At the moment, though, it was only an object to rest his weariness and conceal it from the men. He sat down, pulling his robes around his legs, loosening his stillsuit at the neck.

"The Emperor is still holed up in the remains of his ship," Gurney said.

"For now, contain him there," Paul said. "Have they found the Harkonnens yet?"

"They're still examining the dead."

"What reply from the ships up there?" He jerked his chin toward the ceiling.

"No reply yet, m'Lord."

Paul sighed, resting against the back of his chair. Presently, he said: "Bring me a captive Sardaukar. We must send a message to our Emperor. It's time to discuss terms."

"Yes, m'Lord."

Gurney turned away, dropped a hand signal to one of the Fedaykin who took up close-guard position beside Paul.

"Gurney," Paul whispered. "Since we've been rejoined I've yet to hear you produce the proper quotation for the event." He turned, saw Gurney swallow, saw the sudden grim hardening of the man's jaw.

"As you wish, m'Lord," Gurney said. He cleared his throat, rasped: "'And the victory that day was turned into mourning unto all the people: for the people heard say that day how the king was grieved for his son.'"

Paul closed his eyes, forcing grief out of his mind, letting it wait as he had once waited to mourn his father. Now, he gave his thoughts over to this day's accumulated discoveries—the mixed futures and the hidden *presence* of Alia within his awareness.

Of all the uses of time-vision, this was the strangest. "I have breasted the future to place my words where only you can hear them," Alia had said. "Even you cannot do that, my brother. I find it an interesting play. And . . . oh, yes—I've killed our grandfather, the demented old Baron. He had very little pain."

Silence. His time sense had seen her withdrawal.

"Muad'Dib."

Paul opened his eyes to see Stilgar's black-bearded visage above him, the dark eyes glaring with battle light.

"You've found the body of the old Baron," Paul said.

A hush of the person settled over Stilgar. "How could you know?" he whispered. "We just found the body in that great pile of metal the Emperor built."

Paul ignored the question, seeing Gurney return accompanied by two Fremen who supported a captive Sardaukar.

"Here's one of them, m'Lord," Gurney said. He signed to the guard to hold the captive five paces in front of Paul.

The Sardaukar's eyes, Paul noted, carried a glazed expression of shock. A blue bruise stretched from the bridge of his nose to the corner of his mouth. He was of the blond, chisel-featured caste, the look that seemed synonymous with rank among the Sardaukar, yet there were no insignia on his torn uniform except the gold buttons with the Imperial crest and the tattered braid of his trousers.

"I think this one's an officer, m'Lord," Gurney said.

Paul nodded, said: "I am the Duke Paul Atreides. Do you understand that, man?"

The Sardaukar stared at him unmoving.

"Speak up," Paul said, "or your Emperor may die."

The man blinked, swallowed.

"Who am I?" Paul demanded.

"You are the Duke Paul Atreides," the man husked.

He seemed too submissive to Paul, but then the Sardaukar had never been prepared for such happenings as this day. They'd never known anything but victory which, Paul realized, could be a weakness in itself. He put that thought aside for later consideration in his own training program.

"I have a message for you to carry to the Emperor," Paul said. And he couched his words in the ancient formula: "I, a Duke of a Great House, an Imperial Kinsman, give my word of bond under the Convention. If the Emperor and his people lay down their arms and come to me here I will guard their lives with my own." Paul held up his left hand with the ducal signet for the Sardaukar to see. "I swear it by this."

The man wet his lips with his tongue, glanced at Gurney.

"Yes," Paul said. "Who but an Atreides could command the allegiance of Gurney Halleck."

"I will carry the message," the Sardaukar said.

"Take him to our forward command post and send him in," Paul said.

"Yes, m'Lord." Gurney motioned for the guard to obey, led them out.

Paul turned back to Stilgar.

"Chani and your mother have arrived," Stilgar said. "Chani has asked time to be alone with her grief. The Reverend Mother sought a moment in the weirding room; I know not why."

"My mother's sick with longing for a planet she may never see," Paul said. "Where water falls from the sky and plants grow so thickly you cannot walk between them."

"Water from the sky," Stilgar whispered.

In that instant, Paul saw how Stilgar had been transformed from the Fremen naib to a *creature* of the Lisan al-Gaib, a receptacle for awe and obedience. It was a lessening of the man, and Paul felt the ghost-wind of the jihad in it.

I have seen a friend become a worshiper, he thought.

In a rush of loneliness, Paul glanced around the room, noting how proper and on-review his guards had become in his presence. He sensed the subtle, prideful competition among them—each hoping for notice from Muad'Dib.

Muad'Dib from whom all blessings flow, he thought, and it was the bitterest thought of his life. *They sense that I must take the throne,* he thought. *But they cannot know I do it to prevent the jihad.*

Stilgar cleared his throat, said: "Rabban, too, is dead."

Paul nodded.

Guards to the right suddenly snapped aside, standing at attention to open an aisle for Jessica. She wore her black aba and walked with a hint of striding across sand, but Paul noted how this house had restored to her something of what she had once been here—concubine to a ruling duke. Her presence carried some of its old assertiveness.

Jessica stopped in front of Paul, looked down at him. She saw his fatigue and how he hid it, but found no compassion for him. It was as though she had been rendered incapable of *any* emotion for her son.

Jessica had entered the Great Hall wondering why the place refused to fit itself snugly in to her memories. It remained a foreign room, as though she had never walked here, never walked here with her beloved Leto, never confronted a drunken Duncan Idaho here—never, never, never. . . .

There should be a word-tension directly opposite to adab, the demanding memory, she thought. *There should be a word for memories that deny themselves.*

"Where is Alia?" she asked.

"Out doing what any good Fremen child should be doing in such times," Paul said. "She's killing enemy wounded and marking their bodies for the water-recovery teams."

"Paul!"

"You must understand that she does this out of kindness," he said. "Isn't it odd how we misunderstand the hidden unity of kindness and cruelty?"

Jessica glared at her son, shocked by the profound change in him. *Was it his child's death did this?* she wondered. And she said: "The men tell strange stories of you, Paul. They say you've all the powers of the legend—nothing can be hidden from you, that you see where others cannot see."

"A Bene Gesserit should ask about legends?" he asked.

"I've had a hand in whatever you are," she admitted, "but you mustn't expect me to—"

"How would you like to live billions upon billions of lives?" Paul asked. "There's a fabric of legends for you! Think of all those experiences, the wisdom they'd bring. But wisdom tempers love, doesn't it? And it puts a new shape on hate. How can you tell what's ruthless unless you've plumbed the depths of both cruelty and kindness? You should fear me, Mother. I am the Kwisatz Haderach."

Jessica tried to swallow in a dry throat. Presently, she said: "Once you denied to me that you were the Kwisatz Haderach."

Paul shook his head. "I can deny nothing anymore." He looked up into her eyes. "The Emperor and his people come now. They will be announced any moment. Stand beside me. I wish a clear view of them. My future bride will be among them."

"Paul!" Jessica snapped. "Don't make the mistake your father made!"

"She's a princess," Paul said. "She's my key to the throne, and that's all she'll ever be. Mistake? You think because I'm what you made me that I cannot feel the need for revenge?"

"Even on the innocent?" she asked, and she thought: *He must not make the mistakes I made.*

"There are no innocent anymore," Paul said.

"Tell that to Chani," Jessica said, and gestured toward the passage from the rear of the Residency.

Chani entered the Great Hall there, walking between the Fremen guards as though unaware of them. Her hood and stillsuit cap were thrown back, face mask fastened aside. She walked with a fragile uncertainty as she crossed the room to stand beside Jessica.

Paul saw the marks of tears on her cheeks—*She gives water to the dead.* He felt a pang of grief strike through him, but it was as though he could only feel this thing through Chani's presence.

"He is dead, beloved," Chani said. "Our son is dead."

Holding himself under stiff control, Paul got to his feet. He reached out, touched Chani's cheek, feeling the dampness of her tears. "He cannot be replaced," Paul said, "but there will be other sons. It is Usul who promises this." Gently, he moved her aside, gestured to Stilgar.

"Muad'Dib," Stilgar said.

"They come from the ship, the Emperor and his people," Paul said. "I will stand here. Assemble the captives in an open space in the center of the room. They will be kept at a distance of ten meters from me unless I command otherwise."

"As you command, Muad'Dib."

As Stilgar turned to obey, Paul heard the awed muttering of Fremen guards: "You see? He knew! No one told him, but he knew!"

The Emperor's entourage could be heard approaching now, his Sardaukar humming one of their marching tunes to keep up their spirits. There came a murmur of voices at the entrance and Gurney Halleck passed through the guard, crossed to confer with Stilgar, then moved to Paul's side, a strange look in his eyes.

Will I lose Gurney, too? Paul wondered. *The way I lost Stilgar—losing a friend to gain a creature?*

"They have no throwing weapons," Gurney said. "I've made sure of that myself." He glanced around the room, seeing Paul's preparations. "Feyd-Rautha Harkonnen is with them. Shall I cut him out?"

"Leave him."

"There're some Guild people, too, demanding special privileges, threatening an embargo against Arrakis. I told them I'd give you their message."

"Let them threaten."

"Paul!" Jessica hissed behind him. "He's talking about the Guild!"

"I'll pull their fangs presently," Paul said.

And he thought then about the Guild—the force that had specialized for so long that it had become a parasite, unable to exist independently of the life upon which it fed. They had never dared grasp the sword . . . and now they could not grasp it. They might have taken Arrakis when they realized the error of specializing on the melange awareness-spectrum narcotic for their navigators. They *could* have done this, lived their glorious day and died. Instead, they'd existed from moment to moment, hoping the seas in which they swam might produce a new host when the old one died.

The Guild navigators, gifted with limited prescience, had made the fatal decision: they'd chosen always the clear, safe course that leads ever downward into stagnation.

Let them look closely at their new host, Paul thought.

"There's also a Bene Gesserit Reverend Mother who says she's a friend of your mother," Gurney said.

"My mother has no Bene Gesserit friends."

Again, Gurney glanced around the Great Hall, then bent close to Paul's ear. "Thufir Hawat's with 'em, m'Lord. I had no chance to see him alone, but he used our old hand signs to say he's been working with the Harkonnens, thought you were dead. Says he's to be left among 'em."

"You left Thufir among those—"

"He wanted it . . . and I thought it best. If . . . there's something wrong, he's where we can control him. If not—we've an ear on the other side."

Paul thought then of prescient glimpses into the possibilities of this moment—and one time-line where Thufir carried a poisoned needle which the Emperor commanded he use against "this upstart Duke."

The entrance guards stepped aside, formed a short corridor of lances. There came a murmurous swish of garments, feet rasping the sand that had drifted into the Residency.

The Padishah Emperor Shaddam IV led his people into the hall. His Burseg helmet had been lost and the red hair stood out in disarray. His uniform's left sleeve had been ripped along the inner seam. He was belt-less and without weapons, but his presence moved with him like a force-shield bubble that kept his immediate area open.

A Fremen lance dropped across his path, stopped him where Paul had ordered. The others bunched up behind, a montage of color, of shuffling and of staring faces.

Paul swept his gaze across the group, saw women who hid signs of weeping, saw the lackeys who had come to enjoy grandstand seats at a

Sardaukar victory and now stood choked to silence by defeat. Paul saw the bird-bright eyes of the Reverend Mother Gaius Helen Mohiam glaring beneath her black hood, and beside her the narrow furtiveness of Feyd-Rautha Harkonnen.

There's a face time betrayed to me, Paul thought.

He looked beyond Feyd-Rautha then, attracted by a movement, seeing there a narrow, weaselish face he'd never before encountered—not in time or out of it. It was a face he felt he should know and the feeling carried with it a marker of fear.

Why should I fear that man? he wondered.

He leaned toward his mother, whispered: "That man to the left of the Reverend Mother, the evil-looking one—who is that?"

Jessica looked, recognizing the face from her Duke's dossiers. "Count Fenring," she said. "The one who was here immediately before us. A genetic-eunuch . . . and a killer."

The Emperor's errand boy, Paul thought. And the thought was a shock crashing across his consciousness because he had seen the Emperor in uncounted associations spread through the possible futures—but never once had Count Fenring appeared within those prescient visions.

It occurred to Paul then that he had seen his own dead body along countless reaches of the time web, but never once had he seen his moment of death.

Have I been denied a glimpse of this man because he is the one who kills me? Paul wondered.

The thought sent a pang of foreboding through him. He forced his attention away from Fenring, looked now at the remnants of Sardaukar men and officers, the bitterness on their faces and the desperation. Here and there among them, faces caught Paul's attention briefly: Sardaukar officers measuring the preparations within this room, planning and scheming yet for a way to turn defeat into victory.

Paul's attention came at last to a tall blonde woman, green-eyed, a face of patrician beauty, classic in its hauteur, untouched by tears, completely undefeated. Without being told it, Paul knew her—Princess Royal, Bene Gesserit-trained, a face that time-vision had shown him in many aspects: Irulan.

There's my key, he thought.

Then he saw movement in the clustered people, a face and figure emerged—Thufir Hawat, the seamed old features with darkly stained lips, the hunched shoulders, the look of fragile age about him.

"There's Thufir Hawat," Paul said. "Let him stand free, Gurney."

"M'Lord," Gurney said.

"Let him stand free," Paul repeated.

Gurney nodded.

Hawat shambled forward as a Fremen lance was lifted and replaced behind him. The rheumy eyes peered at Paul, measuring, seeking.

Paul stepped forward one pace, sensed the tense, waiting movement of the Emperor and his people.

Hawat's gaze stabbed past Paul, and the old man said: "Lady Jessica, I but learned this day how I've wronged you in my thoughts. You needn't forgive."

Paul waited, but his mother remained silent.

"Thufir, old friend," Paul said, "as you can see, my back is toward no door."

"The universe is full of doors," Hawat said.

"Am I my father's son?" Paul asked.

"More like your grandfather's," Hawat rasped. "You've his manner and the look of him in your eyes."

"Yet I'm my father's son," Paul said. "For I say to you, Thufir, that in payment for your years of service to my family you may now ask anything you wish of me. Anything at all. Do you need my life now, Thufir? It is yours." Paul stepped forward a pace, hands at his side, seeing the look of awareness grow in Hawat's eyes.

He realizes that I know of the treachery, Paul thought.

Pitching his voice to carry in a half-whisper for Hawat's ears alone, Paul said: "I mean this, Thufir. If you're to strike me, do it now."

"I but wanted to stand before you once more, my Duke," Hawat said. And Paul became aware for the first time of the effort the old man exerted to keep from falling. Paul reached out, supported Hawat by the shoulders, feeling the muscle tremors beneath his hands.

"Is there pain, old friend?" Paul asked.

"There is pain, my Duke," Hawat agreed, "but the pleasure is greater." He half turned in Paul's arms, extended his left hand, palm up, toward the Emperor, exposing the tiny needle cupped against the fingers. "See, Majesty?" he called. "See your traitor's needle? Did you think that I who've given my life to service of the Atreides would give them less now?"

Paul staggered as the old man sagged in his arms, felt the death there, the utter flaccidity. Gently, Paul lowered Hawat to the floor, straightened and signed for guardsmen to carry the body away.

Silence held the hall while his command was obeyed.

A look of deadly waiting held the Emperor's face now. Eyes that had never admitted fear admitted it at last.

"Majesty," Paul said, and noted the jerk of surprised attention in the tall Princess Royal. The words had been uttered with the Bene Gesserit controlled atonals, carrying in it every shade of contempt and scorn that Paul could put there.

Bene Gesserit-trained indeed, Paul thought.

The Emperor cleared his throat, said: "Perhaps my respected kinsman believes he has things all his own way now. Nothing could be more remote from fact. You have violated the Convention, used atomics against—"

"I used atomics against a natural feature of the desert," Paul said. "It was in my way and I was in a hurry to get to you, Majesty, to ask your explanation for some of your strange activities."

"There's a massed armada of the Great Houses in space over Arrakis right now," the Emperor said. "I've but to say the word and they'll—"

"Oh, yes," Paul said, "I almost forgot about them." He searched through the Emperor's suite until he saw the faces of the two Guildsmen, spoke aside to Gurney. "Are those the Guild agents, Gurney, the two fat ones dressed in gray over there?"

"Yes, m'Lord."

"You two," Paul said, pointing. "Get out of there immediately and dispatch messages that will get that fleet on its way home. After this, you'll ask my permission before—"

"The Guild doesn't take your orders!" the taller of the two barked. He and his companion pushed through to the barrier lances, which were raised at a nod from Paul. The two men stepped out and the taller leveled an arm at Paul, said: "You may very well be under embargo for your—"

"If I hear any more nonsense from either of you," Paul said, "I'll give the order that'll destroy all spice production on Arrakis . . . forever."

"Are you mad?" the tall Guildsman demanded. He fell back half a step.

"You grant that I have the power to do this thing, then?" Paul asked.

The Guildsman seemed to stare into space for a moment, then: "Yes, you could do it, but you must not."

"Ah-h-h," Paul said and nodded to himself. "Guild navigators, both of you, eh?"

"Yes!"

The shorter of the pair said: "You would blind yourself, too, and condemn us all to slow death. Have you any idea what it means to be deprived of the spice liquor once you're addicted?"

"The eye that looks ahead to the safe course is closed forever," Paul said. "The Guild is crippled. Humans become little isolated clusters on their isolated planets. You know, I might do this thing out of pure spite . . . or out of ennui."

"Let us talk this over privately," the taller Guildsman said. "I'm sure we can come to some compromise that is—"

"Send the message to your people over Arrakis," Paul said. "I grow tired of this argument. If that fleet over us doesn't leave soon there'll be no need for us to talk." He nodded toward his communications men at the side of the hall. "You may use our equipment."

"First we must discuss this," the tall Guildsman said. "We cannot just—"

"Do it!" Paul barked. "The power to destroy a thing is the absolute control over it. You've agreed I have that power. We are not here to discuss or to negotiate or to compromise. You will obey my orders or suffer the *immediate* consequences!"

"He means it," the shorter Guildsman said. And Paul saw the fear grip them.

Slowly the two crossed to the Fremen communications equipment.

"Will they obey?" Gurney asked.

"They have a narrow vision of time," Paul said. "They can see ahead to a blank wall marking the consequences of disobedience. Every Guild navigator on every ship over us can look ahead to that same wall. They'll obey."

Paul turned back to look at the Emperor, said: "When they permitted you to mount your father's throne, it was only on the assurance that you'd keep the spice flowing. You've failed them, Majesty. Do you know the consequences?"

"Nobody *permitted* me to—"

"Stop playing the fool," Paul barked. "The Guild is like a village beside a river. They need the water, but can only dip out what they require. They cannot dam the river and control it, because that focuses attention on what they take, it brings down eventual destruction. The spice flow, that's their river, and I have built a dam. But my dam is such that you cannot destroy it without destroying the river."

The Emperor brushed a hand through his red hair, glanced at the backs of the two Guildsmen.

"Even your Bene Gesserit Truthsayer is trembling," Paul said. "There are other poisons the Reverend Mothers can use for their tricks, but once they've used the spice liquor, the others no longer work."

The old woman pulled her shapeless black robes around her, pressed forward out of the crowd to stand at the barrier lances.

"Reverend Mother Gaius Helen Mohiam," Paul said. "It has been a long time since Caladan, hasn't it?"

She looked past him at his mother, said: "Well, Jessica, I see that your son is indeed the one. For that you can be forgiven even the abomination of your daughter."

Paul stilled a cold, piercing anger, said: "You've never had the right or cause to forgive my mother anything!"

The old woman locked eyes with him.

"Try your tricks on me, old witch," Paul said. "Where's your gom jabbar? Try looking into that place where you dare not look! You'll find me there staring out at you!"

The old woman dropped her gaze.

"Have you nothing to say?" Paul demanded.

"I welcomed you to the ranks of humans," she muttered. "Don't besmirch that."

Paul raised his voice: "Observe her, comrades! This is a Bene Gesserit Reverend Mother, patient in a patient cause. She could wait with her sisters—ninety generations for the proper combination of genes and environment to produce the one person their schemes required. Observe her! She knows now that the ninety generations have produced that person. Here I stand . . . But . . . I . . . will . . . never . . . do . . . her . . . bidding!"

"Jessica!" the old woman screamed. "Silence him!"

"Silence him yourself," Jessica said.

Paul glared at the old woman. "For your part in all this I could gladly have you strangled," he said. "You couldn't prevent it!" he snapped as she stiffened in rage. "But I think it better punishment that you live out your years never able to touch me or bend me to a single thing your scheming desires."

"Jessica, what have you done?" the old woman demanded.

"I'll give you only one thing," Paul said. "You saw part of what the race needs, but how poorly you saw it. You think to control human breeding and intermix a select few according to your master plan! How little you understand of what—"

"You mustn't speak of these things!" the old woman hissed.

"Silence!" Paul roared. The word seemed to take substance as it twisted through the air between them under Paul's control.

The old woman reeled back into the arms of those behind her, face blank with shock at the power with which he had seized her psyche. "Jessica," she whispered. "Jessica."

"I remember your gom jabbar," Paul said. "You remember mine. I can kill you with a word."

The Fremen around the hall glanced knowingly at each other. Did the legend not say: "And his word shall carry death eternal to those who stand against righteousness."

Paul turned his attention to the tall Princess Royal standing beside her Emperor father. Keeping his eyes focused on her, he said: "Majesty, we both know the way out of our difficulty."

The Emperor glanced at his daughter, back to Paul. "You dare? You! An adventurer without family, a nobody from—"

"You've already admitted who I am," Paul said. "Royal kinsman, you said. Let's stop this nonsense."

"I am your ruler," the Emperor said.

Paul glanced at the Guildsmen standing now at the communications equipment and facing him. One of them nodded.

"I could force it," Paul said.

"You will not dare!" the Emperor grated.

Paul merely stared at him.

The Princess Royal put a hand on her father's arm. "Father," she said, and her voice was silky soft, soothing.

"Don't try your tricks on me," the Emperor said. He looked at her. "You don't need to do this, Daughter. We've other resources that—"

"But here's a man fit to be your son," she said.

The old Reverend Mother, her composure regained, forced her way to the Emperor's side, leaned close to his ear and whispered.

"She pleads your case," Jessica said.

Paul continued to look at the golden-haired Princess. Aside to his mother, he said: "That's Irulan, the oldest, isn't it?"

"Yes."

Chani moved up on Paul's other side, said: "Do you wish me to leave, Muad'Dib?"

He glanced at her. "Leave? You'll never again leave my side."

"There's nothing binding between us," Chani said.

Paul looked down at her for a silent moment, then: "Speak only truth with me, my Sihaya." As she started to reply, he silenced her with a finger to her lips. "That which binds us cannot be loosed," he said. "Now, watch these matters closely for I wish to see this room later through your wisdom."

The Emperor and his Truthsayer were carrying on a heated, low-voiced argument.

Paul spoke to his mother: "She reminds him that it's part of their agreement to place a Bene Gesserit on the throne, and Irulan is the one they've groomed for it."

"Was that their plan?" Jessica said.

"Isn't it obvious?" Paul asked.

"I see the signs!" Jessica snapped. "My question was meant to remind you that you should not try to teach me those matters in which I instructed you."

Paul glanced at her, caught a cold smile on her lips.

Gurney Halleck leaned between them, said: "I remind you, m'Lord, that there's a Harkonnen in that bunch." He nodded toward the dark-haired Feyd-Rautha pressed against a barrier lance on the left. "The one with the squinting eyes there on the left. As evil a face as I ever saw. You promised me once that—"

"Thank you, Gurney," Paul said.

"It's the na-Baron . . . Baron now that the old man's dead," Gurney said. "He'll do for what I've in—"

"Can you take him, Gurney?"

"M'Lord jests!"

"That argument between the Emperor and his witch has gone on long enough, don't you think, Mother?"

She nodded. "Indeed."

Paul raised his voice, called out to the Emperor: "Majesty, is there a Harkonnen among you?"

Royal disdain revealed itself in the way the Emperor turned to look at Paul. "I believe my entourage has been placed under the protection of your ducal word," he said.

"My question was for information only," Paul said. "I wish to know if a Harkonnen is officially a part of your entourage or if a Harkonnen is merely hiding behind a technicality out of cowardice."

The Emperor's smile was calculating. "Anyone accepted into the Imperial company is a member of my entourage."

"You have the word of a Duke," Paul said, "but Muad'Dib is another matter. *He* may not recognize your definition of what constitutes an entourage. My friend Gurney Halleck wishes to kill a Harkonnen. If he—"

"Kanly!" Feyd-Rautha shouted. He pressed against the barrier lance. "Your father named this vendetta, Atreides. You call me coward while you hide among your women and offer to send a lackey against me!"

The old Truthsayer whispered something fiercely into the Emperor's ear, but he pushed her aside, said: "Kanly, is it? There are strict rules for kanly."

"Paul, put a stop to this," Jessica said.

"M'Lord," Gurney said, "you promised me my day against the Harkonnens."

"You've had your day against them," Paul said and he felt a harlequin abandon take over his emotions. He slipped his robe and hood from his shoulders, handed them to his mother with his belt and crysknife, began unstrapping his stillsuit. He sensed now that the universe focused on this moment.

"There's no need for this," Jessica said. "There are easier ways, Paul."

Paul stepped out of his stillsuit, slipped the crysknife from its sheath in his mother's hand. "I know," he said. "Poison, an assassin, all the old familiar ways."

"You promised me a Harkonnen!" Gurney hissed, and Paul marked the rage in the man's face, the way the inkvine scar stood out dark and ridged. "You owe it to me, m'Lord!"

"Have you suffered more from them than I?" Paul asked.

"My sister," Gurney rasped. "My years in the slave pits—"

"My father," Paul said. "My good friends and companions, Thufir Hawat and Duncan Idaho, my years as a fugitive without rank or succor . . . and one more thing: it is now kanly and you know as well as I the rules that must prevail."

Halleck's shoulders sagged. "M'Lord, if that swine . . . he's no more than a beast you'd spurn with your foot and discard the shoe because it'd been contaminated. Call in an executioner, if you must, or let me do it, but don't offer yourself to—"

"Muad'Dib need not do this thing," Chani said.

He glanced at her, saw the fear for him in her eyes. "But the Duke Paul must," he said.

"This is a Harkonnen animal!" Gurney rasped.

Paul hesitated on the point of revealing his own Harkonnen ancestry, stopped at a sharp look from his mother, said merely: "But this being has human shape, Gurney, and deserves human doubt."

Gurney said: "If he so much as—"

"Please stand aside," Paul said. He hefted the crysknife, pushed Gurney gently aside.

"Gurney!" Jessica said. She touched Gurney's arm. "He's like his grandfather in this mood. Don't distract him. It's the only thing you can do for him now." And she thought: *Great Mother! What irony.*

The Emperor was studying Feyd-Rautha, seeing the heavy shoulders, the thick muscles. He turned to look at Paul—a stringy whipcord of a youth, not as desiccated as the Arrakeen natives, but with ribs there to count, and sunken in the flanks so that the ripple and gather of muscles could be followed under the skin.

Jessica leaned close to Paul, pitched her voice for his ears alone: "One thing, Son. Sometimes a dangerous person is prepared by the Bene Gesserit, a word implanted into the deepest recesses by the old pleasure-pain methods. The word-sound most frequently used is Uroshnor. If this one's been prepared, as I strongly suspect, that word uttered in his ear will render his muscles flaccid and—"

"I want no special advantage for this one," Paul said. "Step back out of my way."

Gurney spoke to her: "Why is he doing this? Does he think to get himself killed and achieve martyrdom? This Fremen religious prattle, is that what clouds his reason?"

Jessica hid her face in her hands, realizing that she did not know fully why Paul took this course. She could feel death in the room and knew that the changed Paul was capable of such a thing as Gurney suggested. Every talent within her focused on the need to protect her son, but there was nothing she could do.

"Is it this religious prattle?" Gurney insisted.

"Be silent," Jessica whispered. "And pray."

The Emperor's face was touched by an abrupt smile. "If Feyd-Rautha Harkonnen . . . of my entourage . . . so wishes," he said, "I relieve him of all restraint and give him freedom to choose his own course in this." The Emperor waved a hand toward Paul's Fedaykin guards. "One of your rabble has my belt and short blade. If Feyd-Rautha wishes it, he may meet you with my blade in his hand."

"I wish it," Feyd-Rautha said, and Paul saw the elation on the man's face.

He's overconfident, Paul thought. *There's a natural advantage I can accept.*

"Get the Emperor's blade," Paul said, and watched as his command was obeyed. "Put it on the floor there." He indicated a place with his foot. "Clear the Imperial rabble back against the wall and let the Harkonnen stand clear."

A flurry of robes, scraping of feet, low-voiced commands and protests accompanied obedience to Paul's command. The Guildsmen remained standing near the communications equipment. They frowned at Paul in obvious indecision.

They're accustomed to seeing the future, Paul thought. *In this place and time they're blind . . . even as I am.* And he sampled the time-winds, sensing the turmoil, the storm nexus that now focused on this moment place. Even the faint gaps were closed now. Here was the unborn jihad, he knew. Here was the race consciousness that he had known once as his own terrible purpose. Here was reason enough for a Kwisatz Haderach or a Lisan al-Gaib or even the halting schemes of the Bene Gesserit. The race of humans had felt its own dormancy, sensed itself grown stale and knew now only the need to experience turmoil in which the genes would mingle and the strong new mixtures survive. All humans were alive as an unconscious single organism in this moment, experiencing a kind of sexual heat that could override any barrier.

And Paul saw how futile were any efforts of his to change any smallest bit of this. He had thought to oppose the jihad within himself, but the jihad would be. His legions would rage out from Arrakis even without him. They needed only the legend he already had become. He had shown them the way, given them mastery even over the Guild which must have the spice to exist.

A sense of failure pervaded him, and he saw through it that Feyd-Rautha Harkonnen had slipped out of the torn uniform, stripped down to a fighting girdle with a mail core.

This is the climax, Paul thought. *From here, the future will open, the clouds part onto a kind of glory. And if I die here, they'll say I sacrificed myself that my spirit might lead them. And if I live, they'll say nothing can oppose Muad'Dib.*

"Is the Atreides ready?" Feyd-Rautha called, using the words of the ancient kanly ritual.

Paul chose to answer him in the Fremen way: "May thy knife chip and shatter!" He pointed to the Emperor's blade on the floor, indicating that Feyd-Rautha should advance and take it.

Keeping his attention on Paul, Feyd-Rautha picked up the knife, balancing it a moment in his hand to get the feel of it. Excitement kindled in him. This was a fight he had dreamed about—man against man, skill against skill with no shields intervening. He could see a way to power opening before him because the Emperor surely would reward whoever killed this troublesome Duke. The reward might even be that haughty daughter and a share of the throne. And this yokel Duke, this back-world adventurer could not possibly be a match for a Harkonnen trained in every device and every treachery by a thousand arena combats. And the yokel had no way of knowing he faced more weapons than a knife here.

Let us see if you're proof against poison! Feyd-Rautha thought. He saluted Paul with the Emperor's blade, said: "Meet your death, fool."

"Shall we fight, cousin?" Paul asked. And he cat-footed forward, eyes on the waiting blade, his body crouched low with his own milk-white crysknife pointing out as though an extension of his arm.

They circled each other, bare feet grating on the floor, watching with eyes intent for the slightest opening.

"How beautifully you dance," Feyd-Rautha said.

He's a talker, Paul thought. *There's another weakness. He grows uneasy in the face of silence.*

"Have you been shriven?" Feyd-Rautha asked.

Still, Paul circled in silence.

And the old Reverend Mother, watching the fight from the press of the Emperor's suite, felt herself trembling. The Atreides youth had called the Harkonnen cousin. It could only mean he knew the ancestry they shared, easy to understand because he was the Kwisatz Haderach. But the words forced her to focus on the only thing that mattered to her here.

This could be a major catastrophe for the Bene Gesserit breeding scheme.

She had seen something of what Paul had seen here, that Feyd-Rautha might kill but not be victorious. Another thought, though, almost overwhelmed her. Two end products of this long and costly program faced each other in a fight to the death that might easily claim both of them. If both died here that would leave only Feyd-Rautha's bastard daughter, still a baby, an unknown, an unmeasured factor, and Alia, the abomination.

"Perhaps you have only pagan rites here," Feyd-Rautha said. "Would you like the Emperor's Truthsayer to prepare your spirit for its journey?"

Paul smiled, circling to the right, alert, his black thoughts suppressed by the needs of the moment.

Feyd-Rautha leaped, feinting with right hand, but with the knife shifted in a blur to his left hand.

Paul dodged easily, noting the shield-conditioned hesitation in Feyd-Rautha's thrust. Still, it was not as great a shield conditioning as some Paul had seen, and he sensed that Feyd-Rautha had fought before against unshielded foes.

"Does an Atreides run or stand and fight?" Feyd-Rautha asked.

Paul resumed his silent circling. Idaho's words came back to him, the words of training from the long-ago practice floor on Caladan: *Use the first moments in study. You may miss many an opportunity for quick victory this way, but the moments of study are insurance of success. Take your time and be sure.*

"Perhaps you think this dance prolongs your life a few moments," Feyd-Rautha said. "Well and good." He stopped the circling, straightened.

Paul had seen enough for a first approximation. Feyd-Rautha led to the left side, presenting the right hip as though the mailed fighting girdle could protect his entire side. It was the action of a man trained to the shield and with a knife in both hands.

Or . . . And Paul hesitated. . . . the girdle was more than it *seemed.*

The Harkonnen appeared too confident against a man who'd this day led the forces of victory against Sardaukar legions.

Feyd-Rautha noted the hesitation, said: "Why prolong the inevitable? You but keep me from exercising my rights over this ball of dirt."

If it's a flip-dart, Paul thought, *it's a cunning one. The girdle shows no signs of tampering.*

"Why don't you speak?" Feyd-Rautha demanded.

Paul resumed his probing circle, allowing himself a cold smile at the tone of unease in Feyd-Rautha's voice, evidence that the pressure of silence was building.

"You smile, eh?" Feyd-Rautha asked. And he leaped in midsentence.

Expecting the slight hesitation, Paul almost failed to evade the downflash of blade, felt its tip scratch his left arm. He silenced the sudden pain there, his mind flooded with realization that the earlier hesitation had been a trick—an overfeint. Here was more of an opponent than he had expected. There would be tricks within tricks within tricks.

"Your own Thufir Hawat taught me some of my skills," Feyd-Rautha said. "He gave me first blood. Too bad the old fool didn't live to see it."

And Paul recalled that Idaho had once said, *Expect only what happens in the fight. That way you'll never be surprised.*

Again the two circled each other, crouched, cautious.

Paul saw the return of elation to his opponent, wondered at it. Did a scratch signify that much to the man? Unless there were poison on the blade! But how could there be? His own men had handled the weapon, snooped it before passing it. They were too well trained to miss an obvious thing like that.

"That woman you were talking to over there," Feyd-Rautha said. "The little one. Is she something special to you? A pet perhaps? Will she deserve my special attentions?"

Paul remained silent, probing with his inner senses, examining the blood from the wound, finding a trace of soporific from the Emperor's blade. He realigned his own metabolism to match this threat and change the molecules of the soporific, but he felt a thrill of doubt. They'd been prepared with soporific on a blade. A soporific. Nothing to alert a poison snooper, but strong enough to slow the muscles it touched. His enemies had their own plans within plans, their own stacked treacheries.

Again Feyd-Rautha leaped, stabbing.

Paul, the smile frozen on his face, feinted with slowness as though inhibited by the drug and at the last instant dodged to meet the down-flashing arm on the crysknife's point.

Feyd-Rautha ducked sideways and was out and away, his blade shifted to his left hand, and the measure of him that only a slight paleness of jaw betrayed the acid pain where Paul had cut him.

Let him know his own moment of doubt, Paul thought. *Let him suspect poison.*

"Treachery!" Feyd-Rautha shouted. "He's poisoned me! I do feel poison in my arm!"

Paul dropped his cloak of silence, said: "Only a little acid to counter the soporific on the Emperor's blade."

Feyd-Rautha matched Paul's cold smile, lifted blade in left hand for a mock salute. His eyes glared rage behind the knife.

Paul shifted his crysknife to his left hand, matching his opponent. Again, they circled, probing.

Feyd-Rautha began closing the space between them, edging in, knife held high, anger showing itself in squint of eye and set of jaw. He feinted right and under, and they were pressed against each other, knife hands gripped, straining.

Paul, cautious of Feyd-Rautha's right hip where he suspected a poison flip-dart, forced the turn to the right. He almost failed to see the needle point flick out beneath the belt line. A shift and a giving in Feyd-Rautha's motion warned him. The tiny point missed Paul's flesh by the barest fraction.

On the left hip!

Treachery within treachery within treachery, Paul reminded himself. Using Bene Gesserit-trained muscles, he sagged to catch a reflex in Feyd-Rautha, but the necessity of avoiding the tiny point jutting from his opponent's hip threw Paul off just enough that he missed his footing and found himself thrown hard to the floor, Feyd-Rautha on top.

"You see it there on my hip?" Feyd-Rautha whispered. "Your death, fool." And he began twisting himself around, forcing the poisoned needle closer and closer. "It'll stop your muscles and my knife will finish you. There'll be never a trace left to detect!"

Paul strained, hearing the silent screams in his mind, his cell-stamped ancestors demanding that he use the secret word to slow Feyd-Rautha, to save himself.

"I will not say it!" Paul gasped.

Feyd-Rautha gaped at him, caught in the merest fraction of hesitation. It was enough for Paul to find the weakness of balance in one of his opponent's leg muscles, and their positions were reversed. Feyd-Rautha lay partly underneath with right hip high, unable to turn because of the tiny needle point caught against the floor beneath him.

Paul twisted his left hand free, aided by the lubrication of blood from his arm, thrust once hard up underneath Feyd-Rautha's jaw. The point slid home into the brain. Feyd-Rautha jerked and sagged back, still held partly on his side by the needle imbedded in the floor.

Breathing deeply to restore his calm, Paul pushed himself away and got to his feet. He stood over the body, knife in hand, raised his eyes with deliberate slowness to look across the room at the Emperor.

"Majesty," Paul said, "your force is reduced by one more. Shall we now shed sham and pretense? Shall we now discuss what must be? Your daughter wed to me and the way opened for an Atreides to sit on the throne."

The Emperor turned, looked at Count Fenring. The Count met his stare—gray eyes against green. The thought lay there clearly between them, their association so long that understanding could be achieved with a glance.

Kill this upstart for me, the Emperor was saying. *The Atreides is young and resourceful, yes—but he is also tired from long effort and he'd be no match for you, anyway. Call him out now . . . you know the way of it. Kill him.*

Slowly, Fenring moved his head, a prolonged turning until he faced Paul.

"Do it!" the Emperor hissed.

The Count focused on Paul, seeing with eyes his Lady Margot had trained in the Bene Gesserit Way, aware of the mystery and hidden grandeur about this Atreides youth.

I could kill him, Fenring thought—and he knew this for a truth.

Something in his own secretive depths stayed the Count then, and he glimpsed briefly, inadequately, the advantage he held over Paul—a way of hiding from the youth, a furtiveness of person and motives that no eye could penetrate.

Paul, aware of some of this from the way the time nexus boiled, understood at last why he had never seen Fenring along the webs of prescience. Fenring was one of the might-have-beens, an almost-Kwisatz Haderach, crippled by a flaw in the genetic pattern—a eunuch, his talent concentrated into furtiveness and inner seclusion. A deep compassion for the Count flowed through Paul, the first sense of brotherhood he'd ever experienced.

Fenring, reading Paul's emotion, said, "Majesty, I must refuse."

Rage overcame Shaddam IV. He took two short steps through the entourage, cuffed Fenring viciously across the jaw.

A dark flush spread up and over the Count's face. He looked directly at the Emperor, spoke with deliberate lack of emphasis: "We have been friends, Majesty. What I do now is out of friendship. I shall forget that you struck me."

Paul cleared his throat, said: "We were speaking of the throne, Majesty."

The Emperor whirled, glared at Paul. "I sit on the throne!" he barked.

"You shall have a throne on Salusa Secundus," Paul said.

"I put down my arms and came here on your word of bond!" the Emperor shouted. "You dare threaten—"

"Your person is safe in my presence," Paul said. "An Atreides promised it. Muad'Dib, however, sentences you to your prison planet. But have no fear, Majesty. I will ease the harshness of the place with all the powers at my disposal. It shall become a garden world, full of gentle things."

As the hidden import of Paul's words grew in the Emperor's mind, he glared across the room at Paul. "Now we see true motives," he sneered.

"Indeed," Paul said.

"And what of Arrakis?" the Emperor asked. "Another garden world full of gentle things?"

"The Fremen have the word of Muad'Dib," Paul said. "There will be flowing water here open to the sky and green oases rich with good things. But we have the spice to think of, too. Thus, there will always be desert on Arrakis . . . and fierce winds, and trials to toughen a man. We Fremen have a saying: 'God created Arrakis to train the faithful.' One cannot go against the word of God."

The old Truthsayer, the Reverend Mother Gaius Helen Mohiam, had her own view of the hidden meaning in Paul's words now. She glimpsed the jihad and said: "You cannot loose these people upon the universe!"

"You will think back to the gentle ways of the Sardaukar!" Paul snapped.

"You cannot," she whispered.

"You're a Truthsayer," Paul said. "Review your words." He glanced at the Princess Royal, back to the Emperor. "Best be done quickly, Majesty."

The Emperor turned a stricken look upon his daughter. She touched his arm, spoke soothingly: "For this I was trained, Father."

He took a deep breath.

"You cannot stay this thing," the old Truthsayer muttered.

The Emperor straightened, standing stiffly with a look of remembered dignity. "Who will negotiate for you, kinsman?" he asked.

Paul turned, saw his mother, her eyes heavy-lidded, standing with Chani in a squad of Fedaykin guards. He crossed to them, stood looking down at Chani.

"I know the reasons," Chani whispered. "If it must be . . . Usul."

Paul, hearing the secret tears in her voice, touched her cheek. "My Sihaya need fear nothing, ever," he whispered. He dropped his arm, faced his mother. "You will negotiate for me, Mother, with Chani by your side. She has wisdom and sharp eyes. And it is wisely said that no one bargains tougher than a Fremen. She will be looking through the eyes of her love for me and with the thought of her sons to be, what they will need. Listen to her."

Jessica sensed the harsh calculation in her son, put down a shudder. "What are your instructions?" she asked.

"The Emperor's entire CHOAM Company holdings as dowry," he said.

"Entire?" She was shocked almost speechless.

"He is to be stripped. I'll want an earldom and CHOAM directorship for Gurney Halleck, and him in the fief of Caladan. There will be titles and attendant power for every surviving Atreides man, not excepting the lowliest trooper."

"What of the Fremen?" Jessica asked.

"The Fremen are mine," Paul said. "What they receive shall be dispensed by Muad'Dib. It'll begin with Stilgar as Governor on Arrakis, but that can wait."

"And for me?" Jessica asked.

"Is there something you wish?"

"Perhaps Caladan," she said, looking at Gurney. "I'm not certain. I've become too much the Fremen . . . and the Reverend Mother. I need a time of peace and stillness in which to think."

"*That* you shall have," Paul said, "and anything else that Gurney or I can give you."

Jessica nodded, feeling suddenly old and tired. She looked at Chani. "And for the royal concubine?"

"No title for me," Chani whispered. "Nothing. I beg of you."

Paul stared down into her eyes, remembering her suddenly as she had stood once with little Leto in her arms, their child now dead in this violence. "I swear to you now," he whispered, "that you'll need no title. That woman over there will be my wife and you but a concubine because this is a political thing and we must weld peace out of this moment, enlist the Great Houses of the Landsraad. We must obey the forms. Yet that princess shall have no more of me than my name. No child of mine nor touch nor softness of glance, nor instant of desire."

"So you say now," Chani said. She glanced across the room at the tall princess.

"Do you know so little of my son?" Jessica whispered. "See that princess standing there, so haughty and confident. They say she has pretensions of a literary nature. Let us hope she finds solace in such things; she'll have little else." A bitter laugh escaped Jessica. "Think on it, Chani: that princess will have the name, yet she'll live as less than a concubine—never to know a moment of tenderness from the man to whom she's bound. While we, Chani, we who carry the name of concubine—history will call us wives."

APPENDIXES

APPENDIX I

THE ECOLOGY OF DUNE

Beyond a critical point within a finite space, freedom diminishes as numbers increase. This is as true of humans in the finite space of a planetary ecosystem as it is of gas molecules in a sealed flask. The human question is not how many can possibly survive within the system, but what kind of existence is possible for those who do survive.

—PARDOT KYNES,
FIRST PLANETOLOGIST OF ARRAKIS

The effect of Arrakis on the mind of the newcomer usually is that of overpowering barren land. The stranger might think nothing could live or grow in the open here, that this was the true wasteland that had never been fertile and never would be.

To Pardot Kynes, the planet was merely an expression of energy, a machine being driven by its sun. What it needed was reshaping to fit it to man's needs. His mind went directly to the free-moving human population, the Fremen. What a challenge! What a tool they could be! Fremen: an ecological and geological force of almost unlimited potential.

A direct and simple man in many ways, Pardot Kynes. One must evade Harkonnen restrictions? Excellent. Then one marries a Fremen woman. When she gives you a Fremen son, you begin with him, with Liet-Kynes, and the other children, teaching them ecological literacy, creating a new language with symbols that arm the mind to manipulate an entire landscape, its climate, seasonal limits, and finally to break through all ideas of force into the dazzling awareness of *order*.

"There's an internally recognized beauty of motion and balance on any man-healthy planet," Kynes said. "You see in this beauty a dynamic stabilizing effect essential to all life. Its aim is simple: to maintain and produce coordinated patterns of greater and greater diversity. Life improves the closed system's capacity to sustain life. Life—all life—is in the service of life. Necessary nutrients are made available to life *by* life in greater and greater richness as the diversity of life increases. The entire landscape comes alive, filled with relationships and relationships within relationships."

This was Pardot Kynes lecturing to a sietch warren class.

Before the lectures, though, he had to convince the Fremen. To understand how this came about, you must first understand the enormous single-mindedness, the innocence with which he approached any problem. He was not naive, he merely permitted himself no distractions.

He was exploring the Arrakis landscape in a one-man ground car one hot afternoon when he stumbled onto a deplorably common scene. Six Harkonnen bravos, shielded and fully armed, had trapped three Fremen youths in the open behind the Shield Wall near the village of Windsack. To Kynes, it was a ding-dong battle, more slapstick than real, until he focused on the fact that the Harkonnens intended to kill the Fremen. By this time, one of the youths was down with a severed artery, two of the bravos were down as well, but it was still four armed men against two striplings.

Kynes wasn't brave; he merely had that single-mindedness and caution. The Harkonnens were killing Fremen. They were destroying the tools with which he intended to remake a planet! He triggered his own shield, waded in and had two of the Harkonnens dead with a slip-tip before they knew anyone was behind them. He dodged a sword thrust from one of the others, slit the man's throat with a neat *entrisseur*, and left the lone remaining bravo to the two Fremen youths, turning his full attention to saving the lad on the ground. And save the lad he did . . . while the sixth Harkonnen was being dispatched.

Now here was a pretty kettle of sandtrout! The Fremen didn't know what to make of Kynes. They knew who he was, of course. No man arrived on Arrakis without a full dossier finding its way into the Fremen strongholds. They knew him: he was an Imperial servant.

But he killed Harkonnens!

Adults might have shrugged and, with some regret, sent his shade to join those of the six dead men on the ground. But these Fremen were inexperienced youths and all they could see was that they owed this Imperial servant a mortal obligation.

Kynes wound up two days later in a sietch that looked down on Wind Pass. To him, it was all very natural. He talked to the Fremen about water, about dunes anchored by grass, about palmaries filled with date palms, about open qanats flowing across the desert. He talked and talked and talked.

All around him raged a debate that Kynes never saw. What to do with this madman? He knew the location of a major sietch. What to do? What of his words, this mad talk about a paradise on Arrakis? Just talk. He knows too much. But he killed Harkonnens! What of the water burden? When did we owe the Imperium anything? He killed Harkonnens. Anyone can kill Harkonnens. I have done it myself.

But what of this talk about the flowering of Arrakis?

Very simple: Where is the water for this?

He says it is here! And he *did* save three of ours.

He saved three fools who had put themselves in the way of the Harkonnen fist! And he has seen crysknives!

The necessary decision was known for hours before it was voiced. The tau of a sietch tells its members what they must do; even the most brutal necessity is known. An experienced fighter was sent with a consecrated knife to do the job. Two watermen followed him to get the water from the body. Brutal necessity.

It's doubtful that Kynes even focused on his would-be executioner. He was talking to a group that spread around him at a cautious distance. He walked as he talked: a short circle, gesturing. Open water, Kynes said. Walk in the open without stillsuits. Water for dipping it out of a pond! Portyguls!

The knifeman confronted him.

"Remove yourself," Kynes said, and went on talking about secret windtraps. He brushed past the man. Kynes' back stood open for the ceremonial blow.

What went on in that would-be executioner's mind cannot be known now. Did he finally listen to Kynes and believe? Who knows? But what he did is a matter of record. Uliet was his name, *Older* Liet. Uliet walked three paces and deliberately fell on his own knife, thus "removing" himself. Suicide? Some say Shai-hulud moved him.

Talk about omens!

From that instant, Kynes had but to point, saying "Go there." Entire Fremen tribes went. Men died, women died, children died. But they went.

Kynes returned to his Imperial chores, directing the Biological Testing Stations. And now, Fremen began to appear among the Station personnel. The Fremen looked at each other. They were infiltrating the "system," a possibility they'd never considered. Station tools began finding their way into the sietch warrens—especially cutterays which were used to dig underground catchbasins and hidden windtraps.

Water began collecting in the basins.

It became apparent to the Fremen that Kynes was not a madman totally, just mad enough to be holy. He was one of the umma, the brotherhood of prophets. The shade of Uliet was advanced to the sadus, the throng of heavenly judges.

Kynes—direct, savagely intent Kynes—knew that highly organized research is guaranteed to produce nothing new. He set up small-unit experiments with regular interchange of data for a swift Tansley effect, let each group find its own path. They must accumulate millions of tiny facts. He organized only isolated and rough run-through tests to put their difficulties into perspective.

Core samplings were made throughout the bled. Charts were developed on the long drifts of weather that are called climate. He found that in the wide belt contained by the 70-degree lines, north and south, temperatures for thousands of years hadn't gone outside the 254–332 degrees (absolute) range, and that this belt had long growing seasons where temperatures ranged from 284 to 302 degrees absolute: the "bonanza" range for terraform life . . . once they solved the water problem.

When will we solve it? the Fremen asked. When will we see Arrakis as a paradise?

In the manner of a teacher answering a child who has asked the sum of 2 plus 2, Kynes told them: "From three hundred to five hundred years."

A lesser folk might have howled in dismay. But the Fremen had learned patience from men with whips. It was a bit longer than they had anticipated, but they all could see that the blessed day was coming. They tightened their sashes and went back to work. Somehow, the disappointment made the prospect of paradise more real.

The concern on Arrakis was not with water, but with moisture. Pets were almost unknown, stock animals rare. Some smugglers employed the domesticated desert ass, the kulon, but the water price was high even when the beasts were fitted with modified stillsuits.

Kynes thought of installing reduction plants to recover water from the hydrogen and oxygen locked in native rock, but the energy-cost factor was far too high. The polar caps (disregarding the false sense of water security they gave the pyons) held far too small an amount for his project . . . and he already suspected where the water had to be. There was that consistent increase of moisture at median altitudes, and in certain winds. There was that primary clue in the air balance—23 per cent oxygen, 75.4 per cent nitrogen and .023 per cent carbon dioxide—with the trace gases taking up the rest.

There was a rare native root plant that grew above the 2,500-meter level in the northern temperate zone. A tuber two meters long yielded half a liter of water. And there were the terraform desert plants: the tougher ones showed signs of thriving if planted in depressions lined with dew precipitators.

Then Kynes saw the salt pan.

His 'thopter, flying between stations far out on the bled, was blown off course by a storm. When the storm passed, there was the pan—a giant oval depression some three hundred kilometers on the long axis—

a glaring white surprise in the open desert. Kynes landed, tasted the pan's storm-cleaned surface.

Salt.

Now, he was certain.

There'd been open water on Arrakis—once. He began reexamining the evidence of the dry wells where trickles of water had appeared and vanished, never to return.

Kynes set his newly trained Fremen limnologist to work: their chief clue, leathery scraps of matter sometimes found with the spice mass after a blow. This had been ascribed to a fictional "sandtrout" in Fremen folk stories. As facts grew into evidence, a creature emerged to explain these leathery scraps—a sandswimmer that blocked off water into fertile pockets within the porous lower strata below the 280° (absolute) line.

This "water-stealer" died by the millions in each spice-blow. A five-degree change in temperature could kill it. The few survivors entered a semidormant cyst-hibernation to emerge in six years as small (about three meters long) sandworms. Of these, only a few avoided their larger brothers and pre-spice water pockets to emerge into maturity as the giant shai-hulud. (Water is poisonous to shai-hulud as the Fremen had long known from drowning the rare "stunted worm" of the Minor Erg to produce the awareness-spectrum narcotic they call Water of Life. The "stunted worm" is a primitive form of shai-hulud that reaches a length of only about nine meters.)

Now they had the circular relationship: little maker to pre-spice mass; little maker to shai-hulud; shai-hulud to scatter the spice upon which fed microscopic creatures called sand plankton; the sand plankton, food for shai-hulud, growing, burrowing, becoming little makers.

Kynes and his people turned their attention from these great relationships and focused now on micro-ecology. First, the climate: the sand surface often reached temperatures of 344° to 350° (absolute). A foot below ground it might be 55° cooler; a foot above ground, 25° cooler. Leaves or black shade could provide another 18° of cooling. Next, the nutrients: sand of Arrakis is mostly a product of worm digestion; dust (the truly omnipresent problem there) is produced by the constant surface creep, the "saltation" movement of sand. Coarse grains are found on the downwind sides of dunes. The windward side is packed smooth and hard. Old dunes are yellow (oxidized), young dunes are the color of the parent rock—usually gray.

Downwind sides of old dunes provided the first plantation areas. The Fremen aimed first for a cycle of poverty grass with peatlike hair cilia to intertwine, mat and fix the dunes by depriving the wind of its big weapon: movable grains.

Adaptive zones were laid out in the deep south far from Harkonnen watchers. The mutated poverty grasses were planted first along the downwind (slipface) of the chosen dunes that stood across the path of the prevailing westerlies. With the downwind face anchored, the windward face grew higher and higher and the grass was moved to keep pace. Giant sifs (long dunes with sinuous crests) of more than 1,500 meters height were produced this way.

When barrier dunes reached sufficient height, the windward faces were planted with tougher sword grasses. Each structure on a base about six times as thick as its height was anchored—"fixed."

Now, they came in with deeper plantings—ephemerals (chenopods, pigweeds, and amaranth to begin), then scotch broom, low lupine, vine eucalyptus (the type adapted for Caladan's northern reaches), dwarf tamarisk, shore pine—then the true desert growths: candelilla, saguaro, and bis-naga, the barrel cactus. Where it would grow, they introduced camel sage, onion grass, gobi feather grass, wild alfalfa, burrow bush, sand verbena, evening primrose, incense bush, smoke tree, creosote bush.

They turned then to the necessary animal life—burrowing creatures to open the soil and aerate it: kit fox, kangaroo mouse, desert hare, sand terrapin . . . and the predators to keep them in check: desert hawk, dwarf owl, eagle and desert owl; and insects to fill the niches these couldn't reach: scorpion, centipede, trapdoor spider, the biting wasp and the wormfly . . . and the desert bat to keep watch on these.

Now came the crucial test: date palms, cotton, melons, coffee, medicinals—more than 200 selected food plant types to test and adapt.

"The thing the ecologically illiterate don't realize about an ecosystem," Kynes said, "is that it's a system. A system! A system maintains a certain fluid stability that can be destroyed by a misstep in just one niche. A system has order, a flowing from point to point. If something dams that flow, order collapses. The untrained might miss that collapse until it was too late. That's why the highest function of ecology is the understanding of consequences."

Had they achieved a system?

Kynes and his people watched and waited. The Fremen now knew what he meant by an open-end prediction to five hundred years.

A report came up from the palmaries:

At the desert edge of the plantings, the sand plankton is being poisoned through interaction with the new forms of life. The reason: protein incompatibility. Poisonous water was forming there which the Arrakis life would not touch. A barren zone surrounded the plantings and even shai-hulud would not invade it.

Kynes went down to the palmaries himself—a twenty-thumper trip (in a palanquin like a wounded man or Reverend Mother because he never became a sandrider). He tested the barren zone (it stank to heaven) and came up with a bonus, a gift from Arrakis.

The addition of sulfur and fixed nitrogen converted the barren zone to a rich plant bed for terraform life. The plantings could be advanced at will!

"Does this change the timing?" the Fremen asked.

Kynes went back to his planetary formulae. Windtrap figures were fairly secure by then. He was generous with his allowances, knowing he couldn't draw neat lines around ecological problems. A certain amount of plant cover had to be set aside to hold dunes in place; a certain amount for foodstuffs (both human and animal); a certain amount to lock moisture in root systems and to feed water out into surrounding parched areas. They'd mapped the roving cold spots on the open bled by this time. These had to be figured into the formulae. Even shai-hulud had a place in the charts. He must never be destroyed, else spice wealth would end. But his inner digestive "factory," with its enormous concentrations of aldehydes and acids, was a giant source of oxygen. A medium worm (about 200 meters long) discharged into the atmosphere as much oxygen as ten square kilometers of green-growing photosynthesis surface.

He had the Guild to consider. The spice bribe to the Guild for preventing weather satellites and other watchers in the skies of Arrakis already had reached major proportions.

Nor could the Fremen be ignored. Especially the Fremen, with their windtraps and irregular landholdings organized around water supply; the Fremen with their new ecological literacy and their dream of cycling vast areas of Arrakis through a prairie phase into forest cover.

From the charts emerged a figure. Kynes reported it. Three per cent. If they could get three per cent of the green plant element on Arrakis involved in forming carbon compounds, they'd have their self-sustaining cycle.

"But how long?" the Fremen demanded.

"Oh, that: about three hundred and fifty years."

So it was true as this umma had said in the beginning: the thing would not come in the lifetime of any man now living, nor in the lifetime of their grandchildren eight times removed, but it would come.

The work continued: building, planting, digging, training the children.

Then Kynes-the-Umma was killed in the cave-in at Plaster Basin.

By this time his son, Liet-Kynes, was nineteen, a full Fremen and sandrider who had killed more than a hundred Harkonnens. The Imperial appointment for which the elder Kynes already had applied in the name of his son was delivered as a matter of course. The rigid class structure of the faufreluches had its well-ordered purpose here. The son had been trained to follow the father.

The course had been set by this time, the Ecological-Fremen were aimed along their way. Liet-Kynes had only to watch and nudge and spy upon the Harkonnens . . . until the day his planet was afflicted by a Hero.

APPENDIX II

THE RELIGION OF DUNE

Before the coming of Muad'Dib, the Fremen of Arrakis practiced a religion whose roots in the Maometh Saari are there for any scholar to see. Many have traced the extensive borrowings from other religions. The most common example is the Hymn to Water, a direct copy from the Orange Catholic Liturgical Manual, calling for rain clouds which Arrakis had never seen. But there are more profound points of accord between the Kitab al-Ibar of the Fremen and the teachings of Bible, Ilm, and Fiqh.

Any comparison of the religious beliefs dominant in the Imperium up to the time of Muad'Dib must start with the major forces which shaped those beliefs:

1. The followers of the Fourteen Sages, whose Book was the Orange Catholic Bible, and whose views are expressed in the Commentaries and other literature produced by the Commission of Ecumenical Translators. (C.E.T.);

2. The Bene Gesserit, who privately denied they were a religious order, but who operated behind an almost impenetrable screen of ritual mysticism, and whose training, whose symbolism, organization, and internal teaching methods were almost wholly religious;

3. The agnostic ruling class (including the Guild) for whom religion was a kind of puppet show to amuse the populace and keep it docile, and who believed essentially that all phenomena—even religious phenomena—could be reduced to mechanical explanations;

4. The so-called Ancient Teachings—including those preserved by the Zensunni Wanderers from the first, second, and third Islamic movements; the Navachristianity of Chusuk, the Buddislamic Variants

of the types dominant at Lankiveil and Sikun, the Blend Books of the Mahayana Lankavatara, the Zen Hekiganshu of III Delta Pavonis, the Tawrah and Talmudic Zabur surviving on Salusa Secundus, the pervasive Obeah Ritual, the Muadh Quran with its pure Ilm and Fiqh preserved among the pundi rice farmers of Caladan, the Hindu outcroppings found all through the universe in little pockets of insulated pyons, and finally, the Butlerian Jihad.

There *is* a fifth force which shaped religious belief, but its effect is so universal and profound that it deserves to stand alone.

This is, of course, space travel—and in any discussion of religion, it deserves to be written thus:

SPACE TRAVEL!

Mankind's movement through deep space placed a unique stamp on religion during the one hundred and ten centuries that preceded the Butlerian Jihad. To begin with, early space travel, although widespread, was largely unregulated, slow, and uncertain, and, before the Guild monopoly, was accomplished by a hodgepodge of methods. The first space experiences, poorly communicated and subject to extreme distortion, were a wild inducement to mystical speculation.

Immediately, space gave a different flavor and sense to ideas of Creation. That difference is seen even in the highest religious achievements of the period. All through religion, the feeling of the sacred was touched by anarchy from the outer dark.

It was as though Jupiter in all his descendant forms retreated into the maternal darkness to be superseded by a female immanence filled with ambiguity and with a face of many terrors.

The ancient formulae intertwined, tangled together as they were fitted to the needs of new conquests and new heraldic symbols. It was a time of struggle between beast-demons on the one side and the old prayers and invocations on the other.

There was never a clear decision.

During this period, it was said that Genesis was reinterpreted, permitting God to say:

"Increase and multiply, and fill the *universe*, and subdue it, and rule over all manner of strange beasts and living creatures in the infinite airs, on the infinite earths and beneath them."

It was a time of sorceresses whose powers were real. The measure of them is seen in the fact they never boasted how they grasped the firebrand.

Then came the Butlerian Jihad—two generations of chaos. The god of machine-logic was overthrown among the masses and a new concept was raised:

"Man may not be replaced."

Those two generations of violence were a thalamic pause for all humankind. Men looked at their gods and their rituals and saw that both were filled with that most terrible of all equations: fear over ambition.

Hesitantly, the leaders of religions whose followers had spilled the blood of billions began meeting to exchange views. It was a move encouraged by the Spacing Guild, which was beginning to build its monopoly over all interstellar travel, and by the Bene Gesserit who were banding the sorceresses.

Out of those first ecumenical meetings came two major developments:

1. The realization that all religions had at least one common commandment: "Thou shalt not disfigure the soul."

2. The Commission of Ecumenical Translators.

C.E.T. convened on a neutral island of Old Earth, spawning ground of the mother religions. They met "in the common belief that there exists a Divine Essence in the universe." Every faith with more than a million followers was represented, and they reached a surprisingly immediate agreement on the statement of their common goal:

"We are here to remove a primary weapon from the hands of disputant religions. That weapon—the claim to possession of the one and only revelation."

Jubilation at this "sign of profound accord" proved premature. For more than a Standard year, that statement was the only announcement from C.E.T. Men spoke bitterly of the delay. Troubadours composed witty, biting songs about the one hundred and twenty-one "Old Cranks" as the C.E.T. delegates came to be called. (The name arose from a ribald joke which played on the C.E.T. initials and called the delegates "Cranks—Effing-Turners.") One of the songs, "Brown Repose," has undergone periodic revival and is popular even today:

> "Consider leis.
> Brown repose—and
> The tragedy
> In all of those
> Cranks! All those Cranks!
> So laze—so laze
> Through all your days.
> Time has toll'd for
> M'Lord Sandwich!"

Occasional rumors leaked out of the C.E.T. sessions. It was said they were comparing texts and, irresponsibly, the texts were named. Such rumors inevitably provoked anti-ecumenism riots and, of course, inspired new witticisms.

Two years passed . . . three years.

The Commissioners, nine of their original number having died and been replaced, paused to observe formal installation of the replacements and announced they were laboring to produce one book, weeding out "all the pathological symptoms" of the religious past.

"We are producing an instrument of Love to be played in all ways," they said.

Many consider it odd that this statement provoked the worst outbreaks of violence against ecumenism. Twenty delegates were recalled by their congregations. One committed suicide by stealing a space frigate and diving it into the sun.

Historians estimate the riots took eighty million lives. That works out to about six thousand for each world then in the Landsraad League. Considering the unrest of the time, this may not be an excessive estimate, although any pretense to real accuracy in the figure must be just that—pretense. Communication between worlds was at one of its lowest ebbs.

The troubadours, quite naturally, had a field day. A popular musical comedy of the period had one of the C.E.T. delegates sitting on a white sand beach beneath a palm tree singing:

> *"For God, woman and the splendor of love*
> *We dally here sans fears or cares.*
> *Troubadour! Troubadour, sing another melody*
> *For God, woman and the splendor of love!"*

Riots and comedy are but symptoms of the times, profoundly revealing. They betray the psychological tone, the deep uncertainties . . . and the striving for something better, plus the fear that nothing would come of it all.

The major dams against anarchy in these times were the embryo Guild, the Bene Gesserit and the Landsraad, which continued its 2,000-year record of meeting in spite of the severest obstacles. The Guild's part appears clear: they gave free transport for all Landsraad and C.E.T. business. The Bene Gesserit role is more obscure. Certainly, this is the time in which they consolidated their hold upon the sorceresses, explored the subtle narcotics, developed prana-bindu training and conceived the Missionaria Protectiva, that black arm of superstition. But it is also the period that saw the composing of the Litany Against Fear and the assembly of the Azhar Book, that bibliographic marvel that preserves the great secrets of the most ancient faiths.

Ingsley's comment is perhaps the only one possible:

"Those were times of deep paradox."

For almost seven years, then, C.E.T. labored. And as their seventh anniversary approached, they prepared the human universe for a momentous announcement. On that seventh anniversary, they unveiled the Orange Catholic Bible.

"Here is a work with dignity and meaning," they said. "Here is a way to make humanity aware of itself as a total creation of God."

The men of C.E.T. were likened to archeologists of ideas, inspired by God in the grandeur of rediscovery. It was said they had brought to light "the vitality of great ideals overlaid by the deposits of centuries," that they had "sharpened the moral imperatives that come out of a religious conscience."

With the O.C. Bible, C.E.T. presented the Liturgical Manual and the Commentaries—in many respects a more remarkable work, not only because of its brevity (less than half the size of the O.C. Bible), but also because of its candor and blend of self-pity and self-righteousness.

The beginning is an obvious appeal to the agnostic rulers.

"Men, finding no answers to the *sunnan* [the ten thousand religious questions from the Shari-ah] now apply their own reasoning. All men seek to be enlightened. Religion is but the most ancient and honorable way in which men have striven to make sense out of God's universe. Scientists seek the lawfulness of events. It is the task of Religion to fit man into this lawfulness."

In their conclusion, though, the Commentaries set a harsh tone that very likely foretold their fate.

"Much that was called religion has carried an unconscious attitude of hostility toward life. True religion must teach that life is filled with joys pleasing to the eye of God, that knowledge without action is empty. All men must see that the teaching of religion by rules and rote is largely a hoax. The proper teaching is recognized with ease. You can know it without fail because it awakens within you that sensation which tells you this is something you've always known."

There was an odd sense of calm as the presses and shigawire imprinters rolled and the O.C. Bible spread out through the worlds. Some interpreted this as a sign from God, an omen of unity.

But even the C.E.T. delegates betrayed the fiction of that calm as they returned to their respective congregations. Eighteen of them were lynched within two months. Fifty-three recanted within the year.

The O.C. Bible was denounced as a work produced by "the hubris of reason." It was said that its pages were filled with a seductive interest in logic. Revisions that catered to popular bigotry began appearing. These revisions leaned on accepted symbolisms (Cross, Crescent, Feather Rattle, the Twelve Saints, the thin Buddha, and the like) and it soon became apparent that the ancient superstitions and beliefs had *not* been absorbed by the new ecumenism.

Halloway's label for C.E.T.'s seven-year effort—"Galactophasic Determinism"—was snapped up by eager billions who interpreted the initials G.D. as "God-Damned."

C.E.T. Chairman Toure Bomoko, a Ulema of the Zensunnis and one of the fourteen delegates who never recanted ("The Fourteen Sages" of popular history), appeared to admit finally the C.E.T. had erred.

"We shouldn't have tried to create new symbols," he said. "We should've realized we weren't supposed to introduce uncertainties into accepted belief, that we weren't supposed to stir up curiosity about God. We are daily confronted by the terrifying instability of all things human, yet we permit our religions to grow more rigid and controlled, more conforming and oppressive. What is this shadow across the highway of Divine Command? It is a warning that institutions endure, that symbols endure when their meaning is lost, that there is no summa of all attainable knowledge."

The bitter double edge in this "admission" did not escape Bomoko's critics and he was forced soon afterward to flee into exile, his life dependent upon the Guild's pledge of secrecy. He reportedly died on Tupile, honored and beloved, his last words: "Religion must remain an outlet for people who say to themselves, 'I am not the kind of person I want to be.' It must never sink into an assemblage of the self-satisfied."

It is pleasant to think that Bomoko understood the prophecy in his words: "Institutions endure." Ninety generations later, the O.C. Bible and the Commentaries permeated the religious universe.

When Paul-Muad'Dib stood with his right hand on the rock shrine enclosing his father's skull (the right hand of the blessed, not the left hand of the damned) he quoted word for word from "Bomoko's Legacy"—

"You who have defeated us say to yourselves that Babylon is fallen and its works have been overturned. I say to you still that man remains on trial, each man in his own dock. Each man is a little war."

The Fremen said of Muad'Dib that he was like Abu Zide whose frigate defied the Guild and rode one day *there* and back. *There* used in this way translates directly from the Fremen mythology as the land of the ruh-spirit, the alam al-mithal where all limitations are removed.

The parallel between this and the Kwisatz Haderach is readily seen. The Kwisatz Haderach that the Sisterhood sought through its breeding program was interpreted as "The shortening of the way" or "The one who can be two places simultaneously."

But both of these interpretations can be shown to stem directly from the Commentaries: "When law and religious duty are one, your selfdom encloses the universe."

Of himself, Muad'Dib said: "I am a net in the sea of time, free to sweep future and past. I am a moving membrane from whom no possibility can escape."

These thoughts are all one and the same and they harken to 22 Kalima in the O.C. Bible where it says: "Whether a thought is spoken or not it is a real thing and has powers of reality."

It is when we get into Muad'Dib's own commentaries in "The Pillars of the Universe" as interpreted by his holy men, the Qizara Tafwid, that we see his real debt to C.E.T. and Fremen-Zensunni.

Muad'Dib: "Law and duty are one; so be it. But remember these limitations—Thus are you never fully self-conscious. Thus do you remain immersed in the communal tau. Thus are you always less than an individual."

O.C. Bible: Identical wording. (61 Revelations.)

Muad'Dib: "Religion often partakes of the myth of progress that shields us from the terrors of an uncertain future."

C.E.T. Commentaries: Identical wording. (The Azhar Book traces this statement to the first-century religious writer, Neshou; through a paraphrase.)

Muad'Dib: "If a child, an untrained person, an ignorant person, or an insane person incites trouble, it is the fault of authority for not predicting and preventing that trouble."

O.C. Bible: "Any sin can be ascribed, at least in part, to a natural bad tendency that is an extenuating circumstance acceptable to God." (The Azhar Book traces this to the ancient Semitic Tawra.)

Muad'Dib: "Reach forth thy hand and eat what God has provided thee; and when thou are replenished, praise the Lord."

O.C. Bible: a paraphrase with identical meaning. (The Azhar Book traces this in slightly different form to First Islam.)

Muad'Dib: "Kindness is the beginning of cruelty."

Fremen Kitab al-Ibar: "The weight of a kindly God is a fearful thing. Did not God give us the burning sun (Al-Lat)? Did not God give us the Mothers of Moisture (Reverend Mothers)? Did not God give us Shaitan (Iblis, Satan)? From Shaitan did we not get the hurtfulness of speed?"

(This is the source of the Fremen saying: "Speed comes from Shaitan." Consider: for every one hundred calories of heat generated by exercise [speed] the body evaporates about six ounces of perspiration. The Fremen word for perspiration is bakka or tears and, in one pronunciation, translates: "The life essence that Shaitan squeezes from your soul.")

Muad'Dib's arrival is called "religiously timely" by Koneywell, but timing had little to do with it. As Muad'Dib himself said: "I am here; so. . . ."

It is, however, vital to an understanding of Muad'Dib's religious impact that you never lose sight of one fact: the Fremen were a desert people whose entire ancestry was accustomed to hostile landscapes.

Mysticism isn't difficult when you survive each second by surmounting open hostility. "You are there—so. . . ."

With such a tradition, suffering is accepted—perhaps as unconscious punishment, but accepted. And it's well to note that Fremen ritual gives almost complete freedom from guilt feelings. This isn't necessarily because their law and religion were identical, making disobedience a sin. It's likely closer to the mark to say they cleansed themselves of guilt easily because their everyday existence required brutal judgments (often deadly) which in a softer land would burden men with unbearable guilt.

This is likely one of the roots of Fremen emphasis on superstition (disregarding the Missionaria Protectiva's ministrations). What matter that whistling sands are an omen? What matter that you must make the sign of the fist when first you see First Moon? A man's flesh is his own and his water belongs to the tribe—and the mystery of life isn't a problem to solve but a reality to experience. Omens help you remember this. And because you are *here*, because you have *the* religion, victory cannot evade you in the end.

As the Bene Gesserit taught for centuries, long before they ran afoul of the Fremen:

"When religion and politics ride the same cart, when that cart is driven by a living holy man (baraka), nothing can stand in their path."

REPORT ON BENE GESSERIT MOTIVES AND PURPOSES

Here follows an excerpt from the Summa prepared by her own agents at the request of the Lady Jessica immediately after the Arrakis Affair. The candor of this report amplifies its value far beyond the ordinary.

Because the Bene Gesserit operated for centuries behind the blind of a semimystic school while carrying on their selective breeding program among humans, we tend to award them with more status than they appear to deserve. Analysis of their "trial of fact" on the Arrakis Affair betrays the school's profound ignorance of its own role.

It may be argued that the Bene Gesserit could examine only such facts as were available to them and had no direct access to the person of the Prophet Muad'Dib. But the school had surmounted greater obstacles and its error here goes deeper.

The Bene Gesserit program had as its target the breeding of a person they labeled "Kwisatz Haderach," a term signifying "one who can be many places at once." In simpler terms, what they sought was a human with mental powers permitting him to understand and use higher order dimensions.

They were breeding for a super-Mentat, a human computer with some of the prescient abilities found in Guild navigators. Now, attend these facts carefully:

Muad'Dib, born Paul Atreides, was the son of the Duke Leto, a man whose bloodline had been watched carefully for more than a thousand years. The Prophet's mother, Lady Jessica, was a natural daughter of the

Baron Vladimir Harkonnen and carried gene-markers whose supreme importance to the breeding program was known for almost two thousand years. She was a Bene Gesserit bred and trained, and *should have been a willing tool of the project.*

The Lady Jessica was ordered to produce an Atreides daughter. The plan was to inbreed this daughter with Feyd-Rautha Harkonnen, a nephew of the Baron Vladimir, with the high probability of a Kwisatz Haderach from that union. Instead, for reasons she confesses have never been completely clear to her, the concubine Lady Jessica defied her orders and bore a son.

This alone should have alerted the Bene Gesserit to the possibility that a wild variable had entered their scheme. But there were other far more important indications that they virtually ignored:

1. As a youth, Paul Atreides showed ability to predict the future. He was known to have had prescient visions that were accurate, penetrating, and defied four-dimensional explanation.

2. The Reverend Mother Gaius Helen Mohiam, Bene Gesserit Proctor who tested Paul's humanity when he was fifteen, deposes that he surmounted more agony in the test than any other human of record. Yet she failed to make special note of this in her report!

3. When Family Atreides moved to the planet Arrakis, the Fremen population there hailed the young Paul as a prophet, "the voice from the outer world." The Bene Gesserit were well aware that the rigors of such a planet as Arrakis with its totality of desert landscape, its absolute lack of open water, its emphasis on the most primitive necessities for survival, inevitably produces a high proportion of sensitives. Yet this Fremen reaction and the obvious element of the Arrakeen diet high in spice were glossed over by Bene Gesserit observers.

4. When the Harkonnens and the soldier-fanatics of the Padishah Emperor reoccupied Arrakis, killing Paul's father and most of the Atreides troops, Paul and his mother disappeared. But almost immediately there were reports of a new religious leader among the Fremen, a man called Muad'Dib, who again was hailed as "the voice from the outer world." The reports stated clearly that he was accompanied by a new

Reverend Mother of the Sayyadina Rite "who is the woman who bore him." Records available to the Bene Gesserit stated in plain terms that the Fremen legends of the Prophet contained these words: "He shall be born of a Bene Gesserit witch."

(It may be argued here that the Bene Gesserit sent their Missionaria Protectiva onto Arrakis centuries earlier to implant something like this legend as safeguard should any members of the school be trapped there and require sanctuary, and that this legend of "the voice from the outer world" was properly to be ignored because it appeared to be the standard Bene Gesserit ruse. But this would be true only if you granted that the Bene Gesserit were correct in ignoring the other clues about Paul-Muad'Dib.)

5. When the Arrakis Affair boiled up, the Spacing Guild made overtures to the Bene Gesserit. The Guild hinted that its navigators, who use the spice drug of Arrakis to produce the limited prescience necessary for guiding spaceships through the void, were "bothered about the future" or saw "problems on the horizon." This could only mean they saw a nexus, a meeting place of countless delicate decisions, beyond which the path was hidden from the prescient eye. This was a clear indication that some agency was interfering with higher order dimensions!

(A few of the Bene Gesserit had long been aware that the Guild could not interfere directly with the vital spice source because Guild navigators already were dealing in their own inept way with higher order dimensions, at least to the point where they recognized that the slightest misstep they made on Arrakis could be catastrophic. It was a known fact that Guild navigators could predict no way to take control of the spice without producing just such a nexus. The obvious conclusion was that someone of higher order powers *was* taking control of the spice source, yet the Bene Gesserit missed this point entirely!)

In the face of these facts, one is led to the inescapable conclusion that the inefficient Bene Gesserit behavior in this affair was a product of an even higher plan of which they were completely unaware!

THE ALMANAK EN-ASHRAF
(Selected Excerpts of the Noble Houses)

SHADDAM IV (10,134–10,202)

The Padishah Emperor, 81st of his line (House Corrino) to occupy the Golden Lion Throne, reigned from 10,156 (date his father, Elrood IX, succumbed to chaumurky) until replaced by the 10,196 Regency set up in the name of his eldest daughter, Irulan. His reign is noted chiefly for the Arrakis Revolt, blamed by many historians on Shaddam IV's dalliance with Court functions and the pomp of office. The ranks of Bursegs were doubled in the first sixteen years of his reign. Appropriations for Sardaukar training went down steadily in the final thirty years before the Arrakis Revolt. He had five daughters (Irulan, Chalice, Wensicia, Josifa, and Rugi) and no legal sons. Four of the daughters accompanied him into retirement. His wife, Anirul, a Bene Gesserit of Hidden Rank, died in 10,176.

LETO ATREIDES (10,140–10,191)

A distaff cousin of the Corrinos, he is frequently referred to as the Red Duke. House Atreides ruled Caladan as a siridar-fief for twenty generations until pressured into the move to Arrakis. He is known chiefly as the father of Duke Paul-Muad'Dib, the Umma Regent. The remains of Duke Leto occupy the "Skull Tomb" on Arrakis. His death is attributed to the treachery of a Suk doctor, and is an act laid to the Siridar-Baron, Vladimir Harkonnen.

LADY JESSICA (HON. ATREIDES) (10,154–10,256)

A natural daughter (Bene Gesserit reference) of the Siridar-Baron Vladimir Harkonnen. Mother of Duke Paul-Muad'Dib. She graduated from the Wallach IX B.G. School.

LADY ALIA ATREIDES (10,191–)

Legal daughter of Duke Leto Atreides and his formal concubine, Lady Jessica. Lady Alia was born on Arrakis about eight months after Duke Leto's death. Prenatal exposure to an awareness-spectrum narcotic is the reason generally given for Bene Gesserit references to her as "Accursed One." She is known in popular history as St. Alia or St. Alia-of-the-Knife. (For a detailed history, see *St. Alia, Huntress of a Billion Worlds* by Pander Oulson.)

VLADIMIR HARKONNEN (10,110–10,193)

Commonly referred to as Baron Harkonnen, his title is officially Siridar (planetary governor) Baron. Vladimir Harkonnen is the direct-line male descendant of the Bashar Abulurd Harkonnen who was banished for cowardice after the Battle of Corrin. The return of House Harkonnen to power generally is ascribed to adroit manipulation of the whale fur market and later consolidation with melange wealth from Arrakis. The Siridar-Baron died on Arrakis during the Revolt. Title passed briefly to the na-Baron, Feyd-Rautha Harkonnen.

COUNT HASIMIR FENRING (10,133–10,225)

A distaff cousin of House Corrino, he was a childhood companion of Shaddam IV. (The frequently discredited *Pirate History of Corrino* related the curious story that Fenring was responsible for the chaumurky which disposed of Elrood IX.) All accounts agree that Fenring was the closest friend Shaddam IV possessed. The Imperial chores carried out by Count Fenring included that of Imperial Agent on Arrakis during the Harkonnen regime there and later Siridar-Absentia of Caladan. He joined Shaddam IV in retirement on Salusa Secundus.

COUNT GLOSSU RABBAN (10,132–10,193)

Glossu Rabban, Count of Lankiveil, was the eldest nephew of Vladimir Harkonnen. Glossu Rabban and Feyd-Rautha Rabban (who took the name Harkonnen when chosen for the Siridar-Baron's household) were legal sons of the Siridar-Baron's youngest demibrother, Abulurd. Abulurd renounced the Harkonnen name and all rights to the title when given the subdistrict governorship of Rabban-Lankiveil. Rabban was a distaff name.

TERMINOLOGY OF
THE IMPERIUM

In studying the Imperium, Arrakis, and the whole culture which produced Muad'Dib, many unfamiliar terms occur. To increase understanding is a laudable goal, hence the definitions and explanations given below.

A

ABA: loose robe worn by Fremen women; usually black.

ACH: left turn; a worm steersman's call.

ADAB: the demanding memory that comes upon you of itself.

AKARSO: a plant native to Sikun (of 70 Ophiuchi A) characterized by almost oblong leaves. Its green and white stripes indicate the constant multiple condition of parallel active and dormant chlorophyll regions.

ALAM AL-MITHAL: the mystical world of similitudes where all physical limitations are removed.

AL-LAT: mankind's original sun; by usage: any planet's primary.

AMPOLIROS: the legendary "Flying Dutchman" of space.

AMTAL or **AMTAL RULE:** a common rule on primitive worlds under which something is tested to determine its limits or defects. Commonly: testing to destruction.

AQL: the test of reason. Originally, the "Seven Mystic Questions" beginning: "Who is it that thinks?"

ARRAKEEN: first settlement on Arrakis; long-time seat of planetary government.

ARRAKIS: the planet known as Dune; third planet of Canopus.

ASSASSINS' HANDBOOK: third-century compilation of poisons commonly used in a War of Assassins. Later expanded to include those deadly devices permitted under the Guild Peace and Great Convention.

AULIYA: in the Zensunni Wanderers' religion, the female at the left hand of God; God's handmaiden.

AUMAS: poison administered in food. (Specifically: poison in solid food.) In some dialects: Chaumas.

AYAT: the signs of life. (*See* Burhan.)

B

BAKKA: in Fremen legend, the weeper who mourns for all mankind.

BAKLAWA: a heavy pastry made with date syrup.

BALISET: a nine-stringed musical instrument, lineal descendant of the zithra, tuned to the Chusuk scale and played by strumming. Favorite instrument of Imperial troubadors.

BARADYE PISTOL: a static-charge dust gun developed on Arrakis for laying down a large dye marker area on sand.

BARAKA: a living holy man of magical powers.

BASHAR (often Colonel Bashar): an officer of the Sardaukar a fractional point above Colonel in the standardized military classification. Rank created for military ruler of a planetary subdistrict. (Bashar of the Corps is a title reserved strictly for military use.)

BATTLE LANGUAGE: any special language of restricted etymology developed for clear-speech communication in warfare.

BEDWINE: *see* Ichwan Bedwine.

BELA TEGEUSE: fifth planet of Kuentsing: third stopping place of the Zensunni (Fremen) forced migration.

BENE GESSERIT: the ancient school of mental and physical training established primarily for female students after the Butlerian Jihad destroyed the so-called "thinking machines" and robots.

B.G.: idiomatic for Bene Gesserit except when used with a date. With a date it signifies Before Guild and identifies the Imperial dating system based on the genesis of the Spacing Guild's monopoly.

BHOTANI JIB: *see* Chakobsa.

BI-LA KAIFA: amen. (Literally: "Nothing further need be explained.")

BINDU: relating to the human nervous system, especially to nerve training. Often expressed as Bindu-nervature. (*See* Prana.)

BINDU SUSPENSION: a special form of catalepsis, self-induced.

BLED: flat, open desert.

BOURKA: insulated mantle worn by Fremen in the open desert.

BURHAN: the proofs of life. (Commonly: the ayat and burhan of life. *See* Ayat.)

BURSEG: a commanding general of the Sardaukar.

BUTLERIAN JIHAD: *see* Jihad, Butlerian (*also* Great Revolt).

C

CAID: Sardaukar officer rank given to a military official whose duties call mostly for dealings with civilians; a military governorship over a full planetary district; above the rank of Bashar but not equal to a Burseg.

CALADAN: third planet of Delta Pavonis; birthworld of Paul-Muad'Dib.

CANTO and **RESPONDU:** an invocation rite, part of the panoplia propheticus of the Missionaria Protectiva.

CARRYALL: a flying wing (commonly "wing"), the aerial workhorse of Arrakis, used to transport large spice mining, hunting, and refining equipment.

CATCHPOCKET: any stillsuit pocket where filtered water is caught and stored.

CHAKOBSA: the so-called "magnetic language" derived in part from the ancient Bhotani (Bhotani Jib—jib meaning dialect). A collection of ancient dialects modified by needs of secrecy, but chiefly the hunting language of the Bhotani, the hired assassins of the first War of Assassins.

CHAUMAS: (Aumas in some dialects): poison in solid food as distinguished from poison administered in some other way.

CHAUMURKY (Musky or Murky in some dialects): poison administered in a drink.

CHEOPS: pyramid chess; nine-level chess with the double object of putting your queen at the apex and the opponent's king in check.

CHEREM: a brotherhood of hate (usually for revenge).

CHOAM: acronym for Combine Honnete Ober Advancer Mercantiles—
the universal development corporation controlled by the Emperor
and Great Houses with the Guild and Bene Gesserit as silent partners.

CHUSUK: fourth planet of Theta Shalish; the so-called "Music Planet"
noted for the quality of its musical instruments. (*See* Varota.)

CIELAGO: any modified *Chiroptera* of Arrakis adapted to carry distrans messages.

CONE OF SILENCE: the field of a distorter that limits the carrying
power of the voice or any other vibrator by damping the vibrations
with an image-vibration 180 degrees out of phase.

CORIOLIS STORM: any major sandstorm on Arrakis where winds
across the open flatlands are amplified by the planet's own revolu-
tionary motion to reach speeds up to 700 kilometers per hour.

CORRIN, BATTLE OF: the space battle from which the Imperial House
Corrino took its name. The battle fought near Sigma Draconis in the
year 88 B.G. settled the ascendancy of the ruling House from Salusa
Secundus.

COUSINES: blood relations beyond cousins.

CRUSHERS: military space vessels composed of many smaller vessels
locked together and designed to fall on an enemy position, crushing it.

CRYSKNIFE: the sacred knife of the Fremen on Arrakis. It is manufactured in two forms from teeth taken from dead sandworms. The two
forms are "fixed" and "unfixed." An unfixed knife requires proximity to a human body's electrical field to prevent disintegration. Fixed
knives are treated for storage. All are about 20 centimeters long.

CUTTERAY: short-range version of lasgun used mostly as a cutting tool
and surgeon's scalpel.

D

DAR AL-HIKMAN: school of religious translation or interpretation.

DARK THINGS: idiomatic for the infectious superstitions taught by the
Missionaria Protectiva to susceptible civilizations.

DEATH TRIPOD: originally, the tripod upon which desert executioners hanged their victims. By usage: the three members of a Cherem sworn to the same revenge.

DEMIBROTHERS: sons of concubines in the same household and certified as having the same father.

DERCH: right turn; a worm steersman's call.

DEW COLLECTORS or **DEW PRECIPITATORS:** not to be confused with dew gatherers. Collectors or precipitators are egg-shaped devices about four centimeters on the long axis. They are made of chromoplastic that turns a reflecting white when subjected to light, and reverts to transparency in darkness. The collector forms a markedly cold surface upon which dawn dew will precipitate. They are used by Fremen to line concave planting depressions where they provide a small but reliable source of water.

DEW GATHERERS: workers who reap dew from the plants of Arrakis, using a scythelike dew reaper.

DICTUM FAMILIA: that rule of the Great Convention which prohibits the slaying of a royal person or member of a Great House by informal treachery. The rule sets up the formal outline and limits the means of assassination.

DISTRANS: a device for producing a temporary neural imprint on the nervous system of *Chiroptera* or birds. The creature's normal cry then carries the message imprint which can be sorted from that carrier wave by another distrans.

DOORSEAL: a portable plastic hermetic seal used for moisture security in Fremen overday cave camps.

DRUM SAND: impaction of sand in such a way that any sudden blow against its surface produces a distinct drum sound.

DUMP BOXES: the general term for any cargo container of irregular shape and equipped with ablation surfaces and suspensor damping system. They are used to dump material from space onto a planet's surface.

DUNE MEN: idiomatic for open sandworkers, spice hunters and the like on Arrakis. Sandworkers. Spiceworkers.

DUST CHASM: any deep crevasse or depression on the desert of Arrakis that has been filled with dust not apparently different from the surrounding surface; a deadly trap because human or animal will sink in it and smother. (*See* Tidal Dust Basin.)

E

ECAZ: fourth planet of Alpha Centauri B; the sculptors' paradise, so called because it is the home of *fogwood*, the plant growth capable of being shaped in situ solely by the power of human thought.

EGO-LIKENESS: portraiture reproduced through a shigawire projector that is capable of reproducing subtle movements said to convey the ego essence.

ELACCA DRUG: narcotic formed by burning blood-grained elacca wood of Ecas. Its effect is to remove most of the will to self-preservation. Druggee skin shows a characteristic carrot color. Commonly used to prepare slave-gladiators for the ring.

EL-SAYAL: the "rain of sand." A fall of dust which has been carried to medium altitude (around 2,000 meters) by a coriolis storm. El-sayals frequently bring moisture to ground level.

ERG: an extensive dune area, a sea of sand.

F

FAI: the water tribute, chief specie of tax on Arrakis.

FANMETAL: metal formed by the growing of jasmium crystals in duraluminum; noted for extreme tensile strength in relationship to weight. Name derives from its common use in collapsible structures that are opened by "fanning" them out.

FAUFRELUCHES: the rigid rule of class distinction enforced by the Imperium. "A place for every man and every man in his place."

FEDAYKIN: Fremen death commandos; historically: a group formed and pledged to give their lives to right a wrong.

FILMBOOK: any shigawire imprint used in training and carrying a mnemonic pulse.

FILT-PLUG: a nose filter unit worn with a stillsuit to capture moisture from the exhaled breath.

FIQH: knowledge, religious law; one of the half-legendary origins of the Zensunni Wanderers' religion.

FIRE, PILLAR OF: a simple pyrocket for signaling across the open desert.

FIRST MOON: the major satellite of Arrakis, first to rise in the night; notable for a distinct human fist pattern on its surface.

FREE TRADERS: idiomatic for smugglers.

FREMEN: the free tribes of Arrakis, dwellers in the desert, remnants of the Zensunni Wanderers. ("Sand Pirates" according to the Imperial Dictionary.)

FREMKIT: desert survival kit of Fremen manufacture.

FRIGATE: largest spaceship that can be grounded on a planet and taken off in one piece.

G

GALACH: official language of the Imperium. Hybrid Inglo-Slavic with strong traces of cultural-specialization terms adopted during the long chain of human migrations.

GAMONT: third planet of Niushe; noted for its hedonistic culture and exotic sexual practices.

GARE: butte.

GATHERING: distinguished from Council Gathering. It is a formal convocation of Fremen leaders to witness a combat that determines tribal leadership. (A Council Gathering is an assembly to arrive at decisions involving all the tribes.)

GEYRAT: straight ahead; a worm steersman's call.

GHAFLA: giving oneself up to gadfly distractions. Thus: a changeable person, one not to be trusted.

GHANIMA: something acquired in battle or single combat. Commonly, a memento of combat kept only to stir the memory.

GIEDI PRIME: the planet of Ophiuchi B (36), homeworld of House Harkonnen. A median-viable planet with a low active-photosynthesis range.

GINAZ, HOUSE OF: one-time allies of Duke Leto Atreides. They were defeated in the War of Assassins with Grumman.

GIUDICHAR: a holy truth. (Commonly seen in the expression Giudichar mantene: an original and supporting truth.)

GLOWGLOBE: suspensor-buoyed illuminating device, self-powered (usually by organic batteries).

GOM JABBAR: the high-handed enemy; that specific poison needle tipped with meta-cyanide used by Bene Gesserit Proctors in the death-alternative test of human awareness.

GRABEN: a long geological ditch formed when the ground sinks because of movements in the underlying crustal layers.

GREAT CONVENTION: the universal truce enforced under the power balance maintained by the Guild, the Great Houses, and the Imperium. Its chief rule prohibits the use of atomic weapons against human targets. Each rule of the Great Convention begins: "The forms must be obeyed. . . ."

GREAT MOTHER: the horned goddess, the feminine principle of space (commonly: Mother Space), the feminine face of the male-female-neuter trinity accepted as Supreme Being by many religions within the Imperium.

GREAT REVOLT: common term for the Butlerian Jihad. (*See* Jihad, Butlerian.)

GRIDEX PLANE: a differential-charge separator used to remove sand from the melange spice mass; a device of the second stage in spice refining.

GRUMMAN: second planet of Niushe, noted chiefly for the feud of its ruling House (Moritani) with House Ginaz.

GUILD: the Spacing Guild, one leg of the political tripod maintaining the Great Convention. The Guild was the second mental-physical training school (*see* Bene Gesserit) after the Butlerian Jihad. The Guild monopoly on space travel and transport and upon international banking is taken as the beginning point of the Imperial Calendar.

H

HAGAL: the "Jewel Planet" (II Theta Shaowei), mined out in the time of Shaddam I.

HAIIIII-YOH!: command to action; worm steersman's call.

HAJJ: holy journey.

HAJRA: journey of seeking.

HAL YAWM: "Now! At last!" A Fremen exclamation.

HARJ: desert journey, migration.

HARMONTHEP: Ingsley gives this as the planet name for the sixth stop in the Zensunni migration. It is supposed to have been a no longer existent satellite of Delta Pavonis.

HARVESTER or **HARVESTER FACTORY:** a large (often 120 meters by 40 meters) spice mining machine commonly employed on rich, uncontaminated melange blows. (Often called a "crawler" because of buglike body on independent tracks.)

HEIGHLINER: major cargo carrier of the Spacing Guild's transportation system.

HIEREG: temporary Fremen desert camp on open sand.

HIGH COUNCIL: the Landsraad inner circle empowered to act as supreme tribunal in House to House disputes.

HOLTZMAN EFFECT: the negative repelling effect of a shield generator.

HOOKMAN: Fremen with maker hooks prepared to catch a sandworm.

HOUSE: idiomatic for Ruling Clan of a planet or planetary system.

HOUSES MAJOR: holders of planetary fiefs; interplanetary entrepreneurs. (*See* House *above.*)

HOUSES MINOR: planet-bound entrepreneur class (Galach: "Richece").

HUNTER-SEEKER: a ravening sliver of suspensor-buoyed metal guided as a weapon by a nearby control console; common assassination device.

I

IBAD, EYES OF: characteristic effect of a diet high in melange wherein the whites and pupils of the eyes turn a deep blue (indicative of deep melange addiction).

IBN QIRTAIBA: "Thus go the holy words. . . ." Formal beginning to Fremen religious incantation (derived from panoplia propheticus).

ICHWAN BEDWINE: the brotherhood of all Fremen on Arrakis.

IJAZ: prophecy that by its very nature cannot be denied; immutable prophecy.

IKHUT-EIGH!: cry of the water-seller on Arrakis (etymology uncertain). (*See* Soo-Soo Sook!)

ILM: theology; science of religious tradition; one of the half-legendary origins of the Zensunni Wanderers' faith.

IMPERIAL CONDITIONING: a development of the Suk Medical Schools: the highest conditioning against taking human life. Initiates are marked by a diamond tattoo on the forehead and are permitted to wear their hair long and bound by a silver Suk ring.

INKVINE: a creeping plant native to Giedi Prime and frequently used as a whip in the slave cribs. Victims are marked by beet-colored tattoos that cause residual pain for many years.

ISTISLAH: a rule for the general welfare; usually a preface to brutal necessity.

IX: *see* Richese.

J

JIHAD: a religious crusade; fanatical crusade.

JIHAD, BUTLERIAN: (*see also* Great Revolt)—the crusade against computers, thinking machines, and conscious robots begun in 201 B.G. and concluded in 108 B.G. Its chief commandment remains in the O.C. Bible as "Thou shalt not make a machine in the likeness of a human mind."

JUBBA CLOAK: the all-purpose cloak (it can be set to reflect or admit radiant heat, converts to a hammock or shelter) commonly worn over a stillsuit on Arrakis.

JUDGE OF THE CHANGE: an official appointed by the Landsraad High Council and the Emperor to monitor a change of fief, a kanly negotiation, or formal battle in a War of Assassins. The Judge's arbitral authority may be challenged only before the High Council with the Emperor present.

K

KANLY: formal feud or vendetta under the rules of the Great Convention carried on according to the strictest limitations. (*See* Judge of the Change.) Originally the rules were designed to protect innocent bystanders.

KARAMA: a miracle; an action initiated by the spirit world.

KHALA: traditional invocation to still the angry spirits of a place whose name you mention.

KINDJAL: double-bladed short sword (or long knife) with about 20 centimeters of slightly curved blade.

KISWA: any figure or design from Fremen mythology.

KITAB AL-IBAR: the combined survival handbook-religious manual developed by the Fremen on Arrakis.

KRIMSKELL FIBER or **KRIMSKELL ROPE:** the "claw fiber" woven from strands of the *hufuf* from Ecaz. Knots tied in krimskell will claw tighter and tighter to preset limits when the knot-lines are pulled. (For a more detailed study, see Holjance Vohnbrook's "The Strangler Vines of Ecaz.")

KULL WAHAD!: "I am profoundly stirred!" A sincere exclamation of surprise common in the Imperium. Strict interpretation depends on context. (It is said of Muad'Dib that once he watched a desert hawk chick emerge from its shell and whispered: "Kull wahad!")

KULON: wild ass of Terra's Asiatic steppes adapted for Arrakis.

KWISATZ HADERACH: "Shortening of the Way." This is the label applied by the Bene Gesserit to the *unknown* for which they sought a genetic solution: a male Bene Gesserit whose organic mental powers would bridge space and time.

L

LA, LA, LA: Fremen cry of grief. (La translates as ultimate denial, a "no" from which you cannot appeal.)

LASGUN: continuous-wave laser projector. Its use as a weapon is limited in a field-generator-shield culture because of the explosive pyrotechnics (technically, subatomic fusion) created when its beam intersects a shield.

LEGION, IMPERIAL: ten brigades (about 30,000 men).

LIBAN: Fremen liban is spice water infused with yucca flour. Originally a sour milk drink.

LISAN AL-GAIB: "The Voice from the Outer World." In Fremen messianic legends, an offworld prophet. Sometimes translated as "Giver of Water." (*See* Mahdi.)

LITERJON: a one-liter container for transporting water on Arrakis; made of high-density, shatterproof plastic with positive seal.

LITTLE MAKER: the half-plant-half-animal deep-sand vector of the Arrakis sandworm. The little maker's excretions form the pre-spice mass.

M

MAHDI: in the Fremen messianic legend, "The One Who Will Lead Us to Paradise."

MAKER: *see* Shai-hulud.

MAKER HOOKS: the hooks used for capturing, mounting, and steering a sandworm of Arrakis.

MANTENE: underlying wisdom, supporting argument, first principle. (*See* Giudichar.)

MATING INDEX: the Bene Gesserit master record of its human breeding program aimed at producing the Kwisatz Haderach.

MAULA: slave.

MAULA PISTOL: spring-loaded gun for firing poison darts; range about forty meters.

MELANGE: the "spice of spices," the crop for which Arrakis is the unique source. The spice, chiefly noted for its geriatric qualities, is mildly addictive when taken in small quantities, severely addictive when imbibed in quantities above two grams daily per seventy kilos of body weight. (*See* Ibad, Eyes of; Water of Life; *and* Pre-spice

Mass.) Muad'Dib claimed the spice as a key to his prophetic powers. Guild navigators make similar claims. Its price on the Imperial market has ranged as high as 620,000 solaris the decagram.

MENTAT: that class of Imperial citizens trained for supreme accomplishments of logic. "Human computers."

METAGLASS: glass grown as a high-temperature gas infusion in sheets of jasmium quartz. Noted for extreme tensile strength (about 450,000 kilos per square centimeter at two centimeters' thickness) and capacity as a selective radiation filter.

MIHNA: the season for testing Fremen youths who wish admittance to manhood.

MINIMIC FILM: shigawire of one-micron diameter often used to transmit espionage and counterespionage data.

MISH-MISH: apricots.

MISR: the historical Zensunni (Fremen) term for themselves: "The People."

MISSIONARIA PROTECTIVA: the arm of the Bene Gesserit order charged with sowing infectious superstitions on primitive worlds, thus opening those regions to exploitation by the Bene Gesserit. (*See* Panoplia propheticus.)

MONITOR: a ten-section space warcraft mounting heavy armor and shield protection. It is designed to be separated into its component sections for lift-off after planet-fall.

MUAD'DIB: the adapted kangaroo mouse of Arrakis, a creature associated in the Fremen earth-spirit mythology with a design visible on the planet's second moon. This creature is admired by Fremen for its ability to survive in the open desert.

MUDIR NAHYA: the Fremen name for Beast Rabban (Count Rabban of Lankiveil), the Harkonnen cousin who was siridar governor on Arrakis for many years. The name is often translated as "Demon Ruler."

MUSHTAMAL: a small garden annex or garden courtyard.

MUSKY: poison in a drink. (*See* Chaumurky.)

MU ZEIN WALLAH!: Mu zein literally means "nothing good," and wallah is a reflexive terminal exclamation. In this traditional opening for a Fremen curse against an enemy, Wallah turns the emphasis back upon the words Mu zein, producing the meaning: "Nothing good, never good, good for nothing."

N

NA-: a prefix meaning "nominated" or "next in line." Thus: na-Baron means heir apparent to a barony.

NAIB: one who has sworn never to be taken alive by the enemy; traditional oath of a Fremen leader.

NEZHONI SCARF: the scarf-pad worn at the forehead beneath the stillsuit hood by married or "associated" Fremen women after birth of a son.

NOUKKERS: officers of the Imperial bodyguard who are related to the Emperor by blood. Traditional rank for sons of royal concubines.

O

OIL LENS: hufuf oil held in static tension by an enclosing force field within a viewing tube as part of a magnifying or other lightmanipulation system. Because each lens element can be adjusted individually one micron at a time, the oil lens is considered the ultimate in accuracy for manipulating visible light.

OPAFIRE: one of the rare opaline jewels of Hagal.

ORANGE CATHOLIC BIBLE: the "Accumulated Book," the religious text produced by the Commission of Ecumenical Translators. It contains elements of most ancient religions, including the Maometh Saari, Mahayana Christianity, Zensunni Catholicism and Buddislamic traditions. Its supreme commandment is considered to be: "Thou shalt not disfigure the soul."

ORNITHOPTER (commonly: 'thopter): any aircraft capable of sustained wing-beat flight in the manner of birds.

OUT-FREYN: Galach for "immediately foreign," that is: not of your immediate community, not of the select.

P

PALM LOCK: any lock or seal which may be opened on contact with the palm of the human hand to which it has been keyed.

PAN: on Arrakis, any low-lying region or depression created by the subsiding of the underlying basement complex. (On planets with sufficient water, a pan indicates a region once covered by open water. Arrakis is believed to have at least one such area, although this remains open to argument.)

PANOPLIA PROPHETICUS: term covering the infectious superstitions used by the Bene Gesserit to exploit primitive regions. (*See* Missionaria Protectiva.)

PARACOMPASS: any compass that determines direction by local magnetic anomaly; used where relevant charts are available and where a planet's total magnetic field is unstable or subject to masking by severe magnetic storms.

PENTASHIELD: a five-layer shield-generator field suitable for small areas such as doorways or passages (large reinforcing shields become increasingly unstable with each successive layer) and virtually impassable to anyone not wearing a dissembler tuned to the shield codes. (*See* Prudence Door.)

PLASTEEL: steel which has been stabilized with stravidium fibers grown into its crystal structure.

PLENISCENTA: an exotic green bloom of Ecaz noted for its sweet aroma.

POLING THE SAND: the art of placing plastic and fiber poles in the open desert wastes of Arrakis and reading the patterns etched on the poles by sandstorms as a clue to weather prediction.

PORITRIN: third planet of Epsilon Alangue, considered by many Zensunni Wanderers as their planet of origin, although clues in their language and mythology show far more ancient planetary roots.

PORTYGULS: oranges.

PRANA (Prana-musculature): the body's muscles when considered as units for ultimate training. (*See* Bindu.)

PRE-SPICE MASS: the stage of fungusoid wild growth achieved when water is flooded into the excretions of little makers. At this stage, the spice of Arrakis forms a characteristic "blow," exchanging the material from deep underground for the matter on the surface above it. This mass, after exposure to sun and air, becomes melange. (*See also* Melange *and* Water of Life.)

PROCES VERBAL: a semiformal report alleging a crime against the Imperium. Legally: an action falling between a loose verbal allegation and a formal charge of crime.

PROCTOR SUPERIOR: a Bene Gesserit Reverend Mother who is also regional director of a B.G. school. (Commonly: Bene Gesserit-with-the-Sight.)

PRUDENCE DOOR or **PRUDENCE BARRIER** (idiomatically: pru-door or pru-barrier): any pentashield situated for the escape of selected persons under conditions of pursuit. (*See* Pentashield.)

PUNDI RICE: a mutated rice whose grains, high in natural sugar, achieve lengths up to four centimeters; chief export of Caladan.

PYONS: planet-bound peasants or laborers, one of the base classes under the Faufreluches. Legally: wards of the planet.

PYRETIC CONSCIENCE: so-called "conscience of fire"; that inhibitory level touched by Imperial conditioning. (*See* Imperial conditioning.)

Q

QANAT: an open canal for carrying irrigation water under controlled conditions through a desert.

QIRTAIBA: *see* Ibn Qirtaiba.

QUIZARA TAFWID: Fremen priests (after Muad'Dib).

R

RACHAG: a caffeine-type stimulant from the yellow berries of akarso. (*See* Akarso.)

RAMADHAN: ancient religious period marked by fasting and prayer; traditionally, the ninth month of the solar-lunar calendar. Fremen mark the observance according to the ninth meridian-crossing cycle of the first moon.

RAZZIA: a semipiratical guerrilla raid.

RECATHS: body-function tubes linking the human waste disposal system to the cycling filters of a stillsuit.

REPKIT: repair and replacement essentials for a stillsuit.

RESIDUAL POISON: an innovation attributed to the Mentat Piter de Vries whereby the body is impregnated with a substance for which repeated antidotes must be administered. Withdrawal of the antidote at any time brings death.

REVEREND MOTHER: originally, a proctor of the Bene Gesserit, one who has transformed an "illuminating poison" within her body, raising herself to a higher state of awareness. Title adopted by Fremen for their own religious leaders who accomplished a similar "illumination." (*See also* Bene Gesserit *and* Water of Life.)

RICHESE: fourth planet of Eridani A, classed with Ix as supreme in machine culture. Noted for miniaturization. (For a detailed study on how Richese and Ix escaped the more severe effects of the Butlerian Jihad, see *The Last Jihad* by Sumer and Kautman.)

RIMWALL: second upper step of the protecting bluffs on the Shield Wall of Arrakis. (*See* Shield Wall.)

RUH-SPIRIT: in Fremen belief, that part of the individual which is always rooted in (and capable of sensing) the metaphysical world. (*See* Alam al-Mithal.)

S

SADUS: judges. The Fremen title refers to holy judges, equivalent to saints.

SALUSA SECUNDUS: third planet of Gamma Waiping; designated Imperial Prison Planet after removal of the Royal Court to Kaitain. Salusa Secundus is homeworld of House Corrino, and the second stopping point in migrations of the Wandering Zensunni. Fremen tradition says they were slaves on S.S. for nine generations.

SANDCRAWLER: general term for machinery designed to operate on the Arrakis surface in hunting and collecting melange.

SANDMASTER: general superintendent of spice operations.

SANDRIDER: Fremen term for one who is capable of capturing and riding a sandworm.

SANDSNORK: breathing device for pumping surface air into a sand-covered stilltent.

SANDTIDE: idiomatic for a dust tide: the variation in level within certain dust-filled basins on Arrakis due to gravitational effects of sun and satellites. (*See* Tidal Dust Basin.)

SANDWALKER: any Fremen trained to survive in the open desert.

SANDWORM: *see* Shai-hulud.

SAPHO: high-energy liquid extracted from barrier roots of Ecaz. Commonly used by Mentats who claim it amplifies mental powers. Users develop deep ruby stains on mouth and lips.

SARDAUKAR: the soldier-fanatics of the Padishah Emperor. They were men from an environmental background of such ferocity that it killed six out of thirteen persons before the age of eleven. Their military training emphasized ruthlessness and a near-suicidal disregard for personal safety. They were taught from infancy to use cruelty as a standard weapon, weakening opponents with terror. At the apex of their sway over the affairs of the universe, their swordsmanship was said to match that of the Ginaz tenth level and their cunning abilities at in-fighting were reputed to approach those of a Bene Gesserit adept. Any one of them was rated a match for any ten ordinary Landsraad military conscripts. By the time of Shaddam IV, while they were still formidable, their strength had been sapped by overconfidence, and the sustaining mystique of their warrior religion had been deeply undermined by cynicism.

SARFA: the act of turning away from God.

SAYYADINA: feminine acolyte in the Fremen religious hierarchy.

SCHLAG: animal native to Tupile once hunted almost to extinction for its thin, tough hide.

SECOND MOON: the smaller of the two satellites of Arrakis, note-worthy for the kangaroo mouse figure in its surface markings.

SELAMLIK: Imperial audience chamber.

SEMUTA: the second narcotic derivative (by crystal extraction) from burned residue of elacca wood. The effect (described as timeless, sustained ecstasy) is elicited by certain atonal vibrations referred to as semuta music.

SERVOK: clock-set mechanism to perform simple tasks; one of the limited "automatic" devices permitted after the Butlerian Jihad.

SHADOUT: well-dipper, a Fremen honorific.

SHAH-NAMA: the half-legendary First Book of the Zensunni Wanderers.

SHAI-HULUD: Sandworm of Arrakis, the "Old Man of the Desert," "Old Father Eternity," and "Grandfather of the Desert." Significantly, this name, when referred to in a certain tone or written with capital letters, designates the earth deity of Fremen hearth superstitions. Sandworms grow to enormous size (specimens longer than 400 meters have been seen in the deep desert) and live to great age unless slain by one of their fellows or drowned in water, which is poisonous to them. Most of the sand on Arrakis is credited to sandworm action. (*See* Little maker.)

SHAITAN: Satan.

SHARI-A: that part of the panoplia propheticus which sets forth the superstitious ritual. (*See* Missionaria Protectiva.)

SHIELD, DEFENSIVE: the protective field produced by a Holtzman generator. This field derives from Phase One of the suspensor-nullification effect. A shield will permit entry only to objects moving at slow speeds (depending on setting, this speed ranges from six to nine centimeters per second) and can be shorted out only by a shire-sized electric field. (*See* Lasgun.)

SHIELD WALL: a mountainous geographic feature in the northern reaches of Arrakis which protects a small area from the full force of the planet's coriolis storms.

SHIGAWIRE: metallic extrusion of a ground vine *(Narvi narviium)* grown only on Salusa Secundus and III Delta Kaising. It is noted for extreme tensile strength.

SIETCH: Fremen: "Place of assembly in time of danger." Because the Fremen lived so long in peril, the term came by general usage to designate any cave warren inhabited by one of their tribal communities.

SIHAYA: Fremen: the desert springtime with religious overtones implying the time of fruitfulness and "the paradise to come."

SINK: a habitable lowland area on Arrakis surrounded by high ground that protects it from the prevailing storms.

SINKCHART: map of the Arrakis surface laid out with reference to the most reliable paracompass routes between places of refuge. (*See* Paracompass.)

SIRAT: the passage in the O.C. Bible that describes human life as a journey across a narrow bridge (the Sirat) with "Paradise on my right, Hell on my left, and the Angel of Death behind."

SLIP-TIP: any thin, short blade (often poison-tipped) for left-hand use in shield fighting.

SNOOPER, POISON: radiation analyzer within the olfactory spectrum and keyed to detect poisonous substances.

SOLARI: official monetary unit of the Imperium, its purchasing power set at quatricentennial negotiations between the Guild, the Landsraad, and the Emperor.

SOLIDO: the three-dimensional image from a solido projector using 360-degree reference signals imprinted on a shigawire reel. Ixian solido projectors are commonly considered the best.

SONDAGI: the fern tulip of Tupali.

SOO-SOO SOOK!: water-seller's cry on Arrakis. Sook is a market place. (*See* Ikhut-eigh!)

SPACING GUILD: *see* Guild.

SPICE: *see* Melange.

SPICE DRIVER: any Dune man who controls and directs movable machinery on the desert surface of Arrakis.

SPICE FACTORY: *see* Sandcrawler.

SPOTTER CONTROL: the light ornithopter in a spice-hunting group charged with control of watch and protection.

STILLSUIT: body-enclosing garment invented on Arrakis. Its fabric is a micro-sandwich performing functions of heat dissipation and filter for bodily wastes. Reclaimed moisture is made available by tube from catchpockets.

STILLTENT: small, sealable enclosure of micro-sandwich fabric designed to reclaim as potable water the ambient moisture discharged within it by the breath of its occupants.

STUNNER: slow-pellet projectile weapon throwing a poison- or drug-tipped dart. Effectiveness limited by variations in shield settings and relative motion between target and projectile.

SUBAKH UL KUHAR: "Are you well?": a Fremen greeting.

SUBAKH UN NAR: "I am well. And you?": traditional reply.

SUSPENSOR: secondary (low-drain) phase of a Holtzman field generator. It nullifies gravity within certain limits prescribed by relative mass and energy consumption.

T

TAHADDI AL-BURHAN: an ultimate test from which there can be no appeal (usually because it brings death or destruction).

TAHADDI CHALLENGE: Fremen challenge to mortal combat, usually to test some primal issue.

TAQWA: literally: "The price of freedom." Something of great value. That which a deity demands of a mortal (and the fear provoked by the demand).

TAU, THE: in Fremen terminology, that *oneness* of a sietch community enhanced by spice diet and especially the tau orgy of oneness elicited by drinking the Water of Life.

TEST-MASHAD: any test in which honor (defined as spiritual standing) is at stake.

THUMPER: short stake with spring-driven clapper at one end. The purpose: to be driven into the sand and set "thumping" to summon shai-hulud. (*See* Maker hooks.)

TIDAL DUST BASIN: any of the extensive depressions in the surface of Arrakis which have been filled with dust over the centuries and in which actual dust tides (*see* Sandtide) have been measured.

TLEILAX: lone planet of Thalim, noted as renegade training center for Mentats; source of "twisted" Mentats.

T-P: idiomatic for telepathy.

TRAINING: when applied to Bene Gesserit, this otherwise common term assumes special meaning, referring to that conditioning of nerve and muscle (*see* Bindu *and* Prana) which is carried to the last possible notch permitted by natural function.

TROOP CARRIER: any Guild ship designed specifically for transport of troops between planets.

TRUTHSAYER: a Reverend Mother qualified to enter truthtrance and detect insincerity or falsehood.

TRUTHTRANCE: semihypnotic trance induced by one of several "awareness spectrum" narcotics in which the petit betrayals of deliberate falsehood are apparent to the truthtrance observer. (Note: "awareness spectrum" narcotics are frequently fatal except to desensitized individuals capable of transforming the poison-configuration within their own bodies.)

TUPILE: so-called "sanctuary planet" (probably several planets) for defeated Houses of the Imperium. Location(s) known only to the Guild and maintained inviolate under the Guild Peace.

U

ULEMA: a Zensunni doctor of theology.

UMMA: one of the brotherhood of prophets. (A term of scorn in the Imperium, meaning any "wild" person given to fanatical prediction.)

UROSHNOR: one of several sounds empty of general meaning and which Bene Gesserit implant within the psyches of selected victims for purposes of control. The sensitized person, hearing the sound, is temporarily immobilized.

USUL: Fremen: "The base of the pillar."

V

VAROTA: famed maker of balisets; a native of Chusuk.

VERITE: one of the Ecaz will-destroying narcotics. It renders a person incapable of falsehood.

VOICE: that combined training originated by the Bene Gesserit which permits an adept to control others merely by selected tone shadings of the voice.

W

WALI: an untried Fremen youth.

WALLACH IX: ninth planet of Laoujin, site of the Mother School of the Bene Gesserit.

WAR OF ASSASSINS: the limited form of warfare permitted under the Great Convention and the Guild Peace. The aim is to reduce involvement of innocent bystanders. Rules prescribe formal declaration of intent and restrict permissible weapons.

WATER BURDEN: Fremen: a mortal obligation.

WATERCOUNTERS: metal rings of different size, each designating a specific amount of water payable out of Fremen stores. Watercounters have profound significance (far beyond the idea of money) especially in birth, death, and courtship ritual.

WATER DISCIPLINE: that harsh training which fits the inhabitants of Arrakis for existence there without wasting moisture.

WATERMAN: a Fremen consecrated for and charged with the ritual duties surrounding water and the Water of Life.

WATER OF LIFE: an "illuminating" poison (*see* Reverend Mother). Specifically, that liquid exhalation of a sandworm (*see* Shai-hulud) produced at the moment of its death from drowning which is changed within the body of a Reverend Mother to become the narcotic used in the sietch tau orgy. An "awareness spectrum" narcotic.

WATERTUBE: any tube within a stillsuit or stilltent that carries reclaimed water into a catchpocket or from the catchpocket to the wearer.

WAY, BENE GESSERIT: use of the minutiae of observation.

WEATHER SCANNER: a person trained in the special methods of predicting weather on Arrakis, including ability to pole the sand and read the wind patterns.

WEIRDING: idiomatic: that which partakes of the mystical or of witchcraft.

WINDTRAP: a device placed in the path of a prevailing wind and capable of precipitating moisture from the air caught within it, usually by a sharp and distinct drop in temperature within the trap.

Y

YA HYA CHOUHADA: "Long live the fighters!" The Fedaykin battle cry. Ya (now) in this cry is augmented by the hya form (the ever-extended now). Chouhada (fighters) carries this added meaning of fighters *against* injustice. There is a distinction in this word that specifies the fighters are not struggling *for* anything, but are consecrated *against* a specific thing—that alone.

YALI: a Fremen's personal quarters within the sietch.

YA! YA! YAWM!: Fremen chanting cadence used in time of deep ritual significance. Ya carries the root meaning of "Now pay attention!" The yawm form is a modified term calling for urgent immediacy. The chant is usually translated as "Now, hear this!"

Z

ZENSUNNI: followers of a schismatic sect that broke away from the teachings of Maometh (the so-called "Third Muhammed") about 1381 B.G. The Zensunni religion is noted chiefly for its emphasis on the mystical and a reversion to "the ways of the fathers." Most scholars name Ali Ben Ohashi as leader of the original schism but there is some evidence that Ohashi may have been merely the male spokesman for his second wife, Nisai.

CARTOGRAPHIC NOTES

Baseline for altitude determination: the Great Bled.

Basis for latitude: meridian through Observatory Mountain.

Polar Sink: 500 m. below Bled level.

Carthag: about 200 km. northeast of Arrakeen.

Cave of Birds: in Habbanya Ridge.

Funeral Plain: open erg.

Great Bled: open, flat desert, as opposed to the erg-dune area. Open desert runs from about 60° north to 70° south. It is mostly sand and rock, with occasional outcroppings of basement complex.

Great Flat: an open depression of rock blending into erg. It lies about 100 m. above the Bled. Somewhere in the Flat is the salt pan which Pardot Kynes (father of Liet-Kynes) discovered. There are rock outcroppings rising to 200 m. from Sietch Tabr south to the indicated sietch communities.

Harg Pass: the Shrine of Leto's skull overlooks this pass.

Old Gap: a crevasse in the Arrakeen Shield Wall down to 2240 m.; blasted out by Paul-Muad'Dib.

Palmaries of the South: do not appear on this map. They lie at about 40° south latitude.

Red Chasm: 1582 m. below Bled level.

Rimwall West: a high scarp (4600 m.) rising out of the Arrakeen Shield Wall.

Wind Pass: cliff-walled, this opens into the sink villages.

Wormline: indicating farthest north points where worms have been recorded. (Moisture, not cold, is determining factor.)

AFTERWORD
by Brian Herbert

I knew Frank Herbert for more than thirty-eight years. He was a magnificent human being, a man of great honor and distinction, and the most interesting person at any gathering, drawing listeners around him like a magnet. To say he was an intellectual giant would be an understatement, since he seemed to contain all of the knowledge of the universe in his marvelous mind. He was my father, and I loved him deeply.

Nonetheless, a son's journey to understand this legendary author was not always a smooth one, as I described in my biography of him, *Dreamer of Dune*. Growing up in Frank Herbert's household, I did not understand his need for absolute silence so that he could concentrate, the intense desire he had to complete his important writing projects, or the confidence he had that one day his writing would be a success, despite the steady stream of rejections he received. To my young eyes, the characters he created in *Dune* and his other stories were the children of his mind, and they competed with me for his affections. In the years it took him to write his magnum opus, he spent more time with Paul Atreides than he did with me. His study was off-limits to me, to my brother Bruce, and to Penny, our older half sister from Dad's first marriage. In his household, only my mother Beverly really understood Dad's complexities. Ultimately, it was through her love for him, and the love he gave back to her, that I came to see the nurturing, loving side of the man.

By that time I was in my mid-twenties, having rebelled against his exacting ways for years. When I finally saw the soul of my father and began to appreciate him for the care he gave my mother when she was terminally ill, he and I became the best of friends. He helped me with my own writing career by showing me what editors wanted to see in books; he taught me how to construct interesting characters, build suspense, and keep readers turning the pages. After perusing an early draft of *Sidney's Comet* (which would become my first published novel), he marked up several pages and then wrote me this note: "These pages . . . show how editing tightens the story. Go now and do likewise." It was his way of telling me he could open the door for me and let me peek through, but I would have to complete the immense labors involved with writing myself.

Beverly Herbert was the window into Frank Herbert's soul. He shared that reality with millions of readers when he wrote a loving, three-page tribute to her at the end of *Chapterhouse: Dune*, describing their life together. His writing companion and intellectual equal, she suggested the title for that book and died in 1984 while he was writing it. Earlier in *Dune*, Frank Herbert had modeled Lady Jessica Atreides after Beverly Herbert, with her dignified, gentle ways of influence, and even her prescient abilities, which my mother actually possessed. When he wrote of "Lady Jessica's latent (prophetic) abilities," he was describing my mother, thinking of all the amazing paranormal feats she had accomplished in her lifetime. In an endearing tone, he often referred to her as his "white witch," or good witch. Similarly, throughout the Dune series, he described the heroic Bene Gesserit women as "witches."

Dune is the most admired science fiction novel ever written and has sold tens of millions of copies all over the world, in more than twenty languages. It is to science fiction what the Lord of the Rings trilogy is to fantasy, the most highly regarded works in their respective genres. Of course, *Dune* is not just science fiction. It includes strong elements of fantasy and contains so many important layers beneath the story line that it has become a mainstream classic.

The novel was first published in hardcover in 1965 by Chilton Books, best known for their immense auto-repair novels. No other publisher would touch the book, in part because of the length of the manuscript. They felt it was far too long at 200,000 words, when most novels of the day were only a quarter to a third that length. *Dune* would require immense printing costs and a high hardcover price for the time, in excess of five dollars. No science fiction novel had ever commanded a retail price that high.

Publishers also expressed concern about the complexity of the novel and all of the new, exotic words the author introduced in the beginning, which tended to slow the story down. One editor said he could not get through the first hundred pages without becoming confused and irritated. Another said he was probably making the mistake of his lifetime in not publishing the work, but declined it anyway. Still another said it could attract a cult following, but he didn't want it either.

Initial sales of the book were slow, but Frank Herbert's science fiction–writing peers and readers recognized the genius of the work from the beginning, awarding it the coveted Nebula and Hugo awards for best novel of the year. It was featured in *The Whole Earth Catalog* and began to receive excellent reviews, including one from the *New York Times*. A groundswell of support was building.

In 1969, Frank Herbert published the first sequel, *Dune Messiah*, in which he warned about the dangers of following a charismatic leader and showed the dark side of Paul Atreides. Many fans didn't understand this message, because they didn't want to see their superhero brought down from his pedestal. Still, the book sold well, and so did its predecessor. Looking back at *Dune*, it is clear that Dad laid the seeds of the troublesome direction he intended to take with his hero, but a lot of readers didn't want to see it. John W. Campbell, the editor of *Analog* who made many useful suggestions when *Dune* was being serialized, did not like *Dune Messiah* because of this Paul Atreides issue.

Having studied politics carefully, my father believed that heroes made mistakes . . . mistakes that were amplified by the number of people who followed such leaders slavishly. In a foreshadowing epigraph, Frank Herbert wrote in *Dune*: "Remember, we speak now of the Muad'Dib who ordered battle drums made from his enemies' skins, the Muad'Dib who denied the conventions of his ducal past with a wave of the hand, saying merely: 'I am the Kwisatz Haderach. That is reason enough.'" And in a dramatic scene, as Liet-Kynes lay dying in the desert, he remembered the long-ago words of his own father: "No more terrible disaster could befall your people than for them to fall into the hands of a Hero."

By the early 1970s, sales of *Dune* began to accelerate, largely because the novel was heralded as an environmental handbook, warning about the dangers of destroying the Earth's finite resources. Frank Herbert spoke to more than 30,000 people at the first Earth Day in Philadelphia, and he toured the country, speaking to enthusiastic college audiences. The environmental movement was sweeping the nation, and Dad rode the crest of the wave, a breathtaking trip. When he published *Children of Dune* in 1976, it became a runaway bestseller, hitting every important list in the country.

Children of Dune was the first science fiction novel to become a *New York Times* bestseller in both hardcover and paperback, and sales reached into the millions. After that, other science fiction writers began to have their own bestsellers, but Frank Herbert was the first to obtain such a high level of readership; he brought science fiction out of the ghetto of literature. By 1979, *Dune* itself had sold more than 10 million copies, and sales kept climbing. In early 1985, shortly after David Lynch's movie *Dune* was released, the paperback version of the novel reached #1 on the *New York Times* bestseller list. This was a phenomenal accomplishment, occurring twenty years after its first publication, and sales remain brisk today.

IN 1957, DAD FLEW TO THE OREGON COAST TO WRITE A MAGAZINE article about a U.S. Department of Agriculture project there, in which the government successfully planted poverty grasses on the crests of sand dunes, to keep them from inundating highways. He intended to call the article "They Stopped the Moving Sands," but soon realized he had a much bigger story on his hands.

Frank Herbert's life experiences are layered into the pages of the Dune series, combined with an eclectic assortment of fascinating ideas that sprang from his researches. Among other things, the Dune universe is a spiritual melting pot, a far future in which religious beliefs have combined into interesting forms. Discerning readers will recognize Buddhism, Sufi Mysticism and other Islamic belief systems, Catholicism, Protestantism, Judaism, and Hinduism. In the San Francisco Bay Area, my father even knew Zen Master Alan Watts, who lived on an old ferryboat. Dad drew on a variety of religious influences, without adhering to any one of them. Consistent with this, the stated purpose of the Commission of Ecumenical Translators, as described in an appendix to *Dune*, was to eliminate arguments between religions, each of which claimed to have "the one and only revelation."

When he was a boy, Dad's many Irish Catholic aunts (on his mother's side) tried to force Catholicism on him, but he resisted. Instead, this became the genesis of the Bene Gesserit Sisterhood. This fictional organization would claim it did not believe in organized religion, but the sisters were spiritual nonetheless. Both my father and mother were like that as well.

During the 1950s, Frank Herbert was a political speechwriter and publicity writer for U.S. senatorial and congressional candidates. In that decade, he also journeyed twice to Mexico with his family, where he studied desert conditions and crop cycles, and was subjected unwittingly to the effects of a hallucinogenic drug. All of those experiences, and a great deal from his childhood, found their way onto the pages of *Dune*. The novel became as complex and multilayered as Frank Herbert himself.

As I wrote in *Dreamer of Dune*, the characters in *Dune* fit mythological archetypes. Paul is the hero prince on a quest who weds the daughter of a "king" (he marries Princess Irulan, whose father is the Emperor Shaddam Corrino IV). Reverend Mother Gaius Helen Mohiam is a witch mother archetype, while Paul's sister Alia is a virgin witch, and Pardot Kynes is the wise old man of Dune mythology. Beast Rabban Harkonnen, though evil and aggressive, is essentially a fool.

For the names of heroes, Frank Herbert selected from Greek mythology and other mythological bases. The Greek House Atreus, upon which House Atreides in *Dune* was based, was the ill-fated family of kings Menelaus and Agamemnon. A heroic family, it was beset by tragic flaws and burdened with a curse pronounced against it by Thyestes. This foreshadows the troubles Frank Herbert had in mind for the Atreides family. The evil Harkonnens of *Dune* are related to the Atreides by blood, so when they assassinate Paul's father Duke Leto, it is kinsmen against kinsmen, similar to what occurred in the household of Agamemnon when he was murdered by his wife Clytemnestra.

Dune is a modern-day conglomeration of familiar myths, a tale in which great sandworms guard a precious treasure of melange, the geriatric spice that represents, among other things, the finite resource of oil. The planet Arrakis features immense, ferocious worms that are like dragons of lore, with "great teeth" and a "bellows breath of cinnamon." This resembles the myth described by an unknown English poet in *Beowulf*, the compelling tale of a fearsome fire dragon who guarded a great treasure hoard in a lair under cliffs, at the edge of the sea.

The desert of Frank Herbert's classic novel is a vast ocean of sand, with giant worms diving into the depths, the mysterious and unrevealed domain of Shai-hulud. Dune tops are like the crests of waves, and there are powerful sandstorms out there, creating extreme danger. On Arrakis, life is said to emanate from the Maker (Shai-hulud) in the desert-sea; similarly, all life on Earth is believed to have evolved from our oceans. Frank Herbert drew parallels, used spectacular metaphors, and extrapolated present conditions into world systems that seem entirely alien at first blush. But close examination reveals they aren't so different from systems we know . . . and the book characters of his imagination are not so different from people familiar to us.

Paul Atreides (who is the messianic "Muad'Dib" to the Fremen) resembles Lawrence of Arabia (T. E. Lawrence), a British citizen who led Arab forces in a successful desert revolt against the Turks during World War I. Lawrence employed guerrilla tactics to destroy enemy forces and communication lines, and came close to becoming a messiah figure for the Arabs. This historical event led Frank Herbert to consider the possibility of an outsider leading native forces against the morally corrupt occupiers of a desert world, in the process becoming a godlike figure to them.

One time I asked my father if he identified with any of the characters in his stories, and to my surprise he said it was Stilgar, the rugged leader of the Fremen. I had been thinking of Dad more as the dignified, honorable Duke Leto, or the heroic, swashbuckling Paul, or the loyal Duncan Idaho. Mulling this over, I realized Stilgar was the equivalent of a Native American chief in *Dune*—a person who represented and defended time-honored ways that did not harm the ecology of the planet. Frank Herbert was that, and a great deal more. As a child, he had known a Native American who hinted that he had been banished from his tribe, a man named Indian Henry who taught my father some of the ways of his people, including fishing, the identification of edible and medicinal plants in the forest, and how to find red ants and protein-rich grub worms for food.

When he set up the desert planet of Arrakis and the galactic empire encompassing it, Frank Herbert pitted western and primitive cultures against one another and gave the nod to the latter. In *Dune* he wrote, "Polish comes from the cities; wisdom from the desert." (Later, in his mainstream novel *Soul Catcher*, he would do something similar and would favor old ways over modern ways.) Like the nomadic Bedouins of the Arabian plateau, the Fremen live an admirable, isolated existence, separated from civilization by vast stretches of desert. The Fremen take psychedelic drugs during religious rites, like the Navajo Indians of North America. And like the Jews, the Fremen have been persecuted, driven to hide from authorities and survive in fortified places. Both Jews and Fremen expect to be led to the promised land by a messiah.

The words and names in *Dune* are from many tongues, including Navajo, Latin, Chakobsa (a language found in the Caucasus), the Nahuatl dialect of the Aztecs, Greek, Persian, East Indian, Russian, Turkish, Finnish, Old English, Spanish, and, of course, Arabic.

In *Children of Dune*, Leto II allowed sandtrout to attach themselves to his body, and this was based in part upon my father's own experiences as a boy growing up in Washington State, when he rolled up his trousers and waded into a stream or lake, permitting leeches to attach themselves to his legs.

The legendary life of the divine superhero Muad'Dib is based on themes found in a variety of religious faiths. Frank Herbert even used lore and bits of information from the people of the Gobi Desert in Asia, the Kalahari Desert in Southwest Africa, and the aborigines of the Australian Outback. For centuries such people have survived on very small amounts of water, in environments where water is a more precious resource than gold.

The Butlerian Jihad, occurring ten thousand years before the events described in *Dune*, was a war against thinking machines who at one time had cruelly enslaved humans. For this reason, computers were eventually made illegal by humans, as decreed in the Orange Catholic Bible: "Thou shalt not make a machine in the likeness of a human mind." The roots of the jihad went back to individuals my parents knew, to my mother's grandfather Cooper Landis and to our family friend Ralph Slattery, both of whom abhorred machines.

Still, there are computers in the Dune universe, long after the jihad. As Frank Herbert's series unfolds, it is revealed that the Bene Gesserits have secret computers to keep track of their breeding records. And the Mentats of *Dune*, capable of supreme logic, are "human computers." In large part these organic human calculators were based upon my father's paternal grandmother, Mary Stanley, an illiterate Kentucky hill-woman who performed incredible mathematical calculations in her head. Mentats were the precursors of *Star Trek*'s Spock, First Officer of the starship *Enterprise* . . . and Frank Herbert described the dangers of thinking machines back in the 1960s, years before Arnold Schwarzenegger's Terminator movies.

Remarkably, no aliens populate the Dune universe. Even the exotic, mutant Guild navigators are human. So are the vile genetic wizards, the Tleilaxu, and the gholas grown in their flesh vats. Among the most unusual humans to spring from Frank Herbert's imagination, the women of the Bene Gesserit Sisterhood have a collective memory—a concept based largely upon the writings and teachings of Carl Gustav Jung, who spoke of a "collective unconscious," that supposedly inborn set of "contents and modes of behavior" possessed by all human beings. These were concepts my father discussed at length with Ralph Slattery's wife Irene, a psychologist who had studied with Jung in Switzerland in the 1930s.

Frank Herbert's life reached a crescendo in the years after 1957, when he focused his unusual experiences and knowledge on creating his great novel. In the massive piles of books he read to research *Dune*, he recalled reading somewhere that ecology was the science of understanding consequences. This was not his original concept, but as he learned from Ezra Pound, he "made it new" and put it in a form that was palatable to millions of people. With a worldview similar to that of an American Indian, Dad saw western man inflicting himself on the environment, not living in harmony with it.

Despite all the work *Dune* required, my father said it was his favorite book to write. He used what he called a "technique of enormous detail," in which he studied and prepared notes over a four-year period, between 1957 and 1961, then wrote and rewrote the book between 1961 and 1965.

As Dad expanded and contracted the manuscript, depending upon which editor was giving him advice, an error found its way into the final manuscript. The age of Emperor Shaddam Corrino IV is slightly inconsistent in the novel, but it is one of the few glitches in the entire Dune series. This is remarkable, considering the fact that Frank Herbert wrote *Dune*, *Dune Messiah*, *Children of Dune*, and *God Emperor of Dune* on typewriters . . . hundreds of thousands of words without the use of a computer to keep all of the information straight.

Late in 1961, in the midst of his monumental effort, Dad fired his literary agent Lurton Blassingame, because he didn't feel the agent was supportive enough and because he couldn't bear the thought of sending any more stories into the New York publishing industry, which had been rejecting him for years. A couple of years later, when the new novel was nearly complete, he got back together with Blassingame and went through the ordeal of rejection after rejection—more than twenty of them—until Chilton finally picked up the book and paid an advance of $7,500 for it.

If not for a farsighted editor at Chilton, Sterling Lanier, *Dune* might never have been published, and world literature would be much the poorer for it.

WHEN MY FATHER AND I BECAME CLOSE IN MY ADULTHOOD AND WE began to write together, he spoke to me often of the importance of detail, of density of writing. A student of psychology, he understood the human subconscious, and liked to say that *Dune* could be read on any of several layers that were nested beneath the adventure story of a messiah on a desert planet. Ecology is the most obvious layer, but alongside that are politics, religion, philosophy, history, the evolution of mankind, and even poetry. *Dune* is a marvelous tapestry of words, sounds, and images. Sometimes he wrote passages in poetry first, which he expanded and converted into prose, forming sentences that included elements of the original poems.

Dad told me that you could follow any of the novel's layers as you read it, and then start the book all over again, focusing on an entirely different layer. At the end of his magnificent book, he intentionally left loose ends and said he did this to send the readers spinning out of the story with bits and pieces of it—"detritus," he called it—still clinging to them, so that they would want to go back and read it again. A neat trick, and he pulled it off perfectly.

As his eldest son, I see familial influences in the story. Earlier, I noted that my mother is memorialized in *Dune*, and so is Dad. He must have been thinking of himself when he wrote that Duke Leto's "qualities as a father have long been overlooked." The words have deep significance to me, because at the time he and I were not getting along well at all. I was going through a rebellious teenage phase, reacting to the uncompromising manner in which he ruled the household.

At the beginning of *Dune*, Paul Atreides is fifteen years old, around the same age I was at the time the book was first serialized in *Analog*. I do not see myself much in the characterization of Paul, but I do see Dad in Paul's father, the noble Duke Leto Atreides. In one passage, Frank Herbert wrote: "Yet many facts open the way to this Duke: his abiding love for his Bene Gesserit lady; the dreams he held for his son . . ." Late in his life, Dad responded to interview questions about my own writing career by saying, "The acorn doesn't fall far from the oak tree." He often complimented me to others, more than he did to me directly. To most of his friends he seemed like an extrovert, but in family matters he was often quite the opposite, preferring to retire to his study. Frequently, his strongest emotions went on the page, so I often feel him speaking to me as I read his stories.

Once, I asked my father if he thought his magnum opus would endure. He replied modestly that he didn't know and that the only valid literary critic was time. *Dune* was first published in 1965, and Frank Herbert would be pleased to know that interest in his fantastic novel, and the series it spawned, has never waned. An entire new generation of readers is picking up *Dune* and enjoying it, just as their parents did before them.

Like our own universe, the universe of Dune continues to expand. Frank Herbert wrote six novels in the series, and I have written thirteen more in collaboration with Kevin J. Anderson, including the chronological grand finale that millions of fans were awaiting, the uncompleted project my father called "Dune 7." He was working on that project when he died in 1986, and it would have been the third book in a trilogy he began with *Heretics of Dune* and *Chapterhouse: Dune*. In those novels he set up a great mystery, and years after his death the solution was the most closely guarded secret in science fiction . . . a solution that Kevin and I wrote in two novels: *Hunters of Dune* and *Sandworms of Dune*.

Right now there are nineteen Dune novels (plus one non-canon novel), along with the 1984 movie directed by David Lynch, and two television miniseries that followed Frank Herbert's plotline more closely—"Frank Herbert's Dune" and "Frank Herbert's Children of Dune" (including the *Dune Messiah* story line). As I write this early in 2019, a major new movie of *Dune* is being undertaken by Legendary Pictures, with a top Hollywood director and an exciting A-list cast. I am one of the executive producers, and I've done consultation work on the script. The novel *Dune* is such a massive story that it will now be filmed in two major motion pictures, each covering around half of the book. Dune tabletop and digital games have also been announced, and I have consulted on them as well. There are additional projects underway that have not yet been announced, but when they are it will become clear that Dune has finally become the franchise it has always deserved to be.

Every new project must measure up to the lofty standard my father established with his own novels. When all of the good stories have been told, there might be no more new books, film productions, or other emerging projects. But that will not really be a conclusion, because fans can always go back to *Dune* itself and read it again and again . . . this beloved novel that will be read for centuries to come.

BRIAN HERBERT
Seattle, Washington

FRANK HERBERT is the bestselling author of the Dune saga. He was born in Tacoma, Washington, and educated at the University of Washington, Seattle. He worked a wide variety of jobs—including TV cameraman, radio commentator, oyster diver, jungle survival instructor, lay analyst, creative writing teacher, reporter, and editor of several West Coast newspapers—before becoming a full-time writer.

In 1952, Herbert began publishing science fiction with "Looking for Something?" in *Startling Stories*. But his emergence as a writer of major stature did not occur until 1965, with the publication of *Dune*. This was followed by *Dune Messiah*, *Children of Dune*, *God Emperor of Dune*, *Heretics of Dune*, and *Chapterhouse: Dune* to complete the bestselling saga. Herbert is also the author of some twenty other books, including *The White Plague*, *The Dosadi Experiment*, and *Destination: Void*. He died in 1986.

SIL   Silber Joan.
       In the city

$16.30

DATE			

DISCARD

© THE BAKER & TAYLOR CO.

IN THE CITY

By the same author

HOUSEHOLD WORDS

IN THE CITY

Joan Silber

 50,253

VIKING

VIKING
Viking Penguin Inc., 40 West 23rd Street,
New York, New York 10010, U.S.A.
Penguin Books Ltd, Harmondsworth,
Middlesex, England
Penguin Books Australia Ltd, Ringwood,
Victoria, Australia
Penguin Books Canada Limited, 2801 John Street,
Markham, Ontario, Canada L3R 1B4
Penguin Books (N.Z.) Ltd, 182–190 Wairau Road,
Auckland 10, New Zealand

Copyright © Joan Silber, 1987
First published in 1987 by Viking Penguin Inc.
Published simultaneously in Canada

LIBRARY OF CONGRESS CATALOGING IN PUBLICATION DATA
Silber, Joan.
In the city.
I. Title.
PS3569.I4141I5   1987   813'.54   86-40349
ISBN 0-670-81479-2

Printed in the United States of America by
The Maple-Vail Book Mfg. Group, Binghamton, New York
Set in Garamond No. 3
Design by the Sarabande Press

For Lee

ACKNOWLEDGMENT

I would like to thank the Guggenheim Foundation for its generosity during the writing of this book

IN THE CITY

I

(Summer, 1924)

Pauline had forgotten about the straw seats on the train. She had a half hour's ride from Newark to the Hoboken ferry terminal, and the moment she took her seat she was attacked through her clothing by a vicious meshwork of woven bristles; it was like sitting on a hair shirt. She had dressed for the heat—it was August and near ninety—and she wore a loose voile outfit which, even with her slip under it, provided very skimpy insulation against railroad upholstery.

A woman across the aisle from her had spread a newspaper under herself. Pauline had only a book of poetry with her, which she certainly wasn't going to sit on. She was seventeen and not inclined to be offhand about looking ridiculous in public. And she did think the woman looked ridiculous, settling her skirts over the paper like a hen brooding newsprint.

So she sat on one hand and fanned herself with her book. The train hadn't left the station yet, and outside the window she could see across the street to a theater marquee. Below it there was a poster of a couple about to kiss, a man with a pencil mustache and a woman with marcelled hair. Even from a distance the picture of their profiles leaning toward each other made her smile in recognition, as though she were looking at a picture of herself. She had spent several hours the night before in the front seat of a boy's roadster while it was parked behind the playground of a grammar school. She did not think that the boy, whose name was Harry Bitt, was himself important, except as the agent of certain sensations, but she was in awe of these sensations, and she reviewed them constantly.

It was very hot, and it would be worse in New York, with its reflecting pavements and the massed crowds diffusing their own conglomerate body heat. Pauline didn't mind the weather except that she had to pull at her bangs all the time to keep them from frizzing. All summer she had been going into New York as often as they would let her, on the excuse of running errands for her father's dry-goods store, picking up samples of edge trim and dropping off orders for white cotton batiste. Her visits always pleased her and gave her a great feeling of personal superiority, although they involved a lot of aimless walking in tight shoes, and she generally got lost at some point toward the end of the day; once an oily-haired man in a plaid coat had followed her for blocks, calling out, "You want a map, doll?"

The train began to move, jolting forward so that Pauline was jerked across the raspy seat; then it stopped and began again. Outside the window there was a constant dull flow of scenery—flat-fronted brick buildings. Once they were out of Newark these gave way to a bare and marshy flatland, like a giant vacant lot. Along the horizon there were water towers and crows flying. Pauline liked this part, which gave her a sense of traversing the steppes or the moors, some bleak European wastes.

She took up her book, which she thought she should read since she had brought it with her. It was a copy of Baudelaire in French, and Pauline's French wasn't nearly good enough to read most of it without a dictionary, but she knew some of the shorter poems almost by heart, and she moved her lips over the phrases. In her room at home she read them aloud in a languid chant, trying to absorb into her own personality something of the poems' atmosphere of sonorous corruption and rehearsing her own allegiance with ennui and other delicate monstrosities.

She was trying to figure out what *chevelure* meant when the words *luxe, calme, et volupté* started her thinking about Harry Bitt again and sent her back into that smug nostalgia staying on as aftermath from the night before. She did not resist; she intended to keep thinking about it as much as possible. He was a pale, soft-faced boy, smooth and blond, who went in for soothing hugs and fluttery kisses. With encouragement, a more serious and urgent side of him showed itself, and it was the fact of having worked this transformation in him which lingered most powerfully in her imagination. She kept going over the exact sequence of it; she wanted, if anything, more mental repetition, a more insistent record, since the experience had otherwise all the vagueness of the invisible, witnessed, after all, with her eyes closed. It was to rescue all of it from the blurred realm of private evidence that she always reported everything that happened on dates to her friend Bunny, but these were only lists and lacked the audacious nuance of the real thing.

Bunny was wrongly nicknamed; she was a bulky, solemn girl, burdened with *Bunny* by face-pinching parents when she was young and cute. (Her real name which she still hated anyway, was Roberta.) When she listened to Pauline's descriptions of what happened with Harry (in June it had been Ray), her eyes glistened; she asked intelligent and sometimes peculiar questions. Pauline liked explaining, but she felt there was something too soft, too romantic, in Bunny's attitude.

Still they were really friends—outsiders together—egging each other on in their shared scorn for the monkeyish antics that passed for hilarity in their high school. Minna Green played the piano with her feet at parties; Gilbert Markus had eaten eleven sardine-and-egg sandwiches on a dare in the school cafeteria; the captain of the football team had once set a live chicken loose in the auditorium. Pauline couldn't believe the fatuousness of all this, the "rampant stupidity," as she and Bunny liked to say. It made them style themselves as aloof and eccentric by contrast; they both wore their hair in the same triangular bobs, sometimes wrapped with a ribbon across the forehead, and carried the same knotwork bags; in class they rolled their eyes at each other across the room and passed sarcastic notes.

This avowed indifference did not, of course, make them favorites in most crowds. It was harder on Bunny, who looked so mild and blinking in her middy blouse, and who had once had a balloon filled with ink thrown at her back. Pauline was more convincing—she was a trim, nervously pretty girl, with a clear, slightly nasal voice. She had thin, peaked shoulders and carried herself well; she was also quite vain and a little too eager to be original about her appearance (today she had tied a striped ribbon around her hips for a sash, with somewhat awkward results). Older boys were sometimes drawn to her; she had that slyly knowing look when she was being quick and satirical (always flattering when you were not the target) and a sudden, fresh smile.

The train entered a tunnel and everything went dark inside the car for several minutes; Pauline sat upright, watching the rows of lights bob past the windows. The sensation of this got mingled with the constant physical remembrance of

Harry, and she was feeling excited and reckless. The train came out into daylight and passed through the Hoboken track yards, where it stopped short. The breeze that had been coming through the windows died instantly; all the passengers were sighing and blotting their faces and plucking at their clothing to let the air in, as they lined up to get off. A conductor on the platform reached up to help her step down; he was a fat, white-haired man, who put his hands under her arms, touching her breasts: on purpose, she thought.

She was startled but not angry, since it seemed to her that anyone might want to do that, and it was over in an instant. She followed the crowd through the station—with its great domed ceiling and its dingy skylight—out to the street, and across to the ferry dock. The boat was already waiting, a boxy wooden hulk with peeling paint; beyond the glare of the water, the skyline of the city loomed flat and close, as though she could swim there if she were dressed for it. As soon as the entrance chain was unhooked, she found a seat on deck.

Pauline stood up when the boat got under way. The light cloth of her dress got pressed flat against her stomach and legs and flapped behind her like a sail. Everyone else was sitting down, blinking as though the wind were too much for them, which made her feel very blithe and sturdy, a spirited young thing braving the elements. Near the railing, her face got misted and wet, and she backed away because of her hair.

When she walked out into the Twenty-third Street ferry terminal, she tugged at her dress to pull it down, and a man who was standing under the clock tower smiled at her. She laughed slightly, to show that she was amused at having been caught grooming herself. He said, "Did you ever think about being a model?"

5

He was about thirty (too old for her), a tall man in a straw hat and a summer suit.

"You've certainly got the face for it," he said. Pauline said thank you. He was almost good-looking, except that his freckles made his skin appear splotchy and irritated, and his Adam's apple was too large. "I mean a designer's model," he said. "You didn't think I meant an artist's model, did you?"

"Oh, no," Pauline said.

"The designers are hiring ones like you now, brunettes with little faces, not these horsy blondes. You ever hear of a designer Jean Patou?" He pronounced it more or less correctly, with a soft *j* and the last name a twangy approximation, Patoo as in sweet patootie. "My friend is hiring for him now. He should see you. You could make a lot of money."

"I wouldn't do it for the money," Pauline said.

"It would come in handy, though, right?"

Pauline had heard—who had not?—of girls being "discovered" in odd places, of their piquant expressions and unforgettable complexions striking the commercial hearts of impresarios. She would not have said she wanted to be a model; she had pictured something more singular and Bohemian for herself; she wanted to enter, somehow, a circle of people who did artistic and outrageous things, and to be admired by them, to be famous for being with them. It struck her that being a model would have its own seductive cachet even under those circumstances; no matter what people said, they always wanted to know women like that.

"Do you always wear your hair this way?" he said. "We could just comb it flatter—it's a little messed up now, isn't it?" Pauline had tried pulling spit curls down over her cheeks, and she was disappointed that he thought these weren't deliberate, but she stood still while he brushed them back with his hand and said, "Don't want to hide that face.

"It's a clean business," he said. "There's no monkey

business in it." Pauline thought it was a bit quaint of him to reassure her about that. She did not, after all, object to monkey business, as he so cutely called it. He seemed a little unsophisticated and hokey in his seersucker suit with the pants rolled too low. His shoes were that cheap leather that looked almost orange.

"My name is Earl," he said.

"I'm Pauline Samuels." There was a little silence as they crossed the street, and Pauline asked him where he was from, which was always a good thing to ask new people.

"I've been all over the world. You won't believe me when I tell you where I just came from."

"Where?"

"Paris, France. It's wonderful there except they make you sit with Negroes in cafes and buses."

"What's wrong with that?" Pauline said.

"You're probably very idealistic," he said. "You're young." She hated arguing with people who were so backward in their thinking. Probably he thought Sacco and Vanzetti were just a couple of hooligans too. Bunny would have given him a whole speech.

"We could go over to my friend's office," he said, "if you're not in a hurry. It's around the corner."

If they were hiring right away, she would have to say no; she wasn't graduating until next January. She walked with him down the block; he stopped in front of an office building and held the door for her to follow him inside. The lobby, which was empty, had a cracked marble floor and brown-painted molding. "Wait, here," he said. "Let me go up and see if he's still out to lunch or if he's there." He went up the stairs and came back again in a few minutes. "He's out. You don't mind waiting?"

Pauline shook her head. He edged her under the stairwell, and then he drew her toward him and began kissing

her. He said, "Ah," as though he thought she had been expecting this, which she had not, but she kissed him back by
habit since she was proud of not being cold or timid. His
tongue was much more forceful and probing than Harry's had
been, a technique she did not particularly like but submitted
to quietly; his friend would be arriving soon anyway. They
went on kissing for a minute; then he drew back and took off
his hat, which he put on the radiator. He was balding, with
fine, reddish hair, wispy at the top of his head; he smoothed
it down as though he were sorry she had to see it. He looked
toward the door a moment; then he put his hands down under the neck of her dress, kneaded her breasts, and said,
"Ah," again, as though he had found something. She felt
suddenly foolish and unprepared, shocked that he was really
touching her bare skin, and aware that she was in a public
place and that she didn't like him or find him attractive.

He kissed her very hard and eagerly again, and then he
fumbled with the buttons of his trousers and pulled her hand
down to touch him. Pauline had never done this before, although he seemed to think she had. She was still struck with
something like physical disbelief, alarmed now, and frozen
into a sort of hardened patience with herself, with her own
mistake. It seemed strangest to her that her life contained
this now forever; it awed her beyond everything. He moved
her hand in a tightened grip, thrusting up against her,
and began to shiver all over. "Is it okay?" he said. "Can I put
it in?"

"No," she said.

"No?" he said, and he let her take her hand away. She
turned then so she couldn't see what he was doing. When she
looked back, he was wiping at himself with a handkerchief.

"I have to go," she said. "I have to meet some people."

"Wait," he said, buttoning his pants and tucking his
shirt back under his suspenders. "I'll walk you."

He hooked his arm under her elbow, as though they were strolling through the park, and they walked out through the door of the building. The street was full of noise, busy with the stream of traffic that had been going on the whole time they were inside, and very bright in the afternoon sun. Pauline squinted as though she were coming out of a movie theater.

"You believe in free love, don't you," he said. "I like that. I like a free spirit."

There was an El station by the corner, and Pauline thought she could get away from him there. He said, "Meet me here next Saturday, okay?"

"I can't come into New York any more. I'm not going to be able to for the rest of the summer."

"I could meet you in Hoboken, if you want. Your parents wouldn't have to know. They wouldn't like me, would they? You don't think I'm too old for you, do you?" Pauline shrugged.

He took out an envelope and asked her to write her phone number on it. She gave him a number with one digit wrong, let him kiss her again, and walked up the stairs to the El entrance.

There was a moment while she fumbled for a nickel in her purse when she heard someone running up the stairs after her, but it was only a boy in knickers who pushed ahead of her at the turnstile. She waited on the platform with the others, and no one even looked at her or noticed her especially. When the train came, she took the first seat, next to a woman with an infant in her lap.

She got off at Penn Station and went at once to the ladies' room, where she spent time hiking up her garters and washing her face. Her eyes looked terrible—all hangdog and watery like Bunny's—but she put on powder, which made her cheeks less flushed and swollen, and she pulled the spit

9

curls down again. She walked out into the station until she found a lunch counter, and she sat with her purse and her book balanced on her lap and read the menu, but no one came to wait on her. There didn't even seem to be anyone behind the counter, although other people were eating. She felt clumsy and wincing, laughably timid in all her gestures. A counter boy with crooked teeth came over to her finally, and she ordered a lemonade and drank it down quickly.

When she walked outside again, it had begun to rain. It was only a light rain, which cooled the air and made a soothing, rushing sound on the pavement, but she was wet by the time it was over, and she had to walk the rest of the way with great splotches on the front of her dress, which looked lewdly comical, as though something private had leaked through her clothing.

The office of Art Style Trim was on the second floor, and as soon as she opened the door, a man who was standing up talking to the receptionist called out, "It's the orphan of the storm here. What's the matter, honey, your boyfriend doesn't love you enough to buy you an umbrella?"

A tiny leathery man in glasses who was sitting on one of the armchairs said, "What are you, testing the fabric to see if it runs? That's it, right? I know."

They were salesmen. The older man in fact looked like someone she had seen in offices since she was a child, although she wasn't sure. Pauline hated on principle the heartiness of salesmen, their constant bantering to pass the time, but she sometimes flirted with them to show them they hadn't gotten the best of her. Today she just nodded her head at them: let them think she was shy, a sodden, mincing little thing. She could tell already that was what they thought. They had gone back to talking to the receptionist, a beefy woman with fierce eyebrows and shrimp-colored rouge.

Pauline's errand was to pick up an order of soutache

braid. This would come rolled on a large wheel, and she had planned to stop for it later in the day, since there was nothing to do but go home once she was carrying it. The receptionist told her to take a seat and wait for Mr. Gittelson, who was out.

She took a chair in the corner, next to a wall papered with silhouettes of black swans holding funereal loops of black ribbon in their beaks. The salesmen went back to playing a game of cards, and Pauline picked up a copy of *System: The Magazine of Business* and flipped through it. She read an article on "Bad Debts and Hidden Losses" and the advertisements for correspondence courses. ("Your future depends on yourself. Will you always be a drudge? A few years hence, then what?") The magazine made her feel vexed and vaguely tearful, and she had to put it down, although the encounter in the hallway had left her feeling leaden and dazed, the opposite of weepy.

She waited for a long time, an hour at least, hearing the slapping of the playing cards against the tables and the salesmen's voices. Once it seemed to her that they were saying, "Woes are wild," which could not be right but she let it pass, another piece of oddness from the crackling surface of the world.

By the time she heard the click of the office door opening, her dress had dried where it was stretched between her knees. "Here he is," the receptionist said, "the man of the hour." Pauline had always thought that Mr. Gittelson was handsome in a stocky way, although the stiff collars made his eyes look startled and overeager. There was a shininess near his scalp now where the brilliantine had melted. When he saw her, he said, "Paulie," and then, "So did they give you coffee while you were waiting? A glass of water even? Nothing, right?"

"I was fine," she said.

Mr. Gittelson pinched and wiggled the end of her nose. "A sweetheart." Then he went into the back office. When he returned, a boy came with him carrying the roll of braid wrapped in brown paper. Pauline tore one corner of the package to make sure it was the right kind. "Look at this," Mr. Gittelson said. "She looks before she leaps. This is a very intelligent girl here. You could all of you learn something."

"My father would kill me if I didn't look," Pauline said.

"You're a lovely girl," Mr. Gittelson said. "Your kind I would hire in a minute."

Pauline said, "Thank you," and then she smiled a little. She was thinking, with some appreciation of the irony, that it was the second time that day someone had "offered" her a job. Mr. Gittelson, who thought she was smiling with pleasure at being praised, kissed her on the cheek before she left, rubbing his mustache against her.

On the way back she had to sit on the lower deck of the ferry, so her package wouldn't get wet; the air was close and smelled of gasoline from the engines. When she boarded the train, she dozed off almost at once; once she dreamed someone was holding a fur hat over her face and stifling her, and she woke feeling frightened and slightly ashamed.

When she got off at the Newark station, the downtown streets were thick with people going home from work or shopping. She walked for blocks, shifting her bundle, which was heavy and left marks on her arms.

At home they were already sitting down to dinner; from a block away Pauline could see the yellow light of the citronella candles set out on the screened porch at the side of the house, where they took their meals in hot weather. Pauline rapped on the screen door, and her mother called out from her seat, "We gave up waiting for you already." The porch room seemed very bright and tensely cheerful, with the pink glass plates and the ugly metal fruit bowl and the tablecloth printed with drawings of bananas and sombreros. Solly, who was twelve, banged his fork against the juice pitcher and said, "Time and supper wait for no man." There was cold roast chicken and Harvard beets. Pauline ate slowly, with some pleasure in the tastes but no appetite. She felt as though she had been traveling for a long time; her legs ached, and things were dry in her mouth.

Solly, who had gotten a haircut from his father that day, kept licking his finger and dabbing the back of his neck. He was bleeding in spots from where the clippers had nicked the scalp. "Stop already," his mother said. "Don't touch."

Pauline's father went on gnawing his chicken with that private, inward gaze he had when he was chewing. The upper half of his face was always hawkish and worried, but around the mouth the expression was slack and old, and he lapped at his food when he ate. He was quiet at the table. He could sit still for hours, and then, out of his brooding, he would speak out or dart up suddenly. Sometimes even now he would grab the children and hug them until they squealed. Fits of annoyance came over him without warning. When they were little and he was angry with them, he used to shake them rather than hit them—which was worse, Pauline thought, because there was that hideous feeling of your head rolling over and over in rhythm, as though you were helping.

Her mother said, "You got wet in the rain, right? Next time you'll wear a hat." Pauline had a straw skimmer which she wouldn't wear because it looked like a shellacked waffle.

Solly said, "Ease-play ass-pay the ickles-pay." Pauline reached across and passed the relish dish, because she knew she was the only one who would bother to translate.

Her mother was pouring salt now on a spot where beet juice had gotten on her lap. She wore a kerchief tied around her head in a turban, as she did whenever she was in the

13

house. Sometimes she kept it on even when she was in the
store waiting on customers. She was a patient but unsmiling
salesperson, hauling down bolts of cloth and unfurling them
silently for inspection; she could carry out a sale without
speaking more than a few words. Standing in front of the
shelves of silk chiffons and plaid taffeta ribbons, she was a
plain figure in a shapeless dress, short and solidly built, with
a high mount of bosom. Her looks were marred by an underbite—a jutting chin like a terrier's—which made her say her
s's too thickly. She was cautious by nature—full of warnings
about how eating bread in the morning was the only way to
avoid getting worms in the stomach, afraid of elevators and
uncooked vegetables and drafts in bedrooms—but having
come from Europe as a bride of twenty, she had lived for so
many years in a state of half-understanding and misapprehen-
sion that she had grown shy and hesitant and peevish about
her opinions. Her English was not good, and had it been up
to her, she would not have gone out of the house at all. Every
child on the block could imitate the way she said her own
name—Mrs. Shemuels; they would suck in their lips and
click their front teeth together. Sometimes Pauline and Solly
did it too, beyond her hearing.

Pauline's father said, "Leave the stain on your dress
alone. We'll say you were murdered and sell it for a bundle."

Months before, he had read in the newspaper that the
clothing Abraham Lincoln had on when he was assassinated
had been sold at auction for $6,500, and this had struck him
as so fantastical—an example of enterprise carried to extremes of splendidly grim cleverness—that he brought it up
at every turn. He would cough into a handkerchief and hand
it to one of the children: Here, go sell it when I'm dead.

He said to Pauline, "You got the right ribbon, right?"
Pauline pointed to the package, which she had set in the
corner of the porch.

Her mother said, "So long as she didn't bring back any rotten berries this time." This was a reference to Pauline's having purchased—on Bleecker Street, two weeks ago at least—a basket of blueberries, which had looked very tempting but which had turned out to be soft and spoiled on the bottom. "Miss Millionaire," her mother said. "So you know to look first, then buy?"

"I didn't buy anything this time," Pauline said.

"She learned her lesson," her mother said. Solly rolled his eyes; they did go on about things. Pauline had been made to eat the berries as an instructive exercise, although she had not really minded. She was used to them at home, the way they were fixed and strict about some things and blindly lenient about others.

Pauline had stopped listening anyway. She was thinking about the ferry slip and how the man had seemed better-looking and more intelligent at first; she still had that preoccupation with going over the details as though she could correct them by thinking about them. Her mother was talking about how they should have reported the fruit seller to the police. It struck Pauline that, for all her parents' suspicions, they were full of ignorance about the way things were (which made her feel rather spitefully sorry for them). At the store her mother was always watching old ladies picking over the notions counter, sure that they were going to steal the needles packets. They understood greed, but the rest made no sense to them. Pauline thought of the man Earl (that was probably not really his name) wiping himself with a handkerchief, desperate and methodical, as though he were following some habit of hygiene repeated often before. This went on all the time; the world was full of this. She had kissed him, which made her flinch back in her chair now.

She sat up straight again, but no one was looking at her anyway. Her mother was complaining about how mosquitoes got through the holes in the screen, and Solly was saying the bugs could eat his beets if they wanted, hurry up, come eat. Pauline did not dislike her family at this moment—she was quite relieved, after all, to be back in the house—but they seemed very distant, and at the same time their voices were very loud.

The phone rang then, a long metallic rattle. Maybe Earl had figured out the right digit, or she had written down the right number without thinking. Her father went into the kitchen, and she could hear him saying "Yes?" (that was how he greeted people in the store too—Yes? instead of Can I help you?). It was for the other family on their party line. When he came back he said, "What did you think, it was your friend Mr. Harry?"

Pauline did the dishes while her parents sat in the living room listening to the radio, to a concert of the Philharmonic Orchestra playing Rimsky-Korsakov. The music sounded stiff and silly, with its swelling rushes and dying falls. It annoyed Pauline and made her utterly sure that she was on the other side of things, dry and unfeeling and modern. She began swabbing the dishes in time, as a sort of joke to herself, dipping and lifting them out of the suds on the soaring beat. She didn't really mind kitchen work; she had tied the apron, which was much too big for her, with the strings crossed twice around her waist so she looked tightly bodiced like a tavern wench. She had to heat up another kettle when the water got cold; and although she had been hot all day, she put a dish towel over her head and leaned her face over the spout, because she had heard that the steam was good for her complexion.

For a while Pauline was afraid that the man would be lurking in wait the next time she walked out of the ferry terminal, but then this came to seem more and more unlikely, and childish of her to imagine. She could not go into New York any more now anyway; the August sales were on and she was in the store until late every day.

Pauline worked in the stockroom, which was really a hallway under the stairs, lit by one dangling bulb and heaped with bolts of cloth and cardboard cartons. The window was painted shut and there was no ventilation; all the elastic binding went gummy from the heat and stuck to its spools, and the finish on the chintzes had a gluey feel to it. Pauline pulled things out from under piles and then sat on a stool and made lists. She had devised a way of wearing a strip of flannel around her forehead so it was hidden by her ribbon, to keep the sweat out of her eyes.

Bunny was working at the five-and-ten over the summer, and sometimes she came in on her lunch break, and they went out and sat on the steps at the back of the store. There was a dusty yard and some shade from an overgrown hedge. Bunny always brought a ragged-looking sandwich filled with hacked slices of leftover roast, and they ate together, crackling their waxed paper into little balls for the store cat to play with.

Bunny had gotten fatter over the summer, and she had had her hair cut shorter, which looked mannish instead of boyish on her. Harry Bitt said she looked like an otter that way. He had said that to Pauline in a conversation on the street one night, when he had passed her coming home from work and walked her as far as the schoolyard. He had come into the store once since then and tried to neck with her behind a pile of remnants; after that she hadn't heard from him, and by now he was probably getting ready to go back to engineering school in Pittsburgh.

All summer Bunny had been afraid she was going to get fired from the five-and-ten. Her supervisor kept telling her she was sullen. Bunny wasn't the least bit sullen, but she had a crooked half smile on her face sometimes, which was only faltering and incomplete but which looked sly to some people. Pauline thought that if Bunny wore lipstick it would offset this effect, but Bunny didn't take criticism well so Pauline had stopped suggesting it.

Pauline had waited a week before telling Bunny about the incident with Earl in the hallway. Bunny had listened without interrupting or looking too aghast, and at the end she had even made light of it by joking about how Pauline was always looking for trouble. In many ways she was very sensible. But then later she had said, "Dress models don't earn that much; the ones in stores are exploited worse than clerks." Pauline resented her always bringing her anarcho-syndicalism into everything, nosing it into Pauline's private confession, but she had said, "Oh, I know," politely enough.

Bunny was poking in the dirt with a stick; she drew the lines for tic-tac-toe, and they played a few dullish games. Then the two of them together sketched the figure of an anatomically prodigious naked man. Pauline crossed it out right away in case anybody came by and saw. Bunny said, "You could have just drawn a very large fig leaf over it."

"I would not be so philistyne," Pauline said. This was a pun of long standing between them—there was a girl in their class named Phyllis Stein, and they thought this was funny.

Pauline could hear her father from inside the store, groaning as he hauled something across the floor. Already he was hinting to Pauline that she shouldn't count on working in the store after school was over, she should think about getting work someplace else with a salary. She hadn't mentioned Gittelson yet.

She and Bunny talked about whether rents were really getting higher in Greenwich Village. Bunny thought that two girls could share a furnished room really cheaply if there was a Murphy bed and a sofa in it. A lot of Bunny's ideas of romantic experiment were curiously bound up with finding ways to live ingeniously on very little; it was a kind of ethical adventure for her to think how she might invent methods of curbing her own needs.

Pauline didn't see how with Bunny or someone else there, she would ever be free from a certain strain; even in confiding about Earl she had left out details, and not from delicacy really. She was beginning to think about staying alone in a small, bare white room, with a metal bedstead and a ewer basin and one extravagant object, a Chinese rug or a bronze vase, probably a gift from a lover.

Bunny took off her gray smock from Woolworth's and folded it up under her neck for a pillow. She said, "Wake me up if I fall asleep," and leaned back against the wooden frame of the door. Pauline was just almost closing her eyes when she heard a boy's voice humming Brahms' lullaby, quavering on the notes like an Irish tenor. It was Murray Appelbaum; he was gazing at them over the hedge. "Go back to your naps," he said. "And they talk about the wild, restless fervor of youth today."

"We're warm," Pauline said. "Come fan us with your jacket or something."

Murray crossed into the yard, taking off his jacket as he walked, and then he stood in front of them, flapping it in their faces, until Pauline told him to stop.

"How come you're not working at the bakery?" Bunny said.

"Let them eat crackers," he said. "On Mondays I'm off."

"So you just loaf around," Bunny said.

"Get it?" Pauline said.

He sat down on the grass near them.

Pauline said, "You don't look like you've been outside

too much." He was always white-skinned like that, too pale and bony; he was close to homely, except for his eyes, which were deep-set and slanted, with fine, girlish lashes.

He said, "I'm very rugged and outdoorsy but it's just too subtle for people to grasp."

"You having a good summer?" Bunny said.

"What does that mean? People always ask that, but they don't really want to know. They should say, Are you having a good gozornplatt? Are you having a good gritzilplick? It would open up conversation."

Pauline could never decide whether he was too clumsily whimsical or really unusual. They had been in the same art class last spring; once she had almost agreed to pose for him in the nude. He was always telling her his sketches were as good as Manet's at his age. He was full of quirky arrogance and then streaks of self-parody; at the bakery he would pretend to gauge the perspective of a tray of rolls, edging back from them with his thumb up, with his white hat mashed down like a droopy beret.

Bunny had taken up the stick again and was doodling something in the dirt. Murray said, "Let me see. I'll tell you if it's good or not."

"Toulouse LaDreck here," Pauline said. "He's so modest."

Bunny said, "Draw something yourself," and handed him the stick.

Pauline said, "Wait." She went inside the store and came out again with a box of tailor's chalk she had stolen from the stockroom.

Murray took it and said, "I'm very touched." He rubbed his shoe over the surface of the cement walk, to sweep away loose dirt, and made a few tentative lines and smudged them out. Then he started making big shading strokes with the flat slabs of chalk, until he had produced a pink triangle floating on two brown trapezoids, which (he was disappointed when they did not guess right) turned out to be a cubist version of the Baptist church across the street, with a series of overlapping green ovals for trees and a scribbled purple sky.

"I like it a lot," Bunny said.

"Genius comes to Peshine Avenue," Murray said.

It looked very splashy and vivid on the pavement, next to the scratchy grass and the discarded cardboard boxes. The best thing about it was the way it transformed the yard.

They were all feeling pleased with themselves. Pauline said, "My father will have a fit if he sees it."

Bunny said, "The rhythm of it is really nice."

Murray was wiping the chalk off his hands onto his pants, very workmanlike and casual. He said, "It *is* as good as a Manet." Pauline was sure Manet himself never would have said something like this. It was not bad, but the purple sky wasn't deft so much as sloppy, and he had made the trees too much like the spirals in the Palmer writing exercise. She began to think it might have been better if he had done something funnier, a witty parody or something. The more she looked at it, the more it embarrassed her a little.

They sat quiet awhile, listening to the voices of people passing in the street. Bunny had pulled up a blade of timothy grass and was chewing it absently. Pauline said, "Are you grazing?"

"She was only a farmer's daughter," Murray said, "but she sure knew her oats." Then he said, for Pauline's benefit, "She was only a notion seller's daughter, but she had me on needles and pins."

They heard a lunch whistle from one of the factories, which meant that Bunny was late getting back to work. She started fidgeting with the laces on her shoes, retying them. She still wore those heavy leather oxfords, even in summer. Pauline herself had on scuffed brown pumps (hardly better than Bunny's) over soiled cotton lisle stockings. She was al-most surprised when she looked down and saw them; she always thought of her things as nicer than they really were. She felt that all her own tastes were thwarted now, and that nothing really counted yet.

Bunny left, buttoning her smock, and they waved her off. Pauline yawned and leaned back against the screen door again. Murray stretched over closer to her and pretended to pick a dried leaf out of her hair. He said, "Do you know what a butterfly kiss is?" and then he flicked his eyelashes against her cheek. Pauline thought this was bumpkinish of him and in some way unmanly, but she gave him a flashing smile anyway, out of habit or for practice, with her eyes closed.

II

All that fall Pauline walked to school in the mornings by a longer route, through the park. Since she left the house at the same time she always had, she was almost always late for her first class, but she liked the coolness of the park at that hour—the empty benches and the dusty cement fountains—a landscape that had nothing to do with school.

Sometimes as she was leaving the park she would hear the bell, and then from the next block she could see the schoolyard, already deserted. When she got there she pushed open the heavy, metal-cased doors and walked through the halls, trying not to let her shoes make noise on the corridor tiles. Outside senior Latin she could hear Miss Oughton giving drill and the blurred rumbling of the answers chanted in unison. Sometimes as she slipped through the doorway Miss Oughton would point at her and say, *"Ad principem,"* which meant that Pauline had to go to the office to get a blue slip. Pauline did not see that it mattered how many demerits she got, since it was her last semester, and after a while Miss Oughton didn't bother any more.

In Latin she sat behind Minna Green, who wore beautiful silk-knit sweaters with sappy little piqué collars on them and who got giggly and red-faced when she had to read words like *testis* and *menses*. Once Pauline, without thinking, had actually kicked the back of her seat from annoyance.

Pauline had wanted to take Latin partly, of course, so as not to be left out of knowing what *sine qua non* and *caveat emptor* meant and the phrases that were always interleaved in sentences and used obscurely for titles. She had also been secretly much impressed by the doctrine that through the discipline of Latin the mind attained a certain purity of reasoning and took on classical habits of thought. She had only been thirteen when she'd begun it, and she had liked the idea then of being trained to a sublime and calm logic (she was sorry she was not good at math). It was a kind of whiteness of the mind she wanted, a mental stillness like the sealed expressions on eyeless statues.

She had been disappointed to find that Latin was so involved with military campaigns and letters back and forth from generals, and with learning the idioms for "to pitch camp" and "to lay waste to," and that none of it was useful internally. She still did not hate it; it was too unpopular a subject to feel rebellious toward. It seemed only dull and blockishly masculine, like Miss Oughton herself, and it made Pauline feel wild and futuristic, sitting there with her plastic bangle bracelets and her plucked eyebrows, more ready than ever to slip away from all this.

She had a familiar stock of thoughts which usually occupied her, in the midst of hearing Minna or someone else try to stumble through one of Cicero's orations. She still hadn't done more than hint to her father about the possibility of working for Gittelson. Her father had said nothing so far; it was always hard to know what he thought about things. At times she imagined that he would say no to any job outside of

Newark; she could, of course, not ask him at all and just disappear one morning, get on the train and go. She had already looked at the railroad schedule to see how early a train she would have to take to get out with her luggage before they woke up.

At times she tried to prepare herself to be the sort of person who could do this. After school she took detours on the way home, walking by pool halls and weathered wood-frame houses where men sat out on porches, so that she wouldn't be afraid of strange neighborhoods. Once in the park she made herself watch a cat mauling a sparrow, to harden herself.

The idea of running away (although she did not always think about it directly) kept her distracted and even a little somber. In school this had the effect of actually making her appear more well-mannered. She sat quiet through class, answering most questions by rote in her clear, singsong voice, which carried well. Even in gym she looked earnest, skittering around in her blue serge jumper playing kick soccer.

She felt that she was waiting, that there was nothing in this time but a kind of unprofitable repetition and a prolonged suspense. Bunny was also graduating in January—they had both been skipped a semester in grammar school—and they often greeted each other in the hall by calling out, "Only a hundred and nineteen more days!" (They had argued about whether they should count to the last day of classes or the last exam day.) It braced them both to hear the numbers shrink, as though the march of time were on their side.

At home sometimes she had fits of restless energy, and she would sit in the kitchen and sew, making underwear for herself out of scraps of fabric—silk pongee step-ins and cotton lawn chemises—working the treadle with fierce, slapping rolls until her father complained of the noise and asked her how come she was so busy all of a sudden. She could hardly settle herself to do homework, but during one week she worked feverishly on an essay for a school competition (topic: "What Price Freedom?"), discussing the death of Lord Byron in terms indicating that she would have behaved exactly the same under similar circumstances, as if she were dragging a clubfoot over the cliffs of Greece instead of sitting at the kitchen table eating an apple; she was so distant from her surroundings that any activity in the outside world seemed more possible and more characteristic of her.

On Saturday night she went to the movies with Bunny, although their tastes were very different, and on the way out they had an argument about whether Pola Negri wore too much black stuff on her eyelids. Afterward they went to the candy store, and they were sitting drinking their sodas, making bubbles with their straws rather childishly, when Murray came toward their table, walking pigeon-toed to attract their attention.

Behind him was a short, heavy-chested boy whom Pauline knew only by sight, someone from another neighborhood. "These girls want to beg us to sit down but they're too shy," Murray said.

Pauline said, "If there's one thing I hate, it's begging."

"You see? They can hardly control themselves. Sit down, Cafferty. This is Jim Cafferty. He knows everything, but he's very understated about it."

"That's a nice change," Bunny said. He wasn't bad-looking, Pauline thought.

"You never believe me any more," Murray said. "Cafferty, what's the capital of Nebraska? Whisper."

Cafferty leaned over and pretended to whisper something in Murray's ear. "He says Lincoln," Murray said.

"He's turning you into a talking dog joke," Pauline said. "You ought to bite him."

"Not me," Cafferty said. "I don't get into fights over state capitals."

Murray took a sip from each of the girls' sodas.

"That's a nice ornament you have on," Cafferty said. He meant the scarf ring Pauline had made for herself out of a fake-tortoise belt buckle. "Very unique."

"Thank you," Pauline said.

"How do you boys know each other?" Bunny said.

"We have history together," Murray said. "He's the only other one who thinks the Mexican War got started purely from greed."

"Thoreau thought so," Bunny said.

"He's not in Mr. Klopmeier's class," Murray said. "Probably he studied with him once, though. When they were both in their prime."

"Let us not make fun of the aged," Bunny said.

"Klopmeier's not so old," Cafferty said. "He's just dried up. It's his mental viewpoint is his problem. He has a prune in place of a brain."

"Don't you feel sorry for him?" Bunny said.

"Sure. Someone should slip him a shot of gin in his Ovaltine to perk up his coloring."

Pauline, who did not like practical jokes, stopped smiling.

"She thinks I would really do it," Cafferty said. "I wouldn't—how could I do it? I wouldn't waste the gin anyway." Pauline went on twisting her empty glass in its saucer. "She doesn't believe me. She's going to ask you, Who was that Irish lower-element type you were bringing around to meet us the other night?"

"No, I won't," Pauline said.

"You won't ask?" he said. "Too bad for me."

Bunny started fussing with her coat and talking about how late it was. Murray said he knew she had another date.

Pauline stood up and said, "Bye-bye, boys. Don't get into trouble when we leave."

Bunny said, "So long. Abyssinia."

Murray walked them to the door and waited while they fastened their collars and pulled down their hats. "He's nice, right?" Murray said. "He's very good with girls. He's got five sisters. The oldest sister goes out with a famous gangster, you probably heard about that."

"Stop exaggerating everything all the time," Pauline said.

Jim Cafferty came up then, with a rather adult-looking hat on, and said, "You want a ride home?"

"In what?" Pauline said.

"He's a good driver," Murray said.

They followed the boys to a black Studebaker parked on the corner, and the two girls got in the back seat. "Ooh, this is nice," Bunny said.

Cafferty said, "It belongs to a friend. He lets me use it sometimes."

It was windy once the motor started, but Pauline said she liked riding in the open and it was a nice night, you could see the stars. They dropped Bunny off, and Murray said Pauline should get in the front seat between them. "If she doesn't mind being crowded," Jim said.

"It's all right, we've known each other for years," Murray said, and Pauline settled between them, centering herself so she could just feel the pressure of their knees on either side. She thought Cafferty was pushing his leg against hers on purpose, but she wasn't sure.

Jim said, "Want to go to Philadelphia?"

"I'd rather Miami."

"No, I mean it."

He couldn't really mean it—it was too far, what would they do when they got there? He might have to take them if she said yes (she eyed him as he drove); maybe he was that type. Pauline said, "Not this time." She had only been to Philadelphia once; it depressed her to remember this. She couldn't tell whether she had just failed to be bold—not that she wanted to go—but the whole issue of her own personal courage made her panicky all the time now.

While Murray was going on about how they could visit the Liberty Bell and maybe take Ben Franklin out for a drink, they passed her house and she let them drive around the park, just for the ride. At a bridge just past the turnoff to the river, they stopped to look at the view. "There's a new moon," Pauline said. Jim said that was lucky, and Pauline said good, she needed luck, she was trying to talk her father into something.

Murray, who knew about the Gittelson idea, said, "You should try whispering to your father when he's asleep. Induce autosuggestion."

"Very funny," Pauline said. She was thinking about how nasty her father got when anything interrupted his sleep. Once he had knocked Solly to the floor for bumping into the sofa while he was taking a nap.

Jim said she should wish on a falling star and she would get whatever she wanted.

Pauline said, "What do they look like, falling stars?" Not that this would help—nothing would help if her father said no. She could hear how he would say it. She had no plan really for what she would do, and she was afraid of her own capacity for submission.

They waited by the water, listening to the mild lapping of the river and arguing about whether shooting stars were ever seen in October and whether the steady twinkle in the lower left horizon was really a planet. It was pleasant sitting between the two of them. Jim brought out a flask, and Pauline took down a quick gulp. The two boys passed the flask between them, reaching across her while she gazed over-head, leaning her neck back, as though she could see farther into the night that way.

It was very late when they dropped her off. Cafferty patted her knee before she got out of the car. The street was dead quiet and all the lights were off in all the houses. Pauline had trouble turning the key in the lock; it had gotten chilly out and her fingers were stiff. Tiredness came over her all at once, and she was thinking about how grueling it was going to be getting through a day's work at the store tomor-row. She slipped her shoes off in the hallway.

Often when she came in at night there was a whistling growl all through the house, from someone snoring upstairs, and she listened for it now. In the living room a lamp was still lit by the sofa, and then on the stairs she saw something pale moving by the newel post, and she shuddered. It was her father, standing now in front of the stairway. He was in the heavy long underwear he slept in—gray-white and baggy— his eyes were puffed and fierce, and his hair was matted in tufts. "You know what time it is?" he said. "You don't even know, do you?" His mouth was contorted and sunken with his false teeth out, and his words came out thickly. Pauline stared at him with her shoes still in her hand; she was badly frightened, not knowing whether to answer and wondering if Solly and her mother were awake now and listening.

"What are you standing there for?" he said. Pauline moved toward the stairs, and when she passed him, he grabbed her shoulders and shook her, hard enough so that she bit her lip when her head jerked back. He pushed her as far as the landing, hissing, "Go to bed. Go to sleep, what's the matter with you?"

Pauline ran then, and when she got to her room she could hear him go up to his own bedroom and shut the door. She took off her clothes, and she sat on the bed in her slip, afraid to go downstairs to the bathroom and wondering whether she could fall asleep without peeing first. What time was it? She still didn't know. She felt dangerously stupid. Why had she taken the ride by the river? She had thought something was going to happen with Cafferty but then it hadn't; she had made everything at home much harder and nastier for herself, and for nothing. When she shifted her weight, the bedsprings creaked, and she was afraid once more of her father across the hall, leaping out again with his face raw and twisted. This can't go on, she thought, and the phrase gave her blind comfort, as though it were a plan. She was too old for him to shake like that—a rage of protest went through her. Even now she didn't know whether he was angry because he thought she had done something wild and low and shameful, or only because the sound of the key in the door had broken into his sleep.

For most of the next day he did not speak to her at all. He never mentioned the night or her lateness, and she might almost have talked herself into believing that he had passed it off as a dream, except that when she asked him if she should sort remnants in the stockroom or come out and wait on customers, he said, "Go, do what you want. See if I care."

All the next week he was grim and curt with her, not harsh so much as indifferent. In the store when they were both behind the counter, whenever she brushed past him he stepped aside and grunted. At times she thought he had developed a kind of distaste for her presence. Once at home he picked up a stocking she had left hanging in the bathroom and tossed it on the doorknob with real dislike in the gesture. When he came into the kitchen at night while she was doing her homework at the table, he stood at the stove fixing his tea without seeming to see her. But then he had never been a very sociable person.

For a while she took walks in the evening, to get away from the house. By late November the winds were icy, so that when she came back she was chilled, and she would sit in the kitchen with her coat still on, until her mother told her she would get sick from being overdressed indoors. By then Pauline had decided to write to Gittelson herself. She wrote at some length, explaining her skills in bookkeeping and dwelling on her eagerness to be part of his company. The letter alternated between being very formal and then perky in parts, and in the end she rewrote it so that it was so short it sounded almost rude.

As soon as she sent it she regretted having chosen this prose style. But then that week she found out that she had won the school essay contest, which seemed to prove that even in her simplest utterances she was probably more eloquent than most people.

It was around this time that she had a brief but major quarrel with Bunny. After the news of the essay prize, Pauline mentioned Byron constantly in conversation; his importance as a figure seemed massive and irrefutable now, although at the time she had chosen him more or less at random. Pauline had read in a footnote that Byron had had gonorrhea for most of his adult life—a disease whose effects she understood only vaguely but which she pictured as a sort of glowing decay—and she theorized to Bunny that it had probably enhanced his poetry. Bunny said that disease, no matter who had it, was never beautiful, only ugly and degrading, and that Pauline's attitude showed great shallowness. (Bunny was planning to go work at a settlement house in Philadelphia, and she had started talking all the time about diphtheria prevention campaigns and well-baby clinics and the need for hygiene in tenement neighborhoods.) Pauline said that only trivial people thought that suffering did not have its sublime side and that Bunny was becoming ridiculously prissy and wholesome. Bunny did not eat lunch with her for the rest of the week, and for days she was sulky whenever they spoke.

The essay contest carried a prize of twenty-five dollars, and Pauline bought a New York paper and read through the classified ads for boardinghouses and furnished rooms, trying to calculate how long the money would last her. In magazines she studied recipes for dinners made with condensed soups and canned fish, things that would be cheap to fix in a chafing dish. Solly kept asking whether she was going to buy him some mink long underwear now that she was a millionaire.

Gittelson wrote back that he had been delighted to hear from her; he knew she was a girl who was bound to be a success in whatever she did because she was willing to work hard. He was not hiring any bookkeepers at present but he could find her something as a clerk if she was so inclined.

Pauline's father didn't seem surprised when she told him about the letter. "You like to write letters, I see." He said this in a quietly nasty singsong. "So you'll go be a clerk now," he said. Only her mother looked frightened and asked whether any other girls worked at Gittelson's and whether there was a separate washroom for women. Gittelson had not mentioned salary (which even Pauline could tell was a bad sign), but her father didn't offer any guesses about what she would get; perhaps he thought it was no longer any of his business.

They were finishing dinner at the time, and they all went on spooning up their fruit compote. (Pauline's mother had set out a dish for them to put the plum pits in, a sign that she was trying to copy certain manners Pauline had brought into the house.) Pauline began telling them about the rooming house on West Twenty-second Street where a girl cousin of Murray's lived, very clean and reasonable. Especially the rooms at the top in the attic were very cheap, and then if she got a raise she could probably move down to a lower floor. Also she could easily walk to work, which would save extra on carfare.

"He pays you," her father said. "It's your money." Solly wanted to know if she could see the Statue of Liberty from her room, but Pauline told him it was probably too far south.

It snowed heavily during the week when Pauline was taking her last exams, and on the final afternoon she and Bunny came out of the classroom—where they had spent hours answering questions about Eli Whitney's cotton gin and the mercantile theory—into a schoolyard piled with blinding white. They kicked through the uncleared paths, shrieking to each other; the flakes were still coming down thickly, and the wind kept driving gusts of snow up into their faces. It struck them as hilarious that the weather had gotten this wild. Bunny yelled, "Look at it!" and tossed up a few handfuls like confetti, as though the whole thing proved some point they had both supported, an example of elemental excess unhampered by bourgeois restraint. They wrapped their mufflers across their faces so only their eyes showed, which Pauline thought made them look foreign and heroic, breasting the wind. They could barely see in front of them because of the gusts, and the strangeness of this made them more giddy. When Bunny slipped, Pauline said, "Drunk again, I knew it. What a degenerate." The drifts in some places were as high as their knees, and they walked home, skidding and pushing each other.

It was dark by the time Pauline got home, and when she came into the kitchen Solly was sitting on a chair by the stove, holding one of his galoshes in his lap and whining about a hole in the toe. Her mother was trying to fix it by holding a match to the rubber to melt it together, which did not work at all and made a horrible smell. Pauline patched it with a piece of oilcloth and some glue, and later, when her father came into the kitchen to ask when supper was going to be ready, she held it out to show him. He seemed quite pleased with it. "You could go be a shoemaker," he said. "The world is full of holes you could fix."

For a moment Pauline was terrified that he was going to change his mind; he was not going to let her work in New York at all; he had something else in store and had been waiting to tell her. She started to say, "She was only a shoemaker's daughter, but she had me head over heels," to distract him, and to her own disgust a crooked half smile like Bunny's came over her face. But he was already shuffling out of the kitchen.

Her mother was cutting onions, crying and rubbing her eyes—even Solly knew enough to tell her not to do this, it only made them worse. Her mother said, "It's my eyes, what do you care?" But then she rubbed them again and couldn't open them, so Pauline had to bring her a soaked dishcloth to hold against the lids.

Her mother said, "Pauline, when you go live in New York, don't buy any more fruit from Italians. Maybe they sold you that on purpose before to make a Jewish girl sick."

Pauline said, "It's all right, Ma. Don't worry."

Her mother pushed the dishcloth to the top of her head, like a soldier's bandage, and did the rest of her kitchenwork like that until Solly took it to wipe down the table. Pauline put out plates and they all sat down to supper quietly, with the smell of scorched rubber still around them.

In the end, only Solly went with her to the station to help carry her luggage, although she just had a suitcase and a crate tied with string. "I could carry both," Pauline said. "I carried *you* the whole time when you were little. You were always crying if someone set you down, what a complainer. I could still lift you." She tried to lift him under the arms to show him but she couldn't get him off the ground at all. He squealed, "Stop it, what are you doing?" which made her realize she was behaving childishly in the middle of the station.

She had not slept much the night before, and all the lights along the tracks looked very bright and hotly yellow. The whole station looked different to her, and she was afraid she was going to get on the wrong train. When she finally did take a seat, she gave Solly a nickel for helping her with her things, which surprised him—she had never done anything like that before, and she herself didn't know why she did it. Solly said, "Thanks, I'll get a ice cream," which instantly made her feel jealous and sorry she had given it to him.

She rode the whole way staring out the window; it was bleak skies and stripped trees—everything looked flat and vibrant, the way it did sometimes when she'd been drinking. The river was pearl-gray, a washy streak on the horizon. But it was roiling with whitecaps once she stood at the shoreline, and the ferry pitched and bobbed a great deal, which Pauline liked, although her suitcase slid back and forth and nicked her on the knees a few times.

When she came out into the Twenty-third Street terminal with her luggage, she was hot under her coat from excitement, even in the wind. She walked briskly, brushing past people. She was out on the street before it occurred to her that she had gone past the clock tower without remembering to look to make sure Earl wasn't there. She kept walking, reading the signs on the buildings—advertisements for warehouse storage and grocery supplies—which seemed freshly important.

The rooming house was in the West Twenties—not far—on a block of mostly low, gray stone houses with carved fronts and wide stoops. She went past the right number at first, and then she stood ringing the bell and trying to peer through the curtains at the windows. A very old woman with a mustache shadow on her upper lip answered the door. It was not so nice inside—Pauline could see that already— there was a dark splintery staircase and a purplish-brown flowered carpet. Pauline said, "Mrs. Poganyi?" and was half-way through her speech explaining who she was (Murray's cousin Beatrice was supposed to have told her everything), when the woman said, "Okay. Come, you want the room? Come."

Pauline had only a fleeting impression of the parlor— old plush armchairs and a sepia-toned wallpaper with scenes of shepherdesses—and then Mrs. Poganyi gripped her sleeve to lead her up the stairs. Along the way she said, "Good house, everybody behaves good," and when they got to the top landing she said, "Water is down the hall," and some-thing that sounded like "Do you like windows?" but her chief means of making sure that she was understood was to push and pivot Pauline so that she faced the different features of the room: an iron cot, a framed mirror with a waterfall painted at the bottom, and a set of embroidered valances that matched the dresser scarf on the bureau.

There was a strong odor of mildew in the room, which Pauline tried at first to ignore, and which seemed to be greater once Mrs. Poganyi was gone and she was left by her-self. She had not really thought the room would be any better than this, but the sight of it was embarrassing. She was glad no one was there with her, even Solly; she didn't like the idea of anyone associating the taste of the place with her. Of course it could be described cleverly—she decided already that the plaster molding looked like bird droppings, and she imagined herself repeating this witticism.

She could hear the traffic from Ninth Avenue and the sudden surge of the El going by on its tracks. The rising and ebbing roar of the street made the room seem more still and empty. She got up from sitting on the bare mattress and began unpacking her things; she shook everything out vigorously to get rid of the wrinkles, and this had the added effect of keeping her warm, since the room was distinctly chilly. She thought she shouldn't go outside until she had finished unpacking, and this gave her a pleasantly nervous sense of postponement while she was piling things into drawers. In the end when she put her box of powder on the dresser and her glass beads in the little china dish next to it, the effect was surprisingly artful—sweetly careless—showing she had done much with little.

By then the light in the room had faded. She had already switched on the lamp, which cast rather dramatic shadows on the floor. When she lifted the curtains, a bright blue came through the windows from the early winter dusk. She wanted to go down to walk in the street, and she changed to her wool suit. It was dark when she stepped out the door, and the block was bare and drably quiet under the streetlights.

On Twenty-third Street it was still lively and busy with people, bright from the neon in store windows. A woman passed, wearing a style of Russian boots Pauline thought would look good on her. She peered into the windows of little cheap shops selling ladies' gloves and hosiery, and restaurants where people sat eating supper with their hats on. She wanted to go in somewhere, to order even a cup of tea, but she grew uneasy as she walked farther from the rooming-house—she was not at all sure about the neighborhood and she was wary about walking back too late.

After a few more blocks she turned and went back to the house. Mounting the dim staircase, she could hear people moving behind the doors of some of the rooms; she wondered which one was Beatrice's, but she couldn't very well just go around knocking till she found it. So she stayed in her own room and sat on the cot bed eating the two cheese sandwiches her mother had packed for her.

She had a nice sense of picnicking—of living well in a blithely improvised way—but after that she didn't know what to do with herself. She read a little from a newspaper she had bought, but she kept hearing the screech of the El trains and the occasional rattle of a truck going by. A group of men passed under the window, calling out to each other raucously and laughing about something. She did not want to talk to these particular men, but it hurt her that she was shut away from them, and she opened the window, as though she could enter into the quickened atmosphere of the night by watching it long enough. There was a blast of cold air— which she liked at first; she stood it until she began to shiver—and then the room seemed worse to her when she lowered the window shut.

She lay reading her newspaper, but she couldn't concentrate on the news and she wound up reading the Women's Page, which was full of hints on how to freshen old blouses and add years to your linoleum. Possibly Gittelson would be impressed that she knew about washing black lace in ammonia and coffee. She lay in bed thinking of this and listening to the sounds of taxi horns and buses going by without her, until it was late enough to go to sleep.

On the first day at work she was handed over to Miss Pfeiffer, the stout, unpleasant receptionist, who Mr. Gittelson said knew the whole business from soup to nuts. Miss Pfeiffer spoke rather fiercely about the special ways that the company did things, much better than some places she knew. Pauline was comparing Miss Pfeiffer's blouse to her own and wondering whether she had worn the right thing. At one point she realized that Miss Pfeiffer was giving instructions and she tried harder to follow, but in listening to each part she forgot what had been said just before.

Then she was led to an alleyway of wooden file cabinets and given a stack of invoices to file. She was already hungry for lunch, but on the way back from the washroom she saw that it wasn't even ten thirty yet. Mr. Gittelson stopped by to ask how she was getting along, which made her wonder if she could be doing the filing right; perhaps there was more of a trick to it. One of the salesmen told her if she had any complaints she should come to him, he was in charge of helping all the pretty girls, and Pauline said she would remember.

Miss Pfeiffer did show up finally to ask her what was the matter, wasn't she going to lunch? Pauline put on her coat and walked outside to the first cheap-looking luncheonette she could find, where she ate a bowl of soup sitting at the counter. After lunch she was put to work addressing envelopes, using a horrible little contraption called a stamp affixer. It had a metal plunger that had to be slammed down with the palm of the hand, so that she had a welt from it by the end of the day. She knew that it was the newness of the office routine that made everything go so slowly and seem to take so much time; nothing in the work was harder or more monotonous than what she had done in her father's store, but still it filled her with dread to think that there were four more days left in the week, and weeks after that of five days together.

When she got home there was a note on her door from Murray's cousin Beatrice. The note said: *I'm in the bedroom at the end of the hall on the second floor. If you would like to go eat supper someplace not too pricey, let me know.*

Beatrice was very dark, with large, sleepy features set in a small face, and she said, "Oh, you're here," in such a flat voice that Pauline thought she wasn't very glad to see her, but then it seemed to be her only way of speaking. She was older than Pauline had guessed, twenty-five at least. She wore a dress with a jaunty bow on the shoulder, stylish in a way that Pauline thought was maybe a little overdone but admired nonetheless.

"Your room is bigger," Pauline said, for lack of something else to say. Beatrice said she'd had it for three years, although it looked as bare and unadorned as Pauline's upstairs.

Beatrice warned her that they were only going to a chophouse nearby and it wasn't exactly the Ritz or anything. Once they were outside, Pauline kept trying to guess which it was, and when they walked into the steamy dining room, with its odors of beef and frying onions, she said, "Oh, I could eat a whole cow, couldn't you?"

Beatrice said, while they were looking at the menu, that she worked for a company that packed olives and pickles; she was a typist in the warehouse, and even the elevators smelled of brine. Her boss was always trying to give her bottles of the stuff to take home; he liked to think of himself as wonderfully generous, although he was a petty person who cheated on his partner. Pauline said, "That's terrible," trying to echo Beatrice's outrage, but Beatrice laughed and said, "Everybody does it."

They both ordered stew, which was the cheapest thing on the menu; Beatrice picked out all the fatty parts, but Pauline, who was used to her mother's cooking, ate everything in hers. Beatrice told a long story about a man who had taken her out dancing; the point of the story was his shabbiness in some things and his nervy freshness in others, but Pauline didn't understand all of it and said the wrong things in a few places.

After supper they walked back along the side streets. A man passing them called out, "You're two gorgeous girls. Probably the most beautiful girls in New York." Pauline couldn't help smirking a little, but Beatrice didn't change her expression at all, and it wasn't until she cursed under her breath that Pauline saw she was bitterly annoyed. Pauline thought that she was really a much better sport than Beatrice, and that people probably found her more likable because of it.

. . .

After the first few weeks at Gittelson's the work did get less horribly slow. She stopped feeling dazed and unsteady, and one of the stock boys made her his confidante and came to discuss his problems about his fiancée, and this also helped break up the time. Mr. Gittelson always asked if they were working her hard enough, and Miss Pfeiffer said this was wonderful training for her. Mostly everyone was on the other side of the office and she didn't see them.

What was disappointing was that after she came home and had supper—sometimes with Beatrice and sometimes not—she read or did crossword puzzles and then she went to bed, so that there was nothing much between one day and the next. Once, after she had learned to keep bread and cans of fish and fruit in her room to save money, she went to the movies by herself. She liked watching the picture alone, and she found she concentrated better than she ever had before. But when the lights came on she felt awkward and sorry for herself.

On the way home she saw a man on the street with a blondish mustache; she stared at him without meaning to, and he smiled at her when they passed. She felt that she excited the interest of men wherever she went, but she was never in a position to meet them. She had walked so much through her own neighborhood—and farther south too, all the way down to the harbor—and still there was nothing in it but looking.

She missed Bunny at times, and she wrote her a letter which was full of sarcastic references to herself as the poor working girl heaven was protecting all too well, and in which she described Mrs. Poganyi's mustache and got in the line about the molding in the room being like bird droppings. She had a feeling she was putting in too many laboriously arch expressions, like "I daresay" and "fancy my surprise

43

when," but after she wrote it she felt better.

Beatrice was also impatient with the way things were going in her life—which seemed as uneventful as Pauline's—but it was hard to tell what she was really waiting for; she seemed to want most of what was around her to disappear. She ate her listless dinners with Pauline, complaining that no one in New York ever said anything worth hearing, in a way that Pauline found distinctly unflattering.

Once Beatrice did confess that she would really seriously like to move to Florida, and she brightened when she talked about beaches and cheap bungalows and lucky investments. She already knew Pauline's enthusiasms, and she sometimes teased her and asked if she didn't want to save her dinner roll to bring to some starving artist in a garret who was shivering over his easel by candlelight.

Pauline said, "Not really." She was actually touchy on the subject. She knew better than to ever say anything to Beatrice about the "hunger for freedom" or the "cravings of the spirit," although she and Bunny had used these expressions with perfect sincerity and with a shared sense of their exact meaning. There was no way to voice her ambitions with enough delicacy to avoid sounding precious, but in fact she was full of cravings of the spirit all the time. Beatrice had shown her sketches in the newspaper parodying Village girls as over-earnest and ill-groomed—Bohemia was apparently a well-worn cliché to everyone but her. That it had become all too common only made her feel left out.

Once at night while they were eating supper together, Beatrice said, "Listen, if you really want to, we can go to Vera's sometime and just sit at a table. That's where they all go, those people."

Pauline did not believe that Beatrice could really know this. Probably it was one of those tearooms that fleeced tourists. "What is it—it's a restaurant?" Pauline was finishing a piece of gristly meat loaf, and she kept twirling her fork in the gravy without looking up.

"Sort of. Or you can just sip a cup of something and draw pictures on the tablecloth, they don't care. It's cheap enough. The tea tastes like stewed brooms, but that is only my personal opinion. I'll take you now if you want. I don't mind, it doesn't bother me."

"I love a nice broomstraw taste in my tea," Pauline said.

During the long, chilly walk down to Washington Square, Pauline tried to keep up a brisk conversation about Mrs. Poganyi's eccentricities, and even Beatrice was getting more animated by the time she stopped on a side street and said, "Oh, yes, here it is." They went up a narrow staircase— Pauline could hear the hum of voices, a kind of tinkling monotone—and then they were walking past a tiny kitchen where a black cook stood at the stove with his back to them. They went through another corridor, past a row of coats on pegs; Pauline put hers next to an opera cloak with a ripped lining. There was also a man's sheepskin overcoat, of a kind she had never seen before.

In the main room, small tables had been set impossibly close together. It was crowded and warm and thick with noise—men with longish rumpled hair were sitting with pale, sleek girls, a fat woman with a shrieking laugh was being thumped on the back, and in the corner two old women dressed in identical men's suits were playing chess. There was a log fire, which made the light reddish and intense at that end of the room, and a grouping of copper pots over the mantel, a rustic effect Pauline had not expected at all.

The only seats left were right by the fireplace, and they

had to edge their chairs away to avoid roasting their spines. A man near them said, "It kind of gives you an idea of how Joan of Arc must have felt, doesn't it?"

Pauline said, "Do you suppose if we confessed they'd tamp down the flames or something?"

"If you have anything really good to confess," the man said, "I could speak to the management."

Pauline said, "Wait a minute. I'm searching my conscience."

"I'm dying of thirst," Beatrice said.

"It takes days to get served here," the man said. "I knew a man who keeled over from dehydration and the waiter just stepped over him."

The waiter showed up at their table just then—they both ordered Russian tea with lemon—and the man said, "Adolfo is only human, contrary to popular opinion. Pretty women get faster service."

Beatrice complained of its being smoky in the room. The man said smoke was excellent for digestion, most people got too much oxygen, and then a ruddy-faced blond girl swooped down on their table. "Is he telling you all about mapmaking?" she said. "That's all he ever talks about now."

"Actually he hasn't said a word about it," Pauline said.

"He must be bowled over by your beauty. Normally he goes on about how maps are what we should all be looking at, they're the true distilled vision of the world. Isn't that right, Peter?"

"Don't say anything about distilled too loud," Peter said. "The whole place'll be rummaging through our pockets to see if we brought anything."

"I like maps," Pauline said.

"I just think it changed people's sense of quest once they could see where they were going. It made everything much more concrete and modern. The modern world really begins when they figure out how to gauge longitude."

"Don't listen to him," the girl said. "It just makes him more fanatical. His paintings aren't bad at all, really."

"You've never seen my paintings," he said.

The girl ignored this and asked if any of them read tea leaves and whether they were superstitious.

"I'm sort of skeptical but open-minded on the subject," Pauline said. This was not true at all; her mother had a whole collection of bad-luck-avoidance rituals, all of which disgusted her. The blond girl decided that they should get Rose to come over and read their leaves. "Oh, yes, we need to know our fates badly," Pauline said, "we're about to go astray any minute," and the girl got up from the table and brought back a tall, fine-featured woman with strands of premature gray in her hair.

"You don't look like a gypsy," Beatrice said.

"Oh, I just learned it from someone one time," she said. "I'm not really very good." Pauline would have liked to know how she had met whoever taught her, whether she had traveled or was just the sort of person for whom these contacts were commonplace. The woman poked in their teacups and told Pauline she was going to live to be very old, she had a strong constitution; she told Beatrice she was going to have three children and marry a man she could look in the eyes, which Pauline thought was a nice touch.

Several people had gathered around the table to watch while this was going on. Peter seemed to be a general favorite—he wore icy-looking spectacles and he had soft, boyish cheeks, but he did get more attractive as you looked at him, Pauline thought—there was an outbreak of groaning and clapping when he was told he was going to die rich. A very smartly dressed couple began talking about whether you really drank tea in a way that showed your personality, and they all ordered more tea and a few people burned their tongues demonstrating their sipping techniques. Pauline was wedged between Peter and a dark-haired man who kept suggesting they should really read the imprints left by women's lipstick on the cup rims. He held up Pauline's cup for an example, interrupting Peter, who was telling her about leaf tracings in fossils. Pauline felt that they were both vying for her attention, and she talked at some length about auguries in ancient Rome, so that she wouldn't lose either of them into another conversation. Her voice in her own ears didn't sound altogether like her—she had caught a lilting, slightly petulant way of speaking from the blond girl, and she used bits of slang like "Don't I know it?" and "Tell me another" which were not really native to her—but she liked all this, and there was no one to know it was new except Beatrice, who was on the other side and couldn't hear anyway.

The blond girl announced that she was going to a party at Mickeling's and if anybody wanted to go over with her, this was their chance. Someone wanted to know if Mickeling was still seeing that woman who had thrown the couch cushions out the window the last time, and someone else began imitating the way he hummed arias to himself when he was drunk. Pauline had, of course, no idea who Mickeling was—she gathered, after a while, that he was also a painter—but people seemed eager to recount things they had seen him do; there was a general desire to employ his name familiarly. Peter and several others were already standing up, getting ready to go.

Pauline leaned over to Beatrice. "What do you think?" she said.

"Oh, I'm going home to bed," Beatrice said. "Go on without me, you'll be fine."

It occurred to Pauline that no one had invited her directly, but then Peter was leading her along and the blond woman was chattering about how Mickeling was going to drink all the decent liquor if they didn't get there soon. Pauline got separated from Beatrice while they were all fishing for their coats. She felt that Beatrice disliked her now (just when they'd been getting friendlier), but there was nothing to be done about it; she was probably thinking, quite correctly, that she'd glimpsed Pauline in her true colors.

In the taxi the blond girl and the dark-haired man—who turned out to be the owner of the sheepskin overcoat—kept up a conversation about whether parrots could be taught to whistle two tones at once. When they got to the party, the blond girl was still croaking *Polly want a cracker* in different experimental pitches while they pushed through the doorway. This seemed to amuse the man who had answered the door, who went at once to bring her a cracker, which she nibbled at neatly with little beaklike movements, quite a skillful mimicking of a bird.

A record was playing—something bouncy, with a lot of wailing violins and saxophones—drowned out in places by the din of voices. People clustered in small, bobbing groups, slouching against walls and nodding into each other's faces. A fat man in baggy tweeds pretended to box Peter's ears by way of greeting. A woman in a celery-green dress came by with a tray of drinks. "They look frivolous, I know," she said, "but they're extremely good for cuts and bruises."

Peter sniffed one and gave it to her. Pauline sipped a little and said, "Oh, yes, that was just what I needed."

Across from her, a man teetered and slid against a woman, who pulled him up and said, "I wish you would stop trying to prostrate yourself before me." The woman was wearing a large speckled lily in her hair, and the man leaned forward and nosed the petals. "You'll sneeze," the woman said, rather gently.

A collie was eating some salted almonds off a woman's knee. There were some astonishingly beautiful girls—pretty in clever and interesting ways—in deft makeup and cunningly arranged outfits. Pauline was at once thrilled to be in their company and worried that she looked like some prim office miss in her drab gabardine. But sometimes a neutral appearance was striking in its own way.

"That dog," Peter said, "is the reason no one is dancing."

"He doesn't allow it?" Pauline said.

"He herds people—nips at their ankles and starts yipping and running in circles."

"It's in the blood," the man in baggy tweeds said. "That dog leads a terrible life. Every time the doorbell rings he waits for a sheep to arrive."

A man behind them thought this was extremely funny. He had an awful, high, hiccuping laugh, and he went on for some time, trilling and hawing. The blond girl, who was standing with them again, said, "No more wit, Walter. You see what it does to people."

"That dog," Peter said, "is the proof of nature over nurture. In the middle of Manhattan he still wants to tend a flock. He has to suppress his instincts constantly."

"Oh, that's so bad for you," the girl said.

Walter decided suddenly to introduce himself, and the blond girl, whose name was Nita, said, "Oh, we've known each other for hours already," and shook Pauline's hand, a thing Pauline didn't even know women did with each other.

"Pauline, Pauline, theme of a dream," Walter said. Pauline smiled. She had downed most of her drink, which tasted far less medicinal than anything she'd gotten drunk on in high school, and she was feeling numb around the mouth and pleasantly warm. The room, which she hardly noticed before, seemed to be all white and gray and embellished with oddities—a foot-shaped ashtray made of blue glass, an old puppet hung on the wall, a votary urn used to hold cigarettes; she had never seen furnishings that were funny on purpose (even Mrs. Poganyi's were dead earnest), and it struck her that something had been missing from her aesthetics. The drink had made her a little sentimental, and she felt sorry for her self of the day before who had not understood all this; she pondered the arrangement of the things in Mickeling's apartment with a great feeling of personal satisfaction.

Nita had dragged over a tall, poker-faced boy, and they were all talking about whether an instinct to drink was natural to all humans. Peter said, "Suppose you just put some people on a desert island. Don't you think if you came back in a year you would find them all fermenting passion fruits or distilling wild roots or something?"

Pauline said, "Only if there was a law against it."

This was received with such a chorus of knowing chuckles that Pauline felt she had gotten off a remark that probably bordered on being a stunning paradox. Walter said, "Hear, hear," and patted her on the shoulder.

"In the country, people drink more," the poker-faced boy announced. "I had a friend from boarding school whose parents lived on top of a mountain and they were blotto all the time. The mother used to giggle all through dinner."

Pauline thought fleetingly of her own mother and the timid, sour expression she always had when she stood in her apron and her kerchief, dishing out their supper; she could not be imagined as gaily tipsy. It was true that Solly's ear-wiggling tricks sometimes struck her as funny, but her laugh, when she laughed, did not resemble giggling at all— it was hoarse and hissed through her underbite.

Peter offered a toast to rural life, and Walter went and got them more cocktails. The record had changed to something slow and syrupy—a man's voice singing in a lachrymose tenor—and Nita made faces and sang along in a mocking vibrato. "Let's go tell them we can't stand it," she said to Pauline, and she took her hand and led her across the room. A bald man in evening clothes was by the victrola, and Nita plucked at his sleeve and said, "My friend here is just getting over a very tragic love affair and she can't stand to hear anything too dreary. She's been trying so hard to be brave—but this music—"

Pauline said, "I'll be all right, really. I just need some jazz to make me laugh and forget."

"Oh, in that case," the man said, and he took off the record so quickly it sounded as though the tenor had been throttled. "It's awful, isn't it, how cruel the world is to young girls," he said, giving Pauline a long look. He was apparently not sure whether he was being teased or not, but he wanted them to stay with him. Nita found a louder record, and they bantered for a while about what cads all the men were now. "Oh, not all, don't say all," he said.

"All right, I won't say it then," Pauline said. This made Nita go off into giggles, and Pauline, who was in the midst of sipping her drink, laughed as she was swallowing and sputtered some of it on the man's feet.

"You see what a state she's in," Nita said. "I'm going to take her into the kitchen and feed her dry soda crackers until she calms down." And she took Pauline's hand again and they went back across the room, sliding against each other.

"I missed you terribly," Peter said. "Even the dog wouldn't talk to me."

In the corner near them a group of people was having what was apparently a hilarious discussion in a language Pauline recognized happily as French. A woman shrieked,

"Oh! C'est juste!" Pauline was so pleased at having made this out that she almost translated for Peter, but he wanted to talk now about why he had red paint under his fingernails and about color values in maps and why Canada was always pink. Pauline let the conversation drift around her. Peter seemed full of extraordinarily strong opinions about the color red and its importance in the underlying scheme of almost everything. Pauline did not follow all of what he said, but it made her feel inwardly content to think that there was some latent meaning overflowing even from the colors of things, and she had only to sharpen her own understanding to catch it. She began looking around the room, to check for bits of red in what people were wearing. Nita made them get another round of Manhattans, in honor of the color. Pauline sat down on the arm of a chair, which fit comfortably under her, as though her body had gotten very pliant and light. She heard Nita say, "Oh, look, Garrett's out cold," and she looked up and saw a figure slumped on the sofa with his eyes closed—it was the boy who had been talking about drinking in the country—and a woman was draping a silk shawl over him for a blanket.

"Getting about that time, isn't it?" Peter said. "I'll see you home if you like."

"Oh, yes," Pauline said, getting up. "I've got work tomorrow, isn't that peculiar to think of?"

"Mickeling says his liquor never gives you a hangover, but you know how men lie," Nita said. Pauline said she knew. Nita murmured, "Till next time," while they shook hands good night, and then Pauline and Peter made their way over to the door, where there was a great crush of people in the hall. A sharp-featured man (Bunny would have said he had a Greek profile) came over to ask if she was lost and if she wanted something to drink.

"Too late, Ernest," Peter said, coming up from behind.

"Till next time," Pauline said, shaking hands. She was a little sorry now to be leaving so soon.

"No use trying to say good-bye to the host," Peter said, and he guided her down the stairway.

"I never got to meet him," Pauline said. "I liked his apartment, though. And his dog."

"You did meet him. You made a big hit with him. Walter can be very rude to women sometimes. He's got a nasty streak in him."

"Walter is *Mickeling?*" Pauline said.

"He's got a low opinion of women. He thinks they're all after his money. He behaved awfully well with you."

"I guess he did," Pauline said.

It was a still, icy night, quiet now except for the sound of ferry whistles hooting from the river. They had both drunk too much to feel the cold, and Pauline walked looking down, watching the mica in the pavement glittering ahead of their feet. Peter put her hand in his coat pocket, and they waited at the corner while a bus went by, lit up from inside and ghostly at this time of night. When they got to the block near her rooming house, the buildings looked fatefully familiar, and she felt a great rush of affection for her neighborhood, where she lived at this time of her life.

In front of her doorstep he kissed her fully on the mouth. He pressed her to him, but he wasn't sudden about it (she was used to boys reaching for her as though they had to take her by surprise, before she changed her mind), and there was something hearty and friendly in his passion. Pauline had the passing, exultant thought that all night she had been with people whose assumptions about things were like hers, only in surer form, and this accord made everything simple and natural. He watched while she went up the steps, and they waved to each other before she slipped inside.

. . .

When she came home from work the next day, there was a note by the phone in the hall. One of the boarders had taken down the message with a splotchy fountain pen—it was not Peter who had called her, but Walter. He sounded a little gruff when she called him back; he wanted to know whether she would meet him for dinner at a certain Italian restaurant, and he seemed surprised when she didn't know where it was.

Pauline didn't change clothes before she left; she wanted the feeling that this was her regular evening outing and not something she dressed up for. She brushed her hair until the static turned the bangs wispy, so she had a sense of being very rushed and careless. When she got to the restaurant, Walter was sitting at a table with Nita and the boy who had passed out on the sofa the night before.

"And so we revelers meet again," Walter said. "Don't expect much. You're sitting with a bunch of symptoms here."

Nita said, "What we all need is some food to convince our stomachs that we're sweet people really."

Pauline had felt fine all day, only a little strange and disembodied, as she might after any dense and startling experience. Nor did she think that any of them sounded dull, although they apologized for it all through the spaghetti and while they were downing tumblers of what Walter called blood tonic, which turned out to be sour red wine, inky with sediment, brought by the waiter in an unlabeled bottle.

Pauline, to her own surprise, began a long and giddy description of two boys she had seen having a fistfight on the way over; she was overstimulated and full of nervous brightness. Walter said, "I couldn't stand to walk in the street and see people today. They all looked so god-awful. Some days my dog is the only one I can tolerate being around. My dog and certain rare women. Sweet honest ones like you girls."

Nita said, "Angels of mercy," and snorted, but Pauline

55

was interested in his degree of disillusion and her apparent powers of refreshment. Garrett, who remained wan and expressionless, repeated a long and dirty piece of gossip about a writer's wife. They all made references to people they were sure Pauline knew, and Pauline wasn't sure whether by not saying anything she was pretending she did know them. Nita talked about her job—she worked as a violinist playing for tables at lunch in a midtown restaurant—and about one businessman who danced with a chair whenever she played "The Blue Danube Waltz."

They stayed until very late, when Garrett and Walter started arguing about whether they should go to Vera's or to some cafeteria called Anselm's for coffee. Nita tried to get Pauline to agree that Anselm's was too greasy and noisy. For a moment Pauline wondered whether they had really confused her with a girl seen at these places—people did sometimes mix her up with other wispy-haired brunettes—but it was only their habit of regarding these spots as sites, like the Statue of Liberty or the Paramount Building, too famous and unavoidable for anyone not to know. Pauline would have gone to any of them, but in the end Garrett passed out again, and Walter stayed with him while she and Nita walked each other home.

After that, she almost never stayed in during the evenings. She was often tired and sluggish at work, but as soon as she had come back to her room and eaten her cold, makeshift supper, she felt restless and full of steady energy, and she would walk to Vera's or to Anselm's, usually stopping to pick up Nita from her apartment on Twelfth Street on the way downtown. Pauline liked Anselm's because it was big and open, like a banquet hall, and there was that sudden rush of noise as they walked through the door and the long vista of crowded tables so that they could see who was there as they walked to the back. There was a table by the back wall where they liked to sit and where people sometimes waited for them.

Pauline had let her bangs grow longer, and she had copied Nita's way of wearing a long, flimsy scarf with everything. Peter said she looked loosely gift-wrapped. She and Peter had a brief spell of seeking each other out at large gatherings as though they were bound together romantically, but then they settled instead into a temperate friendship, still marked by certain gallant attentions on Peter's part. It was Mickeling who most often paid for things at the end of the night (although Pauline did frequently pay her share too— she thought Nita was too much of a gold digger the way she always looked around for a man to sit with just before she was ready to leave). Anyway, it was never very much; they did most of their real drinking at parties, unless Walter dragged them off to one of the seedy speakeasies he liked, with spotlit pianos and drab girl singers. Walter said it ruined your health to go to bed too early, your blood got slow. And it was true there was never anything wrong with Pauline's health, despite the fact that she was sleeping so little, and Mrs. Poganyi kept the rooms so cold Pauline could see her breath when she got up in the mornings.

Except to sleep, Pauline was scarcely in her room at all now, and no one ever called for her at the rooming house. The tassel fringe she had tacked around the mirror, part of a plan for refurbishing with small, skillful touches, came undone on one side, and she left it to dangle and get dusty. For a while she was afraid that Mrs. Poganyi was going to speak sternly to her about her late hours, but the landlady apparently slept like a top, and she beamed and nodded when she passed Pauline in the halls.

Sometimes, when Pauline came home from work, she saw Beatrice on the stairway. Beatrice was never rude, but she was decidedly chilly. Pauline would ask her how she was, and Beatrice would say, "Fine, thank you," as though she doubted that Pauline believed her. Pauline wondered whether Beatrice didn't harbor, if not envy, then some admiration for the change in Pauline's prospects. She was not a stuffy girl really; she liked dance music and the idea of travel, she was fearless about a good many things and certainly outspoken. She would not have wanted for herself the sort of social life Pauline was leading, but perhaps she respected the liveliness of it. Pauline would have liked to know if she ever talked about it at all when she saw her family, and whether she ever said anything to her cousin Murray about it.

IV

When the weather grew warmer, Pauline would sometimes walk down to Nita's apartment on weekend
afternoons. Nita lived in two high-ceilinged, underfurnished
rooms in a building that had once been luxurious. There was
still a marble fireplace and—the apartment's best feature—a
tiny balcony that overlooked a small courtyard. Nita, who
generally had a hangover on Sundays, believed in the curative
powers of fresh air, and she would drag out the kitchen chairs
to the balcony and sit there drinking cups of Horlick's malted
milk.

There was a single tree in the yard, overgrown and
sprawling, with big elephant-ear leaves and—for a few weeks
in April—hanging clusters of purple blossoms. Neither of
them knew what kind it was. Nita was from Wilkes-Barre,
which Pauline had thought was in the middle of farmland or
cow country, but Nita said only someone from Newark
would think that. She said Wilkes-Barre did not consider
itself at all socially backward; there were a lot of tea dances
and a local nightclub that featured an all-girl orchestra,

which had given her the idea that she could earn money playing the violin.

By her own account Nita was nothing special as a violinist. It was the homeliness of the girls in the orchestra that had inspired her. She had felt an immediate indignation that girls who were so bovine in their flounced dresses with those silly bertha collars should be paid to do something she would look so much better doing.

She was always reasoning in this way. When they saw newsreels of the young Duchess of York waving to a crowd, Nita was personally affronted by the dowdiness of her hat, and for a week she went around saying it was too bad that one of them hadn't met the duke first. It wasn't so much that Nita thought herself beautiful—by her own estimate she was merely pretty, with her high coloring and her sandy hair. It was only that she believed in a natural ranking that accorded all privileges to the most gloriously attractive, and it shocked her whenever she saw evidence of this order violated.

There were great advantages to this belief; according to this scheme, Nita, whatever her minor lacks, was certainly in line to deserve quite a lot, and it gave her an almost innocent confidence at large social gatherings. Even at the stiffer, dressier parties Walter sometimes took them to farther uptown (where Pauline felt somewhat out of her element), Nita was certain that strangers would welcome them by right.

With all this, she was not vain or apt to fuss unduly over her appearance, and on the afternoons when she stayed out on the balcony with Pauline she wore a faded old cardigan sweater and sat over her malted milk red-eyed, with no face powder even. Pauline admired her forthrightness.

"I bet Peter would know what kind of tree that is," Nita said, as they were looking across into the courtyard. "He knows lots of little useless bits of information like that."

"Doesn't he ever," Pauline said.

"Now Walter, on the other hand, knows nothing. It makes him very restful to be with."

"Walter is not restful," Pauline said.

"I think it's nice for a man to be like that, not always smothering you with information. Walter blusters but he's not boring." She had obviously thought this all out before. "He's really one of my best friends. When I was sick last year, he had the waiter from Tony's bring over a whole pot of soup and a chicken and everything. He's getting kind of soft around the middle now, but it goes with his height; it's more portly than fat. Do you think he's fat?"

Pauline had a fairly good idea where all this was heading. "I think of him as a largish medium in weight," she said.

Nita wanted to know what Pauline thought of her new idea that friends could really make good boyfriends because you knew them already and could tell what you were getting into. "Walter's not a skinflint, for instance," she pointed out. As far as Pauline could tell, Walter hadn't made any passes recently or said anything out of the usual—the idea was strictly Nita's—but there seemed to be no doubt in her mind that Walter would leap at the chance. Pauline thought she was probably right about this.

"Did you ever notice Walter has wonderful shoes?" Nita said.

"You can tell a lot about a man from his feet," Pauline said. "Fallen arches are a sign of weak character."

"I absolutely always check their insteps first," Nita said.

Inwardly, Pauline was appalled that Nita would want to talk herself into a romance with Walter. Imagine having to work yourself up into an attraction instead of having it overtake you by its own force: it made Pauline's flesh crawl; there were things she was quite purist about. It seemed wrong, a betrayal of the higher instincts. Lately she had been thinking

61

rather constantly about Ernest, the man with the Greek profile, who was of course not Greek at all; he was Mid-
dlewestern and Protestant, as almost everyone she met now
seemed to be. Nita said he was really humorless, and it was
true that he was never exactly playful and often hard to talk
to, but Pauline thought that this would change on knowing
him better, and there was something she definitely liked
about his austerity; men who were clownish lacked sex appeal. He wrote poems—once she had talked to him about
Byron but he had said Byron was glib and facile and that had
stopped the discussion.

Whenever she saw him at Anselm's, he was attentive
enough so that she knew he considered her good-looking
—and their conversations always had the flavor of mild flirta-
tions, very promising and yet so far short of the full ambitions of her longing that, when she thought of them, there
was a feeling in her chest as though she were really bleeding
around the heart.

This was not a thing she talked to Nita about. For all
her apparent impulsiveness and flighty reasoning, Nita could
not be imagined entering a situation where she was not at an
advantage, and she always talked as though Pauline were just
the same. This gave their speech when they were together a
special crackling brightness—she always felt very good after
seeing Nita—but they never wavered from that style, and
Pauline had no way within it to talk about her bleeding.

Nita said, "I bet Walter's been married."

"You think so?" Pauline said. "Why do you think so?"

"Oh, the way he talks about how women are. Also one
time we passed a baby carriage on the street and he went into
a song-and-dance about how all infants do for the first year is
smell cheesy and throw up all over you. The Irish don't di-
vorce, you know."

Pauline pictured some hefty Mrs. Mickeling in curling papers chasing Walter with a rolling pin. The wives she knew were not like that at all; they were lively girls who had nicknames for their husbands and who arrived at parties with long stories about how they'd washed all the silverware in bluing for a joke. They treated the details of household routine as things that could be described only with irony but which they were obliged to mention often; you could see they were pleased with themselves. It was not sex that Pauline was curious about in marriage—she was curious about that too, but she felt she was closer to knowing about that: she was so used to thinking of herself as advanced and initiated that it seemed to her that the final knowledge must be an intensification of what she already understood. What seemed harder to imagine in marriage were the domestic arrangements, the constant surveillance of having someone see you at all moments. Nita in her tatty cardigan was obviously not afraid of this.

"I can't picture Walter as a groom," Nita said. "He would look like a black walrus."

"He must have been boiled to the ears at the time," Pauline said. Ernest would look very good in a black morning coat; he was long-waisted and wore clothes nicely.

"You know who looks *boiled* when he drinks?" Nita said. "Garrett does. He turns bright red, and then when he starts to turn pale again, it means he's going to pass out."

"At least he's quiet about it," Pauline said.

"He fell off his chair at Tony's the other night, just like a drunk in a play. Tony was mad; he told him not to come around for a while—go away, go home, dry up."

"Not us too—do we have to stay away too?" Pauline said.

"Of course not us. You think Tony would keep us out?"

Pauline never understood when Nita was going to get

snappish like this. She didn't like being on the receiving end, but she admired the trait in Nita.

For a while there was a fad that spring and summer about taking the ferries all the time. Nita would walk over to Walter's, where there were always three or four people playing cards and drinking shots of peach brandy (Walter's idea of the perfect pick-me-up). Nita would come in and harangue Walter about how he was getting etiolated from lack of sunlight, and then she would coax them all into the great out-of-doors. At first the Staten Island ferry was a great favorite, but once they got to Staten Island there wasn't much to do except eat hot dogs in the station and wait for the next ferry to leave, and so Nita inaugurated other routes, for variety and comparing views—one to Brooklyn and one to Governors Island, a great find because it was free.

Nita had decided not to develop a romance with Walter after all, but they tended to direct so many of their comments to each other that they ended up paired together anyway on most walks. Ernest never went on the ferries with them (he and Walter didn't much like each other, for one thing, so he wasn't likely to be hovering around Walter's kitchen on Sunday mornings). But often as they were pulling out from the dock Pauline was lonely for him, as though his not being with her were unusual.

Nothing in this made her unhappy; on the contrary, she felt very buoyant and hopeful. A friend of Peter's, a sculptor who wore his hair brushed back like a German student's, told her she was eupeptic, a word she had to look up. Later she told him all ax murderers looked that way to the untrained eye. It amused her to think that she was getting a reputation for having a good temperament, a faculty people apparently found desirable and rare.

Frequently they all ended up at a saloon off Greenwich

Avenue that everyone called the Elephants' Graveyard. In the summer weather Pauline stayed out as late as possible. Her room at Mrs. Poganyi's was extremely hot, and she kept hoping that it would cool off if she stayed out further into the night. There was some truth in this theory, but it meant that it was harder to get up in the morning to go to work at Gittelson's, and twice she had her pay docked for coming in late.

Then she found that if she took a nap as soon as she got home from work, she could stay out till whenever she wanted and still get up the next day. She thought there was something very efficient in dividing her sleep into two shifts. It did make her feel a little unstrung at work; she didn't have to be very alert to file things, but she thought her conversation probably sounded strange when people spoke to her, and the office itself seemed flat and oddly lit.

When Pauline went home in July for one of her rare visits, she was amazed at how cool and green Newark seemed. In front of the houses there were maple trees all down the block, a thing she had never taken much notice of before, except when she and Solly had stuck maple pods on their noses when they were little.

For supper they gave her boiled fish with carrots and potatoes. She ate two portions, and her father said, "That's the big fashion in New York now, to eat like a horse." Solly wanted to know what she ate now for all her meals (Pauline lied about this) and what they cost. "She doesn't look like she's starving," her father said.

"Like what does an average banana cost?" Solly asked. He was chewing while he talked, and he reached to get at the plate of bread, leaning sideways so that his elbow stretched across the corner of the table by his father's place. His father gave him a sharp, chopping slap on the back of the neck—

very fast and sudden, with the side of the hand. Solly yelped and jumped back in his seat; Pauline thought she heard him whimpering, but then when he looked up he was trying not to smirk.

Her mother, who was standing up as she always did when they ate, came over to bring more fish. She moved much more slowly than usual, and she spoke in a kind of whisper around Pauline, as though she were cautious of her. She made a face when Pauline asked her about the store, but then she went on at some length about how they couldn't get enough glass buttons in stock this year, there was a big shortage, customers kept asking, they acted like she had them but she was hiding them.

"I saw a girl wearing a beautiful dress with glass buttons in a big slant across the skirt," Pauline said. "It was at a dance I went to at the Lafayette Hotel."

"When you don't have what people want in a store they get like animals," her mother said. "They behave like pigs over buttons."

Her father wanted to know when Gittelson was going to make her a full partner so he could retire already. Solly said she should be careful her scarf didn't fall in the fish broth. It was true that her outfit, which was the same thing she always wore to eat out in New York, was overdone here, too carefully put together. She had not spoken Yiddish since the last time she was home, and she thought there was probably a discordance between it and the way she looked, like those jokes about how Rudolph Valentino was really someone named Rudy Valensky, and that this was why she felt stilted and foolish.

At night she slept in her old room. They were using it for storage now, as a place to keep the off-season fabrics and the old ledgers and invoices, and the floor was all piled with cartons and rolls wrapped in brown paper. The room, which had never been big, was crowded and had a dusty smell— what was oddest about it was that while she was lying in bed with the light still on, looking out at the mounds of packages, she could hardly remember ever staying anywhere else, as if she had made a mistake or dreamed the room at Mrs. Poganyi's.

The first time Pauline read a poem of Ernest's, she was sitting at a table in Vera's drinking tea with Peter and Nita, and someone passed around a little magazine printed on pulpy paper with a dark blue cover. The poem was different from what she would have expected—full of black parrots and metal landscapes—but Pauline thought she liked it. Nita said, "Oh, them," when she saw the magazine. "They're always holding benefits to get more money. Now they want to put on a wild, madcap revue to express their great ideas. They asked me to play the violin in one part—I have to do Chopin's Funeral March. I told them I haven't played it in years. All I know is those slimy Strauss waltzes I play in the restaurant."

"You could practice," Pauline said. Nita said she hated to practice, it gave her rashes under her chin; that was why she had started wearing scarves in the first place.

"I can play musical water glasses," Peter said.

"Well, I'm sure they'll ask you," Nita said, "they're that starved for raw talent."

In the end it was Pauline they asked to do something. Ernest had probably suggested her, or maybe someone else on the staff had been eyeing her. The revue was mostly a series of attacks on literary enemies and stylistic opponents, with a lot of court-martials and hangings in effigy and mock burials. The editor, Dean White, a man she knew from Walter's house, said she only had to stand still dressed as a flame in one scene while someone else did all the work of writhing and perishing.

Pauline went to one rehearsal in the basement of a meeting hall, where she sat smoking cigarettes and flirting with some of Ernest's friends. Ernest came in later. There was no more room on the benches so he sat on the floor, leaning his back against Pauline's knees. The editor gave a speech about old forms and new forms. He said all belief was a disease. "I don't want to even know," he said, "if there have been other human beings before me." Pauline, who knew perfectly well that he had not made all this up himself and had copied it from someone you were supposed to have read, was nonetheless stirred to hear him. What she really liked—what she found truthful—was the coldness in it. It took her own private moments of repudiation and suggested (as she had always suspected) that they were the road to purity.

Ernest looked attentive during the speech—there was an atmosphere of fraternal agreement in the room. At the end he and a few others called out heckling remarks. Pauline would've liked to think of something to call out with them.

The rehearsal was very noisy. People in the middle of the room went through a series of stylized pantomimes, and then someone else practiced an oration in pig Latin. There were references Pauline didn't follow, burlesques of writers she didn't know, but she liked most of it. She had nothing to do until the end, when she stood in a certain spot and someone flashed different lights on her, which she was told would ripple and glimmer over the shiny surface of her costume once it was done.

Ernest said the scene she was in was crucial—the ending was always the most important part of anything. Pauline agreed—she was noticing the shape of his nose, guessing whether it was what you could call aquiline. He left her to go argue with Dean White about how one of the sketches was being directed.

It wasn't until the night of the performance that Pauline saw the costume she had to wear. One of the writers' wives had taken her measurements in a brusque and cursory way, and Pauline had been secretly afraid they were going to give her something that made her look terrible. The costume was really very clever, though; it was a cloak with the sides sewn to drape into sleeves, made of a cheap gauzy red fabric that someone had streaked with gilt paint, and there was an underlayer, an amber taffeta slip that showed through. Nita, who was bustling around backstage in her own black crepe day dress, said, "You look good in that. Probably hell is very flattering to brunettes."

"That's a relief to know," Pauline said. They sat while the writer's wife put makeup on them. Nita got white face powder and silver glitter in her hair. Her eyes were very blue behind the mask of white and her lips were wickedly dark— it was odd to see her smile normally. "You look dangerous," Pauline said. Pauline got gilt greasepaint and red pencil in very fierce-looking flames around her eyes. When she saw her face in the hand mirror she kept looking at it sidelong to try to catch it without seeing herself look. Glimpsed that way, the forked eye was like an animal's markings, brindled and severe.

For most of the performance she was backstage and could see only a small part of what was going on. She stood with the other actors, crowded close next to some men in black tights. It all happened very quickly: the pantomime troupe simulated the motions of a giant typewriter while there were shrieks and the sound of gongs in the background; parodies of certain authors were read; a trial was held in incomprehensible languages. Ernest had written the trial scene—he watched from the wings, nearer to the front than Pauline was. She saw the dark back of his head, blue-tinted in the lights, and the tense angle of his profile. The sharpness of her physical longing for him distracted her; later she realized she had forgotten to watch his scene.

During scene changes, people came out and did card tricks or played tunes on a pocket comb wrapped in Kleenex while staring deadpan at the audience. In the last act a hugely padded green figure meant to represent a dollar bill came out and tried to crush a child by sitting on him. The child (really Bertha Goodwin in short pants) was rescued, and the dollar bill was put in chains and forced to confess his crimes. And then he was condemned to die while Nita played the violin and Pauline stood with her arms upraised under flickering spotlights. She had been afraid that she would start to giggle or smirk onstage, but it all had the opposite effect; her features got very still and solemn—it was almost horrifying to see the rows of faces—she felt incredulous and then flushed and elated, prickly with exhilaration.

When it was over, everyone gathered in the hall upstairs. The editor had originally wanted to have a banquet on the floor with tubs of punch ignited in blue flames, but instead there were barrels of beer on trestles and trays of sandwiches. Most of the cast were still in their makeup and costumes; Nita said if you stopped for cold cream you'd never get anything to eat. The editor was very excited and went around with a gloating expression, and there was a general feeling that things had gone well.

Pauline saw Peter talking to Ernest, and when she brushed past them Peter said, "Here she is, in a literal blaze of glory."

"You were very good," Ernest said.

"I thought your trial scene was really excellent," Pauline said.

"I've heard of red-hot mamas, but this was beyond the pale," Peter said.

"'Nature red in tooth and claw,' that's what you look like with that makeup on," Ernest said.

"We need more of that sort of thing nowadays," Peter said. "Girls with a little fiendish streak in them."

"I'm wild but I'm not violent," Pauline said.

Peter said, "A likely story," and he asked what she wanted to drink after all that sizzling. Pauline said a dainty glass of beer would cool her off nicely, thank you, and she was left with Ernest while Peter went off to get it.

"The attack on MacIver's prose was very good, I thought," Ernest said. "He deserves it. In spades."

"Oh, yes," Pauline said. That had been one of the parodies she had recognized right off; it was an easy one to spot because it had lines like "He held a cigarette carefully between his upper and lower lip," which really did have the overwrought preciseness of MacIver's style. "No one will ever be able to read him again without thinking of it," Pauline said.

"Writing like his is really pestilential. It's a kind of mental corruption to read it."

People—men especially—were always getting extreme like this, ready to beat into the dust all sorts of art that outraged them. Pauline sometimes thought there was something wrong with her that her opinions weren't so impassioned, although she still didn't see that a bad prose style did any harm really.

"I've heard he's very nice," Pauline said. A friend of Nita's went out with someone who knew MacIver, and Pauline was looking to work this into the conversation, but then she thought better of it.

"Oh, nice," Ernest said. "What does nice matter?"

"That's true," Pauline said. "Baudelaire wasn't known for being nice. And Byron was a cad, he kept deserting all his women. And probably giving them gonorrhea."

Nita's friend Rose came up to hug Pauline, just as Pauline was remembering that Ernest didn't like Byron. Rose said, "Everyone loved you in that last scene. A memorable moment." Peter returned with her beer, and with him was the sculptor with the brushed-back hair, who told her she was perfectly cast in the part, a model flame. On the other side of the room someone made a toast to Dean White's magazine and its fiscal serenity. When she looked around again, Ernest had been drawn into another conversation; he gave her a little quick wave when he caught her eye.

A very small band had been hired for the event; the players were all holding glasses during the toast. Pauline didn't want to begin dancing right away, and she stood watching for a while. Peter was talking about which couples on the dance floor looked as if they were really sleeping together, whether you could tell by how they danced. Rose said, "You can't ever tell." She said this very mildly, her voice just audible over the sound of the music, which made it especially convincing.

Pauline didn't dance until later in the evening, when she was fairly drunk and a tall man in white flannels led her onto the floor. The room was crowded now—full of couples swerving and sidling around each other, women in limp, fluttery dresses and men with their jackets flapping. One joker went around picking the men's pockets, pulling out handkerchiefs and fountain pens and handing them to the other dancers. Pauline's partner called out, "Watch out, bozo," and "Look out, it's two-left-feet White," when they passed people he knew, and the editor yelled back at him,

"Go bury yourself in fertilizer, Dewey. Excuse me, Pauline."

"Old friends," the man explained. "We go back a long way."

"How long?" Pauline said.

"Before he could write worth beans. Those first poems were pathetic. He had to bribe Bertha Goodwin to print them in that rag she had then. Well, not a bribe really. More like your basic physical persuasion."

Pauline asked if he was a writer too. "I write plays. Are you an actress?" Pauline said no, not really.

"Too bad. I have a play where there's a girl onstage who has to jump from a ten-foot ladder. You'd be great, you look very agile."

"I think you're going to have a little trouble casting that part," Pauline said. This apparently struck him as very funny—he let out a loud, hawing guffaw—until Pauline recognized the long hiccuping laugh she had overheard at that first party last winter at Walter's. The laugh made him seem oafish, but he was good-looking enough otherwise, Pauline thought. Actually, she wasn't sure. He had gaunt, slightly pitted cheeks and spaniel-brown eyes, so he looked weathered and very young at the same time. He had a tattoo on his arm just above his wrist, a small blue anchor, which he said he had gotten in the navy. Pauline asked him how the navy was, and he said it was dog's work but you got to see good places; Tierra del Fuego was a very good place to see.

They sat out the next dance; they were near the door talking when Pauline saw Ernest coming toward them with his coat over his arm, on his way out. He took her hand and kissed it by way of good night, and Pauline said, "Till next time." Her voice was husky from drinking. She thought it was quite adroit of her to think of saying this. It seemed interesting and somehow richly gratifying that this was becoming a sort of joke between them, a friendly conspiracy of acknowledged undercurrents. He looked rueful as he left, and she was very animated and bright when she turned back to hear more about Tierra del Fuego.

"Is Patagonia in your play, is that what it's about?" she said. Dewey—that was his first name, it had taken her a while to get that straight—said no, his play was a modern retelling of the story of Romulus and Remus, how they were raised by a wolf. "I have a lot of respect for the Greeks and Romans," he said.

"They gave good parties," Pauline said. He laughed his braying laugh again.

It was nice that he thought she was so witty; he was a peculiar mixture, with his spots of intelligence and his mannered roughness and his lapses into showing off. They danced more—he was very supple in his dancing, if not altogether natural—and then Nita came over and whispered that they were all going to Anselm's for breakfast. "About time someone thought of that," Dewey said.

They made a noisy entrance into Anselm's. There were nine or ten of them, all blinking in the sudden bright light; Walter was singing one line of the "Anvil Chorus" over and over, and she and Nita were still in their makeup, with their costumes showing under their coats. Walter complained that he couldn't read the menu, and Nita ordered them all waffles and scrambled eggs.

"Fuel for the machines," Walter said, when the waiter brought the plates. Dewey said, "Grub for the starving crew." They all grew quieter as they ate; Pauline was suddenly tired, and the warmth of the food made her drowsy. She looked down at her waffle for a while—it had a very regular pattern of little diamond grids interlocked—and then she leaned on Dewey's shoulder and let her eyes close. "Baby's gone bye-bye," Dewey said.

.   .   .

It was raining when Pauline got out of the cab in the blue early morning light, and when she woke up the next day it was still raining outside her window. She was lying on top of the covers in a nightgown she had put on backward. The first thing she remembered was walking up the stairs, carrying her shoes and being afraid that Mrs. Poganyi was going to wake up and come out and see her in her flame makeup. This seemed funny even now, and she got out of bed smiling to herself about it.

Pauline never got hangovers really—what she got instead was a rush of recalled scenes from the night before; her own theory was that she was still a little drunk in the mornings. She had a running picture in her mind at the moment of a man with red hair waving his shoe during the dancing and of Nita eating waffles in Anselm's in her dead-white powder and glitter. Pauline was slightly sorry about having spent so much time with Dewey. She didn't think now that she much liked him—he mispronounced words and he had a habit of echoing phrases people had just used. Peter's friend the sculptor would have been better at least, after Ernest drifted off, if she had stopped to think about it. But there was an element of chance in who you ended up with sometimes.

She walked over to Vera's that night, thinking that Nita or Walter would certainly be there, but when she stepped into the room the first person she saw was Dewey, beckoning to her from his table. Out of politeness she went over to him, and he said, "There's the girl. Didn't stay home very long, did you?"

"A few hours," she said. "That's a lot."

"You're like I am," he said. "Don't fence me in."

When the waiter came to their table, he pretended to hit his head when he saw Dewey and he said, "Oh, no, the poor man's Shakespeare is here again." Pauline had never seen the waiter so jolly before. Dewey called him "Adolfo, you dumbbell." Afterward Dewey said, "We're writing a play about his life, Adolfo and me. He used to be a boxer."

A couple Pauline didn't know—a swarthy older man and his painfully thin girlfriend—came and sat with them, and Dewey told stories again about the navy and South America. They were good stories, with grimly comic punch lines, and he cocked his head and looked genial when he told them. He winked at her once while someone else was talking, and he kept patting her hand and trying to buy her more tea. "Tea makes you strong as bull," he said. By the end of the night she was used to him.

It was raining again when he walked her home, and he held his jacket over her head. He said, "You walk like I do. When did you hurt your knee?" She had noticed that he walked with a rolling gait—not a limp exactly but a rocking to one side, very appealing in its way—but she hadn't known she was imitating it. She lied and said she had a stiff muscle from dancing. In front of Mrs. Poganyi's stoop they necked a little in the rain; he had a slow and thorough way of kissing, undulant and persuasive. She was pleased now that all this was happening, although after it went on for a while she was afraid someone was going to look out the window and she began to mind getting wet in the rain.

Later that week, when she came home from work, Dewey was waiting for her in Mrs. Poganyi's parlor, ready to take her to supper as though they had agreed on it. Afterward they went to the Elephants' Graveyard for drinks. Pauline thought she could feel a certain faint surprise from people at seeing them together, although Walter seemed to like him well enough. The two men had a contest about stacking matches, which involved buying each other drinks, and Dewey cawed and clapped when Walter started singing.

She had told Dewey she often had just a tin of sardines and a banana for supper, and in the following weeks whenever they were out having dinner, he always said as he handed her the menu that it was time for her to get some nourishment and fatten up. He was noisy in restaurants, although waiters sometimes seemed to like it. He had a way of arranging at the end of the night when they would meet the next time, so that their times with each other were hooked together.

Once he asked her in a light, teasing voice if she had come into Vera's that Sunday night looking for him. She said, "I was kind of interested in a sandwich actually," and he said, "Oh, I know. Never ask a lady." It was a great issue with him that she was ladylike; when she wore a certain deep-brimmed hat with a velvet band, he kept saying, "Look at the duchess."

She didn't mind spending so much time with him, but she still didn't feel that he really counted. Privately she and Nita called him the Lounge Lizard of Literature, and Pauline would describe with groans his habit of buttonholing strangers to tell them the plots of his plays. Sometimes when he was talking to people, she rolled her eyes so they would know she knew better. He did not seem to notice this; on the contrary, he liked to refer to "Pauline's favorite character" or "the scene Pauline thought was good." He liked to tell her how glad and contented he always was being with her, and he would often look at her as they walked with a grateful, beseeching gaze.

Sometimes he phoned her at work and he would talk a kind of baby-talk lover's slang over the phone, trying to get her to answer in kind. When they saw movies together, he was always comparing the sweetheart couples to themselves. Once he brought her a present—a painted fan he said he had gotten in South America. She put the fan on the dresser in her room; it reminded her of the sort of thing a gently bred child might play with. It lay folded in the china dish next to her beads, a placement that made it look more sentimental than it was, and in the end she was touched sometimes by the sight of it, as a sign of his devotion to her.

V

Dewey liked to try to make light conversation with Mrs. Poganyi when he came to see Pauline. He would stand around the living room saying things like "It's raining cats and dogs and goats outside" or "Sure and begorra, 'tis a dreadful night out there in the peat bog." Pauline wasn't sure what Mrs. Poganyi made of this; she never spoke more than a sentence at a time, except to scold the maid in a language Beatrice had identified as Hungarian. Dewey's opinion was that he brightened things up for Mrs. Poganyi and that she was probably secretly a little sweet on him. Pauline thought that she looked tense and worried when Dewey went on for too long. Perhaps it was only from the effort to understand, but it made Pauline uneasy, and she frequently chose to meet him outside.

Once when he was supposed to meet her in front of a movie theater, he kept her waiting for so long that everyone else in the ticket line went inside and the picture began; she could hear the music. She was afraid he was waiting for her in another place, impatient by now, or even that he was paying her back for being late so often herself. She tried to read from a newspaper she had brought, and that confused her more about how much time had passed, and when she saw him coming toward her, she called out, "Oh, you're here, I'm so glad." He said he had gotten all delayed trying to see a friend about something important, and then they went into the theater and she forgot about it while she watched the film, a comedy with a chase scene and a car falling apart, not her favorite kind of movie but very funny in parts.

Afterward when they were having drinks at the Elephants' Graveyard, Dewey said, "Helene would have screamed bloody murder all over the street if I was late like that." Helene was his old girlfriend; she lived in Chicago now and always sounded like a shrew in his descriptions. "I would've heard about it for months after," he said. He seemed to think that Pauline had shown a fineness of character and also a deeper appreciation of him, a trust in his better side, by waiting. Pauline had a feeling his standards were low—she didn't believe she had really demonstrated anything so substantial as all this, but she was pleased that he thought so.

She did feel loyal to him in some way, and when Nita called him a lout and a clodhopper, Pauline said he was really surprisingly courtly sometimes. She always stressed to Nita how fervent he was in his attentions and how fixedly he had attached himself to her. He did do things like carrying her over puddles in the rain, although she didn't altogether like being hoisted like that in public. With Peter and Walter she emphasized his time in South America or his friendship with Adolfo the waiter. She liked it when Walter called him a tough customer—praise for a side of him Pauline found strongly attractive—although it was possible Walter meant this as a slur against Dewey's "background." Walter always laughed about him in a way Pauline thought was probably affectionate. And Peter wavered—for a while he seemed to think of Dewey as a decent enough person who had for some reason adopted a boorish facade—but then later Peter got very stony and cold whenever Dewey's name was mentioned.

In a way Pauline liked it when people asked her what she saw in Dewey. For one thing, it showed a certain offhandedness on her part in settling herself on an admittedly odd choice. That it was not what she or anyone else would have expected only proved how extensive the possibilities were; she was not, at the moment, in a hurry for anything better. She felt, when people expressed too much puzzlement, that there was something lazy and stubborn in her that mocked their earnestness. Peter gave her speeches on how she was getting in deeper all the time. Sometimes it struck her that this was the nature of a great love, that it drew you against all sense on the least foreseen paths.

Dewey's way of earning money was to work at times as a court reporter. He met her in the evenings still dressed in what he called his working-stiff uniform, a blue suit and a shirt with a high collar. Pauline liked the idea that he was tapping away at a stenotype machine with his anchor tattoo hidden by his shirt cuff, and he looked gratified when she mentioned this. He said someday he was going to throw a stink bomb in the judge's chambers just to see everyone's faces. He would do it now except he had to pay the rent. Pauline rubbed the joints of his fingers to relax them; she didn't know whether this could really help but it pleased him.

He had switched from writing plays to working on short stories. On his urging, she brought home pads and a new fountain pen from Gittelson's. She had never really stolen anything before, and the ease with which she simply walked out with it all under her coat was thrilling in its way. "A little larceny in your soul, my dear," Dewey said, cackling

81

and rubbing his hands like a stage villain. Pauline thought he was overdoing it—she said a small batch of office supplies did not constitute larceny—and this made him hoo-hah more fiendishly; he kept patting her cheek and saying, "Fine work, my pretty."

Dewey lived in a railroad flat, with a curtain in the archway between the two main rooms and a kitchen that always smelled faintly of unlit gas. Sometimes Pauline cooked suppers for them—scrambled eggs or lamb chops. They were cheerful, savory little meals; Dewey called them campfire cookery for wasted youth.

His typewriter was on a table in a corner of the kitchen; possibly he really used it, it wasn't thick with telltale dust or anything. She had never seen a real page of anything he had written and she was hoping not to. She supposed that it would be overdrawn, a copy of things not well understood. As long as he didn't press her about it, she didn't think she cared what his writing was like. She already knew people who were well known and good at what they did—Walter was probably the closest to being truly famous—and her connection to them seemed permanent and settled. But even Walter, who was so forthright and expansive and so maniacally sure of himself in certain ways, did not have Dewey's physical sureness. In that sense, Dewey, with his rolling walk, was from another element. The way he carried himself made him seem very resolute—Pauline was aware that it was not real confidence, but the lack of it in other people seemed unappetizing to her now.

On the nights when she was home alone, she stayed in her room and ate her suppers of sardines and soda crackers with a sense that this was a custom she had invented in a much

82

earlier season; it made her feel her time in New York as very long. Once in the evening she went outside to buy a magazine, and when she came back in the house she saw, on the second floor, that the door to Beatrice's room was open. Beatrice was standing over an open trunk, folding clothes into it. "Hail and farewell," Beatrice said. "You can have my room if you want to. It's bigger."

"You're leaving?" Pauline said. She thought Beatrice must be getting married. She felt unobservant not to have guessed; there must have been signs.

"I can't wait to walk out that door for the last time," Beatrice said. "It's heaven to think of never waking up in that bed again. I can't tell you." She was moving to Brooklyn—a girlfriend of hers had an apartment and was renting her a room in it.

"Moving to the wilds of the outer boroughs, huh?" Pauline said.

"Here it's the wilds," Beatrice said. "It's noisy from the El and it stinks. The mice have a smell. It's worse in warm weather, but I can smell it all the time."

"You'd think Mrs. Poganyi would put out traps," Pauline said, although she didn't care herself; she had only seen mice a few times, and they didn't bother her.

"Oh, Poganyi's a witch. You can see how she walks around shrieking at that girl who's the maid."

Pauline didn't see that any of this justified a move to Brooklyn—the rooming house wasn't so bad for its kind. It seemed wrong that Beatrice wasn't going to be there any more. "I wish you the very best of luck," Pauline said and hugged her.

"Oh, thanks," Beatrice said. She looked happy.

"I'll miss you," Pauline said. "You were my friend when I moved in and I didn't know anybody, and you helped me."

Pauline wondered if she had gotten the habit from Dewey of being a little cheaply false once she got going.

"Oh, I was a saint," Beatrice said.

On Friday Pauline went with Dewey to a dinner at Walter's. Walter's own theory was that he was an inspired cook, not good at everyday meals but gifted at fixing certain stylish and highly seasoned foods. There were about a dozen guests, and they all got very noisy over the punch while Walter was puttering in the kitchen. Dewey kept saying, "Mickeling puts dragon's blood in his punch," and pretending to breathe fire on people. No one minded—in fact, for a while they all went around breathing and hissing at each other. Pauline said, "I love these smart Village soirees with a lot of urbane conversation." Nita, who was passing nearby, made a face and gurgled bubbles into her punch glass. Pauline said, "Same to you," which came out sounding more cutting than she meant it. She had had a long and dispiriting day at Gittelson's, and she was not in a boisterous mood. She watched for a while and then she went into Walter's bedroom to find her cigarettes.

A girl Peter had brought was standing at Walter's dresser, powdering her face. "Getting rambunctious in there, aren't they?" she said. She was a small, child-faced brunette, and she used the powder puff with great energy and system, tapping over her chin and neck. It made Pauline worry that she looked too shiny, and she went to the mirror to check. "Use some, if you want," the girl said and held out her vanity case. When Pauline put the puff back, she saw, next to the little sieve-covered wells of powder and rouge, a small square envelope—it looked like a packet of Alka-Seltzer or some headache powder until she read the brand name, familiar from jokes about it, and she understood that it was a condom.

84

She had a secret desire to ask to unwrap it so she could see it—the woman seemed candid enough. It reminded Pauline that she was still a virgin and that in her own sexual experience a line of distinction still existed, faint but absolute, a border she almost pretended to herself that she had crossed although she had not. She sat on the bed, lighting a cigarette, and when the girl finished combing her hair, they went back into the living room together.

The dinner, when they finally sat down to it, turned out to be veal kidneys—a food Walter said was underappreciated because most people had never had them fixed properly. The kidneys weren't bad, only a little rubbery and close-grained. Dewey was in an especially affectionate mood; he kept nuzzling her neck and calling her Peach of Peaches. An older man, a collector who was a friend of Walter's, told her she looked radiant lately.

Rose said, "She does look good these days, doesn't she?" Pauline wondered if Rose thought she and Dewey were sleeping together. Rose had said you couldn't tell from appearances, but did anyone believe that? Pauline looked over at Peter and the brunette, trying to guess. The girl, spooning her dessert, had a bright, settled look; whatever she was doing she was confident about it. Perhaps it was just the dessert that brought on that expression, a chocolate sponge pudding which everyone agreed had rescued the dinner. In high school Bunny and Pauline had had their discussions about the truth of the senses—philosophically they were both empiricists. Pauline had come up with the formulation that a knowledge of absolute truth was possible in the fullest extension of the senses, probably in sex. Once reasoned, this was a sacred belief of hers. Already she had outgrown some of its earnestness—it meant that in most adults of any experience there had been this contact with the blaze of bare reality, and she wasn't willing to concede this as common to other people. She did feel nonetheless that the brunette's eyes had un-usual lights in them, a quickened depth. Under the table Dewey had his hand on Pauline's knee.

They stayed until late; in the end they all took the dog out to the park for a run. Dewey, who was good with dogs, threw sticks for him. Rose led him to the fountain to drink some water. Garrett climbed a low branch of a tree, which made the dog get very excited and circle the tree, yipping. Nita said, "That's the most excitement Garrett's caused in anyone for years."

Dewey was singing when he walked Pauline home. He sang "Yes! We Have No Bananas"; he only knew a few bars and he kept singing them over and over. He had gotten this from Walter—the idea of singing when he was drunk. A couple passed them, looking amused, and the man tipped his hat. "They admire your beautiful baritone," Pauline said. This made him sing louder, which was not what she wanted.

"Everybody said how good you looked tonight," he said. He was slurring his words on purpose, and he began singing, "Believe me if all those endearing young charms/ Which I gaze on so fondly today."

"People are sleeping," Pauline said. She knew she sounded like someone's mother, but they were on side streets now, moving past quiet half-lighted buildings.

"Were to change by tomorrow," he sang, "and fleet in my arms/ Like fairy gifts fading away."

They were on her block now, and she shushed him out-side the house. "Afraid I'll wake the dead, aren't you?" he said. "This is the street of the dead." He kicked a garbage can, which clanged horribly and fell over. Somebody's house-hold garbage—glass bottles, carrot peelings, old news-papers, coffee grounds—spilled out into the gutter. "You jumped," he said, and kicked the can again, banging it against a metal grate.

Pauline stood quiet, trying not to jump, since that seemed to goad him further. "I scared you," he said. "I didn't mean to." He used the can's lid as a shovel and scooped some of the garbage back. He got the largest pieces back in and then he kicked the rest into a more compact pile by the other cans. "No one will know," he said. "They'll think a dog did it."

"There's a dog on the block that does that," Pauline said.

"I didn't mean to scare you," he said.

"I know that," Pauline said.

"I don't mean anything when I get rowdy," he said.

"I know that," she said.

"You know a lot," he said. "I've never met anyone like you." She thought at first this might be sarcastic, but then he moved forward to hold her and he kissed her neck, he rubbed his cheek against her shoulder. They stayed clasped that way for a while; he rocked her back and forth. She felt awkward but interested at something this stagey happening to her; she stroked his back.

"Go to bed," he said.

The next day was Saturday, and when she first heard knocking at her door, she thought she was dreaming that she had to get up for work and she struggled to shake off the dream and go back to sleep. The knocking went on longer, so that she woke up still hearing it. The door opened while she was tying on her wrapper. Mrs. Poganyi stood on the threshold. "Why you sleep so late?" she said, and she put a piece of paper on Pauline's dresser—a phone message—and left. DOOI IS SICK, it said on the paper. CALL DOOI.

Pauline felt she should be concerned, but there were times when she had to rest from being with Dewey, and he didn't seem to feel that she ever needed this. When she called him from the phone in the hall, the number she reached was the candy store on his corner and she had to wait while a kid was sent to find him. She stood, listening to blurred voices and crackling sounds in the receiver until Dewey came over the line. He said that he'd been in bed all morning with a stomachache—he thought it was from the kidneys at Walter's; he'd been worried that she was sick too. His voice sounded thin and sad, and she ended up offering to come make him some tea and toast.

When he answered the door, he was half dressed, in pants with suspenders over an undershirt. "It's the Visiting Nurse Service," she said. "I'm here to lay my cooling palm on your feverish brow."

"I'm not feverish really," he said. "It's just a slow death from poisoning."

"The coward's way to assassinate," Pauline said. "Who are your enemies? Think."

"Many," he said.

She offered to make him milk toast as a sort of joke, but he liked the idea. They ate a bowl together, spooning up the crusts of buttered bread in the scalded milk. "Hits the spot," he said. He kissed her on the forehead and said he was going to lie down on the sofa, if she didn't mind.

"Want me to read to you?" she said. He thought this was a good suggestion, and she found the funnies section of the paper and read through an episode of Mutt and Jeff.

"Lie down next to me," he said. "I'm lonely."

She settled alongside him on the cushions; it amused her a little that he thought he had to lure her in this way. He was probably not sick at all, only hung over and lazy. She liked the way he looked now, with the leanness of his neck showing and his arms bare. There was less clothing between them than usual—she was wearing a light sweater, which he slipped off almost at once. His mouth tasted of cigarettes and boiled milk. When she opened her eyes, his expression was blurred and slackened, and he looked at her with a fixed sheen in his eyes, reverent and watery. They had shifted so the weight of him was on her; she liked the pressure of it, blanketing and steady. She had a sudden passing remembrance of Harry Bitt, who had liked to lean her against doorways and car seats.

Dewey was stroking the fabric of her slip as though it were her skin; her skin under it seemed eager and thin. They were rocking in place. It reminded her of someone's definition of infinity: constant motion, constant rest. She made a small moaning sound as though she had become as intense and concentrated as the plainest syllable. By degrees they were moving toward the unfamiliar. She said, "Oh," again, more wildly helpless this time. She was quite awed at herself. She thought how the phrase "going all the way" implied something absolute—the part that had been beyond imagining—although the forms of longing within her own body had perhaps been a pantomime, a kind of physical imagining. Dewey was murmuring to her, an endearment she couldn't quite hear; she wanted to say something back. She wanted to hear her voice outside herself, overreaching.

She unhooked her own stockings. She wondered if he was going to ask if she was willing, to ask permission. For a moment, while he was fumbling with the buttons on his pants, the whole thing seemed too personal. Then he was lying on top of her again, he had begun—at first she was startled, not by pain (although there was something like pain), but by the fact that he seemed to be taking himself away almost as soon as he had entered—he had changed his mind, withdrawn for fear of making her pregnant—until she understood that this repetition of leaving and returning was the thing itself, and not a hesitation before the single consummate sliding she had imagined.

Her own confusion humbled her. She lost track of things somewhat; he went on, intent and purposeful.

. . .

Afterward they fell asleep, and it was late afternoon or early evening when they woke up; the room was almost dark. Dewey got up—she could hear him putting on his pants—and then he brought her back a glass of water from the kitchen. She sat up, sipping it. "You look like a siren," he said. "Like the White Rock girl."

"She's not a siren, she's a nymph," Pauline said.

Dewey laughed his guffaw. "You said it, I didn't." He stroked her arm. "You're terrific," he said.

He smoothed her hair. Did she want a cigarette? She was groggy and quiet, waiting to be more alert so she could think; it seemed odd to have him in the room at a time like this. He asked if she were hungry, and when she told him yes, he said he would make supper for them. "Don't move, stay where you are," he said. She leaned back with her arms folded over her breasts, and when he went into the kitchen, she put on her slip.

He made them toasted cheese sandwiches, and he brought out a pot of tea and some whiskey to put in it. "That looks so nice," Pauline said.

She ate eagerly and quickly; there was a kind of blank excitement in her stomach that made her feel hollow and ravenous. Afterward she said she would go wash the dishes, but he said no, they would wait, and put out his hand to keep her from getting up from the couch; he seemed afraid to let her leave the spot. He told her a long story about how in the navy they washed the dishes with cheap soap that made everyone sick at first, and she drank more of the tea with whiskey, and while she was listening she fell asleep again.

When she woke up, he was lifting her off the sofa, starting to walk her toward the bedroom, through the curtained archway. "What time is it?" she said.

"A hair past a freckle," he said, pretending to look at his wrist. She wondered where her shoes were; she would have liked to be back in her room at Mrs. Poganyi's without the labor of getting there, but to leave would be to break away, to make things fall short of what seemed to be their normal sequence. And she was interested, too, to sleep with him literally, to spend the night, to go to bed with him—all the euphemisms that bonded the idea of sex with lying together unconscious. He had tried before to get her to take naps with him, but the notion of it had seemed too sloppy then.

She wanted to brood; she still felt a certain shock in the tissues. Now she would fall asleep before she had a chance to commit the particulars to memory. She had almost forgotten that it was an act she would be repeating.

In the morning, while she was padding around the kitchen barefoot, making breakfast, Dewey told her she was crazy to think of going back to the rooming house now. Poganyi would be waiting for her with a battle-ax. "She knows where you were, she's no fool," he said.

"She doesn't care about anything, she doesn't notice," Pauline said.

"You can't keep sneaking back there in the mornings," he said. "It's a rat-hutch anyway."

"I don't mind it," she said.

"What about me?" he said. "Think about me." He sucked in his cheeks to show how undernourished he was getting on his own cooking. It was his way of suggesting that they live together; she could see he was very tickled with himself at being so offhand in bringing it up. It annoyed her that this was his idea of artful coaxing. She wondered if he had left the phone message yesterday on purpose, a calling card of her whereabouts.

But what struck her more forcibly was that it would be so easy to do it, to move in. She did not fully recognize herself in the person who would do this—it was too sweeping a maneuver, too simple and probably even too bold for her, and it presupposed all sorts of sureties she did not pretend to have—but it bore an irresistible similarity to a hopeful thought. She had a sense of wanting to drive herself to it, to do it over her own objections.

For weeks she brought the more crucial items—toiletries, blouses for work—over in batches, in little paper-wrapped bundles, so that nothing was handy in either place when she wanted it, until the end of the month, when she changed addresses for good and brought the rest over in a taxi.

Pauline's story to Mrs. Poganyi was that she was moving to Chicago—a completely unnecessary lie—which Mrs. Poganyi accepted without comment; her only bit of sullenness was to insist at the very last minute on charging Pauline for a ripped window shade. Dewey said Pauline was a sucker for paying.

"Flapper file clerk vanishes into Village den," she told Nita. Nita alluded to a definite consensus that Dewey had changed, he was much better since he'd been under Pauline's influence. Pauline took this as Nita's version of manners, an attempt at suitable enthusiasm; Pauline could feel her trying to be nice, which was not altogether flattering but did have a kind of loyal tact in it.

The apartment was small and cluttered with both of them in it. Pauline was always hitting her hip against the chairs when she moved around the kitchen. It was messier than she had kept her room at the boardinghouse, but the tumble of things left lying around—newspapers and clothing and shoes—seemed to her to be the effects of movement and abundance and family activity, better than the stillness of a rented room. She got very careless right away, leaving stockings and wrinkled pullovers draped over everything, as though she wanted them to commingle with the background and put their own mark on the look of the apartment.

In bed at night she worried about waking him if she moved when he was asleep. In the daytime she was sometimes stiff in the shoulder from where she had lain cramped and motionless. At work she sat at her desk rubbing her shoulder blade—she liked telling the stock boy she had premature rheumatism.

She would have liked to write to tell Bunny, but they hadn't exchanged letters for a long time and it seemed clumsy to suddenly issue an announcement. There were things she didn't get to tell—passing details, half formulated into thought, dissolved and were forgotten. In a way this seemed right, less girlish. She felt that she lived now in a denser realm, in which events went on continuously, without postponement and without opinion. In her current life her daydreams were more physically graphic—bright with detailed sex—but at the same time more repetitious and formless, less tellable.

In the evening when she came home from work, Dewey was always sitting over the newspaper—he seemed to read three or four papers a day—and she would sit on the sofa with him, taking a section, while they half read and half listened to each other. Pauline found this soothing and companionable, except when items in the news made Dewey angry, and then he would rage in sudden bitterness—it was a joke between them that he swore like a sailor.

By and large he was easier to live with than she would have thought. He told her how lucky he was and how much better she was than any woman he'd known. When they went out at night he tried to neck with her in restaurants; Walter said they were so sweet they made his teeth hurt.

They were only irritable with each other occasionally—about money, which surprised Pauline, since she considered herself unusually free from pettiness on this subject. But on their nights out she noticed now that in restaurants he couldn't seem to order anything but the most expensive dishes, almost on principle; he would pretend to debate, considering pending bills or rent, but he always switched at the last minute when the waiter was there.

His other irritating trait was that he had bouts of being playful in mocking ways—he had pet names for her like Sadie Snob or the Jersey Jewess—and he wouldn't stop, he got more noisily amused the more she protested, so that she had to learn to try not to rise to the bait.

In general, though, it wasn't at all bad to be in his company so much. He could get surprisingly interested in small household matters; he liked to bring home kitchen gadgets—cheese slicers and rubber bottle stoppers—and he liked to recite the recipe for an elaborate cocktail he had invented, based on a bottle of green Chartreuse someone had given them.

Peter had told her that she was playing house (a phrase meant as a dismissal of living together unmarried). And it was true that she had a sense of imitating something, of following out a borrowed form. It was only in the mornings that she felt this as a kind of strain. It bothered her getting dressed when he was there, and there were things she waited to do until he was out of the room.

VI

Dewey's block was full of families—groups of boys who raced around, chasing each other and shrieking, and young girls who brought chairs down from upstairs and sat in front of their doorways watching the street. Dewey had lived there for a year, and he occasionally showed off by using what he said were curse words in Italian, although Pauline wasn't sure he said them right. He also brought home wine from the grocery store on the corner or sometimes from the newsstand; he said everyone on the block was busy fermenting it in their kitchens; in the fall you could see all the mash dumped in the gutters. Pauline had a secret grudge against the wine because it stained her teeth and made her look ghoulish when she drank it, but she was in favor of keeping reserves of it in the house, since it was Dewey's one real effort at buying cheap.

They did not have many visitors, but one night when she came home from work, Garrett was in the living room with Dewey. They were playing cards and drinking the wine out of jelly glasses, and they looked up, dark-lipped, when she came in. "The woiking goil is home from the mines,"

Dewey said. They were both tipsy in a hazy, convivial way. Garrett had that reddish look that Nita said he always got when he drank.

"I hope you boys aren't wagering sums of money on a game of chance," Pauline said.

"Oh, no," Dewey said. "We would never do that, would we, Gar?"

"No, ma'am," Garrett said. He had a flat-voiced, hollow way of speaking, somewhere between politeness and plain listlessness. Pauline thought he was a funny choice as someone for Dewey to take up with. They went on playing cards while Pauline fixed supper. Dewey did all the work of conversation, crowing and snickering and firing off rhetorical insults while Garrett smoked cigarettes and mumbled.

When the food was ready, Dewey said, "Well, eat something with us, you miserable card-sharking bastard," and Garrett went to the table with them. He ate very little—Pauline was afraid he didn't like her cooking—but he said the juice of the grape gave him all the vitamins he needed.

After dinner they went back to their card game. Pauline sat near them, reading. They played for hours—Pauline got sleepy over her book and went into the bedroom. There was only the curtain in the archway between the two rooms, and she could hear them, Dewey's braying laugh and Garrett's swearing when he lost. It annoyed her that she couldn't fall asleep at night in her own house; she was angry that they didn't have a better apartment with separate rooms, a thing she usually didn't think about. She was afraid, too, that Garrett might pass out and have to stay the night. But after a while she heard Dewey walking him to the other end of the apartment, and she could hear their good-byes and the door clicking shut.

"You have fun?" she said, while Dewey sat on the bed, pulling off his shoes and kicking them onto the floor.

"Sure," he said. "It was a bloody massacre. Some people don't have a feel for poker at all. It's like an instinct some people don't have."

"He stayed late," Pauline said.

"He likes us, he likes to be here. He doesn't like people that are phony, like Peter and that whole crew."

"What's wrong with Peter?"

"Garrett thinks I should write that book about Adolfo. He thinks it would be a very powerful story."

"He's probably right," Pauline said. By the time she settled the covers over her again, Dewey had fallen asleep, so she didn't have to hear about it.

Pauline had trouble imagining that Adolfo had ever been a boxer. He seemed much too loose-limbed and shuffling for an athlete—although age might simply have crumpled him: he was close to fifty. Now that Dewey had gotten interested in him again, they had taken to stopping at Vera's very late, just before Adolfo finished his shift, and they would sit and wait until he changed into a clean shirt and different shoes and came out from the kitchen, ready to go drinking with them.

Pauline couldn't tell whether Adolfo really believed Dewey was going to write anything about him. Sometimes he would say, "Did you get that down, scribe?" or "Here's one for the records," but he had a vaguely leering tone when he said this. He could be quiet for long stretches of time— Pauline thought he might be uncomfortable in a place like the Elephants' Graveyard—but then, under Dewey's prodding questions, he had spurts of reminiscence and opinion.

Adolfo's favorite stories were about obscure fights held on barges in the days of his youth before boxing was legal. If Garrett was there, he always made Adolfo talk about Battling Levinsky, Tunney's old rival; it was the name that amused Garrett and he would murmur to himself, "Battling

Levinsky, oh, my, heaven save us." The idea of a Jewish contender struck him as richly humorous, although there were plenty of them, Pauline thought.

Pauline had no interest in boxing anyway, and she would edge over to other parts of the bar, if anyone else she knew at all was there. This gave her a chance to see people she didn't get to talk to otherwise and to have conversations without Dewey.

Nita was there one night, very stirred up, the way she got when she was drunk sometimes. She said, "Oh, it's you, Paulie," and threw her arm over Pauline's shoulder when she saw her. She had just been out on a date that had bored her and put her in a defiant mood—with a stockbroker who had bought a lot of paintings from Walter—and she was full of invectives about skunky old men and how money made people vulgar. Pauline said yes, it was wonderful how poverty was keeping them both so pure and refined, and they went on for a good while about how they weren't getting fat from overrich dinners or drying out their complexions with too many trips on yachts. Pauline said, "Or getting sweaty necks from those nasty furs." The bartender liked this one, and they heard him chuckle from across the counter. Pauline gave a small smile; she was never quite as good at speaking this way as when she was with Nita.

Nita was still stuck on the subject of how she couldn't stand most men with money—a complete turnabout of her usual position—and she got several people around them involved in a debate about whether money ruined character.

"I'd like to get ruined a whole lot more," the bartender said.

"No, you wouldn't," Nita said. "Not if it meant you turned into some odious toad."

"That's not character then," Rose said. She was standing near them at the bar, draped in a silk shawl with an enormous stringy fringe. "Character's the factor that doesn't change," she said. "That's the whole point."

"Why go out of the house if you're not going to change ever?" Pauline said. "Why let anything happen to you at all?"

"I often ask myself that question," Rose said. She laid her hand on her heart for effect. She had a sweet expression naturally and with her shawl swirled around her she gave a good imitation of a D. W. Griffith heroine.

"I'm talking about ruin, not change," Nita said. She could get quite petulant when she got stuck on a point.

The argument had turned silly again by the time Dewey came to look for her. People were voting on their favorite kinds of ruin; dissolution and natural disaster were favorites. Peter was there, with the brunette Pauline had talked to in the bedroom at Walter's, and he was acting out the way they would all look if they got suddenly buried in volcanic ash like the Pompeiians. "Well, not in this hat," Pauline shrieked. "I'm not getting turned into a statue for all time with this hat on. I've never liked it on me."

"You're drunk," Dewey said.

Pauline, who was still gesturing with her hands on her head, said, "Well, that isn't news to anyone." But she was flustered.

Peter said, "I suppose you never are, Dewey. Not you."

"Let's go home," Dewey said. "Let's get out of here."

"I'll go quietly, officer," Pauline said. She was trying to think of a line about how he was the new convert from the Temperance League, but she thought that anything she might say would just be ineffective and sputtering. She kissed Nita and Peter good-bye while Dewey started walking away. He was outside the bar before she caught up to him.

"You're soused," he said.

"That's a new thing for you to comment on," Pauline

said. "No one's ever said anything about my behavior. I don't dance on tables or start drooling or anything."

"Let's just get home," he said. "Go to bed."

"Well, that's what I'm doing. Where do you think I'm walking to?" She walked faster, to get ahead of him, but he kept pace with her, so they moved along the street that way, rushing and hovering at each other's heels.

In the morning, when Pauline got up, Dewey was still asleep. She had an unpleasant sense of smarting under an injustice, and she felt bleak and low-spirited. She thought of calling in sick to work, but there was no phone at Dewey's house, and if she was going to walk to the corner to call, she might as well go to work. And it did freshen her a little, to be up and moving around; she was fine really once she was at Gittelson's.

Sometimes she thought it was an advantage not to have a phone. For one thing, it saved her from the complication of having to explain too much to her parents. They had never called very much anyway. At Mrs. Poganyi's they had always had Solly do all the speaking; he would ask questions relayed by Pauline's mother about how she was doing at work and what she was eating. Pauline told them now that she was sharing a flat with her friend Nita and that this saved money. They didn't believe her that the neighborhood was better, but they liked the idea that she was with another girl. Once when Pauline went home, her mother gave her a length of remnants to take back for both of them to make slips and underwear from.

Dewey thought this was hilarious when she told him, and he paraded around with the fabric wrapped around his hips. He offered to write her mother a note thanking her for adding to his lingerie collection, but Pauline said that was going a little too far.

Most of the time she didn't get much of a chance to feel that living with Dewey was any kind of illicit secret. Occasionally kids on the street ogled her and tittered to each other when she went by, but they did that to anyone dressed like her who was new in the neighborhood. At a party once, someone had introduced her by Dewey's last name—Pauline Franklin—and that had seemed half true in a general way.

The man at the grocery store on the corner had a sales patter that involved pitches like "You bring home this bacon for your man, you going to see a light in his eye," and Pauline found it pleasant to shop in this guise of eager bride. The phrase *my man*—which was both like a popular song and like the readiest term in Yiddish—covered, more or less, the particular, agreeable feeling of being in the house, standing at the sink or setting out food on the table. She had a sense of labor carried out for some natural purpose and of skills flourishing in her, made brighter through use.

One of their quarrels came, in fact, on an evening when she had made fish for supper, and Dewey picked at it and said finally that he didn't like fish. "You don't like any kind?" Pauline said. "You could have told me, I wouldn't have bought it." Well, no, especially this kind, he said, it was the way she cooked it with onions—she was always putting onions in everything. It was true that she used them extensively in cooking; the smell of them in the house was cozy and nostalgic to her. She felt a kind of violent aggravation with him, a thorough and indelible disappointment. She said something sharp and curt, and then she sulked for a long time, bristling when he tried to tease her.

Afterward it was a habit with him to make humorous complaints about her being a novice in the kitchen, and he groaned to Garrett about her charred potatoes and oversalted peas. "The price of nuptial bliss," Garrett said. Only Adolfo told him he was a moron for complaining, he should try being an old man living on restaurant leftovers sometime.

Pauline had gotten to like Adolfo better, just as Dewey was beginning to spend less time with him. Dewey shrugged when she asked him about the book. He said, "Another great idea that'll never see the light of day." Pauline had expected him to bluff or to make more of an excuse—he was quite appealing, looking rueful and raising his eyebrows in that way.

Dewey was apparently used to this sort of thing. He had a whole web of anecdotes about different projects abandoned at the onset of success, and there were people who figured largely in certain episodes he told and who then dropped out of the stories altogether. She had trouble keeping track of the sequence of it all. She could never, for instance, get it clear whether he had served on a ship off Panama during the war or after and on which trip he had been bitten by a pelican.

In Baltimore at some point he had been in business with a friend—selling Addressograph machines—and his stories were sketchy but consistent about how well they had done for themselves. He mentioned always a certain dove-gray linen sports suit he had bought. But then there had been some trouble with the friend, some blowup or betrayal.

Once he said to her that what he liked about Adolfo was that his stories were mostly just lies, that was the reason they got along so well. It was a habit you got into in bars, he said; he used to make up some real fables when he was younger. Pauline was aware that at times she herself altered stories for different tellings and that incidents seemed to change in her memory, edit themselves for later tastes, but to actually invent a falsehood from scratch seemed eerie to her. But really nothing in Dewey's talk was more outlandish than things she saw every day—possibly a few stories were suspect, only because he told them once and never cited them again. It was more likely that he left things out. Once he had been in the midst of telling about Chicago and he'd used the words "my wife" to refer to Helene, and then he'd had to backtrack into telling about the marriage (very brief and her idea) and the annulment (easy because she'd been under twenty-one).

What surprised Pauline finally was that in all his ventures he could stop and begin again so readily. The waste in this bothered her. She thought it was wrong: to have nothing stick, nothing accumulate. There was something chilling in this kind of discontinuity. She assumed, in her own life, that even mistakes and failed experiments accrued toward a purpose, an eventual composite that was not random, and that everything had its later use.

Pauline did miss—even now—the old practice of entering a room and striking up a certain kind of beaming, animated conversation with new men. She was out with Dewey a lot, but it was duller without the potential of winning people to her in that way. Dewey still flirted—he would sidle up to Nita and ruffle her hair—but Pauline had a feeling that it would only be troublesome if she led someone on.

When she was out, people still greeted her as though she were a welcome and decorative arrival (a local sweetheart, as Peter said), although Pauline felt that her looks had declined; her hair had grown out of its cut and she was holding back parts of it with hairpins. She had gotten very penny-pinching lately. In bars she talked mostly to Nita and Rose and Walter or to Peter, who was usually with his brunette friend.

She was at the Elephants' Graveyard one night when Walter announced suddenly, "You know what the problem is?"

"Oh, God," Rose said, "he's going to tell us."

Walter had decided they were all losing their health from ingesting cheap alcohol. For a moment Pauline was really worried—she thought her pallor had somehow evoked this idea—but it was just Walter's way of insisting that they all go to a place he knew where you could get real absinthe. Dewey said, "Lead on," but Pauline was uneasy about spending more money. It was already late. Living with Dewey was more expensive than she had initially calculated. On the other hand, she had never had absinthe. Peter assured her that this was actually Baudelaire's favorite speakeasy they were going to.

They had to walk for a long time in the cold to get there. Peter had a flask which he passed among them. "This stuff is rotgut," Dewey said. "I'm saving you people from slow death by taking it into my own system."

"That's friendship," Peter said.

The place was on a side street, in a building Walter said had been a stable; there were no windows on the ground floor, and there was a high, narrow door that swung open very slightly when Walter knocked. A woman with a loud, peppy voice was singing inside. Walter and Peter both had cards from the time they were there before, and they fished them out of their wallets and passed them to a man inside the door. Walter beckoned them all to follow him in. "Hold it, hold it," the man said. "Four only." No guests without cards: Peter and Walter and their lady friends could go in, but not the others.

"It's all right," Pauline said. "I'm ready to go home, I have to work tomorrow anyway."

"I'm fine, I don't care," Rose said. "It's just as well really."

Walter put his hand on the man's shoulder—he seemed to be trying to offer him money; the man shook his head. "It's all right," Pauline said.

Walter turned back to her and shrugged. "It wasn't this way before," he said.

"Well, go on in," Dewey said. "What the hell do you care, go on in and get so soused you fall flat on the street and freeze to death."

"I think I'll use that as a toast," Peter said.

Nita said, "You don't mind really, do you?" and she hugged Rose and Pauline good night. Pauline waved to Walter and the others and said, "Tell us all about it in the morning," while they went inside.

"I'd like to punch Walter's face in," Dewey said. "He did this on purpose."

"Oh, he did not," Pauline said. She was feeling left out and disappointed herself, but she thought it made it worse to dwell on it too much.

"Let's get out of here," Dewey said.

Dewey started to walk, leaving behind not only Pauline but Rose. Pauline quickened her steps, looking back. "I'm coming," Rose said.

"Walter didn't mean anything," Pauline said. "He considers you a really good friend."

"People like that don't know what they mean," Dewey said. "You know how many times I've helped him get his drunken carcass into a taxi when he was too stewed to see his way home?"

"That was nice of you," Pauline said.

"I didn't do it to be nice. I don't expect much from people, except a little basic human courtesy."

"Don't think about it," Pauline said.

"You know why he's doing this?" Dewey said. "Because I owe him thirty dollars. You make an arrangement with someone and they have to get petty about it." A lot of Dewey's finances had to do with juggling loans. Usually Pauline paid their bills and he paid her back some of the money later.

"Your friends are real rat-fucks," Dewey said.

"Stop it," Pauline said. "I don't want to hear that."

"I'm freezing," Rose said. Her shawl was blowing across her face; she had put it on over her coat.

"Me too," Pauline said.

"At least it's not wet out," Rose said.

Dewey kept moving at a fast clip. He was leaning sideways as he walked—his limp came out more when he'd been drinking. Rose fell behind them again, and then she yelled to them that she had to turn off at a corner to go toward her street. "You have to go?" Pauline said. She was sorry that Rose had seen Dewey like this, and he had been rude to her too.

"It's late," Rose said. "Sleep well, take care, I mean it."

They were near the Square when Dewey said he wanted to go to Vera's, just to get warm before they went home. Pauline thought this might calm him. But when they climbed the stairs to the restaurant, there was a sign on the inside door that said *Closed due to fire. Nothing serious. Will reopen soon.* "I don't believe it," Dewey said. "I hear them moving around. They're in there. You hear that?"

"Probably cleaning up," Pauline said. "You can smell that burnt smell."

"Adolfo," Dewey said. "Hey, it's me. It's okay. Let me in."

"They're closed," Pauline said.

"I know you can hear me," Dewey said. "You fucker. It's cold out. You know that?" He shook the door to make it rattle.

"Let's go," Pauline said.

Dewey was kicking the door. "I know he can hear me. He doesn't goddamned care."

Pauline started to go back down the stairs. She was surprised when Dewey followed her.

"You know what I've done for that creep?" he said.

"The favors I've done? I just can't stand it. He could've given us a cup of coffee, you'd think. It wouldn't have hurt him. You do favors for people, you jump through hoops for them, and they don't see it, it's nothing."

"I know," Pauline said.

"It's nothing to them. If they just appreciated it, I don't care about anything else."

"We'll be home soon," Pauline said.

His voice sounded choked and Pauline saw that he had tears in his eyes; she could hardly believe it. "I can't stand it," he said. As they walked, she put her arm around him, and he stopped where they were and nestled his head against her. "I just can't stand it," he said. He was weeping and sniffling now, and she held him and patted his back.

He was like this for the rest of the way home. He would be quiet for a while and then he would break into speeches that made him stop in the street when he got tearful. "A simple cup of coffee," he said. "You'd think anyone would do that." She kept putting her arms around him, since that was so clearly what she was required to do, but she was horrified that he could sink so readily to this, and for nothing really; she was sickened by all of it. His face, with its pocked cheeks and its gaunt bone structure, got crumpled and red like an infant's. He seemed grateful enough; he burrowed against her shoulder and kissed her neck as they were walking.

For a long time after this, Dewey, in time of affection, seemed to think that one of her great merits was the way she stood by him; she was loyal, that was one thing about her. She wasn't loyal at all; she spoke against him to anyone whenever she could, and she was scornful of any idea that had the least taint of his judgment on it. And yet they were more familiar, more used to each other. He was home almost all the time that she was in the house—he was working less now—and they quarreled easily. She quarreled about how much it cost a month to leave the bathroom light on at night, whether the neighbor below them was Rumanian, whether dogs could be taught not to fight. She had once been more hesitant and more patient, but now she argued readily and sometimes stupidly, not caring if she sounded sensible since he was the only one who heard her. At times she worried that she was becoming less intelligent. There was a low-keyed pettiness that rose up in her. The last time she had been this contrary was a certain stage early in high school when she had picked on Bunny a lot. She felt now that she was speaking out of a reflex that being with Dewey called up in her, and that this was something temporary and artificial, a masking of her actual character.

Dewey didn't seem especially dismayed that she lapsed out of civility so much. He himself was frequently abrasive, full of autocratic pronouncements and menacing sulks. What surprised her was that he had no embarrassment about any of this; he assumed it was common enough—the hidden order of normal things—the "awful truth," to use one of his regular expressions.

She felt that she had declined in certain outer ways too, that she had lost a facility in arranging her appearance. She was down to her older pairs of stockings, and she had gone back to sewing arrow designs on them to cover the runs, a thing she and Bunny had done. At the end of the winter she bought one good new skirt which she wore with everything, so that sometimes when she was out she would find herself in odd colors or strangely paired shapes and she would wonder then why she had thought they matched.

She had toned down her makeup. With her hair in a less definite style, she was afraid that the plucked eyebrows and the dark lip rouge would just look cartoon-like, and it seemed to her that her main chance now was to attempt being handsome in a pale, artless way. It was Dewey who had first made fun of her gravity-defying eyebrows, but he didn't much admire the change in her now either, and he said she looked like she had a skin disease with her stockings that way.

It disappointed her to think that she had failed to keep whatever skill she'd had for displaying herself properly. It seemed to her that it was the sort of pure knack that couldn't ever be regained on the same footing, and that whatever future improvements lifted her out of this spell of plainness, there would always be a gap in her own history, an advantage lost. It hurt her to think that her time of sureness had been so short.

She tried to encourage Dewey to go out at night without her. She had begun reading again, a thing it was hard to do with him in the house. Her tastes ran now to historical novels, gentle epics with plots involving kindly squires and lost wills and sickly nieces. She was aware that if she was going to read junk, she would do better to go in for reading detective stories, as Walter did, but she had tried them and found that even the mildest murder was too harsh to read about, no vacation from the world at all.

Sometimes she remembered living at Mrs. Poganyi's with surprising fondness; she missed the luxury of going out with people and then being alone at the end of the night. She did think at times about what she would do when she wasn't with Dewey any more; she thought she might want to try living in a hotel for a while—Rose had lived at the Walpole for years, and she liked it; she had a room with a nice view. It seemed apparent to Pauline that she was living out the duration of a certain sequence with Dewey and that the conclusion could come of itself, as the term expired.

If Pauline was still reading in bed when Dewey came

home, she would sit up and listen while he talked. He was spending a lot of time with Garrett; they had discovered a speakeasy on Eighteenth Street with a poker game always going on in the back, and Dewey would explain in detail the better moments of the night's playing. Garrett was still a rotten cardplayer, he said. Pauline didn't understand about Garrett—what did he want and why didn't he do a better job of having a good time? "He's an odd bird," Dewey said. "He likes to just sit back and watch everything. But the mind is ticking away. When you get to know him, he has a very active mind, but he only shows certain people."

"Well, he talks to you, he likes you," Pauline said.

"You could say so. We're going to start a literary magazine, him and me, I think."

"Another one?" Pauline said. "When did you decide this?"

"Anything would be better than that crap Dean White publishes."

"I like that one."

"If the pages weren't so stiff, you could use it for toilet paper."

"All right, all right," Pauline said.

"We've been talking about it. The first issue's going to be basically about machines. Anything anybody wants to write about the Machine Age."

"That's good," Pauline said. It was better than she would have thought—a copied idea certainly, but not awful. She was relieved, but then it occurred to her that she was worrying for nothing anyway, since it was unlikely that there was ever going to be any magazine.

Dewey did talk about it a lot, as she might have expected; he brought it up all the time in bars. People who didn't know him so well got interested. Twice he actually got submissions addressed to him in the mail—a set of poems and a scene from an obviously horrendous play. These had the effect of making Dewey act as though the magazine were already in print, and he talked about paper stock and mailing costs. Once he came home from the Elephants' Graveyard complaining that it made him sick the way everyone was trying to get on his good side now that he was an editor.

When they were eating at Anselm's one night, Nita sat down with them while Dewey was holding forth. Pauline gave her a weary, knowing look from across the table. Nita asked Dewey why, if he understood machines so well, he didn't get a machine to go out and raise all the money for the magazine. (Nita could be too rude at times, Pauline thought—she depended too much on her intonation to make everything sound clever.) "Very funny," Dewey said. "You'll eat your goddamned words soon." Pauline had to launch into a plaint about the thinness of the roast beef sandwiches at Anselm's to get everything calm again.

The alarming part, as far as Pauline was concerned, was that the magazine did have some money. Garrett's father had sent a check—possibly he liked the idea of his son being a helpmate to the arts, or perhaps he was just the sort of father who wrote checks when asked. Dewey said the amount from Garrett's father wasn't enough—printers in this country were highway bandits, you wouldn't believe what they charged— but now they were talking about how one good fund-raising party would bring in the rest. (For a while Dewey had wanted Pauline to ask Mr. Gittelson to be another backer—he kept saying it couldn't hurt to ask—but he had finally given up on that.) Dewey wanted to use the hall where Dean White had held the party for his magazine. Pauline tried to tell him it was much too huge, and he got very nasty with her about it. But then Walter, who liked parties and who for some reason had been a fan of the whole magazine scheme from the very beginning, suggested that they use the back room of Tony's restaurant. The room rented cheap and had a small, open floor for dancing.

Pauline was pained every time the idea was mentioned. She kept waiting for the plans to collapse by themselves, and when they didn't, she began to think about how she could escape, how she could break up with Dewey before the event. She picked one fight, an argument about the rent money. She was perfectly sincere; she came home from work one night and complained, with real bitterness of feeling, about how she had paid all the last month's rent and he still hadn't paid her back for his share. Dewey said, "You know I'll get it to you. You know but you just want to rub my nose in it. You see I'm working day and night to get this magazine going. You think this is just the right time to get on my back, don't you?" She held her ground well; she was sullen and hard all through dinner, and she said nothing at all when he finally went out.

But when he came home very late, he sat on the bed and he was so broken-voiced and contrite, he kept talking about all she meant to him and how there was no one like her, that she couldn't think how to answer him cuttingly: it seemed too inhuman, too incongruous a thing to do. For a moment she felt quite angelic in her forgiveness. He got very happy and playful then, and she let him make jokes about how the whole fight was probably based on indigestion from the cauliflower she had made for supper. He said he thought that this was the sort of arguing and making up that would just make the bond between them stronger—which seemed true enough in a general way, if not really true of them. And yet she felt coarse and falsely sweet, mouthing endearments.

Her idea, after that, was that no one really had to think that the fund-raising party—or the magazine itself, for that matter—had anything to do with her, and there was no need to apologize for it. She did occasionally make disavowals, to the effect that it was Dewey's brainchild and all inquiries about it should be addressed to him. She was counseling herself to a state of coolness about the whole thing, and she would sometimes remind herself that everyone had stories about parties that turned out to be fiascoes, and some really legendary flops were recollected very affectionately by those who'd been there.

At times she thought now that she was waiting for the fundraiser to be over so that her time of breaking up with Dewey could begin. She had a sense of the current time not counting, really, and of something disagreeable being put off till later.

At other times it seemed to her that she was already living the way she was going to continue to live, that her present life with Dewey was permanent, that she had gotten settled without really knowing it. There were women like that—always a little surprised at the impractical nature of their own alliances—initiates of a knowledge improbable even to themselves; perhaps she had passed into that state.

VII

On the day of the party, Pauline decided that if she was going to get through the evening at all she was going to have to make an effort to be a better sport about it. She spent the last hours of the afternoon trying on things in her closet; she trimmed the little sidepieces of her hair and stuck them down with lacquer. In the end she looked quite nice, she thought—she wore an old black crepe dress with a yellow glass brooch at the bosom, very classic and impeccable. Dewey had finished dressing and was sitting in the kitchen, fingering the knife pleats in his trousers. She nudged him and said, "How do I look?"

"You look okay."

She kissed him on the back of the neck. "Do you still think I'm pretty?" She was horrified as soon as she heard herself. "I don't know why I asked that," she said.

"Yes, why did you?"

"I sound like we've been together for ninety years, don't I?"

Dewey was putting on his topcoat, smoothing down the muffler. "Only eighty, my dear," he said.

When they got to the restaurant, musicians in dinner jackets were unpacking their instruments, looking listless and bored in advance. Three or four people were hovering around a glass punch bowl set out on a table next to the piano. "Look who's here already," Dewey called out. "It's the starvation army, drinking up the profits."

Pauline recognized one of the writers who had sent poems to the magazine, a bald man with puffed cheeks. He held out his glass and said, "First come, first served. You learn that in life." He pretended to keep Pauline from filling her glass. "It's too strong for the ladies. They'll misbehave."

The back room of Tony's, which Pauline had never seen before, had a décor of potted plants and empty wrought-iron bird cages. On one wall there was a brownish mural of a landscape with hills and Roman ruins. Dewey got busy dragging a table over near the entrance. He seated himself at it and yelled out, "Okay, you deadbeats, pay up. Nobody stays without forking over the admission fee."

"Well, don't threaten them," Pauline said, but they were filing over to Dewey's table, pulling bills out of their wallets. Garrett came through the doorway then, and there was some joking between them over whether he had to buy a ticket or not. Dewey pretended to bend back Garrett's arm to make him pay.

"Pauline, my little pigeon, you know what you can do?" Dewey said. "Go find Tony and see if he'll give us a cashbox or something for the proceeds here."

Pauline went back into the main room of the restaurant, where customers were sitting at tables, eating plates of food and drinking wine; the room smelled of garlic and cooking oil. Pauline envied them all their spaghetti suppers and their conversations. They looked up, annoyed, as groups of people edged past them, heading for the back room.

Tony was standing by the kitchen, drinking a tiny cup of espresso. "What now?" he said. When Pauline told him, he went down to the basement and came back with a black metal box, the size of a Kleenex dispenser, dented and ominous looking. "Tell your boyfriend I'm sorry we don't have a Brink's truck for him," he said.

By the time Pauline went back to the party, clusters of people had gathered in parts of the room and the musicians were tuning up. Garrett tried to introduce her to two men in striped wool suits who he said were the thieves who bilked him at cards every night. "He flatters us," one of the men said.

Pauline kept looking for someone she knew. She waved to Nita's friend Rose across the room and went rushing toward her. "What a great room," Rose said. "I love that mural, don't you? I'd like to hack it off the wall and take it home."

"Perhaps we could leave with it right now," Pauline said.

"Nita's coming later—she said to tell you she would be late. You want some punch? I'll get you some punch."

Rose led her by the elbow—quite gently, Pauline thought; she had never noticed how soothing and maternal Rose was. A noisy group had gathered around the punch bowl, and it was hard to push through. Someone brushed a lit cigarette against Pauline's arm and she cried out.

"Did you get burned?" Rose said.

"That hurt," Pauline said. She held out her arm somewhat childishly to make sure Rose saw the red spot and the smear of black ash.

"I'll get you ice," Rose said. She ladled ice out of the

punch bowl and filled a cup for Pauline. The ice was sticky from the punch but it did take the sting out, as Rose said.

"It's so noisy in here. It's like a barnyard. Company included."

"I've seen worse," Rose said. "In my time."

"The punch tastes like paint remover, doesn't it?"

"You'll get different people later," Rose said. "The crowd always changes. Don't worry."

"Oh, I'm not worried," Pauline said.

The music had started and people were bobbing on the dance floor, smiling open-mouthed at each other or looking foolishly severe and intent. A man came walking across the floor to Pauline—she was afraid he was going to ask her to dance, and she tried to edge away until she saw that it was Ernest.

"I thought that was you," he said. "You've got your hair different." She let him steer her onto the floor. She was startled at being at such close physical range, up against the scent of his Wildroot Cream Oil, feeling the shoulder pads in his suit. She was stiff and not at all light-footed, but he seemed not to notice. He bantered with her about how the literary magazines were all multiplying so much New York was going to be all buried in printed matter soon. "The whole city'll just be submerged under paper," he said. "Like an Atlantis under pages."

"We'll all just have to learn to breathe under paper pulp," Pauline said. Ernest probably thought she still talked this way all the time; she felt as though she were obliged to keep up an impersonation, but the effort made her lively and more cheerful. They tilted and swayed in a slow fox-trot, and then they sat out the next dance at a banquette under the mural. He was still so good-looking, she thought, in that beaky, sharp-chiseled way, although he did seem weaker now. She might have been with him instead of Dewey, if he had been less dilatory, if there had been a little more force in him.

She had a small spot of resentment in her for what had happened because of his hesitation. It was quite possible, of course, that she was going to be with him sometime later on, after she wasn't with Dewey any more. At first this seemed like a satisfying thought: she would be retracing her steps, going back to where she had made a wrong turn before. But wouldn't this be the same as losing ground? She wanted to think that she was weathering everything with Dewey as a price for something better (something less faulty than Ernest). She had the idea that once she was through being tried by a little adversity, she'd be tempered into a subtler understanding that made possible a refinement of happiness not available to her before.

She danced another time with Ernest. A blonde in smeared makeup was waving a coat hanger, lifting her skirt with one hand as she danced and yelling the words to the song the band was playing. From across the floor Pauline could see Dewey, sitting with his cashbox and smiling about something with Garrett. She waved at him and said, "How's it going?" when they danced past, and he pinched her on the bottom.

Ernest had a glass of punch thrown at the back of his pants when they went past an especially rowdy corner of the room. "Who did it?" he said.

A group by the wall was convulsed with laughter. "Hey," one of the men said, "you need diapers?"

"It doesn't show much," Pauline said.

"Yes, it does," Ernest said. "It's a huge stain, isn't it?" He stopped dancing and stood by a pillar. "Christ," he said, looking back at himself. Pauline kept telling him it wasn't bad, but he said she should go dance with someone else, and he left not long afterward.

Nita and Walter arrived very late, just as the blonde with the coat hanger was trying to throw her shoes into the piano. "I can see we're here for the wild, impetuous part," Nita said.

"It was better for a while," Pauline said. Nita wouldn't dance, but Walter found them a table and they all sat watching the dancers on the floor. Adolfo went by, doing an overstated but graceful waltz step with Rose; when he passed the band, he flipped up the blonde's skirt as she leaned over the piano, exposing her garters so that she shrieked.

Dewey whistled through his fingers to get Pauline's attention. When she went over to him, he said, "It's the host's turn for a little sport and frolic," and he led her onto the floor. He was always a good dancer, but now he hammed it up and did a lot of stylized dips and turns that were hard for her to follow. She kept laughing, since people were looking. Then the lights in the room started flickering on and off, which was Tony's way of telling them all it was time to leave. The band stopped playing at the end of a verse and the musicians began packing up their instruments at once.

In the cab on the way home Dewey was in a gleeful mood. He had emptied the contents of the cashbox into his pockets, and then, when he ran out of space, into Pauline's pockets as well, and he kept patting and squeezing the lumps of bills at her hips and saying, "Not a bad night's work." He sang "Good Night, Ladies" into her ear, a song the band hadn't actually played although he seemed to think they had.

For days afterward he kept trying to retell her things that had happened at the party, although she was pointedly not interested and only answered dully. At the time the party hadn't seemed unbearable—she remembered being afraid at every minute that it was going to get worse and feeling reprieved as the night went on—but now the mention of it made her shudder and the thought of it was mortifying to her.

In general now she avoided talking much to Dewey, as far as she could. After dinner she would take her book into the bedroom and read. Garrett was in the house a lot; he sat drinking with Dewey in the kitchen until late, and sometimes he stayed over and spent the night on the couch.

Dewey had taken up Garrett's habit of smoking little cigars; they talked about their "venture" and referred to each other quite seriously as business partners. Pauline was at work the afternoon they took the ticket money and Garrett's father's check to the bank; they had been talking about this for days, arguing about which bank to use. ("Just go to any bank," Pauline had said—she didn't like Dewey keeping so much cash in the house.) In the evening when she came home and there was no one in the apartment, she assumed that they were probably still out celebrating. She waited awhile, and then she ate a piece of leftover roast for supper and read until midnight. She liked the calm and the ease of being in the house without Dewey. In the morning, though, it was confusing when she woke up and saw the bed still empty next to her, as if Dewey had somehow been gone for years without her noticing and her life had long since sealed around his absence.

He came in just as she was leaving for work; they passed each other on the stairs. "It's the old wanderer returned," he said, "making his weary way homeward." He made a sheepish face—he seemed to be waiting for her to scold him, which she had no urge to do.

She said, "There's coffee left if you want to reheat it."

Afterward he was always grateful for this, for the flatness of her modern attitude. He seemed to think she had behaved quite beautifully. They had fewer fights about anything now; they avoided each other, which made for less friction, and Pauline was less prone to bursts of irritation.

They did have one battle at the beginning of the month, when the rent was due. Dewey was hardly going in to work at all now; he claimed that the magazine took all his time and that he was too busy having meetings with Garrett. He did, however, buy himself a wristwatch. He came home one night, pulling back his cuff with great flourishes to show it off. He had picked a simple, rather handsome style—his taste was good, she thought. He said he had gotten it because she was always yelling at him for being late, and she agreed that a watch was a good thing to have. He seemed so foolishly pleased with it; it occurred to her that he got more enjoyment out of objects than she did.

On the dresser later she saw the plush-lined box the watch had come in and the price tag still on it for thirty-five dollars. Thirty-five dollars? That couldn't be right, their rent wasn't that much. How could a watch cost more than shelter for thirty days? Maybe he'd bought it some other way, gotten it hot or at a discount. She didn't really believe this, and secretly she envied him his obliviousness to price and budget, his spurious freedom.

A day later, when he admitted that she was going to have to pay all the rent herself again because he was short on cash, she actually wailed in rage. "I don't have any money," she said. "I make half, less than half, of what you make, and you think I can pay for everything." And then there was a bitter satisfaction in her; she had been proved right about him. She liked the sense of accumulating reasons against him; it made her feel hopeful, as though her leaving were more imminent.

Later in the week, while she was unpacking the groceries in the kitchen, he came over to her and dangled a sheaf of bills in front of her face, flicking them against her nose. "Here it is, the fucking rent," he said. He set the bills on the table. "You want to count it? Why don't you count it?" Pauline took up the money and put it inside her purse; she felt that she looked greedy and coarse as she did this, and yet the money was rightfully hers.

Even so, there were moments, not long after scenes like this, when he would turn to her in bed at night, sometimes waking her out of a sleep, and he would ask, as he moved toward her, before he started taking off her nightgown, if it was all right with her; the asking always seemed poignant to her, and there was a feeling of concord and old bodily understandings between them.

Sometimes, even in the daytime, he showed signs of being about to change for the better. He announced that he was going to look for another job; he hated being a court reporter, that was why he never went to work any more. He had always really had more of a head for business, that was where his real abilities were. His old ventures in Baltimore were on his mind a lot now. He was especially sorry that he didn't have some of the clothes he'd had then—it made a crucial difference in the way people treated you in business. Pauline never understood what *had* happened to his clothes. She herself had garments she'd owned since before puberty; they were a final reserve against really having nothing to wear, although she was always sorry when she resorted to wearing them.

The suit that Dewey bought for himself now was gray with a blue tint, made of a light worsted. Pauline admired the tailoring and the fabric, but beyond that she didn't see what there was to get excited about in men's clothes; they seemed like uniforms to her, subject to only the most minor variations. It didn't surprise her that Dewey was so vain, although it galled her that her own outfits all seemed to center around the same crepe skirt she had bought in the spring, which was getting shapeless from being worn so much.

Dewey wanted to delay the job search until after the summer was over; serious hiring, he said, went on in September. His idleness seemed to make him even more itchy to spend money. She had to stop him from buying a Persian kitten he saw in a pet store window. He did bring home a big, heavy piece of exercise equipment—a rowing machine—which took up most of the floor space in the bedroom.

It was August when Dewey bought the machine, and he would sit in it in his underwear, grunting and sweating; the sinews in his arms looked glazed. Garrett had gone to the country, to a lodge in the Adirondacks that his family had. Occasionally he sent postcards complaining of the boredom and berating Dewey for not writing. "Poor baby," Dewey said. "Never worked a day in his life. And he's getting worn to a frazzle from those brutal croquet matches. My heart bleeds."

With Garrett gone, Dewey had less company in the evenings. He went out by himself to the usual spots and later to the place on Eighteenth Street with the poker game in the back. Once on a Sunday morning when she woke up he had set out a tin of caviar with toast for their breakfast.

She wasn't sure how much the caviar had cost, but she knew he had bought it to spend money. He was training himself in the sport of expenditure. He gave himself missions—forays and retreats of varying boldness.

She had guessed for a while—it was daily more evident—that he was draining money from the magazine's account. She wondered if he assumed she knew. She had a feeling he didn't expect to be questioned about it. To accuse him directly would be like asking to see him with his teeth bared. At best, she would just get taunted for her prig-gishness.

She wondered if other people had suspicions—perhaps everyone knew—perhaps they weren't outraged but only mildly disgusted. It was such a shadowy kind of embezzle-ment, to filch from a nonexistent magazine. Some ticket buyers had been misled, and a few mediocre writers had had their hopes raised for nothing, but the real injured party of course was Garrett, who had signed over his father's check. There was a real ugliness in that, in that buddyship milked for profit. But Garrett was so smooth and unmarked, so sleepy and waxy and removed from the pressures of circum-stance—wasn't there a kind of payment for being in the world that he hadn't stood the cost of yet?

In the days when she had worked in her parents' store, her mother had always been sure that people were going to pilfer things like the packets of needles or the embroidery floss. Pauline had considered this a ridiculous fear: who would want to make off with a skein of thread? To take a thimble without paying seemed like such a violation of nor-mal pride, an admission of the most pitiful kind of greed for something justly withheld. Pauline would have professed in-difference rather than stoop to this sort of cringing grab-biness. But for Dewey the whole matter of pride was reversed. He liked the idea of overcoming refusals and get-ting things by ruses, of gaining consent without the will of the consenter.

It was so unlike her to be linked with anything like this. That a simple romantic attachment—however misguided—could have led her to this still shocked her beyond every-thing. She had a grudge against the unfairness of it, that she was tainted with a mistake that wasn't her own, a stupidity completely different from any she would have committed herself.

As it was, she ate the caviar when Dewey brought it for breakfast. Plundered goods, she thought, but there was no ethical ground to be won by leaving it on the plate: you couldn't put the fish roe back in the ocean. He showed her how to squeeze lemon over it; he talked about how "concentrated" the taste was and how a part of the pleasure in eating it was the texture of the eggs popping against the roof of your mouth. Dewey was not normally so eloquent about food, and she thought he must be repeating this from somewhere. She had not expected a luxurious food to be so salty, but she ate it with considerable interest and mentioned the meal later to Nita.

The day Garrett came back from the country, he and Dewey went out drinking, to celebrate what Garrett called his return to civilization as we know it. At midnight they came back to the apartment and insisted that Pauline come out with them to Vera's. "Back from the hinterlands," Garrett said. "Back from the bush, never to return."

Garrett had a faint, biscuit-colored tan, and he complained of a case of poison ivy. Vera's had reopened with no apparent changes in its furnishings except new, noticeably clean tablecloths. While they were sitting there, Garrett kept reaching under the starched cloth to scratch his shins. "It's our own Nature Boy," Dewey said.

"Maybe I'll write a nature poem for the magazine," Garrett said. "An ode to a horse turd."

"Never get through the mails," Dewey said.

"We forgot mailing costs, didn't we?" Garrett said. "In our budget."

"Don't ask me," Dewey said. "I forget."

"You know what's the worst thing about the country?" Garrett said. "You can't sleep. The birds wake you up."

"And the mosquitoes. Piercing your tender flesh."

"Don't remind me," Garrett said.

"And the wolves," Dewey said. "Weren't there wolves howling at your windows?"

"No wolves," Garrett said.

"Bears? Any bears trying to raid your provisions?"

"They didn't have bears," Garrett said. He was pouring whiskey out of a flask into their teacups, and he looked slightly grumpy now.

"Probably spiders and worms, though," Dewey said. "I don't know how you got out alive."

"He looks alive to me," Pauline said.

"Just barely," Dewey said. "Worn to a shadow after his days with the spiders and the worms."

"Oh, don't talk about worms," Pauline said. "I hate worms."

"Don't move," Dewey said. "I think one's crawling on you now, down your blouse. Just kidding." He got very interested then in describing in grim detail how to dig for night crawlers and the proper way to hook them for bait. He had these little bits of rural knowledge he could call up at times—actually there were two versions of his growing up: he had been raised in a rough section of Baltimore, but then he had really spent most of his time on an uncle's chicken farm in eastern Maryland. This gave him a range of expertise convenient in most discussions.

Garrett said fishing was the world's dullest, most pointless activity, and he and Dewey got into an argument about whether it took any intelligence at all to catch a fish. Pauline thought they were muddled and tedious in what they said; they had both been drinking all day and they were on the verge of being excitable. It occurred to her that she might leave by herself right then, but she knew that Dewey wouldn't want her to go and she thought it wasn't a good idea to cross him now.

"Where's Adolfo?" Dewey said. "Ask an Italian if he thinks fishing is for the feebleminded."

"For the jingle-brains of the world. Strictly," Garrett said.

"Adolfo," Dewey yelled. "Where are you?"

"Don't shout," another waiter said. "Where Adolfo is he can't hear you. He fell off a ladder; he's home in bed with a broken leg." After the fire in Vera's Adolfo had volunteered to fix the stove in the restaurant kitchen so it didn't start a fire again—he had been measuring for putting in a new exhaust pipe when the old one, which he was leaning on, gave way. "Mr. Clever," the waiter said. "Who asked him to show what a great handyman he was? You can see what the kitchen is like. An antique, a relic of former times."

"How bad is his leg?" Pauline said.

"He has to have a cast for a couple of months. Pegleg Pete, you know. Also, he knocked out a front tooth when he fell. But he can eat all right, he says."

"He's home by himself?" Pauline said.

"He can hobble around okay. His problem is you can't wait tables with a cast on."

"He should sue," Dewey said.

"They paid for his bandage, big deal. Vera sends him food, but you can't exist on that."

"Sue," Dewey said.

"Who told him to go on that ladder?" the waiter said. "Nobody told him." He moved away from them to serve another table.

"You think he was snockered when he went up that ladder?" Garrett said. "You think he'd had a few when he took that dive?"

"Who knows?" Dewey said.

"Old people shouldn't drink," Garrett said. "That's what I think."

"Thank you for your opinion," Dewey said.

"I had a broken ankle once," Garrett said. "I broke it ice skating." Garrett lifted his pants cuff, he pulled down his sock and showed them his scar. Dewey said nobody wanted to watch Garrett waving around his hairy ankle in public, and if people really wanted to see scars, Dewey had a few he could show them. He had taken a few falls on shipboard that would make Adolfo's little jump look like the nothing it was. How high up could he have been on that ladder?

Pauline was woozy from the whiskey in her tea. She heard them talking, and she sat until she was almost asleep. Every so often their voices got louder, and she shifted in her seat and opened her eyes.

By the end of the night Garrett had turned sentimental; he wanted to have another party so they could raise money for Adolfo. Dewey said all the guests could come dressed in white like doctors and dentists. "White flowers, white wine," Garrett said. "White suits for the boys, white dresses for the girls."

"The Moby-Dick Cotillion," Dewey said.

"We give great parties, don't we?" Garrett said. "How much did we make at the other party?"

"A mint," Dewey said. "But we still need another whole mint to put out the first issue."

"Fuck the first issue," Garrett said. "Excuse me, Pauline. What is this magazine that it should eat up all our money? That's what I say."

"It's our gift to posterity," Dewey said.

"Do we need posterity? That's what I say. Adolfo's hobbling around with one leg, he doesn't have a goddamned nickel. Let's dump the magazine and just give the money in the account to Adolfo. Give the old codger some relief in his old age."

"He's not old. He could get another job," Dewey said.

"There's things he could do. He's not sick."

"There are not."

"Buy him a keg of brandy. That's the only medicine he likes," Dewey said. "Let him get pickled, he'll forget he has a leg."

"He won't forget," Garrett said. "What's the matter with you?"

"Not everyone can be a great philanthropist like yourself," Dewey said. "A paragon of the higher virtues."

"A broken limb is no joke. I don't suppose you can understand that."

"Don't tell me about understanding broken *limbs*," Dewey said. "You little piss-ass fairy. Mr. Milk of Human Kindness."

"I won't be baited," Garrett said. "You think that'll provoke me, but it won't."

"I think I'm going. If I stayed, I would start to puke from listening to you, and the waiter would just have to clean it up. Some of us think about these things." He got up and left the table. Pauline didn't catch up with him until he was on the staircase. "Why don't you go back and talk to that little shit?" Dewey said. "You like having fascinating discussions."

All the way home Dewey talked about how Garrett was going to get his face punched in if he wasn't careful. Pauline had nothing ready at hand that she could murmur even as background, although she was afraid Dewey would be angry with her for not showing assent. He was quiet for a long time, and then he said grimly, "I'm very disappointed in him."

When she came home from work the next day, Garrett was sitting in their kitchen drinking tomato juice, his favorite hangover remedy. He and Dewey seemed to be talking peaceably. Pauline went into the bedroom to change out of her work dress, and when she came out again, Garrett was gone. She said, "He didn't want to stay for supper?"

"He's out of his mind," Dewey said. "I can't stand it. He hears someone whining about Adolfo, and now he thinks he can just take the magazine money and throw it away on him. You know what it is if you raise money for one thing and then use it for something else? It's fraud. I told him he'll go to jail if he tries something like that."

"He doesn't care about the magazine any more?" Pauline said.

"I would personally see to it that he went to jail if he tried something like that," Dewey said.

Pauline said maybe they could reach a compromise between them eventually (it was the sort of thing Bunny would have said). Dewey said he hadn't busted his ass over that goddamn party so he could make any compromises with a little shit-pants like Garrett. Anyway, Garrett couldn't get to the money without him. "I'm the treasurer," Dewey said. Pauline thought this was funny; he had never said this before—he must have just made it up—but he was serious. His mouth was set in a tight, frowning line; he looked like a cartoon of a scowling baby.

"It'll get settled somehow," Pauline said. She didn't believe this for a moment; it seemed to her that things were getting worse by the instant and that something uglier was going to happen fairly soon. She wasn't sure how much Garrett could do—he would probably lose if it came to just a battle of wills—but he could rage and complain and make the whole dispute very public.

It mortified her to think of this: to have everyone know what Dewey was. Of course she had always been critical of him behind his back—probably no one would assume she was his collaborator—but they would wonder why she lived with him and why she still went home to him every night. She didn't think people would blame her but she would seem inexplicable to them, foolish in a tawdry and senseless way.

All through the next week, Dewey went out at night as usual, and he came home late. If Pauline was still awake, he would go off into long, muttering speeches about certain people who thought they could tell him what to do and how they would be sorry they hadn't shut their mouths. Rose had told Pauline that lots of people were asking Dewey why he didn't want Adolfo to have the money. Dewey said it was a matter of artistic principle, the integrity of the magazine. Peter had hooted very loudly at this idea, and Dewey had threatened him, told him that he was very likely to get jumped and beaten up on his way home some night. Dewey also had pretended to hand Garrett the bankbook—"Looky here, Gar, I changed my mind"—but it turned out to be only an empty pay envelope he gave him. There had been a general outcry then; people booed, and someone from the bar threw a pickled egg.

Dewey said the whole thing was a lesson in how people didn't even have the decency to mind their own business and how a rich kid—even a little fruit like Garrett—always had flunkies around to be his friends.

"I guess that's what happens," Pauline said.

"A lot of labor went into that magazine. Labor and dedication."

"It's too bad."

"There's one thing I didn't want to do but I'm going to have to. It's all over for our friend Garrett," he said. "I'm getting a lawyer. I didn't want to do it. You know how long he'll last in jail? I've seen some things from working in the courts. He'd lose his mind in a week, he'd just be a broken piece of a person. He has no idea. His lovely family won't be any help to him either. With their high ideas."

He's ranting, Pauline thought. She wondered how much longer he was going to stay awake and whether he was going to keep on talking and get worse. She was aware of how late at night it was and that she was shut up with him in the apartment. She had a fear of being drawn into his web of thought, of being held hostage so that she couldn't ever get back to the solid world.

It took him a long time to get to sleep; in bed next to her, he gripped her tightly each time he changed position. Pauline lay looking out at the room. The light was still on; the light fixture in the ceiling was chipped and the string that hung down from it had a pocket comb tied to the end for a weight. Under the window she could see the looming metal frame of the exercise machine. It seemed to her that these were the signs of something dismal and wrongly planned, and that this was a room where unsound people lived.

Sometimes she wondered why Dewey still persisted in going out to the same places at night, since it was clear that the people he knew either avoided him or pressed him now to listen to Garrett and give over the money. Maybe Dewey showed himself in these places out of habit more than defiance, like a job he still reported to. It didn't surprise Pauline, but it seemed stubborn or oblivious. She wouldn't go with him, but she missed seeing people.

Once she called Nita from work—she thought of Nita as the sort of person who was unfazed by things—and they went to an early movie together. Nita said, *"You* look fine anyway," when she hugged Pauline outside the movie theater. They went inside and saw a movie about a nurse in the Crimean War who was in love with a dying soldier. Pauline got very absorbed in the movie; it seemed to her that the expressions on the actress's face were lifelike and complex, and the hot mistiness of the love scenes was an accurate version of a truth everyone in the audience knew. She still felt, despite everything, that sex itself was the purest of wishes. She cried when the soldier died in the movie, not just out of pity for the heroine but out of a general sadness for the bleak endings of things. The nurse put a sheet over the soldier's head and went on making her rounds, rolling men's arms in bandages. She had milky skin and her eyes shone; she seemed to have been ennobled by her ordeal. Pauline wondered what it would be like if Dewey died and how she would behave. The soldier in the film had of course been simple and brave and uncomplaining, not like Dewey at all. And yet Pauline thought she was equal to whatever strength the nurse showed. She felt cheated that all her own tribulations didn't amount to this sort of testing. And the nurse hadn't known the man very long; they had acted out of the same impulses, she and the nurse, only with different consequences.

"Oh, my," Nita said, when they left the theater together. "A three-hanky heart-wrencher. My mascara was in puddles."

"And we pay good money for this," Pauline said. "You'd think we could stay home and be miserable for free."

"It's never as good at home," Nita said.

They had drinks at a tiny, overdecorated speakeasy where the customers were mostly women. Pauline said, "I'm paying this time," as soon as they ordered. She was eager not to have Nita think that she was the kind of person who would be stingy about a check. She wasn't like Dewey: she wanted to make sure Nita knew. She supposed Nita did know, but people couldn't help having suspicions.

Nita talked about her job, how she was getting sick of sawing away at her violin in front of these fatso businessmen.

She was cautious about bringing up Dewey's name; Pauline was grateful for this but it made her nervous. She was afraid the blouse she had worn was too prim, and she had a great desire to be home with no one looking at her.

Nita said, "Peter sends you his love. He said to be sure to tell you."

Pauline tried to think why she had decided that Peter wasn't someone she could ever really be attracted to; she had been awfully arbitrary and spoiled in the early days. She had a passing thought of how she might find refuge now with Peter, how they might have one of those autumnal romances of reunited old flames. But there was still something not believable about this, something falsely soft about the two of them together.

"You know what Peter thinks?" Nita said. "He thinks Dewey's going to run away and disappear. There's a rumor now that he's planning to ship out to sea with his ill-gotten gains. Sail off into the horizon."

Pauline was surprised that no one could follow the real logic of Dewey's obstinacy; the single principle to which he held fast was the simple idea that he wasn't budging. "He's not going anywhere." Apparently she was the only one who understood; it was too hard explaining.

"Are you all right?" Nita said. "You seem all right."

"I'm okay."

"I was going to ask if you wanted to come stay with me." Pauline almost got teary again at this—Nita was really a good sort of person, she thought, in all the ways that counted. But if she began staying in Nita's apartment, it would mean that every day there Nita was being nice to her, and the bright hardness she had when she was with Nita would be ruined and lost. What Pauline wanted, in any case, was to leave Dewey at a time when she could slip off quietly, and now there would be torrents of opposition and accusations of betrayal. She told Nita she would stick it out for the time being. Nita walked with her to the El station and they rode downtown together, without trying to speak over the screech of the train.

When Pauline got back to the apartment, Dewey wasn't home. She heated up a can of soup for herself and she read until she got sleepy. She was dozing in a chair in the living room when she heard the key in the lock. The door pushed open abruptly—she thought from the sound that Dewey must be angry (angry at her, maybe, for not having been home to make dinner). Through the door behind him came Garrett and the bald verse writer who had been one of the first guests at the fund-raising party. Peter was there too, and for some reason he had Walter's dog with him. The dog ran into the room at once; he sniffed Pauline and then he walked through the apartment sniffing at the different pieces of furniture. The others—except for Dewey—were standing around the entrance. "Shut the door, for Christ's sake," Dewey said. "You want to get everybody in the building out here yelling?

"Well, go on," Dewey said. "Search the house. Look in the icebox, open all the books. Get up, Pauline, they're going to want to look under the cushions. See, nothing there. Maybe you want to search Pauline. She's probably got something sewn in her drawers." Dewey groped at Pauline's backside as though he were frisking her there.

"Nobody's making any searches. What's the matter with you?" Garrett said. "I thought you were just going to give us the bankbook if we came over."

"I can't remember where I put it," Dewey said. "I used to know but I forgot."

"When did you forget?" Peter said.

"I'm drunk," Dewey said. "Who got me so drunk?"

The bald man had actually started shuffling through the sofa cushions. He lifted a throw rug to check underneath it. The dog followed, nosing at everything. "Stop it," Garrett said. "What are you doing?"

"This is ridiculous," Peter said.

"I'll sue you for trespassing," Dewey said. "Get your hands off those things. You hear what I'm saying?"

"You better give us the bankbook, Dewey. We want to see what's in there," Garrett said. "Right is right."

The dog was barking. Dewey had smacked the bald man on the back of the neck and he held down the man's head as though he were ducking him in something. "I should throw you out the window," Dewey said. "I'm thinking about it. If I were a certain kind of person, that's what I'd do." He let go his hold and the man stood upright. "I'm sick of this," Dewey said. "You're lucky I don't drop all of you out the window. Nobody leaves me alone. I can't even go to my own house and be alone." (Pauline wondered if he meant her too.) "Look at that dog," Dewey said. "That dog is upset. Here, boy. It's okay." The collie didn't move. Dewey went over and patted its head.

"You won't even think about Adolfo," Garrett said. "You're supposed to be his friend. You don't want him to have whatever's left in the account."

"He can't have it if I say he can't have it," Dewey said. "Poor baby fell off a little ladder. You know how far I fell off a roof one time? I broke a lot more than a shinbone, let me tell you. And I didn't go taking up any charity collections to sponge off people. Don't tell me about poor Adolfo." Dewey spat on the floor (a thing Pauline had made him promise never to do in the house). "Nobody can touch that money unless I say so. Go try. I'd like to see you try."

"Garrett's father wrote a check for two thousand dollars," Peter said. "Remember that? You better give up the bankbook, buddy."

"You tell me how much you need, I might think about going to the bank and getting it."

"You see what it's like talking to him?" Garrett said. "I don't know what to do any more." His voice was getting high and shaky.

"You really want it?" Dewey reached into his jacket and pulled out his wallet. He took a dollar bill from it. "Is that enough?" Pauline had a terrible desire to giggle. She made a faint snorting sound, and Peter gave her a look. "You want more?" Dewey said. He took another bill out. "Not enough?" He shut his billfold. "I'm keeping the rest. You want to see something though?" He opened the wallet again. "See this photograph?" It was a picture of his mother, or so he had always said—a tight-lipped young woman in an 1890s shirtwaist. "You know what this photograph does? It guards the portals, it guards things that belong to me." He reached behind the pocket in his wallet where the photo was, and he pulled out a square brown envelope with NEW YORK SAVINGS printed on it. "See this?" he said, and he threw the bankbook down on the floor. "Why don't you just shove it up your ass?"

When Garrett stooped to pick up the bankbook, Pauline was afraid Dewey was going to kick him—she would have been careful not to turn her back if she had been Garrett. But Dewey only said, "Now, will you please leave?" Pauline felt a great surge of relief that it was over; when the others filed out, it seemed odd to her that she wasn't leaving too.

"What a bunch of pansies," Dewey said, when they were gone. "I don't want you speaking to any of them any more. I mean it. Don't let me see that. Ever."

Pauline walked to the bedroom and began taking off her shoes. She was afraid she would have to answer him if he came into the room and she was frightened that she would say yes, she would swear never to speak to them; she would have to hear herself say it. "Fucking pansies," he said.

She was almost asleep when he got into bed. He reached for her, pressing against her and moving his hands over her breasts. He was urgent but still slow and sinuous in his movements, as though his eagerness made him more thorough. She felt drugged, stirred at some point within her he was moving to reach. She had a thick, feverish sense of something dreamlike and unearthly; then its strangeness made her oddly clear.

When Pauline went to work the next day, the stock boy at Gittelson's tried to joke with her about how pale and "fish-eyed" she looked. "Too much party last night. You got to watch it," he said. "You know what's the best thing for a hangover?" Pauline said she didn't know. "Bromo-Seltzer. You want me to get you a Bromo when I go out?" All day the stock boy made the sounds of a fizzing glass whenever he passed her; he kept doing it until, as he said, he "got a smile out of her."

Dewey was sleeping when she arrived home. He woke up an hour later and she fed him supper. He sat at the table in his undershirt, tearing at the bread in a way that reminded Pauline of her father. "What'd you do to this chicken?" he said. "It's all dry."

"The oven gets too hot," Pauline said.

"I can't eat it. You eat it if you think it's okay."

"I have my own piece."

"No, have another." He put a drumstick on her plate. "You need to practice chewing or you'll lose your front tooth some day like Adolfo. Of course his got knocked out. That's different, isn't it?"

"Very different."

"It's depressing eating with you," Dewey said. "Look at you working over that chicken bone. You're like a dog, you don't care what you eat."

"Yes, I do."

"This is you." Dewey twisted his mouth down on one side and made snapping noises.

Dewey slept on and off all through the next few days. He took long baths and he sat half dressed reading the paper. He was irritable if Pauline went out for any length of time (he said any cripple could do six errands in the time it took her to do one), but in the evenings she stopped at the candy store on the corner and made phone calls to Nita. Nita said, "You're getting so good at these sneak conversations. Maybe we should start leaving messages for each other under rocks."

"In lockers in railway stations," Pauline said. "That's how it's done." She wondered if she did like the intrigue of these calls. She understood perfectly well that the small triumph of doing something without Dewey's knowing was the most misleading kind of victory.

"I saw Peter," Nita said. "You know how much money was left in that bank account? He told me fifty dollars. Dewey ate it up fast, didn't he? Walter thinks it's hilarious—he says that's what happens when you ask a fox to guard the chicken coop, he says it serves everybody right."

"That's like what Dewey thinks." In his better moods Dewey did crow over how well he had done; he made sly remarks about how he had just exercised a little entrepreneurial initiative, and he guessed he had shown them all some of the newer management methods.

"Walter says Garrett ought to pay Dewey for having given him such a great educational experience," Nita said.

"I think he already did," Pauline said. She was about to make a comment about how instruction was really getting expensive nowadays, but she thought the conversation was already getting too brittle. It occurred to her that she was repelled, sometimes, by the idea that the purpose of experience was to provide something so wholesome and unpalatable as *lessons*. She liked it better thinking of experience as something to be acquired, like a wardrobe, a notable collection whose purpose was embellishment.

Nita said, "Is Dewey still hibernating? Walter thinks we should get him a citation from the *Wall Street Journal*. Walter has such a weird sense of humor."

"I'm glad someone's enjoying this."

"Oh, Walter finds a way. You can count on him for that at least. Do you think he's losing weight? I think he is."

Dewey kept the apartment dark while he slept, and because there were no real doors between the rooms, Pauline read her book in the farthest corner of the kitchen. The low light and the straight chair made it hard to concentrate. Once, when Dewey was up, she tried asking him if he wanted to go out to see a movie, but he gave her a disgusted look and said, "What do you think?"

"You're like a troglodyte in a cave," Pauline said. She knew he wouldn't know what this was. "It's a very primitive form of human being."

There was an impulse in her to goad him into being as nasty as possible. She needed it on the record that he had said certain things, so that she could leave with a feeling of justice on her side. She wanted evidence tallied against him, as though the spoken word were always final proof.

"What did you say?" Dewey said.

"Forget it," Pauline said.

"No, I want to hear it again. I'm a what?"

"It's a kind of cave dweller. I just said that because you never go out."

"It sounds like one of Peter's words. Is it?"

"I don't know."

"Then why do you use it?"

"It fits."

"What did you say?" Dewey grabbed her by the arm and jerked her to her feet. She tried to sit down again, but he wouldn't let her.

"Stop it!" Pauline yelled.

He mimicked her, whining in a falsetto, "Sto-op it." He wrenched her arm hard and she cried out. Then he was pulling her away from the kitchen toward the living room. She tried to hold her feet down on the floor to keep from moving but all she did was slide. She kept moving with him, no matter what she did. Under the archway to the living room the bump of the threshold made her stumble. He dragged her, letting her body scrape against the floor. He swayed so she knocked into walls. Pauline was shrieking; she listened to herself making pleading noises. She screamed "Stop" and "No" and "Help," and once she shouted "What are you doing?" as though he were a person you could ask questions. She sounded so shrill and futile. When her shoulder hit the wall near the couch, she could hear herself shriek again and she wondered who in the building could hear. She didn't want them to hear—even at the moment she wanted to erase what was happening—the worst part was a kind of final disappointment that this was in her life.

Dewey dragged her until she was kneeling by the sofa. He lifted her up under the arms—she thought he was trying to get her to stand, perhaps as an ending to the whole thing—but he threw her across the sofa head down and he held her face in the cushions.

"Stop it," she said. "I can't breathe."

"I'll show you caves," he said. "You want to see caves?"

Pauline kept trying to raise her head, but he was pressing her face down against the couch. She thought that if she could just move her face to the side, she could get enough air, but the cushions still smothered her when she swerved. Bunny's brother used to do this, Pauline remembered; he would hold Bunny's head down in the bed pillows until she gave way. She had felt sorry for Bunny, but it had seemed at the time only one out of the many humiliations of childhood.

Pauline's head was shoved so close to the cushions that when she panted she got the fabric of the cushions in her mouth—she was afraid she was stifling herself by trying to open her jaws for air. Dewey would have to let her go soon. She thought of people who died by drowning—how long could you go without breathing?—and then she had a surge of real panic. This was how it happened. She felt that wave of recognition that comes with the onset of horror, a sudden clear sense of having always known about this.

Her gasping was very loud inside her head—which made her think there must be a way to get air in through her ears, only she had never learned the way. It came to her as a terrible regret that she had never learned this. The lapse that couldn't be made up: she would be found later as she was now, forever caught, exposed. The accident that would be a permanent caption for her—she would be fixed in it, it would fix the meaning of what had gone before. Her windpipe was trembling as though it could get air from inside, as though it didn't know.

Dewey took his hand away, and she lifted her head. She gulped at the air—at first she was afraid the lungs in her chest might have jammed but they were pumping as they always did, automatic and normal.

"You all right?" Dewey said.

She sat up on the couch.

"Get up and walk around," Dewey said. "That's how you get your breath back after a run or something in sports."

"I don't want to walk," she said.

Dewey stroked her hair. "You get me so crazy sometimes."

She didn't mind his touching her, it was so usual, but she thought it was grotesque that he had gotten so fond all of a sudden. She felt sickened for both of them. He brought her a glass of water from the kitchen and she took it. The glass was from a set she'd bought at the five-and-ten, ugly yellow-green tumblers—mistakes from the first. It pleased her to think she would leave these behind when she left Dewey.

"Don't you want more water than that?" Dewey said. She could get plain fluted ones like Nita had. It was heartening to her that she was thinking ahead so quickly about practical matters.

VIII

The next day Pauline saw as she was getting dressed that she had bruises on her back from where Dewey had knocked her against the floor and the walls. She had bled in spots without knowing, and there were black-and-blue marks on her shoulders.

At work she had to be careful not to sit back in her chair too sharply, and she kept touching the tender spots through her blouse. It was odd to be walking around with this kind of thing at Gittelson's, as though she really had dropped now into a marginal class. She had a sense of having been involved in some appalling drama, remote from the office atmosphere, of having ventured to extremities, and there was a certain bitter pride in her about this.

When she looked in the mirror in the ladies' room, the marks were already getting more purple and turning yellow at the edges. She thought of Bunny, who must have seen this sort of thing tending all sorts of people in her settlement house. The thought of Bunny's ministrations made her feel a surge of pity for her own back.

On the way home from work she stopped at a pharmacy and picked out a bottle of all-purpose liniment. (The name *liniment* always made her think of that poem of Blake's, which she had misread when she was in high school: "What is it men in women do require?/ The lineaments of Gratified Desire.") "You shouldn't use this if you have cuts," the druggist said, while he was wrapping it. "You have broken skin anywhere?"

"I don't know," Pauline said. She knew this sounded peculiar; she almost wanted to have him guess what had happened or to intuit without saying. And he did give her a kind of anxious glance as he took her money, but perhaps he just had no patience with anyone who didn't know her own symptoms.

Leaving the pharmacy, she cut down a different street than usual, and she passed the Hotel Walpole, where Nita's friend Rose had a room. Rose always said that she had a great view, although the street didn't seem so special to look out on—perhaps she had a room in the back, over a courtyard. She had lived there for years and appeared to have no intention of moving someplace more settled or spacious. Rose was probably not very practical; she had a longtime involvement with a married lover who everyone said was never going to leave his wife. Nita said the trouble with Rose was that she was too lazy.

Pauline thought it would be interesting to live in a hotel—and easy—all you had to do was move in. She was struck by the simplicity of the idea. Perhaps Rose wanted to share, or she might know of a really small room that rented for not too much.

When Pauline walked into the apartment, Dewey was making dinner. He was mixing together some invented dish involving ground beef and macaroni, and he kept tasting it, smacking his lips and saying, "Not bad at all, if I do say so myself." Pauline ate her plateful with appropriate signs of gratitude. She was, in fact, thankful that she didn't have to cook. Dewey made up a long story about how he was going to make his fortune peddling hot lunches in the neighborhood. *Chew at Dewey's,* he would write on the pushcart.

"Where the swank bunch munches," Pauline said. She was aware that it was a mistake to talk with him like this; the worst part of it was that in helping him extend his joke about the lunch wagon, in thinking up names for the hypothetical concoctions he would serve, she was forgiving him. They were sitting over a meal the same way they always did—only with greater cheer, if anything—and there was nothing to mark the fact that he had crossed the line into irredeemable offense. For the first time she was afraid that she would never get away from him, that she had lost her strength and changed for good into someone lesser: that she had grown into her surroundings and this was her place now. Dewey was practicing his street cries as a vendor hawking his ptomaine specials; she did not think that he was charming, but she saw how he might sometimes really be so. When he took the plates away, she said, "I don't feel too good. I think I'm going to just go lie down."

She went to the bedroom and stripped down to her slip and got under the covers. She was almost asleep when Dewey came into the room. He sat on the bed and stroked her shoulder.

"Don't touch," she said. "I'm all sore there."

"Where?"

"All over," she said. "I was bleeding, you know." She felt that she was somehow, in her tone, overplaying this, milking her injuries.

"You got me so mad," he said.

She put her hands over her eyes. "I can't stay here any more," she said. "I have to move out sometime. You know that." She was afraid of what he would do as soon as she said this.

"I know," he said.

"I thought I could live at the Walpole. Rose Brody says it's nice."

"You don't want to live there. For someone like Rose it's fine. She doesn't care where she is."

"No, she really likes it."

"She's a joke. Floating around in those rags she wears for shawls. She looks like a harpy who thinks she's some kind of siren. She has eyes like a cow."

"I like her."

"Well, go and be like her if you want. Do what you want to do. Only you should think about what your situation is going to be. People aren't going to treat you the same as before. You have to face facts, a thing I know you don't like to do."

Her first thought was that people were going to be welcoming her more genuinely once she wasn't with Dewey any more, but that wasn't of course what he meant. He meant that as a girl left over from a "free union" that had been severed, she would slip in her standing to something perilously close to the image he imposed on Rose: weathered and wistful and cowlike, subject to bad luck and unchivalric intentions. It exasperated her to know he thought this. She didn't believe that he was right—his idea of wisdom was always to posit the worst in other people—but he would go on thinking that she had reduced herself in the public judgment, that he had exacted a great sacrifice from her by "taking" her, by sleeping with her. He would believe this no matter what she did.

. . .

The next morning was a Saturday. She and Dewey ate a late, slow breakfast, and then he settled in the living room with the newspapers he would spend all day reading. "I think I might go for a walk," Pauline said. "I don't get outside any more."

"Go and walk if you want," Dewey said. "Who's stopping you?"

It was an overcast day, in that stage of city autumn when the weather gets humid and chilly both at once. She walked through Little Italy, down past the courts where Dewey worked, through the deserted alleys of Wall Street, until she got to the dockyards and the harbor. It was supposed to be soothing to walk near water, and it did give her a sense of purpose to stand by the railing and look down at the currents; the water was a murky green up close, fading to a more decorous gray under the horizon. She noted the gradations of color from near to far—olive drab, pewter gray, oyster white—in an effort to absorb the vista with more intelligence. She wondered why painters found this sort of thing interesting—Peter, for instance—and whether the pleasure they got from this was purely abstract, whether it carried with it an apprehension of natural law that was useful in ordinary life.

She stayed until the wind got too strong, and then she walked back, keeping an eye out for To Rent signs in apartment windows; usually she saw a lot of these, but today there weren't any. She kept west of her own neighborhood, until she was a block from Nita's building. Nita wouldn't be out on her terrace in this weather, but she would be home, moving slowly through the day, and she would make hot malted milk if Pauline went there.

Nita answered the door wearing a yellow silk wrapper. Pauline was afraid she must have woken her up—it was almost two, but you never knew—or interrupted her with a lover—not that Nita had any lovers that Pauline knew about. "Oh, come on in, it's fine," Nita said. "I'm in sort of a hurry but not really."

"It's rotten out," Pauline said. "Very bleak. I'd stay in if I were you. Catch up on your mending or something."

"I could darn all my socks," Nita said, "if I wore socks."

"But could you do it without making them lumpy? That's the question. My mother used to do ours so it was like walking on wads of thread after she was through. Probably deformed my feet forever."

"Did you know Peter got married?" Nita said.

"Who did he marry?" She was acutely embarrassed in front of Nita; the whole world probably had known about this for a long time, but she was no longer part of the world. She had become shadowy or undesirable; even to Peter.

"Well, Marjorie, of course. The brunette with the helmet hairdo. The one who looks about twelve. You always liked her."

"Did they have a nice wedding? Did you go to the wedding?"

"Walter went. It was in Oshkosh or some place. Grand Rapids."

"I didn't know."

"They had some kind of honeymoon at a hunting lodge. They're back now, I saw them."

Pauline pictured Peter at the wedding, smiling behind his glasses, shaking hands with Marjorie's relatives. For Marjorie's sake he would do this—he would wear a cutaway coat and nod at people and be docile and cooperative, and he would find all this reasonable and inevitable. Pauline could imagine Dewey marrying her—once he had publicly referred to them as "engaged"—but she couldn't imagine him doing anything *for her sake.* In this she knew herself to be utterly different from Marjorie.

Nita said, "They got some very lavish presents. From relatives. And Walter gave them a painting that's worth really a lot, I think."

Pauline thought that Marjorie, who was so snappy and self-assured anyway, must feel that she had slipped very easily into her destiny. And it was a pleasant enough purpose to have in life, to be Peter's wife. Unlike Bunny, Pauline held no theory against marriage. And yet it always surprised her when people she knew got married—"so soon," as she phrased it to herself—although at home she had known girls well below her own age who were married, even then.

Nita had changed into a slip and was busy hooking her stockings. Walter was picking her up soon, she said, to go to a tea uptown that somebody was giving for the happy couple. "You could come too," she said. "I could lend you a dress."

"I would just spill something on it," Pauline said. She was genuinely shocked that Nita would expect her to go some place uninvited. Nita of course believed that an extra girl, of the right age and personality, was always welcome; for herself, perhaps she was right.

For a while Pauline thought of leaving the city. Other people had packed up and sailed for Europe or moved to the country. The country seemed more formidable in a way but certainly more within reach. Walter's friend, the sculptor with the brushed-back haircut, was living in upstate New York, and Rose knew a couple who had a place year-round in Provincetown.

In conversations with Nita, Pauline complained about the noise of the El, she said she was sick of being jostled on the street at lunchtime, and she began to mind these things. She did feel put upon, tried by unfair stresses. And what was she here for? She had slipped from the old ties, she was on the periphery. Perhaps, in the country, she was about to be someone plainer and purer. Perhaps that was next, a house with printed curtains, quiet habits.

Nita also knew people who rented in the mountains, and she was ready to look for Pauline. (She said she would do anything so long as Pauline moved out of Dewey's.) Pauline did go so far as to bring up the subject with Dewey. "It'll teach you a lot," Dewey said. "You need more contact with out-of-door things. It'll make you not so spoiled."

The weather was by now getting cold—it was almost November. As she got wet and chilled just walking around in New York, the idea of living in a rural area began to seem more outlandish. She didn't like to imagine being away from heated apartments, nearby shopping. She thought there was something wrong with her that she could have wanted to immure herself in a bare landscape, without friends or promise of work. She was losing her grasp of the most obvious things; there was something wrong with her.

It was Nita, finally, who found her a place to move to in the city—an apartment on Bedford Street, next to where a friend of a friend lived. It had been vacant for weeks and had a smell of damp wood and old paper, like an attic. It *was* almost an attic, a fifth-floor walk-up whose cupboard-sized bedroom actually had an eaved ceiling on one side. From the window of this room you could lean out and see the roofs of other buildings. Walter said it reminded him of apartments in Europe.

Pauline felt panicked when she looked at the place, as though she were about to embark on something utterly foolhardy and had already gone too far to turn back. It was a nice apartment—"picturesque" she and Nita said, only half in jest—but she was overcome with a secret certainty that she was making a mistake in leaving Dewey. He had (whatever his reasons) chosen her, he had taken her in preference to all other people, he had liked her best; to everyone else, she was only secondary.

But the arrangements for moving went on and she let them. She went to the landlord's office, a woebegone chamber in a building in midtown, and signed the lease. She felt hazy and unwell the whole time. She didn't tell Dewey. He had been very genial lately, at his best really. He was working again at the courts, and he left each day looking crisp and resigned in his suit. She dropped hints. "Who'll cook this for you when I'm gone?" she would say, or "You can put that in the closet when I'm not here any more with all my stuff."

In the end, when she told him she was leaving for sure at the end of the month, he seemed to believe it had been his idea all along. "It's better for you," he said. "At first it won't be easy, you won't know what to do. But you'll make progress."

The day she left he wanted to carry the suitcases for her. She had not expected this and was quite horrified at the offer, although it seemed to be impossible to refuse without being ridiculously petulant. She hated the idea of his seeing the apartment. She had expected to disappear into it, to keep it inviolate of his appraisal. It had almost no furniture, only a cot bed the other tenant had left and an enameled metal kitchen table, with one chair, that the super had found for her in the basement.

Dewey was whistling when he walked through the door, showing his insouciance under the weight of the suitcases. He continued whistling while he opened one valise and began putting things away in the closet. "Some of these clothes should probably just get thrown out," he said. "Look at this jacket. How many decades have you had this?"

"Well, I wouldn't throw it *out*." Pauline was sweeping the bare living room.

"What you should do is make the super paint the place. Get rid of that depressing garret look." Dewey fixed a broken chain on a window sash, and then he decided to fix the other windows, a project that took up a good part of the afternoon and involved trips to the hardware store. He made her look at each sash when he was done. "See, up and down, perfectly smooth."

Pauline was nervous around him; she applauded the windows with shrill fake enthusiasm. It was confusing that he was there, as though she hadn't understood something properly. Still, he was being helpful. He went out and got food for supper, and afterward he sat drinking from a flask while she scrubbed out the icebox.

"Gets you tired," she said, when she sat down finally. "Aren't you tired?"

"It's about that time." Dewey went into the bathroom. He was in there for several minutes, and then from the sounds she understood that he was washing himself to get ready for bed. When he came out, he took off all his clothes except for his shorts and his undershirt, and he lay flat on the bed, waiting for her. Even in silhouette, his shape on the bed looked active and factual, despite the fervor of her wishing him away. There was no getting rid of him until the morning; it was too late now.

She undressed quickly and put on her nightgown. When she got into bed, he pulled her next to him and began fondling her breasts. At first she lay still and made no response, but then as he was about to roll on top of her she turned away and slid to the other side of the bed, so that there was no contact between them (or as little contact as there could be in a cot bed). She had not expected to do this, but the instinct of avoidance was so strong in her that she was suddenly clear and forceful. Dewey said, "What's wrong?" and she didn't answer. Later he said, "Are you sure?" And

153

then she could tell he had fallen asleep; she could hear his steady breathing in the room.

The bed was set at an angle aslant from the wall—she hadn't been able to decide how it should go so they'd left it that way—and she had a sense now that the bed was floating. It rose, unanchored to anything; it swayed in the dark. There was an awfulness in the room, from the bleakness of what had just happened. But Dewey would stay away from her now, he would know himself defeated. What seemed terrible to her was the way his physical eagerness for her had become hideous; an old simplicity had been broken.

Even when they had fought all the time she had found him (as she used to tell Nita) "tempting." The continuance of that desire had been a kind of verity to her, an essential truth underneath the imperfect form of her attraction to Dewey. Now she was no longer tempted to anything; a trait had left her; she felt as though her character had contracted and grown shallower.

Pauline, in the days following, spent long stretches of time reading the newspapers—as if she had taken over this job from Dewey. Gangsters had drowned a man in a burlap sack, a dead baby had been found in a garbage can, Sacco and Vanzetti were not getting a new trial no matter who else confessed to the robbery, bums in Battery Park were dying from drinking wood alcohol, whole villages in Asia were starving from famine. The cruelty of these reports blended with her sense of being newly exposed to everything, without advice or company.

The bareness of the apartment reminded her of her room at Mrs. Poganyi's. She was homesick for that time—it depressed her to find herself sinking into nostalgia. It seemed like an illusion—an error in logic—to think of certain periods as counting more, since all time passed at the same rate.

She had begun plucking her eyebrows again, and she wore, as much as possible, the one skirt that didn't look dowdy on her, although it was silk crepe and unseasonably light for winter. She kept it as fresh-looking as she could by sponging the soiled spots with benzine—until one night when she was cleaning it in a hurry before she went out, a cigarette ash fell on the wet fabric and a hole flamed through the front of the skirt. She wept then—the sudden spurt of fire had frightened her—and she was angry with herself for smoking a cigarette near dry-cleaning fluid. How was she ever going to manage to do anything if she didn't have more sense than that? It was the sort of thing her mother would have done (not that her mother smoked). And it was all made worse by knowing that it was ridiculous to cry over an article of clothing, that even her suffering had become small and ignominious.

At work Miss Pfeiffer was out a whole two weeks because her five-year-old niece had died of diphtheria. Pauline had never thought of Miss Pfeiffer as being bound by affection to anything so messy and soft as a small child. It was terrible to think of her secret familial tenderness and her grief. In her absence, Pauline sat at the front desk and stayed extra hours; she was tired from the pileup of work at Gittelson's and from a slow, pressing sense of discouragement. Sometimes she thought of contacting Dewey. She could leave a message by calling the candy store on his corner or she could send him a wire: THE JIG IS UP. LET'S BE FRIENDS AGAIN. Perhaps he had really been her one true friend.

She did remember how much she had wanted to get away from him, and out of respect for this sentiment she waited out the impulse to summon him. She missed having to cook

for him, despite the fact that he had often criticized her cooking. Eating was more haphazard without him. Sometimes she
ate out with Nita; there were different restaurants Nita liked
to go to now, currently in favor and new to Pauline—places
with black-lacquered woodwork, more designed and sleek,
less cheaply cheerful than before. She eyed the men at different tables with twinges of interest—sudden little rises of
erotic longing. But her sense of beginning again made her
slightly cautious. A clean slate: she could take up with someone untainted by anything she already knew, a man who
spoke another language or had habits formed in other circles.

She was walking home from work one night, on her own
block, when she heard someone say, "You gonna fall on your
nose you keep walking like that." She was startled—it was a
moment before she recognized Adolfo. He walked with a
cane, leaning and rocking, and his front tooth was gone—he
looked gruesome and damaged—and then rakish, like a pirate, when he smiled. When he spoke, certain sounds came
out as a lisp, as if he were making fun of someone.

"So you taking care of yourself all right?" he said.

Pauline said she was fine. If not for Dewey he would
have stayed in bed longer, healed better, been less disfigured.
She was ashamed to look at him. What had she done to help?
She had acted as if none of it really mattered. "You okay?"
she said.

"Sure. Too bad about you and Dewey. You couldn't
work out your differences, huh? I always thought you were
such a nice couple."

"Well, you know. That's how it goes sometimes."

"Without a license they can go take a walk whenever
they want."

She had an impulse to offer him money, to make up for

what Dewey had done. She supposed he wouldn't take it, even if she had any to offer.

"So you learned something—get a ring first. You'll probably find another fellow. I got confidence in you. Smile now—let me see you smile. Don't look mopey, that's the main thing. Nobody likes that."

Pauline said, "You look rested. You look good."

"The rest is over," he said. "I'm back to work."

"Where?"

"Vera's, where else? I been there nine years, I'm not leaving. Vera doesn't like my new look too much, but I wasn't getting tips just for my handsome appearance before. Customers ask what happened, I tell them they should see the other guy."

"They believe you?" She was thinking—a waiter with a cane? Maybe he didn't use the cane at work.

"I don't make it up—I tell them a story that's true, it's just not how I broke my leg. The guy I was fighting with— this is thirty years ago—I bet he doesn't have much of a lip even now. It doesn't grow back after certain things. I broke his nose in three places. You can hear when you do that. He was a mess. You should've seen. Nah, you wouldn't want to see stuff like that."

"Not me," Pauline said.

"Blood all around the eyes, he couldn't see for the blood. You don't want to hear."

"No." She didn't.

"I'm sorry."

"Well, you take very, very good care of yourself," she said.

"So go find another fellow fast," Adolfo said. "Just because one ditches you doesn't mean anything. You got time but hurry up, that's my advice."

. . .

Nita had begun an affair with Walter. She announced this to Pauline over supper one night—she was all slyness and mock embarrassment. "You know something else?" she said. "Fat men aren't so bad."

"I never said so."

"Also, Walter's not that fat. It's those Oxford bags he wears for trousers, they make him look wider. I'm trying to talk him into getting something a leetle more tailored."

Pauline supposed they would get married—that would be the end of all this. "It must be nice to be with someone you know so well."

"Well, it's very comfortable. I can just talk to him like a regular person."

It struck Pauline that none of the men she was drawn to was ever a regular person. She didn't associate sexual attraction with direct discourse—she wanted obliqueness, fleeting impressions, hints at hidden mutualities. All the same, she envied Nita now.

She saw Nita and Walter together not long after that, at a new speakeasy. Walter was fairly drunk by the time Pauline saw him—he had his arm around Nita and he was lifting her off the floor in a kind of one-handed bear hug. Nita was saying, "You're hiking up my dress, you're rumpling me," but she was laughing.

Later Walter stood at the bar, playing the match-stacking game with a group of other men, and Nita came over to the table where Pauline was sitting with Rose. "Walter likes his betting, you know," she said. "Look at him. His betting and his crossword puzzles. Yesterday he had me up all night looking up words for him in the dictionary. Till dawn." She seemed somewhat proud of this.

"Woman's work is never done," Rose said.

. . .

Nita seemed very happy at this time. She had developed a great interest in going to formal hotel dining rooms that had supper dancing—places Pauline never would have thought of choosing—and she referred to them by affectionate shortened forms of their names, which at first had to be translated for Pauline. Nita had gotten Walter to buy her an evening cloak, a great sweeping thing, blue-green velvet with a black and white silk lining. Walter referred to it as his walking deficit.

Nita still played violin at the restaurant, and in the midst of her new fondness for more conservative luxuries she decided there was a customer there who would be perfect for Pauline. He was a young business lawyer—quite good-looking, actually much better-looking than Dewey. On Nita's arranging, he took Pauline out to a play and to supper. Pauline didn't dislike him—he wasn't hard to talk to and he was intelligent, although he seemed a bit angry in advance over how she might regard him and he said things like "Of course I'm just one of your Wall Street stick-in-the-muds" or "A materialist like me would say." She wondered how Nita had thought they would suit each other and whether there was a plane of sheer personality on which they were supposed to find enjoyments in common. She let him kiss her at the end of the night—he seemed to think the evening had gone well—and she sank fully into the kiss, as though she were showing off for him.

Twice Dewey had been waiting for her outside the apartment when she'd come home from work. And he had gone upstairs with her, drunk the apricot brandy that Rose had given her as a house gift, talked about how he was thinking of being a news reporter after all his court experiences, and left only when she'd claimed unnamed places she had to go.

On the street she always glanced at the passing shapes of men, relieved when they weren't Dewey. It was amazing how many people looked like him. The capacity for variation within the same type of build and facial features was apparently very great. It made her feel how large the city was and how packed with multiple forms. After a while she began to hope that he had shipped out with the Merchant Marine after all, although there was no real chance of this—he had never talked about it himself; it had only been a rumor invented by other people. She didn't think it was wrong of her to want him to vanish over the horizon, but it worried her that she was so eager to never mention him again, she would have been happy to act as if he'd never happened. In this she was no better than Dewey, who was always stopping and starting over without a trace.

Nita was distinctly annoyed that Pauline hadn't liked the lawyer better, and then she was amused when Pauline took a mild fancy to an actor she met at one of Walter's dinner parties. He was a suavely quiet, slow-speaking sort of person, and they went out with Nita and Walter to a nightclub after the party. The club was in a big room, draped and tented with mauve-colored cloth; a band played light-tempoed jazz, and a woman in a white dress with silver flowers at her hip sang songs about men who had treated her badly. The actor spoke to Pauline in low tones about the crying need for new ideas in the theater; he used clichés with a blind assurance that made them sound solid and full of merit. Pauline liked it when he put his hand over hers; for a while his fingers tapped playfully on her wrist in time to the music. She felt happy in a thin, teenagey way.

"Isn't it nice here?" Nita said. She and Walter had just

had an argument because she had ordered something called a pousse-café, a fussy concoction involving five liqueurs arranged in layers, held in suspension by their different weights. Walter said no serious drinker would be caught within miles of something like that, and he threatened to move to another table to preserve his reputation. Nita was now sipping from her glass with a look of delicate greed. Her expression was more languorous and dreamy than was characteristic of her, and it struck Pauline that Nita must feel that she was living more fully than she ever had. And it was all bound up with the spending of money. The sheer expense of things must be to her like a pushing away from old frontiers, a moving into wider experience.

Pauline tasted Nita's drink with close attention, making approving sounds. It had a full, subtle taste (maybe a little sweet), but she was aware that it didn't thrill her the way it did Nita. Being with Nita made her feel that it should; perhaps there was something stubbornly mediocre in her, unsusceptible. Pauline thought suddenly of her mother, who would have been utterly dumbfounded not only by the arcane mixture of liqueurs with their French names but by the glass, whose narrow bud-vase shape would have been so unlike anything she'd put to her lips before. It wasn't, Pauline thought, just from ignorance that her mother would have found all of this alien—the general arduousness of most of her life would have made it seem bafflingly childish to her.

Nita and Walter had another tiff about whether the waiter was Irish—they squabbled in little spurts, like pigeons. Pauline and the actor danced, moving around the floor in slow gliding shuffles. She felt dimly as though she were having a good time. The actor said, "You have a nose like a Renaissance painting, did anybody ever tell you that?"

·   ·   ·

She saw the actor, whose name was Alfred, several times after that. He had such an irrefutable handsomeness—a well-planed, even face—that it was pleasant just being in public with him.

But she was afraid the whole time of running into Dewey. She had a fear that Dewey might be lurking in the doorway waiting at the end of the night if she ever brought Alfred home. She didn't so much think of Alfred's shock as of the two men flailing at each other, Alfred turned snarling and abusive like Dewey.

Normally Alfred's features were untroubled, almost motionless; he was the sort of person who smiled knowingly. His mouth had a kind of healthy coolness to it when he kissed. At first she thought she was going to sleep with him—he was always very nice to her—but she liked him less and less each time. Still, in being with him she had a sense of getting on with things and moving forward.

She was sorry that she didn't end up with something like a miniature portrait of Alfred to keep, as she might have in another era. As it was, once they no longer saw each other, she had nothing to show for it. And since he had been (to her, at least) so colorless, finally, she retained very little of him.

The whole process seemed too wasteful. She didn't mind forgetting things—she rightly considered herself to have a modern elasticity of temperament—but what vanished out of thought couldn't be of use.

Nita said the important thing was to remain in circulation, although in her own life now she touted the joys of staying still; she seemed quite grateful to have found a resting place in Walter, free of jolts and rude surprises. No more to roam. The sort of peaceful setting in which there wasn't a constant strain to improvise, to rise to the occasion.

· · ·

Now that she wasn't seeing Alfred any more, Pauline spent more time in the apartment. At home after work, she sewed. She made curtains and cushions and even a foolish-looking ruffle for the light fixture. She had frightened her family by admitting that she'd moved one more time—her father believed that she was fleeing to avoid rent bills—but they had let her take back fabric from the store. She had no sewing machine so she stitched by hand like a small girl with a sampler. It was slow work but steadying and soothing. When she went out into the street afterward it was hard to adjust her eyes to distances or to objects moving at the periphery of sight.

She was easily startled; once she thought a discarded heap of brown paper was a dog about to lunge at her, and she froze when a newspaper page blew across her path and grazed her ankles. There was, of course, no shortage of real things to be pained by in the neighborhood. Groups of children foraged through the garbage. Bums slept on the benches in a small park nearby; in winter they tried to cover themselves with flattened cardboard cartons. Once in the same park an old woman suddenly lifted her skirt at Pauline—she was naked underneath, and she kept flapping her skirt up and down; she was making faces and cackling, as though a lifetime of being asked to lift her skirt for sex had reduced her to a harpyish jeering. It's driven her crazy, Pauline thought. The woman turned her back and shook her rear end, as Pauline went farther down the street, and it occurred to Pauline then that she might be the one, after all, that the woman was jeering at.

IX

Pauline could never get used to the fuss people made over Christmas. Nita spent enormous amounts of time shopping, and she thought it had been improvident of Pauline to drop Alfred so soon before the holidays. Nita planned to get a suit made for Walter as his present—something well-tailored in dark wool, which Pauline was sure he would hate.

Nita had gone to Macy's toy department with Walter to help him pick out a gift for his son. The son was ten years old and they sent him a red wagon—Pauline thought he was probably much too old for it, but Nita said he was just an ungrateful brat if he didn't go wild for the one Walter got for him, not a cheap item.

Walter's wife (they were almost divorced, Nita said; there were just some legal things that had to be done) had recently mailed him a copy of the boy's school picture, a gesture Walter considered in the worst possible taste. "He resents that sort of thing; she should've known," Nita said. "The pull at the heartstrings."

They had no pity for the wife; she seemed so old to

them. They both disapproved of her for falling back on methods that were so unattractive. And it was true that neither of them had ever had to resort to an appeal to responsibility.

Nita had decided that Walter should take her to the Ritz-Carlton for Christmas dinner, but Walter kept telling her they were going to a nice cafeteria instead. Nita had refused categorically to spend the day at anyone's house—she said it would only bring back terrible memories of her screamingly boring childhood in Wilkes-Barre—but in the evening she had consented to go to a big, dressy party given by some couple Walter had just met, and she wanted to take Pauline with them.

Pauline was surprised at how much she really couldn't bear this idea. It made her angry to think of working to keep up with a certain kind of conversation. It was Rose who saved her finally. Rose was very eager to have Pauline come to the country with her for Christmas. She had friends with a big house upstate—zillions of guests were coming and there would be lots of people there Pauline would like. Pauline wasn't sure she *would* like them. (Ever since Dewey had spoken against Rose, Pauline had been afraid that Rose wasn't all that discriminating—with her fluttery wardrobe and her breezy amusement at everything, she was maybe too tolerant, too mild and forgiving. This of course made her easy to be with, certainly much easier than Nita.) Rose said they were going to roast a suckling pig in the fireplace, and this finally won Pauline over; it sounded so rollicking and medieval.

It was a pretty ride up on the train, with the Hudson visible outside the window for most of the way, very close and rippling with light. At the station where they got off, everything looked bleak and bare. The ground was all frozen puddles and dingy patches of snow. They took a taxi through the cold, quiet town and past it, down a dirt road. At one point the driver seemed to be turning directly into the woods—they were on a drive that was hardly more than a bridle path. The driver, exposed in his front seat, had to keep pushing away the branches that snapped at him from the sides. Pauline was excited then, elated at going so deep into the pinewoods to a place so secluded, and she gave Rose a pleased look. The taxi stopped suddenly, almost before they saw the house. The house was painted barn red and had ripped screens on the front porch; someone had hung a stuffed deer's head on the door, with plaid ribbons on the antlers for Christmas decorations.

When they rang the bell, they could hear the sound of a baby crying from inside. A girl of about six opened the door for them. "I'm being the butler," she said. "Did you know that?"

"Aren't you Jeeves?" Rose said. "You look just like Jeeves."

"I'm *Martha*."

"She works cheap but she's noisy," a man behind her said. Rose was busy embracing people. A Christmas tree took up a good part of the living room, and Pauline almost fell against it when Rose made a sudden turn. The guests were a mixed group—dressed in everything from tiered chiffon to rusty wools—and they were older, on the whole, than Pauline was used to.

A very pretty woman in an apron walked by carrying the baby who'd been crying when they'd come in. Pauline said, "Calmed down now, has it?"

"For a minute. Are you going to be a good boy now? Yes, you are."

"He's very handsome."

"He is, isn't he? You can hold him, if you like."

Pauline wasn't really eager to hold the baby—from the years with Solly she had a definite fear that he was going to pee on her through his diapers—but she took him and tried to walk through the crowded room jiggling him against her shoulder to keep him from crying.

"He likes that," a man said. "Wants to see what's happening."

Carrying the baby evidently made her very approachable. A couple came over to admire him—she had to explain that he wasn't hers—and she ended up having a long talk with them about whether orphans could ever be happy in later life. Pauline said, "Why not? It's a free country," but the other woman said that the affection of substitute parents was always inadequate. "Great people have been orphans," Pauline said. "Poe was an orphan."

She realized as she said this that he wasn't a good example of serenity in later life, but a man who had just joined them said, "She's right. Don't argue with history, Frances." He was a thick-necked man in his thirties, with a heavy, old-fashioned mustache and beautiful strong teeth. "And Harold agrees with me," he said, patting the baby's arm.

The baby's mother was in no apparent hurry to take him back, and he fell asleep quite sweetly in Pauline's lap when she sat down. The man said, "There he is. The first one to pass out at the party." She felt a little funny using the baby as a prop, like those women who walked dogs to meet men. She noticed that holding the baby made her feel like someone very kindly and reliable. It was quite relaxing, the sensation of being that sort of person.

Someone in the kitchen was banging a pot with a spoon—this was meant to be the dinner gong. The mother came finally to take the baby away, and the man with the mustache, who said his name was Mack, stayed with her as they went in to dinner. He had a nice, courtly way of guiding her to her seat with his hand at her back. Rose, who was at the other end of the table, waved and mouthed the question, How was she doing? and Pauline made a round OK sign. She looked down at the long table, where people were passing dishes of food and cutting up portions for children, and there was a small rush of sadness in her; she was touched at their wholesomeness.

Mack kept piling things on her plate—he was like a playful uncle—he tried to make her take two kinds of soup, extra dumplings, biscuits on the side. Everyone rose and applauded when the suckling pig was brought in on a platter. (Pauline thought it looked disgustingly lifelike, with the apple in its mouth.) There was a contest between two of the men about who could carve better, and they had a mock duel with the carving set. Martha, the six-year-old, thought this was so funny that she got the hiccups. Pauline showed her how to take nine gulps of water from the wrong side of the glass—one of the few remedies from her mother that really worked—but the girl kept giggling before she could get past the first few gulps.

Mack tried to put a giant wedge of pork on her plate but she stopped him. She'd been eating nonkosher food since she left home—she loved shellfish and she didn't mind bacon and once she had even eaten an Italian sausage at a street fair—but fresh pork was still something she couldn't get down; it would've been like eating opossum or camel meat, too alien to be palatable. Mack said he understood and he got her the apple for her plate instead. "My father's like that," he said. "He follows all these health regimens—malted barley and raw vegetables, keeping the temple of the body sacred—and he used to read a lot of Shaw. No feasting on the carcasses of dead animals."

She saw that he had assumed she was a vegetarian. It would be too difficult now to explain that she wasn't without insulting his father.

"I think it's nice to be answerable for everything you do," he said. "To know that you're not sinning with your dinner. I think that's what my father found rewarding about it. Of course, it's a very self-conscious way to live. Chewing every morsel of food twenty times—that's what he does now, it's his latest routine."

"But it's not really possible, the not sinning. I mean you can't go through a whole meal without doing an injury in a way. You're always taking it out of someone else's mouth, aren't you?" She was surprised at what she seemed to be so certain about.

"Oh, I don't know," he said.

"Did they make you chew your food twenty times too?" Pauline said.

"Oh, no, they let me be a noble savage. I had an easy time of it as a kid, a very progressive childhood."

"And look how well you turned out," Pauline said.

"Did I?" He flashed her a half smile from under his mustache—he was really very dazzling when he tried to look sly.

After dinner everyone sat in the living room, a little stupefied from all the food, drinking the brandy that Rose had had the foresight to bring. Martha played "It Came Upon a Midnight Clear" over and over on the piano. Mack said his house was farther down the road, but in the summer with the windows open he could stand in his front yard and hear Martha practicing. "Not from inside, though," he said. "The house is stone. It's like being inside a giant cistern."

"Do you work around here?" Pauline said.

"Well, I don't do anything really. Along those lines. You mean a job—is that what you meant?"

"A job, yes." She sounded too abrupt, like her father.

"For a while I taught Latin and Greek at a boys' boarding school, but I never really meant to make a career out of it."

"I took Latin." She was afraid then that he was going to address something to her in the language and expect her to answer, like Miss Oughton.

"Did you?" he said. "I might have known."

"I've forgotten it all, I think."

"It would come back if you needed it."

When would I need it? Pauline thought. But maybe you did have a need to consult certain authors, the way you might need to do physical exercise or to visit the seashore.

Mack said he was working on a new translation from Epictetus. "It's wonderful working up here. Sometimes when I get snowed in I don't see another living thing for days at a time. It's very peaceful." Pauline wondered if this was meant as light sarcasm but he looked perfectly earnest. And it was nice to think of him sitting over his Epictetus in a room like a rock cavern with white at the windows.

She told him about Miss Oughton and how she used to drill them about things like how many foot soldiers in a legion, how many tribunes in the government. Mack, it turned out, had never gone to high school, had never gone to any school before college. His parents—his father especially—had taught him and his brothers, sometimes they had had tutors, and they had all read a great deal at will. Pauline had never heard of anything like this; it was quite staggering to her, a childhood so emptied of ordinary schooldays. She felt, in looking at him, a faintly superior sense of her own vitality, as though he'd just told her he'd spent his youth as a convalescent. There was a glamour in it too, though, the privilege of that privacy.

The woman whose baby Pauline had held announced that they needed someone to go out to the shed for more firewood. "Want to come with me, just to get a little fresh air?" Mack said. Pauline had no desire at all to go out in the cold but she said yes out of being pleased that he asked.

"Me too. I'm going too," Martha said.

It was still early evening—the sky was a bright, back-lighted blue. Pauline was relieved that it wasn't darker, although they were only going across the yard. She had never really been any place more countrified than the Jersey shore or a Newark reservoir, and she was uneasy, wary of hidden animal life in the trees or in the dirt.

"I can stay up late tonight ," Martha said. "I could stay up as late as I want. Did you know that?"

"No," Pauline said.

"I've been up late a lot."

"You do seem very alert."

"Alice Leidecker always has to go to bed early. Her parents think she's a baby. How old do you think I look?"

"Forty-two," Mack said.

"No, really." Too bad, Pauline thought, that she couldn't tell Martha to get lost the way she could Solly, and Martha was too little to take a hint. Her chaperonage made Pauline feel distinctly deprived; Mack's figure walking next to her seemed all the more silent and electric.

They had reached the shed. Mack handed Martha a stack of branches to carry back. "The birch'll give off a nice smell when it burns," he said.

"I used to know a song about birches," Pauline said. "In Russian. My aunt taught me. I don't really know what the words mean, but it's something about birches."

"You look Russian. The cheekbones."

"I'm not really."

"Are you going back tonight? Do you have to go back? Or are you staying over?"

She was surprised, caught off guard—for him to suggest (as he seemed about to do) that she stay the night with him indicated that he had a completely different nature than she had thought, more sexual and more impatient. It was a little arrogant of him not to expect that he had to spend more time with her first. But there was something very forthright about the suddenness—for a moment she had a kind of pleasurable shock at the audacity of it.

"I'm supposed to stay over at the house with Rose."

Martha was walking ahead of them, singing a song about a little green frog on a log in a bog.

"That's good. I was hoping," he said. "So you'll be here tomorrow."

"For a while. In the morning at least." She got over being disappointed almost at once—she was extremely relieved that she hadn't said anything to give away what she'd thought he meant. But she felt as if she were a rougher sort of person than he was, bulkier and less delicate. She had the natural desire to eradicate this difference between them, to modify and subvert him.

She and Rose were given Martha's room to sleep in—Martha was excited about their being there and she kept rushing in to show them her doll collection until she was finally carted off to her parents' room to sleep.

Rose said, "Well, you did all right for yourself, didn't you? Is he nice? He looks nice."

"I hope he's not too nice."

"With a little coaching I'm sure he'll be fine." They were both undressing as they spoke, undoing hooks and rolling down stockings.

"I think he's kind of a hermit. He stays in all the time and translates. He's a Greek and Latin specialist."

"Well, there you are. His mind is probably seething. Probably reading dirty poems all day about orgies and Nubian slave girls."

"I'll have to ask."

"He probably can't even say some of that stuff in English. It's probably too complicated."

"Maybe he can draw me pictures."

Rose had lit a cigarette and she was sitting on the bed in her underwear. Pauline had never asked Rose's age—she was probably around thirty, with those straggly bits of gray and a tiredness around the eyes. But her figure was perfectly slender and matter-of-fact, no different from Pauline's. For some reason Pauline found this depressing—not that she wished Rose a more matronly shape, but she had always thought of thirty as a stage far enough away to produce marked alterations of some sort. And here was Rose, fresh, unfaded, still waiting.

Rose was moving Martha's dolls off the bed. "She's got so many toys," Pauline said. "I didn't have this many toys."

"They all do now," Rose said. "My friend's kid is even younger. He's always buying her stuff." By friend she meant her lover, the one who was married. Pauline already knew something about him—not facts exactly but the bits of behavior that Rose was always having to interpret. Pauline had by now told her things about Alfred and about Dewey. It was impossible not to talk about men; Pauline didn't mind this—it seemed to her as substantial a field of inquiry as anything, and she was still at an age where nearly all intensities attached to sex.

Rose, lying next to her in Martha's bed, fell asleep within minutes; Pauline listened to her breathing and thought of Mack. She had such a strong sense of his being nearby, as though he were somewhere in the house instead of up the road. She imagined him coming to the room, and Rose sleeping through it all.

Her idea about Mack (it seemed essential to have at least a hypothesis) was that he was very good, very staunch and true-blue, the sort of person who expected himself to behave decently at all times. She was a little worried about his being too unworldly, despite his age—but there was a great longing in her for something pacific and still. She thought of Nita and how she was thriving now because of Walter.

Mack was there when she went down to breakfast. Martha and the baby were making a racket, the baby's father was singing "Jingle Bells" in a goofy voice to distract them, and the mother was at the stove. "You better turn down the heat or the eggs'll get all dry," Mack was saying.

"Happy Boxing Day, all," Rose said.

"It's freezing," Martha said. "Don't you think it's freezing in the house?"

"My nose is an icicle," Rose said. "My behind has turned into two snowballs."

"Watch it," Mack said. "Little pitchers."

"Don't be so stuffy, Mack," the mother said. "It isn't necessary."

"What ravishing six-year-old whose name begins with M is going to drink all her milk today?" the father said. Pauline was bringing the plates to the table.

Mack was not pleased with the way the eggs turned out. He seemed stern today; maybe he'd been jollier than usual the night before from the drinking. His sternness irked her, made her want to change him at once, make him more affable. She hovered over him, taking his plate when he was done, asking him if he wanted more coffee. She was as seductively attentive as she could be with other people present (even so she was probably making a spectacle of herself), and he liked it; by the end of the meal he was conversing amiably about itchy woolen underwear and heating problems in old houses. "Nobody thinks a fireplace takes any trouble to maintain but it does," Mack said.

"It would be fun to be a chimney sweep, don't you

think?" Pauline said. She was saying whatever came into her head. They had shut out the others—who else but two sexually interested people would go on talking about clogged smoke ducts? He offered to show Pauline how he had rebuilt the fireplace at his house. Rose said, "Go ahead. I'm not in a hurry."

Pauline chattered on the way to the house, talking about how it was really healthier to sleep in a cold room (a thing she actively disbelieved) and how she'd never gotten sick the whole winter she lived at Mrs. Poganyi's. From the outside, Mack's house was like a lumpy stone fortress; inside it was plastered and ordinary, small rooms with dusty windows.

He did show her the fireplace—he had done something minor about changing the flue—and then he laughed and said, "You didn't really want to see that." He was reaching out his arms, about to embrace her as he said this—she thought it was ungallant of him to laugh at her for being willing—but she was enormously glad that they were holding each other finally; this part seemed at least simple and clear.

She was very sure of herself, very calm. It surprised her how quickly they moved through the beginning stages—he was quite deft and hasty once he got started; the more aroused she was, the more everything seemed faultless and straightforward and smooth: she knew utterly how to do this. Later, when they were lying down, it struck her that he was unusually graceful, a thing you wouldn't guess to look at him. In a sense, of course, the whole thing was very abstract—he was like the silhouette of a man, a figure moving behind the light, not so singular, almost without a name, despite the intensely specific immediacy of touch. She didn't mind this, it didn't bother her that it wasn't more "personal"; it seemed elevated and featureless. For some reason she kept thinking of the beach, despite the cold—of lying on the beach.

When they were almost asleep in his bedroom afterward (who would have guessed that he had a flannel coverlet with pictures of horses on it, a childhood leftover?), she said, "The light in this room is so nice."

She was very happy and relaxed; it was the most relaxed she had been with him. He said, "I'm so glad you're here." She was sorry they had to get up so she could leave. When they were dressing she could tell he was watching her. She moved easily, stepping into her clothes, still very sure.

On the train ride home Rose had the good sense not to talk to her. She must have seen that Pauline was in that state of reverie and self-congratulation that is too powerful to be interrupted easily. Pauline, although she was too far gone to emerge, felt strange having such highly colored reminiscences with another person present.

She was looking forward to giving the news to Nita— Nita was such a great booster now of the whole concept of forming a couple. She phoned Nita directly from the train station, after she'd said good-bye to Rose. "Well, I had a happy holiday," Pauline said. "Very festive. How did your Christmas go?"

"What Christmas?" Nita said.

"The one yesterday."

"Well, I don't know really. It wasn't on the calendar. I suppose there were people who went to church or exchanged presents in their crass American way. Personally I was taken to a cafeteria. To Rexford's. Walter likes Rexford's."

"For dinner? Why did he do that?"

"He's cheap."

"No, he isn't. He isn't usually."

"He *did* it to save *money*." It was not a good idea to

disagree with Nita now. "He's a very seedy person. I didn't know how seedy he was."

Pauline personally didn't think of cafeterias as a humiliation to eat in. She and Bunny had a favorite one in downtown Newark, where they had liked the huckleberry pie and the mosaic floor. For Nita, though, and for Christmas dinner, it had been mean of Walter.

"I stood in line—I was wearing my beaded crepe in Rexford's, he let me get dressed up—and I got a sliced turkey plate with two vegetables and I handed it to the last person in line and I left. I did not make a scene until Walter ran after me in the street. It was his own fault."

"What kind of scene?"

"Some shouting. I pushed him once but he didn't fall or anything. Many people had some extra holiday entertainment for free. He followed me home later and he tried to make up. He tried to play on my emotions. He brought me a fairly ugly silver cigarette case that he had just gotten somewhere and then we went back to his house and I threw it out the window."

Pauline remembered the sofa cushions that another woman had once reportedly thrown out Walter's window at a party—Pauline had an image of multiple falling objects raining down from the apartment, the overflow of repeated and violent angers. She said something to Nita about how the street under Walter's windows should be declared a danger zone; fortunately Nita thought this was funny.

She seemed in the mood to joke; whenever Pauline said anything directly sympathetic, Nita bristled and got sarcastic ("Mr. Worm" or "Blubber-boy" was how she referred to Walter). Pauline joined in the general blaze of disparagement—it was the least she could do out of loyalty, especially since her own current state was so vastly preferable. She had never been up when Nita was down before; it surprised her that Nita was subject to changes in circumstance. It made Pauline feel more cheerful about her own history, but she wasn't fully prepared to believe that no one was immune to reversals of fortune, and secretly she thought less of Nita for it.

In the weeks to come, she tried not to use Nita too much as an audience for reports about Mack. Nita wasn't all that interested anyway. When she went to dinner with Pauline she was either raging or spiritless; she was distracted by the process of reclaiming items she had left behind in Walter's apartment.

Nita kept forgetting objects she later decided were important—bottles of talcum powder, a broom—and every time she went back there was either a fight or the start of a reconciliation. Once after she'd gone back for some towels she stayed for a week. "It was a very *interesting* week," Nita said when Pauline saw her later. "It's very wearing. It's too exhausting."

All the same Nita did get told everything. She called Mack "your peaceful farmer." (He had said to Pauline that he was like Virgil in the *Georgics,* retiring to the countryside in his post-youthful years—not that Mack was that old.) He did seem peaceful to Pauline. When she went to visit him she always had to bring something to read while he worked, and she spent the days of the weekend in a haze of mild eyestrain, squinting by the fireplace.

Mack tried to coax her into trying to read Latin again but she refused flat out. She liked it when he stopped for tea, as he did several times an afternoon. He was amazed at how hot she could drink tea. She showed him the Russian trick of taking it with a lump of sugar behind the teeth. She had never thought of tea as a beverage that was refreshing, but in the stony cold of the house its heat and its tannic clarity had a brightening effect, a pleasantness associated with childhood or with the teas in English novels. They were very companionable, warming their hands near the teakettle and crunching their Vienna wafers.

Mack would never come to the city to see her. He said it was too loud and too ugly and too full of people. Now when she went home she noticed how noisy and rushed it was.

It was difficult telling him about New York things anyway. She had to repeat and explain the most obvious parts, so that every story was distorted or withered in the telling. For instance when she talked about Nita, Nita sounded shallow or vicious, and when she tried to adjust this ("she's really fun"), she seemed to be bragging about what a colorful, amusing character her little friend Nita was.

Many customs were also foreign to him. He didn't know that marijuana was used by non-gangsters or that bad liquor was called panther piss or that sex could occur during menstruation without infection. He shook his head when she mentioned all this; he looked amused and doubtful. Once she tried describing the costume she had worn to be a flame in the revue for Dean White's magazine—first the dimensions of the skirt sounded ridiculously provocative, and then when she explained it again she bored him with the dressmaking details.

She seemed to be boasting when she described something as simple as one of Walter's dinners—which she had gone to pretty commonly before Nita's break with him—any funny episodes became like cartoons of cosmopolite archness, and her own narratives were clichéd and inexact. And yet it was too hard not to talk about these things—she was stuck up there in Mack's house, huddled uncutely in his old jacket, with chafed cheeks and a runny nose, and there was no sign that she had ever known anything else unless she talked about it. It annoyed her that she spoke so clumsily; she had a sense of self-betrayal, of hurting her own feelings.

Mack sometimes liked to tease her by saying things like "Any friends of yours?" when there was an article in the news about bootleggers arrested, or "You should know about that" when the cat went into heat. Sometimes he was very understanding; he would pat her shoulder while she was talking, as though she had been through something much worse than she really had.

X

When Pauline saw her family again, Solly had changed a lot. He was almost fifteen now, skinny and smart-alecky. His great enthusiasm was military history, and he showed off at the dinner table, expounding on his latest insight into the campaigns of Napoleon. "Nobody knew that before you, right?" Pauline's father said. Solly's manner of explaining—a dogged and condescending patience—and his utter belief in the importance of his subject reminded her of Mack.

At dinner her father was in a bad mood—at one point he smacked his hand on the table to make them all be quiet for the rest of the meal. Pauline reported this to Mack later—she referred to her father as "a real pill," surely one of the milder ways she might have described him—and Mack was taken aback, shocked at this open scorn for a parent. Pauline thought he failed to understand her father's temperament; he seemed to think no one had ever made a sufficient effort with her father or tried to reason with him properly. Pauline said,

"Listen, you can't change the leopard's spots," which only
came out sounding like another of her crudities of feeling.

She hadn't mentioned Mack to her family—they would
have asked questions and found out from his surname alone
that he was part of the unsafe gentile world. (And Mack was
so safe, he was the embodiment of safety.) She told them she
was going to the country sometimes now on weekends with
friends, but that only impressed them as an odd thing to do
in winter. They had always lived in cities; her father resented
the out-of-doors, he was annoyed by most kinds of weather,
and her mother was too timid to venture even into parks.

Pauline herself was starting to feel proprietary about the
particular corner of the Hudson Valley where Mack lived. She
had read a book about the Indians once resident in the region—not that they were current neighbors, but it satisfied
her to see what Mack said were hickory trees after reading
that the Algonquin diet had included hickory nuts.

Even so she had been trying to get Mack to go out more.
There was a roadhouse outside town where Pauline had heard
you could get liquor just by asking for it—Rose's friends
went there when they could get someone to babysit for Martha and Harold. It was a dank, high-ceilinged place where
old men sat together and young men in sports jackets came in
with girls dressed up to look fast (they probably *were* fast). To
Pauline it seemed cheerful, like a wayfarer's inn, an outpost
of sociability. She suspected that Mack secretly liked it—he
talked more when they were there. Once he told her a long
story about a woman he'd gone with in college; he had almost
been engaged to her but they had quarreled about a play
they'd seen together and afterward they had drifted apart.
Pauline was surprised at how well he remembered, for something that had happened fifteen years ago. She wasn't jealous—the relationship sounded to her as though it had been

fairly slight and casual really, but so little else had happened to him that he had pondered it into significance.

Once, another time when they were at the roadhouse, he had looked over at a man who was belting down a jigger of whiskey and said, "See how his profile is? He looks just like Louis the Fourteenth, don't you think?" Since the man lacked long ringlets, Pauline couldn't see the resemblance, but it pleased her that Mack had thought of this, that he was on such familiar terms mentally with the major figures of European history. Another time, a woman who was very drunk stopped at their table and muttered at them for several minutes, and Mack lit her cigarette for her with such beautiful politeness that Pauline had a pang of sudden happiness at being with him.

She tried to get him to stay out at the roadhouse as late as possible. She liked the early morning hours and the feel of a bar thinning out at closing. She was at her most alert late at night. In the day they both carried with them the vague grogginess of new lovers. Mack was surprised at the way their afternoon teas so often trailed off directly into bed; he had expected her to be more retiring or more fragile.

They had only had a few arguments—one about whether aluminum pots should ever be cleaned with scouring powder and one about the mechanization of labor in the twentieth century. Mack hated all machines and thought they always did more harm than good, but Pauline said had he ever made a shirt by hand? Had he ever plowed a field on foot?

They hardly ever saw other people, except in the roadhouse or at the store. Pauline was surprised to find that Mack wasn't all that friendly with Rose's friends. He thought Martha was a brat and he said they were flighty, they lived on credit, they racked up bills at the local store and then made jokes about it. Pauline said feeding a family always cost more than you planned, but Mack thought their fiscal irresponsibility was all the worse for their being parents. He had an annoyingly Thoreau-like view, Pauline thought, of people's ability to do without money.

Pauline was always low on money herself these days. Gittelson had given her only a two-dollar raise at the beginning of the year, and the train trips to see Mack were eating into her salary. Had she been Nita, she would have gotten the ticket money out of Mack, but to ask him for it was offensive to her, like being a hooker or a nagging wife. She made cracks to Rose about how it was so typical of her that being with men always made her poorer while everybody else managed to lean on the male sex as the source of miscellaneous extra luxuries.

Rose was a good person to complain to; she was used to bouts of being broke herself. She did illustrations for fashion ads in the paper and there were slow periods, like now right after the holidays. She was full of advice on budgeting. She went in for what Pauline thought were peculiar economies. She would fast all day and then eat a wedge of Camembert for supper; she went out in winter in an old, thin velvet coat and a fur hat (you were warm, she said, as long as your head was warm). When there was no work at all she passed the time in her hotel room sketching still-lifes of breakfast rolls and wine bottles; she never minded anything and she was never bored or resentful.

She was also the only one of Pauline's friends that Mack had met. (It was probably just as well that he didn't know Nita.) He thought Rose was "endearing," a phrase you would only use, Pauline felt, about someone you didn't think was very bright, and Rose was perfectly intelligent.

Mack liked to give the impression of being extremely

fastidious about whom he spent his time with. (There was an implied compliment to Pauline in this, of course.) He apparently did not require much other company beside hers. But Pauline frequently felt very bottled up just being with him— it was harder to be lively with only one person watching.

So Pauline was glad when she heard a man's voice call out her name at the roadhouse. They were there on a Saturday night, when the place was as crowded as it ever got. A group of teenage boys were telling dirty jokes, a man showing off for his wife was blowing smoke rings, and when Pauline turned around she saw Garrett leaning against a wall. "Pauline," he said. "Little Miss Samuels."

He was wearing a cream-colored overcoat, a little dressy for the surroundings. Pauline hadn't seen him since the days with Dewey—he looked healthier, more fleshed out—or maybe he only looked pinkish the way he did when he was halfway into his drinking. "Well, well, well," he said. "Of all people." Perhaps he hated her. (He certainly hated Dewey.) "Do you live here now?"

"Oh, no. I just visit my friend who lives here." He and Mack shook hands. "I can't believe it," she said.

"Well, believe it," Garrett said.

Garrett said he was on his way down to the city after a week at his family's place in the Adirondacks. "You can't drive in the cold unless you stop a lot. A car needs gas, a human needs alcohol."

Mack lifted his glass. "This'll warm you up." He was being hearty tonight.

"I hate the cold. It's one thing about the mountains," Garrett said. "I notice it every time I go there in winter." He chuckled to himself as though this were a bit of real iconoclasm on his part. "You come here often?" he said. "This a favorite spot of yours?"

"Not really," Mack said.

"You get a real taste of country life here, don't you? Quite the suave crowd."

Mack snorted. "They're all right," Pauline said. The man at the bar was still blowing smoke rings; his wife, who was fat, was leaning on his shoulder. Two men in overalls sat blank-faced next to them, staring straight ahead.

"You know what it is?" Garrett said. "Look at the shapes of those heads. It's inbreeding. It's not their fault. It's just a degeneration that happens."

"They don't look degenerate to me," Pauline said. "They look normal."

"Why don't you go ask them where they get their hair cut? That domed effect would be sweet on you."

"You need a rusty scissors and a bowl to get the look right," Mack said.

"They're not bothering you," Pauline said.

The high school boys across the room were having another outbreak of hilarity. One of them kept repeating the punch line, slapping the wall of the booth. "Look at that boy's teeth," Garrett said. "He looks like a horse."

"He's not a horse," Pauline said.

"Go talk to him," Garrett said. "He's kind of your type."

It surprised Pauline that Garrett's distaste for the people in the roadhouse (his class hatred, Bunny would call it) was so strong. And Mack was joining in. The crowd in the bar seemed altogether ordinary to her, grotesque only insofar as any crowd can be grotesque. In a sense of course she wasn't one of them either. If she had walked into that roadhouse followed by her parents, with their accents and with the mournful old-world cut of their clothes, the place might well have gone silent; the bartender would've found an excuse not to serve them. Or if she had come alone, as a woman she would've been subject to overtures that carried a heavy element of scorn, if not danger. But the men in the room did not look like horses to her; they looked fully like humans. That was the least, the very least, that was required of her.

"Perhaps she should go neigh at him," Mack said.

"I used to have a horse I really liked," Garrett said. "You keep a horse up here?"

"Oh, no. Too expensive."

"They eat a lot. Oats. Hay. That's not what'll eat through your cash, though. It's certain kinds of people that do that. Isn't that right, Pauline?"

"Sometimes."

"She's so pretty. Isn't she pretty?"

"*I* think so," Mack said, a bit huffily.

"She used to live with a swindler, did you know that?"

"I'm not going to answer that," Mack said.

"Oh, well, it's public knowledge, I'm not slandering her. He had a phony magazine and he got people to give money to it. Pauline was sort of the lure. So you'd believe in his artistic purpose. Dewey was totally illiterate, but when you went to their house Pauline was always sitting there in the corner reading reading away." It struck her as especially violating that Garrett remembered her this way, since this was the one activity in which she never thought of anyone observing her. "He was more an athletic type," Garrett said. "When I stayed overnight on the couch I could hear them going at it in the next room. For a lot of women, criminals have sex appeal."

"That's enough," Pauline said.

"That's a nice dress, Pauline. Did Dewey get you that?"

"No."

"I don't object to your wearing nice dresses. It isn't that. What I want to know is who's going to pay me back the money," Garrett said. "That's what I'm asking."

"It's Dewey who took it. I never had any money. I don't have any now. Go ask Dewey. Why are you asking me?" Pauline could tell that this sounded shrill and weak. Mack was wincing; he had a cold, pinched expression.

"I'm sorry it happened," she said to Garrett. This was very true but she said it somewhat bitingly so it seemed insincere or sarcastic. And then she put out her hand—she was surprised herself that she did this—and she and Garrett shook hands. The ceremoniousness of this made it a good cue to leave, and she and Mack made their way out not long after.

Mack had known in a vague way that she'd been involved before with a sort of caddish type. Now he said grimly, "Well, this was interesting."

"He left out the part about Adolfo," Pauline said. This was the heart of the matter, as far as she was concerned— Adolfo's broken leg, his missing tooth, his lost income—it was necessary to tell the fuller version. She told it flatly, as though she were a witness in a trial, one of those worldly, well-dressed women in detective stories who show great coolness in front of the judge. And she did feel cool, narrating it as a string of facts. The telling spilled out on itself, an audible form of remorse. Actually, she felt defiant about it— it was her own business—only she wasn't dignified enough to keep silent.

"That's a charming tale," Mack said. They were in his car, moving slowly along the dark, snow-banked road. "I suppose," Mack said, "that the thing is to keep your eye on the main chance. That's what the smart-money crowd does."

"What smart-money crowd?" Pauline said.

"Your friends," he said. "Rose, Nita, the whole lovely group." He shook his head and laughed soundlessly to himself. She had a great desire to push him out the car door into the snow.

"You're getting it wrong," she said. "You don't have the slightest idea about any of this."

"Yes," he said, "I'm sure I don't."

He seemed satisfied, as though the whole thing confirmed a belief he had held for years about the corruption inherent in most other members of his species. It was certainly possible that he had nothing comparable in his past, that he had managed to avoid the experience of disappointing himself. He had not been tried and found wanting; he had hardly been tried at all. She thought of him as a kind of innocent, although he was thirty-five, a grown man with gray in his mustache and a thickening jawline. She had a grudge against his innocence, which had made him harsh, a champion of unchallenged dogma. How did he know what he knew? He had the intolerance of the untraveled, and he was as unforgiving as an adolescent.

In the morning he argued about how she cooked the eggs. "They're worthless when they're overcooked," he said.

"Eat them or don't eat them. It's your business, brother."

"I'm not usually called brother. My name is Mack."

"Oh, for Christ's sake." She thought for a moment he was going to chide her for taking the name of the Lord in vain, but he didn't.

"Well, I can't eat them this way." He was still harping on the eggs. "And there's no milk for the coffee. What happened to the milk? We didn't get any?"

"I always forget you don't get it delivered," she said. "There's no milkman, right?"

"And it's a good thing," he said, "with you around."

Coming from Mack, this was a considerable insult. She wouldn't answer—he had such scorn for the proverbial antics of the randy housewife and the milkman—Pauline was indignant, suddenly loyal to all bawdiness.

She got up and went into the other room, to sit by the fire with a back section of a day-old newspaper. "That's friendly," Mack said. "Don't say excuse me or anything."

"I'm reading. I do read, despite what they say."

"You must find the *Sentinel* fascinating. Reading the ads for horse serum?"

"I'm riveted."

"I see."

"Maybe you don't think horses should be inoculated," Pauline said. "Too modern."

"I'm not opposed to things of advantage."

"Ain't that the truth?"

Her voice was deeper than usual and she was speaking the way she might speak with Nita or in bars (overdoing it a little, even). Her usual manner with Mack was drier, more like his own (he didn't like girls to be slangy). It was nice to revert, reassuring to hear. Perhaps it was what she would sound like in the future.

They read in separate rooms until the afternoon, when Pauline said she was going for a walk. She would go around to the farm at the end of the road, where they usually bought milk, and bring back a bottle.

"You sure you want to go in the cold?"

"I'm in the mood. I need some money, though."

"I thought I gave you some before."

"It got spent for the cider." He couldn't think she was a gold digger for the milk money: that was too silly. Still, she felt very awkward; she was smiling crookedly at him.

"I only have a twenty," he said.

"I'll take it. Hah, hah, you won't see me again."

He did not think this was funny—he looked miserable as he handed the bill to her. Pauline made a great show of sticking it into her bosom like a dance hall girl.

When she came back with the milk she put the water on to boil and she set out the tea things. "That looks sweet," Mack said. She brought out a bottle of whiskey from the cupboard to spike their tea with.

"Rose used to tell fortunes from tea leaves. She told mine once," Pauline said.

"I hate that. It's such a racket."

"She didn't do it for *money*. She's an *artist*. She didn't go around with earrings and a shawl sitting in storefronts. Is that what you thought?"

Mack shrugged.

"Well, I was going to tell you what she told me, but now there's no point."

"What did she tell you?"

"She said I would live a long life." This did sound pointless. Pauline poured another slug of whiskey in her tea, out of sullenness. "I liked it when she told me that."

"I'm sure she was right," Mack said. "You always seem so strong and healthy."

"Do I?" She wasn't sure how she felt about this.

"You were probably worried about your state of health then. From the kind of life you were leading. It's understandable."

"What life? I had just come to New York."

"It's been good for you to be here," Mack said. "Away from there. You look so much better—well, not just better, I mean much calmer—than when we first met. You were like a little nervous mouse then."

"I was?"

"You know. You talked fast, you couldn't eat—at that dinner you practically tossed your plate in the air every time I put food on it." He winked. "And look at you now."

"Look at *you*," she said. "You hadn't crawled out from under a rock for years until you met me."

He was surprised that she had gotten so testy; she was so volatile, he said. They quarreled all afternoon—it was their longest tea ever, Mack noted at the end. In the early evening he drove her to the train station. "Are you upset?" he said. She was annoyed by the question—she was much too full of animosity to be upset. She had also drunk a fair amount of rye in her repeated cupfuls of tea, and she was in a clear and merciless frame of mind.

"Don't fret," she said (a somewhat artificial phrase for her), and they kissed good-bye. It was a normal, full kiss but with a faint rhythm of mutual suspicion in it.

She liked being somewhat drunk riding the train. She couldn't see much out the windows in the dark—there were the occasional blurry lights of stations passing. She might have been anywhere (it was just the kind of thing she liked); it was a great relief to be away from Mack.

When Mack called later in the week, she said she wouldn't come to the country this time. It was too tiring; maybe he would like to come to the city. "The light fantastic," she said. "The gaiety, the throngs." He was phoning her at work, and she broke off from the conversation a few times to answer people in the office. "Go chase yourself, George," she said to the stock boy. She told Mack that if he couldn't decide then about coming in, he should call her back when he knew.

It was Friday by the time he called again. While she was talking, the stock boy kept walking by her desk singing "I love my baby, my baby loves me," which of course seemed to typify everything peppy that Mack was so remote from. This was unfair of her. Mack often sang jokey little tunes—old Broadway ditties and parodies of hymns with made-up verses—but still she thought of him now as hopelessly dour and stodgy. It was humiliating to her that she had involved herself with someone so old-maidish and conservative.

Mack thought it was out of sheer spite that she was denying herself the peace of a visit to his quiet valley—whereas, in addition to spite, she was sick of the cold and the quiet and the long train trip. "You always say you love the train trip," he said. He was triumphant, having found yet another sign of deception in her. He wouldn't come; they were very stubborn with each other. She felt that she had not been stubborn enough with him before.

At work Pauline flirted with the stock boy. She said things to get his attention each time he went by the desk, calling him Georgie-Porgie even. "Why don't you come into the stockroom and see my etchings?" he said.

"Don't tempt me," she said. He looked startled, afraid she was serious.

On the way home she stopped at the Italian grocery on her street. The owner was complaining that he had lost money betting on a fight. "The wrong guy won. Am I a fool or what?"

"Nobody can tell how these things are going to turn out," Pauline said. "If you could tell before, there'd be nothing to bet on."

He took this as a real piece of consolation. "The truth," he said. She felt very citified and nimble.

For a week there were phone calls back and forth with Mack. She had gotten very uncompromising, he said. Sometimes, in between the calls, she would begin to relent a little. She would picture him—bearish, suffering, wincing at the phone—confused by her, genuinely baffled. But she got an-

gry again when she spoke to him. He agreed finally to come
to New York as proof that he was the more obliging one.

She took him to Tony's for dinner. There was no one she
knew there—the place had apparently gone out of favor—
and it was filled that night with college students. The veal
piccata was oily and underseasoned, and the waiter was indifferent when she made friendly remarks. Mack looked miserable at being there and hardly spoke.

Afterward they went to the Elephants' Graveyard.
Pauline was afraid this might be another mistake—she
hadn't been there for a long time. Walter was at the bar. He
gave her one of his hugs, rocking her off the floor. "Pauline,
Pauline, dream of a dream." His eyes were very small in his
face from drinking. She wasn't sure that it was appropriate to
be friendly with him since she was (always and forever) Nita's
ally, but it was nice being greeted with such enthusiasm.
"You look so sweet tonight," he said.

"That's me," she said. "Sweet all over."

Walter wanted to buy them drinks, but Mack said they
were going to sit down in the back somewhere. "Desert me,"
Walter said. "The hell with you."

The back room had an especially beery smell. "I've gotten some bad hangovers from this place," Pauline said.
"Once I took a bath that lasted the whole day. I couldn't get
out of the tub."

"Who are you waving to?" Mack said. A friend of Peter's had come out of the men's room.

"Someone I know. He's gone now. You can't see him."

Pauline ordered a Manhattan when the waiter showed
up. "You never drink them," Mack said.

"Yes, I do. For the color. I thought it would go well
with my outfit. A potable accessory, don't you think that's a
good idea? Red is a very primary color. The important coun-
tries on maps are always red."

"Why are you being so silly tonight?" Mack said.

"For Christ's sake. Don't be unbearable."

Someone had broken a glass in the front room and there was the sound of applause, and then another glass falling, and more cheering. "Very merry tonight, aren't they?" the waiter said, passing their table.

Walter came into the back room singing. He stuck his chest out at Pauline. *"Toreador-o, la-la, la-la, la. . . ."* Pauline put her hands on her ears. "I need you," Walter said. "The bartender refuses to believe I can stand on one foot and balance a glass of brandy on my head. Great sums of money are riding on this."

"Oh, Walter," she said. "It's so *back*neyed."

"Don't be difficult," Walter said. "We need a reliable person to observe and judge—someone fair-minded like yourself, the soul of honor."

"No bribes, that's right," Pauline said. "I'll be right back," she said to Mack.

The bartender, as it turned out, had decided to prohibit Walter from any more tricks with glasses, but Pauline was given a drink for what Walter called her putative good-sportsmanship. Walter's rowdy moods were not her favorite side of him, but she was glad that Mack was at least getting some proof that a world of social gaiety and freedom really existed and that she had some part in it.

"Nobody appreciates my glass stunt," Walter said. "My dog likes it. He likes to see a human do tricks."

"Rabbits out of hats are probably his favorite," Pauline said.

"I wonder if Houdini had a dog," someone said.

"I admired Houdini so much," a woman said. "Do you think he's dead? I don't think he's dead."

"Perhaps he's come back as Walter's dog," a man said.

There was a discussion about what life form you'd want

to come back as—a woman wanted to be Lake Michigan and someone wanted to be the entire population of Tuscany—and then Pauline got sidetracked into a debate about reincarnation, which did not even interest her but which she had difficulty drawing away from.

When Pauline went into the back room, Mack was gone. It was chilling to see the empty table—the sting of his rebuke. He had left money by the glass; he had taken his coat and hat. She stiffened, as though he had just yelled at her. She was immediately miserable. In a way she didn't blame him, only it had been so petulant and dramatic of him. There were people she knew in the room.

He had never been to her apartment, although he had the address; it seemed unlikely that he would go there. He had probably taken a taxi to the railroad station. In a huff: she could imagine him sitting stern-faced in the cab. She felt deserted then, insulted.

Even in the rudeness of it, though, his going was something like the lightening of a burden. She went back into the front room. A man was trying to explain how Houdini had trained himself to breathe under water. Everyone at the bar made up breathing exercises. When she left much later, no one asked what had happened to her friend, and she couldn't tell what anyone noticed.

It was only when she was back in her apartment that the situation suddenly struck her as agonizing. The place was cleaner than it had been in months, with all the objects on the table and dresser arranged at right angles and a bottle of real Scotch by the sink in the kitchen. She had tied a stocking around the neck of the bottle for a ribbon. It was embarrassing to look at. Her strongest feeling was, in fact, a kind of profound embarrassment. The entire evening was shoddy, she was sorry that she had ever taken up with Mack, she felt grossly mistreated, and she had a distinct sense of having behaved badly. Her life looked formless, without order and without standards.

She considered opening the bottle of Scotch for herself, but the thought of its smell was unappealing after all the Manhattans. Once at a party at Walter's, Dewey had told her that she reeked of Scotch. She was outraged now, thinking of him saying that.

She was sick of all the affronts that had fallen on her in the course of romance. The whole thing seemed full of degradations. (And none of it for love either—it was one thing to be a fool for love—she had not even liked Dewey.)

At least, she thought, I *know* more than Mack does. She had done more, been through more. She contemplated some of the more extreme episodes in her life with considerable secret pride, as though she had been a reporter sent on colorful assignments. She felt very superior to him in this. The glow of this thought did not last very long—she was still smarting from the ugly clumsiness of the evening and she had a general feeling of having compromised herself for a long time in unnamed ways. She leaned very heavily on this idea of *knowing*—but what was it? it was so airy and inexact an accomplishment, and perhaps not even directly useful.

XI

*A*t work on Monday she was dull and slow, weighed down with blank mournfulness over Mack. When she was in this kind of flat mood, it was satisfying to sort and file things, to find receipts. It was almost interesting then—the names on the invoices, the lists of goods sold. Other days she hated it more. She minded the time lost to it, the days gone (the Days of Her Youth). She also minded Mr. Gittelson, who was always patting her cheek and pinching her nose and docking her pay when she wasn't on time.

Late in the morning, just when she was getting hungry for lunch, Mr. Gittelson came around to her corner. "I have a beautiful surprise for you," he said. "Come into my office, you have to see."

It was probably just a new sample he meant, but she was wary.

"Could you guess?" he said.

In the seat by Gittelson's desk was her father. "I gave some orders for the ribbon," he said. "So I came, here I am."

Mr. Gittelson said, "I told him you're a lovely girl only sometimes you sleep too late in the morning, right?"

It was so startling to see her father there. In outline he didn't look that different from any of the men who might be in Gittelson's office—jobbers, salesmen—but his face was too vivid to her, too known, as though she had caught herself talking out loud.

"I was thinking about lunch," her father said. "You're hungry?"

When they walked out through the office together, the stock boy gave Pauline a look. Perhaps he thought she was cozying up to one of the out-of-town buyers. Miss Pfeiffer said, "You're going out now?"

"You have to stay?" her father said. "Stay in, I'll go."

"Is it all right?" Pauline said to Miss Pfeiffer.

Her father was at the door already. "Stay. Go. Just let me know." Pauline couldn't stand it. Miss Pfeiffer said she could go now if she kept it short.

Pauline took him to Schapira's Home Dairy Restaurant on Thirty-first Street. "It looks clean," her father said. "You come here at night too?"

"Oh, no," she said. "I go places near where I live. With my friends."

"That's nice. You go with friends."

"Often."

"Your friends don't cook—you have to go out?"

"I cook sometimes. I made boiled pike one time, they liked it."

A long while passed while her father ate without speaking, the way he did at home. It made her think of Dewey, the silences at meals during the time he wasn't talking, after he had given up the bankbook to Garrett. That was the worst time, she thought. That time is over. She felt with confidence that the most excruciating disasters of her life were finally behind her. In her stubbornness—which was accentuated by being with her father—and in the natural limits of her prescience, she could imagine nothing worse.

"My friends like my cooking," she said. "Nita can't cook at all. Well, maybe fudge. She does fudge well. Rose could cook if she had a kitchen, I think so. She has that kind of personality."

Her father grunted. She dug into her vegetables with sour cream, an enormous portion which her father would yell at her for ordering if she didn't finish.

"How's the store?"

"All right," he said. "Solly helps more now. He's a know-it-all is his problem."

"He is," Pauline said.

"So I'll come back tonight when you're through," her father said. "You can show me your house, before I go back."

For the rest of the afternoon Pauline walked through her apartment mentally, trying to remember what she had left out, what was exposed. It pained her to think of his looking at things—the Scotch with the stocking around it, the ruffled light fixture, the kitchen table with one chair. She had always thought they would send Solly if someone came to see. Still, there was nothing she could do about it.

When her father came at the end of the day she took him on the El, to save the thirty-minute walk. He seemed too old for doing all those blocks on foot, although he was only fifty. In her apartment building, going up the five flights of stairs, she had a wild hope that he would tire and turn back.

She pulled the cord to switch on the light fixture as they went inside. "You want some tea?" she said. "I have tea." He walked through the living room to the bedroom, he opened the door to the bathroom, he looked into the kitchen. "Very small," he said.

"Sit down," she said. "There's a chair."

He was still moving through the rooms like a browser in a store. "If you have bugs," he said, "you should put out boric acid on a potato cut in half."

"I don't have bugs," Pauline said. This was a lie.

She lit the gas and put some water on to boil, to give her something to do while he went on with his inspection of the rooms. Hadn't she outlived this sort of thing already? Wasn't she through with all this? Her rooms looked cramped and dark now, cluttered, embellished unsuccessfully.

"I'm not staying," he said. "I just wanted to look."

"I have Swee-touch-nee," she said. "You like that kind."

"I'm going," he said. He put an arm around one of her shoulders quickly, by way of good-bye, a form of gesture Nita always called a quarter embrace.

At least he hadn't come while she was at Dewey's; it occurred to her after he left to be thankful for that. He wouldn't tell them much at home, whatever he reported; you could never really get information out of him. He would say a few vague things to keep her mother from being any more fretful than she was. But he could come back next week if he decided to—couldn't he?—he could come back any time he wanted.

Mack had once asked her how good Nita really was at the violin. Pauline had said, "Oh, very good, I think," although actually she didn't think that and Nita had certainly never said it. Still, Pauline was sorry she hadn't told her father she had a friend who was a violinist.

Ever since Nita and Walter had broken up, Nita had been practicing five and six hours a day. She played the same pieces over and over, some études her teacher in Wilkes-Barre had given her. The rash came back on her neck, and she wore cake makeup that smeared the handkerchief she tucked under her chin when she played at work.

She was not a person who enjoyed being alone, and she often had people over when she was practicing. Pauline would sit and flip through magazines, waiting for her to finish. Nita looked workmanlike moving her bow, not earnest but fixed on the task. She said she wasn't interested in getting jobs in better places or advancing professionally—she claimed not to like the sound of the instrument. She practiced, she said, because it was one of those urges, like cleaning the house or going shopping, that took hold of you and made you not want to do anything else.

A neighbor complained of the noise, but Nita played louder whenever he banged on the floor. She got cramps in her hand—from bad technique, she said—an early sign of tendonitis, which she believed she could work out by playing more. She would have kept on, but she played at work with a bandage she had contrived out of crossed strips of grosgrain ribbon—the manager of the restaurant said she looked like a boxer without his gloves, and he made her take a week off.

It was not a good week to have off. It was the beginning of March, blustery and cold. She had no money to go away, and she had just lost her one hobby. For a while she talked about getting Walter to lend her some money so she could go to France. She was at a stage where she was impatient with a lot of the things that had diverted her before. There was a French singer in a bar on Cornelia Street, and Nita coaxed Pauline into going there to hear her all the time. Pauline made attempts to translate phrases from the songs. *L'amour est un orage.*

The singer was not a young woman, and when she sang the lyrics to her songs about lost love, she adopted a particular expression of melancholy wisdom—resolute but misty-eyed. She stared into the audience, attempting to convey how well, all too well, she knew the things she was singing about, trying to remind them of their own share in this same knowledge. Coaxed, Pauline thought of Mack and of Dewey; she was aware of Nita sitting next to her, and how they fit into this atmosphere of regretted romances. The torch singer was asking what good it did any of them.

Sometimes the singer did songs like "Varsity Drag" in French. She had to rush to make the lines fit.

"Pack a ukelele when you go to France," Pauline said. "You'll be a big hit."

"I'd never take an instrument. Tony Goodwin had his whole trunk stolen between Le Havre and Paris."

"One of the risks of travel," Pauline said, although she had never been farther away than Pennsylvania.

"It's the same here. It's worse. Rose had her fur hat stolen on the street. Some kids came up and grabbed it off her head. Did you know that?"

"That's horrible."

"Three or four kids. They took it and ran. They tried to take her purse but they couldn't get it."

"Where did this happen?" Pauline knew when she said this that she was pretending that only certain blocks had danger in them, spots where only someone a little foolish or inattentive like Rose would walk. Whereas there was no spot on earth without the possibility of menace. In this respect at least her parents had been right, with their constant suspicions of other people's intentions.

She did think that Rose was the last person who deserved to have anything stolen: she was so ungreedy herself, so content with little. And she had really been very devoted to the hat—a beaver cloche with a band of gray lamb. It was her one impressive garment. "Poor Rose," Pauline said.

"She's so *stubborn*," Nita said. "She won't buy anything else because she says it's too late in the season. She's in mourning, like people who won't get another pet after one dies. So she's running around hatless; the wind is whistling through her ears."

"She'll catch her death," Pauline said. She was kidding, but they had both grown up with the idea that hats were worn at least partly for medical reasons. "I could lend her my old green felt. Do you think she would wear it?"

"No," Nita said.

The French singer was repeating the same repertoire they had heard before—one jaunty street ballad to three gurgling torch songs. Nita was restless; she decided they might as well go to Vera's. She said this with some degree of resignation, but it was clear that she believed that real life was going on at Vera's without them, like the tree falling in the forest. You could only stay away so long.

Pauline also believed this, but she was no longer completely comfortable at Vera's or the other places. And being awkward there made her sentimental about the past, an emotion she considered more or less humiliating at her age. Walking up the stairs to Vera's made her think of the words to a song Bunny used to play on the piano, bowed with the burden of the years.

At the top of the stairs, through the kitchen door, she could see the cook carrying a pot between the stove and the sink—he was yelling something to one of the waiters (not Adolfo, someone younger)—she had a sense of everything happening at a fast, glib pace, on a schedule of urgency. There was the noise of voices from the next room, which also seemed very fast and loud. This was exactly what made her uncomfortable in Vera's—things going too quickly, too mercilessly, to get hold of. You needed a lightness of heart, a thoughtless surety, to keep up.

She and Nita hung their coats on the wall outside the main room. Some of the pegs were chipped and loose—Mack should be here, she thought, he's so good at fixing things. She had a moment of missing him, a quick daydream of Mack.

"I hate March," Nita said. "I hate all months."

"It's one right after another," Pauline said.

Nita was not going to be lively (in her black moods she was intransigent and unpleasable), and there was no one else in the room Pauline knew well enough to talk to, although there were plenty of people she knew by sight; it was distracting to notice them out of the corner of her eye. Vera, the owner, stood in the corner with her arms crossed, a buxom woman in a man's shirt and tie. She nodded hello to Nita; Pauline waved, but Vera had turned away by then. She was watching two men who were chasing the waiter, trying to play tag with him. They bobbed past the tables, ducked behind pillars. Vera, who didn't drink herself, looked sardonic and said nothing. Pauline thought that Vera really wanted people to act like that, that in her own stone-faced way she encouraged it.

"Here comes the Rose," Nita said. "The Rose in bloom."

Rose did look blithe and blooming, or at least flushed. She was swooping down on them—her hair all flyaway and electric—leaning over them in her fluttering, light-bodied way. She hadn't *seen* them in so long. "This is my friend," she said. He looked nineteen or twenty, very collegiate, and he was holding Rose's hand. He corrected her on his last name; they had apparently just met. "How's your country life?" Rose asked.

"I've abandoned it," Pauline said. "I've decided to go in for feverish dissipation and low companions instead."

"Oh, that again," Rose said. She had a cough that snuffed out the last consonants—she was laughing at the same time, so there was a final wheezing effect, like an old person's cough.

"For crying out loud," Nita said. "Get a hat, will you?"

"I'm fine."

"She should be home in bed," Nita said, looking straight at the boy. "She doesn't take care of herself."

"I do," Rose said. "I've been drinking hot lemonade all day and putting mustard plasters on my chest."

"That's disgusting," Nita said. Pauline made a prune face.

"Oh, no, it's the best thing," Rose said. "It always works."

"I'll watch her very carefully," the boy said, and Rose led him back to their table.

"See what happens?" Nita said. "She ditched Mr. Married finally, and look at her today."

"She's free to make a fool of herself in a new way entirely," Pauline said. This came out sounding much sharper than she'd expected—she was surprised at this leak of something bitter-spirited from her: to jeer at Rose, of all people.

A man at a table near them was haranguing his date. "We don't *have* to come here. There's no law that says." The woman stroked his cheek and leaned her head on his shoulder. She blotted her beet-colored lipstick on his collar. "Why did you *do* that?" he said. "You're always doing things like that."

"I bet the logs are wet," Pauline said, thinking of Mack. "It's very smoky. I bet they store their wood someplace where it's damp."

"In Paris they don't have central heating a lot of places," Nita said. "Did you know that?"

"Those girls who do the can-can must get chilly."

There was the sound of someone beating a metal gong. Vera was standing by the fireplace, hitting a copper pot with a spoon. She banged over and over; at first there was a ripple of laughter and a surge of talk—people were asking each other what she was doing. The lights went on and off, which was the usual sign to get out for closing. People groaned and booed. "It's *early,*" someone yelled.

"You all have to leave," Vera said. "Are you listening to me? There's a fire in the kitchen. Walk, do not run. It's not serious."

"Not again," somebody yelled. "It's old hat, Vera."

There's going to be a stampede, Pauline thought. She was much more afraid of being trampled than of the fire itself, which couldn't, she thought, spread that fast (she was still thinking vaguely of wet wood). The waiters were herding people out, getting them to line up. "Is it for the insurance?" a woman said. "Is that why she does this?" One man walked out with a teacup and saucer in his hand. Someone yelled, "Oh, that Vera. *Any*thing to get her name in the papers."

The hallway was foggy with smoke. Pauline had been in this hallway a hundred times—it seemed so unlikely a spot for anything serious to happen. People behind Pauline were pushing. You could breathe but it was like putting sand into your lungs. Nita was handing her someone's coat from the row of hooks—Nita had taken one for herself and put it over her head. Pauline tried to do this too but the coat kept slipping—it was a man's heavy overcoat—and she was holding on to Nita with one hand. Her eyes were tearing from the smoke. She was afraid someone would trip if she dropped it so she toted it under her arm. Her nose ran, and when she touched it her hand came away with black on it. She thought she kept hearing Rose's barking cough behind her, but it might have been anyone.

On the stairs a woman was shouting, "Don't push, we're almost there, don't push." Pauline lost hold of Nita. People were crushing against her from the back. A man who was being shoved toward them actually said, "Excuse me." She heard Nita say, "Don't mention it."

Pauline had gotten over her terror at being at the mercy of other people's behavior, her certainty that they would close ranks against her, that she would be the one to slip to the bottom of the pile. Past the landing there was more room. Somebody made a joke about being ticklish. Now the crowd no longer seemed menacing, they seemed comradely—they were not even a crowd really, only a group of perhaps forty pressing down the stairs with her to the open door and the street.

They stood on the sidewalk in the cold. People milled around in groups, thronging the street. A couple sat on the hood of a parked car, drinking out of a flask. She and Nita were both in men's coats down to their ankles. They could hear the sirens, wailing very loud as they got closer. When the first fire truck turned the corner, people clapped and cheered. Somebody whistled through his fingers. A man with a booming voice started singing, "Oh, say can you see/ By the dawn's early light," and people joined in. They sang in a rowdy, garbled way—they kept it going for several lines. Whatever fright they had felt had been over fast (and not necessary, as it turned out)—as a group they felt celebratory and valiant, pleased at the way they had behaved.

The firemen filed into the building—there were a great many of them, more than could be needed, Pauline thought.

They stomped through the doorway in their rubber boots, hauling a line of canvas hose from the truck. Some hazy smoke was coming from the doorway and blackish puffs rose from the windows. Pauline kept thinking the firemen were going to be angry when they discovered how small a fire it was.

Passersby were already gathering around asking what had happened, and Pauline heard a man explaining that something had flared up in the kitchen. She could tell how proud he was to have information. And she too was already eager to tell about it, glad she had gone there tonight. Even in the worst part on the stairs there had been a wild thrill of interest.

One of the fire trucks was leaving. Vera came out of the building carrying a pile of coats. Pauline took off the man's overcoat—she felt guilty for having put it on. The coats in the pile were soaking wet from the hoses. A couple shook theirs out, joking and sprinkling each other.

Rose was there—she came walking toward Pauline, arm in arm with her collegiate friend. "When he heard the gong he thought it was a raid," Rose said. "He was *so* disappointed."

Pauline scrounged through the pile for her own coat—she was afraid that someone had taken it, her one expensive piece of clothing. When she found it, it was somehow shabbier than she'd remembered, mangled and soggy now.

"Who got hurt?" Rose said. "Somebody got hurt."

The firemen were coming out of the building with a man on a stretcher. Pauline could see part of the head—black hair with gray in it—and the feet sticking out of the blanket. They set him down on the sidewalk and one of the firemen knelt next to him, unpacking what looked like a suitcase; he drew out of it a rubber mask and he clamped the mask over the man's nose and mouth. Pauline wondered whether there was a finite amount of air in the case.

"That's what they do," a man behind Pauline was saying. "See that? That's the procedure."

"It's one of the firemen," someone said. "I bet it is."

Perhaps it was; the fireman who knelt over him showed an intentness that might be personal. It seemed bizarre to Pauline that children always wanted to be firemen. It was more dangerous than any other job, grueling and full of the sight of other people's miseries. She couldn't remember at what age Solly had been old enough not to love fires.

The men were hoisting the stretcher into an ambulance, sliding it through the back like cargo. Vera sat in front with the driver; she looked businesslike and grim.

All around Pauline people were asking each other questions. There was a new theory that the injured man was the cook, but the cook was black and Pauline had glimpsed enough to know the man on the stretcher was a white man. "I've seen burn wounds in the war," a man said. "You ever see anybody really burned? You don't want to see it. This fellow wasn't burned."

Pauline looked back at the building, which was still smoking slightly, wafts of black trailing out the second-story windows. She hated the building—she understood why firemen liked to smash these places, hacking doors and axing through walls. She hated the restaurant, with its cell of a kitchen too small for the volume of business and with its tables crowded so close together—a spark from the fireplace had once burned a hole in her stocking; she was surprised there hadn't been worse fires before now—and she hated, in a fuddled, unreasoning way, the heat of the crowds, all the people coming to mingle together, the friction of their physical presence.

Nita ran after one of the firemen as he was going back into the building. "Who was it?" she said. The fireman shook his head—he didn't know or he wasn't talking. She went to the fire truck and yelled to one of the men; he shouted something down to her.

"A waiter," Nita said, when she was close to Pauline. "He thinks his name was Rudolfo."

"Adolfo," Pauline said. "Don't you think that's who he means? What are the other waiters' names?"

Neither of them knew. Jimmy, they thought, maybe a Henry. "He meant Adolfo," Pauline said.

"Christ," Nita said.

"I forgot about Adolfo," Pauline said.

She was horrified at this, at what had happened while he had slipped from her mind like a lost umbrella. She *had* thought of him on the way into the restaurant, but she hadn't remembered him at all during the fire. She couldn't get over this.

He wasn't burned, a man had said that. "Do you think he's all right?" she asked Nita, although she knew Nita didn't know. She felt too young all of a sudden to know how to behave.

The crowd began to break up. People were edging away, moving slowly as if they'd been chastised. She wanted Nita to ask if there was something they should stay to help with. The firemen were telling people to go home, and Nita said they were both in the way standing there. "Time to call it a night," she said. She steered Pauline by the elbow. "We look like the Wreck of the Hesperus," she said. "All we need is a little seaweed around our collars."

At work the next day Pauline told the stock boy about her "trial by fire"—even Miss Pfeiffer was interested. "Someone got hurt but they said he was okay," Pauline said. "The color of the smoke was so much darker than I would have expected."

It wasn't until the afternoon that she got the phone call from Nita. Nita had been crying—her voice was nasal and weak. "You were right. Not Rudolfo, Adolfo," she said. He had gotten out of the restaurant with everyone else and then he had gone back in to get his shoes. He always kept his street shoes in the back of the kitchen; he wore his old ones for work.

"He died," Nita said.

"I know," Pauline said. She meant that she had known from Nita's voice. She was trying to say something steadying.

"He was always so dapper," Nita said. "He wanted his good pair of shoes." It was true that he had been careful about his appearance, tonic on his hair and starch in his shirts— Pauline hadn't known that Nita noticed. She wouldn't have expected her to be crying for Adolfo—when had they ever had a conversation?—but Nita had strict fidelities and her own points of honor. She was ardent when an event fell into the realm of things for which she had feeling.

"He was fifty-four, did you know that?" Nita said. "He was very youthful." He had tried to help the cook put out the fire, but it was a grease fire and pouring water on it had made it worse. Pauline could picture him, baffled at the rippling of the flames. Salt, he should've used salt: any housewife would know.

"Will you come to the funeral with me?" Nita said. "I want to go."

Are we invited? Pauline thought. She was afraid they didn't belong, they hadn't known him well enough. She thought that it might be too showy of Nita to think they should go. Or perhaps not—maybe it was the staunch and upright thing. Adolfo would've liked it, the young girls in the church for him.

"Somebody I know died," Pauline said when she got off the phone. This was to explain—you were not supposed to be on the phone for more than a minute if it was a personal call—and also to announce a gravity of mood in case anyone was about to talk to her. She knew that it would be a partial lie to say that she would miss Adolfo—when had she ever sought out his company?—but the idea of him gone was a mean surprise. He had sacrificed himself for his shoes—he had gone back in without thinking, he had made a mistake. People who had never known him would know this about him. When had he known what he'd done by going back? It must be like drowning or choking—to be "overcome" by smoke—the rush of realization and then the giving up to it. She didn't know him enough to guess what he would've wanted more time to finish, what he must have thought he'd left undone. The idea of "finishing" meant, of course, a shape you thought your allotted time would assume, all the wastes made use of as spaces in a pattern. Possibly this was another form of vanity: we learn from our mistakes, Pauline thought, frequently things which are never applicable again. Adolfo had learned never to go back for his shoes.

People closer to her than Adolfo had died, before this. Her Aunt Peshie, the one who had taught her the song about birches (really a great-aunt), had died of heart failure, and in school a girl had died of pneumonia in the fifth grade. At the classmate's funeral another girl had sobbed very loudly all through the service and had wailed, "She looks like an angel," at the sight of the figure in the coffin; Pauline had thought this was a terrible way to behave. At Peshie's (where Pauline had been truly anguished—Peshie had been her one relative who liked to play with children), the family had hugged each other afterward and murmured, "What a life she led. No picnic, I tell you." In each case Pauline had felt, among other things, a sense of importance in being at the funeral, a pride that this thing had touched her life. Going to Adolfo's she felt like an impostor, trying to cadge some of the event's importance for herself.

Nita wore the black crepe dress she had worn playing the violin in the revue for Dean White's magazine two years before. The service was in an old, darkened-brick church on a side street in the south Village. When they went in, there were very few people in the pews—two old women whispering in Italian, a couple with a small boy, a very tall black man who was the cook at Vera's, and Vera herself in an odd gray costume that was like an elongated gym smock. Dewey was not there. Maybe he was out of town by now; maybe he hadn't heard or hadn't cared. There was no one there who looked like him. She realized then how much she didn't want to see him; she was frightened that he might mock her even there. She was still glancing toward the door, waiting to see who was coming, when she saw that the priest was walking down the aisle past her, intoning something. She was afraid of not knowing what to do, of doing something "against her religion," of kneeling in compliance or receiving Communion by mistake. One of the pallbearers was another waiter from Vera's, expressionless under his shouldered load.

She had known, of course, that the chanting would be in Latin, but it stirred her to hear ordinary people speaking out responses apparently as familiar to them as any household sayings. She could pick out occasional words. *Et lux perpetua luceat.* They used a soft Italianate *c*—it was all much more rolling than the clipped, hard pronunciation Miss Oughton had taught. The priest had a strong oratorical tenor. It was probably the first time, Pauline thought, that she had "used" her Latin. She had refused to let Mack review it with her, she had been saving it. It seemed right that it should be for this, as though the language—stony, classical, half understood— was designed for mourning, for anything elevated and indistinct.

She did not think of Adolfo directly until the priest began his sermon. The priest made a mistake quoting from a poem; he attributed it to Tennyson when it was really Long- fellow. This struck Pauline as being the sort of thing that would happen to Adolfo even at the last—his name would be mispronounced, he would be laid out in clothes he had hated.

It seemed bitter to her. But then Adolfo in his own time had been good at adapting to random events made perma- nent, had in fact made something of a career of it—he lived in the same hotel room he had checked into casually twenty years before, he went around without the front tooth he was meaning to get fixed when he got some money. Now all those things were his life. She didn't care so much that he had been disappointed—who wasn't disappointed?—but that his life had the quality of still being unformed.

While people lined up for Communion, the cook kept looking down at the church floor, and Pauline copied this. Adolfo had called the cook "our jungle bunny" in conversa- tions with Dewey. There were ways that Adolfo would not have gotten better, things that age would not have corrected. But the cook had overlooked it; a certain amount could be overlooked, was always overlooked at funerals.

For a moment Pauline thought the cook was really clos- ing one eye as he stared down—as if he *were* trying to over- look things, to discern a shape in the whole experiment of Adolfo's life by squinting sideways at it.

It was possible, of course, that the cook had tears in his

eyes; that had not occurred to her at first. As far as she knew, the cook had not been what you could call Adolfo's friend. (Pauline counted eight people at the funeral, including the child, and at least half of them had never seen Adolfo outside a restaurant.) Perhaps the cook's tears, if they were tears, were not from friendship but from something purer, not personal.

She had heard Adolfo describe in detail the contusions on the faces of boxers he'd fought with. He had been very proud of the damage he'd done. It comforted her now to think of his faults, because she couldn't stand there without feeling remorse for certain undefined things in her own past, the funeral had cast an unmistakable tone of regret on everything, and this was not yet an uplifting feeling; she was waiting for it to become so.

The woman with the small child reached over and put her hand on the boy's arm to stop him from fidgeting. She kept him and herself as motionless as possible. Her broad back (you could see through her dress how tightly laced she was into her corset) was rigid and respectful. Pauline saw in everyone else in the room the same solemnity of posture. They wanted to quiet themselves, to be still in the face of Adolfo's stillness—as if by mimicking they could comprehend—but the effort was too much for them; they stirred, they shifted their weights.

The priest was wiping out the inside of the chalice, an act that reminded Pauline of something Adolfo might do in the restaurant, as though the priest were honoring him in the gesture. What order of monks was it that had to do menial labor in the monastery as a form of worship? The priest swirled the cloth around with a bit of a flourish, which made it seem even more like waiter's work, like a gold-lit version of Adolfo on the job.

During the blessing, the small boy stood with his head

up and stared at the altar. And then they were all filing out of the church, following the pallbearers, and the service was over.

On the steps of the church one of the old women stopped to rewrap the shawl around her head. She looked like Queen Victoria, Pauline thought, but with a beakier nose. The other woman spoke to her in a fast, voluble murmur. One of them might have been Adolfo's mother; there was no difference in their expressions.

Miss Oughton had said that modern Italians weren't direct descendants of the Romans but of some other peoples, diluted mixtures; this was to explain the disparity between the lofty Romans and an immigrant group known to be so noisy and emotional. Pauline didn't see now that the Romans had behaved so nobly—parading captives through those triumphal arches they were so proud of, making slaves, crushing revolts, pitching camp, and laying waste to. She was disgusted when she thought of these things, as though they bothered her newly, were freshly offensive.

The old women got into a car. Pauline and Nita had decided in advance not to go to the cemetery, and they slipped away from the group.

Nita waved good-bye to Vera. "Thank you for coming with me," Nita said.

"Well, don't thank me for that," Pauline said. They spoke in very soft voices; they were both tired now in a way that made them gentle.

XII

(Spring, 1927)

Vera's reopened for business the weekend after Adolfo's funeral. They had put a big metal-cased door on the kitchen, which was supposed to make it safer. The sound of the door slapping shut reminded Pauline of the fire doors in the halls in her high school. Vera's was crowded on the night of its opening—people had missed being able to go there—there were lines on the stairs to get in. Pauline thought Adolfo would've liked that, he would've liked the idea of the place continuing, out of the eternal necessity for it. But for Pauline it was too close and noisy, too full of people she didn't know how to behave with.

At the height of the evening she got separated from Nita, who went off to talk to Peter and Marjorie, and then when Ernest came in and Pauline got up to greet him, the man turned out not to be Ernest at all and she lost her seat at the table. She leaned against a wall. A man standing next to her was wearing a coat indoors, a fur coat in April. Pauline thought he was one of the most affected-looking people she had ever seen. "You have intelligent eyes," he said. "It's very unusual for me to like brunettes." She listened to him talk about his childhood in Virginia, about cats he had owned. She couldn't think how to get rid of him. By the time she left she was leaden-eyed and exhausted. She wouldn't let him walk her or take her in a cab, although it was colder outside and drizzling rain. She tied her scarf under her chin like a babushka and walked to a newsstand to get a paper to use as an umbrella (her mother always did that).

A woman in a red hat was in front of her at the newsstand, taking too long getting out her change. Pauline edged behind her to get her to hurry up. And she saw that it was Bunny.

She looked good in red, more spirited than she ever had before, despite the fact that the coat was shapeless and too long. They called out one another's names and threw their arms around each other, blocking the newsstand from another customer.

"I can't believe it," Bunny said.

"Ha," Pauline said. "It's you." She should not have put that scarf on her head. "Well, Miss Roberta," she said, "what are you *doing* here?"

"I just came to see some people. I can't believe I'm just meeting you here like this."

"Well, how's the settlement house business?"

"I'm working someplace else now with indigent alcoholic cases."

"That's wonderful."

"It's a job," Bunny said. Pauline was glad a bunch of old rummies had the benefit of Bunny; Bunny would be nice to them. In a way, she thought, Bunny was more fearless than she was. It occurred to her to admire Bunny.

"So you're still filing at the ribbon place?" Bunny said. This question did not at first make sense to Pauline. In the noise of the rain, which had gotten heavier, it took her a second to make out the words. She and Bunny were huddled under the awning of the newsstand.

"Oh, yes, still there."

"Do you think it's going to keep raining?" Bunny said. "I was on my way to a party for the Young People's Socialist League, but I don't think I want to go now."

"It'll stop."

"You like New York?" Bunny said. "It's not too hectic?"

"Oh, well," Pauline said. "I manage to control my rampant social life."

"I knew you would like it. You always liked those things. You have your own apartment?"

"Now I do. I was living with someone for a while."

"Me too," Bunny said. "Well, not really living with."

Some men would see Bunny as having sex appeal, in a languid, round-eyed way. She had an ardent nature. It had always shown itself in her principles, in the heated logic of her arguments. She had been silly and imitative and frequently right. Often Pauline thought of things Bunny had said—quotes from Gorky and Marx—as though by having known Bunny she had advanced these opinions herself.

"You like Philadelphia?" Pauline said.

"It's okay. I have activities. You know, YPSL, the Sacco-Vanzetti Defense Committee."

"That's a good committee. You help with that? That's good."

"A little." Bunny gave her crooked half smile, proud of herself but careful to convey that she was on the slower fringes of things.

The rain was beginning to let up, as Pauline had said (she was glad to have been proved right, as though New York weather were within her expertise).

"I should show up at the party," Bunny said. "You don't want to go, do you?" Pauline said she didn't think so, but she walked part of the way with Bunny, since her house was in the same direction Bunny was going. Bunny didn't seem to be afraid of being on the street at night, even when they passed a man sleeping on the steps of a building and the man moaned and lurched suddenly in his sleep; Pauline jumped back but she didn't. Bunny on the job saw more alarming things all the time, certainly worse drunks; Bunny wasn't some innocent.

"See my shoes?" Bunny said. "You always said my shoes were oafish but I still like this kind." Pauline still thought they were oafish but she had at least learned not to say everything. "You were mean to me sometimes," Bunny said.

"I know." Pauline was somehow surprised that Bunny knew, although she had complained at the time. Pauline hadn't meant to deliberately torment Bunny but she had been callous; she had been always afraid that Bunny was going to disgrace her. She was not happy at the picture of herself at a certain age, unfocused and wildly out of shape.

"How's Murray?" Pauline said. "What happened to him?"

"He's in France," Bunny said. "He's lives there now. He doesn't speak any French, though—don't you think that's peculiar?"

"Yes," Pauline said. "I'd learn French if it were me." Pauline had stopped; they were standing by her corner. *"Voici* the street I live on," she said. Bunny gazed down it dutifully. "It was great to see you," Pauline said. "You look great."

"I thought you would be different," Bunny said. "I thought you would be more glamorous."

"Oh, well," Pauline said—she pretended to find the very idea of this funny—and they kissed good-bye.

. . .

In the days afterward she kept thinking that New York had become too repetitious for her. She was curious again about France—how could Murray get there and she couldn't? She looked at her Baudelaire again, the perfumed landscapes, the stylized languor. She bought a copy of a French magazine—the ads were the easiest to translate. It was slightly disappointing not to be able to buy the products. Rose said that French tooth powder tasted like burnt vanilla.

Rose had been sick for a week—she had missed Adolfo's funeral because she was laid up in bed with a bad cold. On the night of the fire she had gone off in her wet coat to show the college boy a speakeasy with dancing that was open all night; for a day or so afterward she had mistaken her fever for the ache of a bad hangover.

"She's so dumb sometimes," Nita said. Rose's dumbness, in Nita's eyes, consisted in the first place of exposing herself to germs for the sake of some person in pants. (Nita had spells of being very haughty on the subject.) She thought that Rose fell in love too easily, although Pauline wouldn't have described Rose's latest fling that way; Pauline was always surprised at how freely people used those terms. She herself was careful not to use them, quite scrupulous really. She wouldn't say that she had ever been in love (although sometimes Dewey had made her say it). She was wary about taking the phrase in vain, not because she was "saving herself"—on the contrary she might be said to be blithely throwing herself away—but because she prided herself in making fine distinctions; it upset her, actually, that there was no accurate terminology for the sort of attractions she had had. She was losing her memory of certain things for lack of a mental wording for them—her old, fitful attraction to Ernest, which had had some of the swoon and longing properly associated with love, and her surges of interest in certain men seen in passing or talked to at parties.

However it was true that Rose was impractical—Nita was right about that part of it. Rose was enough to make anyone impatient at times. For her cold she was following a regimen of hot baths with cold showers right after. She wouldn't eat, or she ate things like raw oatmeal and dried figs, and she drank hot salt water. She acted amused when they told her she was going to give herself pneumonia or tuberculosis if she kept this up. She had done all this before, it was the best thing, she would lend them the books if they didn't believe her.

She couldn't do any cooking in her hotel room anyway; the best she could do was to boil water over one of the sconces by the mantel that still had a gas jet that worked. Rose's hotel room showed all through it her efforts to adapt its features to a fuller existence than they were meant to provide. She had draped every surface with a paisley scarf or a piece of cross-stitched embroidery. When friends visited her, she knelt in her kimono and served tea on a trunk covered with one of those Cuban shawls she wore. A few of her dresses always hung along one section of ceiling molding, by way of brightening the wall.

In a way she had succeeded; it was pleasant to sit there with her. She had good afternoon sun from the window that looked over the back yard, and at the end of the afternoons she had the fading shrimp-bisque color of city sunsets. She was very appreciative of the sunsets. The room, when she guided you through it, seemed unusually fortunate and well-situated.

Nita tried to bring her cold broiled steaks to build up her blood, but Rose said red meat wasn't good for you if you were sick. Also she said she didn't believe that large animals that could live for years should be killed for her personal benefit. She had never said this before and Pauline thought of her hiding this opinion, not letting anyone know, perhaps eating nut loaf and carrots in private.

Nita was worried about Rose's cold showers. Rose did seem to believe in heroic measures, rigorous techniques to attack disease and give it no quarter. In a way Pauline was impressed by Rose's courage—Rose didn't mind subjecting her body to rude shocks or denying herself normal comforts. Nita said Rose liked the whole principle of self-punishment, but even allowing for that, there was a physical bravery in it. Pauline wasn't sure, for herself, whether she cared about being physically brave. Still, you never knew what was going to be required of you.

Actually the cold showers seemed to be helping. Pauline's theory was that colds got better in their own time no matter what you did. Solly had gotten colds a lot during one phase of his childhood. Once when she was home alone taking care of him he had disobeyed her by getting up from his bed to watch something out the window, and she had made him stand by the open window for an hour in his underwear. And he had gotten well anyway; he had gone to school the next day. She had been mean to Solly sometimes— irresistibly, in an aimless exercise of power. She had been like Dewey. It surprised her to remember herself like that.

She wouldn't have seen Rose again for a while if she hadn't passed a drugstore with a metal bottle labeled *poudre dentifrice* in the window. She bought one for Rose and one for herself. The label on the back was all extravagant and poetic claims in French about the health of the teeth, the beauty of the mouth.

It was a warm evening, and she was surprised when Rose answered the door with a blanket wrapped around her. Rose was huddled under it and her eyes were glazed. Pauline thought about whether Rose took drugs (Walter liked opium); perhaps her cold had been no cold at all.

"I'm better," Rose said. Her voice didn't sound normal; it sounded distant and thin. "I was so hot this morning. I think that's over, that part."

Pauline showed her the tooth powder and Rose said she hadn't seen any of that in a long time. She was less enthusiastic than Pauline had expected. She lay back on the bed and shivered a little; she still had the blanket wrapped around her. "Do you mind—could you just get me a glass of water from the sink?" she said.

This was so un-Rose-like, this request to be waited on, that Pauline knew then that she was truly sick.

"I'm so thirsty," Rose said. "It's good for you to drink water though, isn't it?"

Pauline put her hand on Rose's forehead, not that she could really tell a fever that way. "Keep drinking," she said. "It's legal."

Rose coughed and sputtered some of it up. Pauline took the glass away.

Rose said, "Do you miss Mack ever?"

"Not really," Pauline said. "Not personally, I don't think."

"I miss my friend," Rose said.

She meant her married lover. Pauline couldn't imagine that he had ever been much help when Rose was sick. "We used to talk a lot about politics," Rose said. "He was very astute, he was good to talk to about that."

"Do you want tea?" Pauline said.

Rose shook her head. This shaking motion continued bizarrely into a great shudder, her head kicked back, and then she was shivering so violently that the bedstead rattled. "Are you all right?" Pauline said. Rose rolled her eyes toward Pauline; her teeth were chattering. The shivering went on for

a long time, as long as ten minutes, during which Pauline
rubbed Rose's arms to get some warmth into her, piled coats
on the bed, and finally began making tea. "I've got the pot
over the flame, I'm holding it," she kept saying. "Is this
right? It's almost boiling, I can hear it."

"Thank you," Rose said a few times, through her teeth,
and, "Don't worry."

When the shivering stopped, Rose was still afraid to
drink the tea for fear of spilling it on herself. What did she
need the tea for anyway? Pauline saw that she was bothering
Rose about the tea to no purpose—she didn't know what she
should be doing. She was alone with Rose, and Rose was not
sick in a minor normal way. Pauline was frightened for both
of them. She felt the weight of Rose's solitude, her days alone
in the room. She was sorry for Rose until it occurred to her
that if she herself were sick she would be no better off. On the
other hand she was younger and healthier than Rose, she
thought, with some vanity. She wondered how Adolfo had
managed with his leg.

Rose had more color in her face and she said she felt
better. "You have to eat," Pauline decided. "When did you
eat? If you're shivering and coughing you should be eating
more than usual, you're using up your strength." Perhaps
this was true. Did Rose want a chicken sandwich? Maybe
some applesauce?

"If you're going out," Rose said. "Maybe you could get
me some Unguentine." Rose had burned herself with the
mustard plaster. She showed Pauline the patches of blistering
skin between her breasts. She hadn't meant to leave the plaster on so long but she had fallen asleep.

"You dumb cluck," Pauline said. Rose said it wasn't so
bad, they used to do that on purpose, blister people to drive
out the toxic fluids. "That was in the Dark Ages, for crying

out loud," Pauline said. Rose didn't know anything about what to do either; her body was wallowing in their ignorance.

I should get a doctor, Pauline thought (she didn't know any doctors except in Newark). Instead she went out and called Nita, and she came back with a chicken sandwich, which she made Rose eat half of before she left.

The doctor Nita called didn't come till the next day. When Pauline got there in the evening, Rose was imitating the doctor's accent, which she said was like the Katzenjammer Kids. Nita said he probably spoke perfect English but was just overwhelmed from getting a peek at Rose's naked chest. Rose was flushed tonight, sweaty and overexcited.

"She's got pee-neu-monie," Nita said.

"I have to go on a soft diet," Rose said. "Don't you think that's insulting for an adult?"

Pauline tried to see from Nita's face how serious this was. Nita gave her one quick glance: not good. Rose's one worry was about the doctor coming again. She didn't want the hotel to know she had something as bad as pneumonia. She was sure they would take her room away. Nita kept saying they *couldn't* throw her out on the street, but Rose thought that she had disqualified herself by falling below a certain level of health. She seemed to think of the hotel as a great blessing rightly bestowed only on the fit. Everybody wanted her room anyway because of the view. She was not sensible on the subject and had to be led off onto other topics.

It was less frightening with Nita there. Still, when Rose was coughing Nita and Pauline both turned away—they couldn't look at each other. Nita left early—they arranged that she would come in the mornings and Pauline would stay on after supper. Pauline was pleased to have something definite apportioned to her. She washed some cups and saucers and rinsed out Rose's nightgowns and then she got the idea that maybe Rose would like to be read to. Rose wanted to hear something from the newspaper. Pauline went down to get a paper, and then she read Rose two articles about the sentencing in the Sacco-Vanzetti case and a feature about April in Central Park. At the end Rose was asleep.

Pauline was satisfied to see this; the atmosphere of reading aloud had made her feel peaceful too. She was full of plans for things she would do for Rose—she would buy her a bed jacket, she would air the room, she would make puddings, she would surprise her with flowers. She had spent her childhood reading books about these things—all the novels where orphaned families lived inventively in terrible poverty, crippled boys were tended by ragged but sweet-tempered sisters, and acts of considerable heroism were performed by children no older than herself at the time. She knew perfectly well that these had been sentimental stories—some of them, when she thought of them now, were downright grotesque—highly dated and beginning to be old-fashioned even then, but there was something in them also which was not purely sentimental and which she had not encountered elsewhere in her childhood. She had been very hurt as a child when her father had made fun of those books. They had given her a taste of a particular kind of glory and left her with secret moral longings.

Nita thought they should get in touch with Rose's parents. She said she felt funny that only Rose's friends knew how she was. The doctor said it wasn't a grave case, but who knew about this doctor anyway?

"It's no good telling them," Rose said. In the first place she wasn't that sick and in the second place there was never any point in bothering them with news. Not that her relations with them weren't cordial—she had a picture of them, a portrait taken in a studio in Wausau, Wisconsin. They were older than you would think—the mother was broad and white-haired and the father had a long, shrunken face. Their eyes had come out pale and moony in the photo; they both look transfixed. There was a brother who lived at home. The father had been in a long gloomy spell some years ago and he had been too timid to do much since then; moving cars made him run. Her mother believed he had weakened his constitution by eating green fruit.

There was plenty Pauline hadn't known before about Rose; in a way they didn't know each other that well. Yet they were intimates—they had told each other strong and indelible details about their private lives, their sexual experiences; they had counseled each other. And Rose was not surprised that Pauline and Nita were the ones in the room with her now, sitting on her bed watching her. She would've been with them if they had been sick (probably coaxing them to drink that miserable hot lemonade of hers). They were bound to each other, for now, not only by the usual ties of friendship but by their shared lots and their understanding (perfectly clear and grim) of how it would go for them without each other.

The next time Pauline came, Rose said she was better, she was well rested, she had been sleeping all the time. She had put on, presumably for Pauline's visit, a pearl rope necklace and a blouse that she wore as a bed jacket. She looked odd, Pauline thought.

Rose said she had been thinking all day about Sacco and Vanzetti. She had had a dream that the air in the room was burning her up, and when she woke up, she realized that she had stolen the idea from Vanzetti, who'd had a violent delusional fit a few years ago about the burning atmosphere in his

229

cell—he had tried to barricade himself and he had smashed furniture. "He was preimagining the electric chair," Rose said. "It's so obvious now." Her eyes teared up.

Pauline, to her own surprise, also got teary. Usually she thought it was not fair in some way that of all the unjustly confined prisoners in the world, people liked Sacco and Vanzetti because they were more eloquent; they could convey what it was like to be in prison. They would probably be dead by July—they had been sentenced now, after seven years. Actually, unlike almost everybody else on both sides, she liked them because they were anarchists.

And she was teary because they reminded her, in a way, of Adolfo. Adolfo would have been insulted by this comparison. He was certainly no radical and he would've considered himself socially several cuts above the level of a shoemaker or a fish peddler. But they reminded her of Adolfo in the way no one listened to them. She pictured Vanzetti gesticulating on street corners, streams of people hurrying past his speeches, and she thought of Adolfo trying to yuk it up with customers or muttering to himself in the kitchen, that vivacity expended in empty space.

Rose was coughing. Pauline thought that pneumonia must be like a kind of claustrophobia within the body, a threat of the lungs closing off and no air getting in—an exitless confinement like Vanzetti's, and like Adolfo's last minutes in the smoky kitchen. Prisoners always longed for things they had barely noticed before. Rose hacked and struggled, marshaling her strength in the simple desire for air.

Pauline tried to arrange the pillows under her so that she could sit up straighter. Nita was much better at this, more deft and better at intuiting what Rose really wanted. Pauline tended to care for her by rote—did she want water? tea? a window opened? Nita was better at thinking of items to bring—silly postcards, an embroidered pillowcase. But

Pauline had more staying power. Nita bustled off to her lunch job after a few hours with Rose in the morning, but Pauline's visits began at supper and went on into the night, when Rose was at her worst.

In the night Rose's fever went up; she still had fits of shivering and she breathed in a wheezy, rapid way; she would grunt suddenly when the breathing hurt her. When she slept, the jolts of her own grunting woke her up. "We could maybe have the doctor in again," Pauline said.

Rose said, "I can't believe you would do that." She was angry then—Pauline had never seen her angry. It was the room—she didn't want to have to give up the room. She had been there for years; her things were there; she had arranged everything the way she liked it. Pauline wondered whether all this was because Rose wanted to make sure her friend could find her if he came looking, but Rose didn't say anything about him. It was the *time* she had been in the room; she was very emphatic about the strength of her sentiment based on a sort of depth of occupancy. "I was here before I even started drawing for the *Journal*," she said. Pauline thought it was nice that Rose felt such an attachment to certain years of her life there (which could hardly have been all pleasant); she seemed to be insisting on their value. Still it startled Pauline that Rose pictured a continuing future in the hotel. So they would all go on as they were, was that it? For herself, Pauline was used to thinking of her current condition as more or less provisional, an introduction to something not invented yet and not really imagined.

"Maybe we can have the doctor show up in disguise," Pauline said. "Camouflage his black bag as a hatbox or something."

Rose didn't laugh. She said, "Don't *talk* about it," and she was getting hoarse and querulous.

．　．　．

Pauline made Nita come with her the next night. By that time Nita had talked to the doctor, who said that Rose was approaching a "crisis"; they should call him if certain symptoms appeared.

"Like what?" Pauline said.

"Turning blue," Nita said.

"No, really," Pauline said. But Nita was serious. It was hard now to tell what could be joked about and what couldn't. Rose was not blue (surely this was a metaphor—how would they know when she approached what was meant by this color?). She was pale and her face was hollowed in parts and swollen in others; she was not herself. She lay without talking to them. When they asked her things she answered in one word and closed her eyes. She seemed to be concentrating on her breathing. Nita said, "Are you warm enough or do you want another blanket?" "Warm," Rose said. Pauline had never seen anyone this sick before. She saw how the downward curl of Rose's mouth was like the sketches done of Keats at his bedside, and then she was ashamed of noticing, of *making comparisons* at such a time. And yet it was not out of heartlessness that she wanted to see, to see clearly. She breathed evenly to try to guide Rose.

Nita tried to give her the hot lemonade she liked, but she made them take the cup away. Rose grunted, a sound of small pain lower than the range of her real voice; in real life she would have begged their pardon.

Nita and Pauline whispered in the corner to each other. Nita thought they should both stay the night; one of them could sleep on the floor and the other one on a chair. Pauline felt a surge of gratitude toward Nita for thinking of this. She was so relieved that they would be doing the right thing it made her believe for a minute that nothing perilous could happen as long as someone was keeping vigil. She smoothed the blanket around Rose's feet; she went around the bed tucking in corners.

Nita turned out the light. Rose made a murmuring noise—perhaps she was saying good night to them. They sat waiting to hear if they could tell when she was asleep. Nita said, "Here," and passed a roll of caramels to Pauline; they chewed in the dark, as though they were at the movies or around a campfire. "To keep our strength up," Nita said. Pauline at that moment did feel their strength, their solid forms in the hotel room and their small careful movements.

Nita got up to wash at Rose's sink. Through the window there was a noise of voices from the courtyard underneath—some old men were standing outside drinking and telling stories. They weren't loud enough to wake Rose, and Pauline thought they were a good omen; their distant sociability was soothing in the room.

"It's nice here at night," Pauline said. She did like Rose's room at night—she had noticed this before in the evenings alone with her. There was a pleasure in staying, a clarity of mind about being in the right place.

Later they heard Rose wake up. She opened her eyes and saw Nita curled up under a shawl on the chair. Nita waved. "All the company passed out," she said. Rose made a little snorting laugh.

When Pauline woke up in the middle of the night, the room was quiet. She was on the floor, with a pillow under her head, and she saw everything from below; the dark columns of the legs of Rose's bed were at eye level. A glass light fixture glimmered overhead; she felt as though she were lying on the deck of a ship. She got up to see how Rose was. She stood as near to the bed as she could, but it was too dark—she could only make out the hump of Rose's body under the covers and the pale blur that was her profile. How could she keep watch if she couldn't see? It struck her as crazy now, what they had thought they could do. She tried to see if Rose's chest was moving under the covers—there seemed to be a motion but perhaps it was a trick of perception, like the vibrations of color people see in total darkness. She stood for a long time, trying to discern what noise or motion was Rose's, waiting, knowing that she was far outside the small realm of what she knew, and hoping that here and now this time she would not be caught out.

In the morning Rose said, "Gads, who was that snoring?" Pauline didn't think that any of them had snored. What sound had come buzzing up through Rose's ears? "I'm just kidding," Rose said. "For Pete's sake. Trying to inject a little humor here."

And she was willing to eat a soft-boiled egg for breakfast. "Isn't that a stirring sight?" Nita said. "Look at how she dribbles that yolk on her chin. It makes my heart spasmodic with joy."

"You eat too," Rose said, in her cracked sick-voice.

Pauline and Nita shared a bowl of shredded wheat with some slightly sour milk that had been left out on the sill. "I have a little sister," Pauline sang softly, "Tries very hard to sleep./ She chews on Father's whiskers/ And thinks they're shredded wheat." She was actually singing out of happiness at hearing Rose talk in whole sentences.

"Don't sing," Nita said. "It's not sporting when you're in a room with someone who can't get up and leave."

"I could leave," Rose said. "I feel better."

Rose had of course announced that she was better every day since she'd gotten sick. But she *wasn't* as bad as she'd been last night. (Unless she was going to waver: better, worse, better, worse.) Still, she seemed with them again; swelled and dried, but herself.

"You don't see me practicing my violin here," Nita said.

"She'd love it," Pauline said. "It would feel so good when you stopped."

They tried to get Rose back to sleep again after breakfast, but she wasn't tired, she said. She wanted them to wash her hair. They had to bend her head into a basin, soap her down like a dog, and try to rinse her off without slopping all the water on the bed. "Aren't you going to work?" Nita said, when they were wrapping the towel around Rose's head. The bed was all soggy on one side, and they sat Rose in a chair with a blanket on her while they changed the sheets. Pauline had assumed she wasn't going to work—it was nine thirty already; if she went she would be leaving Rose alone all through the lunchtime hours while Nita was off playing. Nita's opinion, which she had to whisper and signal, was that Rose would sleep only if they both went away—she was all worked up today.

If Pauline left at once, she could get to Gittelson's before ten and they wouldn't dock her more than an hour's pay. Rose was putting on bracelets, layers on both arms, and she insisted on making Pauline wear a china-bead one for the office. "It looks so nice on you, Pauline, Pauline," she said.

When Pauline walked out into the sudden light of the street, she was conscious that she had slept badly on a wooden floor, that she was wearing the same clothes she had had on since yesterday, and that her own hair needed washing. She was not alert; she let people jostle her. She felt that she had poured her strength into Rose, although she knew that this was not quite true—she was envious of Rose's being able to sleep for the rest of the day. She shuffled, exaggerating the signs of fatigue in her walk. At work she would have to let Miss Pfeiffer know why she was late; she would not make an issue of it but she would tell them: a sick friend. This would be a shallow and reductive summary, like any traveler's report; already the extremes of the night had a visionary quality. The bracelet clinked, a souvenir.

As it turned out, Miss Pfeiffer was not even there, a truly unusual circumstance. Pauline couldn't remember her ever missing work, except after her niece's death. The bookkeeper was at the front desk, trying to cope with the switchboard.

Pauline slipped to her corner in the back, hoping no one would see her and yell at her. The place seemed under-patrolled today. George the stock boy was sitting on a carton sneaking a look at the sports page. Pauline made him stretch out his arm so she could see the front page—something about the health of the economy in one of the headlines. The news, she thought, was always rife with figures of speech about sickness and decline and recovery. In fourth grade her teacher had lectured them about the War and blamed it on the Ottoman Empire, which she said was called the Sick Man of Europe, as though a difficult patient had caused some kind of family havoc. Still, to think of Rose's "crisis" and her "turning point" was for Pauline to feel that she had in the course of things participated in the vocabulary of the race.

There were stacks of invoices waiting for her to file them. She tried to be efficient and fast, so no one would ask her to stay late. She was doing pretty well, she thought, keeping up a good pace. She worked while George went to lunch; the office was quiet. George came back with a printed flyer, which he waved at her. "A present," he said. "Right up your alley."

"If it's a sale, I can't afford it," she said. The flyer said:

RALLY IN UNION SQUARE. THE PEOPLE WILL BE HEARD. SACCO AND VANZETTI MUST NOT DIE.

"Oh, I was going to go," Pauline said. She meant she had been thinking about doing *some*thing. She wondered if Bunny had anything to do with planning this.

"You know what I don't understand?" George said. She hated it when they argued politics. "How many times did they try to get a new trial and get turned down? A lot, right?"

"Seven," Pauline said, reading from the flyer.

"How could they stand that? You think you're going to live, you think you're going to die. Live, die, live, die, et cetera."

"What are you asking me?" she said. "How they could stand it? They stood it, that's it."

"I'm not asking you anything," he said. "It was a rhetorical question."

"They stood it. That's what some people do."

On her late lunch break Pauline went out to smoke a cigarette on a park bench. She didn't smoke outside in public normally, but today she wanted to. The bench was not in a real park, but in a triangle of dirt with one skinny tree. She was very tired once she sat down. It was Murray who had first taught her to smoke in high school. Murray had said it relaxed you. Pauline pictured the blue line of the smoke, taken in, diffusing through the body, making it lighter. She liked the thought of some inner expansion taking place from what she took in, the burning matter transformed. To smoke and think this now made her feel braced for the rest of the day, steadfast.

In the afternoon at Gittelson's she did some of the bookkeeper's job, sitting at the adding machine. She had to work a crank to make the paper roll each time, and the work was physical enough to keep her alert. She worried about how

Rose was—Rose couldn't phone for help unless she went down to the lobby—she would probably rather die than do that and have them see how she was. Nita would be there by three-thirty or quarter to four. Pauline was jumpy until that time came, restless to leave.

In the evening when she went to Rose's, the room smelled of cologne. Rose had given herself a sponge bath and doused herself with some strong flowery scent, jasmine or tuberose, and she had put drops of it on the sheets and blankets.

"Smells like a whorehouse in here, doesn't it?" Nita said.

"Spring is here," Rose said. They seemed to be very short with each other. Pauline took this as a good sign, since Nita would've had to stay agreeable if Rose weren't better.

"They're just some kinds of perfume I don't like," Nita said.

"Otherwise it's like a cell here," Rose said. "I shouldn't say cell. Vanzetti is in a real cell."

"She has a crush on him," Nita said. "An ethical crush."

Pauline showed them the flyer the stock boy had given her. This turned out to be unwise—Rose announced right away that she wanted to go to the rally. "It's this *Saturday*," Nita said. "You're not going anywhere."

"We'll go for you," Pauline said (too brightly—not even Rose was going to fall for that).

"Well, *I'm* going," Nita said. It surprised Pauline that Nita was so eager. Nita said the whole thing made her want to bomb the judge personally. "It would give me great pleasure to see him blown to pieces."

"Don't be disappointed, they're not doing that at the rally," Pauline said. There was a real question, of course, about what they *were* doing. Shouting into the wind? Then—fleetingly—she was happy about the rally, full of the feeling that if Rose could be better, Sacco and Vanzetti could be saved.

Rose said, "I really like Vanzetti."

Pauline knew why she liked him; they had talked about it. Rose's friend had said Vanzetti was the perfect example of a worker more intelligent than anyone wanted him to be. Pauline, having come somewhat late into all this, liked him because of what he had said before the court at the end, that he had never committed a real crime, *"though some sins."* This seemed to her so unflinching in its acknowledgment of things—which no one had asked him about—that he was privately ashamed of; he was so insistent on explaining just which sort of innocence he could claim. It gave her a particular kind of fellow feeling with him.

"Rose," Nita said, "for Christ's sake, stop making that noise with the straw." Pauline had brought a milkshake for Rose, which she was sipping with discouraging slowness. Nita said it probably tasted like soap from the scent in the room.

"You take it," Rose said. "I don't want it any more."

"I don't want it."

Rose coughed for a while, to back up her point, and she closed her eyes, weary with them.

Nita said the rally was going to be a real fresh-air outing for them after all the time spent in Rose's closet of a room with that one crummy window. When they got to Union Square on Saturday, it was already too crowded for them to get very close to the platforms—there were throngs of people spread out on the grounds and out to the sidewalk, people standing on benches, and blocks of people standing in rows holding banners. PERSECUTION OF WORKERS MUST STOP. *Garment Workers for Justice.* TODAY IT IS SACCO AND VANZETTI; TO-MORROW WHO? The closer they got, the more massive the crowd looked. Pauline felt personally triumphant to be joining a gathering that was already so successful. She was sorry they had gotten there late—the speeches had already started, she had missed things, possibly the most important parts had gone on without her. On the platform nearest them a man in a black suit was shouting to be heard; from different sides they could hear the blurred ringing of other speeches being given from other platforms. The black-suited man had to hurl himself forward with each phrase to get volume.

"I can't understand a word he's saying," Nita said. "He's not talking English."

Pauline could understand him fine because he was speaking Yiddish—she had forgotten for a moment that Nita didn't understand. "The powerless are hated and feared," Pauline said. "That's what he's saying. That's kind of a literal translation."

Nita wanted to move—a woman was speaking in English on the other side. "Our mother tongue," Nita said.

"I like it here. It's like being in a giant train station." Pauline said the speakers were rotating from platform to platform, and if they waited the English speaker would come to them. But the next one to mount the podium was an old man who held forth in Italian.

She thought about Rose's "crush" on Vanzetti. Vanzetti was good-looking—the eyes, the mustache—even if he'd gotten balder in his time in prison. Rose said anarchists treated their women well (Rose would believe that). Perhaps they would be a good match, he and Rose. It was odd to be thinking of romance at a time like this—not that it was inappropriate, she thought firmly, as though she were defending Rose's right to happiness (not to mention Vanzetti's), but it seemed on the wrong scale, too particular and specific for the event at hand.

The old man was using impassioned gestures and a spitting manner of delivery; Pauline was quite taken with him. "I can't stand it," Nita said.

"Well, go then," Pauline said. "Go move somewhere without me."

She was mortified that they were having a fight at a time like this. But Nita said, "Look for me at the southwest corner in an hour." Pauline thought it was ingenious of her to think of this; sometimes Nita didn't get mad when you would expect her to.

After Nita left, the crowd felt different; she was packed in closer with them, more similar to them. The old Italian went from the fiery phase of his speech to something more wailing and grief-stricken. All around Pauline, people who were surely not Italian and who could not have understood what he was saying, stood watching him, respectful and even moved. Mostly they looked patient—Pauline thought about the high intentions that had brought them there, that made them wait; she had, with them, a feeling of holding something at bay by simply standing there.

When the woman who was giving her speech in English finally got to the platform, the words at first were too blunt and direct. Pauline disagreed with her about the jury being just a bunch of bigots. She was disappointed—the woman's speech was too unintelligent and it was weakened by cant phrases. The woman was saying that the governor's committee was "too stupid to see its nose in front of its face," a phrase Dewey would have used. Pauline was indignant at the resemblance. She was angry at the woman; she felt so strongly that the speech should be more solemn. Pauline saw then how sure she herself was that Sacco and Vanzetti were going to die.

The woman broke into a suddenly sincere sentence about what had happened since the "terrible accident" of Sacco's and Vanzetti's arrest. "They were taken by surprise," she said, "seven years ago, and what did they do? They didn't yield to fear." (Pauline knew this was not strictly true, they had both had crazy spells in jail—Sacco had beat his head against the wall, Vanzetti had had his fits about the air burning him up—but it was close enough to true.) "In jail all that time, with all their reading and brooding and waiting, they rose to their fates." The crowd burst into a round of clapping, thunderous once it really got started. Pauline clapped and then, when a cheer started, she was shouting too. She felt buoyed up, floating—she was only standing up and making a noise with a lot of people—but in that long shout she had the sense of expansion people feel in the face of great vistas out-of-doors. In the din she couldn't hear her own shout, and she had the odd temporary freedom of doing without her own personality.

After that she kept looking around for Bunny. She wanted Bunny to know she was there. Would she have come from Philadelphia? Pauline thought it would make them both happy to see each other, give them a feeling of reprise and order. But it was impossible to see far enough into the mass to pick out a face more than a few feet away. And Bunny was short, easily hidden.

She didn't think she would ever find Nita either. Someone was halfway through a speech in German, of which she understood bits and pieces, when she spotted Nita just where she was supposed to be, on the sidewalk waving to her. With Nita were two men, a sandy-haired blond with a pug nose whom she recognized from Vera's and a thin man in a brown hat. She had not thought about people from Vera's or Anselm's or the Elephants' Graveyard being here, although if Nita was, lots of the others were bound to be. Not all—some of them wouldn't be at a worker's rally. (Walter had once asked if she soaked her feet in hot water after a long day at the office, and he had asked her in a jeering way; he had been making fun of her for having that kind of job. She had been surprised at that—class snobbery in Bohemia. But then she had expected her own ratings of people, based on taste and flair and currency of style, to reign just as rigidly.) She had almost forgotten about Vera's, so the sight of the men startled her.

"Are you having a good time?" Pauline said. She knew this was a somewhat brainless question, but she needed to know if Nita was going to want to leave right then.

"Did you see the lawyer from Hungary?" Nita said. "On the other side? He was very wonderful."

"I'd like to climb a tree and really see how many people are here," one of the men said.

"Oh, lift me up," Nita said. "I'll sit on your shoulders and count."

Pauline was amazed at the modesty with which Nita managed to get herself hoisted up. The thin man helped, lifting her by the elbows—she was so nimble no one got more than a glimpse of her garters. Still it was quite bold of her to be straddling the blond man's neck like that—perhaps he was a new interest.

"Billions," Nita said. "I see billions. It won't do any good for those poor suckers, but it's a very great sight." They let her slide down. The blond man offered to take Pauline up too, but Pauline said she could get a sense of it from where she was.

"Aren't you glad we learned not to be afraid of crowds?" Nita said.

Pauline couldn't recall that either of them had ever really been afraid of crowds—a good part of the time they liked large groups, the cells of city life—but she thought that Nita meant that they weren't too delicate, that they were hardened and sturdy enough so that they weren't going to fall down at their posts. This was also to say that she intended to stay through to the rest of the rally with Pauline.

It was late in the day when they got to Rose's room. They had let the men buy them coffee at a soda shop off Union Square, and they had all walked west together, bone tired and with a sense of having spent themselves well. Nita was doing a lot of whispering with the blond man before they said good-bye in front of Rose's hotel.

Rose was in bed—she applauded when she saw Nita and Pauline in the doorway. "It's the army of the righteous, back from walking the face of the earth." She had put on a head scarf fastened with a brooch above one ear, and she looked like a very skinny girl playing a pirate in a comic opera. "So how was it?" she said.

"It was huge," Pauline said. "You wouldn't believe how many people."

"I bet my friend was there," Rose said.

"Probably everybody you ever knew was there," Nita said.

For a moment Rose looked sad to hear this. They had come in with all this rush and flurry from the outside world; they were too excited. Rose was propped up with pillows, waiting for them. They had forgotten her till now.

She had made them a punch out of rum and tepid milk. Pauline thought it was the kind of thing Byron might have revived himself with on his travels. "How many do you think were there?" Rose said.

"Zillions," Nita said.

"She had a unique view," Pauline said.

"I saw somebody's hat up in a tree. He threw it and he couldn't get it down."

"Why do people throw things when they get excited?" Rose said. "It's an urge, isn't it?"

"What tree?" Pauline said. "I didn't see."

Rose said, "Tell me something better about it. What was the crowd like?" She twisted in the bed, angry at it, stretching her feet against the bedstead.

"Very varied," Nita said.

They weren't doing a good job of telling her about it. Along with the punch there was a plate of buttered soda crackers. Rose had been moving around much more than she should have been. She had that gloss in her eyes that she got with a fever. She's not that much better, Pauline thought. Why did we think she could get better that fast? "I'm hot," Rose said. When she took off the blouse she wore as a bed jacket, her shoulders under the straps of her nightgown were spindly and birdlike.

"Did you eat?" Pauline said.

"I'm eating a cracker now," Rose said. She was tall, taller than Pauline, and when she sat upright her shoulders looked square. Pauline appraised them, gauging their boniness. She was thinking of how much had passed through Rose's frame. Rose still had something of a hard time breathing—you could see by the way she lifted her chin, putting muscle into the effort.

On the wall above the bed was a watercolor that Rose had done, one of her still-lifes of a wine bottle and a roll. Nita said even in the picture the roll looked stale. It did look inedible, like a yellow-brown stone. Around the roll there were dashes of brush strokes—Rose had pictured the air as full of speckles and vibrations—crowded with threatening, random motion. Pauline had looked at the picture many times before, and the menace of that storming background was connected in her mind with people giving each other hot tea and the sense of being encamped there.

Rose decided now that she wanted the window open. It was a casement window and it stuck at the top, so that to get it open you had to stand on a chair and push at the corner and pray you didn't fling yourself outside when it finally un-jammed. Nita and Rose were both quite brave about doing it. Pauline said she would do it this time. Nita held her feet. She got a good grip on Pauline's ankles; her hands, with their nails kept short for violin playing, were surprisingly strong.

While Pauline was pressing on the pane, she saw straight down to the bottom of the courtyard and she had a twinge of real vertigo—why had she volunteered for this? The window gave way suddenly; it squawked and swung open. Pauline braced herself, with her palms on the wall, and then she had to reach around and hook the window outside so it didn't flap. The chair under her wobbled. Once it was done she was very pleased with herself, hopping down off the chair, but it made her especially admire Rose and Nita, who always did it so casually.

The wind came through in a cool, pleasant gush of air. The light in the room had dimmed and gotten shadowy, but Rose wanted to wait before they turned on the lamp. The line of her dresses hanging against the wall looked friezelike; the skirt of a limp crepe one near the window stirred slightly. In the dimming light the white of the walls was dappled and the varnished woodwork had a dark watery sheen. Nita had gone back to sitting on the edge of the bed; she was settled side-ways, drinking her cloudy white punch out of a teacup. Rose was saying something about the breeze—she liked the breeze from that window—her voice was still thin and raspy and Nita had to lean forward to hear—and Pauline stood for a minute watching them.